Also by Carol Louise Wilde

Books of the Nagaro Chronicle

Gift of Chance (1)

Covenant of the Sword (2)

Return to Lankura (3)

Thief of Slaves (4)

Heir of Darion (5)

Brothers of the Blood (6)

The final volume, Legacy of Loros (7), is forthcoming.

The *Nagaro* Chronicle ⁶

Brothers of the Blood

Carol Louise Wilde

Rivulus Books Trade Paperback Edition

Text, maps, and internal artwork by Carol Louise Wilde

Published in the United States of America by Rivulus Books, Arcadia, CA. The Rivulus Books name and Rivulus Books logo are trademarks of Rivulus Books.

ISBN: 978-1-944492-15-1

Cover art copyright by Cherie Foxley

To the memory of my mother.

She read and genuinely enjoyed what I wrote, and she always believed I could do it even though I often doubted it myself.

Big Farano
Long Harbor
Little Farano
Faranos
Obai
Galenor
Wotana
Great Chanel
Lankura
Edrovir
Farano's Mouth
Soku
Tunapa
Boka
Lapoa
Omei
Oapa
Kel Tierna
Lomoas
Inside Passage
Moluaro
Kapala
Great Chanel
Harmoth
Haru
Pakoa

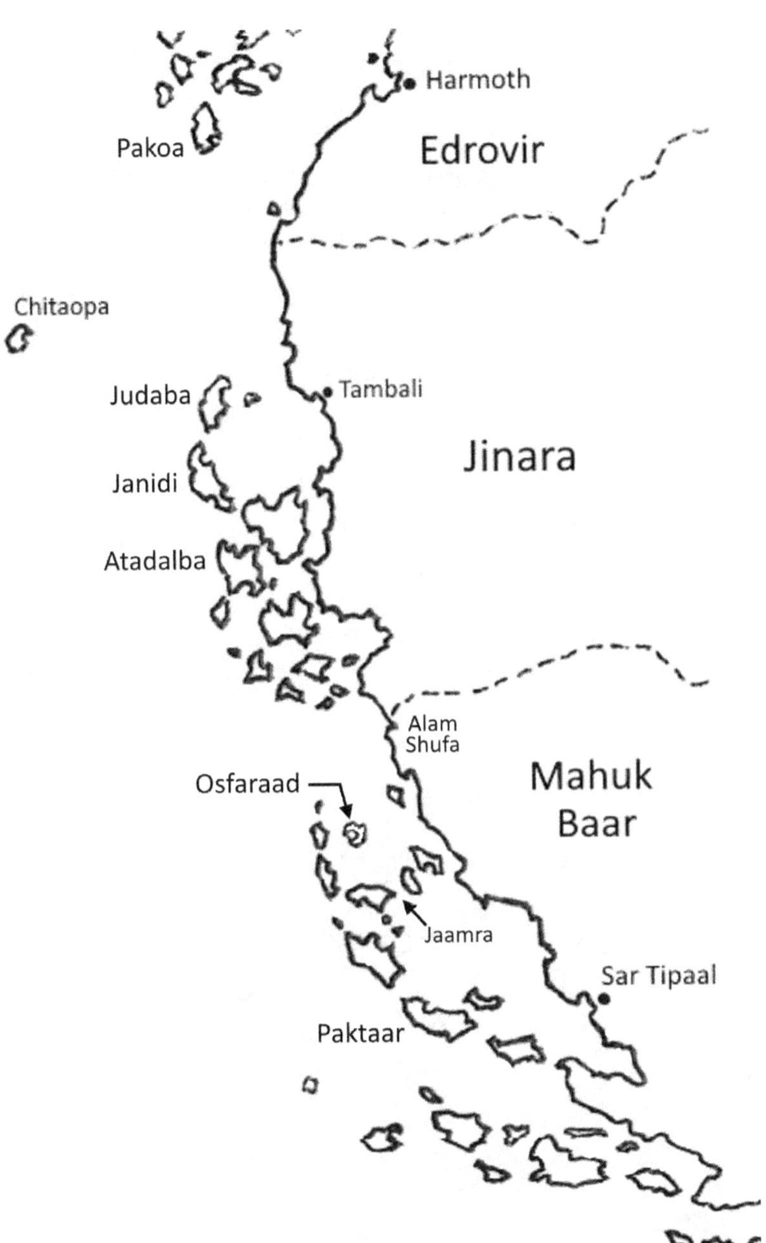

Pakoa
Harmoth
Edrovir
Chitaopa
Judaba
Tambali
Jinara
Janidi
Atadalba
Alam
Shufa
Osfaraad
Mahuk
Baar
Jaamra
Sar Tipaal
Paktaar

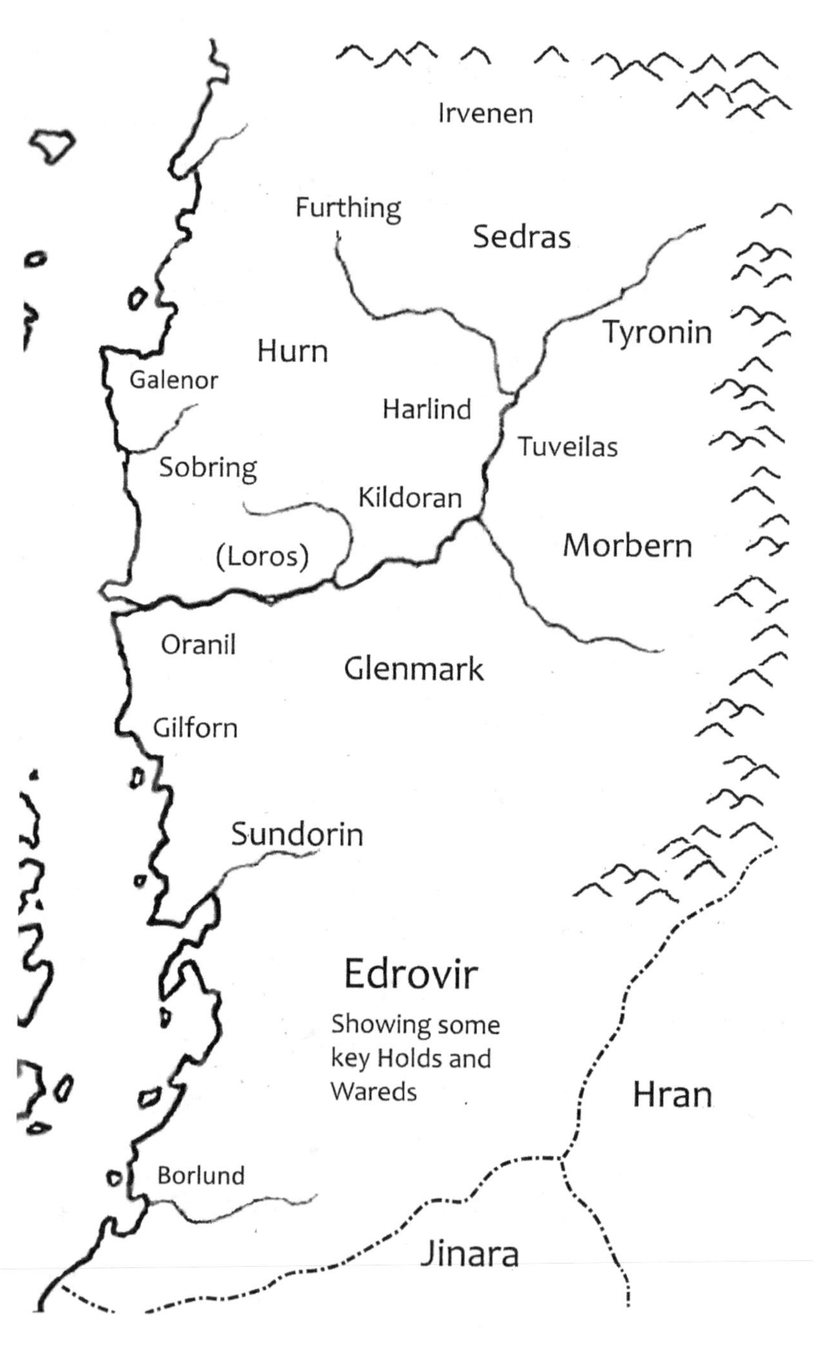

Irvenen
Furthing
Sedras
Tyronin
Hurn
Galenor
Harlind
Sobring
Tuveilas
Kildoran
Morbern
(Loros)
Oranil
Glenmark
Gilforn
Sundorin
Edrovir
Showing some
key Holds and
Wareds
Hran
Borlund
Jinara

Furthing
Hurn
Galenor
Wotana
Lodge
Sobring
Fendred
Virden
Averwin
Kildoran
Kel
(Loros)
Lankura
Glenmark
Oranil
River
Road
Border
Town
Hall
Gilforn
Sundorin

CONTENTS

Chapter 1

Of Marks And Merchants

It was late on a spring afternoon, after hours for most of those employed in the building on Broad Street. The courtyard and cloister-walk were nearly deserted. The sunlight that filtered down into the central courtyard from three stories above was rapidly fading, and the lamps were not yet lit along the encircling cloister walls. Nagaro was glad of the gloom. He had come on foot as he generally did when he wished to move inconspicuously through the streets of Lankura, glad that the blustery late spring day had allowed him the concealment of his cloak and hood. He found Simion waiting in the shadow of the cloister walk just inside the rear entrance of the building where the young Kelorin was a clerk in the employ of Lord Madred Furthing, to whom the building belonged.

Nagaro kept his hood up as he followed Simion along the cloister walk, through a door, and up the stairs. He had arranged this clandestine meeting through Madred's son Brandle Furthing, that being the most reliable and diplomatic way for him to make inquiries of Simion. Brandle was inclined to be highly protective of his lover, and a little jealous despite the fact that he knew Nagaro was categorically uninterested, not being a crossed man.

"I can't tell you how glad I am that you were there to save Kenthos from Lothard's sword," Simion said in a low voice as they emerged into a second floor hallway. "How is he faring?"

"He's recovering well in the Fleet infirmary. Another week and he should be strong enough to ride home." Nagaro also kept his voice low, though the matter was no secret. He didn't really want to talk about the latest would-be heir of the House of Loros, and especially not the part he had played in the man's adventures.

Simion had reached the door of his office and now unlocked it, then stood aside to usher Nagaro through. "Well, that's good, at least. Though it's a shame that he turned out not to be the heir of Darion after all."

Nagaro sighed as he stepped into the office. "Kenthos was misled," he said diffidently. "And he actually seemed rather relieved not to be the missing heir."

"It means the heir is still out there." Simeon's voice had a breathless catch in it. "*Somewhere*. We just have to find him—"

"I suppose that might be true, if anyone knew where to look," Nagaro put in hastily as he hung up his cloak beside the door, which Simeon had closed behind them.

The office was much as he remembered it from his earlier visit. It was none too large and supplied with simple, practical furniture that included a desk, a table, two chairs, and several bookcases. The room was remarkably tidy considering the quantity of books, ledgers, and loose papers it contained. Nagaro sat down on the spare chair without waiting to be invited. Simion paused to turn up the oil lamp on the desk to supplement the struggling light from the window. Then he borrowed the chair from the corner desk for himself and sat down on it.

The light played upon Simion's elfin features, wakening bright highlights in wide eyes of deepest Kelorin blue. He cleared his throat. "Brandle said you wanted me to identify some merchant's marks this time."

"That's right." Nagaro reached into the front of his tirka and pulled out the folded piece of paper he had gotten from the Jinari merchant's agent Utabala more than two months before. It bore copies of three marks that Utabala's spy had seen on papers brought in small boats, by yellow-haired Leithians, to a secret landing near the Jinari port of Patamtala on the island of Judaba. "See if you know any of these." He held out the paper, then hastily added, "It's a potentially delicate matter, entrusted to me by Lord Kuran. We'd appreciate your discretion."

Kuran hadn't yet seen the marks himself. The Lord of the Royal Fleet of Edrovir had thought it better for Nagaro to make the initial inquiries, since Nagaro could do so much less conspicuously. Kuran's instructions had been to pursue the matter at Nagaro's "earliest convenience" after their return from escorting four captured warships and the accompanying sea warriors back to waters controlled by the Emperor of the Mahuk Baar. It was now several weeks since his return, but this really was his earliest opportunity to deal with the matter. The unfortunate affair of the mis-identified heir of Darion had intervened.

"Of course I'll be discrete." Simion smiled tightly as he took the paper. He unfolded it, stood up, and started to turn so as to get the page into a better light. Before he could complete the action, however, he froze. "These aren't merchant's marks," he said. "These are seals of noble houses!"

"*What?*" Nagaro stared at him. "Are you sure?"

Simion stepped towards him, holding up the paper as he stabbed a finger at one of the three little drawings. "This one is the crest of the House of Furthing!"

"The House of *Furthing?*" Nagaro's thoughts spun. *Simion's employer!* He stood up and reached for the paper. "I'd better just take it and go, Simion," he said. "I don't want to put you in a difficult position."

But Simion jerked the paper away. "It's too late for that, Nagaro. I've already seen the seals, and I can easily identify the other two. And besides, I know how serious this could be. Brandle said it had something to do with unlawful trade with Jinara."

"*He* told you that?" Nagaro was dismayed. "He didn't want me to tell you anything!" One of the disadvantages of going through Brandle was that Brandle always insisted on knowing enough to be sure that there was no risk to his beloved Simion. In this case, Nagaro had made a point of explaining that the information he sought was likely to be commonplace and obtainable from many other sources, making it unlikely that anyone would trace it back specifically to Simion.

Simion looked sheepish. "He didn't intend to tell me, but I have ways of getting things out of him, and I was curious. Honestly, Nagaro, it's all right. Just sit down while I get out the book and make sure of them." Without waiting for an answer, he crossed to one of the bookcases and took down a tall leather-bound volume.

Nagaro remained standing, gnawing his lip. He obviously couldn't undo the harm he'd already done, and Simion was clearly not to be deterred.

Simion carried the book to the desk, and Nagaro stepped closer to look over the young man's shoulder. He saw the title: *Noble Houses of Edrovir* emblazoned on the cover in gold letters. Simion glanced at him. "This book has all the seals of all the houses," he said as he set it on its spine on the desktop.

As Simion let the book fall open, Nagaro sucked in a startled breath. "There's a page cut out!" he exclaimed in dismay. A half-inch-wide strip of paper protruded from the binding between the two facing pages of the open book. It's ragged edge had obviously been cut with something sharp like a scissors or a knife.

"Yes." Simion shrugged. "The book always falls open here because of it. But we don't want this section. These are the Kelorin Houses. I think all the ones on your paper are Leithian."

Nagaro's shock was unabated. "Who would cut a page out of a book?"

"Probably Lord Madred's father," Simion said absently, turning pages. "I'm almost certain that page was for the House of Loros. It's in the right place, and Loros is missing. Madred's father was no friend of the House of Loros, so I suppose he had the page removed when King Tevren was slain and that House ceased to exist. But see," he added, pointing to another page. "The wheat sheaf with the crossed spears is the House of Furthing, just as I said." He turned several pages. "And here are the three bull's heads— the House of Hurn. I wasn't sure of that one. And the mounted warrior..." he turned more pages "...is *here*. Yes, I thought so— the House of Sobring."

Nagaro felt a chill. "Furthing, Hurn, and Sobring..." he murmured. "All houses of the Leithian Faction. And it looks like they're dealing *directly...*"

"Dealing directly in what?" Simion asked quickly.

Nagaro shook his head. "No, Simion, I shouldn't involve you."

"I could try to find out on my own—"

"*No!*" Nagaro snatched the paper out of the young Kelorin's hand and thrust it back into his tirka, although it was a little late for that precaution.

Simion frowned. "I know how to be careful," he said, plainly miffed. "And if there's something unlawful going on, something should be done about it!"

Nagaro returned to his chair and sat down heavily. "Kuran will deal with it in whatever way it should be dealt with, Simion." He ran his fingers distractedly through his hair. "It's dangerous to poke around in the affairs of high-born Leithians. And Kuran could have identified those crests himself in a minute, so there's no need to ever mention that I showed them to you. You should just stay out of it."

Simion, however, dragged his chair closer to Nagaro's and sat down facing him. "But I am involved now, Nagaro," he said seriously. "And so are you. So tell me, where did those marks come from?"

Nagaro frowned as he met Simion's deep blue eyes, so very like the Lady Maramine's. Unfortunately Simion had gotten enough clues that his well-developed curiosity had been piqued and he naturally wanted to know more. Nagaro wavered. "They came from Utabala," he said at length. "And the matter involves trafficking with Jinara during time of war— which I've done, myself, in dealing with Utabala. It's likely to be very dangerous to know anything about it, so please don't ask me anything more."

Simion shook his head. "I've kept *your* secret, Nagaro," he said reproachfully. "I haven't even told Brandle. If this is dangerous and you're involved in it, then *you're* in danger too. I'm good at keeping secrets and I'm good at finding things out. Maybe I can help if you'll tell me what's being traded. Is the Leithian Faction buying, or selling?"

Keshaal! Nagaro closed his eyes. Simion was both clever and persistent and it might be better to tell the young Kelorin everything rather than risk having him poke around blindly on his own— especially since the details made the danger even more apparent. "All right," he said, opening his eyes and lowering his voice. "The Leithians are buying—manuscripts on herb lore, herbs for making drugs and poisons, and paraphernalia for that purpose— all things that might be used by a lore master— one interested in that kind of thing. Someone like Dreigen—"

"*Dreigen!*" Simion's dark eyes widened. "By the Eyes—" he began, then stopped as realization spread across his face. "That was it, wasn't it? It was *Dreigen* that hurt you. You must have been *drugged!*"

Nagaro couldn't help flinching as if a spear of ice had shot through him. Desperately he held up a warning hand, signaling Simion to desist. Not trusting his voice, he merely nodded. Then, after a moment, he managed to say, "You don't know what Dreigen can do, Simion. *I do.* Please don't go looking into this. Don't do anything to put yourself in danger!"

"*I* shouldn't?" Simion protested. "What about *you*, Nagaro? What if they find out that this information came from you? What if Dreigen recognizes you?"

Nagaro shook his head. "I'm going to hand it all over to Kuran," he said flatly. "I won't personally take any chances with Dreigen. He has the power to poison a man who's miles away. Or... or make a man go mad!"

Simion looked away, appearing finally to be genuinely daunted. After a moment, he said, "I was a little surprised that you came back— to Lankura, I mean. And you've been in the palace, too. Several times." His eyes returned to Nagaro's face. "Hasn't anyone recognized you?"

Nagaro moved uncomfortably. "No one who seems to mean me any harm. I came face to face once with Dreigen— as close as I am to you—and he didn't know me. He's not likely to, either, since I'm sure he thinks I'm dead. He never cared two rins about me anyway. It could have been... *anyone...* he was experimenting on..." Nagaro shuddered to a stop, unwilling to pursue the thought any further.

Simion had been staring at him wide-eyed, but now he dropped his eyes as if abashed, then rose and went to return the book to its place on the shelf.

Nagaro shook himself. "Thank you for your help, Simion," he said.

Returning from the bookcase, Simion stopped in the middle of the floor, looking pensive. "Maybe you're thinking about this wrong, Nagaro," he said. "Maybe it isn't Dreigen they're buying those things for. Maybe it's some other lore master."

"Some *other* lore master?" Nagaro frowned.

"There *are* other lore masters," Simion pointed out. "Almost all of the lords have one, and the Leithians seem to have a fondness for herb lore that goes beyond medicines— to sleeping droughts, love philters, potions to conjure prophetic dreams— that sort of thing. There was actually a lore master working here for a while—"

"Working *here?* In this building?" Nagaro could feel his thoughts rearranging themselves.

Simion nodded. "His name was Fineas— a decent sort of fellow, I thought. A Kelorin. I never knew exactly what he was working on, and then there was a huge row and he left about two weeks ago."

A Kelorin lore master working for a Leithian..." Nagaro frowned. "What was the row about?"

"I had the impression that he didn't like something they were asking him to do..." Simion's voice slowed to a stop.

They stared at each other.

"By the Eyes," Simion murmured. "I *could* look into it, Nagaro."

But Nagaro shook his head. "I have no right to say that you can't do something, Simion," he said seriously. "But I don't want you to. At least not while Lord Madred is your employer. I wouldn't want to have to face Brandle if anything happened to you because of what I've told you today. Do you understand?" He held the other man's eyes.

This time Simion nodded, almost meekly. "Yes, Nagaro, I do," he said, and then added, "Shall I show you down the stairs?"

"I can find my way, and I'd rather not chance having us seen together." Nagaro retrieved his cloak from the peg by the door. Donning it, he slipped out and exited the building as unobtrusively as he was able.

***

Outside, the wind had stopped gusting but the sun was nearly set and the air was turning chill. The last daylight was waning fast. Nagaro walked as quickly as he could through the dimming canyons of the streets, bundled in his cloak and hood, his thoughts in a dizzying whirl. He was worried about what harm he might have done by confiding in Simion— and about what the Leithian Faction was doing with those herbs and scrolls... *not to mention heskial.* The Jinari High Council's complaint, as presented to Lord Kuran, had specifically mentioned trafficking in that forbidden drug.

He shuddered, glad he hadn't told Simion about the drug... *how it had been used on him...* Simion had guessed accurately that a drug was involved, but he didn't have the *name* of it. The young man had shown some appreciation for the risks involved, but already Nagaro was regretting not having extracted a promise from him. Brandle had said Simion would do anything for him. *Anything except what he was told, it seemed, if it didn't suit him...*

Nagaro frowned harder. He'd imagined that Dreigen was doing business through some Leithian merchants, and that discouraging the merchants could have thwarted Dreigen without anyone becoming a target for the Lore Master's murderous ire. But it wasn't merchants who were acting as intermediaries— *it was the Leithian Faction!* Were the lords of Furthing, Sobring, and Hurn supplying Dreigen? Or were the goods going to their own private lore masters? What might *those* men be doing with them?

He almost walked right past the entrance to Brass Bell Lane, where it opened off of River Street, but he wrenched his thoughts out of their tumble just in time, remembering that he meant to give his favorite book shop more business. It would be a good distraction. He lacked information about the Leithians' activities, after all, and worrying in the absence of facts wasn't likely to get him anywhere. Taking a breath to settle himself, he turned in under the arch with its tarnished, clapper-less bell. The book shop was halfway to the end of the lane, which terminated without any egress at its farther end.

It was a relief to focus on a safer problem, another gift for his friend Pavo. The young Hashtep's literacy was progressing apace and he was ready for something new— something with a longer story, yet simple, that could serve for reading practice. Inside the shop, Nagaro found the perfect thing, a book meant for children that told the story of the young Lord Nevrath and the Princess Minowei. It was a thin volume with a cover only slightly worn, and it had half a dozen engaging illustrations done in pen and ink. The pictures were important because Pavo liked pictures, but what was even better was that Pavo was very taken with that particular story and would be highly motivated to read it. Nagaro purchased the book and the bookseller wrapped it in paper to protect it from the elements.

Nagaro stepped out of the bookshop with his purchase, and found that the little street's single lantern had been lit while he was inside, though the street was quite deserted. The yellow lamplight gleamed on paving stones polished smooth by passing feet. Across the street, it fell on the front of the old, abandoned apothecary's shop and drew Nagaro's eye to the sign over the door. He couldn't help noticing that the word APOTHECARY had been recently touched up with paint. Under it, more newly-painted letters leaped out at him, letters that spelled out: MASTER FINEAS, PROPRIETOR. Apparently the shop was no longer abandoned. In fact, a light glowed behind the curtain covering the window.

Master Finias... It was the same name as the lore master who had recently left Lord Madred's employ due to his unwillingness to do something. Might the man have decided to set himself up as an apothecary to earn his livelihood after losing his previous position? Intrigued, Nagaro crossed the street, arriving just as someone inside the shop was reaching around the window curtain to change the board in the corner of the window from one that read OPEN to one reading CLOSED. Not to be deterred, Nagaro knocked on the door.

The curtain was pulled aside momentarily, and a man's head and shoulders briefly showed, silhouetted by the light of an oil lamp in the shop behind him. A moment later, the curtain fell back as the head and shoulders were withdrawn. This was followed by the sound of a bolt being slid, and the door swung open.

"May I be of assistance, Zirda?"

The speaker's voice was quick and clipped. He was a small man with Kelorin features, wearing spectacles, but that was all that could be made out with the light behind him.

"I see that you're closing," Nagaro ventured, "but I thought perhaps you would take one more customer. Have you anything for headache?" He thought he ought to give the man some business, and it was the first thing that came to mind.

"Headache! Is that all?" The little man sounded disappointed. "Ah but come in, come in!" he added hastily, as if recollecting himself. "A customer is a customer. And no ailment is too trivial for Master Fineas." The last words were uttered with unmistakable bitterness as the proprietor stepped aside and ushered Nagaro into the shop.

The interior was narrow and deep, with the window and door occupying nearly the whole facade. A half dozen feet from the window was a counter that ran nearly the full width of the shop. The space behind it was taken up by an array of long shelves, each rising almost to the ceiling and separated by narrow aisles that offered access to their contents. The latter consisted of jars, vials, and boxes of all sizes and descriptions. The air was heavy with a pungent aroma of desiccated vegetation— an impossibly complex amalgam of different herb smells— mingled with a generous whiff of dust and an overlay of lemon oil. The last addition to the aromatic mix had presumably been employed in effort to control the other two.

Nagaro shook back his hood and set down the cloth-wrapped book on the counter. Gazing about him, he noted several framed pieces of paper hanging on one of the side walls. While Master Fineas closed the door and pattered around behind the counter to disappear among the shelves, Nagaro examined the framed papers by the light of the oil lamp that stood at one end of the counter. The papers included a signed letter of commendation from the Head Master of the Hatherin Lofts School for the Study of Abstruse Arts, as well as certificates of completion "*with Highest Merit*" in such areas of study as Medicinal Chemistry, Historical Herbology, Uncommon Languages, and Astronomy. Obviously the man was indeed a lore master, and how many lore masters named Fineas could there be?

Having finished his perusal of the framed papers, Nagaro went to stand in front of the counter. He could hear Fineas muttering, "Headache, headache... tincture of willow bark... willow bark, willow bark... Ah! Here it is!"

The lore master reappeared, carrying a glass jar filled with what looked like little brown sticks. He set it on the counter and raised his eyes to regard Nagaro through his spectacles. "It would be the tincture that you'd want for immediate use, of course, Zirda, and I regret that I have none of it prepared at this time," he explained with his rapid, precise delivery. "It loses its potency over time, you see, and I've had no reason to make it recently. I shall have to give you a quantity of the bark to take home, with instructions, so you may brew it for yourself."

"That's quite all right," Nagaro said quickly. "I haven't got a headache right now, in any case, and this way I'll be able to make the medicine when I need it."

Master Fineas blinked behind his spectacles. "Most interesting," he said. "You purchase the remedy in advance of the complaint. Do you have headaches often, Zirda? Have you done this before, perhaps?"

"No-o..." Nagaro mentally kicked himself. "Actually I... ah... only just thought of it."

The lore master blinked at him again. "Well," he said. "I must say I commend the strategy." With that, he leaned down and lifted a balance from beneath the counter, placed a square of paper on one of the pans, and set about meticulously weighing out a number of the little brown sticks, which were bits of dried bark.

Nagaro watched with mild curiosity. He had, in fact, seen willow bark before and knew it was used to alleviate pain from his abortive study of the healing arts years before under the tutelage of Tredhold Ferth. By the light of the oil lamp, he saw that the lore master was rather a young man— only in his thirties. The man's dark hair was a little disheveled, and needed cutting, but there was no gray in it. The spectacles made Fineas appear older. Nagaro decided to try to draw him out. "The last time I noticed, this shop was closed up," he ventured. "Have you recently purchased it from the previous owner?"

Fineas' hands, which were in the process of folding the paper containing the willow bark into a small packet, briefly ceased moving. "Yes," he said tersely. "The shop and its contents." He finished the packet and produced pen, ink, and a second little square of paper from somewhere under the counter.

"That purchase must have cost you quite a lot," Nagaro observed conversationally. "But then I suppose you must have had another shop somewhere else that you sold?"

Fineas had just dipped the pen. He stopped with it poised above the paper. "In point of fact, I was previously employed as a lore master," he said acerbically. "Fortunately, I had earned enough funds before leaving my last position to afford the purchase of this shop and the rooms above it."

"Ah." Nagaro nodded. "I thought your credentials—" he gestured towards the framed papers on the wall "— were unusual for a simple apothecary."

This time Fineas put the pen down, and drew himself up to his full height, such as it was. "*This* is the state to which I find myself reduced!" he declared, in a voice that shook with sudden anger. "Peddling powders for dyspepsia, and salves for worts! I— Master Fineas— a meritorious graduate of the esteemed school of Hatherin Lofts. And for *what*, you may ask?" He glared at Nagaro. "For *nothing!* Except that I did what any reputable lore master would have done!"

"What was that? Nagaro asked. It took little effort to appear to be caught up in the little man's passion.

Master Fineas gave a snort, and picked up the pen again. "You couldn't possibly understand," he said bitterly, bending over the paper.

"Well, I certainly understand honesty, and matters of principle—"

That struck a nerve. "*Principle!*" the little man exclaimed. "Yes, it was a matter of principle!" The pen was abandoned on the counter-top once more as Fineas stabbed a fore-finger at Nagaro's face. "Have you ever heard of *heskial?*

Chapter 2

Spirit Magic

The lore master must have mistaken Nagaro's horrified stare for the blankness of startled ignorance, for he continued without pause. "*Of course not!* And well you should not have, Zirda, for it is nothing short of an abomination! A drug so vile and so dangerous that the very folk who invented it have outlawed its use!"

Nagaro swallowed hard, and managed to say, "What does it do?" He knew perfectly well, but he had to hear Master Fineas' answer.

The lore master leaned towards him across the counter-top. "It has the power to do nothing less than *enslave the will!*" he said dramatically. "And do you know how such a feat was accomplished?"

Weakly, Nagaro shook his head. This he did *not* know.

"Then I'll tell you." Fineas was warming to his subject and began to pace back and forth behind the counter as he spoke. "Heskial is one of the drugs that embodies spirit magic in its very essence. Such medicines are very powerful— and very dangerous— if they're not designed in such a way as to be entirely benign. And the man who created heskial— the man who instilled some man's *anim*, some portion of a human spirit, into a *heskia* vine— wasn't wise enough to see what he had done until it was too late!" Fineas stopped pacing and rounded on Nagaro. "Shall I tell you the history?"

Nagaro nodded mutely, as enthralled as he was horrified.

Fineas, clearly in his element, resumed his pacing and his discourse. If he hadn't been so obviously animated by outrage, one might have thought he was enjoying himself.

"I have, myself, read the original texts regarding this— written in the tongue of Jinara. It was a Jinari lore master who created heskial, nearly two hundred years ago. The ruler of Jinara at the time was his employer, and this ruler apparently bade him make a truth-drug— something that, when administered to a man, would absolutely compel him to answer truthfully when so commanded— even if speaking the truth were to his detriment. The drug was intended for use in the interrogation of accused criminals, so accurate confessions could be obtained and mistakes avoided. This was a noble objective, to be sure, but unfortunately the only way the master could contrive to accomplish it was to create a drug that would subjugate the conscious will. So what do you suppose happened?" Master Fineas stopped again to address his audience of one, directly.

Nagaro moistened dry lips, swallowed, and said, "What?"

The lore master seemed not to notice Nagaro's discomfort. He promptly plunged on, now rooted in front of Nagaro. "I'll *tell* you what happened! It was quickly learned that this drug could be abused. A man could be commanded to tell the truth, certainly, but he could also be commanded to lie— even to *lie* when he was commanded by another to tell the truth! He could thus be compelled to confess to a crime he didn't commit! And what is more, since a man under heskial would not only *say* whatever he was commanded, but also *do* whatever he was commanded, the drug could even be used to make a man commit a crime *entirely against his will!* And then *say* that he'd freely chosen to do it!"

Seen through the lenses of his spectacles, Fineas' gray eyes appeared unnaturally large. In the dim room they seemed to glow in the light of the oil lamp as he fixed his piercing gaze upon Nagaro. "And as if all of *that* weren't bad enough," he continued, speaking into the silence that reigned in the shop, "Although it subjugates the will, heskial leaves a man's conscious awareness untouched! Apparently the lore master thought it should be that way, so that the accused man would know that he had spoken the truth, and that justice had been done. But think of the horror of this. The spirit in the drug can divorce the will from the processes of thought and feeling! A man under its sway will say or do anything he's bidden without intervention of his conscious mind. Yet his thoughts and the feelings are still *there*, inside him— and perhaps also the desire *not* to do what he's being commanded to do! Just think what an innocent victim might be forced to endure under the power of heskial in the hands of a wicked man! This is the most abominable kind of enslavement, to be forced to *watch* yourself acting out whatever you might be commanded and unable to do anything about it! Can you *imagine—*"

"*That's enough!*" The two words were wrung from Nagaro's throat, and he clamped his teeth shut to stop himself from blurting more. He was sweating and his heart was pounding.

Fineas stared at him, stunned into silence.

Very deliberately, Nagaro unclenched his teeth, took a deep breath. Trying to keep his voice from shaking, he said, "If you meant to convince me that the experience would be thoroughly unpleasant, you've succeeded." His voice came out sounding rather husky, but at least it was steady.

"I *do* beg your pardon, Zirda!" Fineas exclaimed. "They tell me that in this business, one must never vex the customer. And you, Zirda, are plainly vexed!" He stopped, and peered at Nagaro. "You wouldn't by chance be getting a headache, would you?"

"I... no... I mean, not yet," Nagaro stammered. "But I think I might be going to." This last was not entirely inaccurate.

"Oh dear!" The little man clicked his tongue. "I assure you that I shan't waste any more of your time." And, with that, he picked up the pen, re-dipped it, and set to work meticulously inscribing, in minute handwriting, the instructions for preparing a willow bark infusion on the second little square of paper.

Nagaro took advantage of the interlude to breathe slowly, and calm himself. After a moment, when he felt more composed, he realized that he was losing the opportunity to learn about Lord Madred's plans. Hoping fervently that he wouldn't set the man off on another tirade about heskial, he said in as casual a tone as he could muster, "I assume your previous employer wished you to do something with this... most unpleasant drug?"

This time Fineas didn't even look up. His pen stopped scratching just long enough for him to say, "I was instructed by no less a person than Lord Madred's Chief Minister to have our suppliers procure some of it. I declined on the grounds that it was an unlawful substance in the land of Jinara."

"Were you... sacked for that?"

The pen stopped again, and Fineas elevated his eyes to regard Nagaro over his spectacles. "The man pointed out to me," he said with suppressed outrage, "that in Edrovir we are not bound by the laws of Jinara. To which I responded that the Jinari law nevertheless made good sense, since the use of heskial, even for its original intended purpose, was fraught with great hazard. Whereupon, I was told that I could either do as I was bid or resign my position. And— well, Zirda, here I am." The little man shrugged his shoulders resignedly, and returned his attention to the paper, where he put the finishing touches on the instructions.

"Did you try to find another position as a lore master?"

Fineas signed the bit of paper with an angry flourish and looked up to meet Nagaro's eyes. "Of *course*," he said bitterly, "but I couldn't expect a good letter of reference from Lord Madred, could I? And to heap insult upon injustice, I have learned that the wretched Chief Minister has put the word out to all of the noble houses that I failed to give Lord Madred good service – *which is a bald-faced lie!* Only in the matter of the heskial did I decline to serve Minister Torlung as he wished— and that was on principle. In every other instance he had everything from me that he desired. And I never even *spoke* to Lord Madred!"

Nagaro shook his head in genuine sympathy. "This is certainly a very ill turn, Zirda, and quite undeserved," he said. Then, because he felt he needed to know, he added, "I can't help wondering what use Lord Madred— or his minister— intended to make of the drug."

Fineas sighed. "I have no idea. I hope he's been unable to get it."

"I hope so, as well." Nagaro shivered. In fact, he doubted that Master Fineas' departure would have thwarted the plan.

At this point, the lore master launched into a verbal explication of his written instructions, and Nagaro had to at least appear to pay close attention, although he had learned all about making infusions years before from Tredhold.

When Master Fineas had finished, he handed both the note and the packet of willow bark across the counter to Nagaro. "Here you are, Zirda," he said. "That will be two rins."

"Thank you." Nagaro pocketed the packet and the note, and brought out his purse to pay the man. As he handed over the coins, he added. "And I hope you find a way to return to your proper profession."

Fineas heaved a sigh and murmured his thanks for the money. "It wouldn't be nearly so bad," he remarked dismally, "if only the apothecary business weren't so *desperately* dull. No one ever asks for anything interesting. With nothing on which to practice my cognitive powers, I'm in danger of becoming quite dull myself."

Nagaro felt genuinely sorry for the man. Abruptly, inspiration struck. "Wait a moment," he said, digging into his pocket again. "I have something here that might be a little more interesting." He pulled out Luka's little folded leather keepsake that he always carried. "This was given to me by an old Turowan medicine woman. She said it was for remembrance, but she disappeared before I could ask her what it actually was. I'm rather curious about it. No one has been able to enlighten me."

A gleam appeared in Fineas' eyes and he reached for the little leather book with eager fingers. "I shall certainly endeavor to be of assistance," he said, turning the object over in his hands. "It's an herb-seller's sample, if I'm not mistaken. One uses such a thing to show one's customers what it's possible to obtain."

Nagaro nodded. "Yes, others have told me that much. But can you identify the herb inside?"

"Let me see." The lore master had already untied the ribbon, and he moved closer to the oil lamp as he gently opened the folded scrap of leather. He peered through his lenses at the faded bit of dried herb inside with the air of a cat stalking its prey. "*Hmm...*" he murmured. "Some variety of meadow-wyne, I would say... but not one of the *common* species..." Without taking his eyes from the plant, he fished a small magnifying loop from his pocket and added its power to that of his spectacles as he examined the specimen even more closely. "Yes, definitely in the meadow-wyne family," he affirmed after a moment. "But unusually diminutive— the flowers in particular... And the leaves are more finely-divided..."

Nagaro leaned closer as well. "Of what medicinal use are these meadow-wynes?" he asked.

Fineas shrugged. "None at all, most of them," he said. "Though there are two that do have mild sleep-inducing properties. They're quite different plants from *this* one, however. No, I can't imagine why any herb-seller would carry a sample of *this* plant—" He stopped, abruptly, raising his eyes to stare unseeingly through his spectacles. "*Unless...* unless it were *linjana...* but I wouldn't expect a medicine woman to have knowledge of that plant."

"Why? What's it good for?"

The lore master's eyes came back to focus on Nagaro. "By the strangest coincidence," he said, "linjana is another of the herbs that have been imbued with spirit magic. Unlike heskial, of which I've just told you, however, linjana is entirely benign. It has the power to heal a man's mind of all manner of ills— to restore it to the proper state from which it has become deranged. I've never actually seen a specimen of linjana, though I know it to be a variety of meadow-wyne that grows only in the mountains above a certain elevation. It's very difficult to cultivate. And very old, as well— the product of a lore long since forgotten. Kelorin folk brought it with them from the Isles of Kelor, long ago..."

Fineas was still speaking, but Nagaro was scarcely listening. "*Linjana,*" he murmured. "*The Spirit of the White Flower.*"

The lore master stopped, to stare at him, blinking behind his spectacles. "You *know* of this herb?" he asked in astonishment.

Nagaro hastily shook himself. "I... ah... someone told me, once, about the Spirit of the White Flower, that dwells in a plant with white flowers and has the power to heal minds... to cause a man to forget... or to remember. It sounds rather like linjana. Are they possibly the same?" He didn't think it wise to mention that it was Vothra who had told him. The Benevolent Spirit had re-gathered and was at work in the world once again, but even though Kelorin folk all across Edrovir were becoming aware of Vothra's return, *talking* to Vothra was not commonplace. He waited breathlessly for the lore master's answer.

"Not the *same*, exactly, no, Zirda." Finias was manifestly enjoying himself again. "The name *linjana* refers to the plant, or the medicine distilled from it. The *Spirit of the White Flower* refers to the spirit magic that gives the plant— or the medicine— its potency."

"I see." Nagaro sought to suppress his rising excitement. "And does it have something to do with forgetting? And remembering?"

"It can, Zirda. "The Spirit of the White Flower has power over memory. That is one of the ways linjana works its healing. There are others as well."

Nagaro's heart beat faster, but something puzzled him. "You said a Turowan medicine woman wouldn't be likely to know about linjana."

"I did, yes." Fineas looked thoughtful. "The medicine women are possessed of a very substantial knowledge of herb lore, mind you. They are unquestionably experts in the medicinal uses of the plants that grow naturally in the lands where they practice their art. But linjana doesn't *come* from Edrovir. It came from Kelor, as I said. The Kelorin folk brought it with them, and cultivated it in the mountains of Arlinas. It doesn't grow here in the lowlands where we're standing, but only on the mountain slopes. Irvenen Wared would be our only source of it now, since Arlinas lies under shadow. That is why I thought it unlikely a medicine woman of the lowlands would have knowledge of it."

"Ah." Nagaro nodded. The argument made sense. *How to explain the discrepancy?* "Might the medicine woman who gave me that herb have heard about linjana and gotten some from a Kelorin healer?" he asked. "She said it was for remembering."

Fineas pushed his spectacles up the bridge of his nose with a forefinger. "Well," he said, "If she thought it would simply improve a man's memory, she was mistaken. That isn't the use of it at all. Nor would *this* specimen be of any use to anyone." He gestured with the little leather book. "It's quite dried out. There's no virtue left in it." The lore master closed the little book and re-tied the ribbon.

"But you do think it's linjana?"

Fineas shrugged. "To be honest, I don't know. If you're willing to leave it with me for a time, I know some texts which I believe would resolve the issue."

"Thank you. I'd be pleased to have you do that, Master Fineas."

"Let me write down your name." Fineas rummaged under the counter for another little piece of paper.

Nagaro was wondering whether Luka had imagined that he might have gaps in his memory as a result of what had happened to him. She could easily have guessed that he'd been drugged— even if she didn't know what drug had been used. Her gift, then, would be well-intended, even if quite useless. Thinking, painfully, about having been drugged brought his mind around to another burning question, one that Vothra hadn't been able to answer. He swallowed and tried to keep the tension out of his voice. "Master Fineas, do you think linjana might be able to... to counter the effects of... heskial?"

The lore master had been in the act of dipping his pen, but he stopped to blink at Nagaro. "*By the Eyes!*" he murmured. "*There's* an interesting thought! Heskial and linjana, together in the blood of a single individual..." The lore master's gaze seemed to pass through Nagaro to focus on something beyond. "Two opposing kinds of spirit magic— one that subverts the normal mental process, one that seeks to restore it... What would happen? A battle, surely... *but which would win?* And what would the battle *do* to the mind of the unfortunate man within whose blood it was being waged?" Fineas' focus came back to Nagaro's face. "Truly, Zirda, I wouldn't wish to hazard such a thing. The struggle between the two would burn the brain. It might destroy the man's mind entirely."

"But if it were the only way to save the man's life—" Nagaro caught himself in sudden horror, realizing that Fineas had said nothing to suggest he was aware that heskial could be fatal.

Fineas peered at him. "Save the man's life? What do you mean, Zirda?"

Nagaro spread his hands. "I'm... not sure," he said desperately. "I thought I'd heard somewhere about a man's body becoming *accustomed* to a drug— if it were given over and over. And if the drug were then *withheld*..." He floundered to a halt, gesturing vaguely in the air.

Fineas stood for a moment, blinking at him, then suddenly brightened. "Ah! The habituation effect!" he exclaimed. "Some drugs are indeed like that, though I don't know whether heskial is one of them. Prolonged use of opa, for example, can quite consume a man, and linjana is very effective against that kind of habituation."

"I... see." This was intriguing information. It suggested that linjana might actually have been used to free him. *And as for burning the mind...* His thoughts shied away from that— and then he thought of Kale Fendred and the man's tragic affliction. "How broad is the power of linjana?" he asked. "Could it be used to cure madness?"

"Oh yes." Fineas sounded completely confident. "That was its most common use, historically. Habituating drugs weren't a common thing in ancient Kelor, you see." Fineas still held the pen. "If I might have your name, Zirda?"

"Yes, of course. In a moment, Master Fineas." *If he could find a way to help Kale...* "Do you think you could get me some linjana?"

"*Get you some?*" Fineas stared now, flustered. "I... ah... would be most happy to *try*, Zirda, but I fear... the *expense*... That is, I mean, it comes *very dear*."

"I'm prepared to pay a substantial amount. Whatever you ask, I'll get the money somehow."

Fineas continued to look uncomfortable. He nervously pushed his spectacles up the bridge of his nose, though they had shown no sign of slipping. "I'm afraid, Zirda, I must be very frank. The... ah... purchase of this establishment and its contents has rather depleted my funds. I've a wife and two children upstairs, Zirda, and all of my profit thus far has gone to their support. I'd be very happy to sell you anything in the shop, but as for acquiring any *new* stock, I am not really in a position, Zirda— if you understand me."

"Yes, I think I do." Nagaro appreciated the man's predicament, but this setback stalled him only for a moment. He reached for his purse. "I have five hundred rins, at the moment, that I can spare as an advance upon the purchase— to assist in defraying the cost of procurement." He withdrew five silver trokins from the purse and placed them on the counter-top. "If you find that more is needed, I'll get it for you as soon as I can."

The lore master gaped at him. After several seconds, he managed to close his mouth. "*Five hundred rins!*" he murmured. "Zirda! I couldn't possibly take so much— *in advance*— when I've no idea of the final price!"

"I don't see why you shouldn't," Nagaro observed reasonably. "How else am I to get my linjana?"

"But it could be *more*, or it could be very much *less*."

"In either case, we can easily resolve the matter of who owes what to whom, once the details become clear. I trust to your honesty entirely, Master Fineas, as a man of principle. And as I've said, if you need more, you have but to write to me. I think I should consider also some payment for the information you've given me," he added, thrusting his hand back into his purse.

"What? For *words?*" Fineas protested. "Zirda, I can't allow it!"

Nagaro calmly considered him. "As a lore master, surely knowledge is your stock in trade."

The little man gesticulated with the pen. "Perhaps, yes. But I'm not accustomed to being paid for it piecemeal!"

"Only because you are normally paid for it in wages, which I'm in no position to do. But I've already made use of your knowledge, which normally does not come free, and the information concerning linjana is worth more to me than you know. In all fairness, I think I should pay you for it."

At this, the lore master threw up his hands. "But I have no idea how much it would be fair to ask!"

Nagaro shrugged. "No more have I, but I still have ten rins in my purse, so that will have to suffice." He deposited the copper coins on the counter-top beside the silver ones.

Fineas shook his head, and once again pushed his spectacles up his nose. "Can I not persuade you to reconsider?"

"No, Zirda, you cannot."

The little man swallowed visibly. "In that case," he said faintly. "I'll just write down your name and address." He re-dipped the pen into the ink bottle.

"Certainly, Zirda. My name is Nagaro Nareyo, and I live at the Fleet Compound, number 14, Captain's Row."

The lore master's pen had scratched out the first few letters of this information before it came to halt as the little man looked up, peering at Nagaro with new interest. "*By the Eyes of Vothra's Mind*," he murmured. "You're Captain Nagaro!"

Nagaro heaved a sigh. "As it happens, I am."

Fineas blinked at him. "Well," he said after a moment. "I must say you're not very much what I expected. I confess I'm surprised to find a warrior, and a former pirate captain, to be so interested in herb lore. Still, your identity would explain some things, Captain. You have a great reputation for charity. This wouldn't happen, by any chance, to be pirate silver?" Here Fineas indicated the little stack of trokins.

Nagaro laughed. "It's part of a Fleet captain's wages, if you must know— which they tell me aren't as generous as they should be. I generally find them more than enough to meet my needs, however, and I'm still able to help someone now and then whose need is greater. In this case," he added somewhat sternly, "I don't mean it to be charity at all. I've received good service for the copper coins, and I expect to receive no less for the silver."

"Ah, yes. Of course, of course." Fineas hastily finished recording the information Nagaro had given him. He then rather nervously folded the paper around the little book containing the herb specimen. "I... ah... spoke rather freely, Captain, about the doings of my former employer— more freely than perhaps was wise in the circumstances— owing, I confess, to the freshness of the wrong I have suffered, and the extremity of my indignation. I hope I may count on you to keep what you've heard in confidence."

Nagaro had drawn his hood up to cover his head in preparation for making his departure, and he now reached for his parcel, which had lain on the counter all the while. "I won't swear to speak of it to no one," he said carefully. "This heskial, that you have told me of, sounds quite dangerous, and I might one day find it necessary to repeat some part of what I've heard here to prevent someone from coming to harm. I'd have you rest easy, though," he added, seeing the other man's worried look. "I've every intention of protecting you from hurt, and would avoid associating your name with it to the greatest extent possible."

Fineas nodded then. "Thank you, Captain," he said seriously. "I'm sure I can rely on your discretion." He began rather delicately to pick up the coins one by one from the counter.

Nagaro lingered still, a moment. "I hope I may also rely on yours," he said.

"Captain?" The little man gave him a startled look.

"I'd rather you didn't spread it about that we talked of linjana. And in dealing with any traders or suppliers, I'd rather you didn't mention my name."

"But why? There can be no harm in linjana—" Finias stopped, and a knowing look spread across his face. "You have a specific patient in mind, haven't you— to whom is owed some deference?"

Nagaro nodded. "The man is Leithian, and not of low estate. Leithian folk believe that madness is a curse visited upon men by their gods. His plight is therefore a closely guarded secret, and I would keep it so."

Fineas nodded decisively. "You need say no more, Captain. Let us exchange discretion for discretion. And I am pleased to have had the honor of making your acquaintance." He held out his hand.

Nagaro took it warmly. "You are well met, my friend," he said. "I'm always pleased to meet a man of principle."

***

There was still a light burning in window of Kuran's study when Nagaro reached the Fleet Compound. The clerk, Estevad, was in the act of leaving for the night when he arrived at the door, but the man took note of Nagaro's urgency and reversed course long enough to escort him to Kuran's office and announce him.

The Lord of the Fleet looked up from his desk, pen in hand. There was a sheet of paper half-filled with laboriously tidy writing in front of him and a stack of several pages filled with the same writing beside it. "Ah, Captain," he said, his face losing a little of its weariness. "To what do I owe the pleasure of this interruption?" He motioned for Nagaro to take a seat.

Nagaro drew a chair closer to the desk, sat down on it, and waited just long enough to hear the outer door close behind the departing clerk. "It concerns the matter of certain inquiries that you instructed me to make after we encountered the Jinari envoy on our way back from our meeting with Emperor Baalkir."

"Ah." Kuran put down his pen and leaned back in his chair. "I hadn't entirely forgotten about that, though I confess that the Kenthos affair had pushed it to the edge of my mind. I'm only just now writing the report of our mission to the Mahuk Baar." He paused to gesture at the paper on the desk in front of him. "I hadn't yet gotten to part that will describe our meeting with the Jinari envoy. Have you learned something already?"

Nagaro drew the notorious folded paper from his tirka and leaned forward to place it on one of the few unoccupied areas of the desktop. "Those are the drawings I was given by the Jinari merchant's agent Utabala, My Lord," he said. "I confess I now feel a bit of a fool to have assumed they must be merchant's marks."

Kuran picked up the paper, frowning slightly, and unfolded it. For a moment his face grew very still. Then he looked up to meet Nagaro's eyes, his dark brows constricting sharply. "You now know what they are?"

Nagaro nodded. "My source was more knowledgeable than I. And he also had an entire book of all the noble Houses of Edrovir."

Kuran's mouth tightened. He refolded the paper, then opened a drawer of his desk. He tucked the paper inside and closed it, frowning darkly all the while. His eyes came back to Nagaro. "Who exactly is this source?"

Nagaro swallowed. "You might know him, My Lord, since he was a Fleet warrior briefly, before the plague. His name is Simion."

This elicited a flickering frown. "I recall a Simion Rudrin. A well-meaning young man from a good merchant family, but ill-suited to the service. He took the Plague Amnesty, and I thought it for the best."

Nagaro nodded. "That would be him."

"How much does he know?"

Nagaro shifted uncomfortably in his chair. He was trying to think how he could explain this adequately to Kuran without being too explicit about Simion's private life— or touching on his own secret. "More than I'd like," he admitted cautiously. "Simion and I were slaves together—it's how we know each other— but I located him through Brandle—"

"*Brandle Furthing?*" Kuran's brows shot up. "Are those two still—"

"Yes," Nagaro put in quickly, glad that Kuran already knew of the relationship. "I had mentioned to Brandle that there was illegal trade involved, and... well... Simion has a sharp mind. He made accurate guesses. And then there wasn't much I could do except try to convince him that he shouldn't talk about it or go poking into it on his own."

Kuran's deepening frown relaxed only fractionally. "And you *did* convince him?"

"I hope so, My Lord. I explained that it was political, and potentially very dangerous— and that I'd be handing the matter over to you."

Kuran made a sour face. "Right," he growled. Then he shook his head and passed a hand over his face. "The Houses of Furthing, Sobring, and

Hurn," he murmured. "And we've got Brandle and his paramour mixed up in it."

Nagaro winced. "There's more," he said. "Simion told me that Madred Furthing's lore master had recently been sacked— by one of his ministers. Simion thought it was because the man had refused to obtain some specific item."

Kuran stared at him. "How on earth would Simion know *that?*"

Nagaro winced again. "Simion is living in the building Madred Furthing owns on Broad Street. He works as a book-keeper for Lord Madred."

"*By the bodgering Eyes of Vothra!*" Kuran cast his eyes to the ceiling, then brought them back to focus on Nagaro. "What a mess you've blundered into," he said, then sighed. "If only I'd decided to look at those marks myself."

"Or if only I hadn't assumed they must be merchants' marks." Nagaro put in.

Kuran shook his head. "But they *should* have been," he said. "I'd never have imagined that these lords— or their people— would use the *House seals* on these requisitions! It smacks of extreme brazenness— or complacency. How long have they been engaged in this trade?"

"From what I know, it's probably been going on for several years at least."

"Complacency then." Kuran fingered his well-trimmed beard. "Or perhaps there *are* merchants involved, who are wisely not putting their own marks on anything, for their own protection. But it still means that some highly-placed people within those three Houses are willing to set the House seal on lists of things to be purchased from Jinara. It shows that it's coming from the top of the House— or near the top— and that they either don't think they're doing anything wrong, or think they can get away with it."

For several seconds the two men sat in silence, Kuran gazing down unseeingly at the half-finished page in front of him on the desktop. Finally Nagaro said, "Of course, it's surely a coincidence that the lords of those three Houses happen to be the same Leithians who just raised armies to oppose the Kelorin Faction's claim that Kenthos was the long lost heir of Loros."

Kuran looked up to meet his eyes. "There's not likely to be any *direct* link between illicit trade that's been going on for years and the aspirations of a young blacksmith from Irvenen Wared," he said grimly. "But there could be a connection in the broader sense simply because those three men are all leaders among the Leithians who are determined to preserve the traditional beliefs and practices of their people. I've told you that Lothard Hurn and Grimbold Sobring are central figures among the Brothers of the Blood, who insist that breeding— that is, blood— is the only proper determinant of power, wealth, and privilege. And while Madred Furthing has always denied belonging to the Brothers, he's the tacit leader of the Leithian Faction, and he's clearly in close agreement with Grimbold and Lothard. The three of them obviously share counsel."

Nagaro nodded. "I... ah... understand that some of the Brothers of the Blood were involved in abducting my daughter, Narei, to force my return from exile. And Elgurn himself told me it was Lord Madred who secured her release. He also told me to keep that knowledge close."

Kuran gave him a look as much as to say, *you see?* He picked up his quill pen. "I'm going to have to decide how much of all this to put into my report," he said with a distinct lack of relish. "If there's nothing more to add, Captain, you may go. And I'm sure I don't need to impress upon you how sensitive this is."

Nagaro rose and took his leave, glad that Kuran hadn't asked more about the sacked lore master, sparing him from having to tiptoe around the contents of his discussion with Fineas. Kuran already knew, after all, that there was heskial involved. There was no need to repeat that information.

***

Later that evening, after dinner in the Fleet Compound's dining hall, Nagaro presented the new storybook to Pavo as he and his two friends enjoyed a pot of hot sothiril in the kitchen of his quarters on Captains' Row.

The young Hashtep gazed in admiration at the pen-and-ink illustration showing the Princess Minowei finding the injured and bedraggled Nevrath lying among the ferns on the bank of the River Edro. "Thank you, Nagaro! It is very beautiful book— and very good story! This will be very good for me to practice reading."

Nagaro smiled. "I thought that knowing the story would make it easier for you to figure out the words."

Taru was unpacking the carved playing pieces and game board for *Kasadrin*, or King's Men. "Did ye talk to Simion yet about the merchant's marks?" he asked.

"Yes." Nagaro quickly sketched what Simion had told him about the three little drawings on the piece of paper. Since Taru and Pavo had always known about his dealings with Utabala, he made no effort to withhold anything from them despite Kuran's request to keep the investigation secret. It was far too late to shut his two friends out now, and besides, he valued their counsel.

Taru frowned. "I don't understand, Nagaro," he said. "Wouldn't it be King Elgurn who'd be buying things for Dreigen? Not these Leithian lords?"

Nagaro rubbed the bridge of his nose. "I can easily imagine it happening either way," he said, "*if* the items were even being bought for Dreigen. As Simion pointed out, Dreigen isn't the only lore master in the world."

Pavo set his book aside. "You think maybe Lord Madred have bought poison and other bad thing, for his own lore master?"

Nagaro frowned. "Well, he wasn't buying any of it for the lore master who worked at the house on Broad Street. *That* man was let go for refusing to procure some... heskial. He's now keeping an apothecary shop across the street from the bookseller. I spoke with him, and he knew all about heskial and wanted nothing to do with it." Nagaro reached for his cup of sothiril, to moisten a suddenly dry throat.

Taru stared at him. "You *talked* to him about *heskial?*

Nagaro took a gulp of sothiril and put the cup down. "*He* talked. I listened, mostly. There *is* bad spirit magic in it— just as you always said, Taru. But that's not all we talked about." He proceeded to tell them what he'd learned from Master Fineas concerning the other plant— linjana— as well as about his plan to purchase some in the hopes of helping Kale Fendred.

Pavo spoke first when Nagaro paused. "Do you think you did not die from heskial, all those year ago, because someone have give you linjana?"

Nagaro swallowed. "I... yes, I think it's very possible."

Taru was instantly enthusiastic. "By Hakura Kili, it *has* t' be!" he declared. "Ye've found your Spirit o' the White Flower, Nagaro! The one that took away your memory, and gave it back again. There must have been linjana in the wine ye drank that night in the palace. But who d' ye think put it there?"

Nagaro toyed with the handle of his cup. He'd thought about this quite a bit since leaving Master Fineas' shop. "I don't know. It would have had to be someone who *knew* what was happening to me— or guessed — and wanted to help me. But the person would *also* have had to know about linjana, and I can't think of anyone who fits that description." He was more than a little in awe of the courage of this hypothetical unknown person, whoever it had been.

"Was it not princess who have give you wine?" Pavo asked.

"Yes." Nagaro sighed. "But she knew nothing about what was being done to me."

"And Dreigen knew, o' course, but he wouldn't ha' wanted to help ye," Taru put in.

Nagaro nodded. "Dreigen told Elgurn there was no cure that would help the Lady Maramine— or me. Though I wouldn't be surprised if he knew about linjana and was lying. His knowledge is much greater than his devotion to the truth."

"What about Kale?" Taru asked. "Could *he* have tried t' help ye?"

Nagaro frowned. "He might have wanted to, but I doubt he would have known about linjana, being Leithian. Linjana is a Kelorin herb— and very rare besides. Master Fineas said it grows only in Irvenen Wared, in the far north, and only Kelorin folk live there."

And that was more or less the end of the discussion, since they could shed no further light on the puzzle. They played several games of King's Men before Pavo carefully wrapped up the story book and he and Taru donned their cloaks and went out into a night that was ablaze with spring stars.

Nagaro banked the fire, put out the lamp, and went to his own bed. Lying in the still darkness, his thoughts turned to Kale. If Dreigen had visited the affliction of madness upon Elgurn's boyhood friend, what would have been his motive? It was widely believed that Kale's "death" had been revenge for the killing of Gillard Marchent, but if Dreigen was also responsible for the madness that had driven Gill to jump from the balcony — as Nagaro suspected— this made no sense.

Nagaro frowned in the darkness. Nevien beleived Dreigen had acted on his own against Gill, with her father's anger only an excuse to justify it. And Nagaro knew there had been no love lost between Dreigen and Gillard Marchent. If members of the Leithian faction had seen the king's hand in Gill's death, they might well have sought vengeance against Elgurn by striking someone close to him. Nevien had said that the mad Kale had been found *in his own house*, not in the palace. So perhaps it *had* been some other lore master who had inflicted Kale's madness— although Nagaro suspected that the distance didn't rule Dreigen out.

Nagaro heaved a sigh. He could no more solve this riddle than the riddle of the linjana, and he didn't wish to dwell upon the thought that there were other lore masters besides Dreigen plotting to use heskial. He tried instead to imagine how he could give Kale a dose of linjana— assuming that Master Fineas could obtain some. Kale was kept locked away, his existence a closely guarded secret. *And any such effort could well be thwarting the will of someone possessed of fearsome powers...*

Nagaro again pushed the unwelcome thoughts away. There was nothing he could do immediately about any of this. He resolved to devote himself to his Fleet duties in the days ahead and see what time might bring. After that, he slipped into easy slumber.

Chapter 3

Jila's Tale

As it happened, the following day brought an unexpected diversion. The men were just dispersing after their daily drill on the parade ground, and going to their lunch, when Nagaro was hailed by one of the guards who manned the entrance gate of the Fleet Compound.

"Captain Nagaro! Could ye come talk to this man? He says he has a packet for ye, and he'll give it to no one else!"

Nagaro exchanged questioning looks with Taru and Pavo, then shrugged and went to see what the guard was talking about, with his two friends in tow. Just outside the open gate, he found a large coach waiting, of the kind that regularly carried traffic between Edrovir's towns and cities. The horses were steaming in the salt-tinged air. The driver, a stocky middle-aged Turowan, had gotten down from his seat and was engaged in a loud discussion with the other gate guard.

This second guard, with arms akimbo, was saying, "It's a sad day when folk won't trust a Fleet man with a bit o' mail!"

"And I tell ye, that won't do!" The coachman brandished a large paper-wrapped packet. "The woman made me swear by all the Spirits that I wouldn't put this into any man's hands but the one whose name is on it!" He poked a finger at the front of the packet. "I can read, so I know it says 'Captain Nagaro of the Royal Fleet'. And she give me a description too, and ye don't match it, nor the other man, neither!"

Nagaro stepped up to the driver. "Good morning, Zirda," he said. "I am Captain Nagaro and I'd like very much to see the writing on that envelope." He extended his hand as the coach driver spun around to stare at him.

The coachman quickly regained his composure as he looked Nagaro up and down with a keen eye, taking in the captain's badge on the left shoulder of his uniform tirka. "Well, now," he drawled. "I'll be more than willing t' do that, *Captain*, seeing as how ye do fit the description I was given, hair for hair." And with that, he handed over the packet.

As Nagaro took it, he felt its unexpected weight and heard a muffled clink of metal as some of the contents shifted. He raised a startled eyebrow.

"Aye," the driver said in a low voice. "Ye can guess now, Captain, why I was afeared o' putting it into the wrong hands."

Nagaro nodded. "Yes I can, though you could have trusted these Fleet men—" he stopped as he noticed the writing on the packet. The words were written in elegant, precise strokes, and he immediately recognized the hand. "*Jila,*" he muttered under his breath. He felt Taru's startled movement at his side. It was, in fact, the last thing he had expected. With all that had been happening, he hadn't thought of Jila in many months, though he still very much wished to find her. He raised his eyes to the driver. "Where did you get this?" he asked.

"It was a woman what wrote it, Zirda. A Turowa— and a beauty, I might add, for all that she was confined t' her bed." The man spoke low for privacy's sake, though the two gate guards had by this time returned to their places and were too far away to overhear.

Nagaro frowned. "But where did you encounter her?" he asked urgently. "In what town?"

The man scratched his head. "Not in a town, Zirda. It was an inn on the old South Road. The *Leaping Stag.*"

"Would she be there still, do you think?"

The coachman nodded emphatically. "If she's still among the living, Captain, she would be. She was big with child, and she didn't look likely t' move from her bed. Called me right into her room, she did. She was propped up on a pillow and she wrote that out while I was lookin' on. I was surprised she had the strength t' do it, too. She looked that poorly."

Nagaro's frown deepened. "How long ago was this?"

"Five days, Captain."

"*Five days!* Would it take me so long as that to ride there?"

"We-ll... I had my stops t' make, Zirda. I think ye might do it in three or four."

Nagaro nodded impatiently. "All right," he said. "Can you tell me the way?"

"Aye, that's easy, Captain. Ye take the High Road out o' the east gate 'til ye get t' Stone Island. Cross the river there by way o' the bridge and follow the South Road 'til ye pass the mountain they call Kel Menuwin, on your right hand. It's a steep crag that ye can't miss, with a rocky crest like a broken crown on top. Ye'll see the inn soon after, at the turning that leads t' the town that goes by the same name as the mountain."

Nagaro quickly committed the details to memory and thanked the man, giving him a ten-rin piece for faithfully fulfilling his charge. Then he turned and headed back through the gate, going at a rapid pace and ignoring the curious stares of the guards as the coach pulled away with a jingle of harness. Taru and Pavo barely kept pace with him all the way to his quarters.

At his own doorstep, while digging in his pocket for the key, Nagaro finally became aware that his friends were waiting. He stopped, frowning, long enough to say, "You two should go to your lunch. I'll pack food to carry on the road."

"So ye mean t' try to find her?" Taru sounded worried.

"Yes," Nagaro answered grimly. "For Narei's sake. I only hope Kuran doesn't give me trouble over it. I'd hate to have to chose between this and my orders."

Taru gave him a look that said plainly what he thought of the idea, but seeing the expression on Nagaro's face, he said no more. Instead, he exchanged a significant look with Pavo, and the two of them moved off in the direction of the dining hall while Nagaro unlocked his door and entered his quarters.

Once inside, he tore the packet open and dumped the contents onto the table. As he'd expected, there was a quantity of coins, both silver and copper. There was also a folded letter addressed to him in Jila's unmistakable hand and bearing her name at the bottom. Smoothing it flat, he read:

Captain Nagaro,

I know you are one of Kuran's captains now, and your fame has grown so great that you are known all across the land instead of only in Pakoa. So you have grown more famous, and I less. No doubt it will surprise you to learn that I am now a respectable woman, married to a man of means, an innkeeper, who is honest and kind and who loves me very well. I expect you will not believe it when I tell you that I am content, and love him also, so much so that I have taken my courage in my hands to try to bear him a child, for he has none living and he is not young.

I am now close to my time, and it goes hard with me. At any day it may come and I will either be delivered of this burden or I will lay down my life in trying, and the Spirits alone know which it will be. But if I am to die, I do not wish to die in any man's debt, and yours least of all. So I will put into the packet with this letter an amount of money equal to all that ever I had from you. It is my own money that I have earned by my labor, and none of my husband's. So let this be an end between us.

—Jila

Nagaro stood for several long seconds staring at the page. It was hard to know how much to believe of what Jila had written. From what he knew of her, she hadn't been much devoted to the truth. The part about being with child, and not being well, matched the coachman's account. And the birthing of Narei had not been easy. For Jila's sake, he hoped the part about the husband was true as well. He counted the money and smiled in bitter satisfaction to find that the total came to exactly the sum of what he'd given her outright plus what she'd previously denied having stolen from him— after lying with him while he was drunk. That she had become honest enough to tacitly acknowledge having robbed him was encouraging— until he reflected that her honesty might only be brought on by fear of impending death. *Indeed, she might be dead already.*

He got to his feet and quickly counted out a few hundred rins from the money on the table for traveling money, which went into his purse. The remainder went into the cash box under his bed. From under the bed, he dragged out a pair of saddlebags and hurriedly packed clothes for his intended journey. He then changed from his dark blue uniform into a pair of black pants and a dark gray tirka. He re-buckled his sword belt about his hips, thinking he might meet trouble on the road. Then he took his cloak, locked his door, and set off for Kuran's quarters with long strides.

Kuran looked up from his desk, startled, when Nagaro burst in, out of uniform and with his saddlebags slung across his shoulder.

Nagaro wasted no time. "My Lord," he said, "I need to go on a journey of perhaps a week's duration— and I ask your indulgence. I've just received a letter." He brandished the much-lightened packet as illustration. "I wish to speak to the woman who wrote it, since she could possibly die in childbirth and I would regret it the rest of my days if I had no last chance to talk to her."

Kuran regarded him narrowly. "It appears you mean to go no matter what I say," he remarked dryly. "But I'd prefer to better understand the reason. Who is this woman, and what is she to you?"

Nagaro drew a long breath. "She is my daughter's mother, My Lord," he said. "Her name is Jila."

Kuran steepled his fingers. "Well, I've seen your daughter," he said. "And I've heard the story of her begetting— as it's told in Pakoa Town. I have to say that I found some of the details hard to credit."

Nagaro didn't flinch. "My daughter was gotten out of wedlock, My Lord, because I very stupidly made myself drunk enough to lie with a woman I knew nothing about. I'm not proud of what I did, but I love my daughter dearly, as you know. For her sake, I would make peace with this woman. We did not part on good terms."

"Ah." Kuran un-steepled his fingers and picked up of his quill, toying with it. "It does you credit that you acknowledge this," he said quietly. "I got a girl with child once, long ago, when I was still in my teens. I would have married her, but her parents thought her too young to wed. They sent her away instead, and I never saw her again. Two years later I was told that she'd died in the birthing, and the child— a boy— died soon after. I've never quite shaken the sense that I killed that poor girl, and that my firstborn son was taken as well, to punish me."

Nagaro was gazing, stricken, at the Lord of the Fleet. "My Lord," he murmured, "I'm sorry. I had no idea."

Kuran leaned forward and laid the quill back down on the desk top. "Of course not," he said. "It was hushed up. I don't normally speak of it, and I'm the more impressed by what you're willing to confess. I'm also reminded of how it still grieves me that I had no chance to say goodbye to Rian— that was her name— or hear from her lips that she didn't blame me. That's why I'm inclined to grant your request." He paused, shaking off his dark mood. "Since there's nothing that I can't spare you from for a few days, you have leave to go. Just return as quickly as you can."

Nagaro saluted. "I will, My Lord, and thank you. May I have the use of Thunder-Heels?"

Kuran smiled wanly. "You might as well, since no one else can ride him," he said, then added with a wink. "And have a care of this woman, Captain. I hear she is a notorious temptress."

Nagaro's brows came together. "That may have been true when I knew her," he said. "Her letter says she's married now."

Kuran raised an eyebrow. "In that case, have a care of the husband."

***

Nagaro stopped at the dining hall to load some food into his empty saddle bag and to tell Taru and Pavo that he'd been given leave to go and was leaving immediately. His friends exchanged more looks, but knew better than to argue with him. At the stable he filled a flask with water and a bag with oats from the feed bin, before putting saddle and bridle to Thunder-Heels.

Shortly thereafter, he rode out through the front gate of the Fleet Compound, turning east to ride along the Circle Road where it ran between the city wall and the river, and continuing east onto the High Road at the crossroads in front of the city's east gate. He had to keep Thunder-Heels to a walk as he threaded his way through the normal traffic of farmers and traders who were traveling either afoot or with carts or pack horses. He made fast progress, even at a walk, on the long-legged gray, passing through autumn countryside with the rain-swollen River Edro on his right hand, until he reached Stone Island. There he turned south onto the road that crossed the river by means of the huge bridge, built of hewn stone, that arched in a long span from the northern bank to the stony outcropping of Stone Island in mid-river, and from there to the southern bank in a second span.

Some distance along the South Road, he stopped to sit on a stone wall and eat a lunch of bread and smoked meat while Thunder-Heels grazed. As he was preparing to ride on, he heard a mutter of distant thunder. "Well now, brother of the wind," he observed, speaking aloud to the stallion, "it seems we may expect bad weather. I hope you've rested well, for I fear I will ride you hard these next few days."

He pressed the stallion for speed after that, but by the end of an hour a towering thunder-head filled the western sky and the other travelers on the road had grown few and were glancing west with anxious faces. A mile further on, the rain began, and within minutes became a drenching downpour. Nagaro rode blindly on, bent low over his horse's neck with his hood dripping water, pressing Thunder-Heels as hard as he dared into the deepening gloom. Twilight came early under the storm-dark sky and they would have fared even worse if not for the lightning that came, along with deafening thunder, to give sudden startling views of the road ahead. Nagaro was cold, wet, and weary by the time the lights of a village inn appeared dimly ahead to show the way to a warm bed for him and a dry stall for Thunder-Heels.

That first night was the worst for weather, but not by much. The rain continued intermittently the next tday and was sometimes heavy, slowing his pace. There were two such days and two nights, one spent in an inn and one in a farmer's barn. After that he began to seriously look for the mountain named Kel Menuwin.

In the middle of that gloomy, drizzly fourth day, he at last caught a brief glimpse of it when the clouds parted above the trees long enough to reveal the looming crag with the unmistakable crown of jagged rocks on its crest. Half a mile farther on, Nagaro drew rein in front of a building with the image of a leaping stag on a large wooden sign hanging from a beam above the solid oak door. He swung stiffly from his horse and tied the weary stallion to the hitching rail beside three other horses, all standing dispiritedly with their heads down. He was surprised to see the other beasts. It had been a lonely stretch of road. The presence of the horses in front of the inn meant either that their owners were just passing through or else that they'd arrived so recently that their mounts hadn't yet been taken to the stable.

The inn was a substantial building, with two stories at the front and an arched opening beside the door that lead into a stable yard. Though he didn't intend to stay long, himself, Nagaro did mean to see that Thunder-Heels had at least a few hours in a dry place to rest and be fed. First, however, he needed to enter the building by the front door and announce himself to the innkeeper—Jila's presumptive husband. He squared his shoulders.

The door swung open to his hand and he stepped into a small entry hall, closing the door again behind him to keep out the weather. He paused to savor the warm air and the complete absence of dampness and dripping water, not to mention the lingering aromas of baking bread, spices, and roast meat. The entry hall was empty at the moment. There was a counter directly in front of the door with a needlework image of a stag on the wall above it, but no one behind it. Nor was anyone immediately visible through the open doorway to his left that apparently led into the inn's common room. Nagaro was just about to call out when he heard a man's voice speaking from the adjoining room. The voice was unpleasant and grating, and it carried an obvious threat.

"Come now, Thenden. We knows ye can spare us a bag o' silver. Ye just go into yer back room, there, an' fetch it while we keep an eye on these two here, t' see that there's no tricks. Then we'll be on our way, and no harm to anyone."

"And I tell ye again, ye'll get nothing, Baku! Now be off with ye!"

The second voice was deeper than the first, resolute on the surface, though with an undercurrent of tension. Nagaro's brows descended sharply. *The inn was being robbed!* Feeling intensely glad that he'd made no sound to announce his presence, he stealthily approached the open common room doorway, stopping just outside as he got a view of the space beyond.

It was a large room, with stone walls, a wood plank floor, and a raftered ceiling. Several long tables looked as if they'd been hastily thrust aside. Nagaro could see six men. The three closest were only a dozen feet from the doorway, with their backs to him. They were rough-looking Turowan men with damp traveling cloaks still on their shoulders. At least the nearest one held a long naked knife in his hand, and the postures of all three were menacing. One of them presumably was Baku.

Three more men stood beyond the intruders, facing them defensively from behind one of the tables. Two were Kelorin and Nagaro guessed the one standing front and center must be Thenden, the man who'd just spoken. He was of middle years, gray at the temples and a bit thick in the waist, but not ill-favored. Anger smoldered in his eyes and there was a set to his jaw, not to mention a heavy iron poker clenched in his fist. He was flanked by two others, one a much older Kelorin, very gray and a little bent, but with an expression no less defiant as he brandished a heavy wine bottle. The third was a weedy Turowan youth— little more than a boy— armed only with a broom and looking quite terrified. The attention of all three of the inn's defenders was focused on the intruders. None of the men had noticed Nagaro's arrival.

Nagaro took only an instant to assess the scene. Then he stepped through the doorway before the robber chief could respond to the innkeeper's defiance. He was careful to keep his cloak around him to conceal his sword. "Well met, friend Thenden," he said, trying for a jovial tone. "I'm Captain Nagaro, as you see, and I have traveled far seeking this house. But who are these men with knives in their hands?"

The men all started at the sound of Nagaro's voice, as well as the mention of his name. The old man with the wine bottle lowered his arm, gawking. The youth nearly dropped his broom. The man named Thenden didn't relax his grip on the poker, nor alter his stance, but his eyes widened in astonishment. He recovered quickly, however.

"They are thieves, Captain!" he cried. "They've come to rob us! That's Bloody-Hand Baku, there." The innkeeper gestured at the man in the middle. "He's a murderer *and* a thief! Ye must help us be rid o' them!"

The three thieves immediately shifted positions so that they could brandish their knives simultaneously at the innkeeper and at Nagaro, who stood between them and the door. The middle man of the three, Bloody-Hand Baku, was older than his fellows, in his thirties. He was heavier and broader in the shoulders, with an ugly scar along his jaw, and he was clearly the leader, judging by the way the younger two men glanced at him as if seeking direction.

Baku fixed Nagaro with a challenging stare. "*Captain Nagaro*," he mimicked, disparagingly. "*If* that's who ye are. What would ye be doin' so far from the sea, I'd like t' know?"

Nagaro stood his ground, doing his best to appear indifferent to the ten-inch knives the ruffians were holding. "That," he said coolly, "is my affair." Behind his studied calm, he was weighing his options. While he might be able to disarm the thieves, he couldn't single-handedly subdue them all, and he was uncertain how much help to expect from the innkeeper and his two unimposing employees. Alternatively, he could probably chase the ruffians off, or he might be able to kill them, but he had only the innkeeper's word concerning the murder charge against Baku. He heaved an inward sigh. *Perhaps they would decide their own fates.*

He twitched the cloak from his left shoulder, exposing the sword that hung at his hip. The light of the room's oil lamps glinted on the weapon's gold-inlayed hand guard and kindled a green spark in the heart of the smooth stone in the pommel. "It seems that you and your men aren't welcome here," he said, "I suggest you depart."

Baku made no move to go, and his eyes narrowed as he took in the sword along with Nagaro's wet and travel-stained attire. "*If* ye're Captain Nagaro," he sneered, "then ye're a pirate, and who are ye to be tellin' us t' be off when ye're a thief yerself!"

Nagaro heaved another silent sigh. The man apparently knew his name but had heard no description of him or of his distinctive weapon. *So much for his reputation.* It seemed that a demonstration would be needed. He smiled his best pirate smile—a flash of teeth in his black beard. "If you knew anything about me," he said with deadly calm, "you'd know better than to say that. And you'd also know that I don't kill men without a good reason. I suggest that you don't give me one. You know the way to the door." He moved a bit to one side, gesturing for the men to pass and make their exit.

Baku and his two henchmen exchanged glances. One of the two muttered something under his breath. Baku gave the man the very slightest nod before returning his attention to Nagaro.

"*Well, now...*" he drawled, lowering his knife a little, but not sheathing it. "Perhaps we will, at that. We was just goin' anyway. But ye'll excuse me an' the lads if we keeps our knives ready. That's a nasty long sword ye've got there."

The three thieves began to move, circling around Nagaro as if to pass him, still with their knives in their hands and their eyes firmly fixed on him. Nagaro stood ready, turning only enough to follow the movement of the men and keep Baku directly in front of him. He had very nearly turned so that his back was to the innkeeper before Baku made a very slight movement of his head, and all three men charged him at once.

The events that followed were over in a matter of seconds.

Quick as thought, Nagaro drew his sword as he dodged the young thief on his left. He struck the knife from the hand of the one on his right with the flat of his blade, then brought it around, level with their leader's chest. Baku tried to check his charge, but the effort came too late. His momentum carried him onto the point of the sword and Nagaro had only to lean into it to pierce the villain's heart. Bloody-Hand Baku fell dead at the feet of his intended victim with his knife underneath him.

Nagaro yanked his sword free and spun to face the young thief he had dodged, who was gazing in frozen horror at the body of his fallen leader. With a ringing blow of his sword, Nagaro struck the man's knife from his hand and sent it skidding across the floor among the tables. "I believe," he said coldly, "that you and your friend were on the *point* of leaving." He drew a little circle in the air in front of the man's face with the tip of his bloodied sword for emphasis.

The young ruffian gave Nagaro a terrified look and bolted for the door, nearly colliding with his comrade who was frantically doing the same.

"Look to your horse, Zirda!" cried Thenden. "They're horse thieves as well!"

The fleeing men must have left the outer door open in their haste, for those inside all plainly heard an angry neigh, followed by a human cry of pain and a string of curses. One of the men shouted, "Leave the bloody brute!" and seconds later there came the sound of receding hoof beats.

Nagaro turned to the innkeeper. "It appears," he said grimly, "that my horse can look after himself."

The innkeeper and his two employees had stepped from behind the table and all three of them now approached Nagaro. The old man jauntily wagged his wine bottle. "Oy, Zirda!" he exclaimed, grinning. "That were a pretty piece o' work!"

The boy poked at the body on the floor with his broom. "Were ye *hoping'* that they'd go for ye, Zirda?" he asked.

Nagaro let his breath out. "No," he said. "I was hoping they'd be sensible."

Thenden gave him a shrewd glance. "So ye are indeed Captain Nagaro? I confess I wasn't sure, but I can well believe it after seeing how ye dispatched those scum."

Nagaro stooped to wipe his sword on the dead man's tirka, then straightened and returned the blade to its scabbard. "I regret spilling blood in your common room," he said soberly. "And I hope you are sure about that murder charge."

Thenden dismissed Nagaro's concern with a wave of his hand. "Baku wasn't called 'Bloody-Hand' for nothing, Captain," he said. "He's slain three men just in these parts— *with* witnesses— and he would ha' slain ye too, if he could have. I sent my stable boy to fetch the town watch as soon as I saw him and his louts ride up. I thought I could hold them in talk 'til the watch got here." He shook his head ruefully. "I'll admit I was doubting the wisdom o' that plan. It might ha' gone ill with us if ye hadn't come when ye did. I would at the very least have had t' give them the silver they wanted."

Nagaro was frowning. "What about the two I let go?"

Thenden shook his head. "They're local lads that Baku must have lured in with promises o' riches— too new to the game to have blood on their hands. I hope they'll now go back to honest work. We're all well rid o' Baku, and the watchmen will be glad to carry his corpse away." Thenden turned and addressed the older man. "Ye'd best fetch some sacking, Orlad, to cover him up so we don't have t' look at him— then a bucket t' mop the floor. And gather those knives for the watchmen, as well." He turned to the boy. "Nilo, would ye please take care o' this gentleman's horse."

The youth looked worried. "Will he kick, Zirda?" he asked Nagaro. "Or bite?"

Nagaro smiled. "Not if you handle him gently and speak to him respectfully. He goes by 'Thunder,' and fancies himself the brother of the wind."

Once the other two had gone about their tasks, Thenden asked whether Nagaro meant to dine before continuing on his way, or whether he wanted lodgings for the night.

Nagaro hesitated, wondering how best to explain his purpose. "My business is here," he said at last. "And I expect it will be brief, though I'd be glad to purchase provisions for my journey back to Lankura."

Thenden looked surprised. "Your business is *here?* Do ye mean in the town?"

"I mean under this roof, unless I have been misled." Nagaro shifted his feet. "Is there a place where we might speak more privately?"

Thenden looked somewhat dismayed at this, but said, "This way, Zirda," and led Nagaro through a doorway, across a hall, and into a small room used for bookkeeping. There the innkeeper pulled one chair away from a desk that stood against a wall, and another from a long table under the room's window. He motioned for Nagaro to sit on one, and seated himself on the other with an air of puzzled expectation.

Nagaro sat down and cleared his throat. "I have a request to make of you," he began.

Thenden spread his hands. "I'm in your debt, Captain. Ye've but to name your desire."

But Nagaro shook his head. "I won't hold you to that when you haven't heard what I'm going to ask." He paused, searching for the right words. "The matter is somewhat delicate," he said at length. "You are the keeper of this inn?"

Thenden nodded.

"And you have a wife named Jila?"

Now Thenden sat up straight in his chair, his expression guarded. "I have," he said, "though I wonder how ye come to know it."

Nagaro drew the flattened packet from his tirka. "I know it by virtue of this letter that she sent to me, and I've ridden in haste from Lankura to speak with her privately, if you will permit it."

The innkeeper frowned. "My wife has but yester-eve delivered a child— my son— and I wouldn't willingly disturb her rest," he said severely. "At the very least, I'd want to know more about your purpose."

Nagaro ran a hand through his hair. He was relieved to learn that Jila had safely delivered her child, though much of his anxiety on that score had already been eased by Thenden's demeanor. The innkeeper didn't look like a man who had just lost his wife or felt in immediate danger of losing her. "I assure you that I mean no harm to her or to you," he ventured. "You may read the letter, if you wish, as far as I'm concerned. Though I suppose you should ask her first."

The innkeeper continued to give him a hard look. "I trust my wife enough that I needn't be reading her letters," he said stiffly. "I assume that ye two must be known to each other, having both dwelt on Pakoa Island. But since she's said no word to me of your coming, I think it's for ye to explain yourself."

Nagaro sighed. "I hope you won't think me rude if I ask how much Jila has told you of her history," he said, and he saw the muscles of Thenden's jaw tighten.

The innkeeper looked him squarely in the eye. "I know what she's been," he said. "But that's all in the past, and the Writings say we're to give a man— or a woman— grace to make a change for the better."

Nagaro smiled fleetingly. "I can't argue with that," he said. "But I wonder if she's told you that she has a daughter— named Narei?"

"She mentioned it." Suspicion was dawning in Thenden's eyes.

Nagaro plunged ahead. "Narei is my daughter as well," he said simply. "We parted on rather ill terms, and for my daughter's sake I'd like to mend the rift if I can."

Thenden's eyes widened in astonishment. "This isn't what I expected, Captain," he said. "And I'll not pry into your affairs to ask ye how it came t' be. Ye've something of a reputation as a man of high character, so I beg your pardon when I say that Jila described the father of her daughter somewhat... *differently*."

Nagaro sighed. "As I said, we parted on ill terms. I was very angry with her, and if she's unwilling to see me, I must accept it. But I hope that you will at least tell her that I'm here, and that I wish to speak to her."

Thenden rose. "That much I'll do," he said soberly, and made for the door.

***

A short time later, Nagaro found himself outside the door of Jila's bedchamber. Thenden had left him at the landing, halfway up the stairs, after first requesting that he say nothing about Baku and his henchmen. The innkeeper had then gone back downstairs, though Nagaro suspected the man had not gone far. Thenden didn't seem the sort to eavesdrop but he was very protective of his wife.

The bedroom door wasn't closed, but Nagaro paused to knock on the doorframe. A voice that he recognized— throaty and low— answered, bidding him enter. As he started forward, a girl of about fourteen with a sleeping infant in her arms appeared in front of him. The girl gave him a shy, wide-eyed look as she slipped past him into the hallway with her precious burden. Beyond her, Nagaro had a view of a large, comfortably furnished room. The bed stood with its head against the farther wall, beside a window that let in the gray light of the cloud-shrouded day. A lamp burned on a nearby table, making a warmer glow.

Jila was in the bed, propped up with pillows to a sitting position. There was a little hollowness to her cheeks, and shadows under her eyes, but otherwise she was much as he remembered her— still beautiful, with her cascade of dark hair, cherry lips, and wide, deep, brown eyes in a heart-shaped face. He stepped into the room, leaving the door open as he'd found it, both for Thenden's reassurance and for the sake of ventilation. The room still smelled of the birthing, the cleansing scents of lavender and sage not quite masking the odors of sweat and blood.

Jila's eyes had settled on him as he entered and remained fixed on his face as he crossed the room and came to a halt a discreet distance from the bed. He hesitated there, searching for words.

Jila didn't give him time to find them. "Well, Captain Nagaro," she said tartly, "I didn't mean for you to find me— since ye said ye wished never to set eyes on me again. But seeing that you've come of your own choosing, at least I can't be blamed for it. I don't know *why* you've come, though. I've only done as ye commanded. I've made no trouble for any man— or do you begrudge me having married?"

Nagaro shook his head. "I haven't come to judge you, Jila," he said. "And I don't begrudge you anything that you've honestly undertaken. If your marriage is as you described it in your letter, I am glad of it."

She eyed him skeptically. "Is it the money then? Was that coachman less honest than he looked?"

"The coachman was both honest and diligent, but the money isn't important. I've come because there can never be an end between us, Jila, as long as there's a child between us."

Jila's face became guarded. "I left the child with Ani, not with you!"

Nagaro sighed. "She lives with Ani still, but I visit her as often as I can, since I love her dearly. Narei is a precious gift. One for which I never thanked you."

"*Thanked me?*" Jila's eyes were wide now. "I thought it was plain ye didn't want her!"

"I thought I didn't," he admitted. "But it was really *you* I wanted no part of. I was angry about the way you used me. And, though I still say that you used me, I think I understand things better. And I'm not angry anymore."

At this, Jila put her head on one side, speculatively. "Tell me what ye think ye understand."

Nagaro met her probing gaze with a direct one of his own. "I believe you thought that all men are alike," he said. "And that if a man had his pleasure with you, he wouldn't care if there was a child— especially if he didn't need to be bothered with it. And if all men thought that way... well, then why shouldn't you do as you did with me? And what would it matter if I were drunk or sober?"

She was studying him now. "Are you saying that you're not like other men?"

He shook his head. "There are many different kinds of men," he said. "But I was raised to follow the teachings of Vothra, which say that a man shouldn't lie with a woman he doesn't intend to marry— exactly because there could be a child who would suffer as a result. When you took advantage of finding me drunk, you led me to do something I believed was wrong— something I wouldn't have done if I were sober. And when you pretended to fancy me, and didn't tell me that you meant to get a child from me..."

He let the words hang.

Jila's brow had furrowed into a frown as she listened. Her dark eyes were luminous when she spoke into the silence. "I did wrong," she said. And she gave him a look that was so open and devoid of guile that he was reminded of her sister, Animara. "Do you remember what ye said to me when I brought ye the child?" she asked. "You said you hoped that I would come to know I had done wrong before I died. I always *did* know that I used you. But it is as ye said. I didn't think it was wrong. Why shouldn't a woman use a man, after all, if men use women?"

She paused and reached for a cup that stood on her bedside table. She drank a little from it and set it down again. Turning her eyes back to him, she sighed. "That's how I used to think," she said. "But I've come to see that there are good men in the world. Thenden is one of them, and I see that ye're another."

Nagaro made her a small bow. "Thenden does indeed seem to be a good man," he said, "And I think that, in marrying you, he hasn't gotten less than he deserves."

She gave him a wan smile. "Would ye like to hear how I came to marry him?"

"I confess that I'm curious."

She drew a long breath. "It takes a little time to tell," she said. "You know, of course, how I came by ship to the city of Kel Tierna, in the company of Mendorel the candlemaker." She stopped, and smiled wryly. "You made that possible. And I never thanked you for it because I thought you only wanted to be rid of me. I told myself that what ye said about everyone deserving a chance to be happy was just words."

Nagaro shrugged. "I *did* want to be rid of you— because I was angry. But I could also see how desperate you were to leave Pakoa. I confess that I hoped you might find a different path in a different place."

She laughed, a low, musical ripple of sound. "It happened almost that way," she said, "but let me tell it." She paused for another swallow of water, then took up her narrative.

"I passed the winter at an inn, earning my keep by helping with the cooking." She laughed again at the look he gave her. "Yes, I do know how to cook. Mama taught both Ani and me. I kept myself out of trouble, too. I was afraid you might come after me, just for spite. It got easier, though— not having men— the longer I kept to it, and by the spring I was thinking that I could do very well without any man at all."

She sighed. "But I still wanted to travel and see the world, so when the traveling players came—"

Nagaro nodded. "I heard you'd taken up with a band of players."

Jila gave him a startled look. "Did you? I thought ye'd likely forgotten all about me by that time." She shifted her position on the pillows. "The players stayed at the inn," she continued. "And I went to watch them. I envied the way they went about the country, and acting out tales seemed an easy way to make one's way in the world. So when I heard that they needed someone to cook and to sew their costumes, I told the leader of the troop I wanted the job. He already knew I could cook, and when I told him that I made all my own clothes, he hired me."

Here she stopped again in response to the look on his face. "You don't believe I can sew," she said accusingly. "But Mama taught me that as well as cooking, and I'm very good at it!"

Nagaro immediately shook his head. "No," he said, "I was remembering what you were wearing the night I first saw you. It was, ah… very flattering."

"*Flattering?*" She put her head on one side. "You're saying that I needed flattering?"

He felt himself blushing. "I, no… I meant—"

Her laughter rippled again. "Ye meant it for a compliment, so I'll take it for one. But I pity any woman you ever try courting, Captain. Ye've no notion of how to flatter a woman, do ye?"

Nagaro frowned. "I've never really tried."

Jila crooked a perfectly arched eyebrow. "Because you haven't found a woman that ye fancy?"

Nagaro felt a wrenching pang, and he paused uncomfortably. He had no intention of laying himself bare to Jila. "I meant that I prefer the truth," he said a little stiffly. "And if I admired a woman a great deal, I think she might find the truth flattering enough."

She considered him. "Well, I suppose if she admired *you* enough, she might at that," she said after a moment. "But, let me finish my tale."

She took another sip of water, and continued. "The leader of the troop was long past his lusty youth," she said. "But there were other men in the troop whose heads turned my way. One or two tried to woo me, but I had decided I didn't need a man, so I turned them away." She sighed. "I stayed with the players for three years, without having a man. I traveled up and down the whole length of the South Road. I did some acting too, and I was good at it. It was a good life."

Jila stopped speaking, gazing unseeingly before her, her thoughts far away. Presently she sighed again, and shook herself out of her reverie. "I expect I would be doing that still, if I hadn't taken sick," she said. "We were on our way south one autumn, and we stopped at this inn just as my illness was coming on. I've never been so sick in my life. The troop stayed as long as they could, but in the end they had to move on without me. They left some money with Thenden for my lodging and for the healer, but I think it probably ran out long before I came to the end of my need."

Jila paused again, toying with the bedclothes, running a finger along the stitching on the quilt. "Thenden took care of me when the healer couldn't be here," she said. "At first I'm sure that he was just showing me the hospitality of the house. But by the time I was feeling well enough to notice, I could see by the way he looked at me that it was more than that. Still, he waited 'til I was almost completely well before proposing marriage." Jila raised her eyes to meet Nagaro's.

"I didn't know what to do," she continued. "I had no wish to marry, and I still wanted to rejoin the players. I tried to put him off by telling him things I thought would change his mind. In the end I told him every wicked thing I'd ever done, and *still* it made no difference! He said I had plainly changed my ways, so none of it mattered."

Jila reached for her water cup and held it before her eyes as if it were an object of great fascination. "I thought he was the greatest fool I'd ever met," she said quietly. "I told him so, and he forgave me for that as well." She took a drink of water, but still kept the cup in her hands, though now she met Nagaro's eyes. "By this time, winter had come, and it was too late for me to find my players before spring. So I set to work in the kitchen to earn my keep. All winter long Thenden kept asking me to marry him. I must have said no a score of times." She let out her breath and set the cup back on the bedside table, then turned to face him again. "I don't really know what happened," she said. "But somehow, by the time spring came, something had changed inside of me. One day, when he asked me, I said yes. And I meant it, too. Isn't that strange?"

Nagaro had listened with more sympathy than he dared to show. He thought he knew exactly how such a thing could have happened, and a part of him envied Jila her happiness. What he said was, "No, I don't think it's strange. I'm glad for you— and for Thenden."

She stared at him for a long moment as if trying to decide whether he were entirely sincere. "Tell me about Narei," she said at last. "How is she growing, and what is she like?"

And now Nagaro smiled. "She's growing very well. She's clever, and pretty, bold as brass, and quite fearless."

Jila laughed. "That sounds like me when I was a girl."

"If all goes well, I mean to bring her to Lankura in a year or two. After that, I'd like to bring her here to meet you, if you're willing and your husband will allow it."

Jila nodded. "I'd like that," she said. "And I'm sure Thenden won't mind." Her expression turned rueful. "This is better than I deserve. I'm ashamed that I gave her up so easily. I know I have no right to claim her now, and it's only right that she's more your child than mine. But how did you come to change your mind about her?"

Nagaro smiled again, more wryly. "Animara sent for me when she found that you'd taken the money I meant for Narei. And I went because I meant to see the child was provided for. When I got there, Ani told me I was a member of her family and insisted I stay for dinner. She told me your family's story, too— how much your mother loved your father, and how he stopped coming back to her. Then Tavo and Pilo called me uncle, and Bahiri put the baby into my arms, and... what could I do? I'd never had a family before— at least not one I was joined to by blood."

Jila's laughter rippled yet again. "Is that all it took to win you?" she asked, shaking her head. "It does sound like Ani, too. I must write to her— now that I know how things stand—" She stopped abruptly, tensing and turning an ear towards the door, listening. "I heard the baby cry," she said. "And the girl will be bringing him back to me. It's time for you to go."

At the door he paused and made Jila a bow that brought a smile to her lips and an arch to her eyebrow. He bade her farewell then, and hastily made his exit, passing the girl coming in with the baby in her arms. He glanced back in time to see the infant settled at his mother's breast and to witness the expression of contentment that stole across Jila's face.

∗∗∗

Below in the common room, Nagaro found that the watchmen from the village had removed the corpse and were waiting to shake his hand and present him with a purse containing three hundred rins— the reward for bringing down Bloody-Hand Baku.

Nagaro didn't like taking money for killing a man, so he presented the money to Thenden as a gift for his newborn son. "After all," he pointed out. "It's only fitting I should give your child a gift, since I'm a sort of half-uncle."

Thenden frowned at first, then laughed. "Well, why not," he said. "Ye can indeed claim to be a relation, and my son will have a story to tell to his own children."

After that, Nagaro availed himself of water to wash, then purchased a hearty lunch. He ate it in the common room, after which he bought supplies for his return journey, reclaimed Thunder-Heels, and set off just as the rain began again. The road home was likely to be wet and cold, but at least he went with a lighter heart, having written a new ending to a chapter of his life that had long troubled him.

Three days later, he rode into the Fleet Compound under a clear blue sky with a crisp breeze off of the sea blowing into his face. He found Kuran leaning on the rail at the edge of the practice field, watching the new recruits.

The Lord of the Fleet turned at Nagaro's hail, and looked him up and down. "I see you're still in one piece," he said. "Though I'm wondering if the woman and her husband fared as well."

"I found the woman changed for the better," Nagaro replied. "And the husband was a very reasonable man."

"Ah. Good. You encountered no other difficulties?"

Nagaro shrugged. "There was an altercation involving some thieves, at the inn, and the weather was wretchedly wet— until last night— but that is all."

Kuran smiled. "In that case, all is well that ends so. And you'll be glad to know that the princess has arranged an outing to River House, to which you are, of course, invited. It's set for this week's end— in four days' time."

Nagaro's heart leaped at the thought of having a chance to talk to Nevien. It leaped, but then it plunged, as he remembered how distressed she was— the anguish in her voice that day in the palace, outside the Compass Room, when she had told him of her father's plan to let the courtships begin again— *with the pain of the queen's death still an open, gaping wound.* The king apparently believed that the country would benefit from the distraction provided by the ritualized dance of the suitors— the parade of men vying for the chance to wed Edrovir's princess, and perhaps one day, also, to rule the kingdom.

Nagaro managed to give Kuran some innocuous response and hastily turned away, hiding his own pain. None of Nevien's suitors were, so far as he knew, motivated by love. *And as a commoner of unknown parentage, his own feelings were entirely irrelevant.*

Chapter 4

Clues

Nagaro stood in front of one of the windows in Lady Maramine's treasured library at River House— or Averwin, as he had known it in his childhood. He was holding a book and turning pages at what he hoped were convincing intervals while waiting for Rianine, Alisset, and the Lady Merriel to finish making their selections and depart. This was the first outing to River House since Nagaro's return from exile. The princess's party had just arrived a short time before lunch was to be served, and he had decided to use that time to see whether he could shed any more light on the mystery of his own origins.

The library was a pleasant room on the villa's second floor, with light provided by two north-facing windows that overlooked the garden. It smelled of old leather, and its comfortable furnishings were decorated in hues that suggested sunlight, earth, and growing things, but Nagaro was much too tense at the moment to enjoy the pleasing ambiance. The library had also served as Maramine's study, and his real interest was in the contents of a secret compartment in the lady's desk, which stood against the wall at the farther end of the room.

At last Rianine brandished a slim volume aloft. "I'm going to take this one, Merriel," she announced.

Lady Merriel gave the younger woman a bright, if slightly harried, smile. "All right, Rian. You just go back downstairs with it, then, while I finish helping Alisset find what she's looking for."

Rianine rolled her eyes, then relented enough to give Alisset a brief sympathetic glance before disappearing through the door with a swish of rose-colored silk.

"Now then, dear." Merriel returned her attention to Alisset. "Surely out of this whole shelf of Leithian poetry there must be something that will serve."

Alisset blinked, her wide blue eyes a little teary. She had a book open in her hands which she now thrust at the other woman. "What do you think of this verse, Merriel? Is it talking about Lady Lissafel?"

Merriel read two lines aloud: "'*The heart o'er-leaps the guardian fences of the day, To find the garden where the Lady of the Night holds sway.*' Yes, I know that one, dear. It's quite lovely, and the 'Lady of the Night' is one the ways that poets refer to Lissafel."

"Oh good." Alliset hugged the book, keeping one finger in it to mark the place, her eyes now shining moistly. "It's *ever* so romantic! If I copy it out onto a piece of paper and fold it three times and put it under my pillow, the Lady will surely hear my prayer, won't she?"

"*Well...*" Merriel was cautious. "That's a very old charm— my grandmother used to swear by it. And the gods always *do* hear us, I'm sure. They just don't always give us what we ask for. You must try to be strong, child." Merriel put a comforting arm around Alisset's shoulders and steered her in the direction of the door.

Nagaro heaved a sigh of relief as the two women exited the library. From the hallway he could hear their retreating footsteps and Alisset's anguished voice, saying, "The king mustn't choose Nile for Nevien— he just *mustn't!* It would be all wrong, when I love *him*, and he loves *me*—"

Nagaro wondered whether King Elgurn had any idea how much distress he had caused by officially declaring that Nevien's suitors might resume their pursuit of her hand. Alisset was in a panic. And he knew that she was right: Nile Fendred was no willing suitor, but merely a dutiful pawn in the hands of the Leithian Elders. *Poor Alliset. And poor Nevien...* He frowned as he dragged his mind back to the matter at hand. This was his chance to re-examine the secret contents of his Lady Guardian's desk.

The mystery surrounding his birth had been nibbling at the edge of his mind for months— ever since Varsyl Virden had confided his conviction that Leyel Virden had been the Lady Maramine's child by her lover, the minstrel Beloras. And then, more recently, the wounded Kenthos had offered to help him seek his origins in the northern Wared of Irvenen from which the man hailed. Kenthos' wound had finally healed to the point where Kuran had no more excuse to keep the young blacksmith in Lankura. Nagaro had watched Kenthos ride out of the Fleet Compound that very morning with a small escort of Fleet warriors. The man, whose misguided claim to be the heir of Loros had roiled the political waters so badly as to bring the country to the brink of war, had thus slipped away so quietly that his departure had caused scarcely a ripple.

Nagaro had declined Kenthos' offer when it was given, partly because it would likely have been a futile effort, and also because he was needed in Lankura— by Nevien, among others. But there was nothing to prevent him from searching for clues closer to home if the opportunity presented itself.

Hastily he replaced the book he'd been pretending to read on the shelf and crossed to the desk at the other end of the room. He leaned down and ran his fingers along the underside until he found the little dimple that marked the catch, pressed the right spot, and heard the faint click. What had appeared to be a fixed panel at the front of the desk, between two sliding ones, tilted forward a little and he quickly swung it open the rest of the way. The papers inside were exactly as he had left them months before, some loose and some in bundles tied with ribbon. He smiled fleetingly. He was quite sure that no one else knew about the desk's secret compartment or the existence of this trove of the lady's private papers. He felt less guilty this time for the intrusion. If Maramine had in fact been his mother, he had a right to know. And since she'd been his guardian in any case, and had left no other living child, he was for all practical purposes her only heir— even if it turned out there was no blood-tie.

He began his investigation by setting aside the uppermost thick bundle of folded papers tied with a white ribbon. He knew they were letters written to Maramine by her lover, Beloras, the man Varsyl Virden believed to be his father. Since Beloras had been slain before Nagaro was born, there was no chance that the minstrel's letters would refer to him directly. He went through the other papers systematically, moving each one to the desktop once he decided it wasn't useful. He tried to move quickly, examining most items just long enough to determine what they were and only looking longer at those that held some interest.

Most of the papers had no relation to him at all. There was the Lady Maramine's bound ledger, containing various records of money spent to repair or improve the house and grounds. Tucked into it were terse letters from Maramine's father authorizing a number of the larger expenses. There were also a great many notes— making a thick bundle tied with string— from a bookseller in Lankura, each describing one or more volumes the merchant thought might be of interest to the lady. Nagaro recognized quite a few of the books as being in the library's collection. Most of them he had read.

Other items dealt with things that concerned him somewhat, but they told him nothing he hadn't already known or suspected. Most of these were related to his instruction in swordsmanship. There was, for example, an elliptically-worded receipt signed by Master Fendar stating that the man had done "all that is possible to be done in the contracted matter," that in his opinion, "further service would not result in further improvement," and that payment had been "received in full for all rendered services." The document conspicuously failed to specify the nature of the services or the amount of the payment. Nor did it name anyone other than the Lady Maramine and Fendar himself. Nagaro's suspicion that Maramine had sold some of her jewelry to pay the swordmaster was confirmed by records from a jeweler detailing the valuing or purchase of items, with dates corresponding to the years of his training.

Nagaro's disappointment grew as the stack of unexamined papers shrank. Surely, he thought, there must be *something* here? But in the end, he found himself reduced to re-examining the collection of Beloras' letters. He expected nothing more from them than confirmation of what Varsyl had told him, that Maramine and Beloras had plotted together to conceive a child, but he decided to look, nonetheless. He undid the white ribbon and scanned the letters quickly, turning each one over to go on to the next. The passionate outpouring that he glimpsed in this way smote his heart. This man— who was possibly his father— had been very deeply in love. No one reading the words Beloras had penned could possibly believe otherwise. The letters had been ordered by date with the earliest ones on top, and the evidence Nagaro sought unfolded among those in the bottom third of the stack.

The references were cautious and oblique. The lovers must have conducted their most explicit discussions of the delicate subject verbally whenever they were able to meet, obviously not wishing to commit anything damning to paper. There were, however, several references to the responsibilities of parenthood together with expressions of hope and concern regarding the success of what Beloras referred to as either *our plan*, or *our intent*. It wasn't clear which of the two lovers had first made the suggestion, though it appeared that Maramine had played the part of the persuader. Beloras showed ambivalence in the beginning, but came to embrace the idea in the end. The final letter contained words whose meaning was wrenchingly clear. Nagaro read:

My dearest love, my heart beats faster with joy and trepidation as I read your words, that you are certain we have been successful in our intent! Oh, Maramine, I fear Lokundas, that trickster, who gives with one hand and takes with the other. But still I would not undo it. Whatever may come of this, my love, I can only feel that we have been blessed.

Nagaro stood for a long moment holding the letter, the confirmation of Varsyl's tale. He had never doubted the man's sincerity but it had occurred to him that Maramine's brother might have been mistaken, or deceived. It turned out there had indeed been a child— conceived at least.

Oh Vothra! Had he been that child whose begetting had made Beloras feel so blessed? It had proven more of a curse than a blessing, as it turned out. The man had died for it. Had he still, in the moment of his death, felt it was a thing he wouldn't have undone? And what of Maramine? Had she regretted persuading her true love to do this thing? Had she found it hard to love the son whose begetting had led to his father's death— especially when that son had come in some ways to resemble her own brother— Beloras' slayer— as Varsyl Virden believed?

A voice came distantly but clearly, cutting short his thoughts.

"Captain Nagaro! Will you come down? The luncheon is about to be served."

It was Lady Merriel calling from the foot of the stairs.

Shaking himself, he raised his own voice to answer. "I will come directly!"

Hastily he refolded the letter, returned it to its place with the others, and began to retie the white silk ribbon with trembling fingers. As he did so, he discovered a loose note that he must have inadvertently picked up with the bundle of letters. It was a small piece of paper, folded twice, and had been sealed with ordinary candle wax. Nagaro finished quickly with the ribbon and put the bundle back into the secret compartment. Then he picked up the little note. The seal was broken, of course, and was quite plain, having borne no intentional impression. Curious, he opened the note. The message inside was brief and written in a graceful, flowing hand that he immediately imagined to be a woman's. It said simply:

Look for him at your door at dawn of the third day, and all my love and gratitude go with you always.

There was neither the name of an addressee at the top, nor of the sender at the bottom. In place of a signature there was only a small pen drawing of a rose.

Nagaro stared at the words on the little piece of paper. They struck him very oddly. The writer's intent had clearly been to be secretive, and the mystery intrigued him. To whom might the word "him" refer? Perhaps to Beloras? The note might have been written by some go-between. But why, then, would the writer express her gratitude? And dawn didn't seem a very appropriate time for romance. Evening would be better for a lovers' tryst, wouldn't it?

...at your door at dawn of the third day...

Abruptly he drew breath as he remembered that Maramine had always told him he'd been found at her door in the early morning of the third day of Evril. His mind reeled as it spun away in a new direction. The lady Maramine had never given him the impression that she'd been expecting to find a baby on her doorstep. He'd always assumed the discovery had been a surprise. Yet, when he thought about it, he couldn't recall that she'd ever actually described the event in enough detail to indicate either one or the other.

But if *he* had been found on the doorstep, after all, what had become of the child she had conceived with Beloras?

Standing there at the desk he felt he was drowning in a sea of mingled excitement and uncertainty. With an effort, he steadied himself. He surely wouldn't solve this mystery by standing here, and he needed to go downstairs since the luncheon was ready. He hesitated a moment more before re-folding the little note and thrusting it into the front of his shirt. Then he closed the secret panel, making sure that he heard the latch click into place.

***

The meal was served on the terrace, as was usual when the weather was warm. The latticed roof and the leafy trellises supporting it made the place pleasantly shaded and open to the afternoon breeze. Nagaro arrived late and had to take the last remaining seat, which was not at the princess's table. One look at Nevien was more than enough, however. She still wore a black veil, in mourning for her mother, covering her hair. Her face was pale. Knowing her as he did, he could read tension in her face, though she was obviously making an effort to appear cheerful. He knew she would want to talk— to meet him in the secret place they'd found— and he very much wanted to do the same. But for now, he looked quickly away. He was determined not to betray his interest— a resolution facilitated by his own unsettled thoughts.

The other guests at his table fortunately seemed to have no shortage of things to talk about, and his inner turmoil gradually eased as he went through the motions of eating while trying to focus his mind. By the end of the meal, he had concluded that his knowledge hadn't been advanced by what he'd found in the library. He had come to River House with two conflicting tales of his origin— Varsyl's assumption that he was Maramine's son, and Maramine's assertion that he was a foundling. He had found two concrete pieces of evidence, one that appeared to fall on each side, and neither one was conclusive— thus only raising more questions. He needed more information and it occurred to him that Chula might be able to help. The old Turowan gardener was the only person he knew of who had been at Averwin at the time of his appearance and he resolved to seek the man at the earliest opportunity.

As the luncheon concluded, he rose and excused himself, murmuring something to the other guests at his table about intending to go for a ride. Since this had been his habit on every other visit he had made to River House, no one was surprised. He fleetingly caught Nevien's eye across the terrace as he turned to go and knew that she would follow after a discreet interval and expect to find him in their secret glade. He therefore didn't have much time if he wanted to speak to Chula before meeting the princess. Accordingly, he turned right instead of left as he exited the terrace, making for the garden with long, swift strides.

He was fortunate to find Chula almost at once. The old Turo was down on his knees in the kitchen garden, pulling weeds. Nagaro dropped to one knee beside the old man. Chula looked up, startled, but broke into a broad grin when he saw who it was.

"Good day t' ye, Master," he said. "I mean, Capt'n, that is, o' course. Have ye come t' pass the time with ol' Chula?"

"I'm sorry, Chula. I wish I had time just to talk, but I'll need to get to the stable and be gone before the princess comes to get her horse."

"Ahhh... I sees the way of it." Chula nodded wisely and gave Nagaro a broad wink.

Nagaro shook his head, frowning. "It's not like that—" he began, but then he broke off and waved the words aside. "Never mind. I just need to ask you some questions."

Chula shrugged and gave him a sly look. "Suit yerself, Capt'n. What d' ye want t' be askin' me?

"You were here already, Chula, when... I came? When I was a baby?"

"Aye."

"Do you remember if there was anything to show that the Lady might have been... well... *expecting* me?"

The old Turo's face constricted. "Oh, now, Capt'n!" he exclaimed. "I know ye must ha' heard that tale— 'bout how ye was *her* child, got on the wrong side o' the blanket. But I never believed it, 'cause she surely would ha' said so. Never bein' the kind t' tell lies."

"I know she wasn't," Nagaro agreed. "But that's not quite what I meant—"

Chula took no notice. "All she ever said was she found ye on th' doorstep. An' that's what I'll always believe."

"But... you don't really *know* how it came about?"

The gardener looked uncomfortable. "Well... *no*... Zirda. Not if ye puts it like *that*. She was just new come t' the place— not more 'n three months, I'd say. An' I was kind o' shy of her, on account o' she was real stern an' quiet. Kind o' *secret*, she was, at first, if ye know what I mean. All I know is, one day there was a baby in th' house. An'... an' it was *you*. I'm sorry, lad."

Nagaro sighed. There was no help there. But he needed to make haste.

"Was there ever a wet nurse? A woman who had a baby of her own, so she had milk—"

"Ye mean a woman t' have *fed* ye, is that it?"

"That's right."

Chula rubbed his graying beard. "Now don't that beat the wind an' the rain," he murmured. "I never thought o' that! I wonder how she managed it."

"There was no wet nurse, then?"

Chula shook his head. "None that I ever seen. Though it seems like women must have some way o' gettin' around that." He frowned. "But there *was* a woman I *did* see, now that I thinks of it. It was just th' one time. I seen her leavin' the house by th' front door one morning."

Nagaro stiffened. "When was *that?*"

"Oh, Master— I mean, Capt'n— I don't know! It was a terrible long time ago."

"I'm sorry, Chula. Try to remember if you can. Was it just before you first heard there was a baby in the house?"

"I'm not sure..." Chula's brow wrinkled painfully with the effort of trying to recall. "I guess it *could* ha' been."

"What was she like? Young? Old?"

Chula threw up his hands. "I don't remember after all these years. I don't suppose she could ha' been very young or very old or I'd remember it. She warn't nothin' special that I can recall. I wouldn't ha' marked it at all, except that I didn't *know* her. 'Cause we never got many visitors up at th' house that I didn't know."

"Was she Kelorin?"

Chula shrugged. "I 'spect so. If she'd ha' been a Turowa, I'd have stopped t' talk to her, and I didn't. An' if she'd been a yellow-hair Leithian, I'd remember it for sure!"

"I see." Nagaro gnawed his lip. If Maramine's child hadn't been him, there remained the question of what had become of it. "I've just one more question," he said. "Do you remember whether the Lady Maramine had anyone bury anything anywhere about the place? Around the time that she found me? Within a few days or week before or after?"

"Bury something?" Chula squinted at him. "Well, she never asked *me* t' bury nothin', that's sure."

Nagaro frowned. It wouldn't necessarily have been Chula who had done the burying. "Were there any unusual signs of digging?" he asked desperately, fearing he was asking a great deal of the old gardener's memory. "Around the grounds, in the garden, or in one of the pastures, maybe?"

But Chula shook his head emphatically. "Oh no, Cap'n. There was never any diggin' what I didn't know about. Th' lady knew better'n to let anyone be muckin' about with my dirt! And I'd ha' knowed if she'd tried t' sneek around me, too. I looks after my dirt, I does!"

So Chula had seen no grave. If Maramine's baby had died, then, where had it been buried? Somewhere in the woods maybe?

Nagaro stood up, aware that more time had passed than he had meant to spend. "Thank you, Chula," he said gravely.

The gardener grinned. "Any time I can be o' service, Capt'n, ye've only t' ask.

Chapter 5

Confidences

Thankfully, the stable was empty when he got there except for the horses, and the princess's white mare was still in her stall. The mare wickered softly as Nagaro hastily saddled Thunder-Heels. "Be easy, Snowdrift," he murmured distractedly. "Your mistress is coming." Then he swung astride his big gray stallion.

Indeed, he heard the voices of Nevien and Brandle approaching as he was riding out of the stable yard. He pressed for a brisk trot and urged the stallion into gallop as soon as he knew he was out of sight of the house. Thunder-Heels was more than willing.

His thoughts were spinning. *There had been no grave— at least none that Chula knew of— and no wet nurse! But an unknown Kelorin woman had come to the house...*

The road beside the river, with its overarching trees, passed in a blur. He reined in the stallion when he came to the bridge, almost by reflex. He'd stopped there so many times as a child and as a youth when Averwin had been his home. Then, he had ridden a tall black stallion, a stallion he had tethered to the big oak that shaded the nearer end of the bridge. He longed to cross the bridge now and ascend the narrow path to the little ledge— his "stone seat"— high on the cliff that rose on the river's farther bank. It had always been his favorite place to go whenever he wanted to be alone. But the princess and her bodyguard were too close behind him. He needed more distance.

He let Thunder-Heels have his head once more, and sped on until he reached the place where his chosen path left the road to follow a rivulet under the trees. There he slowed the big gray out of necessity. The way was not so broad, the footing less certain for the horse, and an occasional low branch presented a hazard for the rider.

There had been no wet nurse. Unless there was another way to feed a baby, Maramine must have nursed him herself. And what of the strange Kelorin woman? Could she have been the writer of the mysterious little note?

He followed the path out of the trees, across a green meadow laced with white and yellow flowers, then forded the stream and re-entered the woods. At last he reined to a halt in the cool, dim quiet of a stand of mature cedar trees. He had almost reached the little glade where he and Nevien went to talk. She was certain to seek him there, but he thought he had given himself a little time. He dismounted under the trees and stood beside Thunder-Heels, holding the horse's bridle. He let out one breath in a long sigh and drew another, trying to let the serenity of the place flow into him. The dark trunks, hoary with moss, stood all around him like the pillars of some ancient, lofty hall. No wind stirred, and the still air was laden with the scents of damp earth and cedar needles. There was no sound, save for his own breathing and the snorting breath of the gray stallion beside him.

He stood there for perhaps a full minute, seeking calm and eventually finding it. Then he stepped deliberately forward, passing between the trees, his boots making scarcely any sound on the thick bed of needles that covered the ground. He moved unerringly towards a place where a thick meshwork of branches descended towards the earth, meeting a tall stand of undergrowth to form a kind of curtain, lit by sunlight from behind so that it glowed in emerald hues. He knew the best place to part that curtain and pass through it. Shouldering the boughs aside and pushing through the undergrowth, drawing the stallion after him, he emerged into the brilliant splendor of the glade.

It was a little oval meadow with a stream running through it, forming a still pool near one edge of the grassy space. The sunlight poured down into that quiet place, so bright after the dimness under the trees that the meadow grass glowed like pale green flame. Blue lupin, scarlet columbine, and white queen's lace were nearly lost in the dazzle, while the little pool lay like a cool emerald, mirroring the darker green of the trees on the farther side of the glade.

Nagaro stood for a moment, taking it in. Then he sighed. There were two weathered wooden benches set with their backs to the trees, one on either edge of the glade, east and west. He loosened Thunder-Heels' bridle, slipping the bit, and turned the stallion loose to graze. Since the day was warm, he chose the east bench that was in the shade, and sat down on it. Leaning back, he let his thoughts run as he waited for Nevien.

If Maramine had nursed him, wasn't it the simplest thing to suppose that she had also borne him? There still might have been another child, and a secret burial, but in seventeen years the lady had never mentioned anything about it. Of course, she had also never called him "son," and never heard him call her "mother." And there was the cryptic little note, and the strange woman that Chula had seen. Could that woman have been the messenger who had brought him to Maramine's door? Or had she been the writer of the mysterious note? *Had that mysterious woman been his mother?*

"Nagaro! What's wrong?"

He started, to find Nevien suddenly standing beside him. He had been so deep in his thoughts that he had ben unaware of her approach. She wore traditional Kelorin riding clothes. Her *shapas*, or riding pantaloons, were dark green, and the long flowing *shilka* she wore over them and belted about her slender waist was of pale gray-green silk with dark green trim. She had dispensed with the veil, and her honey-colored hair hung loose about her shoulders. Here in the shadow of the trees, the highlights on her tresses were dark amber rather than sun-gold.

"Nothing," he said reflexively as he looked into her face. And looking, he suddenly forgot everything else when he read the deep concern in her sea-green eyes. She mustn't worry about him. "Nothing," he repeated. "I was thinking, that's all."

Her brow relaxed, though doubt lingered in her eyes.

"Sit with me, Nevien," he said. "Talk to me."

Abruptly, then, she folded up, dropping onto the bench beside him and leaning her shoulder against his. "Oh, Nagaro!" The words seemed to be wrung from her. "It's such a relief to be with someone that I *can* just talk to— someone I can say anything to, because I know you'll understand. Nagaro, I'm so *tired!*"

He had prepared himself for the familiar thrill of physical contact and had steeled himself against it. Cautiously, deliberately, he put his arm around her shoulders. Here in this place, he must not push her away— not if he was to be of any use to her. He couldn't tell her what he was feeling— must try to suppress those feelings, for his own sake— but if he seemed to be more distant it would surely hurt her because she wouldn't understand.

"Just rest a moment," he said. He could feel the tension in her body, could feel how thin she was. "Are you managing to eat?"

She nodded. "Yes. Enough, anyway."

"I thought your face didn't look quite so thin." He cradled her and felt her melt against him as the tension ran out of her. He resisted an urge to reach up with his free hand and stroke her hair.

"I'm getting back my strength," she said. "At least my body is. But inside... I don't know." She sighed. "It seems that I used to be so much stronger— just a few years ago. When my mother was alive and well, and—" Her voice caught.

Looking down on her face from above, he saw that she had closed her eyes and that tears were welling under her lashes. Very slightly, very gently, he tightened his encircling arm.

She sniffed loudly and wiped at the tears, unashamedly. "Sometimes I think I just can't do it again... without her... Not another marriage."

"I thought you told me that you didn't talk to her about unpleasant things. Because she became too upset."

She shifted, pulling a little away from him, and he loosened his arm again, allowing the movement.

"Upset isn't the right word," she said, and now that she was focused on something that she needed to explain, her tears subsided. "Saying it that way is just easier than trying to explain it. Mother never fussed, or cried, or shouted about anything. She would just be quiet, and she would look at me, and I could see how deep her trouble was by looking into her eyes. And I knew that she was thinking very hard— thinking about what was to be done. She would set her mind to it and she wouldn't rest until she'd figured out what was *right*. What was honest, and honorable, and... *noble*. And then of course she expected me— or, more likely, Father— to *do* it, no matter how hard it was or what it cost, even if it wasn't at all practical. We *couldn't* always do what she thought was right. So sometimes it was just easier not to tell her about the worst things."

"But you told her about the smaller things sometimes?"

"Oh yes." Nevien wiped at her cheek again, unconsciously. "She was so strong. And so *good*. And she had so much knowledge of the world. She didn't just tell me what I ought to do, either, she showed me by her example. I wanted so much to be like her."

Nagaro swallowed. "I think you are," he said. "Or at least you're coming to be."

She gave him a bright, brittle smile. "It's kind of you to say so."

"I mean it," he said seriously. "You're very strong, Nevien. It's just that you've been through too much all at once. A less strong person would have broken."

"You really think so?"

"Yes, I do."

They sat in silence. In the bright meadow, Thunder-Heels and Snowdrift were becoming reacquainted.

"Is there anyone you can talk to in the palace?" he asked at length. "I know you've said your own ladies aren't much use, but what about Lady Merriel? Or any of the rest of your mother's ladies?

"Merriel's the only one left. The others have all gone— they were Mother's friends. And I do try to talk to Merriel, but she hasn't much to offer— about the marriage— except to hope. Her marriage was arranged, after all, and it turned out well. She just keeps hoping that will happen for me. The only other person I talk to at all is Rianine. She's the only one of my ladies I would dare to tell about the complicated and messy things.

And she listens well. It's just that her answers are often so flippant— or just impractical."

"Oh." He couldn't think what else to say. *If only she didn't have to marry again at all...*

Nevien sighed. "I just pray that *this* time— *this* marriage— won't be so bad. And that this one will be the last."

Nagaro winced. "Maybe Lokundas is saving the best one for last."

She shot him a look even as her shoulders sagged. "The best? *That* wouldn't be hard. But... out of *this* lot?"

He winced again, wondering if *he* had been the worst. *Or had the worst one been Gill Marchent?* "What are the choices?" he asked desperately. "Maybe if you try to look for the best in each of them..."

At this she laughed without mirth. "It's the same old list," and she began to tell them off on her fingers. "There's Lothard Hurn... Nile Fendred... Devral Sedras... and Ferenan Eyilas."

And he knew them all. Lothard was arrogant, ambitious, and a complete cad. Nile was young and naive and in love with Alisset. Devral was gray and battle-scarred, and older than Nevien's father. And Ferenan was a middle-aged widower whose chief recommendation seemed to be that he was half Kelorin and half Leithian so that neither side could say he belonged entirely to the other.

He drew a long breath. As hard as this must be for Nevien, he wasn't finding it easy either. Imagining her wedded to anyone else was like putting a knife through his own chest. But he wanted to keep her talking. "Has no one else declared an interest, then?"

She shook her head wearily. "No. At least not yet. And I don't know whether to be glad or sorry. Every time I catch myself thinking that *anything* would be better than the choices I've got, I'm afraid to wish for another for fear that he'd be the worst of all!"

Nagaro felt his gloom deepening. Her responses echoed his own thoughts too closely. He could only try to help her find any happiness that she could. "Which one do you find the least objectionable?"

Nevien groaned. "Oh, Nagaro, I don't know!"

"Well, not Lothard, certainly."

"Of course not! Lothard is the worst. I'm just a prize to him. A way to get at the throne. And he's typical of the worst of the Leithian men who follow the old ways— the ones who think women should stay in their place. The other three would at least respect me, but there are arguments against each of them. Ferenan is personable and not too old, and Nile is young, of course, and handsome. But neither one of them wants to marry me. Ferenan misses his dead wife too much, and I could never feel good about taking Nile away from Alisset. Devral, on the other hand, would rather like having a new, young wife, though he tries not to show it for fear of seeming a lecher. But he's so old, and stiff, and crotchety. I could run circles around him! The best I can say for him is that when he died and left me alone, I wouldn't be quite an old woman. But then of course I might have to marry again!"

"Which one does your father favor?" While it mattered very much to Nagaro what Nevien wanted, he knew it was the king who would make the decision.

She frowned. "Ferenan, I think— if he can be persuaded. But I keep hearing hints that the man may decide to bow out of the competition. After that, Father's choice most probably would fall on Nile. Devral is a last resort, because Devral is a Signer of the Pact and so can't be king— unless the Pact were somehow voided. The first assumption is that if I married Devral, I wouldn't be queen. And Father has his heart set on my being queen."

For a long moment they sat in silence, contemplating the dismal prospects while gazing at the incongruously peaceful sun-drenched meadow where the two horses now grazed contentedly side by side.

Nagaro tried imagining Nevien as queen, which wasn't hard. She would make a wonderful queen, he thought. But when he tried to stand any of the suitors beside her as king, he couldn't quite manage to do it. Unconsciously he spoke his thought aloud. "If only there were someone else— someone that you *liked*."

"Well there isn't, so I shall just have to make the best of it!" She sounded bitter, but in the next instant she seemed to cast that bitterness aside and to find her strength because she spoke with resolution. "I've always managed before, and I suppose I shall find a way this time. I can't very well let everyone down. I've been preparing to be queen my entire life."

Nagaro drew breath. *She was so brave! Oh, he found her admirable!*

And sitting there with his arm around her— feeling her against him— he was suddenly overwhelmed by desire as strong as the rising tide. He wanted to take her in his arms, to kiss her of course, and to lie with her somewhere in the private darkness of a night that belonged to them alone. But more than anything else, he wanted to protect her. He wanted to stand between her and all the ills of the world... *until his life ended, or there was no more world, or she was no longer in it...*

"Nevien..."

She turned her face up to his. "Yes, Nagaro?"

Her eyes were deep green under velvet-black lashes. There was a question in them, and concern— and a spark like the sun glancing off a wave, or morning light shining through the leaves of a forest. Her lips were tempting. He leaned towards them. *He could feel himself starting to fall...*

With an effort he drew back from the precipice, straightening, and wrenching his own eyes away before he could lose himself— or she could read his heart in them.

Vothra! What had he imagined he was going to do? To say?

"Nagaro, what is it?"

"I... nothing."

She pulled away from him and shifted, turning so that she could face him more directly on the bench. "There it is again!" she exclaimed. "That's the second time you've said that, and I know you well enough to see that whatever is on your mind it surely isn't nothing. And I think you'd better tell me about it. You've been listening to me while I've gone on and on about my troubles. Now it's time I listened to you. So come, now. Out with it!"

Nagaro guiltily retrieved his arm. It felt as if a spell had been broken, and he had to answer her with something plausible. But outright lies never worked. If he tried to make something up it would only come around again to trip him. He fell back on the strategy that always worked best for him— the careful half-truth.

"All right," he said, without looking at her. "I found out something recently about a man who might have been my father."

"Your father? Nagaro, that's wonderful!"

His head came around to face her. "I said he *might* have been my father. The evidence is inconclusive, and he's dead in any case. He died before I was born. I was offered a chance to have some help in seeking to learn more of him—"

"Then you should take it!" Nevien's eyes were alight with eager excitement.

"It's too late. The chance is past. It was Kenthos who offered to help me, and he's already gone. He left this morning."

"Oh!" She looked quite crestfallen. And then she frowned. "Nagaro," she said reproachfully, "I hope you didn't turn him down because you'd agreed to come to River House today."

"No, no!" He made haste to reassure her. "There just seemed to be too little hope in it. The only clues I have are his given name and the fact that he was a minstrel. And he came from Irvenen— which is such a big Wared. I don't even know if I could have gotten leave from my duties to go."

"You didn't ask?"

He shook his head. "I'd made up my mind not to go. I would probably just have ridden hopelessly about the countryside and learned nothing. But I find myself wondering whether it's true, and it preys on my mind."

She nodded, with a sigh. "I see. You've been distracted."

"Just a little, yes. But I'm here, and I'll go on being here— at least until the end of the summer when I have to sail with Kuran to Chitaopa to meet the Emperor of the Mahuk Baar again. The Emperor is supposed to surrender a hundred slaves to Lord Kuran and he specifically asked that I be there."

Her brows met in a worried frown. "Aren't you afraid the Emperor might try to seize you again?"

Nagaro shook his head. "I trust his honor. And it seems that he trusts mine. But that's at the end of the summer. For now, I am here, and I'll be able to accompany you on your charitable missions if you want me to—whenever my duties allow. Or to talk again if we can manage it."

She gave him a fragile smile. "Dear Nagaro! I'm very glad that you're here. And I *will* want you to come with me on those missions. I'll be going to another orphanage next week, and I hope you can come. The children are the hardest. They need more distraction than I can give them, and you were so good the last time. I had to go visit the Home for Fishermen's Widows while you were away in the south and the women kept fussing over me as if I were a child! I couldn't keep from weeping. But at least they understood, being mothers."

"Lady Merriel gave me a list, with the dates. I'll check them with Kuran."

"Will you be able to attend the Feast of Midsummer?"

"Probably. If Kuran comes, himself, I'm sure I'll be allowed to."

She'd been continuing to face him, looking earnestly into his eyes. Now she looked away. "And will you... will you be dancing on Devral's behalf again, do you think?"

He heard the falter in her voice and wondered at it. "I really don't know," he replied after a moment's hesitation. "Lord Devral hasn't said anything to me. Of course I wouldn't expect him to, but after what happened at Loros Hall, I'm not sure he'll think it's a good idea."

"I heard about that." Her eyes came back to him. "They say you were magnificent— the way you stepped in and stopped Lothard from killing Kenthos."

He felt himself blushing under his kuma stain. "I was officially following orders."

"Yes. They say that too."

This time he looked away. Her glance was too admiring and he was having trouble deciding whether he was embarrassed or pleased. "It's rather important that you repeat the part about the orders," he said a little stiffly.

"I know. And I do. But I don't believe it for a moment."

There was an awkward silence. Looking down, Nagaro traced the weathered grain of the cedar-wood bench with his fingers.

Nevien spoke again. "Is there someone I should invite to sit across from you at the match table?" Her tone was almost brisk.

He looked up, startled. "Someone to sit—

"Yes. You know... a woman?" She was studying him, a little tensely, he thought. "It's just that I'll be sitting there again, instead of on the dais, because of the courtships starting again. If you'd... ah... like to be there too, we'll have to find someone to pair you with, since you didn't get on with Delasin. You haven't found anyone you'd like to court in all of your travels?"

"Oh. No. Not really." The curse of his honesty made him add, "Well, no one you could *invite*." And then he kicked himself when he saw the sharp flash of interest in her eyes.

"Then there *is* someone!"

"Well, there's Hamani," he said quickly. "But I only told her I might court her if Taru married her sister instead."

For a moment Nevien seemed only able to stare at him.

"If *Taru* marries her *sister*... This is your friend Taru? The one who left you alone with a bottle of Southern Borlundian?"

"Yes."

She was looking perplexed, so he felt he had to explain. "Hamani is in love with Taru, you see. But he's courting her younger sister."

"And you offered yourself as a *consolation prize? Nagaro!* Has it occurred to you that this woman could hold you to such an offer?"

"She never would if she thought it would make me unhappy. But I was quite serious. I'd like to try to make her happy because she deserves to be."

Nevien had been leaning forward, searching his face, but now she drew back and seemed to withdraw a little into herself. Her brows knit together making the sharp line between them that he never liked to see. "You must think very highly of her," she said after a moment. "This... Hamani. What is she like?"

Nagaro was thinking fast. He realized there could be an advantage in allowing the princess to think that he had a serious interest in Hamani even though he really very much hoped Taru would see his error. It might cause her to put aside her efforts at matchmaking on his behalf. *And he wouldn't need to lie.*

He allowed himself to look introspective, glad that he didn't find it difficult to praise Hamani. "Well," he said seriously. "She's very warm-hearted. And very kind— besides being intelligent and sensible. She's the kind of person you can really talk to. And she's a marvelous cook."

"A marvelous cook..." Nevien looked as if she were trying to picture Hamani in her mind's eye. "And she must be Turowan, judging by her name. And... is she pretty?"

"Most folk consider her rather plain, actually, but I don't see her that way. Her sister's the beauty in the family, but she can't compare with Hamani in any other way. And appearance isn't really important, is it?'

"No, of course not." Nevien was studying him and appeared to be thinking hard. "And you said I couldn't invite her. Why not? Wouldn't she come?"

Nagaro laughed. "To begin with, she lives twenty miles away in Wotana, and besides, she's a fisherman's daughter. She'd feel completely out of place at one of the palace feasts. It really wouldn't be at all kind to invite her."

"Oh. No, I suppose not."

Nevien fell silent and sat staring off across the glade. Nagaro had just begun to think that maybe he ought to mention that it was growing late, when she turned back.

"Will you be going to Wotana, then, to see her?"

"I mean to the next time Taru goes. He's there right now, actually. He was able to get two days' leave."

"You let your friend Taru go without you? You stayed here? While Taru is there with Hamani?"

"He didn't go alone. My other friend, Pavo, went with him— for friendship's sake. And I stayed here— for friendship's sake. And Hamani loves Taru—"

"— and you want her to be happy."

"Yes."

Nevien sat for moment, studying her hands. Finally she said, "Well, I hope it all works out for the best. But perhaps you don't really want to be at the match table."

"Oh, but I do," he said hurriedly. "If I must be paired with someone, there's Rianine."

Her head came up, her eyes uncertain. "I thought Rianine made you nervous."

He frowned. Rianine did make him nervous, but if the alternative was not to be at the match table... "It would be all right. We both know it isn't real. And... folk may already have noticed that I danced with her the last time." He stopped, watching her face because there was something odd about her expression. "If she doesn't mind, that is," he added quickly, thinking that perhaps he was presuming too much.

Nevien's mouth twitched into a feeble smile. "As a matter of fact, she volunteered for the duty. I'm afraid she enjoys harassing you."

He shrugged. "I'm beginning to get used to it."

This time Nevien actually laughed, a little shakily. "I mustn't tell her *that*. She'll think she has to try harder." She glanced at the sun. "The afternoon is getting late. We should catch the horses."

He followed her look. "Yes. We had better."

***

Brandle met them earlier than usual. The big blond guardsman on his liver chestnut horse appeared from among the trees as they were fording the stream. He gave Nagaro a penetrating look but said nothing, and they all rode in silence until they reached the road that led back to River House. Once on the road, Nevien urged her mare into a canter, making conversation impossible in any case.

At the house, they found that preparations for departure had begun but that the other guests had yet to emerge. Nevien looked preoccupied as she dismounted and tied her mare. "I'm going in for a minute," she said. "But there's no need for either of you to come if you'd rather wait out here."

Sitting astride Thunder-Heels in the stable yard, Nagaro would have been glad to have been left to his own thoughts. Brandle, however, sidled his horse until their stirrups nearly touched and addressed him in a low tone.

"Correct me if I'm wrong, Captain, but it seems to me the wind has shifted."

"The wind?" Nagaro gave the other man a puzzled frown.

The Leithian regarded him archly. "You may recall that on the occasion of your first outing to this house I told you that I like to know which way the wind is blowing..." The sentence dangled expectantly.

Nagaro did remember. Brandle was Nevien's bodyguard, and while he was no slave to propriety, he liked to know how things stood. *And Brandle had witnessed Nagaro's interaction with Nevien outside the Compass Room at the palace while Kenthos and the warring parties had faced judgement in the Audience Chamber. That encounter must have appeared rather intimate.* He looked away, feeling the blood in his face and hoping it didn't show. "If the wind has changed," he said carefully, "it blows only one way. And there's nothing I can do about it in any case, so you've nothing to worry about, Lieutenant."

"Ah. All right then, Captain. I'm glad to have your word on it." Brandle nudged his horse away to a comfortable distance.

Nagaro returned to his thoughts. He was trying not to dwell on the fact that other men would be courting Nevien. He'd be watching it soon enough. Before he could settle on a safer topic, however, Nevien and the rest of her guests emerged from the house. The ones who didn't ride on horseback took their places in the carriage, while Nevien remounted her mare. Kuran and Rianine mounted their horses as well, and the four other members of the Princess's Guard appeared from the direction of the guard house, already astride their mounts.

Nagaro had no desire to be drawn into talk, so he held Thunder-Heels back and allowed the rest of the party to exit the stable yard before letting out the reins and giving the stallion a quick squeeze with his knees that sent the big gray eagerly cantering after them.

Chapter 6

Trouble On The Road

Nagaro found that staying close to the carriage without having someone try to draw him into conversation wasn't easy. Kuran wanted to talk about the officers' postings for the upcoming mission to Chitaopa. The guardsmen tried to press him for the details of what had *really* happened with Kenthos at Loros Hall. And Rianine, who was riding beside the carriage with a distracted and introspective Nevien, kept looking at him and smiling in a disquieting way. In the end, he resorted to what he called riding circles, leaving the road to explore the surrounding terrain while allowing the carriage with its entourage to get a bit ahead of him, then circling back to catch up.

The princess's party traveled southward at first along a narrow, rutted road that followed Averwin's river, the Tenorin. This road eventually joined a wider, more traveled one that promptly crossed the river on a sturdy bridge and ran on in a more westerly direction. The wider road wound through gently rolling hills. Scattered farms and pastures were interspersed with bits of woodland. The afternoon was waning and the coach and company passed in and out of the shadows of trees, cast across their path by the westward-sinking sun. The driver of the carriage shook the reins to hurry the pace and the riders pressed their mounts as well. While there had been no recent reports of highwaymen, the driver presumably didn't relish having to find his way by the light of the carriage lanterns. The crossroads and side-lanes would all look very much alike if dusk overtook them.

The road continued south-westerly, until they neared the place where it would join the High Road, that broad, raised way that ran almost due west along the River Edro, straight to the east gate of the capital city of Lankura. In that last stretch, the old country road was flanked on its western side by a number of groves of trees, all casting shadows across it, before it made a final S-curve and climbed the embankment to reach the High Road.

Nagaro knew he would have to stay with the carriage once they were on the raised bed of the High Road. Accordingly, he turned to Kuran, who was riding beside him, and said, "I want to give Thunder-Heels one last run, My Lord. I mean to make a long circle west of the road, along the other side of the trees where the light is better. If I don't come back to you sooner, I'll rejoin you where the road swings west just past the last stand of trees."

Kuran shrugged and raised a hand lazily in a half salute. "Very good, Captain. I'll look for you."

Nagaro turned the stallion off of the road and let the horse have his head across a wild bit of open pasture. After that he turned and rode parallel to the road, allowing Thunder-Heels to exercise himself by leaping over the occasional low wall or derelict fence that divided the fields. The series of small groves of trees often hid the roadway from his view, but he caught glimpses of the carriage and the other riders and so could mark their progress. He rode on more quickly when he reached the final, largest stand of trees and began to pass along the edge of it. He might out-distance the princess's party before reaching the far end of the wood, but he knew he could always wait for the carriage to catch up.

The air was cooling, but the sun was still warm, and the land lay in repose. Nagaro let his eyes drink in the sight. The waning sunlight touched the land with a glorious golden light that woke a rich color in everything it fell upon. There were the deep browns of exposed earth, the dark gray or pale silver of tree trunks, the myriad vibrant greens of leaves of every kind, and the jewel-like hues of wildflowers winking in the grass. Over the far hills, the pale blue haze of distance was deepening towards violet.

All was very peaceful, the more so because the land here was very nearly deserted, being part of the old Loros Wared that was now held by the crown. This land, Nagaro now knew, had been depopulated years before by the strife surrounding the death of King Tevren, and it had never fully recovered. There were very few dwellings to be seen, all a long way off, and no folk visible at this hour. For some time, the only sounds besides those made by the stallion's hooves on hardened earth had been the light rustle of the breeze in the grass and the calls of birds that flitted among the trees as he rode past.

Nagaro was therefore surprised when he thought he heard the sound of voices.

Curious, he reined Thunder-Heels to a halt and sat in the saddle, listening. Yes, there definitely were voices— men's voices. They came from the woods a little way ahead on his left, but he could see nothing owing to a screen of thick bushes at the edge of the trees that stood as high as a man's head, crowding each other and straining for the sunlight.

Presumably the same bushes had prevented the men from noticing his approach, for the voices continued as they had without any modulation. It sounded like more than one or two men, but they were speaking low and more than one at a time, and he couldn't make out what they were saying. Thunder-Heels pricked his ears in the direction of the sounds and gave a low wicker, evidence that there were horses among the trees as well.

Nagaro frowned. He could think of a few reasons why a small group of men with horses might be gathered in conversation in a grove of trees. Some of them were quite harmless, others less so. He decided that he should investigate, and he was in the act of dismounting quietly when someone among the group of men under the trees must have said something funny, because laughter followed. The quantity of laughter made it clear that there were more than a half a dozen men doing the laughing, perhaps two or three times that number. Nagaro froze with his hand on the stallion's bridle. Some of the more harmless possibilities had just become very much less likely.

In the next instant, the laughter was cut short by a voice that was raised enough for the words to finally be plain.

"Quiet, you lot!"

The laughter immediately died and the same voice spoke again, this time in a lower tone that Nagaro still heard perfectly in the sudden silence.

"The carriage is coming, idiots! If they hear you, it'll ruin everything. Now mount up!"

Nagaro didn't wait to hear any more. He had been intending to surreptitiously approach the gathering, observe the men, and address them if necessary. Now he retreated back along the edge of the trees, pulling Thunder-Heels after him as he made for a narrower part of the woods that he had just passed. His heart was racing. He needed to get through the trees and back to the road quickly and without being seen. He had to warn the princess and her party, or failing that, come to their aid.

He found the narrow place and began to thrust his way between the bushes. Thunder-Heels balked briefly at the unfamiliar wall of greenery, but came when Nagaro spoke reassuringly. Once through the bushes and under the trees, where the sun didn't reach, there was little undergrowth, but their progress was slowed by the narrowly-spaced trunks and low-hanging branches and hampered by the sudden dimness, as well.

The width of the grove at this point was about thirty feet. Nagaro could make out the farther side of it through the gloom, marked by another dense screen of bushes with the light shining through. He worked his way towards it. Branches snagged his clothing, and Thunder-Heels snorted his displeasure.

"Steady, brother of the wind," he murmured under his breath. "Just a little farther."

But he still had several feet to go when he heard the rumble of the carriage wheels, the clop of hooves, and the jingle of harness as the carriage and its party passed on the road. Immediately he raised his voice, crying, "*Look out! Ambush!*" He struggled forward, as his cry was nearly drowned by a chorus of loud whoops and a crashing in the bushes away to his right. This was followed by shouts of alarm from the road, the frightened neighing of horses, and the shrieks of the women.

Nagaro swore as he fought his way through the last branches that barred his way, pulling Thunder-Heels after him. As he emerged from the deep gloom under the trees into the open shade of the road, he heard the first clash of swords. He saw at once that the carriage had halted not fifty feet away. He didn't stop to try to decipher the melee around it, but sprang into the saddle and drew his sword. With an angry cry of his own, he urged the big gray into a gallop and bore down on the tangle of men and horses.

The highwaymen had surrounded the princess's party. There were at least twenty of them, enough to prevent anyone from escaping. Kuran, Brandle, and the other five guardsmen were valiantly defending the carriage, while the unarmed young men who were courting the princess's ladies were using their horses' bodies to shelter Nevien and Rianine against the side of the vehicle. The coach driver cowered on his seat. The carriage horses, unused to so much shouting and clashing of metal, appeared on the verge of panic and might have bolted if two of the brigands hadn't caught the lead horses by their bridles in an effort to restrain them.

As Nagaro swept towards them, one of the carriage's guardsmen, a red-haired Leithian, cupped his hands to his mouth and shouted in the direction of the High Road. "*Help! We're being attacked!*"

Nagaro saw that Kuran and Brandle were trying to engage five men at once, and he rode straight at the knot of ruffians. The two closest attackers promptly shifted their attention and came at him together, only to be met by Nagaro's steel. He wasn't accustomed to fighting on horseback, but his skill and speed still served him well and the two assailants both hauled on their reins, backing off in alarm, and then seemed to at last take a good look at him.

"Oi! That's Capt'n Nagaro!" cried the smaller of the two, a grizzled old Turo. "I'll not be fighting *him!*"

"Aye!" exclaimed the other, who was taller and younger and had startlingly blue eyes in a pale face under matted black hair. "Nobody said *he'd* be here!"

Nagaro urged Thunder-Heels to advance on the two men, menacing them with his sword. *There was something not quite right about the fair-skinned man.* "Be off!" he cried. "If you don't mean to fight!"

"To me, lads! To me!" The old Turo waved his sword aloft like a flag. "It's Capt'n Nagaro! This is no place for us!"

Roughly half of the men around the carriage were brown-skinned Turowans, and these now began backing their horses out of the fight, shouting, "It's Capt'n Nagaro!"

"*Cowards!*" bellowed a big, burly, light-skinned man with an unkempt thatch of black hair, who was pressing Kuran hard. "He's only one man! We still outnumber them!"

The Turowans hesitated in response to the big man's rallying cry, milling about uncertainly until several cries of "It *is* Capt'n Nagaro!" apparently convinced their grizzled leader, who shouted, "Turo, to me!" This time, his folk obeyed with speed, and a moment later they were in full flight down the road in the direction from which the carriage had come.

"*We're being attacked! Help! Help!* The red-haired guardsman was shouting again, more frantically this time. Despite the desertion of the Turo, there were still nearly a dozen attackers, and the guardsman's cries were echoed by one of his fellows, a tall, blond youth with an incipient mustache.

Another brigand with pale skin and black hair left the assault on the carriage to come at Nagaro, slashing at him wildly. This man didn't look right either, but Nagaro had no time to think about it. Lightning-quick, he parried several strokes, then caught the man's weapon and sent it spinning into the grass at the side of the road.

"*Ai!*" the man cried as he swung out of the saddle and stumbled into the ditch to scrabble for his sword.

Nagaro let the disarmed man go, as yet another light-skinned, black-haired man peeled away from the group around the carriage and came at him. He reined Thunder-Heels around, twisting in the saddle to meet this new attack. His sword flashed once to turn the man's blade and a second time to leave him bleeding from a cut on his upper arm.

"*By Hel!*" the man swore, backing his mount. "He moves like a bloody demon!"

Nagaro pressed his knees to Thunder-Heels, advancing on the man. *There was something about this man's face...*

By this time, the fight around the carriage was slackening, what with the loss of the Turo and those who'd been drawn off by Nagaro's assault. The remaining highwaymen were beginning to falter as the defenders pressed their advantage. "Go to it, Captain!" Brandle called cheerily, not missing a stroke as he helped Kuran engage the burly ruffian who seemed to be the leader of the assailants.

"You bleeding cowards!" the big man thundered. "He's just a man! Go after him!"

"Go after him yourself!" retorted the man Nagaro had wounded. "He's Captain Nagaro! Even Lothard couldn't touch him!" And with that, the wounded man spun his mount and galloped off up the road after the disappearing Turo.

"Bloody bodjering Hel!" The leader of the brigands swore violently, pulling away from Kuran. The big man appeared nearly beside himself. He threw a glance in the direction of the High Road, then back at the rest of his men, most of whom were now in various degrees of retreat. *"Stand!"* the man bellowed. *"Stand and fight!"* But it was no use. The big man glanced again towards the High Road. This time there were shouts from that direction, and a party of mounted men in red, white, and black livery galloped into view around the bend in the road at the end of the woods.

The brigand leader's eyes flicked back to Nagaro, who was still sitting his horse with his sword in his hand and a dangerous gleam in his eye. The big man cast a glance after his fleeing men, then back at the approaching force, and back again at Nagaro. *"Oh, to Hel with it!"* he muttered as he spun his horse and put his spurs to the beast's sides.

By the time the company of liveried horsemen pulled up beside the carriage, several seconds later, the rump of the brigand leader's horse was rapidly disappearing in a cloud of dust.

Nagaro had turned his attention to the approaching group of riders as soon as the last of the highwayman turned tail. He recognized the colors they wore as those of Hurn Hold and so wasn't surprised to see that the company was composed of a dozen fair-skinned, fair-haired men-at-arms. He was only slightly surprised to discover that the man riding in the vanguard was none other than Lothard Hurn.

The tall, muscular Leithian lord was staring hard after the fleeing brigands with a scowl on his face as he drew rein. He managed to reduce the scowl to a frown as he brought his gaze around to sweep over the carriage's defenders and fasten upon the Princess Nevien. "My Lady," he said with an effort at grace. "We heard cries for help as we were passing on the High Road. We came as quickly as we could."

Kuran pointedly cleared his throat. "We are grateful, My Lord, for your good intentions," he said smoothly. "We were set upon by a band of highwaymen, but as you can see, they've been put to flight owing to a stalwart defense by the Princess's Guards, assisted by myself as well as by the swordsmanship and reputation of Captain Nagaro, here."

Lothard's gaze was transferred from Kuran to Nagaro, whom he raked up and down with an angry glare. His eyes narrowed. "You again!" he exclaimed with some heat, then seemed to catch himself and continued more coldly. "How fortunate for you that these highwaymen proved to be such a pack of cowards. But then low-born filth usually are when faced with a few trained swordsmen."

The Leithian lord paused pointedly as if expecting a response.

Nagaro, who'd been wiping the blood from his sword on a corner of his saddle blanket, ignored the comment. He expected nothing better than insults from Lothard and knew better than to take the bait. His sword slid back into its sheath with a decisive chink that was plainly audible in the pregnant silence.

A look of annoyance crossed Lothard's face, but he managed to replace it with his accustomed hauteur as he looked past Nagaro to focus on Kuran and Brandle.

"We shall accompany the princess back to Lankura, Zirdas," he said. "I and my men will ensure her safety."

Nevien was sitting erect in the saddle, regarding Lothard coolly. "That won't be necessary, My Lord, though the offer is gracious." she said calmly. "I have six well-trained guards as you can see, and two other gentlemen who are armed and both fine swordsmen, not to mention these others who have bravely stood their ground despite having no weapons. It's only a few miles to Lankura, and there's no more cover for thieves. I'm sure you must have important affairs of your own. Please don't let us keep you from them."

Lothard frowned and dismissed her words with a wave of his hand. "This is a matter for men to decide, My Lady," he said shifting his gaze to Kuran. "And I insist. The safety of the king's daughter is of greatest importance. Those highwaymen might come back."

"Surely that's unlikely, since they were— as you pointed out— nothing but low-born cowards," Nevien put in sweetly, giving him a smile that was purest honey.

At this, Lothard's frown deepened and his face began to redden.

Before there could be any outburst, however, Kuran spoke. "If you wish to be of assistance, My Lord," he said in the blandest of tones and with a studiously neutral expression, "we would be obliged if you and your men went in pursuit of our attackers. They fled up the road in disarray. Perhaps you may catch some of the miscreants."

"Ha!" Lothard's unpleasant frown turned into an equally unpleasant smile. "Perhaps we may indeed," he said gloatingly. "And when we do, it will please me to teach them their error! Forward, men!"

With that, the Leithian lord drew his sword, flourished it, and goaded his horse into a gallop. With a scattering of shouts, the troop of liveried men-at-arms thundered after him.

Nagaro, Kuran, and the rest of the princess's company sat and watched until the departing riders were a good distance up the road.

"Well," Kuran observed. "I must say he took a fancy to that notion. Though I notice he didn't ask us for a description."

"He doesn't need one," Brandle muttered darkly.

Kuran gave the Leithian a startled look. "You think he might arrest any poor peasant he stumbles across?

Brandle was frowning. "Let's hope not. Though that's not what I meant." He turned to Nevien. "My Lady Princess, we shouldn't linger. We've lost time and the afternoon is growing late."

Nevien nodded agreement. "You're quite right." She turned to the driver who was sitting on his seat and now sagging with relief. "Set us the fastest pace you deem prudent, driver."

As the carriage started to roll, Brandle made a sign to Kuran and Nagaro. "Stay with the carriage, Zirdas," he said in a low voice. "I'm going to look at something and I'll catch you up. I shouldn't be long."

Kuran raised an eyebrow but nodded. "All right."

As Kuran and Nagaro set off at a brisk trot at the rear of the company, Kuran shook his head. "I'm surprised to have encountered highwaymen here, within hailing distance of the High Road," he murmured. "It's been nearly a year since there were any reports of banditry in this part of the country, let alone on this stretch of road." He sighed. "I did hear you shout a warning, by the way, but I didn't see where you were."

"I was in the trees when I shouted. I'd heard the men talking when I was on the other side of the woods. It was plain they were lying in wait for the carriage, so I tried to cut through, but there was no path and it was tangled, and I had my horse. I'm sorry my warning came too late."

"It wasn't entirely so. I'd been lagging, and your shout gave me just time to catch up with the carriage. Otherwise I might have been cut off from the others."

"Well, I'm glad of that at least."

At this point Brandle came cantering up to join them. "Did either of you notice anything strange about those highwaymen?" he asked, pitching his voice so that no one else in the party would hear.

Nagaro frowned. Something *had* bothered him about those men.

Kuran spoke first. "I thought some of them seemed rather well-spoken for common thieves."

"You're right." Nagaro's mind pounced. "It was the fair-skinned ones. And they should have been Kelorin by their hair, but their features looked more Leithian to me. And they swore like Leithians, besides."

"That's because they *were* Leithians. One of them lost this."

Brandle held up an object that had been tucked under his arm. It was a mass of black strings attached to a cloth cap.

Kuran reached for it and examined it as he rode. "A wig," he muttered. "It seems to be made of fine wool yarn. And all of them had hair that looked like this, disheveled and of the same color. But how did you know?"

"I had my eye on the man when he lost it, searching the ditch for his sword after Nagaro disarmed him. He didn't notice right away, and when he did, he ducked into the trees— horse and all— but not before I saw that he had blond hair, cut short so it wouldn't show."

"Ha!" Kuran's laugh was grim. "So we're attacked by Leithians disguised as Kelorin, and then Lothard and his men just happen to come by so they can rescue us. I call that convenient! And the Turo were hired, of course—"

"And not told the whole story by the sound of it," Nagaro put in. "They didn't expect me to be here, for one thing."

Brandle grunted agreement. "Some of the Leithians didn't sound as if they expected you, either. Their leader may have been the only one who knew everything. Did you notice that he began looking towards the High Road before Lothard and his men came into sight?"

Kuran nodded. "He sounded like a military man, now that I think of it— a sergeant trying to rally his troops. But they must have all had some notion of the plan. Lothard wouldn't have wanted us to be hurt— or really robbed, for that matter. I expect they were supposed to make a show of attacking us, keep it up until Lothard arrived, and then make a show of being routed by Lothard and his men."

Brandle chuckled. "Except Nagaro spoiled the plan. That's quite a reputation you have, Captain. The little affair at Loros Hall hasn't done it any harm either."

Nagaro frowned. "It doesn't always work so well," he said, remembering Bloody-Hand Baku. "But some of those here clearly knew me by sight, and some, at least, among the Turo consider me a friend. These didn't want to be fighting on the wrong side."

"It didn't seem to bother them until you arrived," Kuran observed archly. "Lothard's plan might have worked if not for your presence and your reputation, though he'll likely be more careful in the future. And of course we don't have proof of everything we've guessed." Kuran handed the black wig back to Brandle. "You retrieved that evidence," he said. "And this affair falls more properly within your jurisdiction than mine, though I'll make sure that Elgurn and the Council hear of it. For now, though, it's best that none of us accuse Lothard openly of anything. We should, however, make sure the story gets out that we were attacked by men, some of whom were Leithians disguised as Kelorin, and that we drove them off ourselves. I don't want Lothard to profit from this if it can be helped. Though he may claim to have chased them all over the countryside."

"He can't very well bring any of those Leithians in for questioning," Nagaro ventured. "Or any of the Turo, either, if they were all in his employ."

Brandle's face darkened. "You mean he can't bring any of them in *alive.*"

They had by this time reached the raised surface of the High Road. The way lay straight before them now, into the west under the setting sun with the river on their left and a wide green sweep of pasture land on their right, dotted with farms. It was no more than five miles to the East Gate of Lankura. The driver of the carriage shook the reins and the horses hastened their trot, eager for their comfortable stable and their feed troughs.

Presently the princess reined in her mare and dropped back to join them.

"What have you three been whispering about?" she inquired with an arched eyebrow.

"Our little adventure, of course," Kuran replied. "But before I say more, I'd like to know what the other members of our company have had to say about it."

"Those who were inside the carriage didn't see a great deal," Nevien told them. "They were all too frightened to look, although Merriel told them she's been in carriages that were attacked by highwaymen before, years ago, and that such men generally only want your jewelry and aren't inclined to hurt ladies. She did think that some of these seemed unusually persistent, however, especially their leader. As for the men in our party, the guests are all berating themselves for not having brought their swords. They and the guards seem to be evenly divided on the question of whether the fair-skinned robbers were Kelorin or not, and their opinions tend to correspond to the color of their own hair. Rees, Vanhold, and that red-haired Leithian guardsman are all particularly insistent that the robbers must have been Kelorin, while Hendrel and Geivian are just as insistent they weren't. And Rianine is adamant that she saw one of them lose a wig and that he had blond hair underneath."

At this, Brandle promptly produced the wig. "I saw it too," he said. "And this should put an end to any argument."

Nevien examined the wig. "So," she said, handing it back. "The attack was probably set up by Leithians. Do you think Lothard was behind it? It's a remarkable coincidence that he just happened to be near at hand with a body of armed men."

"I don't doubt that it was done for Lothard's benefit," Kuran responded gravely. "Though others might have done the planning. It *is* the sort of thing Lothard would do, however— trying to improve his position in the competition for your hand by being able to boast of having gallantly rescued you from a band of robbers."

Nevien rolled her eyes. "I don't think Lothard knows what the word 'gallant' means." She turned to Brandle. "Will you show that thing to the others and tell them what you saw?"

"I'm going to do that right now," he said, spurring his horse. "I mean to put an end to the argument about the identity of our attackers before we get to Lankura."

It wasn't long before the party reached the city gate, where Brandle called a halt while he and Kuran made a report to the captain of the City Garrison who commanded the gate house. Nor were the other members of the party silent as they waited for the two men. Several passers-by stopped to ask questions. The carriage driver was ready enough to answer and was joined by members of the Princess's Guard, as well as by Hendrel and Geivian.

Nagaro sat his big gray in silence a little apart from the rest of the group, not wishing to participate. He heard his own name mentioned rather more often than he liked, and several glances were cast in his direction. By the time Brandle and Kuran emerged from the gate house he suspected that the tale of what had happened was already spreading through the city. He said as much to Kuran.

"Good." The Lord of the Fleet smiled grimly as they rode through the streets behind the carriage. "Is everyone quite clear about the disguises?"

"Oh yes. I've also noticed that most of the Leithians in our company are being rather quiet— Rees, Vanhold, and that red-haired guard that Nevien mentioned."

Kuran grunted in satisfaction, then frowned. "I hope none of them had any part in the plot. I think the big red-haired fellow was the one who first shouted for help. Did you mark it, Brandle?"

Brandle had been listening intently and was frowning darkly. "I believe you're right, My Lord," he said. "Though he's been under my command for a number of years and I've never had any complaint about him before."

"Has he ever given any indication of his political sympathies?"

Brandle shook his head. "No. Members of the Guard are expected to keep their views to themselves, and they're generally careful to appear neutral. Still, I think I can tell which are sincerely neutral and which are covering something. This fellow has just been silent." Brandle rode on thoughtfully, then added, "I think I'll be making a few... *inquiries*."

Dusk was gathering as the princess's party passed through the city. In spite of the late hour, crowds had begun to gather along the sides of the street. Nagaro noted Kelorin, Leithian, and Turo represented among them. The people of Lankura always enjoyed a good show, and this time there were some particularly juicy rumors afloat. Some of the townspeople hailed the royal party as they passed, to wish the princess well. Some called out Nagaro's name, and Kuran's, hailing them as her defenders.

In due course, they passed through the city's western gate, crossed the broad paved courtyard in front of the palace, and came at last to the stable yard where the carriage disembarked its passengers. Kuran dismounted, telling Nagaro not to wait, and went immediately into the palace to report to King Elgurn and any of his Council who were presently in residence.

The sun was already set and the air growing distinctly cool as Nagaro rode back to the Fleet Compound. He pulled up his hood and passed through the shadowed streets at a brisk trot, hoping not to attract attention. The crowds had largely dissipated as folk had gone home to their dinners. A few of those he passed did call his name. To these he raised a hand in acknowledgment. Arriving at last at the compound, he stabled Thunder-Heels and then went to see if Taru and Pavo had returned from Wotana.

Chapter 7

Puzzles And Politics

He found his friends in the Fleet dining hall where they had apparently just joined the line of men waiting to get their dinners. Taru hailed him immediately.

"Hoy, Nagaro! What's this about ye fighting off a band o' highway thieves that attacked the princess's carriage?"

Nagaro motioned for him to speak more softly as he hastily joined them in line. "Not so loud," he muttered. "How did you learn about it so quickly?"

Taru lowered his voice even as his grin spread wider. "We stopped in town at a tavern, for a sip o' ale and some news. So it's true, then, about the attack?"

"Everyone is talk about it," Pavo put in. "But they do not always tell same story."

Nagaro frowned. "I wasn't the only defender, obviously, but there was an attack. Let's get our dinner in a basket and take it back to my quarters. Then I can tell you everything you want to know."

An hour later, the three friends had finished their dinner in the seclusion of Nagaro's kitchen-dining room at number 14 Captain's Row. Nagaro had provided all the known details of what had befallen the princess's party on the road home from River House. He was now washing the dishes while Taru dried. Pavo was at the table setting up the board and the playing pieces for a game of King's Men.

Taru was grinning as he plied the dish towel. "Finding that black wig puts the nail in it, Nagaro. That attack was set up to put the blame on the Kelorin and Turowan folk, and Lothard must have been behind it! His men must ha' told those poor Turo a pack o' lies."

Nagaro, already frowning, frowned harder. "I am fairly sure the fair-skinned men were all Leithians disguised as Kelorin. The wig, together with what Brandle and Rianine saw, supports that, but laying the blame on Lothard isn't so easy. Although it certainly looked as if the 'highwaymen' were expecting someone to intervene, coming from the direction of the High Road."

Pavo shot Nagaro a sideways glance from where he was sitting. "I also think it is Lothard who have send these man," he said. "So he can come with all his soldier and drive them away and look like hero."

Nagaro paused with a dripping plate in his hands. "That's one interpretation," he said carefully. "We just don't have any actual proof—"

"Except that it's so obvious!" Taru interjected. "Lothard was tryin' to make himself look good, and he only made *ye* look good instead. I'll wager he's fit t' be tied!

Nagaro sighed. "There were a dozen of us defending the carriage," he pointed out. "There were seven others besides me who were armed."

Taru's delight remained undiminished. "Aye, but ye said the Turo wouldn't fight against ye, and it sounds like the Leithians hadn't the nerve t' face ye without the Turo. Now, are ye going t' hand me that last plate, or stand there washing it all night?"

Nagaro bit back further protest and handed over the plate. Taru was notoriously stubborn when he thought he was right. What was worse was that Pavo was nodding his shaggy head in agreement. The young Hashtep's belief in Nagaro's heroic destiny amounted to an unshakable conviction. *And what these two believed would likely be believed by a great many other folk once the tale got about.* "I'd rather you didn't make too much of the part I played when you talk about it publicly," he said seriously. "And you mustn't accuse Lothard while there's no better proof of his involvement."

Pavo was regarding him calmly with his dark eyes. "Always you are such good man, Nagaro," he observed. "Because you do not like to boast."

Nagaro sighed as he picked up the wash basin— since the dishes were done. "It's more than that," he said. "I really don't need more attention from Lothard right now, and Kuran as much as ordered Brandle and me not to accuse him. So I'm giving you the same order."

He fixed his friends, each in turn, with a stern gaze until each gave a nod of acquiescence— Taru with reluctant ill grace, Pavo with stoic equanimity. Then he went out into his little back garden to empty the wash basin. When he returned, he found the other two men sitting at the table with the game board between them. He sat in the third chair and said, "Now you two have to tell me about your adventures."

Taru gave a rueful laugh. "There weren't any. We didn't meet a single scheming lord on the road to Wotana— going or coming. There weren't even any honest highwaymen." He extended his hand towards a playing piece to make his opening move.

"How are you doing with courting Jitali?"

Taru's hand paused. "Well enough," he said with a smug smile, before returning his attention to the board and completing his move.

"Ah. Good." Nagaro nodded easily, though inwardly he wasn't so pleased by the news. He waited until Pavo had made his answering move before he asked, teasingly, "What wonderful thing did Jitali cook for you, then?"

This time the question brought a flicker of a frown to Taru's handsome face. "Hamani made apple fritters," he said without looking up. He appeared to be concentrating on the game board. "But," he added a little too quickly, "She's teaching Jitali how to do it, and Jitali will make ones every bit as good when she's learned."

"Of course she will." Nagaro kept his tone neutral. At least this time Taru knew who had made the fritters. "How is Hamani?" he asked, as casually as he could.

Taru reached for one of his horsemen. "She seemed t' be well." He picked up the piece and finished his move without turning. "But she was busy with cooking and such."

Pavo had been silently watching his two friend's faces. "Hamani say she have missed seeing you, Nagaro," he put in, his own broad face betraying nothing. "You should come with us next time we go to Wotana. Hamani would like that very much."

Nagaro was relieved to have Pavo playing the same game he was—trying to make Hamani appear more desirable than her sister. He and Pavo both thought Taru would be better matched with Hamani than Jitali, but they knew that saying so directly would be poison. *Pavo also knew about Nagaro's feelings for Nevien, but he obviously hadn't yet said anything to Taru.*

Nagaro picked up Pavo's dangling thread, managing to sigh with genuine regret. "I missed seeing her too," he said. "I hope I can come next time. Hamani is so good to talk to, so generous and warmhearted.."

"Oh yes," said Pavo. "And when she smile, and her eye light up, she remind me of my Tenepti."

Taru hadn't taken his eyes from the board, but now he cut in. "When are you going to bring Tenepti here from Pakoa, Pavo? So ye don't have to miss her pretty smiles?"

Pavo didn't hesitate over his answer or look at Nagaro. "Maybe at end of summer when we come back from Chitaopa," he said. "Or maybe in springtime."

Taru waved impatiently at the board. "It's your move, Pavo."

"That is so." Pavo calmly studied the board. " The subject had been turned and it would be suspicious to try to turn it back.

While awaiting Pavo's move, Taru turned to Nagaro. "So," he asked pointedly. "Did you look for clues about your parents at River House?"

Nagaro, who had been thinking about what he'd said to Nevien regarding Hamani, had to hastily refocus on Taru's question. "I did, and I almost forgot. The attack put it out of my mind."

"Did ye learn anything?"

Taru was obviously keenly curious and Pavo was looking at him expectantly as well. Nagaro sighed. "Nothing certain," he said. "It seems there was a child gotten between Beloras and Maramine, as Varsyl told me. But there was nothing to prove that I was that child."

"What sort o' proof d' ye need?" Taru asked.

Nagaro frowned. "I don't know. Something to make it *feel* right, I suppose. Something written about me— or to me— by Maramine, saying she'd meant to tell me, or *wanted* to tell me. I looked at everything hidden in her writing desk, and there was nothing like that. But..." He hesitated. "I did find *this*."

He reached into his tirka and drew out the little note. He unfolded it and laid it on the table beside the game board. Taru bent over it avidly, his of lips moving as he deciphered the writing. Having come late to his letters, he wasn't a facile reader. Nagaro waited with some trepidation. He had begun to fear that he was reading too much into it.

Presently Taru had gotten the sense of the message and read it out aloud for Pavo's benefit. "*Look for him at your door at dawn of the third day, and all my love and gratitude go with you always.*" When he had finished, he looked at Nagaro uncertainly and back at the paper, puzzled.

Pavo was the first to speak. "I do not understand, Nagaro. What does it mean?"

Nagaro's heart sank. "I don't know for certain, of course," he admitted. "What do you think of it, Taru?"

Taru shook his head and shrugged. "Someone is thanking someone for meeting with a man— or maybe for doing the man a favor? Why ever did ye bother t' take it, Nagaro?"

Nagaro shifted in his seat. "*Well...*" he began uncomfortably, "I... ah... *thought* it sounded like the sort of thing a woman might write if she was giving up her child to another woman to raise..." He stopped because now they were both staring at him.

Taru took the note and bent over it, his lips moving again as he silently re-read it. "I suppose ye might be right, Nagaro," he said after he had finished. "But I thought ye said your lady guardian found ye at her door."

Nagaro sighed. "That's what I always believed. But I don't remember exactly what she said— except that she *didn't* say that a woman sent her a note that told her to look on her doorstep."

Pavo was frowning. "I do not know if 'on third day' means on third day of week," he said, "because Droviri do not have name for day of week like Hashtep do."

Taru snorted. Pavo had told them about the Hashtep custom. "Who ever had such a silly idea as naming days after things?" he demanded. "Like sun-day, moon-day, earth-day, and sky-day?"

"There is not any sky-day," Pavo reminded him severely. "The day are named for sun, moon, star, wind, fire, earth, sea, and stone. And always you know what is day a person means." He poked a finger at the note on the table. "In Droviri way, you cannot tell if it mean third day of week or third day of month."

Nagaro intervened. "You're not entirely wrong, Pavo, though generally we say 'on the third day of Madrel', for example, if we mean the third of the month. And if we mean the third day of the week, we just say 'on Third Day'." He sighed. "Of course, the third day of the month is always *also* the third day of the week, because of how the calendar is set up. All the months have exactly four weeks of eight days each— except for Idrin, of course, which only has seven."

Taru suddenly slapped the table. "Nagaro!" he cried. "Ye told me ye've always marked your birthday on the third day of Evrel, because that's the day your lady guardian found ye! So ye were found on the third day, whether it's the week *or* the month!"

Nagaro sighed. "I already thought of that, Taru." He reached for the note and drew it towards him, smoothing the paper under his fingers.

"Do you think maybe your mother have written it?" Pavo asked.

Nagaro found his throat inexplicably tight. "I'd like that to be true, of course—"

"But Nagaro, it *has* t' be!" Taru was entirely taken with his new idea and seemed to have forgotten all about the game of Kasadrin. "That note was meant t' tell your Lady Maramine to look on her doorstep on the third of Evrel!"

Nagaro frowned because Taru's thinking was too simple. "The third day can mean the third day of *any* month, or of *any* week. Do you know how many Third Days there were during the seventeen years that the Lady Maramine lived at Averwin? There are forty-nine in every single year."

Taru's face acquired an expression of concentration as he tried to multiply forty-nine by seventeen. Under other circumstances Nagaro might have laughed. Instead, he said, "I worked it out, Taru. It comes to more than eight hundred."

"Well, yes, but *still...*"

Nagaro heaved another sigh. "I'd have to find more than just this, Taru." He tapped the note. "It doesn't say nearly enough. If it was as you're thinking, there should have been something to explain exactly what it was the... *person*... wanted done on that third day. And Maramine would have had to have already said yes to whatever was being proposed. But there was nothing else about it in the desk. Nothing at all."

"Maybe the rest wasn't written down," Taru suggested. "Maybe they just talked about it."

"Well, yes, they *could* have," Nagaro conceded. "But that's another point. The way this note is written doesn't sound as if the writer was some farmer's daughter. It sounds more like someone talking to an equal— as if the two people knew each other. A noble lady doesn't just give her child away to another noble lady to raise. It doesn't make sense. And if there *were* all those arrangements made, and if it *had* been anything to do with me, I, well, I think Maramine would have told me about it. If she knew who my mother was, why would she have kept it from me?"

Taru frowned. "Ye argue first one way and then the other, Nagaro. Which is it ye want to believe?"

Nagaro pressed a hand to his brow. "I want to know which is *true*, Taru, but there isn't enough evidence to decide! I did ask some questions of old Chula the gardener. He actually remembered seeing a woman leaving the house one morning, some time at the beginning of Evrel. That women might have been the messenger who brought the note. Or she might have been the one who brought me. She might even have been my mother. But she also might have been the midwife— or someone who had nothing to do with any of this. Chula wasn't even sure whether she was Kelorin. He has an amazing memory sometimes for odd facts but it's hardly surprising he's a bit vague on these details considering it was twenty-seven years ago. He *was* quite clear that there was never any wet nurse, though."

Nagaro paused, seeing Pavo's questioning expression. "That means she didn't have another woman in to nurse me, Pavo. But it doesn't prove that she bore me. If her own baby had died she would have still had milk."

"But then there should be grave somewhere," Pavo pointed out.

Nagaro sighed. "And there isn't one that I've ever seen. I asked Chula, and he was very emphatic that there had been no digging done on the grounds at about that time by anyone but him. But that would only include the areas he considers to be his domain as gardener. Someone could have dug a small child's grave in the woods without Chula having been aware of it. And there'd be little hope of finding it now without knowing where to look."

"I'm sorry, Nagaro." Taru's sympathy was genuine. "Maybe ye should ha' gone to Irvenen with Kenthos."

"Maybe..."

There was a long pause during which the cracking of a burning branch in the fireplace sounded unnaturally loud.

Taru cleared his throat. "It's a shame whoever wrote that note didn't put their name to it," he said. "Ye might ha' learned something from that."

Nagaro touched the little drawing of a rose. "It's likely it was written by a woman named Rian. That means 'rose' in old Kelorin. Or maybe Rianine—'little rose'," he added with a grimace, thinking of the distinctly prickly Lady Rianine. "So it wouldn't help much even if it had been signed. There aren't many Kelorin names you'd call common, but Rian is as common as they come."

Pavo spoke into the pause that followed. "Do you think maybe Vothra know which thing is true, Nagaro?"

Nagaro sighed wearily. "Vothra knows anything that Maramine knew, Pavo, so I suppose so."

"Then..." Pavo hesitated, uncharacteristically abashed. "Why you do not ask Vothra to tell you?"

Nagaro drew a long breath. "Because it's exactly the kind of question Vothra doesn't answer," he said. "The Writings tell us we should turn to Vothra to seek knowledge that leads to wisdom, not to satisfy our curiosity."

"Oh." Pavo nodded sagely. "It is like that also with Sheptuum."

There was another silence.

Finally Taru said, with a cheerfulness that sounded forced, "Well if it's not t' be solved, we might as well play a few games of King's Men. Ye have the next move, Pavo."

Nagaro sighed. "Right." He refolded the note and thrust it back into his tirka. Pavo's eyes followed the movement, but then the young Hashtep shrugged and returned his attention to the board and the playing pieces.

Nagaro sat through the game, trying to give it his attention. Then, according to their custom, he played a second game against the winner, who was Taru. He found it hard to keep his mind on the game, however, and lost rather badly to a ploy he felt he should have seen coming. Custom would then have pitted the two losers against one another for a third game, but all three men were tired, though it wasn't very late. They folded up the board, put the pieces back into their bag and Taru and Pavo gathered the things up and said good night.

After closing the door, Nagaro banked the fire in the kitchen grate and carried the lamp into his room to undress for bed. The little note came into his hands again when he removed his tirka. He stowed it in his sea chest for safe keeping, tucked in at one edge next to the little collection of invitations addressed to him in the princess's elegant hand. He heaved a sigh as he closed the lid. He should probably return the note to Maramine's desk, since he had no evidence that it had anything to do with him.

He wanted very much to believe in a mother who had given him up out of love or out of necessity, rather than one who simply hadn't wanted him— or one who had raised him for seventeen years without ever telling him he was her son. It was hard, thinking he probably would never know the truth. There weren't likely to be any more clues at Averwin. And going to Irvenen Wared with nothing but the name Beloras to go on, would likely only risk revealing that he had once been Leyel Virden, the idiot prince.

He was just preparing to unbutton his shirt when he heard a knock at his front door. He took up the lamp and went see who it was, thinking it might be Taru or Pavo, returning for some reason. When he opened the door he was astonished to find no less a person than Lord Kuran standing cloaked and hooded on his front porch.

"My Lord!" he said in surprise. His commander had never paid him such a visit before.

Kuran motioned him to silence and gestured his desire to enter.

Obediently Nagaro stepped aside to let the older man pass, closing the door as soon as he was inside.

Kuran shed his cloak, draping it hastily on one of several pegs set in the wall for the purpose. "I'm glad to find you still dressed," he said. "I have things to tell you. The kitchen, I think, will suit."

Nagaro quickly led the way to the room his friends had so recently vacated. "I was just preparing for bed," he said. "But I would have come to your office if you'd sent word."

"This is quicker," Kuran replied easily. "I've only just returned from the palace and will want to be in my own bed before another hour is spent. Besides," he added more significantly. "This way is less likely to draw attention. I'm fairly certain no one noticed me as I passed through the compound." He took a seat in one of the chairs at the table.

Nagaro replaced the lamp on its hook and sat down in the chair opposite. "What's this about?" he asked.

Kuran ran a hand through black hair that was beginning to gray at the temples. "I thought it best that you know what Lothard has done— and said— this evening."

"Did he come to the palace after his hunt for the robbers?"

"Yes. Less than an hour after we parted in the stable yard. I'd made my report to Elgurn, and we'd summoned the Council and they had all just come when Brandle brought us the news that Lothard and his men were outside and they'd brought three men's bodies on their saddle bows 'as a present for the king.'"

Nagaro stared in shock. "He *killed* three of them? These men we think he hired?" Then he remembered Brandle's words. "Were they even the right men?"

"By the look of it they were." Kuran wearily massaged his neck. "They were all Turowan, of course, and one of them was surely the seasoned old fellow that spoke to you."

"The one who wouldn't fight me and who called the others away?"

Kuran nodded. "I asked Lothard why he thought they were the right men and he said that they were Turowan curs with swords and horses, caught hiding in a barn, and so they must be rogues." Kuran sighed. "Of course, if he or his agent hired them, as we suspect, he knew exactly what they were guilty of— and quite possibly where to find them. And what they were guilty of was failing to do what they'd been hired to do. Naturally Elgurn explained to Lothard rather pointedly that slaying them was inappropriate without first proving their offence, especially since we would have liked to question them."

"What did Lothard say to that?"

"That the men had resisted being taken, and so had been slain. But it was plain he thought nothing of having killed them, because they were common folk, and Turo besides."

Nagaro frowned, feeling acutely the weight of these men's deaths, men who hadn't wished to fight against him. Who had they been, he wondered, and what circumstances had led them to involve themselves in the attack on the princess's carriage? "There were more than three Turo," he murmured. "There must have been at least seven—"

"Which means that the others are out there somewhere and could bear witness, I know." Kuran finished his thought. "But they won't come forward. They've seen the punishment for incurring Lothard's displeasure." Kuran paused. "And there's more."

"My Lord?"

"Remember the wig?" Kuran rubbed his forehead. "We let Lothard do some talking before we showed him the wig, just saying we thought the men looked like Leithians, that one had blond hair, and so on. He said it was getting dark, and we must have been mistaken. And then he volunteered the opinion that these supposed robbers were some of Kenthos' followers."

Nagaro's brows drew together. "He's trying to drag *Kenthos* into this?"

Kuran waved a hand. "I suppose it still rankles him not to have been allowed to kill the man. But mostly I think he wants to blame this on the Kelorin Faction— on folk who think like the men who were with Kenthos. 'Kenthos' rabble' was what he called them."

"But Kenthos' followers were all Kelorin, and the men Lothard brought in were Turowan. It doesn't even make sense!"

Kuran sighed. "I'm afraid Lothard considers Kelorin and Turo all of a feather, at least within the borders of the old Loros Wared. He also claims he saw some Kelorin at this barn where they were hiding, but that they all got away— conveniently. But— here's the part that concerns you." Kuran looked at him keenly. "He said it was suspicious that these highwaymen all ran away so quickly when you came out of the woods."

Nagaro stared back at the older man. "He's trying to involve *me* with the robbers?"

Kuran sighed. "Or he's trying to tie you to the Kelorin Faction. First you prevented him from killing Kenthos, after all, and then these Kelorin 'highwaymen' from Loros Wared refused to fight and ran away after you came out of the woods to join the defense of the princess and her party."

"They didn't run away very fast!" Nagaro was indignant. "Not all of them, anyway. And besides, how did he know I came out of the woods? He arrived too late to witness it."

For an instant, Kuran stared. Then he laughed. "Do you know, you're right!" he exclaimed. "He shouldn't have known that, and I missed it. He could only have learned it from the robbers themselves, and why would they have told him unless they were trying to account to him for their actions?"

"Did you eventually show him the wig?"

Kuran's laughter died. "Yes. It pulled him up short, just for a moment. I could see his mind working. And then he waved his hands and said that anyone could drop a wig on the ground to try to fool us. So I reminded him that Brandle and Rianine both had seen blond hair on one of the men, but he said that a man might wear a blond wig as easily as a black one."

"But Brandle said the blond man's hair was cut short," Nagaro protested. "You could never make a wig of that sort that would be at all convincing."

"I know." Kuran sighed again. "But I didn't press the matter further. We haven't proof that any of it was Lothard's doing, so we have no one to accuse."

Nagaro frowned darkly. "I don't like the idea of Lothard trying to stir up the same trouble we just smoothed over," he said. "And I like it even less that he's trying to accuse me of doing something similar."

Kuran nodded. "Yes, it is worrisome," he said. "We can't let him rekindle all of that. But I don't think you need to worry greatly as long as you go carefully. The notion of black wigs on top of blond ones is quite preposterous. Few people will take it seriously, and few will believe ill of you, for that matter. The only allies Lothard is likely to find in this are those who already think the same way he does. But I came here tonight because I wanted you to hear about this first from me. Lothard can be really quite unpleasant, and you'll need to keep your temper no matter how he tries to provoke you. And you must be careful not to appear to give too much sympathy to the Kelorin Faction."

Nagaro heaved a sigh. "Thank you for the warning," he said. "I've already had some experience of Lothard's twisted ways. And there are genuine limits to my sympathy for those members of the Kelorin Faction that I've met so far. Still, I will be careful."

Kuran rose to his feet. "Good enough," he said grimly. "And now I'll wish you good night and be off to my bed."

After Kuran had gone, Nagaro mulled over what the Lord of the Fleet had told him as he undressed. He reviewed his past encounters with Lothard. The man was arrogant and vindictive, and displayed very few scruples. And Lothard had caused him to lose his temper rather badly on one occasion. He still winced at the way he had shouted at Kendira after Lothard had goaded her into digging into his past and had impugned the high character of his Lady Guardian. He knew he mustn't vent such anger directly on the Leithian lord. The asymmetry of their social positions meant that he must avoid accusing or insulting Lothard to his face. He couldn't risk anything that might end in a fight, for his own sake as well as for the sake of the peace of Edrovir.

Chapter 8

Being A Princess

Nevien stood in front of the wardrobe that contained her gowns. They hung arrayed on hangers like so many brightly-colored soldiers. A row of shoes marched across the wardrobe's floor, each pair aligned beneath its matching gown.

She had gotten as far as changing from her nightgown into her shift and then her progress had stalled. She was officially out of mourning— far too soon— and so could not retreat into the necessity of wearing gray. This left her too many choices.

Frowning, she reached out and put her hand on the shoulder of a dark blue-green gown trimmed around the neck and hem in black and silver. She imagined sitting in her carriage in the blue-green dress *...with Nagaro sitting across from her.* That dark blue-green seemed rather a gloomy color. If he thought she looked sad, he might become distressed on her account. She frowned harder and withdrew her hand. A moment later she stretched it out again, this time to finger the sleeve of a deep red gown, its bodice embroidered with curling tendrils of green, gold, and ivory. *Cranberry red certainly wasn't sad.* But with such a strong color, might it seem as if she were trying to draw his attention?

"What's this, Nevien? Not dressed yet?"

The voice came from a few feet behind her and belonged to Lady Merriel. Nevien had been so lost in thought that she hadn't heard the older woman approach.

"I... can't decide which dress to wear."

"For the orphans?" Merriel stepped closer and briefly gave the matter her focused attention. "Why not the gold one, dear? It's so warm and cheerful looking."

Nevien sighed. She didn't feel warm and cheerful. "I don't know," she murmured. "Sometimes the children want me to play games and that light color will show any soil so easily."

"Well, if you're worried about that, any one of the dark colors should suit. Why not the dark brown one? Nothing will show on that color— and you scarcely ever wear it."

"Mmm." The argument made sense, but... "I've never really liked that dress."

"Well, do whatever you please then," Merriel said lightly. "But do be quick about it. We should be getting into the carriage in a little less than an hour and I still have to see to the gifts. I'd be glad of any help you can give me."

Nevien felt instantly guilty. "I promise I'll come soon."

Merriel, on her way out the door, nearly collided with Rianine coming in. The diminutive, flaxen-haired chaperon stepped aside to allow the tall, slim, raven-haired young Kelorin woman to pass. Turning back, she said, "Well, here's Rian. Maybe she can help you decide. And don't forget to bring your cloak, dear, since we mean to stop at the Temple Compound afterwards." With that she hurried out.

"Decide what?" Rianine crossed the room with rather unladylike strides.

"Which dress to wear. Merriel has suggested either the gold or the brown."

"No no no!" Rianine came to halt beside Nevien, shaking her head emphatically. "The gold says everything is all sunshine and there's no need for more sympathy. And the brown is much too severe. You'd have to carry yourself like a queen the whole time in that one. If you drooped for even a moment you'd look like a mud puddle."

"I was thinking about the dark red one."

"Cranberry?" Rianine pursed her lips. "No, that's almost as bad as the gold. The color will reflect into your face and make you look rosy. You're still on the mend and entitled to milk it for all the sympathy you can get."

Nevien gave the other young woman a look of dismay. "From the *orphans?*"

"No, silly! You're going to be riding with Captain Nagaro again, aren't you?"

Nevien felt her cheeks starting to burn. "*Ye-es...*"

"Well then," Rianine declared triumphantly, "With a man like *that* to look at you, I hardly think you'd be dressing for the orphans!"

Sweet Lissafel! Nevien tried to fight down the blush. Rianine had hit uncomfortably close to the mark. "But I *should* be dressing for the orphans," she said, with what dignity she could muster.

"Well, please yourself." Rianine waved a hand in the air.

"Actually, what I was thinking was that the red one would be too distracting... would draw too much attention..."

"To itself?" Rianine arched a brow. "Or to *you?*"

"Either. Or both." Nevien did her best to shrug, then added defensively, "Really, Rian, Captain Nagaro is just a friend and I'm sure he won't care what I wear."

"Of course he won't *care*." Rianine turned back to the array of gowns. "Men don't *care* about clothes— but that doesn't mean they don't notice the effect." She reached into the wardrobe and pulled out one of the gowns on its carved wooden hanger. "Here," she said decisively. "Wear this."

Nevien took the hanger. The gown was dark green with fine accents of gold embroidery around the neck and at the ends of the long sleeves. She had always liked it. She felt good in it, too. It was a comfortable choice. "All right," she said. "But why this one?"

Rianine shrugged. "Dark enough not to show the dirt from dealing with those urchins. Pretty, but doesn't scream at one from across the room. You'll still look a little pale in it, too, so everyone will be careful not to overtax you." Rianine dusted her hands together in indication of a completed task.

Nevien nodded as she slipped the gown off the hanger. It really was one of her favorites. It was fairly old by now and she no longer wore it often for fear of wearing it out. Still, this time it should be all right. She gathered the garment up in her hands and dropped it over her head, thrusting her arms into the sleeves and unceremoniously tugging the bodice and skirt down into place.

Rianine helped her straighten it. "There," the other young woman said, then gave her a cattish glance. "And of course, green is also your best color. He'll be sure to notice your eyes."

"Rianine, you are *awful!*"

"You don't find him attractive? Honestly. I've no use for men, but *that* one? If only he were a woman, I'd eat him up! You can't say you haven't noticed."

Nevien looked away, biting her lip. "Of course I've noticed," she said. "But he's only a friend, and he can never be more than that... *and you're not helping...*"

Rianine, standing beside her, abruptly dropped all trace of mockery. "Do you want to tell me about it?" she asked.

Nevien started to shake her head. But really, who else could she tell?

She went to the bed and sat down on the edge of it. "It's just that... well..." she faltered, "...he's a very dear friend, and he's been so good to me."

Rianine came and sat beside her. "He must be good to you," she said seriously. "Because he so plainly is good *for* you. Every time you spend time with him you come away glowing. And each time it lasts a little longer."

Nevien looked at the floor. He did make her feel warm inside. "You remember that I told you he was there when my mother died?"

"Yes."

"Well, I... I asked him to hold me that night. Just for comfort. And he put his arms around me and held me. I needed it, and he did it, and it was all right. He'd done it once before, too— put his arm around me to comfort me because I asked him to. And it was all right then too. But *now*..." She paused. Then continued haltingly. "I... I find myself wanting to ask him to hold me even when I don't really need comforting all that much. And the last time we were at River House— sitting alone together in the place we've found— I actually thought for a moment that he was going to kiss me! I... I must have been wrong, of course— because, why would he? But I caught myself thinking how nice it would have been if he *had*." She looked up into the other young woman's face. "Am I being terribly wicked, Rian?"

Rianine regarded her earnestly. "What you're being," she said, "is perfectly ridiculous— to worry about it so much. He's a man, and you're a woman, and you're not crossed like me. So it's only natural to feel that way. If he pleases you so much, I don't know why you don't just lie with him under a tree somewhere—"

"*Rian!*" Nevien was horrified. "I couldn't do *that!* And he *wouldn't!* He's very proper."

"Proper!" Rianine rolled her eyes. "In my experience, men only worry about being proper when they're afraid of being caught. It's bad enough that you're going to have to marry a man you *don't* want. You shouldn't have to go to your grave without ever once having lain with one you *do!*"

"But he's my *friend*, Rian! Even supposing he would do it, we could never go back to just being friends after that. It would ruin everything!"

Rianine gave her a look of sympathetic exasperation. "It's not as if you have anything to lose," she said. "Being friends with him will have to end soon, anyway. You can't very well go on sneaking off alone with him when you're married to somebody else."

And that, Nevien realized, was exactly what she'd been trying not to think about ever since that last outing to River House: that her inevitable marriage would raise a wall between her and Nagaro. They would be reduced to exchanging mundane pleasantries when their paths crossed at one of the palace celebrations. She might be allowed the luxury of a single dance with him now and then. Maybe a serious word or two might pass between them if no one seemed to be listening. But there could be no more invitations to River House... no more long talks in the little glade beside the cedar grove.

She felt a terrible emptiness at the prospect. Yet it had to be so. *Unless he were courting one of her ladies again...* But the desperate little hope that sprang with that thought died with the next. "He's found a woman in Wotana," she murmured, speaking her thought aloud. "A Turowan woman named Hamani..." She stared across the room, unseeing.

"All Right. But even if he goes and weds some other woman, you could still bed him *once*, surely, before he's married," Rianine suggested.. "This... Hamani... would never have to know."

Nevien was aware that the other young woman had spoken, but the words didn't register. Her own thoughts still held her in thrall. "He said she isn't beautiful," she murmured. "That other folk call her plain, but he doesn't see her so. He said he wants her to be happy. But she's in love with his friend Taru, and he wants *them* to marry— so she'll be happy. He's being so *noble*..." Her voice trailed.

There was silence for several heartbeats.

"And what do *you* want, Nevien?" Rianine's words seemed to come from far away.

Nevien frowned. "I... want him to be happy too," she said slowly. "So I hope that Taru marries Hamani's pretty sister instead. If Taru thinks beauty is all that matters, it's what the fool deserves. And then Nagaro can marry Hamani, and he'll be happy. And I know he'll make *her* happy, too, in time, because he's so very kind... and so very good..."

"But it means you must lose him."

"I... I know. But... it's just as you said. I'm going to lose him anyway. And at least he'll be happy." She blinked. "Oh Rian! I've fallen in love with him, haven't I?"

Her vision blurred and suddenly there were tears streaming down her face, and in the next instant she felt Rianine's arms around her, giving her a sisterly hug.

"Poor dear Nevien," Rianine murmured. "I *do* know how it feels to be in love. And I'm sorry I teased you."

Nevien sniffed, wiping at the tears as Rianine released her. "I don't think I really knew it until just now. I think I didn't want to admit it."

"I know about *that*, too."

"Here I've always thought that falling in love was something only silly young girls did. You won't tell anyone, will you— especially not *him!*"

"Of course I won't!" Rianine was affronted. "Now go wash your face while I get your shoes and stockings. Merriel will be missing you. If she notices anything, we can say the tears were for your mother. She'll believe that."

***

Nevien and Merriel were already in the carriage waiting when Captain Nagaro cantered into the stable yard on his tall gray stallion. Nevien watched as he reined his horse to a halt and swung down from the saddle in one continuous motion, stepping from stirrup to ground with feline grace. He handed the reins to a waiting groom with whom he exchanged some quick words before turning and crossing to the carriage in three long strides.

Nevien saw the frown on his face, but she'd planned what she was going to say and decided to go through with it anyway. "You could ride beside the carriage, Captain," she said through the window. "You don't have to sit inside."

He only shook his head at her and gave the guard holding the door handle a perfunctory nod. As soon as the door was opened for him, he stepped in and dropped unceremoniously onto the seat opposite the two women.

"I'm sorry I'm late," he said. "I had to stop several times on the way to tell people to stop calling me *'Defender of Loros'* —that I was just doing my duty, defending Edrovir. But when I said *that*, they started shouting *Defender of Edrovir!'*" His slim black brows constricted more sharply. "I'll be glad to go to Chitaopa in a few months and be rid of all this!" He leaned back against the velvet cushions, then seemed to recollect himself and his brow relaxed. "Or I would be glad, if it wasn't that I'll miss the company of you two gentle ladies," he added, and favored them with a smile that showed a flash of white teeth in his dark, bearded face.

Nevien found watching Nagaro's features pass from thunder to sunshine as exhilarating as witnessing a summer thunderstorm. *Some men's good looks were spoiled by a frown, but not his...* She pulled herself up short. Thoughts like those could only lead to trouble. She'd managed to collect herself after her revealing talk with Rianine, but now she was afraid all the bits would fly apart again, sitting in close quarters with Nagaro— hence her suggestion that he ride outside. Hurriedly she tried to find a way to continue the conversation.

"At least they're shouting those things at *you*, Captain, rather than at Kenthos," she said. "You're a Fleet officer, and not a member of any faction. So in focusing on you, they've put aside their preoccupation with the heir of Loros.

Nagaro's expression immediately turned serious. "They haven't put it very far aside, since the 'Defender of Loros' refers to my having stood between Kenthos and Lothard Hurn."

"At least Lothard seems to have turned *his* attention to the re-opening of the courtship— assuming that the attack on my carriage was his work."

"That's true." He sounded relieved, but a shadow darkened his face.

Nevien smiled as bravely as she could. "When the courtship gets into full swing, the shouts will all be for me. You'll be able to ride through the streets without anyone taking any notice at all."

"I could wish for a happier reason to be left in peace." The shadow deepened, but after a moment he shrugged it off and added, "Lothard hasn't completely forgotten politics, I'm afraid. He's been trying to link me to Kenthos, and to planning the attack on the carriage."

"So I've heard. But I don't think anyone believes him."

Merriel spoke. "I hope you don't think that all Leithian folk care what Lothard says. There's only a few that do. Not even all of those who agree with his political position actually like him."

Nagaro turned to address the chaperon. "I know there are many Leithians who have no love for Lothard," he said. "There was one who came up to me on the street just this morning who told me he was sure I had nothing to do with the attack— that he wouldn't be surprised if Lothard had planned it himself!"

Nevien had to laugh at this, and Merriel joined her.

Their mirth quickly subsided, however, and Merriel abruptly put her hand to her mouth. "Oh dear, Captain!" she said. "I forgot to tell you that Nevien and I mean to stop at the Temple Compound after we finish our visit with the orphans. "If you'd ridden your horse, you could have just gone home your own way."

He considered. "I still could. I could walk."

"But then all the folk in the street would see you," Nevien pointed out, remembering how annoyed he had been in the stable yard.

He frowned. "That's true, though they don't notice me nearly as much when I'm not on horseback. But Kuran has given me the whole morning. How long do you expect to be at the temples?"

"Not long. What do you think, Merriel? Will we be longer there than half an hour?"

"I shouldn't think so." Merriel dropped her eyes and her cheeks went a little pink. "I certainly won't be."

Nevien thought that she knew the cause of the older woman's embarrassment and hoped that Nagaro wouldn't notice. Indeed it didn't seem that he had.

"Well then," he said seriously. "If there's no objection, I'll just ride along with you. I certainly don't mind sitting in the carriage for half an hour."

"That would be fine," Nevien told him quickly. "No one will pay any attention to you in here, I'm sure." And then she hastily turned the conversation to the subject of what might be expected when they reached the orphanage, and Merriel stepped back into the discussion with evident relief.

By the time they neared their destination, the harmless talk had put them all at ease and Nevien felt safe in allowing herself to surreptitiously watch Nagaro. As the carriage rolled around the last corner, she was reflecting that it was a small miracle that he hadn't ever suffered any crippling or disfiguring wounds, considering all that he'd lived through. Not that it would have mattered to her if he had. It was his earnestness that she loved, his intelligence, and his honesty— not his good looks. When he'd said at River House that physical beauty wasn't important, he had spoken truly.

When the carriage drew up outside the Sailor's Child Orphanage, Nagaro got out and handed first Merriel and then Nevien down onto the cobbles, bowing to each as he did so. Nevien felt a very gentle thrill as he took her hand, but nothing more alarming. He bent close to her ear and asked, "Should I escort you on my arm?"

She nodded.

It's quite all right, she thought as she lightly placed her hand on the forearm he held ready for her, *I can manage this.* And then he bent to her ear again and said, "I remember when I first saw you in that dress on the day of the Mautep attack, three years ago. It's a good color for you because it matches your eyes."

Her heart did a somersault. Rianine had said he wouldn't notice! Though he *had* made his remark in the most matter-of-fact way imaginable...

The carriage driver and the two guards who had accompanied them were unpacking the gifts they'd brought. Lady Merriel beckoned, and led the way up the steps and through the wide front door. Nevien followed on Nagaro's arm, desperately trying to regain her mental equilibrium. And then the children came running to meet them and she dropped his arm to reach for their welcoming hands as they shouted, *"Princess Nevien!"* and *"Captain Nagaro!"*

***

The orphan children were being taught trades and crafts that might serve them when they were grown. Since it was important to reinforce with the orphans how important this was, Nevien and Lady Merriel dutifully sat with a group of girls who were practicing spinning with spindle and distaff. She and Merriel allowed the girls to give them a lesson and then did their own practice, just like the children.

As far as Nevien knew, Nagaro was somewhere else learning something to do with furniture making. Nevien frowned. Furniture making would have to be easier than *this*. Try as she might, she couldn't get the thread even.

An eight-year-old watched her critically. "It's not supposed to have thick parts and thin parts," she said as if she thought Nevien might not know any better.

One of the older girls shot the younger one a look and said, "*I* wasn't any better when I just started, and neither were *you!*"

"But she's all grown up!"

Nevien sighed and turned to Lady Merriel, whose thread ran smooth and even. "Why are you so much better at this than I am?"

The older woman looked up from her work. "I was taught to do it as a girl," she said. "Though it's been years. I suppose it's something you never forget once you've learned."

Nevien sighed again. "Unfortunately *princesses* aren't taught to spin."

In fact, she realized, princesses weren't taught anything very useful— just embroidery and a little sewing. She frowned. She had embroidered the gown she was wearing but she hadn't sewn it. That would likely have been beyond her skill. She *did* know how to sew a shirt. She had sewed shirts for each of her three husbands. *And she'd given one that she'd sewn for her third husband to Nagaro. It had been the morning after they'd first met. He had worn it to River House once or twice, though not on their most recent outing.*

She shook her head, thinking about the early days of their acquaintance. She'd once told him rather smugly that princesses didn't fall in love. She blushed now to think how naive she'd been. *He* had been skeptical, of course, and her feelings for him now were proving him right. She frowned again. Nagaro had never done anything the least bit flirtatious. All he'd done was talk to her, and listen, and show her that he was prepared to be her friend. It was her own heart that had betrayed her.

It struck Nevien that she now had another hopeless love to pray for at the Temple of Lissafel, the Maiden Goddess. But in the next instant she reminded herself that it was selfish folly to ask the goddess to help her wed Nagaro when his heart lay elsewhere. It would surely tempt some twist of fate that would bring all her hopes to ruin. *Not that she had any hopes.*

She would have to do her best to be strong. She'd been offering prayers on Alisset's behalf for some time. It wasn't selfish to wish that Alisset might wed Nile Fendred. It was just a wish for their happiness, since they both loved each other. She could pray that Nagaro would wed Hamani—but no! That wouldn't do either, because then Hamani couldn't have Taru. Nor could she pray that Hamani would wed Taru, because then Nagaro couldn't have Hamani...

While Nevien was marveling at how complicated love could be, the spinning practice came to an end, and it was time to hand out the gifts they had brought. There were shoes and handkerchiefs, and wooden tops to play with, and of course there were fruits, and nuts, and sugar buns.

***

Back in the carriage at last, Nevien sat watching Nagaro, now completely at his ease as he stretched and beamed at her.

"It's good to see you smile, My Lady," he said.

And when he said it, she realized that she was indeed smiling. And she knew why. "It's good to see *you* smile," she said."

He laughed. "I enjoy the children. Talking to them makes me forget all the serious grown-up things that trouble me."

"I'll wager the chair you made was the best, too."

He looked thoughtful. "I don't know. And it's not as if I really made it either. Someone else made the pieces and I just put them together. The children all said it was the best, but I think they would have said so whether it was true or not."

"Oh, no." Nevien shook her head emphatically. "In my experience, children are much more honest than that— the younger ones, at least. Some of them were quite unimpressed with my spinning."

They rode on a little way, talking about what they had done at the orphanage, until the carriage turned onto the street that led to the Temple Compound. Merriel had been sitting quietly, letting the two of them talk, but when there came a lull in the conversation, she stirred. Turning to Nagaro, she asked, "Do Kelorin folk have any temples?"

He shook his head. "No. They used to say the whole world was a temple, but you don't hear that very often anymore."

"Where do they go to pray then?" Merriel asked, her blue eyes innocently curious.

Nevien felt compelled to say something, for she remembered what her mother had taught her. "Vothrin people don't pray the way Leithians do, Merriel."

"They don't pray?" Merriel looked shocked.

Nagaro leaned towards her, suddenly also very serious. "Vothrin people do pray," he said. "But we don't pray to ask for things, because we don't believe that some power is going to rearrange the workings of the world for our personal benefit. And we can pray anywhere, because all we do is think about what we really want— what's important and appropriate to hope for— and then we hope for it with all our hearts."

Merriel suddenly laughed, and the mood lightened. "Oh *well*," she said. "That's not so very different then. Maybe you stop short of *asking*, and we don't, but we Leithians know we had better think carefully about what we ought to hope for before we ask. They say the gods have a way of turning your wishes against you."

Nagaro grinned. "We say the same thing about Lokundas, the Turner of Worlds, who sends men their fates. That's why we don't even *try* to pray to Lokundas."

"And Leithians can pray in lots of places besides temples, too," Nevien put in quickly. "Anywhere, really."

He frowned and asked, "Why do you go to the temples then? If you could pray anywhere?"

She smiled. "Simple folk believe the gods listen better there, I'm sure," she said. "And also, of course, we bring offerings to show the gods our sincerity. In the old days it used to be food or wine, but now the priests and priestesses encourage everyone to bring coins. I'm sure they've found that they can more easily put money to good use." She read the question in his face and answered it before he could ask. "The money contributes to the upkeep of the temples, and the needs of the priests and priestesses—and quite a lot of it is used for charity."

"Oh," he said, nodding. "I see. And I certainly can't quarrel with doing charity."

The carriage had rolled into the Temple Compound and Merriel leaned out of the window to instruct the driver to find a stopping place that was close to both the Temple of Lissafel and the Temple of Solbrid. As the driver carefully threaded a course through the hurrying folk, Nevien studied Nagaro's profile as he stared curiously out the window.

Presently he turned to look at her. "I've never been here before," he said. "Why do so many of the folk go cloaked and hooded? The day is warm, but I'd say almost half of them are bundled up as if it were winter."

"It's supposed to be a way to humble yourself before the gods," she told him. "Those who are cloaked are mostly the wealthy and the high-born, covering their fine clothes lest the gods look askance at them for flaunting their good fortune and decide to take them down a peg. But I think most of them do it also so they won't be recognized." She fished a basket from under the seat and pulled two cloaks out of it, one of which she handed to Merriel. "After all, who wants to have folk pointing at you and whispering when you go to the temples?"

For answer Nagaro merely nodded, both understanding and sympathy in his eyes. As the carriage creaked to a stop, he settled himself to wait while the two women put on their cloaks and disembarked.

Merriel drew close to Nevien as they climbed the steps of the Temple of Lissafel. "With all that talk about what it's appropriate to ask for, I've been thinking that maybe I should change the words of my prayer a little bit," she said in a worried voice.

"What words were you going to use?"

Merriel gave her nervous glance. "I meant to ask that Kuran might... ah... look upon me with favor."

"That's... fairly direct, if not exactly *specific*."

"Oh, Nevien!" Merriel's hands fluttered. "How can I be specific? I'm so ashamed! A woman at my time of life shouldn't be asking for such a thing!"

They were passing under the temple portico into the high, dim central hall. Nevien lowered her voice to a whisper. "Why don't you just pray that he may find a good wife to be a comfort to him in his remaining years? That's what you want for him, isn't it? And you know you'd make him a good wife."

"Of course I would!"

"Then the Lady will surely know that too."

***

A short time later, when she knelt on the thin cushion before the Listening Wall in one of the little prayer rooms, Nevien had to laugh at herself. It was so easy to think of a good, cautious, unselfish prayer for someone else. She'd thought of one easily for Merriel. And to express Alisset's hopes, she had asked the Lady to bless both Alisset and Nile with happiness by bringing them together— if it could be done without doing harm to anyone. Now she was thinking of Nagaro, and Hamani, and of course his friend Taru. *She didn't really want anyone to be unhappy...*

A cool breath of air stirred in the room, not enough to carry away the mingled scents of the herbs that poor women used as perfumes because they couldn't afford the floral essences favored by the high-born. It was very quiet. Not even an echo of the sounds from the central hall managed to pass the great stone baffles around which the supplicants had to thread their way to reach the four-by-four-foot cubicles. Only the goddess would hear her words. Nevien frowned as she tried to find words that would say what it was safe to say, and nothing more. Presently she bowed her head and murmured, "Sweet Lissafel, Queen of the Night, please bless everyone who loves, wherever they may be, with as much happiness as can be spared."

She sighed. She felt it lacked both poetry and precision. And it was much too big in scope for the size of her offering. Still it would have to do. She rose, leaving her coins on the offering stone. As she left the little room, she caught herself wondering whether the Maiden Goddess really had been listening to her words. *And if she can hear my words, can't she also hear the thoughts behind them?* She shook her head at herself. There was no escaping her own heart, and no peace or safety anywhere.

Lady Merriel was waiting for her in the central hall. The older woman looked much more composed than she had before going in to make her prayer. "I took your advice," the little Leithian woman told her in a hushed voice. "It was a good, unselfish prayer, and I feel much better for it."

Outside in the sun, they turned automatically towards the Temple of Solbrid, for Merriel knew that Nevien always stopped at the Altar of the Lost, which was enclosed within a little annex built under the high portico of temple of the Mother Goddess. The two women climbed the steps to the portico in silence, each lost in her own thoughts. At the doorway of the altar Merriel stood aside and spoke at last.

"I'll just wait here."

Nevien nodded and stepped through the doorway into the familiar gloom where a single candle glowed in a tiny niche above the altar. The altar stone was pale and smooth and unadorned, its upper surface broken only by the small round hole through which traditionally a single coin was meant to be dropped. She didn't linger long. It took only a moment for her to draw her thoughts together and recite the prayer she had composed, years ago, for her first husband who had disappeared during an attack on Lankura and whose body had never been found.

"This is for Leyel, wherever he may wander, be he living or dead. Wherever his spirit may dwell, keep him safe and bring him peace."

She dropped a silver trokin through the hole before bowing her head briefly and going out again to rejoin Lady Merriel.

Chapter 9

Echos Of The Past

As they approached the carriage, Nevien saw Nagaro's face framed in the window, watching them. She frowned as she realized that he must have picked them out among the crowd despite the cover of their cloaks and hoods. He knew what to look for, of course, two women walking together, one tall, one short; she with her plain black leather slippers, Merriel with her dainty shoes with the gilt buckles peeping from beneath her skirt.

Nagaro swung the carriage door open for them and they climbed in, gratefully shaking off their cloaks, for the day was really too warm for such covering.

As the carriage began to roll, he asked, "What was the second place you went to, outside the door of Solbrid's temple? I couldn't make out the name above the door."

"The Altar of the Lost." Nevien answered absently. "I always say a prayer and make an offering there for Leyel Virden."

It was as if something froze in his face for an instant. Then he moved again, but guardedly. "Surely you don't think he's still lost somewhere," he said seriously. "I thought he'd been declared dead, and I'm quite sure I saw a grave marker for him in the palace garden."

"Well, his body isn't there, of course, though he must be dead," Merriel put in. "But even so his spirit could still be lost."

Nagaro turned on the chaperon, his gaze stabbing her. "You don't think his spirit would have had enough sense to find a new life?" he asked sharply.

"Well, I... no—" Merriel was flustered. "But Leithians don't believe that people's spirits live more than one life."

Nevien, surprised by Nagaro's sudden intensity, tried to smooth the waters. "No one knows if he's alive or dead," she said quickly. "They never found his body."

Nagaro appeared to become aware of her eyes on him and his face relaxed a little, though he avoided her gaze. "I beg your pardon, My Lady," he said to Merriel, speaking levelly. "It's just that according to Vothrin teaching, the body shapes the spirit that dwells in it for as long as the flesh holds that spirit. Spirit by itself can't be simpleminded, or blind, or crippled— or male or female, or anything else for that matter." He turned an earnest gaze to Nevien. "So you needn't worry about Leyel Virden's spirit, My Lady."

Nevien had begun to frown. The turn of the conversation was causing her to remember things she preferred not to think about. "But what if he is still alive?" she asked quietly.

His dark brows came instantly together. "In that case, he would do well enough as long as folk left him alone and didn't make sport of him!"

Neven was stung. "I never made sport of him!"

"Of course you didn't!" Despite the vehement tone, this was spoken as if it were an established fact. "But nearly everyone else did."

"Well some people did laugh and make jests, I know, but—"

"*Some people?*" Nagaro's eyes fairly blazed. "He was the laughing stock of Edrovir, My Lady! Even now I hear folk as far away as the southern isles use his name as a synonym for idiot!"

"Oh surely not!"

Merriel coughed. "You would never have heard the worst of it, Nevien," she said. "I've heard things like that said— everywhere from the royal kitchens, to the marketplace, to my father's Hold."

"Not *still*, surely!"

Merriel nodded ruefully. "Not as often, but yes."

Nevien sat, stunned, looking from one of them to the other. Merriel looked uncomfortable. Nagaro's expression betrayed no hint of victory. He looked, if anything, as if he felt a little ill, and he didn't quite meet her eyes.

"Surely you don't still think he would have been better off dead than living in Lankura, do you, Captain?" she asked. "You said that to me once."

She thought he flinched a little, but he didn't immediately answer.

Merriel stirred. "I suppose that would be all right by Kelorin thinking," she said. "Since they don't have a ban on seeking their own deaths, as other folk do."

Nagaro shot the Leithian woman a frowning look, then dropped his gaze to stare at his hands where they lay clasped in his lap. "I've seen men of every race seek death," he said quietly. "There was a Kelorin man, a slave, who refused food rather than try to recover from the plague. He said he'd rather die in the open air than in the black hole of the oar deck. But there was also Taru's father, a Turo, who saw his wife killed by a Mautep raider. He struck the man in the face to draw his wrath, and then turned his chest to the man's sword. There was the Jinari who starved himself rather than eat food he thought his god had forbidden him to eat. And there was the Hranji who was beaten to death by the slave-driver because he refused to row. I've seen more than one Mautep warrior die rather than surrender. And young Peldred sought an honorable death in battle rather than live with the memory of his shame, even though Leithians say that seeking death is a sin. We all have things we're unwilling to bear. And who is anyone to say what the right choice is for another?"

The carriage rattled on. No one spoke.

Nevien shivered. Nagaro had refrained from mentioning the two members of the royal household— Prince Elyan and Queen Semorel— who had sought his help in ending their pain by letting go of life. Neither of those deaths had seemed wrong to her. She'd even been present at her mother's passing, had participated, but the fact wasn't generally known.

She looked hastily at Merriel. The older woman was sitting, frozen, staring at Nagaro and looking rather pale after listening to his catalog of horrors. Nevien cleared her throat. "I suppose there are some things that no one should have to endure," she conceded. "And I suppose it's hard to say exactly what all those things might be. But as far as Leyel is concerned, I'm sure he had no idea he was being made fun of, so I don't think I'm doing him any disservice by hoping he might still be alive."

Nagaro's head came up. "How do you know what he understood?" he asked sharply.

"Well he never protested. He gave no sign..." Her voice trailed under the intensity of his gaze.

Abruptly he dropped his eyes and turned towards the window, hunching down into the carriage seat. "If you're sure of that, you should let it give you comfort," he said. His voice sounded taut, as if he were trying to keep it even. After a moment's awkward silence he added, still without looking at her, "But you of all people shouldn't have to make offerings for him, My Lady. You surely never did him any harm and have no need to make amends."

And because he wasn't looking at her, he didn't see how she dropped her eyes and bit her lip.

Inwardly, Nevien writhed, wishing he wouldn't sound so certain that she was blameless. "I didn't care for him as I should have," she murmured, though that didn't go nearly far enough, and she knew it.

A moment later she risked raising her eyes and saw that he was still turned rigidly towards the window.

Merriel said, "I'm sure you did your best, dear."

Still Captain Nagaro said nothing.

The carriage rolled on along Broad Street and thence to Market Street, while its occupants sat in silence. Nevien spent most of that time in a stew of unpleasant memories complicated by Nagaro's recent responses and current stony silence.

He couldn't know how miserable she had been... how much she'd wished to escape from that first marriage. *She'd tried everything she could think of in an effort to get some genuine response from Leyel, but he'd remained as wooden as a post. Half of what he'd said had been completely inappropriate to the situation and the other half had sounded as if someone had told him what to say and he had no idea what it meant.*

Nevien bit her lip again. She was tremendously grateful at that moment that Nagaro wasn't looking at her. It meant he couldn't see her face— couldn't read her trouble in her eyes. *If he were to ask her the cause...* She squeezed her eyes shut. It was true, as she had said, that Leyel had never complained, but it wasn't entirely true that he'd never given any sign that he was unhappy. On several occasions she'd thought she had read something like anger or resentment in his eyes. Always it had been before one of his fits, so that she'd begun to wonder if emotions were what brought them on. She'd begun to imagine that if a way could just be found to forestall the fits, the emotions might be able to come through. *It was that kind of thinking that had tempted her to—*

The carriage lurched to a stop and her eyes sprang open to see that they were in the stable yard. Across from her, Nagaro stirred and finally turned to look at her. He gave her a furtively apologetic look and hurriedly rose to open the door. Stepping down, he turned to offer her his hand and assisted her to alight, then turned his attention to doing the same for Merriel.

Nevien stood waiting, her thoughts still running. *She'd never told anyone. She'd locked the guilty secret away...* It would have been a relief, she suddenly realized, to be able to tell Nagaro, this person with whom she'd come to feel so comfortable. She wouldn't have done it with Merriel there, of course, and now she wasn't sure she'd ever dare to. What if he thought less of her for it? He seemed to feel so strongly about Leyel, and his good will meant everything to her.

Nagaro had finished helping Merriel out of the carriage, and he turned from the chaperon to Nevien, giving her a wry smile. "I'm sorry, My Lady," he said. "You wanted me in part for my company, I think, and I've been rather poor company the whole way back from the Temple Compound."

His gray eyes were serious, not angry, and she felt a rush of warmth and an ache in her heart. "Please don't worry about it," she said quickly. "I think it's quite wonderful that you care so much about the welfare of a stranger."

Something flickered in his eyes and he looked away. "I don't like to see anyone made sport of," he said tightly. Then he raised his hand to signal to one of the grooms. "Would you bring my horse, please, Zirda?"

"You needn't go straight away, Captain," Merriel put in. "You could come up and sit with us for a while."

But he shook his head. "I'm sorry, My Lady. I can't stay today." He spoke lightly, but it seemed a little forced. "I've just remembered an errand, and I still have time to do it if I hurry."

"Oh, well, by all means." Merriel was gracious.

In the next moment, the groom appeared leading the big gray stallion and Nagaro made his farewells, swung lightly into the saddle, and trotted briskly out of the stable yard.

The two women watched him until he was out of sight, then turned and entered the palace by the small side door that adjoined the rear corner of the stable yard. As they climbed the back stairs, Merriel turned to Nevien.

"Captain Nagaro certainly takes a great interest in Leyel Virden, doesn't he?"

"Yes, he does."

Merriel pursed her lips. "Come to think of it, I remember now that he snapped at Delasin Virden when she said she was no relation to Leyel."

Nevien knew of the incident only because Merriel and Rianine had told her about it. "I wasn't at the match table that day," she said, frowning. "What did he say exactly?"

"Oh goodness, I don't know. *She* had said that Leyel was adopted, and he said he'd heard that Leyel was actually Maramine's son— a love child, I think— and that she shouldn't try to distance herself because none of it had been his fault. Some such thing."

"Well he's right about that last part, but still it was a little hard on Delasin. She must have been only a child when Leyel was in Lankura."

"Yes she was. And I think Captain Nagaro must have realized it too. He tried to apologize— said it was only something he'd heard— but she ran away in tears. And now of course Varsyl Virden is going about saying that it's true after all." Merriel shook her head. "It's only a turn of chance, I'm sure, that the captain had heard the right tale. But after today, I don't think it was chance the way he snapped at her. I wonder why he cares so much."

They had reached the second floor landing and Nevien paused to catch her breath, not having fully recovered from the long ordeal of caring for her dying mother. Merriel of course paused with her. Nevien stood frowning thoughtfully. "So do I," she said. Then after breathing for a moment, she added. "He said he doesn't like to see others made sport of... and he himself is very sensitive to ridicule..."

"What, *him?*" Merriel's eyebrows shot up. "A man like that? What could anyone possibly find about him to make fun of?"

"I don't know. But the first time he asked me to dance it was only to spare me from having to dance again with Lothard, and when he realized he was actually going to have to do it, he was nearly in a panic for fear he wouldn't remember the steps."

"*Really?*" Merriel put a hand to her mouth to stifle her mirth. "And then he danced like a dream."

Nevien nodded. "It's strange, isn't it? He's a man who can face a forest of swords, by all accounts, or offer up his life to the Emperor of the Mahuk Baar; but he was terrified of making a fool of himself on the dance floor. And he made off afterwards in a hurry when he heard people laughing."

"Now that you mention it," Merriel mused. "Kendira did tell me that he misunderstood what they were laughing about."

Nevien was frowning. If someone were excessively sensitive about something there was usually a reason. "Perhaps he was made fun of a great deal for something when he was a child," she said, thinking aloud. "Or perhaps he saw someone else made fun of— someone he cared about."

"It must have been someone else," Merriel said with conviction. "I can't imagine him, as a child, being any less intelligent, less dextrous, or less good-looking."

Nevien glanced up at the portrait that hung on the wall. Leyel Virden's face, serious, thoughtful— and exquisitely molded— looked down at her. "That's it!" she exclaimed with sudden insight. "He must have been *too* handsome! Too pretty for a boy— and so was Leyel!" *Hadn't she once thought that the two of them could almost have been brothers?* "They would have been very nearly the same age, too," she went on. "I imagine some folk couldn't resist pointing out that he was as pretty as the simple-minded prince whom everyone was laughing at." She turned away from the painting and started up the final flight of stairs.

Merriel hurried after her. "Do you really think that's it? I mean, it does seem to make sense."

"Well, it could explain a great deal." Nevien didn't wish to sound too certain. She knew better than to assume that something must be true merely because it made sense. Still, it did feel right...

And then she thought of the beard he wore, and the kuma stain that he used to darken his skin— the stain that he used in all seasons and never allowed to fade. Were these efforts to make his appearance more manly? Or to make him less like Leyel Virden? It could be either— or both, of course. *So he was a man who was unsure of himself. Still trying keep the laughter at bay...*

As she continued up the stairs, she realized that some people would have seen Nagaro's behavior as evidence of weakness, but she only felt more strongly drawn to him. She didn't like men who were too sure of themselves. And some men, finding themselves subjected to such ridicule, would have turned their anger into resentment of Leyel Virden for making their own lives miserable. But Nagaro was a man who could see the suffering of another and be moved, not to resentment, but to sympathy. One who would turn his anger not on Leyel, but on those who caused such pain.

***

Nagaro rode furiously through the streets, mechanically acknowledging waves and hails from folk as he passed— although these weren't many. Indeed he went by so quickly that most of the folk in the streets would have had no chance to react even if they'd recognized his face.

Fool! he told himself. *Idiot!*

When would he learn to simply hold his tongue when others spoke of Leyel Virden?

He was quite sure that no one would ever think to connect him with the idiot prince if only he could manage not to betray himself through his own stupidity. Yet here it was, ten years after the fact, and the memories still made him writhe. He still felt rage boil up inside of him at the memory of how he'd been treated. *And to hear anyone suggest that they knew what he'd been going through—*

He'd even been short with Nevien. That hurt.

He shouldn't blame her... couldn't blame her. He knew how badly she had suffered. He must learn to curb these feelings! Whatever had possessed him to speak so revealingly? Maybe he'd become too comfortable with Nevien... too much at ease. Or maybe he cared too much about what she thought... what she felt. She was berating herself— feeling guilty— because she hadn't 'cared properly' for her wooden puppet of a husband! As if anyone could have cared for him as he'd been while under the influence of heskial! She was too good... too kind... too noble...

Distracted as he was by his thoughts, he nearly missed the entrance into Brass Bell Lane, but caught himself just in time and drew on the reins. He'd told Lady Merriel he had an errand to do, and he wanted there to be some truth to it. This was the only errand he could think of. He hadn't heard from Fineas, and it was too soon to think that lore master might have succeeded with the linjana, but there was always the hope of finding some new book to read in the little bookshop. Hurriedly dismounting, he tried to walk in Thunder-Heels' shadow as he passed under the arch, where the old brass bell hung, and moved down the cobbled lane.

Half an hour later, he was feeling considerably calmer when he rode out through the city's South Gate into the paved space between Lankura's city wall and the wall of the Fleet Compound. It was early afternoon, and the space was thronged with people, horses, and laden carts. Most of this traffic was coming and going between the city and the quays where the ships of the Royal Fleet were moored, or between the city and the road that ran eastward along the River Edro, into the interior of the land of Edrovir. One of the vehicles present on this occasion, however, was a carriage drawn up directly in front of the gate of the Fleet Compound, implying that its occupant had business there.

Nagaro couldn't help noticing the carriage since he had to go around it to pass through the Fleet Compound's gate. The vehicle was rather ornate, sporting some unnecessary carved embellishments and flourishes of scarlet paint. It must have arrived recently, too, for the horses were lathered with sweat. The driver was sprawled, exhausted, on his seat. The carriage's passenger, an elderly man with snow-white hair was leaning out of the window, remonstrating loudly with one of the Fleet warriors guarding the gate.

Nagaro, not wishing to intrude on the rather heated exchange, was doing his best to slip past the disputants unnoticed when the Fleet warrior suddenly cut short his expostulation and exclaimed, "But here he is, now! Captain Nagaro, this man wishes to speak to you!"

Nagaro reined Thunder-Heels to a halt and turned in the saddle to take his first real look at the owner of the carriage. He had just time to recognize Burdal Korinos before the man flung open the carriage door and hailed him, excitedly brandishing a silver-tipped cane.

"Captain Nagaro! By the Eyes, I'm glad you've come at last!"

"Why? What's the matter, Tor Burdal?" Nagaro turned the gray stallion around so he could face the old merchant.

"It's about my grandson. Is he here with you?"

"Sindar? No. I thought he would have been with you in Vered Mahir."

The old man contrived to wring his hands without dropping his cane. "He *was*— until four days ago! We... ah... had quarreled the night before over how soon he might leave us to go to Lankura to join the Fleet. I wanted him to stay until midsummer so we could help him be more prepared, but he said he was tired of everyone helping him. It appears that he took a little money, some food, and a change of clothes, and left early in the morning on a west-bound river boat. Someone saw a man matching his description in Granath the following afternoon, but there's been no other trace. I was *sure* he would have come to Lankura! I hoped I would find him here with you!"

Nagaro's heart had been sinking steadily as he listened. "I'm afraid I haven't seen him," he said gravely, then turned to the guard, who was still listening. "Have you seen a Kelorin man of about my age and height hanging about recently? You might have recognized him. He used to work in the stables."

The guard shook his head. "No, Captain."

"Oh dear! Oh dear!" Burdal was beside himself. "Whatever can have happened to him?"

Nagaro sat chewing his lip thoughtfully. "I don't think there's reason to fear for him yet just because he hasn't come to the compound or asked for me," he said after a moment. "I'm sure he was making for Lankura as you say, but he wouldn't come to me if he doesn't want help. He'll look for work and lodgings— but not in the Fleet stables this time. He'll be trying to make his own way until he presents himself at the muster of new recruits at midsummer. Has his speech improved?"

"His speech? Yes." Burdal had calmed a little. "He still doesn't speak like you or I, but he does better than he did, and he understands a great deal more."

"Well, that's good. Let's hope he gets his wish this time."

"But what am I to *do* about this, Captain?" The old man's distress was quite piteous.

Nagaro considered. "We can't do more than wait and watch, and make inquiries perhaps. If you wish to take lodgings and stay in the city for a few days, we may get some word of him. But if you return to Vered Mahir without any word, you may be sure I will write to you with any news as soon as it comes to me."

"But is there nothing else? He'll be having such a difficult time! I could easily pay for his lodgings so he wouldn't have to work."

Nagaro shook his head. "You mean to be kind, I know, Tor Burdal, but he wouldn't like that. I know it's hard when he rejects all your offers of help, but I think I understand him. He's a grown man and doesn't want to feel that he's being treated like a stripling. One day I hope he'll come to appreciate all you've done for him."

"Do you really think he'll be all right, then?" Burdal's voice still quavered.

"There's a good chance of it. He traveled all the way from the Mahuk Baar to Jinara on his own, after all."

"Well then, I'll try to trust what you say." The old man heaved a sigh. "I'll have to stay here in Lankura for a few days to rest myself. I've come a long way in great haste and I am no longer young. Perhaps, as you say, we'll learn something before I must return to Vered Mahir. But if not, I'll put my trust in you, Captain."

***

Nagaro was feeling very sober as he rode through the Fleet Compound. All his earlier concerns were, for the time, forgotten. He was more worried about Sindar than he'd admitted to Tor Burdal. The young Kelorin had indeed traveled from the Baar to Jinara, but he'd subsisted along the way by means of petty thievery. Nagaro hoped the young man wouldn't be driven to return to that practice, which, if he were caught, might bar him from a place in the Royal Fleet. How, he wondered, could he possibly find Sindar in a city as large as Lankura?

At the stable, he gave Thunder-Heels a quick rub-down, then sought out the stable master and appraised him of the situation. "If Sindar comes asking for a reference," he finished, "or if anyone asks about his having worked for you, I'd appreciate it if you'd send word to me."

The stable master nodded. "Aye, Capt'n, I'll do that. He was a good worker. I'll do anything I can."

As Nagaro turned to go, one of the stablemen, a middle-aged Turo named Kinu, stepped up to him, and said, "Beggin' your pardon, Capt'n, but I couldn't help overhearing what ye said t' the master. I'd like to make a suggestion, if I may."

"Of course, Zirda."

"Sindar 'll be looking for work in a stable or horse-barn, or maybe in the cattle-yards. There's a lot o' Turo what works in such places. Ye could do worse than t' put the word out among the Turo."

"That's a good suggestion. Thank you, Kinu."

The man ducked his head. "The truth is, Capt'n, I've a message for ye."

Nagaro frowned. "A message? From whom?"

"From my mother's sister's first cousin. Her name is Omei an' she said ye'd remember her."

"Omei? The Turowa who worked for some of the Leithians on Broad Street?"

"Aye. That's the one." Kinu grinned. "She wants to meet with ye as soon as ye finds it convenient. She's got somethin' t' tell ye about those Turo what attacked the princess's carriage t'other day."

"Oh. Of course. You can tell her that I'll meet her whenever and wherever she wants." A sudden thought struck him. "Do you think she could help me find Sindar? I had the impression that she might know a lot of the Turowan folk that live in this part of Edrovir."

The man's face lit up. "Aye, that she does." He beamed. "An' those she knows will know the ones she doesn't. D'ye want me t' ask her about it?"

"Yes, please, Zirda." Nagaro felt immensely relieved. "Tell her I'd like to ask her help as a favor."

Moments later he was crossing the Fleet Compound on the way to the dining hall, feeling better than he had at any time since leaving the orphanage. He hoped Kinu could quickly arrange a meeting with Omei. If Sindar was anywhere in the city, Omei would surely know how to find him. He glanced at the sun and increased his pace. If he hurried, he could eat a quick lunch before joining the other men for sword practice.

Chapter 10

More Politics

Nagaro shivered, though not from cold, as he moved cautiously down the narrow dark street. Kinu had indeed been able to quickly arrange a meeting with Tira Omei, and Nagaro was now in the act of following the stable man's directions to the Turowa's dwelling. He hadn't worn his sword because he was only going to meet Omei, but he now realized that this part of the city had a somewhat unsavory reputation. He didn't like sneaking about, either, on general principle, but he'd had to put up his hood because he didn't want to be identified. Now he was worrying that this made him look suspicious.

He'd also come on foot because he knew that a horse— any horse— would attract attention here. People who lived in places like this didn't own horses. There was nowhere to stable them and not even a post to tie one to while paying a call. Indeed, a horse tied to a post would have very nearly blocked the entire street. The upper floors of the buildings beetled out over the lower floors. There was a strip of sky overhead if you craned your neck to look, but when Nagaro had looked for stars, he'd found his eyes blinded to them by the pale yellow light shining through curtains or spilling around the edges of shutters on upper floor windows.

Evidently people lived on those upper floors. He'd seen a curtain twitched back into place and the shadow of a head withdrawn. The windows on the bottom floors were all dark. They seemed to belong to workrooms, storehouses, or pitifully tiny shop fronts, and all of these appeared to be shut up for the night. The street was all but deserted. The only other person in this block of it besides Nagaro was an old man who shuffled along up ahead of him, then finally turned a corner and disappeared.

Nagaro counted the doorways along the right-hand side of the street. *Three... four... five... six.* The sixth doorway was, as expected, a kind of alcove containing a bolted first-floor door and the bottom of a narrow stairway leading upward into darkness. Nagaro hesitated only fractionally before starting up the stairs. Kinu's directions had so far been excellent. The street itself had no name. If you wanted something delivered here, Kinu had explained, you called it "third lane off Potato Street."

The stairway was so dark that Nagaro had to find the steps by feel. At the top was a door, confirmed by the touch of his fingers on worn wood and the cold metal of a door handle. He raised his hand and knocked, then waited. He wasn't quite sure that he heard a step, but suddenly there was a rattle and a squeak, and a tiny door about two inches square was opened in the larger door, about level with his chin. A voice spoke to him.

"Who do ye be, there, knocking?" It was a woman's voice and it could have been Omei's.

Nagaro bent a little to bring his eye to the opening, but the woman's face was lit from behind and he couldn't make out her features. "I am Nagaro," he said simply. "I've come as I was bidden, to speak with Omei."

"Bidden, eh?" There was irony in the way she said it. He heard a bolt being slid back. "Well, ye'd best come in then, Zirda."

The door opened, and the woman ushered him into a tiny entryway. The only light there came from the room beyond, but there wasn't much to see in the little hall in any case, just a narrow bench, a neatly-placed pair of worn shoes, and a rough wool cloak hung on one of several pegs set in one wall. The woman was indeed Omei. Even in the dim light, he was struck by how much she looked like a younger version of her mother, the old medicine woman, Luka, whom he'd known as a boy. She was dressed very simply, in an unbleached linen blouse and a brown skirt. Her dark hair was pulled back into a single braid and her weathered brown face was beginning to be etched with lines across her brow and at the corners of her eyes.

He took off his own cloak and hung it on one of the other pegs, then turned to her and said, "Good evening, Tira Omei," inclining his head respectfully. He would have done more than that if he'd thought she would accept it. He knew that Omei was a person of some importance among her own people, a *Ku Taihana*, one of a handful of women who kept in their heads the names, histories, and whereabouts of the descendants of the scattered people of the old Loros Wared— both Turo and Kelorin.

"Good evening t' ye, too, Zirda," she said, turning to lead the way. "Will ye join me in a cup o' sothiril?"

"I'd be very pleased to, Zirdyn."

She led him into a very modest room of the kind that was kitchen, dining room, and sitting room all in one. It was typical of a Turowan kitchen in that it was scrubbed spotless and still managed to smell very pleasantly of good things to eat. Besides the door by which they had entered, there were two ways leading out. One apparently opened into a combined pantry and general storage area, the other he could see plainly communicated with a small bedroom. These appeared to make up the entire premises.

The kitchen was illuminated by a lamp, which hung on a hook at the end of a length of chain set into a ceiling beam. The lamp hung over a small table and a pair of chairs that occupied the center of the floor. The table was already set with two cups and a steeping teapot.

Omei motioned to one of the chairs. "Sit ye down," she said, though she herself remained standing long enough to pour the sothiril.

Nagaro seated himself and reached for the cup in front of him, glad to have something to occupy his hands. "Is this where you live then?" he asked, for he was surprised by the modestness of the place.

Omei settled herself in her chair. The bright black eyes in her square brown face shot him an unreadable glance. "Sometimes," she said equivocally.

"You live alone?"

She nodded as she reached for her own cup, then shut her eyes as she took a long luxurious sip.

"And you're not afraid? To live here alone, in this part of the city?"

She opened her eyes to regard him steadily over her cup. "Oh, no," she said. "No one ever troubles me." And then, as if guessing the root of his question, she said, "This is the Turo-Town, Captain. Some folk what aren't Turowan sometimes find themselves unwelcome here, and then they go about givin' the place a bad name, that's all."

"Oh." He winced inwardly and was quite sure that she read his chagrin. "I didn't realize." He took a quick swallow of his sothiril.

She took another sip of hers without taking her eyes off of him, then said matter-of-factly, "This man that ye've lost— this Sindar— has been working as a stableman at the *Golden Tankard* tavern in High Street since Seventh Day, last."

He stared at her. "You've found him *already?*"

"It wasn't hard," she said with a shrug, her black eyes laughing. "I had a stroke o' luck. I put the word out to a handful o' my best lads, and one o' them found him the first place he looked."

"Still, I am obliged to you for your trouble," he said seriously. "I haven't got men I could set to such a task. I would have had to do the searching myself."

"It wasn't much trouble. Besides, my mother always said ye were worth any amount o' that."

Nagaro shifted uncomfortably in his chair. Omei's words had sounded serious, but there was the hint of mockery in her eyes. *Was she laughing at him?* But Omei was Luka's daughter and knew his history. *She wouldn't be so unkind.* He tried to relax. "It was kind of her to say that," he ventured cautiously, "though I would hardly agree."

"Aye." Her smile widened even as her eyes narrowed. "I'm still waitin' to see the whole of it. Ye've a fine reputation, Captain Nagaro. But reputations don't catch fish— as the fishermen say."

"You're a wise woman not to believe everything you hear," he said. "And where I grew up, they used to say that reputations don't do the ploughing. It's pretty much the same idea but more fair, I think, because any man with a horse and a plough and a will to work can do the ploughing. Catching fish depends at least in part upon the will of the fish."

Omei's brow furrowed thoughtfully. "Ye have a point, there," she said. Then she waved the matter aside with a motion of her cup, and said, "This man, Sindar, isn't one o' the children of Loros."

Nagaro frowned. "No. His father's people dwell up the river in Vered Mahir, his mother's to the south around Kel Tierna."

"How did ye come t' take an interest in him?"

"It's a long story." He sketched the tale as briefly as he could, casting it from Sindar's point of view as much as possible and omitting any mention of the blood debt and how Roheed jir-Akaan had eventually paid it. "So the High Council of Jinara made him officially my responsibility when I signed that paper," he finished.

She put her head on one side. "But this isn't Jinara, an' ye're no Jinari."

"I know, but I feel bound to help his relatives deal with him, because, well, who else is there to do it? Besides, I can help with his Fleet ambitions— he knows me and trusts me. And there's a young woman in Pakoa who's in love with him. I try to look out for him for her sake."

Omei gestured impatiently with her cup. "So ye've got yourself tangled up with his troubles, and I can see that ye're a good man, Zirda. It's no concern o' mine, really. I only asked 'cause I was curious. But I have to admit that right at the beginning I did wonder if findin' him had something t' do with your plan for bringin' the children o' Loros back to Loros Wared."

"*My* plan?" Nagaro was so taken aback that he set his cup down rather noisily on the table. "That was Kenthos' plan! Whoever told you I had anything to do with it?"

Omei regarded him with unnerving equanimity. "Ye put Kenthos on the path to finding *me*, didn't ye?"

"Well... yes... Because he asked. And I can see that he must have done it, too."

Omei sipped her sothiril. "I've never met Kenthos," she said. "It was his man, Venerev, that came t' me. He got word t' me through a Turowan mate o' his named Mundabo. Mundabo turned out t' be my son's wife's brother-in-law, ye see. 'Tis funny how small the world is."

"I think I remember Venerev. A broad-shouldered Kelorin man, with a scar on his chin?"

She nodded. "Aye. He said ye gave Kenthos a peck of advice. About bringin' folk back t' Loros Wared slow and quiet, and about the law and choosing a new lord an' so on. He said ye made Kenthos swear to wait a year before doing the choosing."

"I thought it a good idea to let all the excitement die down."

"And ye wouldn't call that a plan?" She was studying him with those bright black eyes.

He shrugged. "Just advice."

"*And* ye took his oath."

"Yes. For the sake of the peace of Edrovir— which I am sworn to defend. It was my price for giving him your name." He hesitated. "Have I done ill, Tira Omei? I thought you could help Kenthos realize his dream of restoring Loros Wared. It's a good, honest dream. A noble dream. But I didn't stop first to ask you what you thought about it."

The black eyes were on him still, and now there came that slightly enigmatic smile. "Ye have not done ill, Captain Nagaro," she said quietly. "No, ye have not done ill."

"I told Kenthos not to ask you about Tevren's son."

She nodded. "And the man Venerev didn't ask. He just did everything but. Hinted north, south, east, an' west."

He hesitated. "You're... sure you know the answer?"

"Aye." The response was matter-of-fact "But I wasn't going t' tell Venerev. How would ye like it if everyone in the world knew who ye were afore ye knew it yourself?"

"I don't think I'd like it at all," he said, "but does he really not know?"

A little secret smile played about her lips. "He hasn't a shred of a clue."

"And do you ever intend to tell him?"

It seemed a very obvious question to Nagaro, but Omei's answer didn't come immediately. She withdrew her gaze and appeared to study her sothiril, swirling the liquid gently in her cup. "If the time seems right," she said at length, then raised her eyes back to meet his. "But it may be that he'll find it out for himself."

Nagaro frowned. "Are you watching over him in the meantime? Looking out for him, I mean?"

Omei was suddenly brisk. "Aye. Him and his line. We lost him for a while, but we found him again. But lately he hasn't needed much looking after. He's been doing quite well all by himself."

"Oh. Well, that's good, I guess." Nagaro reached for his sothiril, uncomfortable under her gaze.

"I'd say so," she said, quietly sipping her sothiril.

Nagaro drank from his cup as well, and frowned again. The conversation had strayed rather far from the direction he'd expected it to take. "You haven't said anything about what you called me here to discuss," he said as he lowered his cup. "Kinu said something about the Turo that were among those who attacked the princess's carriage."

"Oh, aye," she said, as if this were as good a topic as any other. "There were three o' them that came by t' see me. They seemed to want to explain themselves an' to be sure the explanation reached your ears— without them havin' to come face t' face with ye themselves, if ye know what I mean."

"Ah." He knew what it meant. It meant that the men wouldn't be willing to give testimony before the king. "But why did they come to you?" he asked. "I hope it wasn't because I talked to Kenthos about you. I'd rather that didn't get about. Peace will not be well-served if it appears that a Fleet man like me is taking sides."

But she shook her head. "They'd heard about me havin' looked after your little girl when she was taken from Pakoa Island. They figured ye'd remember me an' I'd have your ear on account of it."

"Oh." This reason at least sounded safe. "What did they have to say for themselves?"

Omei pursed her lips. "Well, o' course they wanted ye to know they were sorry. There's not many Turo-folk that'd want to be fightin' on t'other side from ye, Zirda."

Nagaro's brows came together. "Well they wouldn't be likely to if they stayed on the right side of the law," he said sharply.

"I told them ye'd likely say as much. But they said the law had served them ill an' so they'd a bone t' pick with the law— an' with the Crown— and if it hadn't been for that, they'd never have had any truck with a pack o' Leithians."

Nagaro leaned forward. "So the others *were* Leithians."

"Oh, aye." Omei waved airily. "I'd heard that much before. Leithians disguised as Kelorin. Half the folk in that part o' the country seem t' know about it. But that was only when they went in for the attack accordin' to what my three visitors had to say. They'd made no secret o' bein' Leithians when they made their pact wi' the Turo band. Said the law had done them dirty too, so they was all like brothers— Turo and Leithians together. But these three Turo said it was all lies. They found that out when Lothard came after 'em with his soldiers. Seems that their Leithian 'brothers' were ridin' with the soldiers. An' to look at 'em grinning, ye'd ha' thought it was the Leithians an' the soldiers that was brothers. And they all hunted the Turo down an' killed them like dogs."

Omei's eyes shone in the lamp light as she finished speaking.

Nagaro sat for a moment with his cup in his hands, staring into the dark amber liquid. "It's a tale that doesn't surprise me," he said at length. "Unfortunately, it's both a tale that might well be true and a tale you would expect these men to tell. If they won't come forward and speak, they can't hope to prove the truth of it."

He looked up to find that Omei was studying him with her bright dark eyes. Her expression, however, was otherwise opaque. "I know," she said. "But they believe they wouldn't live long if they were t' speak out."

He looked back down at his sothiril, swirling it in the cup. "That doesn't surprise me either." He raised his eyes. "Did you ask them what kind of grievance they had that set them against the law?"

"Aye." She nodded soberly. "They said they'd all been soldiers, called up by their lords for the border war— they came from several different Holds an' Wareds, mostly away t' the south. They claimed they'd all done their duty an' then come home t' find that something o' theirs had been taken— a house, or a boat, or a bit o' land— and they couldn't get it back."

"Taken?" He frowned. "Taken by whom?"

Omei shrugged. "There were different tales. A stranger that moved in, or a neighbor. Maybe one what'd had his eye on the thing."

"And why couldn't they get it back?"

"On account o' not bein' able to prove it was theirs, Zirda." Her voice was now tinged with bitterness. "Their lords wouldn't help on account o' them not having words writ on paper. Turo don't mostly know their letters. Our folk aren't used to thinking that they need words on paper t' say a thing is theirs."

Nagaro sighed. He knew this last part was true. "Had they tried bringing a petition before the king?"

"Aye. Some o' them, at least. They said that was why they'd come t' Lankura. But King Elgurn said it was a matter for their lords. And anyway, he couldn't make the lords do anything without proof. And the proof he wanted was words writ on paper."

Nagaro ran a hand through his hair, his brows knit sharply. "It's a serious matter," he said, "if their complaints are true. And the Crown ought to give them redress since it's the Crown that decrees that the lords call up men to send to war. If there is no written document, there must at least be witnesses. A simple edict from the Crown to the lords saying that they must hear witnesses in such cases would go far towards setting this right. I'd be glad to present a petition to King Elgurn concerning this, myself," he added. "But I would need a number of specific cases to present as examples— stating names, places, what was taken, and listing witnesses of good repute who could be called, and so forth."

Omei's eyes were very bright. "And if some men were to come to ye with their tales, ye'd not be askin' them to account for their whereabouts on a certain afternoon?" she ventured.

He met her gaze steadily, considering. "There would be no reason for me to ask them about anything but the details of their complaints," he said at length.

Omei nodded decisively. "Well," she said, and her voice registered satisfaction. "The hour is gettin' late, Zirda." She set her cup down with an air of finality. "I'd not want t' be keepin' ye."

Nagaro hastily drained his cup. He was becoming accustomed to Omei's occasional abruptness and he quite clearly understood that the interview was at an end. He stood up. "Nor would I wish to keep you from your rest. Thank you, Zirdyn."

He gave her a little bow, which she waved aside with one hand. Then she led him back to the little entry hall. As he was donning his cloak, she slid back the bolt, but she paused with her hand poised on the door handle. She turned her face up to him, though it was too dark there to read her expression.

"Do ye know," she said. "I do think ye might be worth any amount o' trouble, after all. Will ye be comin' to dwell with us in the new Loros Wared one day when it's all new-made again?"

He stared, caught completely off his guard by the suggestion. "I hadn't thought about it."

"It's not as if ye've a Wared t' your name."

"Well, no. I mean, I've considered Pakoa to be the only home I have for several years now, but I probably won't be spending much time there in the future."

She gave a little soft chuckle in the darkness. "Well, we'd be glad t' have ye," she said. "Do think about it."

"I consider that a compliment," he said. "And I will."

A moment later he was standing outside, slightly bemused, and the door was closed. Shaking his head, he put up his hood and pulled his cloak about him, then descended to the street. Once there, he set off with a long stride, eager to put Turo-town behind him. The hour was not so very late, despite Omei's assertion, and he had two letters he wanted to write before he sought his bed. One would be to Burdal Korinos, reassuring the old man that his grandson had been found. The other would be to Lissel, telling her that Sindar had left Vered Mahir earlier than planned and had come to Lankura, where he would likely try to join the Royal Fleet at midsummer.

***

He reached the Fleet Compound without incident. The guard at the gate waved him through with a perfunctory salute. As he rounded the corner into Captain's Row, however, he was surprised to find Taru waiting for him on his doorstep. The young Turo jumped to his feet when he saw him.

"Nagaro!" he cried. "Here ye are at last! Kuran's been looking for ye. He was so put out not t' find ye where he expected ye to be that he came 'round to our quarters t' look for ye there. And he was on at Pavo and me about where ye'd gone. We didn't know what t' tell him!"

Nagaro frowned. "It's after hours, and I'm off duty, and therefore not required to be where Kuran expects me to be," he said rather testily. "And as for where I've been, I don't mind telling him— at a reasonable hour."

Taru threw up his hands. "Well, ye'd better go tell him now," he said exasperatedly. "He said he'd be *obliged* if we sent ye to him— if we set eyes on ye any time before midnight. And it didn't like he meant he'd just be *grateful*, so I told him I'd be watchin' for ye."

Nagaro heaved a sigh. "All right," he said. "I had something I meant to do, but it can wait."

"Did Tira Omei say she'd look for Sindar?"

Nagaro gave a short laugh. "She'd already *found* him, Taru. I was going to write to Tor Burdal about it tonight. Now go back to your quarters and tell Pavo that I suggest he look in at the *Golden Tankard* in High Street where Sindar is working. Tell him to see if he can learn where the man is lodging, see how he's faring and whether he's in good spirits. Just make sure he doesn't mention the word 'help' in Sindar's hearing under any circumstances."

"Aye Capt'n!"

Nagaro caught the quick flash of Taru's teeth in the darkness and the young Turo was striding away. He heaved a sigh and turned in the direction of the building that housed Lord Kuran's modest office, or study. Even before he reached it he could tell that the Lord of the Fleet was still working because a light was plainly visible glowing in the office window. Estevad, the clerk, had apparently gone to his quarters, however, for it was Kuran himself who answered Nagaro's knock.

"Ah, Captain. Did Taru find you then? I'm glad you could come."

Kuran sounded tired. Nagaro followed him into the study and dropped into a chair. "He was waiting at my door. He seemed to think there might be trouble if he didn't make sure I saw you tonight."

Kuran smiled wanly as he sprawled in the padded chair behind his desk. "I'm afraid Taru must have been hearing my frustration— which wasn't with you, or with him. The matter could have waited until the morning. Where were you, by the way, if you don't mind telling? I had the distinct impression that both of your officers knew and for some reason didn't wish to tell me, and of course that only piqued my curiosity."

"I imagine they thought they were protecting the confidence of the Turowan woman I went to meet."

Kuran raised an eyebrow. "Not a romantic interest at last?"

Nagaro frowned. "Hardly, My Lord. Tira Omei is old enough to be my mother. I went to see her about some information. It turned out she's already located Sindar."

Disappointment, followed quickly by relief, flickered behind Kuran's eyes. "Has she? That's good news. You'll contact Tor Burdal, won't you?"

"I was planning to."

"Good. And thank you. I had old Burdal in here twice while he was in town, pestering me about it. I would have liked to help the old man, but I really didn't need another thing on my desk. I'll do my best to look favorably on Sindar's candidacy come midsummer." Kuran paused, then added, "I have to say, though, that finding him hardly seems to require confidentiality."

Nagaro shrugged. "That was only one matter that we discussed. The other concerned some of the Turo who were involved in the attack on the princess's carriage. Apparently several of them came to see her and specifically wanted their words passed on to me." Nagaro proceeded to outline his conversation with Tira Omei concerning the Turowan men.

Kuran listened with interest. "Well," he said when Nagaro had finished. "None of that surprises me either, and I think you handled it as well as you reasonably could have. It's been clear from the beginning that there'll be no formal charges in this matter. It would be very bad politics right now to embarrass Lothard." He sighed heavily. "Always it seems it's politics. But I might as well tell you the reason why I came looking for you. There's politics involved in it, too, more's the pity."

The Lord of the Fleet leaned forward, clasping his hands on his desktop. "You remember our little encounter with the Jinari envoy concerning trafficking in illegal goods?"

Nagaro shifted in his chair. "Of course," he said. "I confess I hadn't thought about it much since I told you what I learned from Simion."

"Which implicated the Houses of Sobring, Hurn, and Furthing. My report included those details, and it engendered some considerable discussion in the Council as you might imagine. Though it was more because it suggested some long-standing collusion between those three Houses than because there was any great concern about what was being purchased."

Nagaro frowned darkly. "They should be concerned about both!"

"Perhaps." Kuran raised a placating hand. "But they would need to see more reason to be worried about what these men were buying than what they've heard so far. That's just the fact of the matter. They do, however, understand the need to satisfy the Jinari about the illicit trade, and so they've decided to issue an edict, addressed to all the Edroviran lords, officially forbidding all traffic in objects or substances that have been declared unlawful by the High Council of Jinara. We'll need a list, of course, but more about that in a moment. The edict won't mention any House by name, but will state that it comes in response to a Jinari complaint about the activities of some unidentified Edroviran citizens, and it will state that any and all such activity is to cease forthwith. I think that was more or less the wording."

Nagaro shook his head. "I hardly think that will persuade these people to stop what they're doing," he said. "Though it *will* likely cause them to be more careful to conceal themselves. Utabala thought they'd already moved their operation once in response to the Jinari High Council's investigations.

Kuran nodded grimly. "I agree. But the edict is a reasonable action for the King and the Council to take. It puts the Crown of Edrovir in the official position of disapproving of these activities."

"I suppose that's true." Nagaro sighed. "Are they going to take any other action?"

"Yes. But not openly. The matter is too sensitive politically for that. Essentially, I've been charged with trying to gather more information, both here and in Jinari waters. I have been told that I should appear to act autonomously so the King and the Council can deny knowledge of the investigation if it should prove politically necessary to do so."

"I see," Nagaro observed bitterly. "I don't envy you, My Lord."

Kuran returned him a sour smile. "I have been authorized to assign personnel to the effort as I see fit. That being the case, I'm assigning you to command a small expedition to the Jinari coast."

Nagaro sat up straight. "To what end, My Lord?"

"Officially to obtain from the Jinari a list of unlawful objects and substances— to find out whether there's anything else besides this heskial that our citizens should know they're forbidden to buy. But *unofficially*, it's to see whether the Jinari authorities have learned anything more about the unlawful trade, to perhaps look around a bit yourself and see what can be seen. Elgurn and the Council have authorized the mission, and there was unanimous agreement that you were the best man for the task when I put the suggestion to them."

Nagaro frowned. "How often are their decisions ever unanimous?"

Kuran snorted. "I didn't say they all wanted it for the same reason, but oddly enough they all seemed to be seeing reason— if in different ways. Elgurn and Devral saw the sense of sending a man who already knew something about the matter and who had a contact in Jinara. Pendrik pointed out that by using you and your men, we wouldn't have to spread the knowledge around any further, as he put it. And Odus surprised me by saying you were plainly a man who knew how to handle himself in a delicate situation. I was less surprised when I realized that Odus' remark was a jibe at Anduar. It appears they all know you saved the day at Loros Hall by acting without waiting for Anduar's order."

Nagaro winced. "And what about Anduar?"

"Him? *He* sat there as cool as chilled sothiril until everyone else had stopped speaking, at which point he very diplomatically told them how astute they all were. And *then* he said he personally thought the mission wasn't likely to yield much useful information but that it would at least serve the purpose of getting you out of Lankura for a while."

"*Getting me out of Lankura?*" Nagaro was taken aback "What, then? Is he afraid I'll do something else on my own initiative?

Kuran shook his head. "Odus accused him of that, of course, but I think it does him a discredit. He said he's concerned for your safely, and I believe him. I confess I am a little concerned myself. You've crossed Lothard twice in less than a month. And men who cross Lothard have a way of turning up dead."

Nagaro frowned. "Surely Lothard wouldn't think I was worth that much trouble."

"Let's hope not." Kuran heaved a small sigh. "But sending you where you can't possibly cross his path for a while doesn't seem amiss. Unfortunately, we can only afford to send two ships. You would lead as a Captain-in-Command. I've wanted to advance you to the rank of commander for some time, but I'm afraid it will have to wait awhile yet. Politics again. You'd be, in a sense, replacing Commander Strad. He was a Leithian, whereas you are, well, whatever you are— but clearly not Leithian."

Nagaro swallowed. "I... appreciate your confidence in me, My Lord," he said. "But really there's no need to think of advancing me. Rank isn't important."

Kuran's sharp black eyes bored into him. "Rank is *always* important, Captain. It's how we establish the chain of command." His eyes narrowed. "But I think perhaps you mean it isn't important to *you?*"

"Well of course that's what I mean. Captain-in-Command suits me perfectly well."

Kuran considered him. "Not more than one man in ten who says such a thing actually means it," he said. "And you're that tenth man. It truly confounds me how you've achieved so much when you seem to have no personal ambition."

"I haven't achieved so very much, My Lord, and I do have things I wish to accomplish."

Kuran waved his words away. "I've no desire to argue with you," he said briskly. "Especially since your modesty is so becoming. Now, can you suggest a second captain?"

Nagaro didn't need to cudgel his brain. "I'd like to suggest Landros, My Lord," he said without hesitation. "If you'll restore him to the *Sea Eagle* for the duration of this mission. He's accustomed to following my lead, and he can be trusted to keep secrets if need be."

"Landros and the *Sea Eagle*... and her old crew, I suppose?"

"Yes, My Lord. That would be appreciated."

"Good enough, then." Kuran picked up a pen, dipped it, and scratched a note on a piece of paper. "I want you to sail as soon as possible. I expect you to see to the details."

"Aye Zirda." Nagaro gave him a salute. Then he asked, "When do you wish to see us return?"

"Shall we say in four weeks?"

Nagaro nodded, but frowned. "That won't allow us to do much scouting in Jinari waters," he said. "But I think Lord Anduar is right that we're unlikely to learn very much— at least from our own efforts and with only two ships. The amount of territory to be searched is too large. Also, the trade was being carried out at night with small boats. We'd have to be lucky indeed to catch them at it by setting a night watch with a spyglass, and the Jinari likely wouldn't be pleased to have us stopping and searching fishing boats in their territorial waters, even if they approved of the purpose. Really I think we must hope that the Jinari themselves have learned something."

Kuran nodded. "I expect that's an astute assessment," he said. "You'll have a letter to show them, bearing the royal seal and explaining what you're about, and we'll see what that gains you." He leaned back in his chair. "There's one more thing. I may be conducting some covert investigations of my own here in our own territory, and I'd appreciate any help you can give me. For example, would you happen to know the name of the lore master who was sacked for refusing to acquire something for Lord Madred's minister?"

Nagaro frowned. "I can do more than that, since I met him... ah.. by chance. His name is Master Fineas, and he's been reduced to keeping an apothecary shop in Brass Bell Lane. He lives above the shop. I'm sure he'll help you if you explain that I have reason to believe someone has brought heskial into this country. These men won't have bought it if they don't mean to use it, and being a man of principle, I believe Fineas will want to help prevent them from harming anyone. Just please try not to get him into any more trouble for whatever help he gives you."

"Of course." Kuran made some more notes on his paper. "And I suppose I can contact Simion through Brandle Furthing?"

Nagaro hesitated. "Yes... but you'd best be very careful if you don't want to endanger Simion. And you may have to give some details to the Lieutenant in order to persuade him to arrange a meeting."

"Say no more." Kuran scratched yet another note.

"Simion will likely be willing to do almost anything for my sake. You may have to restrain him to prevent him from putting himself in unnecessary danger."

Kuran's eyebrow went up again, but all he said was, "I shall make a mental note. Is there anyone else?"

Nagaro considered. "There's no one else who knows anything about it, My Lord. If you could make use of some unobtrusive people with sharp eyes, you might try the Turo, and Tira Omei— whom I talked to earlier this evening— seems to have access to most of the Turo in Lankura. Kinu, who works in the stables, can arrange for you to speak with her if she is willing."

"If *she* is willing?" Kuran frowned. "Am I to wait upon her pleasure? And what if she's *not* willing?"

Nagaro raised his shoulders in an apologetic shrug. "She may not be willing to get her folk mixed up in this, and I don't think you could force her to help. She's chiefly concerned with the scattered folk of the old Loros Wared, but she'll probably be willing to at least talk to you if you mention my name."

Kuran looked sour. "Ah, yes. *Your* name, Captain. Not mine, I notice, even though I have the governance of a piece of the old Loros Wared and my mother is a Turowa from the northern isles."

Nagaro winced. He was thinking of Omei's puzzling words, "*worth any amount of trouble*", but he decided not to repeat the words to the Lord of the Fleet. "I seem to have made a favorable impression on Tira Omei," he said uncomfortably. "It's almost as if she wants to adopt me as one of her 'children of Loros.'"

"Adopt you, eh?" Kuran gave him a speculative look. "*There's* something to think about."

"I really don't know why..."

"Don't you?" Kuran leaned back in his chair, interlacing his fingers behind his head. "I would think it's obvious. If Loros Wared is reinstated, they'll be needing to choose a lord."

"Well of course they will, but..." He stopped as the light dawned. "You're thinking they'd try to choose *me?*"

"And why not?"

"I don't want to be lord of anything!"

"I know. That's one of the reasons why you'd make a good one. Don't dismiss the idea out of hand, Captain. And now,"— he unlaced his fingers to cover a yawn— "I really must douse the lamp and lock up this office. I hear my bed calling."

Moments later Nagaro was re-crossing the compound on his way to his quarters, firmly forcing Kuran's parting suggestion to the most obscure corner of his mind. He still had two letters to write before he might lay his head on his own pillow. And tomorrow he would have to begin preparations for the mission to the Jinari coast. *And,* he realized with a sudden stab of disappointment, he'd also have to send word to the palace to Nevien and Lady Merriel explaining that he'd be unable to take part in any charitable outings for the next four weeks.

He sighed. *Four weeks away from Nevien...*

Chapter II

Night Shadows

"Fire burns tree in spite of the numbers, and stones dam the river. Put one counter on the Tree Card and one on the Water Card, Clarimel." Kendira made her play, placing her cards on top of two of the four cards arrayed in the center of the table— the three of fire on the nine of trees, and the seven of stone on the two of water. Then she drew two more cards from the deck to replace the one's she had played. Clarimel laid the counters. They were small polished disks of wood and one went on top of the beautiful drawing of a tree on the Primal Tree card in front of Delasin while the other went on top of a similar large card in front of Alisset bearing the image of an elegantly cresting wave.

Nevien settled herself more comfortably onto the cushions of the window seat and decided to watch the game for a while. The book she was supposed to be reading was in her lap. Lady Merriel, seated beside her, was busy with some embroidery.

The five young women who were referred to as the Princess's ladies were seated around a square table in the library on the palace's third floor, where they were passing the time until supper with *Oskampo*. Theys were teaching Delasin, the newest and youngest of them, how to play the game, since she'd admitted with some embarrassment that she had never learned. She had said her Father had forbidden it— something about her Aunt Maramine, who she'd never met, and who had died.

"All right, Delasin, it's your turn now." Rianine said. She was seated behind Delasin and was coaching her. "Look at the cards that are up, see what you can do. And remember that you're the keeper of the Primal Tree."

Delasin frowned over her cards. "Well..." she hazarded, "Water always drowns fire when you're playing a water card, so that's easy enough. But my stone card would need a higher number to break that tree card, and I know I mustn't play this fire card on it."

"That's right," Rianine affirmed. "You don't want to play your fire card on a tree card. You want to play it on a water card with a lower number."

"Delasin nodded. "Then I could say 'fire boils water,' but this time it's the water that drowns the fire." She laid down her water card on top of the exposed fire card, and drew another card from the deck to replace it.

Again Clarimel laid a token, this time on Kendira's Primal Fire card with its flame-rayed sun. She looked back and forth between the cards on the table and the ones she was holding. "Oh fiddle!" she said, her delicately-arched blond eyebrows coming together in annoyance. "I can't do a single thing! I guess it's your turn, Alisset."

Alisset must have already seen her move because she made her play with scarcely a glance at the new cards that were showing. "Ten of water beats eight of stone," she announced, smiling cherubically. "So flood sweeps the stones away!"

The play proceeded with Clarimel placing a token on her own primal card, which bore a drawing of a pair of standing stones atop a green hill. Nevien watched through another round before returning to her book. Oskampo was not a highly challenging game. The outcome was determined largely by chance and only a little by the decisions of the players— at least once one got past the point where one made gross blunders like playing against one's own Primal. The game was best suited to whiling away time when one had nothing better to do and didn't wish to think very hard.

Nevien, however, did have something better to do. The book she was holding, Gobrig's *History of the Holds*, was an account of the doings of all the noble houses of Edrovir, their migrations, the changes in their holdings, and some of the more noteworthy conflicts that had occurred between them in the period prior to the unification of the country under Darion the Great. She was supposed to "familiarize" herself with it. "Don't try to read the whole thing," her father had told her. "Just look it over. Get the sense of it." Clearly this wasn't going to be easy.

She had begun perusing it the previous evening and had found herself nodding within five minutes. The bulk of the book was essentially a single long rambling narrative broken more or less arbitrarily into chapters. There were three maps at the end of the volume representing different stages in the country's colonization, the last of which corresponded roughly to the current state of affairs. The maps at least appeared to be straightforward, but how things had progressed from the first map to the second and then to the third could only be learned by searching through the narrative for the bits that explained the changes, and the author's style was excessively detailed and very tedious.

Nevien struggled valiantly with the first chapter for nearly fifteen minutes before giving up temporarily and trying to commit one of the maps to memory instead. She was just reflecting that, compared to the book, the Oskampo game was scintillatingly interesting, when a light knock sounded on the library door. The young women at the table were so intent on their game that they failed to notice, but Nevien and Merriel exchanged questioning glances. The knock sounded again, this time distinctly louder and the game came to a startled halt as all eyes turned to the door.

Merriel hastily put down her embroidery and stood up. "I'll just see what it's about," she said firmly, and crossed to the door. When opened, it revealed the imposing figure of Brandle, the Commander of the Princess's Guard, accompanied by a young messenger boy. A few low words were exchanged, the door was closed once more, and Merriel started back across the room holding a small rectangle of folded paper. "It's nothing urgent," she said. "Just a note for My Lady Nevien."

The game, and the babble of the young women's voices, resumed as Merriel approached the window seat and handed Nevien the folded paper. She leaned close as she handed it over and whispered, "It's from Captain Nagaro."

"Oh!" Nevien's heart soared as she reached for the note. Folded roughly in three, it was sealed with what appeared to be ordinary candle wax. She broke the seal, opened it, and read:

My Lady Princess,

I regret I will be unable to accompany you and Lady Merriel next week, or at any time during the remainder of this month. I have been assigned a mission in the south. With apology and my regards, —Nagaro Nareyo

Her heart plummeted. The news was most unwelcome. And the note, which a few months ago would have seemed merely appropriate, now felt cruelly terse. "He can't come next week," she said bleakly, passing the note to Merriel. "He has a mission."

"For the rest of the month, it seems," Merriel noted after glancing over the small paper. She sighed. "Well, we have to expect that sort of thing. He's a Fleet officer, after all."

"Yes..."

Nevien sat staring at the words, written in the fine, precise hand that she'd come to recognize at a glance. His handwriting had never struck her as unmanly, though it was unlike any other man's she'd ever encountered. It suited him. It was what one would expect from those fine-boned, long-fingered hands. She wished he could have told her to keep up her spirits... or that he would miss her. But of course it wouldn't be appropriate for him to put anything like that in writing.

If he felt that way, of course.

Nevien frowned. "Merriel," she said anxiously. "Do you think he could be angry with me after everything that was said in the carriage?"

"Angry with you?" Merriel looked surprised. "I hardly think so. He seemed a little upset when he left us, but he surely wouldn't still be. And if he should be angry with anyone, it should be me. I'm the one who said those ignorant things about Vothrin beliefs."

Nevien shook her head. "It wasn't that. It was what I said about Leyel that upset him. And now he sends me *this*."

Merriel looked even more surprised. "You can't mean that you think he's making it up about being sent on a mission!"

"Of course not! He would never lie. But he might have had a choice about whether to accept the mission, or when to go. That sort of thing."

Merriel gave her an exasperated look. "I think you're making a cake out of crumbs," she said. Her little rose-bud of a mouth set into a firm line as she picked up her embroidery.

"You're right, of course." Nevien folded the note guiltily and hastily reopened her book. *You're acting like an idiot,* she told herself. *Like a giddy little milkmaid... And if you don't stop it you'll have Merriel guessing everything!*

She tried to focus again on memorizing the first of the three maps, but her thoughts slid sideways. What kind of mission was it? The note said it was in the south. Was it going to be in Mahuk waters? Would it be dangerous?

Clarimel's voice rose above the rest, interrupting Nevien's wayward thoughts.

"That's *twice* you've done 'tree splits rock', Alisset! There's nothing else you could have done with the *one* of trees, I know, but the *eight* of trees tops the seven of fire. You could have done 'tree blocks out the sun!'"

Nevien looked up to see Alisset blinking her round, corn-flower blue eyes. "But I didn't *want* to do that to poor Kendira," the Leithian maid protested. "There are so many counters on the Primal Fire card already!"

"It's all right, Alisset," Kendira put in hastily. "Please don't' worry about me."

Rianiine turned sternly to Clarimel and said, "And you know she's allowed to do whatever she likes!"

Clarimel pouted. "And *you* know that you don't get anywhere in this game if you insist on being *nice!*"

Nevien heaved a sigh. The end of the afternoon promised to be very tedious.

***

Dinner, when at last it came, was served in the Great Hall. The normal residents of the palace, together with the current assortment of guests, took their places at three tables located near the head of the hall, adjacent to the kitchens but spaced apart sufficiently to allow private conversation at each table. The princess's ladies had a table all to themselves, as was customary, but Nevien wasn't seated there. She was placed instead at the table reserved for the king and the members of the council.

Being seated at that table meant relief from her ladies' rather silly conversation. Indeed, conversation at the king's table often resembled that of the Council Chamber, though usually lighter in tone. It wasn't uncommon for Elgurn to take reports from some of those present. Nevien would never have been placed there while her mother was alive. With the queen gone, however, there was no longer any need to maintain the fiction that Nevien was being sheltered from the details of the kingdom's governance as Semrel had been.

Nevien frowned and firmly pushed the thought of her mother away. Memories of that kind still tended to bring the shadow of grief stealing in their wake. With an effort, she re-ordered her thoughts. These dinner discussions could be quite interesting. Some of what was said might even prove important.

The conversation at that moment, when she forced herself to listen to it, turned out to be centered around the food— which was sliced venison with creamed leeks and spring potatoes. On this particular occasion, there were only four others besides Nevien at the table. Her father and Lord Devral were on her right, with Lords Anduar and Pendrik seated across the table. The fourth Council member, Lord Odus, was currently absent from Lankura.

To keep her thoughts from straying once again in undesirable directions, Nevien amused herself by considering the four men as they ate and imagining what animal each of them most resembled. Pendrik was easy— loading up his plate with second helpings. He was a big blond bear of a man— jovial and well fed, and still vigorous even though the gold of his hair was paler now for being shot with silver. Devral was older than Pendrik, the oldest of the four. He was a grizzled black wolf, she decided, a pack leader, scarred from many a battle fought to maintain his place. He was no longer as fit and hale as he once had been, but still game for a fight. And of course Anduar couldn't be anything but some kind of cat, a big, sleek, black one she decided, despite the scattering of gray that shot through his raven hair. He ate his dinner fastidiously, ever alert and watchful, silent and self-contained. Odus, who wasn't present, would have been a deerhound, or perhaps a terrier.

Her father gave her the greatest difficulty, perhaps because she knew him best, but in the end she settled on the image of an aging lion.

His close-cut hair had once been red-gold, and now was nearly gray. His neatly-trimmed beard that had been redder than his hair, was gray completely. Still, he sat erect, carrying himself like the king that he was. The lines of care were deeply etched in his face, but his ice-blue eyes were as sharp and shrewd as ever. He had recovered well from the passing of his queen.

Nevien had thought it strange at first, even unnatural, that he had seemed to emerge from a shadow the very morning after Semrel's death. She'd been hurt at first, until she'd realized that her father had begun to grieve for his queen from the moment he'd accepted the inevitability of her impending death. Her illness had been so protracted that he'd used up all of his grief before the end had come. Her death, for him, had brought only relief that her suffering had ended...

Nevien bit her lip. *More treacherous thoughts.* Fortunately she was spared the need to wrestle with them because, at that moment, her father set down his wine glass with a decisive clink and addressed his dinner guests.

"Is the peace holding?" he inquired. "What do your spies say, Anduar?" Then in a lower voice he added, "Pass me the venison, Pendrik, will you please?"

Anduar deftly speared a modest piece of meat from the platter as Pendrik handed it across the table and answered with his customary coolness. "All is quiet *so far*, My Lord. There are one or two newcomers reported in the region around Loros Hall, but no massive migration."

"What of Irvenen Wared?"

Anduar had begun meticulously to cut his meat, and he answered without looking up. "All is quiet there as well. Kenthos was returned safely to his home, and the escort has returned to Lankura."

"There was no celebration at his homecoming?"

"I believe Lord Rastyl made it clear that there should be none." Anduar was still intent on his meat, though his features fleetingly registered a small, hard smile. "And of course Kenthos has been giving out that it was all a mistake— that he is no heir of Loros." And here at last the knife and fork stopped moving and the steel-gray eyes were lifted. "Although there is a rumor that he's hired a local carter of his acquaintance to build him a rather large wagon."

"A rumor!" The exclamation came from Devral. He had paused with a fork-full of potatoes halfway to his mouth, his scarred face twisted into a frown. "Come, now. Has he, or hasn't he?"

Anduar had placed a morsel of cut meat into his mouth in the interim and he proceeded to chew and swallow at his leisure before making his reply. "There is unquestionably a wagon being made. The carter declines to say who it is for."

"Well then it must be for Kenthos! Why else this bloody secrecy?"

Anduar poked the air pointedly with his fork. "That kind of reasoning," he said, "undoubtedly explains why there is a rumor. In this instance it may actually be true, but we shall have to wait and see."

Nevien smiled a little at this and it drew a guffaw from Lord Pendrik. The big Leithian shook so hard with laughter that he very nearly spilled his wine. "By the Gods, Devral," he gasped when he'd caught his breath. "You must have become a fool in your old age, not to know better than to try to second-guess our friend Anduar!"

Devral glowered, then shook his head with a wheezing chuckle. "I'll wager you a bottle of wine to a leg of mutton," he growled, "that you'll have to take that back— when it turns out the wagon *is* for Kenthos."

Anduar regarded the two lords archly, then returned his gaze to Elgurn. "That is my report, My Lord."

The king inclined his head. "Thank you, My Lord Anduar." he said, then addressed himself once more to the table at large. "How goes the collection of the monies to pay the recompense for the lives of those killed in our recent abortive civil war? Will the exchange take place according to the agreement?"

Devral put down his fork. "I can speak for the Kelorin Faction, My Lord. Rathdar will be ready. He's collected most of the money from the appropriate sources and means to make up the rest out of his personal coffers— part of which is to be repaid in the future by those still owing." The old Kelorin covered a cough. "Kenthos, himself, will be among that number."

Elgurn nodded. "Odus isn't here to speak for the Leithian side," he observed. "But I know he confides in you, Pendrik. What can you tell us?"

Pendrik frowned, and appeared to consider his answer.

Nevien, sitting quietly beside her father, thought this said quite a lot, considering how much wine the Leithian lord had consumed. Drink usually tended to make Pendrik more garrulous.

"Lothard has done what Devral just described— more or less," Pendrik ventured at length with a hint of caution. "Save that he's apparently suggesting the levying of... a tax... to reimburse himself and those other highborn men who've had to pay."

"A tax?" Elgurn raised an eyebrow. "A tax on the people of his hold?"

Pendrik nodded uncomfortably. "He's suggested it— on the grounds that it was an expense incurred in the defense of the Hold." Pendrik gestured vaguely with his wine glass. "Or some such. Odus has gone to investigate, but you may recall that it was... ah... decided that the lords might raise the money as they saw fit."

Devral scowled. "I knew we should have been more explicit about that. This means that the common folk will bear the cost, rather than the men responsible!"

Pendrik drained his glass and reached for the bottle. "Unfortunately, yes."

Elgurn shook his head, frowning. "At least we did specify that the money received is to go to the families of the dead men. We can hope that Lothard will follow that directive."

There was a moment's silence as the four men considered the likelihood of this event. Then the king turned to Nevien.

"You're very quiet this evening, Daughter. Have you anything to report?"

Nevien shook her head. "No, Father. I've only begun to read the book by Gobrig, and my ladies have been speaking of nothing but frivolities. In fact, I could scarcely concentrate on the book this afternoon because they were chattering so over their game of Oskampo."

"I'm not surprised you've made little progress with *that* book under such conditions," Devral observed with a pointed glance at Pendrik. "It is exceedingly dull. Leithians have no notion of how to write history."

Pendrik smiled expansively, and saluted the old Kelorin warrior with his newly-filled glass. "That's because we'd rather be making it! Ha, ha! Making history. Do you see?"

Anduar pushed his plate away and leaned back in his chair. "We all make history," he observed coolly. "The question is, *what kind?*"

Devral smirked. "Now you see, My Lord Pendrik, that it is you who ought to know better than to attempt a jest when Anduar is seated at the same table. But if I might make a suggestion," he added, turning back to Elgurn. "Perhaps our dear princess would fare better with her studies if she spent less time with these frivolous ladies of hers."

"We could send the silly girls home," Pendrik offered.

Nevien frowned. She knew very well what was wrong with this idea, though she didn't wish to appear to instruct the members of the council. Fortunately, her father spared her the need.

"I'm afraid that Nevien must spend the greater part of her time with her ladies," he explained patiently. "They're supposed to be her companions. It's their excuse for being here, although in fact their fathers send them because the society of Lankura offers an unparalleled opportunity for young ladies to find husbands. We would incur the wrath of quite a few fathers if we were even to suggest ending the practice."

Devral and Pendrik both shook their heads over this. Anduar actually looked bored.

Nevien decided to see if she might gain some information. "I have a question," she said. "I wondered what the Fleet mission is that will shortly send Captain Nagaro to the south. I don't recall anything having been mentioned in the Council. Is it a routine patrol?"

This time Anduar's eyes narrowed fractionally, though he continued to lounge in his chair. Devral and Pendrik had returned their attention to their dinners and didn't bother to look up. It was her father who answered.

"It's a small diplomatic mission concerning trade with Jinara. The Jinari have made complaints concerning illicit trade. Captain Nagaro has some relevant knowledge, and we requested that he be entrusted with the mission. Lord Kuran has complied. That's the whole of it."

"There's no danger then?" She did her best to make it sound like a casual question.

"There shouldn't be."

Nevien nodded, relieved, though trying not to show it. *He could hardly have turned down the mission when the King and Council had asked for him specifically.*

"May I ask how you learned of this mission, My Lady?"

Anduar hadn't altered his languid slouch as he asked the question, though his steel-gray eyes were on her. His tone, however, was apparently as casual as her own. So she explained that Nagaro had meant to accompany her on one of her charitable visits, but had sent her a note saying he couldn't come. "He said it was because he had a mission in the south, and I was curious."

"So he won't be available to serve as your defender? I've heard him so styled since the attack on your carriage— that in addition, of course, to 'Defender of Loros'." Anduar's gray gaze was level. He didn't seem to insinuate, but the mere fact that he chose to raise the issue prompted Nevien to say, "He does everything he can to discourage such talk."

"Does he indeed?"

"Yes." She tried not to frown. "He doesn't like to have people saying such things."

"I see." Anduar's voice was still level, but he was sitting just a little straighter. "Are his efforts successful?"

Nevien couldn't help frowning this time. "Not as much as he'd like them to be."

"Ah." And now it seemed to her that there was just the slightest upward twitch of the lips, a trace of mirth in the steel-gray eyes. Anduar leaned back once more and his gaze grew momentarily introspective. Nevien had just decided that he'd finished his interrogation when he refocused on her face and said, "You're rather fond of the good Captain, aren't you?"

At this, she felt a jolt of apprehension— though really it was a harmless question. *At least it should be.* "Well, yes," she said lightly. "We've become quite good friends."

"Ah," he said again, and already it seemed that his thoughts had moved to other things. "Good."

And that was the end of it. In the next moment, the serving women arrived to clear away the dishes and the remains of the main course and to bring the dessert. The latter in this case was a pudding of a dark brown color and a remarkably rich and wonderful flavor, which none of them had ever had before. When Nevien asked what it was, the serving woman smiled a bit smugly.

"It's a new delicacy, My Lady— from Jinara. I believe they call it *jokolata.*"

And then dinner was over and Lady Merriel shepherded all the young ladies out into the twilit garden, "For a bit of air." Nevien was, of course, expected to go too, and she was quite glad of the chance to inhale the cool, salt-tinged breeze and clear the cobwebs from her head before returning to the library to take up Gobrig's *History of the Holds* once more. Fortunately, once in the library, Rianine correctly interpreted her pleading glance and persuaded the other ladies to pass the evening with reading instead of playing any more Oskampo.

***

Nevien couldn't get back to sleep. She lay in her bed, trying to ignore all the mysterious little night noises. She could never quite explain them, and now they were setting her on edge even though the same sounds, heard by day, would have caused her no concern. She preferred to sleep with the heavy window curtains open, because she liked to be awakened by the early morning sun. There was no sun now, of course, but Talebra, the bright moon, was westering, with small, dark Naru close behind, and the moonlight shining through the two high windows made a pair of pale, cold rectangles on her bedroom floor, one on either side of the bed. From where she lay, curled on her side under the quilted covers, she could see the entire outline of one of those rectangles and gage the passage of time by it's slow creep across the polished floorboards.

She had originally crawled into bed with a mind weary from the struggle of making sense of Gobrig's convoluted sentences and graceless prose. She'd fallen asleep out of weariness and boredom, but had awakened out of a dream. She couldn't remember all of the dream, but some bits still hung in her mind with vivid clarity.

She'd been going to meet Nagaro in the woods at River House, or so it seemed, except that she'd found herself following him instead, on foot. He'd been walking on ahead of her, not turning, not seeing her. She'd tried to call to him, but hadn't been able to get any sound to come out of her mouth. They had reached the little glade— and then she'd seen the other woman— the woman he was obviously going to meet! Nevien had been right behind him, as if looking over his shoulder, as he'd approached that other woman. She'd been so close that she'd gotten a clear view of the young woman's face. It had been a plain, brown, Turowan face, with gentle, dark eyes. Eyes that had lit up when she smiled— *at Nagaro—*

Nevien had never met Hamani, the Turowan woman of whom Nagaro had spoken with such enthusiasm that day at River House. Hamani lived in the little village of Wotana, twenty miles away along the coast to the north. Nevien had never visited Wotana, and Hamani had surely never been to Lankura, yet Nevien couldn't shake off the notion that the dream had shown her the face of the actual woman.

Nevien pulled the covers tighter around herself with a guilty shiver. *She'd been thinking about Nagaro all afternoon, and she'd completely forgotten about Hamani.*

She wished she had someone to talk to about this, someone in whom she could *really* confide. Obviously, she could never tell Nagaro about it, and Rianine's often cynical approach to matters of the heart ran completely counter to Nevien's sensibilities. She had sometimes shared things with Lady Merriel, and the older woman would surely be sympathetic since she herself was enamored of Kuran. But Merriel was of a different generation, and was such a proper Leithian woman. Nevien could easily imagine the kind of useless things that Merriel would say.

And her mother was gone.

Years ago, when she was girl, and before the beginning of her mother's illness, she could have told her mother about this. *If only...*

She felt her throat tighten, and the hot tears begin to well in her eyes. Hurriedly she wiped at them with her hand, but they wouldn't stop. They were running onto her pillow and she needed to blow her nose. With an exasperated sniffle, she threw the covers off and got out of bed to get herself a handkerchief. Crossing the cold floor, treading on the patch of moonlight with bare feet, she fumbled several handkerchiefs out of the top drawer of her dresser. Then, because she was thoroughly awake anyway and because it was so lonely in the dark, she lit the candle on her bedside table and sat cross-legged on the bed, dabbing at her eyes.

Eventually the tears passed, and she was just about to get up again and go to her wash basin to wash the salt from her cheeks, when she heard quiet footsteps in the hall outside her bedchamber door. Startled, she sat listening as the sound went past her door, coming from the left, and dwindled away to the right. She frowned. There was a guard in the hall, and of course a second one would come for the changing of the shifts, but the footsteps she had heard hadn't been the measured, booted tread of a guard. They'd been rather slower, softer, and a little shuffling.

She couldn't think of anyone who ought to be on the third floor after dark whose walk would have sounded like that. On the other hand, the footsteps had sounded as if they were going in the direction of the main stairway and the guard was posted there. She hadn't heard the guard challenge anyone, so whoever it was, the person must not be any sort of threat. Perhaps it was a servant sent to replenish the oil in the lamp near the stairs or bring some food to the guard. Nevien shrugged mentally, dismissing the matter.

Still, she didn't feel like trying to go back to sleep. She was much too wide awake. *Perhaps a little walk in the hallway would help. She might even try going out onto the south-facing balcony for a little air, if the guard would allow it.* She got up, slipped her feet into her slippers, and put her dressing gown on over her nightdress. The dressing gown was of a deep, dusky rose color. It looked almost red where the candlelight fell on it, but in the shadows it was just another shade of gray. She put out the candle before leaving the room so as not to leave it burning unattended. The lamp in the hallway would light her way.

The end of the east hall, where her bedroom lay, was very close to the back stairs and quite a long way from the single lamp at the crossing of the halls near the main stairway. The lamp was turned down low, besides, with the result that the light was quite dim outside her door. Nevien had to pause for a moment to let her eyes adjust after the relative brightness of the candle and the moonlight. After a moment, however, she began her walk. She could make out clearly the low balustrade, enclosing the top of the main stairs on three sides, and also the figure in profile that was the guard in his alcove, just before the crossing where the long east hallway met the other three shorter halls.

Her slippers were shod with soft leather. They made almost no sound as she walked, and she smiled a little at the thought that she might actually catch the guard unawares and startle him. *She could say she was making a test.* He'd be one of the elite corps known as the Princess's Guard— but not Brandel. The lieutenant had once told her laughingly that a major advantage of being the commander of that corps was that he could order other men to take the night shifts.

She was about halfway down the hall, having passed the vacant chamber that would house whatever man she eventually married, and the equally vacant queen's chamber, when she stopped dead in her tracks. She had just identified the guard— it turned out to be the tall, red-haired Leithian who had first shouted for help when her carriage was attacked, but that wasn't what stopped her. Rather, it was sound of a door opening (the hinges creaked a little), and some footfalls— and a voice. The voice was cold and hard and lacked any modulation. Nevien knew instantly to whom it belonged.

"I still want to know what happened to my powdered still-heart root. It was quite plain in my last order, and I know they can get it."

"Ye can ask 'em yourself, Zirda." The responding voice was truculent. It had a noticeable quaver, but this seemed to be due to age rather than fear. "I just takes 'em your list and brings ye back whatever they gives me. I been doin' it for twenty years, and I ain't about t' start asking 'em questions. That ain't my job."

Nevien instinctively crouched down and pressed her body against the wall, trying to make herself invisible. She couldn't see either of the speakers in the shadows of the west hall, but she knew they must be there, beyond the dimly burning lamp, on the other side of the stairs that were a little way ahead of her. The door she'd heard must have been the door leading to the chambers of Dreigen the Lore Master, because the first voice she had heard was certainly his. The second voice sounded like that of one of the servants— an old man, a Leithian— who helped around the kitchens, turning spits and sweeping floors and so on.

Nevien frowned. The two men weren't speaking loudly. Clearly they intended their conversation to be private, but the silence of the third floor hallways was otherwise so complete that the words had come to her ears with perfect clarity. *What on earth were they about?*

"*That ain't your job?*" The cold voice spoke again, now dripping sarcasm. "It's your *job* to please me as much as to please them, old man. You're just a go-between. I say they've shorted me, and I'll not stand for it. You tell them they'll get no more advice from me about the heskial until I get my still-heart root powder. They must get me what I want if they expect my cooperation."

Nevien had been straining her eyes to see into the shadows on the other side of the lamp and now she could just make out the shapes of two figures exactly where she expected them to be. *What did the guard think of this? Why didn't he intervene, or question the two men?* She cast a hurried glance at the man where he stood in his alcove. No, he wasn't asleep on his feet. She could read the tension in his stance. She saw him move a little. His gaze appeared to be fixed on the part of the shadows where the two men stood.

"*Hach—*" A rasping hack drew Nevien's attention back to the shadow-figures. The sound was followed by a more complex one, rather wet and ballistic, which she interpreted as indicating that the old man had spat on the floor. Then he said, rather non-committally, "Ye can put it in writing on the list, if ye like, and I'll carry it."

"Huh! Do you think I don't know that trick, dotard?" The cold voice of the Lore Master took on an unpleasant edge. "If I put anything about the heskial in writing, it has to be in the code— which they'll pretend to misunderstand."

"Please yourself, Zirda." The old man's voice had a shrug in it. "But it's more 'n my job is worth t' be tellin' that lot what they *must* be doing."

"Spineless fool!" Dreigen hissed, his voice lowered dangerously. "Do you fear them so? What can they do to you compared to what *I* can do? There will be more than your job at stake if you don't do what I say!"

"*Spineless*, ye say? *Fool*, is it?" The old servant was indignant now, and his voice rose with his ire. "I'm a warrior, I'll have ye know! I fought in the border wars. And I don't have t' take that from the likes o' *you!* For all your fancy chambers an' your fancy title, ye're nothing but hired help like the rest of us. What'll ye do? Kill me? Who'll be bringin' ye your little packages then? There's not another one downstairs is willing t' come near ye!"

The old man turned with an angry jerk that Nevien's eyes caught plainly in spite of the dimness of the light. In the next instant, he started in the direction of the stairs with a rapid shuffling gate. Hastily Nevien sought to withdraw, though not before catching a clearer glimpse of the man as he moved closer to the lamp— enough to tell that she'd been right about his identity. She backed away, still crouching, then turned and glided swiftly on her slippered feet back to her room. She slipped through the door, closed it, and leaned against it. Despite the pounding of her heart, she heard the old man's shuffling footsteps and the harsh wheeze of his breath as he passed outside in the hallway, a few feet from where she stood.

She continued to lean against the door until she had calmed a little. She wasn't sure exactly what she had witnessed, or why she'd felt so strongly that she didn't want to be seen by the old servant. He was quite harmless, had worked in the palace for as long as she could remember. And although Dreigen had been suspected of crimes in the past, nothing had ever been proven. In recent years, he'd become so reclusive that she sometimes forgot that he lived on the third floor. He was only the Royal Lore Master. He did experiments. Obviously he must get his supplies delivered by some means, and if he chose to have them brought after dark when others were abed, well, that was consistent with the man's secretive nature, but it wasn't a crime. The servant had said he'd been doing this for years, and the guard had been interested but apparently not surprised. Was it only because Dreigen was so cold and sinister-sounding that she was so unsettled by her experience?

She shivered as she crossed to her bed and re-lit the candle, feeling better for it's light. There was also the fact that the guard happened to be one about whom Brandle had raised some suspicions... *and there was Dreigen's talk about using a code...*

Altogether, she was in no mood to sleep, so she picked up the *History of the Holds* from her bedside table and propped herself up in the bed on some pillows to try to read it. The book had put her to sleep once already, perhaps it would serve her a second time as well.

Yet she was still awake about a quarter of an hour later when she heard a familiar booted tread in the hall, and her father's voice as he exchanged a word with the guard. On an impulse, she jumped out of bed and ran to the door. Opening it, she was just in time to catch the king with his hand on the handle of his own chamber door.

"Father!" she whispered urgently.

He turned at the sound. "What is it Nevien?"

Remembering that the guard might hear, she said, "I've had a bad dream, Father. Can you sit with me a while?" It was all that she could think of.

Fortunately, he didn't simply tell her not to be foolish. He cocked his head a little, puzzled, but he came. When they were both standing in her chamber with the door closed behind them, he asked gently, "Do you want to tell me about the dream?"

She made a small impatient gesture. "I did have a dream a little while ago, but that's not really what I wanted to talk to you about. I've just seen something that I don't quite understand."

"Seen... something?" The candlelight was kind to him, casting a ruddy glow on his hair and beard, and softening the lines of his face so that he looked at that moment very much as he had in the days of her childhood. His glance was every bit as piercing as he looked at her, questioning.

"Yes. Out there. In the hallway, just past the stairs." She took a breath. "Do you and the members of the Council supply Master Dreigen with the things that he uses in his studies?"

She thought she saw his face stiffen. "Yes, we do," he said, his voice perfectly level. "I used to handle Dreigen's keep myself, years ago, but lately I've involved the Council. Why do you ask this? What did you see?"

"It was more *heard* than *saw*," she told him. "But I know Dreigen's voice. He was talking to one of the servants outside the door of his chambers. They were arguing— about something that had been in Dreigen's 'order' and that he hadn't received. He was very annoyed that the servant wouldn't pass on his complaint to 'them'— I suppose he meant to you and the Council. The servant was the old Leithian man who sweeps floors in the kitchens. I suppose, then, that you employ the man as the go-between?"

Now the king was frowning, his gaze abstracted. "I don't know who makes the exchanges," he murmured. "I leave that to my Chamberlain— taking the orders and sending them out to the appropriate merchants and apothecaries... receiving the deliveries, and so on. Of course the paperwork comes to my desk— the orders and the bills. I like to know what my Lore Master is costing me..." His voice trailed off and his eyes came back to focus on her face. "What was the thing he claimed he hadn't received? Do you recall?"

Nevien frowned in her turn with the effort of remembering. "Still-heart something... yes... powdered still-heart root— that was it. There was something about something else, too. Some foreign-sounding word— I can't remember— but he said he wouldn't help 'them' with it if they kept 'shorting' him. And he said that if he put his complaint it in writing, he'd have to put it in a code. Does all of that make sense to you, Father?"

His eyes slid away, this time to the window where the two moons, one nipping at the other's heel, were beginning to sink behind the black silhouette of the rocky peninsula on which the palace stood. "Not entirely," he said darkly. "But I'm sure I shall once I've looked into it." Then abruptly he looked at her and smiled, a quick, tight flash of his teeth. "I'm glad you've told me this, Nevien," he said with unaccustomed earnestness. "It raises some minor questions. Nothing of any great importance, I'm sure, and I don't want you to worry any more about it. Can you go back to sleep now?"

She smiled back ruefully. "I'll read myself to sleep. With Gobrig's book it shouldn't take long." She paused. Something in his face or his stance seemed to suggest tension— or perhaps it was just weariness. "Are you tired, Father," she asked. "I hope you also can sleep. What on earth are you doing still awake and dressed at this hour?"

"I'm quite all right." He straightened his shoulders. "Anduar was expounding upon another one of his schemes. Rather a far-fetched one, I thought, but he was insistent that I hear him out. You know how Anduar can be."

Nevien sighed and nodded. She was suddenly very tired herself. "Good night then, Father," she said.

"Good night, Daughter."

He turned to the door as she moved towards the bed, but he turned back at the threshold, pausing with the door half open. "I'd be happier if you didn't wander about the halls at night, Nevien," he said. "Not if Dreigen might be about."

"But why, Father?" she asked, surprised. "You surely don't think he would harm me?"

"Of course not." The answer might have come too quickly. But he was too far from her and the candlelight too feeble, and she couldn't read his face.

He was still speaking to her.

"Dreigen is a cold creature, Nevien. He has no heart. He cares for nothing but himself— while you are so very kind. See how this little adventure has unsettled you? I'd rather you didn't risk confronting him, that's all."

With that, he bade her goodnight once more and went out, closing the door.

Nevien stifled a yawn. It was good to have her father being so solicitous, and if there were anything to be dealt with, he would surely deal with it. And she was really very tired— too tired to think about any of it any more. *It's all caught up with me*, she thought. *I shan't need Grobig's book after all.*

She was so confident, in fact, that she left the book on the bedside table and pinched out the candle. Nor was her confidence misplaced. Whatever other dreams she had that night, she didn't remember them when she awoke in the morning. The sun was already up by then. Her chamber was completely suffused with the warm light of day, and the shadows of the previous night seemed absurdly insubstantial.

Chapter 12

Mission To Jinara

"Welcome, Captain Nagaro! I am most glad to see you again, and may de Unnamed One keep you ever in his favor." Utabala inclined his head and touched the heel of his hand to his forehead in the formal Jinari gesture of reverence. When he raised his face again, his black eyes in his smooth, dark countenance were alight with genuine pleasure as he continued in his accented but fluent Common Speech. "And I have to say dat it is most especially good to see you here in my es-study, wit-out any official persons looking over our shoulders, as dey say."

Nagaro nodded, returning the smile with equal pleasure. "May you have prosperity and long life, my friend. And yes, it is both a pleasure and a relief to be here speaking to you."

The two men were seated on comfortably padded chairs on either side of the small table in Utabala's modest study. They were sipping chilled Jinari tokabi-leaf tea that a clerk had brought in on a tray along with a plate of thin, crisp, cinnamon-sprinkled biscuits. Being able to pursue this meeting so openly was a novel pleasure for both of them. Nagaro had brought the two ships under his command right up to the docks where the Jinari merchants moored their craft, and in broad daylight. Previously he had come under his own white sword banner with its sable field. This time they flew the flag of Edrovir, the white hawk on a field of blue. Nagaro had also presented himself at the main front entrance of the counting house instead of creeping around to the back door.

"So, you must tell me, Captain, what it is dat brings you to my humble place of employment. I do not suppose dat dis time it is business dat will bring eider one of us any profit?"

"You're right about that." Nagaro took a swallow of the tea. It had a rather musty flavor compared to sothiril, but was not an unpleasant change. "I'm here on an official mission from the Kingdom of Edrovir concerning Jinara's complaint of illegal trade. I have a letter from King Elgurn addressed to the High Council of Jinara that explains what has already been done and what else we mean to do, including the details of the purpose of this mission. The letter will need to be translated and then delivered to the High Council. I'm sure you can help me with the first part of that and possibly with the second as well."

"Yes, yes." Utabal nodded his sleek head and his teeth flashed in his dark face. "Most assuredly I can assist you wit dese tings. It will be my pleasure, and for a matter of such importance, I am sure dat my esteemed master, Mundata Punda— blessing be upon his name— will be happy to have me attend to it at once."

"Excellent." Nagaro had brought a small leather satchel, which he now opened, drawing out the letter. "I'm authorized to pay for the translation as well as for courier service, and I urge you not to stint in naming your fee. My superiors are anxious to show their generosity and will only be distressed if they think they haven't paid enough."

Nagaro excused himself to go outside and take some air while Utabala prepared the translation. There he paced the broad paved way that edged the piers of Tambali's waterfront. The road was busy with passing folk and he threaded his way among them, drawing glances from dark-skinned, hawk-nosed Jinari, who eyed him with studiously restrained curiosity. Many met his eyes, nodding politely and murmuring some standard phrase of greeting. It struck him that the Jinari were an exceptionally well-mannered people. Even the sailors were too polite to jostle him.

He paused to lean against a railing and gazed out across the harbor. He couldn't help remembering that the illegal trade he was investigating had been carried out from this very port. It could be going on right now, he realized, and he would be none the wiser. The docks were thronged and the harbor was dotted with vessels of various kinds, all going about their affairs. The *Sword* and the *Sea Eagle* were rocking gently at their moorings a short distance away, flanked by Jinari merchantmen taking on cargo. As he stood and watched, all manor of barrels, boxes, and bales were being moved up gangways and lowered into various hatches.

Those containers could have held anything, and the thought gave a somber turn to his thoughts, although it was hard to believe there was anything sinister going on around him on such a day as this. The sun was high and bright, the sky a peerless blue. The breeze was brisk and clean out of the west with a salt tang that tugged at his slumbering wanderlust. Gold and silver highlights danced on the deep green swells.

His contemplation was interrupted by a polite cough, and he turned to find Utabala's clerk beside him. The man bowed unctuously and issued a staccato stream of incomprehensible Jinari while pantomiming his intention that Nagaro should follow him back to Mundata Punda's counting house.

Once back in the study, Nagaro returned to his seat and helped himself to a biscuit. Utabala smiled in welcome before returning his attention to putting the finishing touches on his translation of the letter. As Nagaro had expected, knowing the Jinari custom, the translated document took the form of a small scroll.

Presently the merchant's agent looked up. "I tink it is all in good order," he said as he dusted the ink with fine sand, paused, and then blew the sand away. "And I have arranged dat a message rider will come soon to take it quickly to de capital, and deliver it directly to de Chamber of de High Council— may de One Whose Name We Do Not es-Speak give dem long life." He carefully inspected the writing to make sure that the ink was dry, and having satisfied himself on that point, rolled the scroll tightly and tied it with a short length of black ribbon. He then sealed the ribbon with wax and proceeded with meticulous care to inscribe the address information on the outer curve of the parchment. Finally, he put down the pen, dusted this last bit of writing, blew on it, and looked up.

His black eyes met Nagaro's. "Now dat I have read what is in de letter," he said seriously. "Dere are some tings dat I tink I had better tell you."

Nagaro leaned forward. "I am listening, my friend."

Utabala bobbed his head. "It is a good letter," he said carefully. "De High Council— blessings be upon dem— will be pleased. It is good dat your King Elgurn— may his ways be es-straight under de sun— has asked for a list of all de tings dat it is illegal to buy and to sell. Dis means dat de Droviri want to please de Jinari, not only in de present, but in de future as well. But de High Council— may dey ever prosper— will not be pleased to permit Droviri ships to search very freely in Jinari waters."

Nagaro lifted his shoulders. "I didn't expect them to be," he said mildly. "And we don't intend to do what the High Council doesn't wish us to do. Never-the-less, we are anxious for additional information. We cannot really do very much without it."

Utabala regarded him with eyes as sharp and bright as polished obsidian. "So," he said, "You are wondering maybe what de most honorable and official Inquisitors— may dey be blessed wit long life— have learned about where de trade has gone?"

Nagaro made an equivocal gesture. "I don't care whether it comes from the official investigation or from your own inquiries, Utabala. If there is information that Edrovir can use to stop the trafficking or prevent it from being restarted, I would very much like to hear it."

Utabala nodded. "One of dose dat is investigating happens to be a good friend of mine, and so de information comes to me," he said. "Dat is why I can tell you dat Droviri gold is es-still being paid for heskial. But de

Inquisitors— may de Unnamed One grant dem clear sight— have been unable to find out how de trade is going in and out of de country."

Nagaro's brows came together upon hearing this. He found the idea of heskial flowing into Edrovir quite intolerable. "Can't your government put a stop to the production of this drug?" he asked sharply.

Utabala spread his hands. "Dey do try, Captain. But it is too easy to grow de plant and to make de drug. All dat is needed are a few pots in de back garden for de plants and a back room of de house for de preparation. And de price dat it brings is very high. So as long as dere are people who are willing to buy it, dere will be people who will find a way to make it."

"I'm sorry." Nagaro sighed and rubbed his forehead. "I didn't mean to suggest that your people aren't doing everything they can. I just want to find a way to stop it."

The bright black eyes regarded him keenly. "I tink," Utabala said slowly, "dat maybe you have some personal ek-es-sperience wit dis heskial. But if it is better dat I do not know about dis, I pray dat you do not tell me."

Nagaro's stomach gave a sickening wrench that he managed, with an effort, not to manifest. "I've had the effects described to me in very graphic terms," he said. This was true as far as it went, which wasn't nearly as far as it could have.

"I under-es-stand, Captain." The response was as smooth as satin. "I will send de letter today, as soon as de rider comes, and I tink it will be in de capital by sunset. De High Council— may de Unnamed One es-smile upon dem— will take deir time to consider and to discuss. Deir answer will not come back for a few days at least. And when it comes, I do not tink it will give permission for you to be es-stopping boats in Jinari waters to make de search. But," and here Utabala paused significantly, "while you are waiting to hear de word from de capital, dere is no-ting to prevent you from sailing wit your ships wherever you wish to sail, and putting down de anchor, and looking wit de es-spy glass. And if you happen by chance to see a man wit yellow hair, I am sure dat dere would be no objection if you catch him and make him answer your questions."

"Yes, I ... see."

"And aldough I have every confidence in de es-skill of de official Inquisitors— may deir days be long— I es-still will keep my own eyes open and my ears unsealed, as dey say. And if any information should come to me, you may be assured dat I will see dat it comes to you as quickly as possible. And whatever else may happen, I will send word to you when de message rider comes from de capital wit de answer." Utabala rose and extended his hand. "Blessings be upon you. And may de Unnamed One make es-straight your ways."

Nagaro stood up also and took the hand and shook it warmly. "Thank you, friend Utabala. May your fortunes be always fair."

***

A sleepy dusk was settling over the harbor town of Patamtala on the island of Judaba. The anchorage was sheltered from the worst weather by virtue of facing east, away from the open sea from whence came the storms. It was scarcely a bay, being little more than a crescent-shaped scoop in the shoreline with a low headland at the southern end of it and a bit of a sandy spit at the north end. The *Sword* and the *Sea Eagle* rode peacefully at anchor, well out from shore, a little distance from the cluster of small boats that represented Patamtala's fishing fleet.

The air was balmy, with only a light breeze wafting from the shore, carrying the pungent smell of wood smoke with a hint of spicy Jinari cooking. The sun was sinking into the sea beyond the island's verdant hills, which stood as dark silhouettes against a sky that was deepening towards violet. The harbor swells were taking on the hue of midnight jade, save where they reflected the golden glimmers of the lights starting to show in the windows of the town of Patamtala.

Nagaro was leaning on the rail of the *Sword*'s stern castle with his spyglass to his eye, carefully scanning the shore at the base of the sand spit.

Landros slouched against the rail beside him. The old sea warrior had rowed across from the *Sea Eagle* to join Nagaro. Presently he cleared his throat and asked, "Have ye seen anything, lad?"

"No. But I didn't really expect to." Nagaro ignored the familiarity. He was used to hearing it from Landros, who had known him since he was little more than a lad. "Even if they had resumed the traffic to and from Patamtala, it would take a stroke of luck to see anything on any particular night from this vantage point. I can make out the warehouse, and we already know it's in use from having gone ashore this afternoon, but that use may be completely legitimate. I have a clear view of a short stretch of the path that leads to the cove on the other side of the sand spit, but I've seen no one moving on it. It's Taru's expedition to the cove that will give us the real answer."

"I can't help thinking they'd be fools to come back here, after it got hot enough once to scare 'em off."

Nagaro nodded, lowering his glass but keeping his eyes fixed on the shore. "I agree. The only reason they might have come back, really, is that this location is best suited to their purpose. Still, I think it likely that Taru,

Nanu, and Haruda will tell us that the hut we saw on the other side of the sand spit— near that little makeshift dock— is as deserted on the inside as it appeared to be on the outside." He sighed. "But that won't mean the trade has stopped."

Landros cocked his head. "Ye think not? Ye don't trust those yellow-haired keel-rotters, either?"

At this, Nagaro turned to face the other captain, and fixed the grizzled Kelorin with a penetrating gaze. "That's not a good way to talk, Landros," he said coolly. "We both have Leithian friends."

"Well, aye." Landros was taken aback. "But our Leithian friends are good men."

Nagaro shook his head. "The Leithians who were coming here to carry on this trade were probably underlings— loyal to their lord and acting under orders. I'm guessing there have never been more than a few who knew what was being traded, and fewer still who knew why. And while the trade is traceable to three Houses, two of whose lords are Brothers of the Blood, there are other Leithian lords who have openly distanced themselves from that brotherhood. No, it's not because we're dealing with Leithians that I doubt the illicit trade will have stopped. It's because Utabala has known about it for years. It's unlikely that something that's been going on for so long could be stopped so easily."

Landros sighed. "Point taken, Captain," he said hastily, "about the sympathies o' Leithians, great and small. And I take your other point as well about the trade going on for years. But ye should go and eat something now. I smelled some good cooking from the galley when I came aboard. Old Rubo's done himself proud again. If ye'll hand me the glass, I'll watch for a spell while ye have your dinner, then hand it back and go to get mine."

Nagaro laughed. "It will very soon be too dark to see anything with the glass, at least until moonrise— and Taru should have returned by then. But you can stay and watch if you like."

It was indeed quite dark when the longboat under Taru's command slid in beside the *Sword*'s long hull, bumping gently as the men steadied it and found the rope ladder. Soon all three Turo were on deck, and a short time after that, Taru joined Landros and Nagaro in the great cabin. He had come by way of the galley and brought his dinner with him. He sat at the table devouring a freshly-baked flatbread folded around a helping of seasoned meat and onions while he made his report.

"It was empty, all right, Nagaro, and it looked to have been that way for months. One o' the windows had a great hole torn in the oiled skin so's ye could look right in and see almost the whole inside o' the place. We peeked in that way first and saw there was nobody there. And the door wasn't locked or barred, either. So we went in an' poked around— even though there was hardly anything ye'd call furniture."

Landros was sitting across from Taru. "Are ye sure they couldn't have just cleaned her out well?" he ventured.

But Taru shook his head. "I'd say no. There was naught but a broken stool, an empty crate, and a table that had one leg nearly off. And we could see where the roof must ha' leaked when it rained and got the table wet— it was black with mold, an' nobody had taken any care t' clean it up or move it out o' the way. The water had splashed onto the floor— it was nothing more'n hard-packed sand. Ye could see plainly where the drops had fallen. And there weren't any footprints on top o' the splash marks."

Nagaro had been pacing the floor as he listened. Now he stopped. "Well done, Taru," he said. "Those are good observations. You and the men were very thorough."

Landros leaned back in his chair. "Did ye see any sign that there had ever been trafficking going on there o' the kind we've been told about? I know Nagaro trusts our old friend Utabala, but I'd feel better knowing ye were lookin' in the right hut."

Taru had finished the last scrap of the flatbread and started to reach for his cup of sothiril, but he stuck his hand into his pocket instead. "Well, Haruda did find *this* on the floor in a corner." He tossed a small, flat bit of something red onto the table. It was no bigger than a fingernail.

Landros picked it up and held it in his cupped palm under the lamp that hung from a ceiling beam. "Seems to be wax," he said.

Nagaro came close to examine the find. "It looks like sealing wax. See how it's flat on this side— that would be where it was stuck to the paper. And *these* parts are smooth, just the way the wax hardened— while it's plainly broken *here*, and *here*. It's just the kind of bit that might crack off when a seal is broken."

"A pity there's no part o' the stamp on it," Landros observed.

"True." Nagaro frowned as he picked the fragment out of Landros' palm and pocketed it. "But it's not something you'd expect to find in an abandoned fisherman's hut. I'll have to tell Haruda that he has sharp eyes."

"Ye think they're really gone, then, Nagaro?" Taru made another reach for his sothiril.

"From here, yes."

"They might be taking the loot overland to the other side o' the island," Landros offered. "It'd be more bother than just trotting 'round to the other side o' the sand spit, but there's a lot o' little coves with fishermen's huts on this island."

"Keshaal!" Nagaro swore with sudden vehemence. "You're right, Landros!" He resumed his pacing. "I was thinking about places where that kind of cove was *close* to an anchorage suitable for ships. There wouldn't be many such places in these islands, and this one is easily the best— here at the northern edge of Jinari waters. But if they're willing to go *overland*— that makes it like looking for a needle in the straw!"

Landros cocked his head at him. "Ye're taking this mission awfully serious, lad," he said. "And I know it's the first time Kuran's put you in command of more than your own ship, but this is just a bit o' politics and diplomacy. No need to let the wind ruffle your sails."

Nagaro stopped pacing, aware that his scowl was like thunder. He'd been keeping his emotions at some distance up until that moment by telling himself that the Jinari would find the new trade route, if there was one. Now he could feel Taru's eyes on him and he struggled to compose himself. "I don't like what they've been doing," he said defensively. "I want to see it stopped."

Landros raised an eyebrow. "A bit of illegal trade?"

Nagaro managed to rearrange his features into what he hoped was a concerned frown. "It's *what* they've been trading, Landros. And what the Brothers of the Blood might do with it."

"Ye know something that I don't? Ye know what they're trading?"

Nagaro sagged inwardly. He didn't want to talk about heskial to anyone who didn't already know about it. The subject was too painful. In this case, Taru knew, but Landros didn't. He cast about for some other way to explain himself. "Did I ever show you those scrolls we found among the loot on this ship after we first took her?" he asked. "There were dried plants as well. Dangerous ones. I don't know whether that shipment was meant for our Leithians, but it's the kind of thing that Utabala found was being traded— poisons and things of that kind."

"Well, I admit that sounds bad," Landros conceded. "But ye can only do what ye can do. There's others whose task it is to catch the scoundrels, so I say let them do their task and ye do yours. But I'll go out and ply the glass some more, if ye like. Talebra should be rising soon."

Nagaro sighed and waved a hand. "Yes, Landros, by all means. Go keep the watch. It may have little chance of accomplishing anything, but at least we should be able to say we tried."

After Landros had gone, Nagaro sank into the chair the older man had vacated and took his head in his hands. "Am I taking this too seriously, Taru?"

Taru considered him over his cup of sothiril. "Aye," he said after a moment. "But I know *why* ye are. And I wouldn't worry about how it looks t' Landros. Everyone knows ye always take things too serious when ye see that something's not right."

Nagaro gave his friend a wry look. "I didn't really expect we'd catch anyone on this mission. We've only got two ships, and there's too much territory to search and too little time. But I *was* really hoping the Jinari would catch them. Now I'm wondering whether the Jinari can even do it. And I feel guilty because I've known about this for years and never told anyone. I was afraid of giving myself away. If Utabala hadn't decided he had to go to the Jinari authorities I might still be waiting."

Taru shrugged. "It's not as if ye knew they were trading heskial. As soon as ye found *that* out, ye told Kuran, didn't ye?"

"Well... *ye-es...*"

Taru had finished his sothiril. Now he set down his cup and changed the subject. "I tell ye Nagaro, I'm glad there was nobody in that hut t' see us sneakin' around. Leithians might take Turo for Jinari at a distance, but not up close. And we'd ha' never fooled the local folk. There were plenty o' Jinari out and about in the harbor in boats an' they gave us the eye while we were rowing. We just eyed 'em right back. The last thing ye want t' do when ye're doing something ye shouldn't is to *look* like ye shouldn't be doing it."

Nagaro laughed. "You'd have made a good thief, Taru. Though I shouldn't give you ideas."

"No fear o' that. I like being a Fleet officer. Sometimes I still can't believe that's what I am. I wonder what my father would think if he could see me now."

"He'd be proud of you, Taru. Your mother too. Of course they always were proud of you, but they'd be even more so now." Nagaro paused, then added, "Is Jitali's father impressed?"

Taru's glance slid away. A frown fleetingly crossed his face. "Oh, aye. Very impressed," he said. Then he pulled his eyes back to Nagaro. "There's something I was wondering while I was rowing about among all those fishing boats," he said. "If the Jinari don't eat any meat, why do they have so many fishermen?"

Nagaro decided to let the second change of subject pass. "I asked Utabala about that once. It took a little while for him to understand what I was getting at, but when he did, he explained to me that, to the Jinari, fish aren't animals."

"Not animals! What d' they figure they are then?"

Nagaro shrugged. "The best word he had was just 'fish.' There are animals and there are fish, he said. Animals have legs to walk with and fish don't. That's the distinction. So birds are animals, and crabs and lobsters are animals, but clams and oysters and cod and mackerel are fish."

Taru stared. "What about snakes?" he asked.

"I didn't ask about snakes. By the definition, they would seem to be fish. I don't know whether the Jinari eat them."

"What about porpoises?" Taru's eyes were going wider. "They don't eat *porpoises*, do they?"

Nagaro shook his head. "That I did ask about, and they don't. It seems that porpoises aren't ordinary fish, they're sacred fish, 'blessed by the Unnamed One,' because they're friends to sailors."

Taru looked relieved, but he said, "It's bloody *stupid* saying fishes aren't animals!"

Nagaro sighed. "The Jinari just have a different way of dividing the world into bits, Taru. They have two categories of what we call animals— the ones with legs, which they're not allowed to eat; and the ones without, which are fair game, mostly. We don't have words in the common speech for those two categories because we don't divide things up that way. So Utabala had to chose words to use, and the words he chose were 'animals' and 'fish.' It feels wrong to us because to us, fish are a *kind* of animal."

"R-right..." Taru looked a bit dazed. Then he shook his head as if to clear it. "It's all right for *you*, Nagaro. Ye've got the right kind o' head for that sort o' thinking. *I* still say it's bloody stupid." He stood up. "And now I'm going t' go and find Pavo. He may have some strange ideas of his own, but at least he knows what an animal is!"

Nagaro sighed again as the cabin door closed behind Taru. He had hoped to learn more about the progress of Taru's courtship, but there was no drawing Taru out on a subject if he didn't wish to be drawn.

He shook his head and frowned. He still had their mission to worry about. All he could think of was to make a circuit of the island of Judaba in case Landros was right, to look for other potential places where the small boats might land. It would be slow going, but at least the island wasn't very large.

Two days later, as they were nearing the completion of their circumnavigation of Judaba, Matapili found them. Utabala's courier hailed them and pulled his small craft along side. Nagaro was waiting at the rail. He smiled a little to note the black and white ribbons flying from one of the small craft's mast stays. It was the signal that Utabala had devised years before to indicate that the messenger sought Captain Nagaro, specifically. They were pirate colors and so no longer appropriate, but they still served their purpose.

Matapili raised his voice and called over the water. "Cap-i-tan Nagaro! May de Unnamed One smile on you! My master say he have answer from High Council— praise to deir names. You come back to Tambali— get answer."

Nagaro glanced along the curving shore in the direction they'd been sailing. He could see the rocky point that marked the southern boundary of the Patamtala Harbor in the distance with nothing but beach in between. Anyone coming ashore on the beach would be visible for miles.

There was no place that would serve for illegal trading purposes along the remaining stretch of coast.

"Very good, Matapili," he said. "And good health to you. We will set course for Tambali at once."

Matapili's smile split is face. "Den you follow me, Cap-i-tan!" he cried. "I go back dere too. Blessings of de Un-Named One!" The Jinari touched the heel of his hand to his forehead, pushed his boat away from the *Sword*'s hull, and put the tiller over as the wind caught his sail.

Nagaro gave the order to follow the courier. Then he sighed. They had found several places where a small craft could come to shore without being in direct view from any town or village but where there were huts or other structures about. He'd marked the places on his charts, but there was no reason to be particularly suspicious of any of them. He could only hope that Utabala's 'answer' would prove more useful.

***

"I have received de letter from de High Council— blessings of de Unnamed One be upon dem— and de list of all de tings in which it is forbidden to trade. Also I have dis map of de islands on which I have marked de places dat most especially we tink dey might try to use for dis traffic." Utabala laid several papers on the table and spread them out so that they were fully displayed. "Already I have done all de translation. In de case of de list, as you can see, dis most often means rendering of de words into de characters you Droviri use to write your Common es-Speech."

Nagaro picked up the indicated paper and scanned the list of about two dozen items. "The set of letters we use is called the Reivinkor," he said absently. "I see that you've included alternative names for some of these things, and some physical descriptions. Would it be possible to include information concerning exactly what each of these things *does*— or why it's been placed on this list? Is this something that you know, Utabala?"

"Oh, yes. I know what dey all do, and I can add dat information if you will give de paper back to me. It will not take very long."

Nagaro handed the paper back and waited while Utabala dipped a quill and added a series of annotations. When he had finished, Utabala once more proffered the paper.

Looking over what the merchant's agent had added, Nagaro saw that most of the substances were poisons, as he had expected, but not all. Heskial was an exception (although it could indeed kill), and there was one that caused erotic dreams, and several that could cause madness—

temporary or permanent— with or without being potentially fatal in larger doses. He couldn't help but wonder how many of these things Dreigen had in his arsenal. The thought made him shiver.

"Dey are all tings dat have no known medicinal use," Utabala observed conversationally.

"I see. Very good. Thank you."

"De letter you will want to read carefully at your leisure I am sure, Captain, but I can tell you dat dey have asked dat you not interfere wit de Jinari fishing boats or question Jinari citizens. Dat is for de Inquisitors to do— blessings be upon dem. But if you see any people who look like dey are Droviri, you have permission to es-stop deir boats and ask dem as many questions as you wish."

Nagaro smiled wryly. "So it's just as you said it would be, my friend. But what is the purpose of the map? Does it come from the High Council, or the Inquisitors? Or is it something of your own devising?"

Utabala smiled from ear to ear, revealing strong white teeth. "De information was conveyed to me from de Inquisitors by de one dat I know, but de map I have made for you myself. You see how I have made a red mark in all de places dat we tink are most possible to use for dis trade."

Nagaro bent over the map. His heart sank as he noted no fewer than nine red marks, scattered widely on five of the six major Jinari islands. Only one of them was on the island of Judaba— at the cove near Patamtala where they had already looked. "I'm very glad to have this," he said, doing his best to sound sincere since it was better than having nothing at all. "We've already sailed all the way around Judaba," he added. "We saw no Leithians anywhere, nor any sign of anything to warrant further attention. Can you tell me whether any of these spots seem more likely than the others? Have the Inquisitors seen any suspicious activity at any of them?"

"As for dat, I do not tink so. De Inquisitors— may dey have long life— have made very little progress." Utabala leaned over the map. "Dese are all places where it is possible to make landing wit a small boat witout being widely seen. Besides dat, dey all have a house or oder es-structure dat is close by so dat de business may be conducted out of sight and out of de rain. And also dere is in every case a harbor dat is not too far away, for de use of de big merchant ships. I tink dat is why dey were chosen. But if you want my most humble opinion, I would say you should try first here on Dronobo Island, and den here on Janidi, and maybe also dis one on Atadalba." Utabala indicated the three spots with his finger. "Dese places are on de sea-ward side of de islands. If de yellow-haired Droviri go to any of dese places, dey will not have to sail where so many of our fishermen may see dem."

Nagaro nodded. He could only agree with this assessment. "I wish I could talk to the fishermen— just to ask if they had seen any yellow-haired men," he said with a sigh. "I can't see why there should be an objection to that. But of course I don't know the language."

Utabala immediately brightened. "Oh, I do not tink de High Council— blessings be upon dem— would object to de asking of dat question only," he said. "And es-specially not if you have a Jinari wit you to ask it. If you wish, I will arrange for you to take Matapili wit you when you make your search."

"Could you do that?" Nagaro's spirits rose. "It would be most welcome— if he can be spared, of course."

Utabala waved a hand. "For a ting of such importance, I am sure my master will agree. I will go at once to see to de matter. If you will be so good as to wait here, I will return as quickly as I can."

Left alone in the office, Nagaro took the opportunity to quickly read over the letter that contained the High Council's response to the letter he had brought from Edrovir. It was couched in flowery diplomatic language, but seemed to contain no great surprises— and no language that would prohibit Matapili from questioning Jinari citizens on Nagaro's behalf. Near the end of the letter there was a paragraph that caused him to smile faintly because it concerned negotiations between Edrovir and the Mahuk Baar on the matter of raiding merchant ships and taking slaves. The Jinari High Council politely pointed out that Jinari interests were similar to those of Edrovir and expressed a hope that this fact "might be conveyed to the Mautep Emperor during any future discussion of these matters." He had just finished his perusal of the letter and was placing it in his leather pouch when Utabala returned.

"De arrangements have been made," the merchant's agent informed him. "It will require a delay of one hour while Matapili obtains de provisions for his boat."

"Excellent." Nagaro reached for the map, then paused to consider it. With Matapili's help there was actually a chance that they might learn something during their search, but he was thinking of what Landros had said at Patamtala.

"There is really too much area to cover properly in the time we have left," he said. "I wish we could be sure that we only need to worry about the places you have marked. But if the Jinari traders are willing to go overland to meet the Leithians, there are surely many more places they might be using."

"Over-land?" Utabala looked puzzled. "Do you mean over de land— in de islands?"

"Yes. If they're willing to walk from *here* to *here*, for example." Nagaro tapped an obvious harbor on the south side of one of the islands and a small cove on the northern shore, roughly across from it.

Utabala's eyes widened. "Oh dat is not good," he said. "If dey are willing to do dat, dey could be making deir trade almost anywhere in de islands!"

"Yes, I know..." Nagaro's voice trailed. Then, "Vothra's Eyes!" he exclaimed, as a new thought struck him. "If the Leithians are willing to travel overland, there's no reason we should be searching in the islands at all! They could be going *anywhere* that a man or a horse can go!"

Utabala blinked at him. "A man can go... or a horse?" he said. Then understanding dawned. "Oh, I see. You mean dat dey do not need to come in little boats by way of de sea. Dey can come on de mainland. Dey can come on de roads, or off de roads."

"Yes. Exactly." Nagaro was staring past the other man, frowning. "Why didn't any of us think of that before? The most southern coastal district of Edrovir is the Leithian Hold of Borlund. Since we aren't at war right now, what is there to stop any of our folk from trading with your folk across the border? And it could be legal or illegal trade. How would anyone know?"

"I do not tink dere is as yet very much legal trade between de people of Jinara and of Edrovir," Utabala observed dryly. "De peace has not been so very long, and de people along de border remember de fighting, and dey do not feel so very friendly to one anoder."

Nagaro had an image in his mind of Leithians creeping through the Jinari woods, ducking into an abandoned farmhouse. His alarm was rising. With an effort, he forced his thoughts to focus on what the merchant's agent was saying. "That might make illicit overland trade a little easier to discover," he ventured. "Since any activity at all would potentially be suspect."

"Yes, yes." Utabala was nodding vigorously. "I will tell dis at once to de man dat I know who is one of de Inquisitors. De unlawful traders will try to hide what dey are doing, of course, but de Inquisitors— blessings be upon dem— are not great fools. If only dey know where dey should be looking, I tink dey will find what is dere to find. But until now dey have been looking only in de islands."

Nagaro frowned. "I don't *know* that the trade is coming overland. It's just a possibility."

"Dis I under-es-stand." Utabala waved a placating hand. "But it is a most promising possibility, and one dat we had not tought about. How long are you able to es-stay in Jinari waters, Captain?"

"About three more weeks. We have orders to return to Lankura by midsummer."

"Den I will tell you what you should do. You should sail around de islands with Matapili, looking for your yellow-haired men and asking de fishermen. If you look in all dese places dat I have marked, you can tell your Lord of de Fleet dat you have been torough. Maybe you will learn someting, even if it is only dat no one has seen dese men in dese places. Den, when you have es-spent all de time dat you have, you come back here to me and I will tell you if de Inquisitors have found any sign dat de trade is going over de land."

Nagaro nodded. "Yes," he said, "This is the most we can do." Then he remembered the attack on the princess's carriage, and added, "Tell the man you know that the Leithians might be wearing disguises. They might have black wigs." He gestured with his hand when Utabala looked blank. "False hair on their heads. Made of black wool. They might even darken their skins, as I do, with kuma stain— although the stain doesn't wear off quickly. A man who uses it must be prepared to have his disguise last for weeks."

Utabala nodded gravely. "I will tell my friend dis also." His black eyes were shrewdly fixed on Nagaro's face, but he refrained from comment or question regarding what reasons his Droviri friend might have for his own use of kuma stain.

Chapter 13

Needles In The Straw

Nevien was a vision in dark green silk, her honey-gold hair flowing loose over her shoulders. She was coming towards him... smiling as she raised a hand to beckon. She continued to move, yet somehow was never nearer— but always she beckoned him on. He was struggling to close the gap between them, struggling as if trying to push through water, to move against the flow. He cried out to her— called her by name— but a figure stepped between and he was confronted by Lothard Hurn...

The man came at him with a drawn sword, face contorted with rage, shouting for him to defend himself. But his own hands were empty! He had no sword! Desperately he felt for the scabbard at his waist, but found nothing there. Then Lothard lunged... and he fell... landing on his back. He lay looking up, unable to move, as the Leithian stood over him— laughing...

Lothard's yellow hair was imperfectly covered by a thick, black wig, straw-blond strands sticking out from under it as he held aloft a vial of what looked like dirty water. *"Do you see this?"* the Leithian exulted. *"I needed only half a dram to put you in your present state!"* Now the face looming over him was dark-skinned, the hair naturally black. The features were those of Dreigen— hawk-nosed, black eyes burning in their shadowed sockets. The man was leaning closer....

"Vothra!" Nagaro was jolted awake. He lay shuddering, his heart pounding. *That man.... that horrible man!*

The memory of the dream-image was fading, leaving him aware that he was lying in his bunk, clutching at his left arm— at the places where the bladder-thorn had pierced his skin when the hated Lore Master had injected heskial's poison into his veins— where the faint scars left by those dreaded needles were still visible to a well-trained eye. With a shudder, he released his fingers. He knew he had spoken the name of Vothra, the Benevolent Spirit, aloud— that speaking the name had awakened him— and he was intensely glad that he slept alone in the *Sword*'s great cabin. There was no one here to ask unwelcome questions.

The cabin was suffused with the light of early morning. He shook himself and disentangled himself from the covers, then rose, and went unsteadily to the wash basin where he poured some water and splashed his face. He dried himself, shivering. The lingering shadow of the dream's ending still lay upon his spirit, and he tried briefly to call up the image of a smiling Nevien to dispel it— which only reminded him of how, in the dream, he'd been unable to reach her.

The dream had been compounded of his old fears and his current frustrations, and he stood for a long moment, breathing in and out in a slow, deliberate measure until he felt calmer. *Best to let all those memories go.* With a sigh, he set about getting dressed, and tied his hair, then took his spyglass from its hook and went out onto the deck to find something else to occupy his mind.

The *Sword of Freedom* was riding quietly at anchor in the smaller of Atadalba's two harbors, which lay on the northern shore of the southernmost of Jinara's seaward isles. The harbor was deep and narrow, formed by the intersection of a sharply-folded valley with the ocean's edge. It embraced a modest fishing village with an accompanying fleet of small craft.

The thin morning mist was evaporating, and the fishermen were readying their boats for the day's work. Nagaro shielded his eyes, frowning, as he scanned the bobbing flotilla, then relaxed a little when his eyes found Matapili's slim craft edging in among the others, the identifying black and white tell-tales still fluttering from her mast stay. They had come to the anchorage the previous evening too late for Matapili to make his inquiries. This morning the Jinari courier was already remedying that situation.

Relieved that he would soon have Matapili's report, Nagaro turned his gaze to the long, sloping headland on the harbor's western side. The undulating hills that formed it were forested, and the trees came down almost to the margin of the narrow beach that skirted its edge. On the other side of those hills, and that forest, he knew there was a much smaller anchorage, suitable only for small craft, and beyond that an estuary and an expanse of mud flats. It was the small anchorage— together with the wooded hillsides— adjacent to the larger harbor where the *Sword* now lay, that had apparently caused Utabala to mark this spot on his map. The Inquisitors presumably had reasoned that a merchant ship bearing secret goods might anchor in the harbor while a small Leithian craft could anchor on the other side of the hills. By walking just a little way, the Jinari traders and the Leithians could potentially find a meeting place under the cover of the trees.

Nagaro narrowed his eyes. From where he stood, he could make out a number of figures moving along the edge of the woods. With a muttered exclamation, he raised his spyglass for a better look. He was in the process of scanning the border of the woods with the glass, checking each figure in turn, when he heard a quiet step at his side.

Pavo's voice said, "There are people walking there, where tree meet beach."

Nagaro marveled, not for the first time, that the big Hastep could move so lightly. "Yes, I see them," he replied. "Some are women, and the others are mostly well-grown children. They're carrying sacks and most of them have what look like shovels on their shoulders."

"So they go to dig up something?"

Nagaro lowered the glass. "So I would assume. They certainly don't look like illegal traders. And there aren't any merchant ships in the harbor right now, anyway."

Pavo nodded his shaggy head. "That is true. But there could be digging now and trading later. When there is ship."

It was at this point that Taru sauntered across the deck to join them, yawning and stretching. "What would ye two say to a bit o' breakfast?" he asked. "Rubo's making pancakes."

Nagaro grinned. "I'd say it's a good idea. By the time we're finished eating, Matapili may have finished questioning the fishermen."

The ship's galley had a single long bench-like table with enough space to accommodate about a quarter of the crew at one sitting. The men tended to eat in irregular shifts, unless they took their food out onto the deck or to the crowded crew quarters in the forecastle. Officers, on the other hand, had the luxury of taking their food to their less-crowded cabin if they chose, or if invited, to the great cabin which was the captain's quarters. On this occasion, Nagaro led the way to his cabin with his two friends close on his heels. All three carried plates of steaming pancakes spread with honey, and mugs of hot sothiril. Once seated at the table in the great cabin, there were several minutes of silence marred only by the clink of utensils.

Pavo was the first to speak. Pausing with a fork-full halfway to his mouth, he said, "This place is last place that is marked on map. We have look in all of them, and we have not find anything."

Taru leaned back in his chair and wiped his mouth with the back of his hand. "Except that there were some Leithians seen around Patamtala nearly a year ago," he observed. "Which is no more'n we expected. And I don't expect that Matapili will have any more luck in this harbor."

Nagaro was focused on mopping up a puddle of warm honey with the last bite of pancake. "It may be significant that none have been seen for a year," he said. "Not around Patamtala, or anywhere else."

Taru's dark eyes narrowed. "Ye really think they've been going overland?"

Nagaro put down his fork and pushed his empty plate aside. "The more I think about it, the more it makes sense," he said earnestly. "It's much less trouble, and much less conspicuous. An Edroviran fishing boat this far south couldn't just be off its course. But a Leithian seen a quarter mile across the border of Borlund into Jinara might be looking for a lost goat or gathering wood. Going overland is what I'd do if I were in their place."

Taru pushed back his chair and stood up. "Well," he said, "If they're going overland, it's not for us t' worry about. We're sea warriors."

Nagaro didn't respond. He was frowning as he stood up and picked up his plate and cup. "Come on," he said. "I want to hear what Matapili has to tell us."

Matapili, as it turned out, had nothing unexpected to tell. "I talk to a dozen of de fishermen, Cap-i-tan," he said. "No one have seen man wit yellow hair. Not in any place where dey take de fish."

"Have they seen any strange Jinari on the island? Any men they didn't know, who might have crossed from another part of the island?"

Matapili shook his head. "Dis I have ask also. Dey only see Jinari men who live here. Some of dem make trade, but dey live here too. On oder side of island."

Nagaro chewed his lip. "What do they trade?"

"Pots for de cooking. Cloth for make de clothes. Ordinary tings. Not so many merchant ship come to dis harbor. More come to harbor on oder side of island."

"Does anyone ever go to the shore on the other side of those hills?" They were standing on the *Sword*'s deck and Nagaro pointed to the wooded headland.

Matapili nodded vigorously. "Yes. Dey go to dig de clams."

Nagaro frowned. "And the ones who dig clams haven't seen any yellow-haired men? Or any other strangers?"

"No, Cap-i-tan. Dey see no-ting dat is strange."

Nagaro sighed. He glanced at Taru and Pavo, and at Landros who had come across from the *Sea Eagle* to hear the courier's report. "Can any of you think of anything else?

Pavo shook his great head. Taru shrugged. "I think ye've asked it all," he said.

Landros squinted at the sun. "I've nothing to add. It's the same here as everywhere else. We might as well heave up the anchor and be away."

Nagaro sighed again and nodded. "All right," he said. "We sail in an hour's time. Have you had any breakfast, Matapili?"

The Jinari shook his head. "No, Cap-i-tan."

"Then go to Rubo and get some. It's pancakes this morning. No part of an animal."

Matapili smiled broadly. "Aye, Cap-i-tan," he said, then made a passable imitation of a Fleet salute and made off in the direction of the galley.

The other four men watched the Jinari go. "And fish aren't animals," Taru muttered. Then he shrugged. "I'll tell the rowers," he said, and struck off across the deck without bothering to salute. Pavo shook his head at the first mate's informality. "I will make ready to sail, Captain," he said, saluting smartly before striding off after Taru.

Nagaro felt Landros' eyes on him. The older man cleared his throat . "Don't ye fret, lad," he ventured, "on account o' not finding anything. We did everything we could."

Nagaro frowned. "We're not quite finished, Landros. We have to go back to Utabala for one last report, and he may well tell us that there's evidence the illegal trade is going overland."

"Well if he does, ye can report it to Lord Kuran, and he can tell the king. And then it's Elgurn's problem to deal with. Overland trade isn't a Fleet matter."

"No, it isn't." Nagaro pulled his eyes away. "You'd best get back to the *Sea Eagle*, Landros. Your crew will need to make ready to sail."

"Aye, Zirda." Landros saluted easily and made for the rope ladder that marked the position of his longboat.

Nagaro stood frowning beside the rail, watching Pavo give orders to the main deck crew. He knew that overland trade was not a Fleet matter, and he found no comfort in the fact whatsoever.

***

"De Inquisitors are most impressed— may deir lives be long. Dey have seen dat my friend, Captain Nagaro, is indeed a very smart man."

Utabala was transferring a plate of sugared biscuits and two cups of dark tokabi tea from the lacquered tray to the table top. Nagaro sat grimly on one of the padded chairs. He could guess what was coming, and he would rather have been wrong.

The Jinari sat down and took a decorous bite from one of the biscuits. He chewed the mouthful precisely, washed it down with an equally decorous sip of tea, and continued. "Dere is trade dat goes in many different directions, you see. Already dey had known dat some of it was going trough de area close to de border. Dey had not tought dat any of de tings being traded dere were passing into de hands of Droviri, but after hearing what you have told me, Captain, dey have looked along de border for yellow-haired men wearing de tings you call wigs— de false black hair on deir heads. What do you suppose dey have found?"

Nagaro smiled a small, tight smile. "Yellow-haired Leithians wearing black wigs?"

"Yes! Precisely! Dey have seen some of dese men making meetings wit Jinari in de hut of a woodcutter where nobody is living any more because of de war."

Nagaro took a swallow of tea for the sake of appearances. His stomach was in a knot and he had no appetite for sugared biscuits. "Have they succeeded in arresting anyone?"

Utabala looked uncomfortable. "Not at dis time. De Inquisitors— blessings be upon dem— have seen two of dese meetings, but dey are not sure what de men are trading. It might be only lawful tings. De men meet in de hut, but when dey are not dere, dey leave no-ting dat anyone can find."

Nagaro scowled. "Then the Jinari involved must have a different location that serves as their base. Your Inquisitors must find that location. They must search it for evidence."

Utabala made a small placating gesture with the hand that held his biscuit. "Of course. Dis dey are trying to do. But de Jinari traders are very careful. To find de oder location will take time. And in de meantime it has been pointed out dat dere must be a similar location on de Droviri side of de border. You have Droviri inquisitors perhaps?" Utabala's question was accompanied by a significantly raised eyebrow.

Nagaro sighed. He had spoken too harshly, and he knew it. This entire matter fretted him to the point of distraction. "I'm sorry I spoke so strongly," he said. "While I'm confident that the King and Council of Edrovir will wish to make a similar effort on our side of the border, we unfortunately have nothing equivalent to your inquisitors. We have many lords in Edrovir, and each lord has jurisdiction within his own lands. The king may attempt to tell the lords what to do, but if any of them choose to defy him, he can only call upon the other lords to support him, and things can then become... political."

"Ah. I see." Utabala nodded his sleek, dark head. "I had tought dat since you have such a very fine fleet of warships, you must have also very fine inquisitors. We Jinari do not have any warships at all."

Nagaro grimaced. "You have inquisitors, but no warships. We have warships, but no inquisitors. The King and the Council may see the wisdom of creating inquisitors after hearing my report, but all I can really tell you is that once the trade moved from sea to land, it ceased to be a matter to be dealt with by the Royal Fleet." He twisted in his chair to rummage in the leather pouch he was carrying, and brought out

Utabala's map. He unfolded it and spread it on the table, pushing the plate of biscuits to one side to make room. "Can you show me where the woodcutter's hut is located?"

"Let me see." Utabala leaned over the map. "Dere is not so much detail here, but I know what my friend has told me. It is near to where dis river crosses over de border." He tapped the map with a finger. "Let me get my pen and I will mark de place."

The merchant's agent crossed to his desk and returned with ink and pen.

"Dere is a little es-stream dat joins de river about a half a mile on dis side of de border. De es-stream flows like *dis*." He drew a line for the stream, then made a small x. "De hut is described to be *here*. It is a little less dan a mile up de es-stream, on de sout side of de water."

Nagaro studied the marks and repeated the description aloud to fix it in his mind.

Utabala nodded. "Yes, Captain. You have got it right."

"In that case I should take leave of you, my friend. This information must be carried to Lankura without delay." Nagaro returned the map to the pouch and stood up.

Utabala came around the table to take his hand. "I under-es-stand, Captain. But dere is one ting I want to ask before you go. Whatever has happened to de man dat you took from here— de man wit a Droviri face who es-spoke only Hashti? I have wondered what is his tale."

For the first time during the course of the meeting, Nagaro really smiled. "The man you speak of is named Sindar," he said. "He is in Lankura, and he's quite well. As for his tale, the Mautep killed his father and took his mother captive while he was still in her womb. He was separated from her at birth, and kept as a slave in the Mahuk Baar. That's how he came to speak only Hashti. Fortunately, I've found members of his family in Edrovir who were able to identify him and I expect he will become a member of the Royal Fleet in just a few days time, when we hold the annual induction of new recruits."

"I am glad dat he is well. But de promise you made, to make sure dat he does never any harm to Jinara? It will be kept?"

"In the event that the High Council of Jinara were to decide to build a fleet of warships and to use them to wage war on Edrovir, keeping the promise might become an issue. But not otherwise."

Utabala smiled broadly as he shook Nagaro's hand. "In dat case, I do not tink we have need to worry. I bid you farewell, and may de Unnamed One make your ways ever es-straight under de sun."

***

As soon as Nagaro was back on the deck of the *Sword of Freedom*, he gave the order to sail, and within the hour the two ships had weighed anchor and put the port of Tambali astern. Nagaro, standing in his place on the captain's platform atop the stern castle, gazed tensely ahead as if he could measure the distance to Lankura with his eyes.

Nor did his tension abate in the days that followed. He could scarcely contain his anxiousness to return to the Edroviran capital. He argued the need for haste to Taru, Pavo, and Landros by saying that the Jinari High Council would be waiting to see what action Edrovir would take, and that the action couldn't come until Elgurn and the Council had worked out what to do. His two mates and his fellow captain had to concede the truth of this, although Landros in particular wasn't convinced that the matter was of such great importance to Jinara— or, by extension, to Edrovir.

"Ye've acquitted yourself well, lad," the grizzled Kelorin opined. "Ye've completed your mission, learned all ye could, and ye'll be returning on time to make your report. Ye can relax now. Pull in your oars and let the wind carry ye."

Nagaro smiled weakly at the figure of speech. So far that day, he'd resisted the urge to order the use of the oars.

In truth, there was more behind his urgency than his fear of what the Leithians might do with heskial. The slender, beckoning figure of Nevien continued to haunt his dreams. On the out-bound voyage, he'd had the mission in front of him to distract him from what he had left behind in Lankura. Now that the city lay ahead, his thoughts constantly strayed there.

When the ships were passing Pakoa, and Pavo spoke in his calm, steady way of his regret that they couldn't stop to visit, Nagaro realized with a shock that he hadn't even thought of it. His concern for Nevien— as well as memories of her face, her voice— were calling him back to the place that had become his heart's new home.

They approached Lankura on a bright, warm, windswept afternoon, the day before the summer solstice. Standing on the captain's platform, Nagaro's heart leaped at the first sight of the royal palace on its promontory. White as cream, its marble walls cast back a blaze of sunlight. As the two ships drew closer, he could make out windows and the elegantly patterned courses of green and black stone that embellished the structure's strong, graceful lines. His eyes sought the third floor balcony where he had once stood watching with his spyglass for Kuran's returning fleet and had found that Nevien was watching him.

On this day, at this hour, the balcony was empty. He felt only a fleeting disappointment. The palace's inhabitants would have had no advance warning of the return of the *Sword* and the *Sea Eagle*. The two ships had already been hailed by fishermen, and the news of their coming would have been shouted from boat to boat. But the highborn folk of Lankura were not adept at using this nautical grapevine. So it didn't matter that Nevien wasn't standing on the balcony. She would be near. She might be somewhere in the city, making one of her charitable visitations. Most likely she was in the palace.

But there were others in the palace, as well. His eyes slid upwards from the vacant balcony to the building's two short towers. The nearer one, the west tower, he knew contained the chambers of the cold and cunning Lore Master, Dreigen. The farther one, the north tower, held Kale Fendred— boyhood companion of King Elgurn, turned murderous madman— imprisoned in its topmost chamber. *Two very different men, though almost certainly their lives were connected. Perpetrator and victim... both potential dangers, under the same roof as his beloved.*

The palace loomed closer. Abruptly recalling where he was, Nagaro shook himself and shouted the orders for a change of heading and for the rowers on the oar deck to make ready to assist in negotiating the river's current.

The two ships turned gracefully under the coordinated efforts of their helmsmen and first mates, sailing into the mouth of the river Edro, gliding past the nearly sheer outcropping of native rock that bore the palace on its shoulders. The palace slid away to stern as the oars bit the water, and the two craft plied their way upstream to come to rest in their familiar berths at the high stone quay just before the river bend that encircled the walls if the Fleet Compound.

Nagaro called for the gangplank to be extended as soon as the ropes had been made fast to the quay's iron cleats. He bade Taru and Pavo make sure that the *Sword* was ship-shape and secure before dismissing the crew, and left the matter in their capable hands. He paused just long enough to arrange to have his sea chest delivered to his quarters. Then he disembarked with his leather diplomatic pouch over his shoulder, intending to seek Lord Kuran without delay and make his report immediately. The sooner he communicated the little he had learned, the better he would feel.

A small crowd had gathered on the quay. Some had undoubtedly gotten wind of the ships' coming. Others had merely been passing by and stopped to see who the new arrivals might be. Now these folk pressed around him, calling, "Captain Nagaro! Captain Nagaro!" Hands reached out to touch his shoulder or his sleeve.

"Please, good people! Let me pass!" Nagaro raised his hand to acknowledge the crowd, smiling as best he could despite his sense of urgency as he gestured for them to stand aside. "I must make my report to the Lord of the Fleet."

A path opened before him, and he strode along it, still waving in response to the people's enthusiasm. As he approached the gate of the Fleet Compound, a stocky Turowan man stepped out of the crowd and fell in beside him. Nagaro frowned fleetingly until he recognized Kinu, the Fleet stableman.

"Beggin' your pardon, Capt'n," the man said apologetically. "I'd not trouble ye in goin' about your important business, but I happened t' be passing, and I heard 'em shouting your name. An' there's something I ought to tell ye, seein' as how I think ye'd want to hear it."

"What is it, Kinu?"

"Well, Capt'n, I'm not sure what t' make of it. But it seems that Sindar has disappeared."

"Disappeared?" Nagaro's feet slowed. He glanced up and he found that they were already at the gate and that some of the crowd had followed him, hoping to catch his attention or perhaps merely to get a better look. With a hasty salute to the guard, and a final wave to his admirers, he hurriedly gestured the stableman through the gate so that they might continue the conversation on the other side.

"What do you mean, disappeared?" he asked once they were safely inside the walls of the compound.

"I mean that he seems t' be gone from his little loft room at the *Golden Tankard*, Zirda. No one's seen him for nearly a week."

Nagaro frowned. "Could he have realized that he was being watched? He wanted to be completely independent, after all. Maybe he's moved to other lodgings."

Kinu shrugged. "I don't know about that, Zirda. All I know is, he left his tasks undone, and he didn't give no notice. He left some of his things, too. The Landlord was good enough t' let me take 'em to keep for him. They look like the same things he had when he used t' sleep in the stable, here, sometimes."

Nagaro's frown deepened. "So they were old things he'd brought from Pakoa," he murmured, trying to think. "Why would he leave things like that?"

Kinu shrugged again. "Maybe he earned enough, muckin' out stalls, t' buy himself some better ones."

"Maybe." Nagaro chewed his lip. When leaving his grandfather's house, Sindar might have left things that his new-found family had given him in favor of things he'd owned for some time, though even the older things had been given to him as well. Once he could buy new things with money he'd earned, he might very well have discarded these older ones without a thought.

As for leaving without giving notice, well, Sindar had spent his youth in an isolated Hashtep village where he'd been beaten, hobbled with a rope, and made to do whatever menial labor the villagers had chosen. As a free man, he'd taken a little time to understand that he could do whatever *he* chose. Having once mastered the general concept, however, he tended sometimes to take it too literally. Perhaps he'd come to realize that he had been "found" at the *Golden Tankard* and had simply dropped his job and sought other lodgings, knowing that the midsummer muster was only a few days away.

Nagaro sighed. "I expect we'll see him tomorrow at the muster."

"Aye." Kinu nodded emphatically. "He'll not want t' miss that." He looked suddenly thoughtful. "Would ye be wantin' to keep the bag o' things for him, yourself, Zirda? He was staying with ye before, an' I expect he'll come around lookin' for ye after he joins up."

"That's a good idea, Kinu. Just bring it around to my quarters when you have a chance. And thank you for bringing me the news."

Nagaro bade the stableman good day, and then set off with his diplomatic pouch to seek the Lord of the Fleet. Kuran, who was in his study, looked somber upon hearing the news that the illicit trade had shifted to going overland.

"It's not surprising," he grumbled. "If you make things too hot in the kitchen, the rats can be trusted to move to the scullery. I'll have to see what the Council wants to do about it, since it no longer involves boats."

"Have you learned anything while I've been gone, My Lord?" Nagaro asked hopefully.

But Kuran shook his head. "I was instructed to wait and see what you discovered," he said sourly. "Lords have a distinct reluctance to investigate other lords, in my experience, and I'm afraid the principle applies in this case."

Concerning the matter of Sindar's disappearance, Kuran was inclined to agree with Nagaro that the former slave would probably turn up at the midsummer muster.

Chapter 14

Midsummer's Eve

It was the end of the last day of Dunrel, the eve of midsummer's day, and the walls of the Great Hall were decked with leafy boughs that ringed the room in a myriad shades of summer green. All the fresh-cut greenery lent the atmosphere a fragrance resembling that of new-mown hay. The tall windows in the north wall were aglow with the light of the year's longest afternoon. The tables were set with gleaming white china, gilt-edged green cloth napkins, and lavish centerpieces composed of sunflowers— dark-eyed rosettes of golden petals— nested in frothy clouds of queen's lace as white as the china. All around, the pillars and furnishings were hung with satin ribbons that echoed the same colors: purest white, summer green, and sunflower gold.

The visual impact of the decorations was all but lost on Nagaro, however, as he finished bowing to Lady Merriel and began to make his way up the long axis of the room to his appointed seat at the match table. He hadn't come particularly early on this occasion, and the room was already becoming crowded. He frowned as he threaded his way among the tables, seeking his destination while absent-mindedly dodging other guests.

He was worried about Sindar. The former slave hadn't appeared at the muster of new recruits that had taken up most of the day at the Fleet Compound. Nagaro had only been spared from other duties to attend a portion of it, but Lord Kuran had informed him of Sindar's absence shortly before he and Nagaro had set out for the midsummer festivities at the palace.

Sindar's failure to attend the midsummer's day muster was not a catastrophe. He could still be included in the year's crop of new recruits if he appeared at any time in the next two months. The natural range of skills and knowledge among the newly recruited sea-warriors-in-training meant that they could never be treated as a uniform cohort, and Sindar's experience with sailing on the *Sword*, as well as the training he already had in swordsmanship, should make it easy for him to catch up. All the same, his absence from the muster was disquieting considering how eager he'd always been to join the Fleet.

As Nagaro passed between the tables, he was telling himself that Sindar's failure to appear needn't necessarily be connected with his disappearance from his room at the *Golden Tankard*. The young man could have changed his lodgings, for whatever reason, and then suffered some temporary illness that had kept him from the muster. So Nagaro's thoughts were running— until his gaze chanced to light on Nevien standing near the match table, at which point all thought of Sindar fluttered way like a leaf in the breeze.

She was wearing a gown of sunflower gold embroidered in green. Her golden-brown hair flowed freely over her shoulders except for the foremost tresses on either side, which were swept up and caught by a pair of ivory combs. An emerald necklace flashed at her throat. She was standing among a group of ladies, listening to something and frowning in concentration, until she turned her head in his direction as if in answer to his unspoken prayer. When their gazes met across the intervening space, her face lit up with a beaming smile.

For an instant Nagaro came to a complete halt, transfixed. Then he pressed urgently forward, threading the throng, only to find his path suddenly blocked by the tall, broad, golden-haired figure of Lothard Hurn, resplendent in black britches and a rust-colored satin tirka. The encounter was so unexpected that both men had to pull themselves up short to avoid a collision.

Mutual recognition required but an instant. Then the Leithian lord's face contorted into a thunderous scowl. "*You!*" he exclaimed, and then added, "Stay out of my way, you insolent pirate!"

Nagaro wanted nothing more than to get past the other man so that he could reach Nevien. "Believe me, My Lord," he said, "Nothing would give me greater pleasure."

He attempted to step around Lothard to the right, but the big man immediately shifted sideways to block his path. "I'm not finished!" the Leithian snarled. "You interfering oaf! You upstart! *You bastard son-of-a-fisherman!*"

Behind him, Nagaro heard a number of gasps. Someone on his right murmured, "*Oh my!*" Under other circumstances, Nagaro might have paused long enough to devise some pointed rejoinder, but Nevien was waiting by the match table and he was in a hurry. "Farmer," he said, by way of amendment.

"*What?*" Lothard's frown was displaced by an expression of utter bafflement.

"More probably a farmer than a fisherman," Nagaro observed by way of explanation. "He might have been a traveling minstrel, but really it's quite immaterial."

"In-*material?*" Surprise was now struggling with confusion, while wrath threatened to make a comeback.

"It doesn't matter." Nagaro translated. "I really don't care. And now, if you will excuse me—" He attempted to move around Lothard to the left.

The Leithian, however, side-stepped immediately to block his path again, the scowl returning to his face. "*Ha!*" he barked. "You see how it feels to have someone always in your way? And how dare you suggest that what I say doesn't matter!"

It was Nagaro's turn to be astonished. The childishness of Lothard's behavior was scarcely to be believed! He recovered very quickly however. "In fact, I did not say that, My Lord," he said with as neutral an expression as he could manage. Then, recalling the direction of the Leithian's movement at the time of their near collision, he added, "I believe you were on your way to the head of the Hall. Please proceed." And with that he bowed low, making a sweeping gesture with his arm as he did so.

Lothard must have been so accustomed to being ushered about with such elaborate obeisance that he responded automatically by taking a step in the indicated direction. This was all that Nagaro needed. He promptly straightened and slipped behind the other man's back to continue on his path to the match table.

Unfortunately, Nevien was no longer there. A quick sweep of the room with his eyes revealed that the princess was at that moment taking her place at the High Table on the raised dais at the head of the hall. He felt a surge of disappointment, then heaved a resigned sigh. It wasn't as if they would have had any chance to speak privately, and it was clear that dinner would soon be served in any case.

He slowed his steps, since there was now no need to hurry, and became aware of Lady Merriel at his elbow. "Captain Nagaro," she said a little breathlessly. "I heard what Lothard called you, and I must say it was *extremely* rude. Really, it's a marvel that you kept your temper!"

Nagaro offered her his arm, seeing that she was unescorted, and she took it. "It wasn't very difficult, really," he said. "I really *don't* care who or what my father was. It was harder to keep from laughing when it appeared that he didn't know the meaning of the word 'immaterial'."

They had reached the match table, and Nagaro assisted Merriel in taking her seat at the head of it, then went to his own seat, which was on her right hand and identifiable because Rianine was seated directly across from it. The other guests were already seated and Nagaro felt their eyes on him.

Rianine leaned forward to address him. "We were all watching, Captain," she said with obvious relish. "For a moment it looked as if Lothard was actually going to come after you. But I guess he had wit enough to see how ridiculous that would have looked."

Hendrel, seated on Nagaro's right, laughed approvingly. "I gather he made you some insult. What did the oaf say?"

With a shrug, Nagaro told him.

"And you didn't strike him?" This came from Vanhold, one of the two Leithian men at the match table.

"Of course he didn't!" retorted Rees, the other Leithian. "Lothard would have called it a challenge and used the opportunity to try to kill him!"

"Little good it would have done him," put in Geivian from the far end of the table. "The Captain would have beaten him handily. You should have seen how Nagaro dealt with him at Loros Hall!"

"That's right," Hendrel affirmed. "It was a sight to see!"

Nagaro was listening with a gathering frown and he now reached for his fork and struck his glass so that it rang a single sharp note that instantly turned all eyes to him. "If I might speak for myself, Zirdas," he said. "I don't think it is at all certain that I could best Lothard in a fair fight. He's highly skilled, very fast, and he outreaches me besides."

"But you turned his every stroke!" Geivian blurted.

Nagaro turned to the young Kelorin. "Those strokes weren't intended for me, except perhaps the last one, and Lord Anduar intervened at that point."

"*Yes... finally!*" muttered Hendrel.

Nagaro ignored this. "Lothard was in a blind fury— which is never good for a man's swordsmanship— and it was all directed at Kenthos. If I were to face him when he was cool-headed, in a fair bout, I expect I would be pressed to my utmost, and I am in no way sure how it would end."

"But—" Geivian began.

At that moment, however, a bell sounded three times, ringing out over the babble of a hundred conversations. Voices died as the king rose from his seat on the dais at the head of the hall. All eyes were turned to him as he began a speech of welcome.

Nagaro's eyes were drawn, like everyone else's, to the High Table. Unlike most of the other guests, however, his gaze didn't linger on the king, but slid sideways to where the princess was seated. He couldn't afterwards have repeated a single word of what Elgurn said. Nevien was at first watching her father with obvious pride, her expression rapt and admiring. Nagaro watched her with admiration of his own. As her father's oration wore on, however, Nevien's attention eventually strayed. Her head turned, her gaze wandered across the tables, to come to rest upon *him.*

Oh Vothra! Nagaro guiltily yanked his eyes away, bringing them back to the table in front of him where the first thing that caught his attention was his glass of sothiril. Desperate for something to appear to be doing, he reached for it, took a sip, and swallowed. As he put the glass down again he glanced furtively around the table to make sure the others seated there were still intent on Elgurn's words, only to find that Rianine was watching him, her gray eyes narrowed with interest.

Caught! Writhing inside like an insect on a pin, Nagaro did his best to smile innocently at her. The way her eyes narrowed even further told him how little she'd been taken in.

Fortunately, the king's speech ended at this point and everyone rose to applaud. The servants bearing the first course of the dinner were already positioned and waiting, and almost before the guests had returned to their seats, the first of the steaming dishes were being laid upon the tables. The babble of voices rose again in the hall, and the topic of conversation at the match table turned immediately to the subject of food— much to Nagaro's relief.

He gave his attention to his dinner, outwardly at least. Almost the only thing he could remember about it later was that there had been roast lamb. Inwardly, he was engaged in a review of everything he knew about Nevien's four suitors— all of whom were likely to be present. The table conversation went on around him unheeded, until he abruptly became aware that he'd heard Lothard's name mentioned once again and he emerged from the dark cavern of his thoughts.

"I think it's quite horrid!" Alisset's round, pink face fairly radiated disapproval.

"I hear he's in trouble with his own people over it," Merriel put in.

"Well if he isn't, My Lady, he should be," interjected Geivian. "First he taxed them to raise the recompense he had to pay to Rathgar, and now that he's gotten most of the money back from what from Rathgar received from the Kelorin Faction, he's keeping the lion's share of it! And the families of the men who were slain— *his own men*, mind you— are getting only three hundred rins apiece! It amounts to even less when you figure in the tax they paid."

Nagaro knew all about what was being discussed. He'd heard the gist of it the day before. "Does anyone know what Lothard's rationale is for keeping most of the money?" he asked. "It's in direct defiance of the king's order, after all."

Vanhold, two seats down, leaned forward, the better to address him. "He says he needs the money to pay for defending Hurn Hold."

Nagaro raised an eyebrow. "Defending it from whom?"

"Bands of marauding Kelorin, I suppose." Vanhold waved his hand. "I didn't say it made sense."

"I heard he's claimed that the lives of commoners aren't worth more than three hundred rins anyway, " added Rees.

Clarimel sniffed. "Well, you have to admit that five thousand rins *is* rather a lot."

"For the worth of the dead man's labor over the entire remainder of his life?" Geivian was indignant. "What are his wife and children supposed to live on? It's an outrage! Especially since it could be claimed that these men actually died fighting in the Hold's defense."

Rees paused with a forkful of food halfway to his mouth. "Lothard *does* claim they were fighting to defend Hurn Hold."

"*What?*" The word was uttered by a chorus of voices all along the table.

"Then how can he justify paying the families so little?" Geivian demanded.

"He says they were fighting voluntarily."

"What difference does *that* make?"

"It's a well-established Leithian custom. The families of men killed fighting in defense of their own lands are paid only burial costs. They're compensated three times as much if the men were formally conscripted."

"But that isn't fair! We Kelorin say a life is a life— and if it's lost in a just cause—"

From that point on, the men's discussion degenerated rapidly into an argument over the relative merits of Leithian versus Kelorin practices. The women seated across from them, in the meantime, struck up a conversation of their own revolving around the arrival of the musicians and the question of how soon the dancing might begin.

Nagaro had tried to follow what the men were saying, because he thought he should, but he was listening with only half an ear and a quarter of his mind. The rest of his mind was wandering, and his eyes with it. Both eventually found their way to the High Table— only to find that the princess was no longer there. Nor was her father. Nagaro frowned and began to search for the golden yellow gown, but he suddenly became aware of Rianine's face in front of him as she leaned far across the table.

"*She isn't there because Elgurn told her she should mingle,*" the young Kelorin woman informed him in a carefully modulated whisper.

"Mingle?" He stared at Rianine, quite forgetting to pretend that her guess was off the mark.

"Nevien is supposed to *mingle* with the guests." Rianine airily waved a hand.

"Yes," put in Merriel. "Both she and Elgurn intend to go from table to table to make a little light conversation to bid the guests welcome more personally. It's a new idea."

"Personally, I don't think much of it," Rianine observed loftily, "Since it means the two of them have scarcely had time to finish their dinner, and I think they're going to miss dessert. The servers are only just now bringing it to us. And it's not a dessert to be missed, either. It's *jokolata* pudding. Do we have you to thank for it, Captain?"

"Me?" Nagaro was resisting the urge to look past Rianine and search for Nevien's figure among the tables. "I hardly think so. I've never heard of it before."

"No? But it's a Jinari delicacy, and you've just returned from a mission concerning trade with Jinara."

This gave him pause. He wondered how one of the princess's ladies came by such detailed information. "It wasn't that kind of trade," he said weakly.

"Oh, I see." Rianine's tone seemed to dismiss the matter, and she took a spoonful of the pudding that had just appeared in front of her. Then abruptly she leaned across the table again. "Are you going to dance with me tonight?"

Nagaro had just picked up his spoon to try the pudding. He came to a halt, managing with an effort not to gape at her. "Yes... of course."

"That's good. Do try to remember that I asked you first."

"First?"

"*Before* anyone else." Rianine showed her teeth in a brittle smile while a subtle movement of her head and redirection of her gaze suggested that he ought to look to his left. At the same time, he heard a rustle of silk from that direction. When he turned, he discovered that Nevien was standing there at the corner of the table, between his chair and Lady Merriel's.

She wasn't looking at him, although the tail end of a movement of her head suggested that she had been. She was resplendent in her sunflower gold and smiling a very well-studied smile that belied the tired lines around her eyes. All conversation at the table now stopped and every eye was on her.

"Dear people," she said in a voice to match the smile. "I wish to welcome you to this celebration of Midsummer. I hope you've enjoyed the feast and that you're looking forward as much as I am to the entertainment provided by our musicians. For those of you who wish, there will be dancing in just a few minutes."

Clarimel smiled indulgently. "Oh *really*, Nevien," she said. "You *know* we're all enjoying ourselves."

"Oh, yes!" Delasin gushed. "We're having a *lovely* time."

"And I can't *wait* for the dancing to begin," Kendira put in.

Nagaro rose from his chair. He stepped aside and gestured to it. "Will you sit, My Lady, and rest for a little while?"

But she shook her head. "I can't stay," she said with studied politeness. "There are still a few more tables." Then her shoulders sagged, and she dropped her voice so that it carried only to Merriel, Nagaro, and Rianine. "I'm *so* tired of that speech. I hope it didn't sound as if I were."

"Oh no, of course not," Nagaro said hastily.

Merriel gave the princess an encouraging smile. "It was perfect, dear, but you shouldn't over-tire yourself. You should finish as quickly as you can and sit down for a while."

"But not before you agree to grant me the honor of the first dance, My Lady," said a gravely voice from behind Nagaro's back. "If Lothard hasn't already commandeered it, that is."

They all turned, to find that Lord Devral had approached while they were conversing. The scarred old Kelorin warrior bowed stiffly to Nevien.

Nevien acknowledged the bow with a gracious inclination of her head. "As it happens, My Lord Devral, I seem to have missed Lothard. He'd apparently stepped out for a moment when I got to his table." She smiled in a way that suggested this was not a tragedy. "The first dance is therefore yours."

"Excellent." Devral covered a cough with a thorny fist. "It will, of course, be Captain Nagaro here who'll do the dancing. You will be my proxy as usual, won't you, Captain?"

Nagaro caught Nevien's look of hopeful expectancy. He was also aware of Rianine's eyes boring into him. "I, ah..." he began. "Are you sure that's wise, My Lord? I seem to have thwarted Lothard's purpose twice of late. I thought the Council might consider it too... well... *provocative,* if I continue to take your courtship dances. Or hasn't it been discussed?" He was carefully keeping his eyes on Devral's face, not looking at any of the three watching women.

Devral smiled a smile like a hungry wolf. "Oh, it's been discussed all right," he said meaningfully. "We concluded that to change my proxy now would be an unacceptable retreat. You don't represent the Kelorin Faction, after all. You're a Fleet man, meaning you belong to the Crown. And you *are* just a proxy. If Lothard accuses you of thwarting him again, you just refer him to me. *I'm* the one who'll be in his way this time."

Nagaro still hesitated. It wasn't just that he wasn't looking forward to another confrontation with Lothard. He could also feel the heat of Rianine's gaze. *Or was it that Nevien was so close...* "But I've already promised to dance with the Lady Rianine," he said.

"And so you shall." Devral gestured expansively. "She shall have the second dance, and I dare say some others as well. There'll be plenty of dances tonight to go around. What do you say to that, My Lady?" he added, addressing Rianine.

Rianine gave the old lord a smile as sweet as syrup and as brittle as glass. "I must of course defer to My Lady Princess," she said, with a prim inclination of her head.

"There. You see, Captain? What do you say now?"

"Well..." He made the mistake of looking at Nevien and found her suddenly demure, her eyes cast down. He heard himself say, "In that case, I shall be delighted to escort My Lady Princess in the first dance."

"Good man!" Devral clapped him on the back, then bowed to the ladies and turned to limp off across the hall in the direction of the table reserved for the members of the King's Council.

Nagaro's eyes hadn't left Nevien's face. She seemed strangely abashed as her lashes lifted and her eyes came up to meet his. There was a healthy and becoming blush of color in her cheeks, which had lately been so pale.

"Thank you, dear Captain," she said and held out her hand to him.

He took one step closer, took the hand, bent over it and kissed it formally. But as he raised his eyes again, her fingers slipped through his and she was gone, hurrying away towards the next table. He stood looking after her for several heart beats before he recollected himself and took his seat once more.

Merriel leaned towards him, smiling reassuringly. "Don't worry, Captain. I'm sure Devral will see to it that Lothard doesn't trouble you."

"And I can make do quite as easily with the second dance as with the first," Rianine added pointedly.

"Oh. Good." Inwardly Nagaro squirmed. Rianine was pinning him with a concentrated stare that gave him the distinct impression he was being dissected. *Had he transgressed?* If so, he wasn't sure how. He dragged his eyes away from Rianine's face and attempted to look as if he were giving his full attention to his jokolata pudding. In fact he was so distracted that he'd gotten down to the last spoonful before he really noticed the flavor, at which point he belatedly wished he'd begun paying attention to it a good deal sooner.

By this time, however, it seemed that everyone else had already finished their dessert, and many of the guests had begun to get up and move about so that they could greet and converse with acquaintances seated at other tables. The musicians had also taken their seats and were beginning to tune their instruments. He noticed with relief that Rianine was no longer sitting across from him. A number of the others who had been seated at the match table were gone as well, including Lady Merriel. His eyes sought the High Table, but the moving figures of other guests were in the way. Frowning, he pushed back his chair and stood up.

"I'm right here, *Captain Dear*. Not that I think it's me you're looking for."

He spun to find Rianine standing beside him in the same spot where Nevien had made her earlier appearance. "I... was looking for Nevien," he said a little stiffly. "I have to find her before the music starts. After all, I did agree to have the first dance with her."

"Oh, *yes*." Rianine rolled her eyes. "'*I shall be delighted to escort My Lady Princess in the first dance,*'" she mimicked, her voice dripping syrup.

"What was I supposed to say?" he demanded, stung. "'I suppose I can do it if I must?' She was standing right there! And I *did* remember that you'd spoken to me first. And besides, you said you would defer to her!"

Rianine, however, shook her head at him and stepped a little closer. "It wasn't *what* you said, it was the *way* you said it," she informed him, lowering her voice a notch. "It was the tone of your voice, the gleam in your eye..."

He stared at her. "*The gleam in my eye?* What are you talking about?"

He tried to draw away from her, but she moved closer still, placing a slim hand on his arm in a proprietary way, with a grip that allowed no ambiguity. At the same time, she brought her lips close to his ear, and— lowering her voice still further— murmured, "*You've fallen for her, heels over head. And you're not a good liar, so don't try to deny it!*"

For a moment Nagaro felt as if his stomach had dropped right out of him. He sought for some plausible words of denial, but he knew she was right. He sagged in defeat. "All right then," he said, "I won't."

She cocked her head at him. "Smart man," she said. "Yes, smarter than most. I'll give you that."

"Is it so obvious then?" he muttered, his eyes on the floor.

"Only to those who know how to *see*. Fortunately for you, most people don't."

He risked looking at her and found that she was regarding him much less unkindly than he'd expected. "*Please* don't tell anyone," he said desperately. "Whatever you do, don't tell *her!*"

"Don't tell her?" Rianine slyly arched an eyebrow. "Are you sure? I could easily arrange to smuggle you secretly to her bedchamber— in and out before dawn. I'd make the perfect go-between."

"*No!*" He shook his head violently, then lowered his voice as several heads turned in their direction. "She's a princess, not a tavern woman! Even if she were willing, she deserves better than that— sneaking about and keeping secret trysts with a man who can never court her properly. No good could possibly come of it!"

Rianine rolled her eyes. "Suit yourself," she said. "And I might have known. You really are two of a kind."

"What do you mean?"

Rianine dismissed the words with a flick of her hand. "Consider the subject closed," she said. "Your secret is safe with me. And now you *had* better find Nevien. Those musicians will be starting any minute."

"Yes, of course." Eagerly he started forward and began to rake the room with his eyes, only to feel her restraining hand on his arm.

"Not so fast, Captain," she chided. "You're supposed to be more interested in *me* than in *her*, remember? I'm coming with you. You just concentrate on talking to me, and I'll find Nevien. And don't worry; I *will* find her. She's my friend after all, and I know she'd rather dance with you than with any of her suitors."

Nagaro frowned, trying not to look around as he let Rianine steer him by a gentle pressure on his arm.

"Am I really behaving so badly?" he asked, keeping his voice low.

"Let's just say that if I *were* interested in you, the way you're behaving would be making me extremely jealous."

"Oh. I'm sorry...

"Don't be. I'm *not* interested, remember?"

"Ah... what should I talk about?"

"It doesn't matter as long as you say it to *me*." Rianine paused. "There she is," she murmured under her breath. "At the last table by the door to the kitchens— talking to Dreigen."

"*Dreigen!*" He jerked to a halt with an involuntary shudder that made Rianine turn to him in astonishment. "What is *he* doing here? She shouldn't talk to him!" The panicked words spilled out. He was deliberately not looking for Nevien now... *in case the terrible, fierce-eyed Lore Master was looking this way.*

As he had told Simion, he'd come face to face with Dreigen once, shortly after he first returned to Lankura— several years ago— and the Lore Master hadn't recognized him then. There was no reason to imagine that the man would now, either, but it scarcely mattered. The mere thought of Dreigen conjured memories of the worst period of Nagaro's life, worse by far than the eighteen months he'd spent as a galley slave.

Rianine was shaking her head at him in bafflement. "Dreigen isn't one of your rivals," she said. "Nor is he likely to be. He's no more high-born than you are, and you couldn't warm *that* man's blood if you lit a fire under him."

"I... I know..." Nagaro was at a loss to explain himself. "But he's... well... I think he may be dangerous," he finished lamely. "Why would Nevien be talking to *him?*"

Rianine shrugged. "I suppose she's just being kind. *Mingling.* Personally I agree with you about him, but Nevien is such a sop. She insists on trying to see good in everyone. Come on, now. Let's rescue her from her folly."

Nagaro allowed himself to be drawn forward again, and risked a furtive glance in the direction they were going. He saw Nevien immediately. She was about twenty feet away with her back turned to him, and there was a table in the way that he and Rianine would have to go around. His heart leaped at the sight of her, but in the next moment his feet faltered when she moved to one side and Dreigen came into view. The dark-haired, sallow-skinned, hawk-nosed man was seated at the table just beyond where Nevien was standing, facing Nagaro. His deep-set eyes were fixed on Nevien with a cold avidity that laid a chill across Nagaro's soul.

"What's the matter with you?" Rianine was impatient. "This way." She was trying to steer him around the intervening table.

Nagaro yanked his eyes away, and somehow managed to get his feet moving once more. "Why is Dreigen here tonight?" he muttered. "I haven't seen him at one of these feasts in years. I didn't think he liked them."

"He has to come now if he want's to eat. None of the servants are willing to go near his chambers since the old serving man who took him his food died of a fit."

"*Died of a fit?*" Nagaro's mind seized on the words and recoiled in horror. *But surely folk sometimes suffered fits without any unnatural intervention*, he told himself. *Surely old men sometimes just died...*

"I know. It sounds rather awful, doesn't it?" They were just rounding the end of the table, having had to weave their way between moving guests, and Rianine must have been keeping one eye on Nevien because now she murmured, "Ah, she's turning around. There! She's seen us. She's coming this way." And Nagaro breathed a sigh of relief, knowing that he wouldn't have to confront the dreaded Lore Master.

Then Nevien was in front of him, smiling, and looking in perfect health and completely unscathed.

"Well," said Rianine, "Here's your proxy, Nevien. Shall I hand him over to you?"

Nevien laughed. "Thank you, Rian. You're a dear. You make a handsome pair, by the way. Both of you in dark blue."

Nagaro hadn't even noticed what color Rianine was wearing. She might even have chosen it on purpose to match the color of his uniform, but it was far too late to comment on it now. Rianine had released his arm and was stepping away. Realizing that something was expected of him, he gave her a bow, then turned and gave Nevien another one, trying not to make it any deeper. "My Lady Princess," he said formally for the sake of any listening ears. "On behalf of My Lord Devral, I would like to claim the honor of the first dance."

She inclined her head, then raised her eyes, beaming. "I would be charmed," she said, and moved to take the place that Rianine had vacated at his side. Her slim fingers curled around the arm he offered her, and he felt his pulse quicken.

"Shall we go to the dance floor then?" he asked as he began to turn about in order to conduct her towards the other end of the hall. His attention was all on her face, turned up to his. Rianine was already forgotten.

"Eventually," she said. "But we needn't hurry. Before the first dance there's going to be a song."

"A song?"

"Yes. See? The woman there in dark green is going to sing it."

Nevien pointed and he followed the gesture— just as the musicians struck up the opening bars of a familiar melody— to where a pale, dark-haired young Kelorin woman was standing among the players.

A hush fell over the Great Hall. The high, pure notes of a flute soared into the sudden stillness, and now the singer opened her lips and began to sing in a clear, sweet voice. The words Nagaro knew well.

"My love he was a Leithian, golden as the sun,
And good and kind as any man that ever maiden won..."

"It was one of my mother's favorites," Nevien continued. "It's called *Karidei's Lament.* It's about the love of a Kelorin woman for a Leithian man..." Her voice trailed and she looked away, brushing at her cheek with her free hand.

"Yes, I know—" he began, before he caught himself.

"You *know* this song?" Her eyes came back to his, questioning, the moisture on her cheek forgotten.

Nagaro was thinking fast and decided that in this case the truth— or at least part of it— would probably do him no harm. "It was a favorite of my Lady Guardian's," he said. "Because it's about a hopeless love."

"Oh? Did she love a Leithian man?" Nevien's expression was very serious, her voice resonant with compassion.

He shook his head. "No. Her love was Kelorin, as was she. But their love was hopeless all the same. They weren't allowed to wed..." He faltered under her earnest gaze. "And he... he died. So she lived all the rest of her life alone. Except for raising me, of course."

"Oh. That's terribly sad." Her sea-green eyes brimmed with sympathy.

He felt a sudden catch in his throat, and this time it was he who looked away. *If only he could tell her about Maramine... how blamelessly his Lady Guardian had lived... how horribly she had died.*

The singer was wending her way through the lyric, but Nagaro wasn't listening. He was lost in his own thoughts, gazing across the hall— which was why he saw the two men in close conversation near the farther wall of the room, under one of the tall windows. Even so, he probably wouldn't have noticed them, rapt as he was, except that one of them was Lothard Hurn. The rust-colored tirka leapt at him, and his eyes narrowed. There was something about the way the two men had their heads together that made him instantly suspicious. But who was the other man?

Now the two separated. Lothard moved quickly to a place at one of the tables, but the second man didn't join him. Instead, he continued to move in a series of short advances that didn't carry him in a straight line, but always in the same general direction. In this way, the man— who was also Leithian— passed along the wall under the windows in the direction of the dais. This course inevitably brought him closer to where Nagaro was standing so that his face came more clearly into focus, until, with a start, Nagaro realized that he'd seen the man before. It had been more than a year ago and in a very different place— the courtyard of the large building on Broad Street that was Lord Madred's Lankura residence. The sleek-haired Leithian with the well-oiled mustache was unmistakable. On that occasion, Madred had addressed the man by name— *and the name had been Torlung!*

Nagaro realized that he was looking at the same man who had dismissed Master Fineas for refusing to procure him some heskial! He drew in his breath. Torlung was nothing less than Lord Madred's Chief Minister. Why had he been talking so intimately with Lothard? And where was he going now?

Torlung had changed direction, meanwhile. He was now moving across the head of the hall among the tables. Watching him, Nagaro realized that the man kept glancing at a particular spot even as he moved by fits and starts, apparently trying to be unobtrusive. Nagaro followed the direction of the glances, tracing them to their target, and found—

"—*Dreigen!*" he whispered under his breath.

At that moment, Nevien moved, where she stood beside him, pulling his attention back to her. The singer was drawing towards the song's conclusion, her voice now laced with pain, rising to the emotional climax.

"The day that I may seek for him will be the day I find,
That all the world has all gone deaf, and dumb, and also blind.
While eyes may see and tongues may speak, I cannot be my own.
Until some day that ne'er can be, we both must walk alone."

As the final note died away, the audience breathed and there was a flurry of applause. Nagaro hastily joined in. Nevien turned to address him.

"Well, what did you think of it?" she asked, and her eyes were misty.

"I—" he cast about, for he'd only half heard the performance. "It's a beautiful song, and she sang it very well."

She blinked and brushed at her cheek. "Do you think the message will be heard?" she asked urgently. "That Kelorin and Leithian shouldn't let their differences drive them apart?"

"Oh." Now he understood. "Yes, I think some of them at least will surely get the point."

He risked another glance in the direction of the table where Dreigen was sitting. Torlung was there now— *talking to Dreigen*. The Leithian was standing beside the seated Lore Master, bending in conversation. As Nagaro watched them, Dreigen produced a bundle of what looked like papers and passed then to the minister. Torlung slipped the bundle into his tirka, drawing out a flattish package that he, in turn, passed to Dreigen, and which Dreigen sequestered within the front of his robe.

"What was that all about?" Nevien asked.

Glancing at her, Nagaro realized that she had followed his gaze and seen what he'd just seen. She was still watching the two men, although they seemed to have finished their exchange and Torlung was moving away again.

"I don't know for certain," Nagaro said grimly. "But I'm afraid I may be able to guess."

"Why? What do you mean?"

The musicians had moved their chairs to the edge of the dance floor and now the flute played the opening bars of *The Ivy Vine*, signaling that those who wished to dance should begin to assemble. Nagaro crooked his arm for Nevien and started across the floor. He bent his lips to her ear. "I think we've just seen how Dreigen gets some of his supplies," he murmured. "And from whom he gets them. And just before that conversation with Dreigen, I saw Minister Torlung talking to Lothard."

"*Lothard?*" Nevien was so startled that she came up short, pulling Nagaro to a stop. "But Torlung works for Lord Madred!"

"I know." Nagaro motioned for her to lower her voice and tugged her forward again. "I wonder what Madred's involvement is— whether it's only the Brothers of the Blood who are in this, or whether it extends to the wider Leithian Faction as well. I wonder whether Madred is with the Brothers, even though he says he isn't."

"Wait!" Once more Nevien came to a halt. "You make it sound like there's a... a *conspiracy!* Just because you saw *one* exchange involving Dreigen and Torlung— and Lothard—"

"But there *is* a conspiracy!" Nagaro spoke fast and low. "There's been secret traffic with Jinara for years, in poisons and all manner of things that Dreigen uses, and it can all be traced to three Houses— *Furthing, Hurn, and Sobring!*"

Nevien's eyes went wide, even as Nagaro pulled her forward again. A hasty glance had shown him that the circles were nearly complete for *The*

Ivy Vine and they were in danger of being too late to join one. Nevien had noticed this too, and she now began to hurry. "Is *that* why you were sent on that mission to Jinara?" she whispered urgently.

Nagaro found them a place in the nearest circle, politely insinuating himself with murmured apologies, and drawing her after. "*Yes,*" he said between clenched teeth.

"But do you have any *other* evidence that Dreigen is involved?"

Any other evidence? He stared at her, but he couldn't speak, couldn't explain. "I... think we had better dance," he said, as the musicians launched themselves enthusiastically into the melody.

The Ivy Vine was a circle dance, breaking at intervals in its pattern to allow the members of each couple to do a turn about each other, first clockwise with right hands pressed palm-to-palm, then counterclockwise with left hands pressed palm-to-palm. The dance afforded limited opportunity for conversation. Nagaro's mind was in a whirl, even while his body moved flawlessly through the figures. *Had he really just seen evidence of the connection he had always feared existed between Dreigen and the mysterious Leithian traders?* He found it hard to believe that what he'd witnessed could mean anything else... *and yet...* Whenever they did their turns he saw that Nevien was frowning in puzzled disapproval. She wouldn't believe him without more evidence, and he couldn't give her any more. *And if he couldn't persuade her, would anyone else believe him?* Perhaps if he could find Lord Kuran...

The dance ran its inevitable course. The couples completed their last turns and recreated the circle for the final time, joining hands all around and setting their feet to the pattern that spun the circle counterclockwise as the music played itself out. Looking around the circle in the direction of its turning, Nagaro's eyes ran over the crowd of guests who had gathered to watch the dance, as he tried to gage how far the music would carry them. What he saw, there at the end of their path, was Lothard, with a scowl on his face, and Grimbold Sobring beside him.

A little beyond the two Leithians, he saw Ferenan Eyilas, the king's favorite among the princess's suitors. A glance at Nevien's expression told him that she had also seen Lothard and had performed the mental calculation of their trajectory. The frown she was wearing had shifted from mild disapproval to frank distaste.

Suddenly the idea of having to hand Nevien over to Lothard became unbearable. *So... just a small adjustment...* With the faintest of satisfied smiles, Nagaro subtly lengthened his strides, pulling the circle with him. And as it broke up with the closing notes of the melody, he took Nevien by the hand and deftly turned her under his arm in a final flourish that carried them past Lothard and brought them to a halt in front of Ferenan instead.

The man gaped at them, then glanced nervously in the direction of the thunderously scowling Lothard. Clearly he'd expected to have to yield the next dance to Lothard, and the prospect didn't distress him nearly as much as the risk of angering the Leithian lord. Ferenan's interest in Nevien was, after all, entirely manufactured.

Compared to Lothard, a blond giant, Ferenan was unimpressive. He was of middle height and middle years, and his mixed Kelorin and Leithian blood had produced facial features that averaged the characteristics of those two races in a way that was entirely unspectacular. His medium-brown hair was very lightly sprinkled with gray, his eyes were a watery blue— and worried. His expression was irresolute.

Nagaro didn't wait for Ferenan to say anything. "Ah, My Lord," he said. "I assume you were waiting to ask this lady for the next dance?"

Ferenan licked his lips nervously. "Well... ah... yes..." He flicked another glance at Lothard, who was trying to shoulder his way in Nevien's direction through the milling crowd.

Nevien wisely didn't wait for anything more decisive. "Why *thank you*, My Lord Ferenan," she said with a smile that gave every appearance of sincerity. "I would be delighted." And she relinquished Nagaro's arm to take Ferenan's, which the man tentatively extended to her.

Nagaro bowed to both of them with a flourish. "Very good, My Lord. My Lady, thank you," he said, and contrived to back away in such a manner as to place himself squarely in Lothard's path, while at the same time mouthing at Ferenan to *Go!*

Ferenan evidently saw the merit in this advice. In any case, he took it, making off hurriedly across the dance floor with the princess on his arm.

"Out of my way, farmer's bastard!"

Lothard shoved Nagaro roughly aside, only to find that he was too late. He immediately rounded on Nagaro. "*Idiot!* The next dance should have been *mine!* Didn't you see me standing there?"

Nagaro felt a surge of indignation, but he mastered it. Managing to return the big Leithian a level glance, he said innocently, "If I see you, My Lord, you may be sure that I will do something appropriate." Beyond Lothard, he noticed Grimbold loitering with an avid look in his eye and a frown on his florid face.

Lothard's eyes narrowed. "Ha!" he said with obvious satisfaction. "You're beginning to learn your place, pirate. Except that it isn't the place of a bastard half-breed like you to be dancing with a lady of quality in the first place! If you do it again, there will be *consequences*—"

"Captain Nagaro dances with the princess on my behalf."

Neither Nagaro nor Lothard had been aware of Devral's approach, and Nagaro recalled having seen the old warrior earlier about a quarter turn farther around the circle. Considering his game leg, the Pact Signer had managed to cover the distance with remarkable speed. The man now eyed Lothard coolly.

Lothard's lip twisted into a sneer. "I'm surprised you stoop so low, Devral," he said. "Letting this commoner stand in for you. His kind shouldn't be allowed to dance with the princess as if he were a suitor. It's a disgrace to her and a dishonor to all the noble men who are courting her!"

"I cannot agree." Devral smiled, an expression that inevitably acquired a sinister twist owing to the scar that marred his countenance. "Captain Nagaro has proven his honor, his worth, and his courtesy on numerous occasions. Besides which, he dances better than any man in this room. When I find one who is his equal, I will consider changing my proxy." He turned to Nagaro. "The task was very well executed, Captain. I commend you. But you need not trouble yourself with this." A flick of his hand indicated his exchange with Lothard. "I will deal with it."

"The way Anduar *dealt* with things at Loros Hall?" Lothard sneered at Devral, then turned on Nagaro, who still held his ground. "Anduar stepped in to rescue his little pirate, didn't he? You fancy yourself a great swordsman, farmer's bastard? I could gut you like a rabbit!"

In spite of himself Nagaro felt his anger rise. Behind him the music was playing and the next dance had begun. In front of him, Devral was shaking his head in warning, but Nagaro couldn't just walk away. Nor did he wish to let Devral do all the talking for him. "Here in this room?" he asked tightly. "Where you carry a sword, while I go unarmed? That would be a fitting show of honor for a lord of a noble house, would it?"

Lothard's hand moved to his sword hilt as his lips curled in a smile. "Do you challenge me, half-breed?" he purred.

This time Nagaro didn't need Devral's head-shake to tell him he was on dangerous ground. Lothard had all the subtlety of a serpent reared to strike. "No," he said, biting back a retort.

"Are you a coward, then?" the Leithian jeered. "Because you know you'd lose? Or is it as I've always said— that a commoner has no honor to defend!"

Nagaro's teeth flashed ferally, but still he restrained himself. "It's been explained to me," he said coldly, "that— win or lose— a common man risks far more in challenging a high-born than the other way around. I'm not such a fool as to do it. And," he added, "I see little honor in baiting a man whose position doesn't allow him to defend himself."

For the space of several seconds, Lothard stood still with a frown gathering like an approaching thunderstorm. Then he exploded. "*You filthy pirate bastard!* By the Gods, someone should teach you a lesson!"

Before Nagaro could make any response, Devral stepped decisively between them.

"What the Captain *meant*—" Devral began, but he was interrupted by Grimbold who had obviously been listening and who now shouldered his way into the conversation.

"We know what he meant!" Grimbold snapped, but then he seemed to catch himself. The lord of Sobring Hold tended always to appear angry because his face was perpetually red, and indeed he was widely known for his temper. On this occasion, however, he abruptly twisted his face into an unctuous smile. "But we have betterr things to do," he said, "than stand here bandying words on such *unimportant matters*."

Lothard had stopped in mid-scowl, momentarily derailed. "*Better* things?"

Grimbold gave the other Leithian a surreptitious jab in the ribs. "Yes! *Much* better things. Come away so we may speak of them."

The two men exchanged glances, Lothard's questioning, Grimbold's full of unspoken meaning. Lothard's eyebrows went up, but then came down again in another scowl. "Oh, very well," he conceded with ill grace. Pointedly turning his shoulder to Nagaro he gave Devral a perfunctory bow. "We must leave you, My Lord," he said, and added with fine contempt, "And if you're too infirm to do you own dancing, and won't find another stand-in, at least teach your dog some less offensive tricks!"

He turned on his heel, and both Leithians were quickly lost to view in the milling crowd, though not before they were seen to put their heads together for an exchange of words that didn't appear to be entirely amicable.

Devral stared after them. "Humph," he said scratching his grizzled chin. "*That's* something new— Grimbold stepping in to end an argument? It can't be that he means to teach Lothard better manners. I'm sorry to have put you through that, Captain," he added. "Lothard is an arrogant idiot, but he's also dangerous, and I'm glad to see you know the risks of challenging him." He shook his head. "Elgurn can decree that the lives of both noble and commoner be valued at five thousand rins, but he can't force Lothard or Grimbold to pay their own people that sum. Those two are making a mockery of the king's good intentions." He sighed."You'd best stay out of Lothard's way for the rest of the night, Captain. You've taken the first dance for me. That keeps me in the play."

Nagaro managed to nod, though in fact he'd been looking forward to another dance with Nevien later. There'd hardly been a chance to enjoy the first one. *And watching Lothard dance with her wasn't going to be pleasant.* "Very good, My Lord," he said, and bowed.

Excusing himself, he skirted the dance floor as the music was winding down. A surreptitious glance over his shoulder revealed that

Nevien's third partner would be Nile Fendred, not Lothard. Strangely, the big Leithian was nowhere to be seen at the crucial moment, and young Nile all but leaped in to intercept Ferenan and the princess. Nagaro smiled to himself humorlessly. The youth had no more enthusiasm for the courtship than Ferenan, but he knew his duty and had wit enough to make his move safely in Lothard's absence.

He was just turning away again, remembering that he wanted to find Kuran, when he saw Rianine bearing down on him, midnight blue skirts in full sail. He muttered an oath to himself as he realized that he was supposed to have given her the second dance.

"There you are, Captain!" she exclaimed, flashing him a brilliant smile. "Looking for me, no doubt?"

"No doubt," he murmured resignedly as he gave her his arm.

She put her lips close to his ear. "*Smile*, Captain," she murmured. "You're supposed to be glad to see me."

Somehow he managed to comply. "I've just had Lothard try to pick a fight with me," he said through his teeth. "I side-stepped it, but I had Devral taking my part as well. And I'm sure that tomorrow Lothard will be spreading the word about my 'cowardly retreat'."

"*You poor thing!*" Rinanine spoke with exaggerated sympathy, pulling him towards the nearest dance circle in a most unladylike fashion.

"And Devral has forbidden me to dance again with Nevien tonight." he added. "*That* should make you happy."

The dancers were forming up into pairs for the third dance. Nagaro hadn't been paying attention and had no idea what the dance was, but he didn't care.

"That's rather unkind." Rianine spoke into his ear. "And not at all true. It doesn't please me to see you suffer. In fact, I rather like you. Would you consider marriage?"

"*What?*" Nagaro twisted around to stare at his partner in astonishment.

The music was starting, and it was *Tavinskala*, which fortunately had a rather long lead-in.

"A marriage of convenience, of course," she said. "People do it all the time, you know."

"But... but... You're *crossed*. Aren't you?"

"If we must put a word on it, yes. I wouldn't expect you to be faithful, as long as you didn't expect me to be."

Nagaro gaped at her. "Are you *serious?*"

"Perfectly." She pulled him into the couple position and his feet remembered the steps, which was fortunate because mentally he was completely off balance.

"We'll talk later," she said, smiling archly. "Let's enjoy the dance."

It would have been enjoyable too, under other circumstances. Rianine danced well, as ususal, with a kind of dreamy, abstracted expression on her face, and she didn't spoil things with attempted conversation. Nagaro, however, had too many thoughts vying for his attention. First, there was what Dreigen was up to. Then there was the regrettable fact that Nevien must eventually dance with Lothard. And now there was this unorthodox and thoroughly unwelcome marriage proposal.

Distracted though he was, he still couldn't help noticing Kendira's new dance partner. Nevien and Nile were in a different circle, sparing him from having to watch them together, but the circle Rianine had chosen included Kendira, and her partner was one Nagaro hadn't seen before. He was a tall, lithe, Leithian youth with pale blond hair and a thin mustache. He was an excellent and rather flamboyant dancer, making him hard to miss. Nagaro couldn't help noticing that Kendira's expression as she danced with the young man was rapturous, her eyes aglow, a spot of pink rising in each cheek.

Rianine must have noticed as well, or perhaps she noticed that Nagaro had noticed. "That one means to steal your title of King of the Dance Floor," she said as they spun to a stop and Kendira's young man swung past them spinning Kendira with a final flourish.

"He can have it." Nagaro spoke with feeling. "I never wanted it in the first place. But who is the young man? I don't remember seeing him before."

"His name is Groft, I think. Something like that. He's a new member of the Palace Guard. Good family, I hear, from somewhere in the south. He's been making eyes at Kendira ever since he arrived. She was trying to ignore him because he's a Leithian and she's being courted by Geivian, but after tonight I'm afraid Geivian doesn't stand a chance."

"Oh. Yes, I think you may be right."

"And now we need to talk."

Nagaro felt an immediate stab of alarm. "I have to look for Kuran," he said hurriedly. "There's something I should tell him that could be very important."

Rianine shook a finger at him. "Not right now," she chided. "You can't, anyway. Kuran went out with Elgurn before the last dance. I suppose they had something private to discuss. And so do we. Besides, it's about time we were seen having an intimate conversation." She gave him a broad wink, and added, in a stilted voice as if reciting from a book of manners, "*Somewhere in the public eye, so as not to cause scandal.* At one of the tables where no one is sitting, I think."

"Must we do this right *now?*" Nagaro twisted about, looking back over his shoulder in the direction of the other end of the dance floor, searching for a gown of sunflower gold.

Rianine reached up, grasped his chin, and turned his head back towards her. "Yes, *now,*" she said sternly. Then, lowering her voice, she added, "She'll have to dance with Lothard sooner or later, Captain. Really you shouldn't be so jealous."

"I'm not jealous! I'd only be *jealous* if I thought she actually liked him! I just don't want her to have to dance with someone she detests."

Rianine gave him an exasperated look. "Nevien's used to it, and she can take care of herself. Now, come *on!* It looks as if the musicians are going to have a rest, anyway."

Indeed the musicians had put aside their instruments and were being served some refreshment. Reluctantly Nagaro gave in, since the alternative was to stand at the edge of the dance floor where they were much more likely to be overheard. He escorted Rianine back to their seats at the match table, hoping they would find too many others there to allow a private conversation. Instead, they found themselves quite alone, at least initially. Fresh pitchers of cold sothiril had been brought and he resignedly poured a glass for Rianine and another for himself.

Rianine took a perfunctory sip and leaned across the table. "Now," she said, fixing him with cool gray eyes. "What have you got against marrying me— besides the fact that we don't love each other? Neither of us can marry the one we do love, after all."

Nagaro frowned. Rianine had him in a weak position after the confession he'd been forced to make earlier. "Well," he said cautiously. "For one thing, I've already made the suggestion to another woman."

"The one Nevien fancies you're in love with? The Turowa? What was her name, Hamani?"

Nagaro was momentarily nonplused, but realized that Nevien must have confided these details to her friend. "Yes, that's right," he said. "If my friend Taru marries her sister—"

"*If,* you say! What if he doesn't? And even if he does, what has this Hamani got to offer you?"

"At least I like her—" Nagaro caught himself and winced as he saw Rianine's glance sharpen. "I... What I mean is, I just don't think that you and I are... very... compatible."

"I don't see what—" Rianine began. But then she stopped as her gaze shifted, looking past him. "Oh drat," she said. "Here come Nile and Nevien."

In the next instant, Nevien settled with a rustle of golden-yellow silk into the chair at the end of the table that had been Lady Merriel's. Nile bowed over her, murmuring something unintelligible, then quickly took his leave. Nevien reached for one of the fresh glasses standing inverted at intervals along the table, righted it, and poured herself some sothiril. "Well," she said brightly as she put down the pitcher. "And what were you two talking about?"

Rianine responded without so much as batting an eye. "We were just discussing the prospects for our marriage."

Nevien's hand jerked so that she nearly spilled her sothiril. She cast Nagaro a dismayed look that became less dismayed when she saw the look he was giving her, which said very plainly that this wasn't his idea. "Oh," she said, with a slightly brittle smile. "That's... nice. I didn't mean to interrupt."

"It's quite all right." Rianine waved an airy hand. "Devral has forbidden the Captain to dance with you again tonight, by the way."

Nevien cast Nagaro a questioning glance. "I'm afraid it's true," he said. "I think he wants to avoid rubbing Lothard too much the wrong way."

"Oh. Well... that's probably wise." Nevien's disappointment was obvious.

Rianine eyed her disapprovingly. "How is it that you're here without the company of a suitor?" she inquired.

Nevien grimaced. "I told Nile I had to go upstairs and change my shoes. They *are* new, and they *do* pinch, so it isn't a lie. If I wait until the next dance is about to start before I go, I'll be able to sit with you for a while, and I'll have one less dance with one of *them*."

"That's very clever—" Rianine broke off as a shadow fell across the table.

"What must I do to be served dinner in this hall, My Lady?" The cold, flat voice of Dreigen the Lore Master cut across the conversation.

Chapter 15

Dreigen

Nagaro froze. He had neither seen nor heard Dreien's approach, not with Nevien to look at and listen to. Now the gaunt figure of the half-Jinari seemed to loom over them like a huge carrion crow. Fortunately, Dreigen's attention was all on Nevien, whom he had addressed, and the two women were both looking at Dreigen. No one had noticed Nagaro's sudden rigidity or the hunted look in his eyes as he stared at the half-cast Jinari in horrified fascination, unable to pull his gaze away.

Dreigen's hard, black eyes were the same as he remembered them. They still glittered evilly in their deep sockets. Otherwise, however, the man had visibly aged. His hair was longer, and lank, its dull black marred by strands of gray. The skin of his face looked paper-thin, stretched over his sharp cheekbones, beaklike nose, and knife-sharp chin.

"They haven't served you yet, Zirda?" Nevien's gentle response was accompanied by a sincere smile. "I'm sure it's only because you requested them to cook you a special dish, but when next I see a serving person I will be sure to inquire."

"I am obliged." The Lore Master inclined his upper body very slightly— it could hardly be called a bow. His facial muscles twitched briefly into what was apparently intended to be a smile, but which lacked any suggestion of the feeling that ought to accompany one. Then he turned without another word— and without ever having looked at Nagaro or Rianine— and glided away.

Nagaro let out a breath, and shivered. He reached for his glass and took a gulp of sothiril to cover his discomfort and realized that Rianine was speaking.

"He treats you like one of the servants. I don't know why you put up with it."

"He only speaks to me because no one else will speak to him." Nevien was frowning. "The servants avoid him, so how is he to live?"

"I'd just as soon he didn't." Rianine sniffed. "They avoid him because they're afraid of him— and well they should be. Everyone knows he's done murder, whether it's been proven or not."

"It *hasn't* been proven, and so everyone *doesn't* know it. They only think they do."

Rianine gave her friend an exasperated look. "The kitchen staff believe he murdered that old man who used to take him his food. And your father seems to think so too by the look of things. He had those brooms burnt after Dreigen had been seen handling them."

"I'm sure that was just to humor the staff."

"He had the brooms taken away by men wearing *gloves*, Nevien. And he had the gloves burnt, too! They said Dreigen was wearing gloves when he touched the brooms, and that he'd asked specifically about things the old man used every day."

Nevien had begun to look increasingly upset. "But this is ridiculous!" she cried. "How can a broom poison anyone? I know it all looks suspicious, but why would Dreigen kill that old man? Now there's no one to bring him his dinner!"

Rianine arched an eyebrow. "Well you *did* say you heard them arguing."

Nagaro had been listening with mounting dread. Now he leaned forward in his seat. "You heard Dreigen and the old man arguing, Nevien?" he asked urgently. "What were they arguing about?"

"It didn't seem to be anything very serious." Nevien gestured vaguely. "The old servant didn't want to pass some message along. He was accustomed to bring Dreigen things besides food— things on a list. Dreigen said he'd been shorted. Something was missing, some kind of powdered root. He was annoyed that the old man wouldn't complain about the missing item to whoever got him the things on the list. He did say something that sounded a bit like a threat, but the old man pooh-poohed it—"

She broke off, frowning, then shook her head at the memory. "The servant was just the go-between! If Dreigen was really angry, he ought to have taken it out on the people who shorted him, surely— not the old man who brought him the things."

"Ha!" Rianine gave a short laugh. "Maybe he didn't think of that. Or maybe he wanted to show those other people that they had better take him seriously."

Nevien's frown returned. "He... *did* say they'd better get him what he wanted if they wanted his cooperation. But to kill a man over it? That just doesn't make sense!"

Rianine shook her head. "Maybe not to you, because *you'd* never kill anyone. But to a cold-blooded murderer it makes perfect sense. It was just an old man. A servant. Someone of no account. But it sends a message doesn't it?"

Nagaro cleared his throat, which was feeling oddly tight. He was trying to think how he could convince Nevien of the danger. "It's consistent with the way folk have cast Dreigen in the histories," he pointed out. "As a man who kills with a cool-headed purpose, without compunction. Many believe he poisoned Darion for the Leithian Faction when they wanted a Leithian on the throne. Berinar Sundorin was one of the chief advocates of that view, and Dreigen is thought to have poisoned *him* when it became necessary to even-up the numbers of Pact Signers."

Nevien gave him a reproachful look. "There's no proof of any of that!"

Rianine leaned forward, her eyes narrowing conspiratorially. "That's because he's working for people who make sure there isn't any evidence!"

Nagaro frowned. "If only someone could look in his journals—" he began, and stopped dead, in horror, as he realized what he had just revealed.

"His journals?" Nevien turned to him, startled. "Why do you think he has journals?"

"I...ah..." He cast about wildly, at a loss to explain himself.

Fortunately Rianine came to his rescue. "Of course he has journals!" she declared. "He's a lore master. They always write everything down."

"You think he would murder people in cold blood and then *write* about it?"

"I don't see why not. He's perfectly safe up there, after all. Everyone is much too terrified of him to go snooping about in his rooms."

Nevien abruptly stood up. "Well *I'm* not," she declared. "And look, Filora and two of the kitchen maids just walked in with Dreigen's dinner. While he's busy eating, I'm going to go see for myself whether there's any truth to any of this."

"*No!*" Nagaro was on his feet. "Nevien, you mustn't! It's too dangerous!"

Nevien turned to him as if to chide him, but then her look softened as she registered the depth of his distress. "It's kind of you to be so concerned, Nagaro," she said, shaking her head at him. "But, what danger can there be when the man is here, rather than there?"

"I don't know..." He waved a hand vaguely and swallowed past the narrowing of his throat. He felt sick with dread. "He... might have set traps..."

Nevien brushed the idea aside. "When he knows that everyone is afraid to enter his chambers? I hardly think so."

Rianine was frowning. "What will you tell the guard in the hallway?" she asked.

"I'll say I'm thinking of redecorating Dreigen's rooms and want to look at the furnishings. I've done several of the other rooms upstairs, after all."

Rianine's brow relaxed fractionally. "Yes, that might work. But I do think I should go with you." She stood up.

"Well, if you insist, Rian."

Nagaro was looking from one of the women to the other. Two were better than one, and Rianine would be careful, but... His mouth felt terribly dry. His heart was pounding. "Then... then I should come too—" he began.

He had started to move away from his chair, but Rianine emitted a peal of laughter. "No, no, *no*, Captain!" she cried. "Just think how that would look!"

Nevien was already moving in the direction of the door that led to the main stairs. "Come on, Rian," she said over her shoulder. "We need to be done and back here before he's finished."

Rianine started after her, turning back long enough to give Nagaro a sympathetic look. "Don't worry," she said, keeping her voice low. "I'll see that she's careful." Another thought apparently struck her. "And if Dreigen starts to leave before we get back, we'll need you here to stall him."

And then she was gone too, both women making the best speed that skirts would decorously allow.

Nagaro stood looking after them, staring at the door through which they had just vanished, in an agony of indecision. His thoughts spun wildly. He ought to go after them, try to stop them. Two women alone in Dreigen's chambers... *If anything were to happen to Nevien...to either one of them... when he had known what they meant to do...*

He took a step after them and brought himself up short. How could he hope to stop them when Nevien was so determined? And the guards would surely prevent him. They wouldn't ignore a man who wasn't a household member wandering about the hallways. Rianine was right about the appearance of impropriety.

With a guilty sense of relief, he sat down again, trying to breathe slowly to calm himself. Nevien was probably right about the traps— that Dreigen would be too complacent to bother with such precautions. He reminded himself that the man had lived in the palace for thirty years, unmolested. And Rianine was right, too, about the need for someone to keep an eye on Dreigen.

With a shiver, he tore his eyes away from the empty doorway and forced himself to turn his gaze in Dreigen's direction. The lore master was seated just two tables away. Filora and the serving maids were still attending him. They had brought him his own dishes, including a bowl and spoon. There was a steaming tureen and fresh bread in a basket. Filora was just finishing ladling something from the tureen into the bowl. Nagaro knew the Mistress of the Royal Kitchens. She was a woman who had once been prepared to defend those kitchens with a kitchen knife and who had conducted a contingent of his pirates through the palace hallways on a hunt for invading Mautep raiders. The woman had nerve, but he could see from the way she moved now how tense she was. Her face was frozen in a mask of polite officiousness. The two young serving women appeared to be trying to hide behind her skirts, keeping as far away from Dreigen as possible, while still managing to minimally fulfill their duty.

At last, the three women appeared to be finished. Dreigen dismissed them with a negligent wave of his hand, and they withdrew with rather more alacrity than was properly called for. Dreigen began his repast, his hands moving with deliberate precision while his eyes scanned the room with a mixture of disdain and chilling curiosity.

When the glance of those eyes moved in Nagaro's direction, he hastily picked up his glass of sothiril and made an elaborate show of taking a swallow, of savoring it. After a while, he glanced at the doorway again— where there was of course no sign of the two women— then risked another cautious glance at Dreigen. The man was still eating.

And so it went. The musicians took up their instruments once more. The dancers began to spin. Outside the palace walls, the soft, warm midsummer's eve was falling. The glow from the tall windows was ebbing, and inside the Great Hall the servants began to make the rounds to light the ornate lamps that encircled the room, nestled among the decorative greenery.

Nagaro's attention jerked nervously back and forth between the doorway and the seated Dreigen. He watched as the Lore Master sopped his bread in his soup and sucked the crusts. He watched the man empty his bowl and fill it again from the tureen the serving women had left with him. Other guests from the match table came and went— Kendira and the young Leithian, Groft, came, laughing and breathless. Geivian came a little later, looking glum. Nagaro scarcely took heed of any of them, paying them the minimum courtesy required.

As he watched the second bowl of soup disappearing spoonful by spoonful, Nagaro's anxiety began to mount. He wondered what was keeping Nevien and Rianine. How long had they actually been gone? The music was playing again, but was it the second dance or the third? *And what on earth would he do if Dreigen got up to leave?* Nagaro shuddered at the idea of meerly going near the man, and the thought of actually speaking to the Lore Master frankly terrified him. Even if he could bring himself to approach Dreigen, what could he possibly say that would hold the man in conversation for any length of time?

"Captain?"

Nagaro started violently, but it was only Lady Merriel who had come up behind him.

"I'm so sorry," she said. "I didn't mean to startle you, but I can't seem to find Nevien, and the last place I can remember seeing her was here. This is the second dance she's missed and some of the suitors are looking for her."

Nagaro swallowed. "She... ah... went upstairs a little while ago. To change her shoes. I think she might not be in a hurry to come down again."

Merriel nodded knowingly. "I can't blame her. Still, I know she's a responsible person, so I expect we'll see her soon."

"I... certainly hope so."

He had risen out of respect for Lady Merriel. Now, as she departed, he started to sit down again. At the same time, he turned his attention back to the table where Dreigen had been sitting— and froze in horror. *The Lore Master's seat was empty!*

He spun towards the doorway that led to the stairs, scanning the space in between until his eyes found what they were seeking. Dreigen was a few feet from the door and moving in its direction with purposeful gliding steps.

Keshaal! He was going to have to do something to stop the man— and quickly!

Trying not to give himself time to think, he struck out on a course to intercept the gliding figure. Dreigen, however, had a considerable head start. By the time Nagaro was within range to hail him, the Lore Master had already passed the threshold and was in the short hallway, beyond it, that led to the bottom of the main stairs. As Nagaro passed that same threshold, a dozen feet from the dreaded man, he knew he was going to have to speak. He drew a shaky breath past a tightness in his throat that threatened to choke him.

"Master Dreigen!"

The words came out sounding half-strangled, but the Lore Master heard them nevertheless for he stopped and turned around, impaling Nagaro with his piercing, dark stare.

"Yes?" he said, with a voice like a fall of ice in a winter wood. "What do you want, pirate?"

Vothra help me now, Nagaro thought desperately. *What can I say to him?* As if in answer, words seemed to come into his mind: *You have three scrolls.*

Of course. Yes. The three scrolls were under his bed back in the house he'd shared with his friends on Pakoa Island.

"I... I have three scrolls..."

"So? You have three scrolls." Dreigen was clearly unimpressed. "What of it? I have dozens."

Nagaro's mind floundered, terror flooding it, until he saw Nevien in his mind's eye— *standing in the Lore Master's chamber with one of the accursed journals in her hands.* He *had* to keep the man talking. "I... I thought they might interest you," he managed. "They're Jinari scrolls."

"Of *course* they're Jinari scrolls." Dreigen was disdainful. "The Jinari are the only folk who *make* scrolls. If you knew what was *in* them, perhaps? If they concerned herb lore or medicines, for example—"

"Oh, but they do!"

"*Really?*" The Lore Master's dark brows arched skeptically. "And you know this... *how?*" he inquired. "Surely you don't mean to suggest that you read Jinari."

"No. No, I... I don't—"

"Of course not." Dreigen began to turn away contemptuously.

"But I know a man who does! He's a... a friend of mine. He told me what was in them."

Dreigen stopped. "You have a *friend* who reads Jinari?" He uttered the word "friend" as if it referred to something faintly disgusting, and the tone of the entire sentence was such as to suggest that he considered the claim highly suspect.

"Yes! Yes, I do. He's... he's a Jinari, you see—" Nagaro knew that he was babbling. Fear was making a fool of him— making him appear almost as much an idiot as he must have seemed under the influence of heskial— but at that moment he didn't care as long as he could keep the other man from walking away.

For the first time, a spark of interest had appeared in the Lore Master's sunken eyes. "*You* are acquainted with a Jinari?"

"Yes! He's... a...a merchant's agent."

Dreigen took two steps towards him, his black eyes suddenly avid. Nagaro had to resist a nearly overpowering urge to back away. He was sweating and his heart was thudding against his ribs. *Where were Nevien and Rianine? He could see the bottom of the stairs from were he stood.*

"And what did this *Jinari* tell you about these scrolls?" The Lore Master came yet another step closer and smiled a rabid, hungry smile.

Desperately Nagaro cudgeled his brain even as he still fought the urge to flee. He was trying to remember what Utabala had said about the scrolls all those years ago. "He... he... said... one of them was about... about antidotes to poisons. And another was... was... about the dangers of misuse of certain medicines. Both of those were by a master called Obiari— though one was only a copy—"

"Those are my scrolls!" Dreigen's burning eyes had been fixing Nagaro ever more intensely as he listened, and now the words suddenly burst hissing from his lips. *"They were coming to me!"* The Lore Master extended his arm and leveled an accusing finger. "Pirate! Thief! Was it *you* who stole them from the ship that was bringing them to me?"

Nagaro backed away, but not very far. What he wanted to do was run, but he couldn't take his eyes off the man. It was like watching a snake about to strike. *"No!"* he gasped. It seemed as if he could hardly breathe. "I swear it! The Mautep stole them! The scrolls were on the ship— when we were slaves— we found them after we took the Mahuk ship!"

"And I suppose you now think that I will pay you a lot of money to get them back? Is that it?" The finger was withdrawn but the Lore Master's eyes and voice were still accusing.

"We never... found a market for them. I– I thought you might want them. I didn't know they were being sent to you!" At that moment, Nagaro would have flung the scrolls at Dreigen's feet and fled had they been in his hands. As it was, he managed to hold his ground, but only just. He was aware of the sweat trickling down his sides, and there was a nasty prickling all along the insides of both his forearms as if every one of the bladder-thorn scars were an ant that was biting him.

Dreigen appeared to be considering, and the accusation retreated from his eyes. "I suppose there would have been something paid upon delivery," he said grudgingly. "So I *suppose* you may be due some payment for delivering them to me. Provided that you do it promptly."

"They're... not here. They're on Pakoa—"

Dreigen emitted a hiss of frustration that made him seem all the more snake-like. He began to advance once more upon Nagaro, who found himself now rooted to the spot from sheer terror. Still he somehow managed to say, "When next I go there... I can bring them—"

"See that you do!" The Lore Master's voice was low and cold and commanding as he closed the distance between them. *"Bring them to me, and only to me. And you will receive what you deserve!"*

And with that, Dreigen thrust out his skeletal arm and poked Nagaro once, hard, in the chest as if he meant to drive the words into his listener's heart with his bony finger. Then he turned without another word and stalked away.

Nagaro staggered back, gasping at the blow. His feet stumbled and he came up hard against the wall of the hallway. He stood there, leaning against it, panting for air. The blood was pounding in his ears and his heart was beating so hard against his ribs it seemed it would shake his bones apart. Little points of light began to dance in his vision as the world seemed to recede, the sounds dying away and images fading to gray...

The next thing he knew, he was on the floor, his head spinning. *Fool,* he thought, thoroughly ashamed of himself. *The man didn't hurt you!* He remembered now, belatedly, what Tred had told him years before about breathing slowly if he didn't want to faint. He pulled himself to a sitting position with his back against the wall, and clamped his mouth shut on a wave of nausea. He closed his eyes, then, and tried to take long, slow breaths. But in the next moment he became aware of the sound of light footsteps approaching, and a rustle of fabric.

He opened his eyes, only to find that it was Rianine standing over him, and she was alone.

"What's the matter, Nagaro?" she asked urgently. "Are you ill?"

Embarrassed, he clambered to his feet, then clutched at the wall as the points of light reappeared and the world threatened to fade again. "*Where's Nevien?*" he gasped. "Is she all right?"

"Oh, yes. She seemed a bit shaken by what she'd read, but that's all. She went to find her father while I came down this way so you wouldn't worry. But whatever is the matter?"

"I... I was talking to Dreigen—"

"Vothra!" She was suddenly alarmed. "He didn't *touch* you, did he?"

"Yes..." He saw her look. "It's all right. He wouldn't hurt me. He wouldn't get his precious scrolls if he hurt me."

"His *scrolls? What* scrolls?"

Nagaro gestured impatiently and passed a hand across his brow. He was still trying to control his breathing. "It was... all I could think of. I was trying to... to keep him from going upstairs."

"Oh. I see. In that case, I think you saved us from being caught in the act. I passed him going up the stairs as I was coming down."

"*Oh Vothra!*" He shut his eyes again at the horror of this narrow escape.

"Captain!"

His eyes snapped open as he felt her hand on his arm. Her expression was unmistakably worried. "Are you sure he didn't do something to you?" she asked urgently. "You don't look at all well."

"No, I'm all right. This is just... just..." He floundered, embarrassed and uncertain how to explain the extremity of his reaction.

"Nerves?" she suggested. He nodded sheepishly.

"Don't worry," she said, patting his arm. "I understand. When I had to get past him on the stairs, he looked at me and I felt as if I were going to choke— after reading about the cold way he planned and carried out the murder of that old serving man! *That* was as much as I could stand to read. I felt so sick I went and stood in the doorway where I could see the top of the stairs while Nevien kept reading. You're absolutely right that Dreigen is dangerous, and we were both right about the journals. There are *volumes* of them, and he describes everything in detail as if he were bragging about it! But you just wait here while I find Kuran. He'll know what to do with you, and you wanted to talk to him anyway. If you and I were to be seen walking out of here together, it would simply *ruin* my reputation!"

She rolled her eyes dramatically, gave him a wink, and was gone with a swish of skirts.

Nagaro waited, grateful for her understanding but worried about how long it might take for her to find Kuran. And even more worried about exactly what she might tell the Lord of the Fleet. As it turned out, Kuran must have been no farther away than the Fleet table.

The Lord of the Fleet came quickly, looking very grave. "What's this all about?" he asked. "Rianine hinted at all sorts of things."

By this time Nagaro had largely composed himself, though the after-effects of having had a bad shock were now catching up with him, causing his hands to shake and his legs to feel like water. Kuran noticed his unsteadiness as soon as Nagaro abandoned the support of the wall in order to approach him. "By the Eyes!" the older man exclaimed. "If I didn't know better, I'd say you'd been in a fight— one that didn't go well. You're not hurt, are you?"

"No." Nagaro made haste to reassure him. "I'll be all right. I just need a little time, but I have no wish to see more of the festivities." He needed to talk to Kuran, but there was too much to say and he didn't want to begin by explaining why merely talking to Dreigen affected him so severely. In fact, he wasn't at all sure that he *could* explain it.

Kuran considered him narrowly, clearly aware that his original question hadn't been answered. Apparently he decided not to immediately probe any further, however, for he said, "In that case, we can go out by way of the main hallway. I'll send word to the other Fleet men to say that we left early."

They traversed the main central hall together in silence, for which Nagaro was grateful. As he walked, he found himself growing steadier. He could feel Kuran's eyes on him and knew that the older man must be observing his improving condition. Nevertheless, Kuran insisted on calling for a carriage when they reached the front door. Nagaro protested that Thunder-Heels was waiting for him and that he was quite able to ride, but Kuran looked at him sternly. "I want a carriage," he said. "The horses can be led behind." The door guard accepted the request with a disinterested salute.

A moment later, they emerged to stand within the portico at the top of the stairs that led down to the stable yard and the broad expanse of the courtyard separating the palace from the city of Lankura. The cool evening air struck Nagaro like a wave of cleansing water and he breathed deeply, raising his eyes to the twilit sky and trying to distance himself from his recent ordeal. The evening had not begun auspiciously, and it had ended very nearly in a nightmare.

Kuran still refrained from questioning him, and Nagaro was grateful again for the older man's forbearance. In spite of his earlier protests, he was grateful also when the carriage arrived. He climbed in and sank onto a cushioned seat. It was a tremendous relief just to sit comfortably, to lean his back against the cushions, and not to have to worry about balancing to a horse's stride. He would have shut his eyes as well, but it soon became apparent that Kuran's purpose in ordering the carriage was not entirely humanitarian. The Lord of the Fleet had settled into the seat across from him, and as the carriage began to move, he leaned forward, his sharp black eyes probing Nagaro's face. "Now, Captain," he said, "Since we're alone and, I hope, comfortable, I want you to tell me what this is all about—starting from the beginning. And I'm quite prepared to make that an order if it should prove necessary."

Fortunately, by this time Nagaro had figured out what he was going to say. He began at the beginning of the evening's strange events, starting with how he'd seen Lothard in conversation with Madred's Minister Torlung and how Torlung had then gone to Dreigen and given the Lore Master a packet of some kind. Then there had been the odd way that Grimbold had persuaded Lothard to abandon a quarrel so that the two of them could go off together and talk about "more important things." And finally, there was Nevien's determination to test all the frightening rumors about Dreigen by going upstairs and trying to read the man's journals while the Lore Master was eating his dinner.

Kuran had been listening with a gathering frown until this last part, but when Nagaro described Nevien's plan, he suddenly leaned forward and exclaimed, "Vothra's Eyes, man, don't tell me you *allowed* this!"

Nagaro felt as if he'd been slapped. "How was I to stop her?" he demanded. "I tried to talk her out of it, but she's the *princess!* I don't command her! Rianine went with her—and told me to stay behind to stall Dreigen if necessary. It *was* necessary too, as it turned out."

Kuran was immediately conciliatory. "Is that how you ended up sitting on the floor at the bottom of the stairs?"

Nagaro drew a deep breath. He hoped that any difficulty he displayed in telling this part of the tale would be attributed to the shame he might be feeling for his weakness. "I... I'm afraid I must have fainted, My Lord," he confessed. "In my defense, I can only say I have a terrible fear of what that man can do. I was terribly afraid for the princess— for both of those ladies. When I had to go after him, to stall him, it was all I could do to stand there and keep him in conversation for a minute or two. And when he...

stabbed me in the chest with his finger, I... well... the next thing I knew I was on the floor, feeling dizzy and sick."

Kuran regarded him intently from the opposite carriage seat by the light of the small carriage lantern that hung from a hook beside the door. "Rianine said you looked quite ill," he ventured. "That you stood up and looked like you were going to fall down again."

"I'm afraid it's true, My Lord. Rianine asked if it was just nerves... and I suppose it was." He looked down at his hands where they lay in his lap, while the carriage rattled on through the darkness.

Kuran's voice when next the older man spoke was gently probing. "He actually touched you with his finger? I think we should have your shirt off and take a look at the spot."

"It wasn't so hard as to hurt me, My Lord," Nagaro protested. "It was just a poke in the chest."

Kuran however wasn't satisfied until Nagaro had unbuttoned his tirka, and the shirt underneath, and allowed the skin of his chest to be inspected. There wasn't a mark to be seen.

"Hnnh." The Lord of the Fleet sat frowning while Nagaro re-buttoned his clothing. After a moment, he added, "I wonder if you might be one of those that my mother used to call 'truth-feelers'. Ones who can sense evil— or who are affected by it's presence. I confess I'd never given the notion much credence until now."

Nagaro didn't want it thought that he might have such a gift. He shook his head. "I've never heard of such a thing. The Writings make no mention of it."

Kuran raised an equivocal eyebrow. "There may be more things in the world than Vothra has knowledge of," he observed.

"Well, that may be true," Nagaro conceded, but he was thinking of how the words *you have three scrolls* had flickered through his panicked brain just when he'd needed something to say to Dreigen. He suspected that Vothra had been very much aware of the situation. "But I think that in this case it was simply the power of my fear working against me," he added quickly. "I was breathing too fast, and I made myself faint." And then, because he wished to turn the subject, he said, "What do you make of all the other things? Of who was speaking to whom, and that packet being handed to Dreigen by Minister Torlung?"

Kuran had been looking abstracted but he came instantly back to focus. "It certainly could have been a delivery to Dreigen from the Brothers of the Blood— or from the Leithian Faction. Unfortunately, it's still impossible to say whether Lord Madred is directly involved. You may be sure that I will... ah... pass the information along. In any case, I hope you'll go to bed and get some rest, and try not to trouble yourself any more about it. This water is too deep for such small boats as ours."

And at that point the carriage rolled into the Fleet Compound and the conversation, like the carriage ride, was at an end.

Chapter 16

The Road Again

"He told you not to *trouble yourself?*" Taru was incredulous. "When Dreigen has been poisoning people for years? And it looks like he's working for the Leithians?"

Pavo nodded agreement. "And I am afraid princess maybe is in danger now, because she have found out what he is doing," he added.

The three friends were breakfasting together in Nagaro's quarters. It was a week after the Midsummer feast. Taru and Pavo had returned very late the night before, and very weary, from a week-long furlough spent in Wotana. Rather than keep them from their beds, Nagaro had asked them to join him for breakfast early the following morning. Not only did he have a great deal to tell them, but he also had an invitation for another outing to River House later that same morning. He had just described his adventures at the palace and this had been their response.

He toyed with a slice of toast spread with jam, and frowned. "Kuran said these waters are too deep for us," he said. "Meaning that he and I aren't in a position to deal with it. It's Elgurn and the Pact Signers who must decide what's to be done. And as long as no one tells Dreigen what Nevien did, she's as safe as she ever was." His frown deepened as he took a bite of toast and reached for his sothiril to wash it down. He'd been trying to convince himself of that for the last several days.

"Well that's so, I suppose." Taru had already finished his toast and jam, and his sothiril, and now he leaned back in his chair. "Can ye believe that Dreigen still remembered those scrolls after all this time? It's been how long? Seven years?"

"Almost nine. Dreigen must have the kind of mind that holds on to things like that forever."

"Are ye going t' take the scrolls to him?"

Nagaro's face clouded. "I'd rather not," he said darkly. "And not just because I don't want to face him again. I really don't want to give him anything—knowing what it might be used for. I did say that I would bring them from Pakoa the next time I went there, and I'll keep my word to that extent. I just won't go out of my way to do it."

Taru looked worried. "What if he... well... comes after ye about it?"

Nagaro felt a chill at the thought. "Then I suppose I might have to hand them over to placate him," he conceded. "But I don't think he ever leaves the palace anymore."

Taru looked relieved, but then another thought seemed to strike him. "What did the princess find out, anyway?"

"Rianine didn't say. But she wouldn't have read at random. There are too many notebooks. She would have looked for known events—things she had dates for. Years and seasons, at least. And I have another clue." Nagaro reached into the front of his tirka and brought out the princess's invitation to River House, a small folded piece of parchment, which he opened so that his friends could read what was written there. Below the usual formal wording, and above her signature, Nevien had written: *All the tales are true. Please come.*

"*All* the tales!" Taru gave a low whistle. "Does that mean Dreigen really *did* murder Darion?"

"I assume she learned that much at least, since that's the oldest tale involving Dreigen's misdeeds. When I see her, I'll ask her."

Taru shook his head. "Just the thought o' standing face t' face with Dreigen gives me shivers!"

Nagaro set his half-eaten slice of toast on his plate and studied his hands. "It did more than give me shivers," he said. "That's why Rianine found me sitting on the floor. I don't know if I could face Dreigen again like that. And of course she told Kuran all about it, so I had to explain it to him as well— without telling him the *real* reason why Dreigen scares me so. He thought I might somehow be sensitive to evil, but I told him it was just fear, and that was that. Since it's rather embarrassing to have fainted, I don't imagine he'll press me further about it. Or spread it about."

Taru stood up and went to the window, where he twitched the curtain aside. "Ye'd best be on your way, Nagaro," he said, "if ye don't want t' be late for that your outing."

"Yes," put in Pavo. "We will wash all these dish for you."

Nagaro glanced at the window. The morning light was brightening. "Bishka! You're right." Hurriedly he drained his sothiril. "Thank you for helping." He dug his key out of his pocket and put it on the table. "Be sure to lock the door when you leave. I'll get the key from you tonight." He rose and started for the front door, but turned back at the kitchen threshold. "By the way, Taru, how is the courtship going?"

Taru had picked up his knife and plate and was moving toward the washstand. "It's going just fine," he mumbled, without turning around.

Pavo gave Nagaro a broad wink behind Taru's back. "Next time you really should come with us, Nagaro," he said brightly. "It sound to me as if it is much more safe for you in Wotana than in Lankura."

At this, Taru shot a look in Pavo's direction before returning his attention to the wash basin.

Nagaro laughed. "I think you're right, Pavo."

He snatched his cloak from its hook beside the door and went out into the crisp, clear morning, turning in the direction of the stables where Thunder-Heels was waiting for him. He'd have liked to have asked for more details of Taru's courtship, but that would have to wait for another time.

***

When he arrived at the palace stable yard, he found that the party bound for River House had already assembled. Some were mounted and some weren't, and most of the women who didn't ride were already sitting in the carriage. Nevien, clad in her dark green riding clothes, was still afoot, looking fretful and preoccupied. She brightened when she saw him and approached, leading her white mare by the bridle.

"We're having to wait a little," she explained. "Anduar just came out and told Kuran that he's needed at an unscheduled Council meeting, so he won't be able to join us. Merriel just went upstairs to find us another chaperon."

"Oh." Nagaro found the news unsettling, partly because he wondered what the meeting was about, and partly out of concern that the outing might have to be cancelled. "Will that be difficult?"

Nevien shook her head. "Merriel didn't think so. She means to ask one of my mother's ladies who's staying here this week with her husband. She says Lady Reineth won't mind being imposed upon and would probably enjoy an outing in the country."

"I see. That's good, then."

Nagaro dismounted and stood, chewing his lip and frowning at the ground as Nevien hurried away again to answer some question from one of her own ladies. This would be the first time in his experience that an outing to River House didn't include Lord Kuran.

"There you are, you handsome beast. Have you decided when our wedding is to be?"

It was Rianine, of course, speaking from right next to him. Rudely jolted out of his thoughts, Nagaro turned to meet her teasing eyes. Rianine also had her horse by the bridle, so they were flanked by their mounts on either side. No one else appeared to be paying them any attention. He rallied his thoughts and tried for a jesting response.

"The Turo have an expression— When fishes fly and birds swim under the sea."

"Oh, now that's cruel!" she said, pouting. "Especially since you haven't given me a good reason for refusing. Not being compatible is quite irrelevant when a marriage is only for appearances."

Nagaro's frown returned. "If it's only for appearances, I'm afraid I don't see the point."

"Don't you, you silly man? It keeps folk from wondering what's wrong with you. Do you really think they won't begin to wonder just because you have a daughter? And if you do want me in your bed, I think you're pretty enough that I could manage it from time to time— do you know that you tend to get a helpless look when you're off balance that's really quite charming?"

Nagaro strongly suspected he was wearing such a look at that very moment. "But," he protested, "how can I lie with a woman if my heart isn't in it?"

"You did it once before, didn't you?" She asked archly.

Nagaro felt the blood in his face. She was obviously speaking of the episode that had given him his daughter, Narei.

"I was very drunk when I did that. And I... I thought the woman had a genuine interest in me."

Rianine pouted and fluttered her lashes in an exaggerated display of coyness. "*My* interest couldn't be more genuine," she purred. "And if you must be drunk, that can be easily arranged."

"No, it can't! I've promised myself it would never happen again. I've sworn to keep the ban."

This only earned him another exaggerated pout. "Oh, how you wound me, Captain! Would it be so terrible to lie with me?"

Fortunately the call to mount spared him the need to respond. Merriel had returned with Lady Reineth, a tall, gracious, Kelorin woman who cast smiles and greetings liberally about her as she was ushered to the carriage. Rianine promptly mounted, and he hurriedly swung into the saddle, even as she gave him a sugary parting smile and guided her sorrel mare to a place beside the princess.

From the Thunder-Heels' back, Nagaro surveyed the company as the carriage rolled out of the stable yard. Something was nagging at him, and he soon realized what it was. Brandle was nowhere to be seen. The order to mount had come from one of the other guards, of whom there were only five. Those five guardsmen had exchanged questioning glances as if the absence of the sixth caused them some concern.

One of the five men was new to the uniform of the Princess's Guard, though well known to Nagaro. As the party crossed the wide courtyard in front of the palace, Nagaro spurred forward to bring himself abreast of the new man. "Good morning, Delvin," he said. "Did you grow weary of manning the palace's front door?"

The young Kelorin grinned at him. "Weary indeed, Captain!" He laughed. "All I did all day long was take men's swords away and give 'em back again. That, and bow a lot. So when I heard there was an opening in Lieutenant Brandle's troop, I put in for it. The Princess's Guards may spend a lot of time guarding the third floor hallway, but we also get t' go for rides in the country."

Nagaro cocked an eyebrow, suddenly curious. "There was an opening, you say? Who are you replacing— if you know— and what happened to the man?"

"I don't know his name. A big, silent, red-haired fellow. He's gone t' the City Guard. That's all I know."

Nagaro nodded. He'd already noted the absence of the red-haired man, and this confirmed his suspicions.

"And where is Brandle?"

Delvin frowned. "Off about some business of his own, I think. He left the guard chambers early this morning, saying we should leave without him if need be— that he'd catch us up. Some o' the men don't like going without him. I guess we all thought he'd be here by now."

Nagaro nodded again, trying not to let his concern show in his face. He thought he understood what it was that worried the other men, though it seemed unlikely that Lothard would try to repeat the ploy that had failed on the first attempt.

As if in answer to the thought, Delvin asked, "Ye don't suppose there are any more brigands on the road, do ye?"

"I doubt it." Nagaro gave the young man a reassuring smile. "But keep your eyes open and watch the land all around as we ride." In fact, he thought they really should be quite safe even if Lothard *did* make a second try. The Leithian surely hadn't meant to harm Nevien or the other women. *Still, with neither Kuran nor Brandle, there were fewer to put up a defense.*

He and Delvin were riding near the rear of the party as they passed through the city gate, and Nagaro took stock of the mounted men who were with them rode under its arch. Besides himself, there were the five guards, riding three at the front of the little cavalcade and two at the rear, one of those being Delvin. He knew that Rees and Vanhold were riding ahead of the carriage with the lead guards, and he could see Hendrik riding on one side of it. Not surprisingly, the young Leithian named Groft was riding on the other side where Nagaro could see Kendira's head leaning out of the window, her hand sometimes gesturing animatedly.

Groft appeared very attentive to her, turning in the saddle and bending his head sometimes as if to hear better.

Geivian was conspicuously absent, which didn't surprise Nagaro at all after what he'd seen at the Midsummer Festival. He knew Geivian to be a fair hand with a sword, a far better swordsman than a dancer. He wondered fleetingly whether Groft's skill with a blade was any match for his prowess on the dance floor.

Soon they were passing at a good pace along Market Street. Nevien and Rianine, the two mounted women, were riding immediately behind the carriage and therefore just in front of him. Since his conversation with Delvin had lapsed, Nagaro passed the time by admiring the way Nevien sat her horse. She was lithe and supple, and very sure of her seat as her hips moved with swing of the white mare's stride.

The princess was deep in conversation with Rianine. Now and then the two women frowned or laughed at some joke they shared, though it seemed to Nagaro that Nevien's laughter was fleeting and that her smile faded too quickly. He had begun to watch her with concern, when suddenly both women twisted around to look back at *him*. Two pairs of earnest eyes impaled him with their gaze and he felt as exposed as a lizard on a rock. He barely managed to maintain enough composure to make a small bow over his saddle bow. He swore to himself and shook his head. *At least they didn't seem to laughing at him.*

As the party neared an intersection where a choice of routes through the city had to be made, the lead guard, a sergeant, turned his horse about and rode back to speak briefly with Nevien before returning to his place. A short time later, the cavalcade made the turn to the right, which was south. At this point, Nevien drew rein and dropped back to speak to Nagaro and the rear guard.

"We've decided to leave the city by the South Gate," she informed them. "We'll ride around by the outer Circle Road. It's a little longer but less in the public eye, which pleases me more. We'll stop at the Main Gate to see if there's been any word of Brandle."

The two guards acknowledged her news with a salute. She answered them with a gracious inclination of her head, then gave Nagaro a quick smile and rode back to her place with Rianine.

When they reached the Main Gate a quarter of an hour later, they all came to a halt where the Circle Road joined the eastward-running High Road, taking care to be out of the way of the early morning traffic of carts and peasants leading animals with loads on their backs. Delvin drew rein, looking about and frowning. Brandle was not immediately to be seen.

"Perhaps he's already passed through and gone," Nagaro suggested.

Delvin shook his head. "He would have asked whether we'd been seen going either past the gate, or through it. Since we haven't done either, he'd have waited. Maybe he's in the guard house."

The lead guard had dismounted and tied his horse to a hitching post in preparation to enter the guard house. Delvin swung down from the saddle and handed his reins to Nagaro. "Would ye hold my horse, Captain?" he said. "I'm going t' see what I can find out," and he trotted after the sergeant.

Nagaro held the reins as the two guards disappeared through a door located under the gate's great arch. He then tried to keep one eye on the folk who were leaving the city by way of the gate while at the same time watching Nevien speaking to her ladies through the carriage window. A member of the City Guard emerged from the gate house and hailed Groft, who rode over to apparently exchange pleasantries.

After a few minutes, Delvin reappeared wearing a puzzled frown. "There's been no word of him," he said as he retrieved the reins of his horse. "The sergeant is telling the duty officer what to tell Brandle when he comes. He doesn't mean to wait."

The other man who'd been riding rear guard, a Leithian named Orl, shook his head. "It's not like the Lieutenant to let personal matters interfere with his duties. I've been expecting t' see him come through that gate, but— Wait a minute! *There he is!*"

It was true. Brandle had just ridden through the gate, going at a hard trot, his face set in angry lines. His expression changed when he saw the princess's party to a look of relief. His glance briefly found Nagaro, and he mouthed something before riding to the princess, who had remounted. There followed an animated conversation of which Nagaro was able to catch enough to tell that Brandle was making abject apologies for his absence, and Nevien was reassuring him that they hadn't been waiting long. Presently the sergeant joined them and had to add his two rins' worth.

When at length the cavalcade got under way again, Brandle allowed his sergeant to continue in the lead position and fell in with the rear guard that included Nagaro. The big Leithian had resumed the stone-faced demeanor of a guardsman on duty. Several minutes passed as the party started along the High Road, before Nagaro managed to catch Brandle's eye, thinking the man might have something to say to him. Brandle's response, however, was to swing his horse closer and mutter through his teeth, "*Not here!*"

Nagaro shrugged, determined to let the other man choose his time to talk.

The day was fair and beginning to grow warm, though a thin, late mist still lingered in places over the cultivated fields on either side of the road. Much of the traffic on the High Road was outward-bound from Lankura at this time of day and was moving more slowly than the princess's party, so it wasn't long before they had outdistanced most of it. Even so, Brandle held his peace until after they'd made the northward turn off of the High Road and had put the grove of trees from which Lothard's simulated attack had been launched well behind them. By that time, Delvin and Orl had dropped back a bit because the road wasn't wide enough to let four horsemen comfortably ride abreast.

At last, Brandle swung his horse closer to Thunder-Heels. "Do you know what Simion has been working on these past few weeks?" he asked, in a low voice.

Nagaro frowned. "No, I have no idea."

"It's not some assignment of yours or Kuran's?"

"We haven't—" Nagaro stopped as a dark premonition hovered. "Why do you ask?"

Brandle was watching his face. "Because Simion has disappeared."

The shadow moved closer. "What do you mean?" Nagaro asked cautiously. "How exactly has he 'disappeared'?"

"I haven't seen him since the day before yesterday and it looks as if he didn't return to his room last night. I was just in his office this morning and there were several books left open on his desk. I know he had some communication from Kuran at least once, a few weeks ago, and you're very close with Kuran."

Nagaro swallowed uncomfortably. "Do you remember what the books were?" he asked, with grave misgivings.

Brandle's brow furrowed. "They were all about Sobring Hold. There were maps, descriptions of the holdings—"

"*Bishka!*"

"What is it, Captain?" Brandle's eyes bored into him. "What exactly do you know?"

Nagaro had inadvertently pulled up on the reins, thinking his fears might be justified. He urged Thunder-Heels forward again. The matter was sensitive, but Brandle didn't deserve to be kept in the dark. "Do you remember those merchant's marks I wanted to ask Simion about?" he asked.

"*Ye-es...*" Brandle was frowning. "There was something about trafficking with Jinara in time of war."

Nagaro drew a long breath. "I'd known about the trade for some time, and that it involved Leithians. I got hold of the marks during my exile, and had no chance to pursue them. Then, two months ago, the Jinari sent an envoy to complain to Kuran that an illegal drug had been sold to yellow-haired Droviri, and Kuran charged me with identifying the marks." He paused, glancing at Brandle.

Brandle's frown had deepened and he sat his horse stiffly, posting automatically to the animal's trot. "So you went to Simion because they were merchant's marks?"

Nagaro drew another breath. "Yes," he said. "Except they weren't. They were the seals of the Houses of Sobring, Hurn, and Furthing. Simion knew it at a glance and he wanted to know what it was all about. I didn't want to tell him, but he got it out of me."

"*Ha!*" Brandle barked a short, mirthless laugh. "He's good at that."

"I told him the information would go to Kuran, and I asked him not to pursue it on his own because it was potentially dangerous. I thought he accepted that. And of course I had to tell Kuran what Simion knew. Kuran may have approached Simion about it, but I'm not aware of Kuran having set Simion any kind of task or assignment."

Brandle's frown darkened alarmingly. "*Bloody bodgering Hel!*" he muttered. "There needn't have *been* any task. If Simion takes it into his head to poke his nose into something, he just does. I wish you hadn't involved him."

Nagaro sighed. "So do I. But I truly thought they were merchants' marks that any number of people could have identified. I didn't think there would have been any danger in that. And maybe Simion is off poking his nose into something else, something quite harmless," he added hopefully.

But Brandle shook his head, unmollified. "I'd like to believe that, Captain, but there's more I haven't told you. He was last seen in the company of three Leithians. One of the grooms saw him talking to them in the street behind our building on Broad Street, the day before yesterday."

Nagaro chewed his lip. "That building is full of Leithians, Brandle."

"That's what I thought— at first. But the groom said he didn't recognize these men, and when he looked again a short time later, all four were gone. I tell you, I have a bad feeling. What if Simion thought the men were doing something suspicious and decided to follow them—"

"— and got caught?" Nagaro finished the thought, with a shiver. "I don't like that at all! I hope we're imagining things. And I'll ask Kuran if he knows anything about it the first chance I get."

"Excuse me, Zirdas." Delvin's voice cut across their conversation. "I don't like to interrupt, but it seems there's a man following us." The young Kelorin had brought his horse as close up behind them as he was able.

"*Where?*" Brandle was instantly alert, twisting in his saddle to look behind. "I don't see anyone."

"Not on the road." This was from Orl, who had also pressed his horse forward.

"Aye," Delvin concurred. "He's riding cross-country, off there t' the right and a little bit behind. He was on the left, but he crossed the road a ways back to find cover. Right now he'll be on the other side of this bit o' woods." With a gesture, Delvin indicated an irregular stand of trees running along the right-hand side of the road.

Nagaro quickly swung his gaze around to survey their surroundings. He'd been so intent on his conversation with Brandle that he'd been heedless of anything else— which he now regretted. They were passing through gently rolling country with scattered farms, and he knew the stand of trees well. It was the last bit of woods of any size before the road crossed the Yuna River. It extended for fifty or sixty yards and most of that length still lay before them. "We should ride ahead," he said, "and catch this fellow when he comes to the other end. Do you suppose, Brandle, that Lothard has resorted to this because you sent that big red-haired Leithian to the City Guard?"

Brandle was staring keenly up the road, his eyed narrowed. "That's exactly what I was thinking," he said. "What does this fellow look like, Delvin?"

"We never got a good look at his face. But he looks to have dark hair."

Brandle snorted. "That proves nothing. He could be wearing one of those wigs."

"And he's wearing a cloak with his hood up, even though the sun is getting rather warm."

"Which is suspicious." Brandle nodded decisively. "We should catch him and get a good look at him— and ask him to explain himself. But I think Captain Nagaro and I should attend to this. It might require some *delicacy*." The Lieutenant saluted Delvin and Orl. "Carry on, lads, and well done," he said, then added ruefully, "I'm glad *someone* here was paying attention."

Brandle proceeded to set his heels to his horse, cantering past the two mounted women, who gave him startled looks. Nagaro urged Thunder-Heels to follow but slowed as he came up beside the princess. "It seems a man is tracking us," he told her, keeping his voice low. "Ride on as if nothing were amiss." He saw her eyes widen, but didn't wait for her response as he gave the stallion his head. Within a few strides the big gray had caught up with Brandle's dark chestnut gelding.

They quickly passed the carriage, and the lead guard, drawing rein just long enough to let the sergeant know what they were about. When they reached the farther end of the stand of trees, they pulled their horses down to a walk. They crossed a shallow ditch at the side of the road, then rode cautiously just under the verge of the woods, working their way around the end of it.

Brandle, in the lead, abruptly reined his horse and drew his sword, signing Nagaro to silence with a finger to his lips. Nagaro drew Thunder-Heels to a halt at Brandle's flank. He unsheathed his own blade and waited tensely, peering past dark trunks, through the bright green foliage, as the sound of hooves and wheels on the road behind them drew closer and then moved past.

Abruptly he saw the man, a dark, cloaked shape moving between the trees, almost upon them. In the same instant Brandle drew a sharp breath and signaled him to ride forward. Their horses leaped ahead in unison. The unknown man gave a startled cry. His horse tried to rear, but Brandle caught the beast by the bridle even as Nagaro swung Thunder-Heels into position on the other side to block the rider's escape.

"Mercy!" the man gasped. "Put up your swords! It's only me!"

"*Geivian?*" Brandle and Nagaro spoke in simultaneous disbelief. Both were staring at the man whom they could see clearly for the first time. Brandle released his hold on the bridle. "What are you doing here, Zirda?" he demanded. "We took you for some spy of Lothard's."

"I—" Geivian looked nervously from one to the other of them. "I... ah... wanted to go for a ride—"

"By *this* road? But not *on* the road?" Brandle was sarcastic. "Keeping pace with us and moving from tree to tree? I'll wager you've been following us all the way from Lankura."

Geivian hung his head and nodded shamefacedly. "I... I heard there was to be an outing," he said haltingly. "And I... well... I thought at first it was just a mistake that I hadn't gotten an invitation. So I came early to the palace, but the stablemen showed me the list, and there was that young rake— Groft— on it, instead of me."

"So you're spying on Groft?"

Geivian's head came up. "I just want to be sure he's treating her right," he said defiantly. "Kendira, I mean. If she chooses him over me, well, so be it. But I want to see that he's treating her right."

Brandle looked disgusted. "What were you going to do, follow us all the way to River House and hide in the garden? You know there's no good cover for miles on the other side of the river. You'd be seen for certain— and not just by us in the rear guard. Go home, Geivian. You're only making yourself look a fool."

Nagaro had sat silently watching Geivian's face. Now, seeing the beginnings of a belligerent look, he finally spoke. "I think you should go back, too, Geivian. You'll do yourself no good this way if Kendira finds out what you've been doing. You can trust us not to tell her, and we'll also keep an eye on Groft."

"That's right," Brandle put in. "It's my duty to watch the behavior of all the young men who come on these outings."

Geivian looked uncertainly from one to the other of them. "Will you give me a report?"

Brandle's teeth flashed briefly. "It would exceed my duty to do that," he said, "but there's nothing to stop the captain from giving you one."

"You'll do that, Captain?"

Nagaro nodded. "Of course I will."

Geivian sagged a little. "Well... all right then." He turned his horse about. "Don't tell anyone you saw me— unless they have to know," he said over his shoulder, and a moment later he and his horse were a shadow disappearing under the trees.

Brandle shook his head and laughed shortly. "Can you believe he followed us all this way?" he said, though not altogether unkindly. "Love can make such a fool of a man."

Nagaro smiled ruefully. He was thinking of some of the things Rianine had said to him at the Midsummer Festival. "That's the truth," he said. "But come, we have to catch the carriage."

When they did catch up, Delvin and Orl had to be told what they'd learned. Then Brandle rode ahead to inform the sergeant while Nagaro explained briefly to Nevien and Rianine.

"Don't tell the other ladies or the guests that it was Geivian," he admonished them. If they saw or heard anything, say it turned out not to be a brigand or spy, but only a man on horseback who meant no harm."

Nevien nodded soberly. "Of course. I understand."

Rianine's teeth flashed in a feline smile. "Oh I *understand*, too," she said tartly. "A man must protect the pride of other men if he wishes to have his own pride protected. But I have no wish to see any trouble come of this, so I'll keep mum."

The rest of the journey was uneventful. Nagaro made some effort to watch Groft, but the young Leithian's behavior continued very much as before, and his mind tended to wander. The news about Simion had unsettled him. Brandle said nothing more about it as they rode, but Nagaro knew the lieutenant wasn't satisfied, only chastened by the embarrassment of not having spotted Geivian.

Chapter 17

The Lily And The Rose

Nagaro managed to exchange a glance with old Chula, who served as stableman at River House, while the horses were being tended to. Then it was into the house, where the guests milled about in the sitting room or spilled out onto the terrace. When he saw Rianine moving purposefully in his direction, he bolted back into the hallway, then up the stairs, hoping to avoid further matrimonial discourse. As he reached the second floor landing, he could hear the voices of Rianine and Lady Reineth, and their footsteps starting up the stairs behind him.

"*Bishka!*" He swore under his breath. The library was the usual destination on the second floor. The idea of discussing marriage there with Rianine while Lady Reineth stood by as chaperon— and audience— didn't appeal to him in the slightest. In desperation, he dashed past the door of the library, and pulled open the next door that presented itself, hastily stepping through and closing it behind him.

The decision was made in an instant, without any thought to what room he was entering. It was only as his feet crossed the threshold that he realized he was in the Lady Maramine's bedchamber— the room where she had died! He immediately clamped his eyes shut to avoid making matters worse, then groped for the wall to steady himself as a wave of memories washed over him.

This was the room where he'd been forced, under the grip of heskial, to witness Maramine Virden's's death. He could picture her final agony vividly... *the way she had writhed, screaming, on the bed... the king's arrival and outraged anger when Dreigen told him the woman's death couldn't be prevented... how Elgurn had smothered her with a bed pillow to end her suffering... how Dreigen had coldly felt for a pulse and dispassionately pronounced the outcome...*

Leaning against the wall, Nagaro convulsively gulped air, sucking in a breath, then letting it out again. It came out sounding like a sob. He drew another breath, almost choking. "Vothra," he gasped. "Spirit, give me strength!"

Words instantly flowed into his mind.

Death is not an end, but a path to a new beginning, and this death was long awaited. Do not think it was unwelcome, despite the manner of it.

He shook his head. "Not... unwelcome," he murmured, "but still horrible..." The pillow had cut short the escalating pain that came when the drug was withheld, but it must have added the terror of suffocation to her final seconds of agony.

Look past the horror, Spirit that calls itself Nagaro, and find the serenity.

With the Spirit's words came the memory of the Death Dream Maramine had sent to him all those years ago. He saw her figure standing before him, heard her voice— calm, gentle, and reassuring— telling him not to weep, that she would soon be joined with Vothra.

And he knew it was true, just as her spirit had foretold. Maramine *was* part of Vothra. And if the Benevolent Spirit told him that her death shouldn't trouble him so, then he ought to believe it. Determined to try, he let out a final breath and opened his eyes, forcing himself to see at what the room actually contained.

The room was the same, and not the same. All the old furniture was there, placed just as it had been, the wood stained a deep red-brown and polished to a ruddy glow. But the fabric fittings, which had been in somber shades of deep blue and storm-cloud gray, had all been replaced. The new coverlet on the bed was saffron yellow, trimmed with white and sapphire blue. The window curtains were white, as were the runners on the table, night stand, and chest of drawers, all trimmed with an embroidered pattern of blue and yellow flowers. The new rug was blue with a floral border worked in yellow, white, and green. The changes shifted the mood of the entire room from melancholy to cheerful. Even the light that entered through the window seemed brighter.

Nagaro stood for a long moment gazing in grateful astonishment at the transformation.

This must be Nevien's doing, he realized. Chula had told him that she'd redecorated the room— just as she had redecorated and transformed the horrible little room in the palace where he'd been made to sleep years ago while a slave to heskial. And here, again, her touch brought healing. He crossed the room as if in a dream, treading the sapphire carpet gently, letting the new brightness of the place push his troubling memories into the darker corners of his mind. He stood briefly at the window, which overlooked the garden, inhaling peace.

But then he shook himself. Rianine and Lady Reineth must have reached the library by now, but they probably wouldn't linger long. He should take advantage of the moment to return to the sitting room below.

What he needed, though, was something with which he could appear occupied once he got there. Something like a book. He frowned as his eyes swept the room, then brightened as he discovered a stack of books on the night stand. They must have been borrowed from the library and not yet returned.

There was no time to examine the books, so he took the bottom one, thinking it least likely to be missed. Then he went hurriedly to the door, opened it a crack, and peered out. As he had expected, the hall was empty. He left his shelter, darting past the library door. From within, Rianine's voice could be heard saying, "I really thought I saw him go up the stairs…" He made his way down those stairs as quickly and as quietly as he could.

Back in the sitting room he circumnavigated the table where a game of Oskampo was in progress, doing his best not to look at Nevien, and found a chair by the fireplace. Then, and only then, did he open the book he'd chosen. The title page proclaimed it to be *Words of Wisdom and Solace: A Personal Companion*. The title was vaguely familiar. He must have seen it in the library years before but never perused it. It wasn't the sort of thing that had interested him as a youth, though it was very much the kind of thing that Maramine would have read. Thinking of her, he felt his throat tighten as he examined it. The volume wasn't very thick, though it had fair-sized pages. It appeared to consist of quotations from the Writings along with other short passages offering inspiration or advice, all strung together with short bits of commentary authored by the anonymous compiler.

As he flipped through it, trying to appear interested, he discovered something tucked between the pages about midway through the book. Mildly curious, he pulled it out and found that it was a single sheet of fine, thin paper, folded once and a little darkened around the edges with age. Now genuinely intrigued, he unfolded the paper to reveal writing— apparently a verse— in a hand he recognized instantly as that of his Lady Guardian. Frowning, he read with growing agitation:

Dear heart, true heart, none truer that I know,
The rose is fallen. All her petals blow
Before the wind of memory, beneath the rain of tears
I shed for her, dear confidant and friend across the years.
Two flowers from a single stem were sprung,
To intertwine, one song together sung.
Across the miles between, our words have flown,
To find each other's hearts with comfort sown.
The mother lost, the sister never born,
Could not be more to me than her I mourn.
A wiser head the world may never see,
A hand more gentle, or a soul more free.

Together we had breasted hope and pain.
Now she is gone and, lonely, I remain.
Poor poet I, I struggle to compose
These lines for our memorial, the Lily and the Rose.

Nagaro blinked and brushed at the moisture that blurred his eyes, still focusing on those final words: *The Lily and the Rose...*

"She must have lost a very dear friend."

"*What?*" He started at the sound of Nevien's voice, speaking close to him, and turned to find her standing beside his chair, looking over his shoulder at the piece of paper lying open on the pages of the book.

"I'm sorry." She gave him a tight little smile. "I didn't mean to startle you. I only meant that Maramine Virden must have written that when a dear friend died. I was reading the book several months ago, looking for comfort, and I found that poem in it. Trying to puzzle out the meaning of it was a welcome distraction at the time. The hand is Maramine's. Her mother died when she was a child, so that's the 'mother lost.' And she never had a sister as far as I know, so that's the 'sister never born.' Maramine herself would be the 'Lily'— there are lilies all over her garden, after all, and not a rose in sight. Which means her friend would be the 'Rose.' Notice how she's likened to a rose in the second line. I wonder, though, who she could have been."

"I... have no idea." He was thinking of the little note he'd found, the one signed only with a drawing of a rose, but of course he dared not mention it.

Looking at Nevien and seeing the tenseness in her face and in her hand that gripped the chair arm, he felt the urgency of her desire to talk— at that moment— about anything.

"Wasn't there anything else written about it?" he asked, to keep the conversation going. "Any letters or correspondence?"

Nevien shook her head. "If the Lady Maramine kept any of her correspondence, I never found it. It's odd, too, since that bit about words flying 'across the miles between' certainly suggests letters. I thought perhaps her family had taken them."

"Perhaps..." He knew exactly where Maramine had kept her private correspondence. He knew what was there and what was not. It was so tempting to imagine that the poem eulogized his mother. He longed to slip it into his tirka and take it with him, but obviously he dared not for fear it would be missed. "Shouldn't you put the poem somewhere else," he suggested. "For safekeeping?"

Nevien's brow puckered. "I thought about it, but I think she chose specifically to put it in that book because of what the book is, and what the poem is— a memorial to her friend and to their friendship. There are other things in the book of a similar kind."

"Oh."

There was a stirring among the other guests and Nevien started and looked up. "There's the cook" she said, sounding relieved. "Our lunch must be ready for us." She bent close again, and now her eyes were haunted. "I mean to ride as soon after lunch as I can. There are so many things I need to tell you—terrible things. I tried to tell Rian, but she made me stop because she didn't want to hear any more. But I know you'll listen—"

And she was gone, as if in a hurry to have lunch be over and done with.

The other guests were rising and making for the door that led out onto the terrace.

Frowning, Nagaro re-folded the paper and tucked it back between the pages, the emotion it had engendered all but forgotten amid his rising concern for Nevien. Hurriedly closing the book, he put it down on the nearest end table and rose to follow the others— only to find Rianine suddenly beside him and pointedly taking his arm. She arched an eyebrow at him. "*Really*," she said in a voice that was obviously intended to carry, "I thought Nevien would *never* finish with you."

Realizing that whatever he said was likely to be overheard, he choked down his protests and managed to say, "I... ah... didn't want to be rude to her."

On this occasion, there was a single long table set up on the terrace. Not surprisingly, Rianine held back long enough to see which end Nevien chose to sit at and then steered Nagaro towards the other one. The best he could do was to maneuver them to seats on the opposite side of the table so he could see the princess clearly. The result was that he found himself seated between Alisset and Rianine with Groft and Kendira across the table from him. Their half of the table was presided over by Lady Reineth, seated in the end seat, while Lady Merriel occupied the seat at the other end.

Lady Reineth had no sooner settled in her chair than she launched into a discussion of the pleasantness of their journey and the attractiveness of their surroundings, just as the food began to be passed around. Nagaro did his best to appear to give his attention to the meal, letting the conversation wash over him largely unheeded. He was utterly distracted by recent events— Simion's disappearance, the mysterious poem, Nevien's desire to share her discoveries.

He was aware that Rianine, beside him, was speaking from time to time, and once or twice she prompted him for some innocuous comment. But he was caught completely off guard when he suddenly heard Clarimel say, "So, Captain, I'm sure we would all like to hear what *you* think," and realized that everyone was looking at him.

"I'm sorry," he began, feeling the blood in his face. "I'm afraid I—"

Fortunately, Rianine stepped in. "Yes, you *must* give us your opinion, Captain," she admonished. "Which are the most beautiful women, Kelorin or Leithian? We have opinions from Rees, Hendrel, and Vanhold— all quite predictable. But you have traveled the larger world."

Nagaro gave silent thanks to Rianine for this rescue, even as he balked at the absurdity of the question. His glance strayed to Nevien, who rolled her eyes, clearly indicating what she thought of it. He cleared his throat. "It doesn't seem to be a very useful question," he said. "Especially if the answer is predictable." He would have said he thought it a rather stupid question, but he didn't know who had asked it. "What do you think, Groft?" he added, hoping to hand the ball to someone else.

The young Leithian fidgeted a little as all eyes now turned to him. "I think Kelorin women and Leithian women are both beautiful," he ventured and flashed an ingratiating smile at Kendira, who smiled back adoringly.

"What, equally so?" exclaimed Vanhold.

"Well, yes, I suppose." Groft shrugged.

Clarimel flung up her hands. "How can they be equally beautiful when they're so *different?*" she demanded.

Rianine promptly waved this aside. "Groft was obviously just being diplomatic, Clarimel. He can't to be disloyal to his own kind— which is Leithian— but he has a Kelorin woman sitting beside him."

"Is that what you meant, Captain?" inquired Lady Reineth, turning to Nagaro. "That the question isn't useful because men just answer it diplomatically rather than honestly?"

"Nagaro frowned. "Partly. But even an honest answer is only one man's opinion, which is colored by what is familiar to him. Why do you ask only about Kelorin and Leithian? Why don't you include Turowan women?"

This caused a stir all around the table, though what caught Nagaro's eye was the way Nevien straightened and looked hard at him— then dropped her gaze as soon as their eyes met.

Clarimel was indignant. "Surely you can't compare them to fair-skinned folk!"

While Vanhold pounced. "Aha! The Captain has revealed his true preference!"

Nagaro ignored Clarimel and answered Vanhold's presumption. "No," he said. "I could as easily have used the example of Hashtep women. When my friend Pavo brings his wife to Lankura at the end of the summer, you'll have the opportunity of seeing an example of a Hashtep beauty."

"What are Hashtep?" asked Alisset with round-eyed curiosity.

"He means folk from the *Mahuk Baar,*" Rianine explained with obvious relish.

"Oh, surely not *them!*"

"How absurd!"

Nagaro raised his voice to speak over the storm of protests. "What I'm trying to say is that beauty isn't only one thing. There are many beautiful things in the world, and most of them are so different that it makes no sense to compare them to each other. You can't say a butterfly is more beautiful than a flower. Or a flower more beautiful than a gemstone. You can't even compare one flower to another— a lily to a rose, for example."

"Are you saying that women are like flowers or gems, Captain?" Hendrel inquired from the farther end of the table.

"In that they exhibit different kinds of beauty, yes." Nagaro frowned. "You might say that one is like a diamond and another like a pearl. The one glitters, while the other glows with a soft luster. How can you say that one is inherently more beautiful than the other? Is the opal that My Lady Princess is wearing on her finger more beautiful, because it contains every color of the rainbow? I could complain that the opal changes color with every turning of the light, while the blue stone in My Lady Reineth's pendant is more pure because it has a single hue."

Nevien had been watching him fixedly and now she blushed a little and then frowned as she fingered her opal ring. Lady Reineth merely smiled, touching the stone at her throat. "It's a sapphire," she said. "I chose it to complement my dress. Had I known that I would be coming here today, I would have worn my string of lapis lazuli instead, as being more suitable to this rustic place. But I understand what the captain means. If you say my sapphire is fairer than Lady Merriel's green tourmaline, it's only because you prefer blue to green, and another person might say the opposite."

At this, Rees spoke for the first time. "Yet we count a sapphire more precious than a pearl, and a pearl more precious than a piece of lapis."

"Only because the sapphire is the rarest of the three," Hendrel pointed out. "And the lapis the most common."

Vanhold leaned forward and turned to fix his gaze on Nagaro. "Since you used to be a pirate, I yield to your authority on the subject of gems, Captain," he said pointedly. "But you surely can't say that all women are equally beautiful."

Nagaro returned him a shrug. "Perhaps not," he conceded. "But the matter isn't simple, and judgement is very individual."

"And will you answer Lady Clarimel's question? Will you give us your individual judgement, since, as Lady Rianine pointed out, you've seen so much of the world?"

Nagaro sighed. "I've learned to see beauty in the women everywhere I've been," he said earnestly. "Sometimes it's taken a while, which is why I believe it has a lot to do with familiarity as opposed to strangeness. Really, though, I don't think physical appearance is very important."

"Of course it isn't." Lady Reineth smiled benignly. "Beauty fades with time, after all, and we would hope that love does not fade with it. The Vothrin Writings speak of a beauty of the spirit."

Nagaro nodded. "Yes, and I also think that if a man truly cares for a woman because of the beauty of her spirit, he will come to see physical beauty in her as well."

He stopped speaking under their astonished gazes and reached for his glass of sothiril to hide his embarrassment. Fortunately he was spared hearing their reactions by the arrival of the dessert. Suddenly all anyone could talk about was the crisp little biscuits with raspberry filling.

Chapter 18

A Nest Of Secrets

The air in the glade shimmered in the summer heat. Bees droned lazily among the blue and white flowers scattered in the grass, while the two horses grazed contentedly. A butterfly, bright yellow with black stripes and spots of azure, did an erratic dance against the backdrop of dark cedar trees that ringed the little circle of meadow with its tiny stream and limpid pool.

"Dreigen is a monster!"

Nevien shuddered. She was sitting stiffly beside him on the cedar-wood bench with her legs drawn up, hugging her shapa-clad knees to her chest, not touching him and not looking at him either. "I've never wanted to believe that anyone could be like that! And it's not just *what* he's done, it's the way he writes about it— so detached and cold— as if he were writing about... *swatting insects!*" She released her knees just long enough to swat at a fly with her hand.

"Then he did poison Darion, as many folk believe?"

Nagaro had arrived at the little glade about a quarter of an hour after Nevien. It was a quarter hour he had spent trying to get away from Rianine, who had made it no secret that she was trying to prevent him from rushing off immediately after Nevien and causing undesirable speculation. It was probably a sensible precaution, but he suspected the delay had contributed to Nevien's mood being so completely at odds with the peaceful summer afternoon. She was so tense and agitated that he wanted to put his arms around her. Since she also seemed to have suddenly decided to observe proprieties, the best he could do under the circumstances was to listen, and keep her talking.

"*Yes*, he killed Darion! *And* Berinar Sundorin! *And* the old man who used to take him his meals!" Nevien tightened her arms around her knees again, digging her fingernails into her calves. "You know how some folk doubt that he killed Berinar because the man wasn't taken sick until several hours after he'd left the palace? Well, that's *nothing* to Dreigen!

Dreigen has poisons that will kill a man in less than a minute, and poisons that take two days to do it— and everything in between! I thought a broom couldn't kill anyone. Do you know how he did that?" She shot Nagaro a look. "It was a powder that he had on his left glove— so he could handle anything he wanted with his right hand— and when he found the thing he wanted to poison, all he had to do was pass it into his left hand and set it down without touching it again with his right!"

Nagaro made a face. "That's... clever... I suppose—"

"*Clever?*" She shuddered again. "Oh yes, *he* thought it was! He went on about it for well over a page! Do you know that he was responsible for Gillard Marchent's madness as well? And Kale Fendred's?"

"Really?" Nagaro tried to sound surprised, though in fact he had long suspected as much.

"With Gillard, it was another one of his powders. Something that makes you see horrible things— whatever you're most afraid of. Dreigen sprinkled it on Gillard's pillow, so when he lay down at night, hewould breathe it. Then he'd wake up seeing things that weren't there. The guards kept him from hurting himself the first night, and the effect wore off during the day. But the second night they couldn't hold him, and he jumped from the third floor balcony! I suppose he was trying to get away from whatever frightful things the powder made him see."

Nevien stopped speaking and sat, biting her lip and staring unseeingly across the little meadow. Her face was deeply troubled. After a long moment, she bowed her head, and said, "I never liked Gillard. You know that. He wasn't a good man, and he was cruel to me. And I confess I was relieved to have him gone. But the *way* he died was awful! And Dreigen *gloated* over it in his journal! He wrote that Gillard would never be disrespectful to him again. Disrespectful! The man died, not for mistreating me, but for being *disrespectful* to Dreigen! And from what the journals say, being disrespectful was part of why Dreigen decided to kill the old serving man. That, and to show the man's 'masters' that he wasn't to be trifled with!"

Once again, she stopped speaking and sat still with her head up and her shoulders rigid.

Out over the meadow, the butterfly had been joined by a second of its kind. The two jewel-like creatures fluttered and danced, but Nevien's eyes weren't seeing them. Nagaro again resisted the urge to put his arm around her shoulders. "Did he say who those 'masters' were?" he asked. It was a question that led in a less disturbing direction, but also one he wanted answered.

She gave her head a tight little shake, without looking at him. "Not in what I read. But my father believes they're members of the Leithian Faction."

"The Leithian Faction." Nagaro nodded. "That makes sense. Everyone knows it was members of the Leithian Faction who presented Dreigen to Darion at the beginning of his reign." In fact, he knew that Dreigen had originally worked for Harl Sobring, but it was a fact he had learned directly from Dreigen himself and he dared not mention it. "What else did your father say?" he asked. "Rianine said you went to speak to him immediately after reading the journals."

She dropped her eyes as she gripped her legs more tightly, and it appeared that she was searching for words as she made a minute study the dusty green fabric of her shapas where it was stretched over the twin curves of her knees.

"I thoight I had so much news to tell him," she said at last in a voice that was flat, yet tense with controlled emotion. "I thought that when he heard it, it would make a difference— that something would have to be done about Dreigen." She paused to brush a strand of hair out of her eyes with a nervous flick of her hand. "But I don't think he was surprised by anything I told him! It seemed he either knew it straight out, or had guessed it long ago. He was upset— terribly upset, and angry— that I'd gone into Dreigen's chambers and read parts of his journals. He forbade me to ever do it again— as if I'd ever want to!"

She broke off, releasing her knees. Then she wrapped her arms around her body and began to rock gently, forward and back. "Reading those journals was almost the last thing Kale did before he went mad. The madness was Dreigen's way of punishing him for it. And do you know how he made Kale go mad?"

She was still rocking and her voice was rising, spiraling towards hysteria. "He knew Kale would handle his leather bookmark! So he soaked it in something horrible that goes right through the skin! The poison took several hours to work its way to the brain." She shuddered. "So Kale had time to go home, before he... before the... the madness took him. And he must have strangled his wife, after all! *And... and I... I touched the bookmark too!*"

"Nevien!" Nagaro put an urgent hand on the princess's shoulder, trying to shake her loose from her train of thought— only to have her burst into sobs and suddenly turn and fling her arms around his neck. He could feel her body shaking against his, her breath coming in gasps.

"Nevien!" he said again, laying his hands on her, gently but firmly. "It was a different bookmark! Do you hear me? He would have thrown the other one away!

"I... I... I *know!*" She gulped, still clinging to him. "But it was so *horrible*— t–touching the bookmark— after reading that! And thinking about Kale touching one just like it! *And there was what Dreigen wrote about it*— how it had worked out better than he'd hoped! And no one would ever tamper with his notebooks again... and... and— *Oh that poor woman! And poor, poor Kale!*"

He wanted to stroke her hair. To kiss away her tears. To hold her in an embrace that would go on forever— He felt himself flushing with the heat of his blood and the rising of desire.

"Nevien, I—"

"I'm sorry! I'm sorry!" She was struggling to extricate herself, seeming not to notice in her embarrassment how reluctant he was to let her go.

But he did let her go. And in an instant she was sitting apart from him again, hugging herself and not looking at him. And he was trying to find something to do with his hands.

She hung her head. "I'm so sorry, Nagaro. I promised myself I wouldn't do that."

"It's all right," he managed. "Don't worry about it."

She sniffed and wiped at her eyes. "It's just that I've been so scared ever since reading the part about Kale. It was the last thing I read, and it was all I could do to close the book properly and put it back in the right place on the shelf! I–I mean... I've lived my entire life in the palace. And I was never, in all those years, afraid to go to sleep alone in my chamber. And now it seems I've been living in a nest of terrible secrets!"

She paused to tug a handkerchief out of her sleeve and wipe her nose with it. "I always knew my father didn't tell me everything," she went on. "But I never imagined anything like this! All I can think of now at night, is how *that* man lives just down at the end of the hall and around the corner. I lie awake imagining that he might be sneaking about! Or imagining what he might be doing in that horrible room of his! Do you know he has *cages* in there— with mice, and rats, and pigeons in them? And some of them didn't look healthy at all! I wanted to let them go, but if I'd done that, he would have known someone had been there. And all Father did was tell me to try not to think about it! *How can I possibly not think about it?*"

Nagaro had by this time fully regained his equilibrium. It was Nevien's need, as much as anything, that brought him back— the thought of what she was facing. "The best way to *not* think about something is to think about something else," he said, speaking from extensive personal experience. "That's really all you can do."

She gave him a wan smile. "It must work," she said. "Since I came out of Dreigen's chambers, I don't think I've thought about my mother once! So if I want to stop thinking about Dreigen, should I think about my mother instead? Being sad seems better to me than being so afraid."

"It doesn't sound like much of a choice."

She shrugged. "No. But I suppose I'll get used to it." She squared her shoulders. "I suppose I *have* to."

Nagaro shifted uncomfortably on the bench. He knew she was strong. It was part of what he admired about her. And it was good to hear her sounding more like herself after her earlier outburst, but there was more that needed to be said. "The important thing, is that you mustn't treat Dreigen any differently. As long as you appear to show him respect and deference, he'll have no reason to harm you."

Nevien's face clouded. "Father said that too, and I know you're both right," she said. "In all these years, he's never touched me. But it isn't going to be easy— knowing what I know now about him. I don't want to be anywhere near the man!"

Nagaro swallowed and looked away. How could he expect her to do something he doubted he could do himself? He struggled for something to offer her and found the answer in her own words. "Do you remember what you told me once?" he asked. "About how Dreigen's birth was the result of a cruel rape? You said you felt sorry for him because he couldn't feel anything. Very likely his father was the same way, and Dreigen just inherited the trait. As horrible as the man is, it may not be entirely his fault."

He looked back, and saw that her expression had turned thoughtful. She bit her lip. "*Yes*, that's true..." she said. "If I can just remember that... And maybe it won't be for very long. After all, Father says Dreigen is getting old, and he won't live forever. And he has no ambition beyond his lore and his studies— no lust for power. If we can just wait him out, give him what he wants for his work, and leave him alone... maybe he'll leave us alone. And if the Leithians find another go-between to take him his dinner, we won't be having him in the Great Hall anymore—"

"The Leithians!" Nagaro straightened with a jerk. "I almost forgot about them! Dreigen may have no ambition for himself, but what do the Leithians want with him?"

Nevien wearily passed a hand across her eyes. "I don't know. Father said he'd always assumed the Leithian Faction had access to Dreigen— had some influence with him— but that what I witnessed in the hallway that night was the most direct evidence he'd ever had of how it works. He also said it was a relief to know that the Leithians have to *buy* Dreigen's services by supplying him with things— that he doesn't favor their cause, and that they don't always get his cooperation."

Nagaro frowned. "Now that your father knows what they're doing, is he going to do anything about it?"

Nevien hunched her shoulders and looked at the ground. "There's not much he *can* do. It's been going on since before he became king, and the Leithian Faction still has a lot of power."

Nagaro felt his indignation rise. "But some of this surely involves the illegal trade I was sent to investigate! If I'm right, they've been dealing in a drug the Jinari have declared an abomination!" An alarming thought crossed his mind. "When you heard Dreigen and the old man talking, did they happen to mention something called—" he swallowed "— *heskial?*"

"*Heskial?*" She stared at him. "*Heskial...*" Suddenly her eyes went wide. "Do you know," she said, "I think Dreigen *did* say that word! I couldn't remember it exactly afterwards, because it's unfamiliar. But it was something like that."

"What did he say about it? What was the context?"

She smiled tightly. "*That* I do remember. He said he wouldn't help them any more with it if they didn't get him what he wanted."

"Then Dreigen didn't want it for himself?"

She shook her head. "No. He wanted something else. Something called still-heart root powder— or something like that. I remember something else too," she added, with a catch of excitement in her voice. "He said that if he wrote anything down about the thing he was helping them with, he'd have to use a *code*. That would make sense if it was something being traded illegally."

Nagaro stared past her across the sunlit glade. Warm though it was, he felt a chill. *Still-heart root... Did that still the heart, perhaps? And the Brothers of the Blood had been getting Dreigen's help with heskial...* He shook himself. At least it didn't sound as if the heskial was making its way into the palace. He didn't need to fear for Nevien in *that* way...

"Nagaro? What's the matter?"

When he turned to look at her, he found that she was searching his face with her eyes. He ran a hand through his hair. "Do you remember what we saw at the Midsummer Festival?" he asked.

"You mean when Lord Madred's minister, Torlung, exchanged things with Dreigen?"

He nodded. "And before that, I saw Lothard talking to Torlung. And you've just told me that Dreigen has been helping someone with heskial. It's not what I'd call *proof*, but when you consider that the illegal trade is traceable to the Leithian Houses of Hurn, Furthing, and Sobring, it's pretty clear what's been going on. If your father is serious about stopping the illegal trade— and he sent a letter to Jinara to that effect— I don't see how he can do it without confronting the lords of those houses— and exposing Dreigen's involvement, for that matter."

Nevien sighed. "He won't do anything openly," she said. "He may let them know that he knows what they're doing, and that he doesn't approve of it. But it will all be done in back rooms, behind closed doors. And how much effect it will have, I couldn't say."

Nagaro shifted uneasily. "Does your father ever try to make use of Dreigen's knowledge, himself?"

Nevien frowned. "No. I asked him about that, and he said he hasn't been— not for many years. He said that a long time ago he did try to use Dreigen once, but it all went wrong. He said the man is too unpredictable— too hard to control— and that he has no honor or scruples of any kind."

Nagaro shivered. He thought he knew *exactly* how things had gone wrong for Elgurn. *If the king regretted that... if the man had learned enough wisdom not to try to use Dreigen...* "I should think he would want to be rid of the man," he said, thinking aloud. "Get him out of the palace, no matter what the Leithian Faction might say."

Nevien was studying her hands where they rested on her knees. "It isn't just the Leithians, Nagaro," she said quietly. "I think my father might stand up to the Leithians if that's all it was. But he believes any effort to dismiss Dreigen would bring some reprisal from Dreigen himself. He's *afraid* of Dreigen— terrified of what that man might do if he was threatened removal from the palace. And Father has reason to be afraid, Nagaro. He told me that Kale wanted to get rid of Dreigen. It's why he was reading Dreigen's journals, to find proof of his crimes!"

Nagaro felt a stone drop into his stomach. The image came vividly into his mind of the first day of his enslavement with heskial. He had watched while Kale, sitting across the table from him, had opened one of Dreigen's notebooks and read some of what was written there, some of the most recent entries. He'd seen the look on the man's face— extreme distaste verging on horror.

So poor, honest, right-minded Kale had wanted to put a stop to such horrors— to see justice done, perhaps. *And he had paid.*

He looked away. "I see," he said, swallowing to moisten a mouth that had gone dry as dust. He believed there might be a cure for Kale's condition, but he dared not mention it now. It would raise too many questions. *And what would Dreigen do to anyone who tried to use that cure?* He tried to put that thought out of his mind.

He was intensely grateful that Nevien clearly hadn't read any of the things he had watched Kale read that day, or any of the other descriptions of the 'experiments' Dreigen had performed on Leyel Virden— or on the gentle Lady Maramine. There'd been more than enough horrors revealed to her already without that. He dreaded to think what Nevien's reaction might be if she ever learned the full truth— considering the sympathy she'd already voiced for her simple-minded first husband.

And Nagaro realized that she might also look at him with clearer vision... see through the veneer of his disguise... He mustn't let that happen. She must never know—

"I know that my father has been trying to protect me by keeping me in ignorance," Nevien murmured. "I'm trying to forgive him for that."

Nagaro flinched at the interruption of his thoughts. "I think you should forgive him," he said, and was surprised to find that he meant it.

She turned a thoughtful gaze upon him. "You tried to protect me too by telling me I shouldn't go into Dreigen's rooms— that it was too dangerous— even though reading his journals for myself was the only thing that would have convinced me you were right about him. And you *were* right. About everything."

"I just didn't want you to come to any harm."

"Of course not," she said earnestly. "And I *would* have come to harm, if you hadn't gone after him and delayed him. He would have caught us. Rianine would have tried to warn me, of course, as soon as she saw him at the top of the stairs, and I could have tried to put the journals back. But we could never have gotten away from the room in time. He would have known we had been there. It was very brave of you to go after him."

He stared at her. "I'm not brave at all when it comes to Dreigen," he confessed. "Not compared to you, Nevien. I fainted from fright. Didn't Rianine tell you that she found me on the floor? He put his finger on my chest, right over my heart— to drive home his point— and I panicked."

But she shook her head at him. "You had to be very brave indeed if you were *that* afraid. And it *might* have been more than panic. I can't tell you how relieved I was to see you this morning—looking perfectly well— after what happened. I was so afraid he'd done something to you! But I don't understand how you knew enough to be so afraid of Dreigen just from speculations in the history books. You're not one to judge a man by appearances." She frowned. "Is there something else you know about him?"

Vothra! He looked hastily away, his gaze fleeing from her even as his body remained rooted to the bench. *She mustn't guess!* He could feel her staring at him. *Idiot! Say something!* But he couldn't bring himself to lie to her outright. In desperation, he took refuge in telling part of the truth, the most distracting and misleading part.

"Someone I cared about died because of Dreigen," he said huskily.

"Someone you cared about? But *how?* Dreigen never leaves the palace!"

"It was a long time ago. There... was a time when he did." He still wasn't looking at her. "I don't want to talk about it. It wouldn't do you any good to know."

"Of course, of course! I'm sorry, Nagaro." Suddenly she had her arms around him, giving him a quick squeeze and just as quickly letting go. "You don't need to say any more."

Relief flooded through him, but it was relief tinged with guilt. He'd successfully steered her clear of the truth, but only by misleading her—much as he'd done that day in the carriage with her and Merriel. *But it had to be done. He didn't really have a choice.*

Feeling a need to escape from the moment, he stood up, giving her a forced smile and a glance that didn't quite connect with hers. "Come on," he said. "Let's forget about Dreigen and the Leithians and who you're going to have to marry. Let's just ride!"

"All right!" She laughed as if trying to dispel the shadows, and followed him as he strode across the meadow to where the horses grazed.

Moments later they were under the cedar trees, where they paused only long enough to mount. From astride her white mare, Nevien gave him a crooked smile. "Do you know?" she said, "I don't believe I've thought about my marriage these last few days, either."

"I'm sorry." He frowned as he urged Thunder-Heels into the lead along the path under the trees. "I shouldn't have reminded you."

"It's all right. Ferenan is much less frightening than Dreigen."

He reined in, slowing the big gray, feeling as if something had just struck him in the chest. "Is it... to be Ferenan, then?"

"Yes." She'd drawn up beside him. "It's been decided. Father only needs to make the announcement."

"Ferenan." He couldn't bring himself to look at her. "He scarcely even tries to look as if he's courting you!"

Nevien laughed lightly. "That's because he has about as much enthusiasm for it as I have. At least it should be an easy marriage. He already has grown children— heirs, to inherit. He won't want much from me."

Nagaro gave Thunder-Heels an angry squeeze with his legs. The horses' hooves splashed across the little stream as they broke out from under the trees and turned along the watercourse that wended its way back towards the road. The sun-washed day seemed dark around him. *Nevien in another loveless marriage!* It was impossible to dislike Ferenan, or to blame him, but that didn't make it any easier to bear. *Lokundas was so cruel!* "There must be someone better than that," he muttered under his breath. "Someone who cares at least a *little*."

"Like who, for instance?"

He hadn't intended her to hear, but apparently she had. She had urged her own horse forward and was riding beside him again, giving him a wry glance.

"I don't know." He struggled to explain himself. "Someone you care about a little, too, maybe—" He cast about and seized upon the only unmarried male he could think of who seemed to be any sort of friend to the princess. "What about Kuran?"

"*Kuran?*" She sounded almost horrified. "Oh no, Nagaro, not Kuran! I've known him since I was a little girl. It would be like... like marrying my uncle! Besides," she added. "I couldn't spoil Merriel's hopes."

"*Merriel's hopes?*" His hand jerked the reins again at this non sequitur, causing Thunder-Heels to toss his head. And then understanding dawned and astonishment displaced all other thoughts. "Lady Merriel has her eye on *Kuran?*"

"Now I've done it!" Nevien sounded chagrined. "And I promised her I wouldn't tell anyone."

He turned in the saddle to stare at her. "Has she said anything to him? He was imagining Merriel and Kuran standing side by side, and he rather liked the picture. They had both lost spouses to the plague, years ago, and... well, why not?

Nevien looked faintly exasperated. "Of *course* not," she said, shaking her head. "She's much too proper a Leithian woman to do anything so forward. Instead she's worked her way up to praying to the gods that Kuran will find a new wife— and hoping it might be her."

"But that won't do! She should *say* something to him— or get someone else to drop him a hint. He probably has no inkling, and he might very well like the idea if he only knew she was interested."

Nevien sighed. "Actually, I agree," she said. "But that isn't the Leithian way."

By this time they had passed through a final stand of trees and emerged onto the road. Nagaro reined to a halt. "Thank goodness *I* haven't promised not to tell anyone," he muttered, as he looked left and right, considering the two directions they might go.

Nevien brought her mare up beside him. "I should make you promise—"

"No, you shouldn't! And if you don't try, I won't have to refuse. I wouldn't mention it to anyone but Kuran, and I can truthfully say I found out by accident. And I wouldn't just blurt it out, either. I'd wait for the right moment." He turned his horse decisively to the right. "Come on! I'll race you to the end of the road."

Chapter 19

What Geivian Saw

It was a wild, breathless gallop to where the road ran out in a little stand of ancient oak trees beside the river. Several paths ran on from that point in various directions and Nagaro would have liked to go "exploring," but the afternoon was advancing. So they let the horses breathe and splash and slake their thirst at the river's edge, before turning about for another good canter back along the rutted, shade-dappled road. They were very nearly at the bridge when they met Brandle, riding towards them so fast that they all had to come careening to a halt to avoid a collision.

"*Here* you are!" Brandle exclaimed exasperatedly while he was still hauling on the reins. "Kroneg's Blood! You two will cost me my posting—or worse! I tried to give you a little privacy, and when I came back, you weren't where I'd left you! So I went all the way back to the house looking for you, and then all the way back here again!"

"I'm sorry, Lieutenant." Nevien was flushed from the excitement of the ride. A moment before, she'd been laughing for pure joy, but now her eyes were serious and her tone contrite. "We just rode to the end of the road and back."

"It was my idea," Nagaro put in apologetically. "We were talking about such serious things that I felt we needed to lighten our mood."

Brandle looked from one to the other of them, and sagged. "Well, all right," he said, then added, "But I want you to come at once. Geivian's here. He says he's seen Simion, and that it looks like he's in trouble." He wheeled his horse about and set his heels to its flanks without waiting for a response, setting off at a rapid trot.

"Geivian here?" Nevien urged her mare forward to bring her abreast of Brandle's mount. "I thought you sent him back to Lankura."

"And what did he see?" Nagaro maneuvered Thunder-Heels into position on Brandle's other side.

The big Leithian pressed his horse into a canter. "He went back by a different road, and passed a carriage with Simion inside. But I'll let him tell it."

"How does he happen to know Simion?" Nagaro asked breathlessly over the drum of the hooves.

"They're cousins— used to be playmates when they were boys! Enough talk. Just ride!"

They found Geivian in the stable yard, sitting sitting on one of the hitching rails while his horse appreciatively munched mouthfuls of hay from a fork-full that had been tossed onto the ground beside the water trough. Delvin and Groft were hitching up the carriage horses while the rest of the guardsmen were saddling the other mounts.

Nagaro, Brandle, and Nevien all dismounted and converged on Geivian, who slid off the hitching rail and came to meet them. The three horses were left to find their own way to the water.

"It was a covered carriage— all the windows tightly curtained," Geivian explained in response to their questions. "There were four armed Leithians escorting it, wearing white and black livery with purple baldrics."

"Grimbold's colors!" Brandle and Nagaro spoke at once.

Geivian nodded. "I thought so," he murmured, then resumed his tale. "I reined my horse right over to the side to let the carriage pass and that's when I saw him. One of the curtains was twitched aside and almost immediately jerked back. It was only for a second, but I had a clear view and I'm sure it was him. I could see he hadn't shaved for several days, and he looked scared."

Nagaro and Brandle exchanged grim glances. Simion unshaven was definitely not normal.

"Where was this?" Brandle asked. "Which way were they going?"

"The carriage was northbound on the North Road. I rode on by, going south— the way I'd been going— but as soon as I dared, I turned around and followed them."

Brandle frowned at this. "I hope you did a better job of not being spotted than you did this morning," he said sharply.

Geivian looked hurt. "I was careful!" he protested. "I stayed well back, and it's wooded country. There was plenty of cover."

"That's good, Geivian," Nagaro put in, with a chiding glance at Brandle. "I'm sure you did your best, and that's all anyone can ask."

"All right then." Brandle spoke more kindly. "Where did they go? Have they taken him to Sobring Hall? That's one place that's up the North Road."

But Geivian shook his head. "They turned off of the North Road before they got there, and I thought it best not to follow any farther. A local farmer told me the road they turned into was one that leads into Sobring Wood. It was wild-looking country, and the man said there'd been highwaymen about besides."

Nagaro started a little on hearing the name of Sobring Wood and covered it by reaching up to scratch his ear.

Nevien turned to him. "Has this got anything to do with that illegal trading we were talking about?" she asked.

"Very possibly, since Simion knew about it. But I don't know exactly how this kidnaping may be connected."

"Well whether it's connected or not, kidnaping is a serious matter," she observed. "Will his family be willing to make a claim against the House of Sobring, Lieutenant, if there is strong evidence that members of that House, or their agents, are holding him?"

Brandle was standing with his head down, nervously chewing a thumbnail. "I think so," he said. "Maybe not publicly, since the House of Sobring is pretty powerful. But Simion's family name is Rudrin. It's a well-respected merchant family. The Rudrins do have some standing in Lankura."

"What would qualify as strong evidence?" Geivian asked.

Nevien answered him. "What you saw probably isn't good enough by itself, but it's a start. One or two more reliable witnesses—"

"—such as officers of the Fleet, or of the Palace Guard." Brandle finished for her. He frowned. "Blast it! I can't go after them right now. I've already missed time today, and the princess's party should have a full escort."

Nagaro squinted at the sky. "There are probably still three hours of daylight at this season," he said. "That's not very much time, but it would probably serve for Geivian to show me the way to this road they turned down, if he's willing."

Geivian drew himself up. "I'd be glad to, Captain."

Nagaro nodded his thanks, then turned back to Brandle. "Then you and I could go back when you're free, and there's more time, to see what we can find."

Brandle was still frowning, but he nodded. "I guess that's the best we can do." He squared his shoulders. "Everyone should get ready to mount up." He turned away and began giving orders to the other guardsmen.

Nevien sighed. "I'll go tell the women to get ready," she said, and turned away also, though not before she gave Nagaro one last glance filled with understanding and sympathy for his friend's plight. "The Gods speed you," she said over her shoulder. Then she was gone, moving in the direction of the house.

Nagaro let his breath out in a long sigh and looked about for Thunder-Heels and the white mare, Snowdrift. He stopped short when he discovered that Groft had come up behind him. He frowned. *Had the man overheard any of the conversation? And was it any concern if he had?*

The young Leithian's face at that moment, however, was a picture of startled innocence. He took an apologetic step backward. "I beg your pardon, Captain," he said deferentially. "I wanted to talk to you for a moment."

"Well? What about, then?" Nagaro's impatience caused him to speak more shortly than usual.

"Oh, well," Groft looked at the ground and scuffed at the dirt with one boot. "It's... ah... about Kendira."

"Kendira?" Nagaro was momentarily mystified.

"Yes. I, ah, understand that you were courting her at one time. I wanted to be sure I wasn't, well, stepping on your toes, so to speak. You have quite a reputation." The young Leithian finished and stood waiting with the air of one who has just stuck his hand into an animal's den and is waiting to see if he'll get bitten.

"Is that all?" Nagaro almost laughed. "I spent some time trying to decide whether I wanted to court her and decided that she and I were not well suited to one another. You needn't worry on my account." He might have said that Groft ought rather to worry about Geivian, but he doubted that would help Kendira's other suitor. Geivian must seem much less intimidating.

"Ah. I see. Thank you." Groft looked relieved. Then, before Nagaro could excuse himself, he added, "Is something amiss, Captain? It seems that you and the Lieutenant have just gotten some bad news."

Nagaro frowned in annoyance, but Groft's expression appeared innocently interested and solicitous. Most likely he'd just read their faces and gestures from a distance. Cautious truth was usually the best response.

"There's a man who's been missing, and our news suggests he may be in trouble."

"A man? You mean the lieutenant's *friend?*"

Nagaro didn't entirely like the knowing and faintly indulgent tone that had accompanied the last word. "I have reason to count him as a friend also," he responded, somewhat stiffly.

Groft's eyebrows shot up. "Your friend... *too?*" he stammered.

Nagaro's teeth flashed in his best pirate smile. "He was one among the slaves at the Straight of Jaamra. One who wielded a sword that day when we won our freedom."

This time he was gratified to see that the young Leithian looked embarrassed.

"I beg your pardon, Captain." Groft spoke hastily and made a little bow. "I imagine something like that must create a sense of, ah... *comradery.*"

"You might say that." Nagaro smiled his smile again. "And now I have things to attend to."

***

Less than half an hour later, Nagaro and Geivian were turning off of the familiar north-south running road that led to Averwin. Nagaro had taken little more than idle note of the turning on previous visits to River House, and had never considered where it might lead. In answer to his inquiry, Geivian shrugged. "It runs more or less west, and eventually connects to the North Road," he explained."It does wind around some, but it's the shortest way I know."

They had left River House quietly, before the other guests had even emerged into the stable yard. Nagaro thought this was just as well, since it saved them the trouble of making any explanation. Brandle planned simply to tell the others that there had been a messenger and that Nagaro had been called away on some private errand of his own. Prior to Nagaro's question about the turning, they had ridden in silence, pressing the horses as hard as they dared. The question having been answered, they continued in silence until they paused briefly to let the horses rest a little and drink from a stream that flowed beside the road. Here Geivian again broke the silence.

Standing and holding his horse's bridle while the animal drank, he looked up at Nagaro, who had already re-mounted, and hesitantly asked, "So, Captain, what can you tell me about how Groft has been behaving?"

Nagaro felt a small twinge of guilt, knowing that he'd spent a large part of the afternoon with Nevien in places where he hadn't been able to keep an eye on Groft. "I'm afraid I didn't make a very close study of it," he confessed. "But I saw nothing one could take offense at. He seems a pleasant enough young man— if a bit superficial in his thinking." He rather doubted that Kendira was looking for depth, but decided not to say so. As it was, he still felt a pang on seeing Geivian's disgruntled look.

"And Kendira is... happy with him?" There was still a trace of hope in Geivian's voice, overlying a deeper vein of resignation.

"She seems so." *Smitten would be a more accurate word for it.* "But she hasn't known him very long, Geivian. Her mind could change after she's seen more of him. He might say or do something that puts her off."

For several seconds, Nagaro watched hope and guilt at war on Geivian's face before the young Kelorin hastily turned away and busied himself with mounting his horse. Once in the saddle, he led the way back onto the road and they set off once more at a trot.

Nagaro maneuvered Thunder-Heels so that they were riding stirrup to stirrup. "I think I know how you feel," he said in as low a voice as would be heard over the clip of hooves and jingle of harness. "You want her to be happy, but you'd rather she was happy with you."

Geivian shot him a grateful glance. After posting on for several more strides, he said, "I just wish I knew what to do."

Nagaro sighed. "There's nothing much you *can* do— except make sure that your own behavior is exemplary. That way, she'll find herself thinking well of you if she should turn away from him."

Geivian gave a sad little shake of his head. "If only I was a better dancer," he said morosely. "She was starting to teach me, you know, but I learn so *slowly*. I just don't have much talent for it. Not like you. Or Groft."

"Talent or not, practice can't hurt, Geivian, and it would be something to keep you occupied."

"But now I have no one to teach me, or to practice with!"

Nagaro sighed. This was an undeniable difficulty. He rode on for a little ways, and a thought struck him. "I'll wager Rianine could teach you."

"*Rianine?*" Geivian reined in abruptly, dropping from trot to walk, and turned Nagaro a look of utter dismay. "Not the tiger lady!"

Nagaro also drew rein. "The *tiger lady?*" He stared at Geivian in astonishment. The other man's expression of complete consternation was so comical that he nearly burst out laughing. "Do people call her that?"

"I... that is..." Geivian stammered. "Some people do. I've heard it, but I really shouldn't have repeated it. I was actually paired with her— at the match table— back at the beginning. But it lasted less than two months. She seemed to enjoy making me squirm."

Nagaro grinned. "Don't take it personally." he said. "She enjoys making everybody squirm, and 'tiger lady' is so perfect! I'll have to tell her. I'm sure she'll be gratified. But really she's not so bad when you get to know her— if she lets you. She can be quite decent when she wants to be."

Geivian looked doubtful. "I don't know, Captain. I suppose she's different with you. Since you've tamed her."

This time Nagaro did laugh, but he sobered again quickly. "No one tames Rianine," he said seriously. "Except Rianine. If she wants to help you out of the goodness of her heart, she will. And I would never send you into her clutches without first being confident that she was going to be decent to you."

"Well… all right, I guess." Geivian didn't sound entirely convinced, but he obviously had too much respect for Nagaro to say so. He urged his horse back to a trot. Nagaro squeezed Thunder-Heels' flanks to follow.

"I suppose," Geivian added, "that a man like you must prefer a woman with a bit of fire. That's probably why you didn't get on with Kendira. She's so timid and sweet."

A bit of fire? That was amusing. Nagaro grimaced inwardly and decided it was best to let his silence be taken for agreement.

They rode on again briskly but without speaking, passing through open country that was dominated by gentle, rolling hills, liberally sprinkled with large boulders and small thickets of thorn bushes. The areas that were in use were given over mostly to grazing land, with here and there a dwelling or a small farm nestled in a hollow. There were few folk to be seen, and almost none on the road. Most were at such a distance that they appeared as small dots. It was possibly part of the old Loros Wared, and Nagaro thought this might have contributed to the sparseness of the population. Still, there was a gentle haze that softened the harshness of the landscape. And everything was awash in the warm golden light of a late summer afternoon, lending a certain charm to a land that might otherwise have seemed forlorn and desolate.

As they rode on and the sun sank lower, the land began to change. Trees began to appear and to become increasingly common as they progressed. The hills became gradually more rugged, and the tide of golden light that flowed out of the west was interrupted more and more frequently by swatches of violet shadow. At last they reached the North Road and turned onto it, going to the right, which was northward.

As they continued, Nagaro began to understand what Geivian had meant when he'd called it wild country. The landscape was more wooded than otherwise, and the land itself was becoming ever more deeply folded. The ridges of the hills rose steeply, with prominent outcrops of dark gray stone like huge buttresses. The valleys were deeply cut. Farms were infrequent, being restricted to the rare land that wasn't too steep, and any pastures there were had been carved out by clearing patches of the ancient trees and tangled undergrowth.

There would have been many more shadows here even at noontide, and now those shadows were lengthening as the sun descended towards the western sea beyond the hills. The result was that, increasingly, the two men found themselves riding in a deepening gloom that weighed upon their spirits. They spoke only occasionally and their scant conversation was now entirely focused on the location of the road that Geivian had seen the carriage turn onto several hours before.

"I hope we find it soon." Nagaro looked about him as Geivian pulled his horse to a halt after rounding a bend in the road. "The daylight won't last much longer here."

The road, at that stretch, ran along the bottom of a deep valley. Everything around them was in shadow.

Geivian was intently scanning their surroundings. "Actually, we're almost there," he said, "if I don't mistake myself. I remember this great rock that nearly beetles over the road. And that little farmhouse among the trees across the way, where you can see the light in the window, would be where the man lives who told me the road led to Sobring Wood. I came around that bend behind us just in time to see the carriage turn off of the roadway and into the trees up ahead. There, on the left."

Nagaro considered the landmarks, such as they were. The huge outcropping of rock was the best marker. It thrust out of the steeply sloping hillside on the right-hand side of the road, not far beyond the bend they had rounded. The nearer end of it stood a dozen feet high and did very nearly overhang the road, while the farther end disappeared among the trees. Some of the trees, being rooted higher on the slope, were tall enough to overarch it with their boughs. "All right, then," he said. "Show me the road to Sobring Wood."

Geivian led the way forward about fifty yards and slowed his horse to a walk, searching the ground and the trees along the left-hand side of the road with his eyes. "It should be here... somewhere..." he muttered. "There! No, wait... Yes! Yes, that's it!"

The road that Geivian indicated was no more than a pair of well-worn wheel-ruts with weeds growing in the space between them. It would have been easier to see if the daylight had been brighter, but it would have been easily missed even then since it plunged immediately into the shadows under the trees. Raising his eyes, Nagaro could see that it apparently ran into a narrow, densely wooded valley that joined the wider valley traversed by the North Road.

He cleared his throat. "Well, I'm certainly glad I have you to show it to me. I would never have found it otherwise."

Geivian nodded. "I'm sure this is the place. I marked it well."

Nagaro turned his horse around, scanning the road, the trees, and the wooded hillsides. "Are we close to Sobring Hall, do you think?" he asked.

"It can't be far. I never saw a marker for the border, but I know we must be in Sobring Hold by now. The hall is farther on, along this road. It could be only a few miles."

Nagaro was still gazing northward along the road. Abruptly he started. "Did you see something move, there, among the trees?" he asked, pointing.

"Where?" Geivian turned his mount and followed Nagaro's outstretched hand.

At that moment, three men quietly stepped out of the trees at exactly the point Nagaro had indicated.

"*Vothra!*" Geivian sounded alarmed. "The farmer said there were highwaymen!"

The men were less than fifty feet away. They were big, burly men, roughly clad. From what Nagaro could see of their coloring in the waning light, they appeared to be Leithians. They also were armed with swords and long knives, and the way they moved was distinctly menacing.

"We should just ride away," Nagaro said in a low voice. "They're on foot. They'll never catch us." He twisted in the saddle to look behind him and immediately swore. "*Keshaal!*"

A row of four horsemen barred the south-bound road not a dozen yards from where their horses stood.

"*By the Eyes!* Where did they come from?" Geivian had half turned his horse and twisted his neck to look behind him.

Nagaro tightened his reins, causing Thunder-Heels to dance, turning the big gray to stand athwart the roadway so that his horse and Geivian's stood shoulder to shoulder, facing in opposite directions. His mind was racing. The horsemen were cast from the same mold as the three unmounted men in every respect except that they were mounted. There was no reason not to assume that all seven men were working together. It was late. He and Geivian had seen no other travelers on the road for several miles. A shout for help might be heard by the farmer whose lighted window they had seen, but the man was unlikely to be able to give much assistance even if he were inclined to come to the aid of strangers.

Geivian, wore a sword, and Nagaro knew he had some skill with it, having sought to wield it in support of Kenthos. But he wasn't a trained military man and Nagaro knew nothing of his mettle in a fight. *In any case, two against seven wasn't good odds.*

Both groups of men had begun to advance, closing in on their quarry. Some had drawn their weapons, and now one of the riders spoke. "Well, well, *well*," he drawled. "What have we here, lads? Looks like a pair o' fine gentlemen. Do they have fine purses, d' ye think?"

"They have fine *horses*," one of the others put in, leering.

"Aye, that they do. A pair o' fine horses for two of our lads what's got none."

"*Captain!*" Geivian hissed. His horse was dancing now, too, under the tenseness of its rider's hand on the reins. "*What are we going to do?*"

Nagaro leaned towards him, speaking low out of the side of his mouth. "Stay close to me, and be ready to move fast! I'm going to try to drive through the riders. If you see a chance to get clear, take it."

The horseman who had spoken first, a particularly big man with a crooked nose whose bearing suggested he was the leader, was getting quite close. He had his sword in his hand and he was smiling most unpleasantly.

The rider next to him, a slim young man with an incipient mustache, seemed to be holding back. "I don't know about this, Grobend," he said uneasily. "I think one o' them might be Captain Nagaro."

"Nagaro the pirate?" The big man sneered. "What would *he* be doing here?

"I—I've heard what he's supposed t' look like. And he's supposed to ride a big gray horse!"

"Pawh!" Grobend spat. "You're a milk-livered ninny, Tolbert. By the Mark! There's just two o' them an' seven of us, and I don't care what ye've heard." The big man shifted his grip on his sword. "*At em' lads!*" He spurred forward, and the other horsemen followed, even the one called Tolbert, who came on a fraction of a second after the rest.

Nagaro had already turned Thunder-Heels to face the advancing horsemen. He was awaiting his moment, knowing that success would depend greatly on catching his adversary by surprise. His focus never left the four riders, though he was aware of Geivian. The young Kelorin was on his right-hand side, stirrup to stirrup, as the highway came at them.

Nagaro hissed, "*Now!*" and squeezed the gray stallion's flanks, giving the horse his head. At the same time, and in one swift movement, he drew his sword. He drove straight at the one called Grobend, praying that Geivian would stay close and not be cut off.

Grobend's face registered surprise for only a second before the expression was transformed into an exultant snarl. The man swung his sword, only to find it met by steel where there had been no steel an instant before. The sharp metallic ring of blade on blade shattered the still air.

Beside Grobend, the man named Tolbert hesitated, jerking his reins reflexively, checking his horse's speed a little, creating a gap. Geivian drove his mount towards it with a cry. His sword rang against Tolbert's as he shot through.

Shouts of rage erupted on both sides as the other two riders closed in on Thunder-Heels. Nagaro's sword was a blur— parrying Grobend's second thrust, sending another man's blade spinning away, then slicing more than the air—

With a cry and an oath, Grobend dropped his weapon, clutching at his sword arm where already dark blood was staining his shirt-sleeve. Nagaro swept past the brigand leader, his sword still in his hand. Geivian was before him, waiting, his horse dancing.

"*Go! Go!*" Nagaro's heels spurred the gray stallion into a full gallop. Geivian gave a wild shout that was nearly a scream as he spun his horse to follow. An instant later, they were pounding down the road together in the gathering twilight, Thunder-Heels in the lead, Geivian's mount struggling valiantly to keep up. Oaths and shouted curses followed them, but nothing more.

It was long after sunset by the time Nagaro and Geivian reached Lankura, and they were both bone weary. Nagaro sent the obviously drooping Geivian home, while he himself went immediately to the palace to seek out Brandle in his quarters and give him a report of what they had learned. This took some time, much of it expended in arguing the virtues of caution and patience with the understandably distraught Leithian.

When he returned at last to the Fleet Compound, Nagaro found Taru and Pavo waiting anxiously for him on the little porch outside the door of his quarters. Inside, he found two notes that had been slipped under his door. The first was a message from Kuran requesting his presence in the Fleet Lord's study the following day at the second hour of the morning. This wasn't particularly unusual, and Nagaro was grateful for it because it would give him a chance to talk to Kuran about Simion.

The second note was something completely different. It took Nagaro a moment to recognize the close, tidy writing on the outside of the sealed message, which said simply: *Number 14, Captain's Row, The Fleet Compound.* Then his heart jumped and he hastily broke the seal and opened it.

"It's from Master Fineas," he explained excitedly to his friends. "With everything that's happened, I'd almost forgotten that I should be looking for word from him." He opened the note and read:

Zirda: The headache medicament you requested is available at your earliest convenience. —F, Apothecary.

Taru was reading over his shoulder. "Headache *me-di-ca-ment?*" he asked.

"It must be the linjana." Nagaro did his best to suppress his elation. After all, having the linjana in his hand and being in position to use it were two very different things. "I told Fineas to keep my request in close confidence, so he's being careful not to give too much away with his wording. It's quite clever, really. Anyone else reading this wouldn't think it was anything important or mysterious."

"Will you go tonight to get it?" Pavo inquired.

Nagaro let his breath out in a long sigh. "No, I'm too tired," he said. "Let's get some dinner and I'll tell you about my day's adventures while we eat. If I go to bed early, I should be able to rise early enough tomorrow to make a visit to the apothecary shop before meeting Kuran."

Chapter 20

Master Fineas' Medicament

Nagaro rose at dawn the next morning after a night of the sound slumber reserved for the truly weary. He breakfasted on the previous night's left over bread and some hastily brewed sothiril, donned his cloak, and went to the Fleet stable where he arrived before any of the stablemen had made their appearance. Walking to the apothecary shop was out of the question this time because he didn't want to keep Kuran waiting. On the other hand, Thunder-Heels was too well known in the city with him in the saddle. Accordingly, he chose a nondescript brown gelding that stood in docile boredom while Nagaro buckled on saddle and bridle and swung astride. Out in the compound, the morning was cool, with a light mist, and the guard at the Fleet's gatehouse noted his passing with barely a raised eyebrow.

Nagaro rode through the streets with his hood up and his head down, at a pace calculated not to draw attention. Fortunately, the few folk abroad at that hour mostly didn't give him a second glance. Depending on how long his business took, he might well have to ride faster on his return journey. By then there would be more people about, and he might hope to lose himself in the traffic. For now, hurrying would only make it more likely that Master Fineas' shop would still be closed when he reached it.

His thoughts were on Kuran's investigation as he rode. He wanted to believe that Simion's plight wasn't related to the illicit trade with Jinara, but he was finding it increasingly difficult. And the knowledge that he was the one who had involved Simion in the investigation was preying on his mind. He also worried that Fineas might become more entangled in the affair as well.

By the time he reached the entrance to Brass Bell Lane, the mist had burned away, the air was clear as crystal, and the number of passers-by in the wider adjoining street had significantly increased. Nagaro dragged his thoughts back to the matter at hand. He sincerely hoped he wasn't being watched, and he restrained himself from looking about as he dismounted, trying to move naturally as he passed under the arch with its old brass bell. He moved down the cobbled lane as quickly as he dared, and arrived at Master Fineas' apothecary shop without being hailed.

When he looked surreptitiously about, he found that the short, narrow street was deserted except for an elderly woman at the far end of it who was sweeping off her front doorstep. Many folk were probably still taking their breakfast or getting ready for the day's activities. The card in the apothecary's window read CLOSED, so he dropped the horse's bridle and told the animal to "stand." The horse gave him a look that told him the admonition was unnecessary.

He knocked on the door, then stood and waited. After a while, when nothing happened, he knocked again a bit harder and waited some more. When he eventually knocked a third time, he finally heard a muffled voice from within and thought he caught the words "I'm coming" in the midst of the indistinct utterance. As last, the door opened a little way and Master Fineas' bespectacled face appeared around the edge of it, looking rather flustered.

"Pray give me a moment, Zirda," the little man was in the midst of saying. "If you will have but a modicum of patience, I will attend to you directly."

Nagaro suppressed a smile. He still had his hood up and apparently Fineas had yet to recognize him. "Have you any more of that excellent headache medicine you sold me?" he inquired.

The lore master straightened, blinking. "Captain Nagaro? Is that you under that hood?"

Nagaro lowered his voice. "It is. And I'm sorry to disturb you so early, Master Fineas. Although you did say I might come at my earliest convenience."

Master Fineas stared at him. "Well... yes... but I didn't expect—" He stopped and collected himself. "Never mind, Zirda. Please come in." And the little man stepped aside as he opened the door wider to usher Nagaro into the shop.

Nagaro quickly brushed past him, and Fineas swung the door closed.

"I'll just leave that sign in the window as it is for now," the lore master added. "That way we shouldn't be disturbed."

Light from the shop's single front window illuminated the deep, narrow room, revealing it just as Nagaro remembered from his earlier visit, with the long counter in front of him, the certificates of commendation from the highly regarded Hatherin Lofts School on one side wall, and the ranks of shelves piled with bottles, pots, and vials that reached nearly to the ceiling and ran back into the shop's dim recesses. The musty aroma of the place was equally familiar.

Nagaro stepped up to the counter as Master Fineas moved around the end to take his place behind it. The small, thin Kelorin man blinked gray eyes behind his spectacles. "It is good to see you again, Captain," he ventured. "I assume you have come about the linjana, since you obviously received my note."

Nagaro inclined his head. "Well met again, Master Fineas," he said. "And, yes, I assumed that your note referred to the linjana. I apologize for coming at an hour when I didn't really expect you to be open for business. I am very eager to have the linjana in my hand— and also Lord Kuran is expecting me in his study this morning at the second hour."

"Oh, tut tut!" The lore master dismissed this with a wave of his fine-boned hand. "A shopkeeper should always be ready to do business, I am told. And I'm sure your Fleet duties are more important in any case. It didn't take quite as long to get the linjana as I had feared it might, though it was difficult to find a supplier with whom I was quite comfortable— one who was willing to simply quote me what he thought was a fair price, rather than first asking how much I had to spend. Or else quoting a price that was inordinately high with the obvious aim of letting me think I was bargaining him down. Really, I have to say that the business of making money by buying and selling things is an invitation to the dishonest and dishonorable."

The lore master made a little huffing sound to emphasize the fact that he found such practices deplorable. "But, I *was* able to obtain the linjana," he continued, "and if you'll just wait here a minute, Captain, I will go upstairs and fetch it. I've been keeping it locked away in a safe place, as you may well imagine."

The little man turned about and pattered away down one of the narrow aisles between the laden shelves. Presently his tread could be heard mounting some rather creaky stairs somewhere at the back of the shop. Nagaro stood at the counter, his mind racing. Fortunately he didn't have long to wait before the lore master's steps sounded again on the stairs and Fineas reemerged from between the shelves, coming to a halt behind the counter.

The lore master held up a small cloth bag made of plain gray material and closed with a simple drawstring. "Here it is, Zirda," he said, then loosened the drawstring and carefully drew forth a clear glass vial. It was scarcely two inches tall, securely stoppered, and sealed with hard wax. "This is very important," he said, tapping the wax with a long finger. "It prevents evaporation as well as keeping the stopper in place. When you wish to open the vial, you must simply break the wax by twisting the stopper." He held up vial. "It isn't much to look at, I'm afraid," he added apologetically, "considering the time and effort required to obtain it— not to mention the expense. Still I'm assured that it is of the purest quality and highest potency. The liquid contains the distilled essence of freshly-gathered linjana leaves and stems and will retain its virtue so long as it remains in liquid form." Without more ado, Master Fineal held out the vial in the palm of his hand.

Linjana!

Nagaro reached out and took the vial. At that moment he had no words. He was all but certain it had been the spirit magic in this drug that had saved him from the living hell of heskial, at a time when he had believed that death was his only escape. Mutely he stared at the vial he was holding in his fingers. The liquid inside had to be as clear as water. He couldn't easily tell how much there was.

Turning toward the window, he held the vial up to the light. As he did so, he couldn't keep his hand from trembling. With the sunlight behind it, he could see that the liquid in the vial had a faint tint of yellow-green— just enough to say that it was not plain water. He could also see that the walls of the vial were quite thick and the space inside quite small. There couldn't be more than a rather small spoonful. "There isn't very much here," he murmured, scarcely realizing that he spoke aloud.

"The vial contained two drams when it was sealed." Fineas answered his spoken thought. "That is one full dose for a grown man if taken by mouth. And of course it would be two doses if delivered by means of a bladder-thorn, because—"

Nagaro's shudder was entirely involuntary. He lowered his hand and turned quickly around in an effort to cover it. "— because drugs are always more potent when delivered directly into the blood," he said, meeting Fineas' startled eyes. "I know."

"Exactly so!" The little man bobbed his head in acknowledgment. "But however do you come to know it, Captain?"

Nagaro's mouth twisted grimly. "Let's say there was a time when I found it a matter of some interest." He pocketed the vial. "I'm very well pleased, Master Fineas. Was the amount I gave you sufficient for the purchase? Is there more that I still owe you for this service?"

Fineas blinked at him. "I have a little more than a hundred rins remaining of what you gave me, Zirda, that I can return to you."

"But surely you're entitled to some profit. I think you should keep whatever remains."

"Well, some perhaps... but, *all* of it? That's rather a lot for a single item."

Nagaro shifted impatiently. "It seems to me that the single item in question has cost you considerable time and effort— including the effort of getting a fair price. None of which I knew how to do. But if you wish to give me some more of your headache remedy and include that as part of the exchange, I won't quarrel with you about it."

The lore master's mouth hung open for a moment, and it looked as if he might have been considering a protest, but past experience must have been instructive because in the end he swallowed and said, "Very well, Zirda, I will fetch you some willow bark. And I suppose you will be wanting your little herb sample back as well— it is indeed linjana, by the way."

The sample was duly fetched, and the container of willow bark, and Fineas set about weighing out a portion of the bark and wrapping it up in paper.

"How has your business been faring?" Nagaro inquired as the little man worked with the balance.

"Not as well as it might be, but getting better. Thank you for asking, Zirda. The folk living on this street are well-meaning and kind, and they've given me what custom they can, and passed the word amongst those they know who live nearby. They've assured me that it takes time to acquire regular customers. My wife does the books, and she was telling me just yesterday that both the amount and frequency of sales have been increasing over-all, at least in a general way."

"I'm glad to hear that, and I will be sure to recommend you to anyone I know who is in need of an apothecary."

"Thank you, Zirda." Fineas blinked behind his spectacles as he handed over the packet of willow bark.

Nagaro paused with the packet in his hand. He was thinking of how Fineas and Simion were connected— of what he knew that he had— and had not— told Kuran. "I fear I should warn you, Master Fineas," he said seriously, "that there is an investigation underway, under the direction of Lord Kuran, into certain illicit trade that has been going on between Edroviran citizens and citizens of Jinara. The Jinari High Council has complained of it to King Elgurn, and specifically mentioned... heskial—"

Fineas stiffened. "You know I refused to procure any of that!"

"Yes, yes. You were extremely clear regarding your feelings on the matter." Nagaro felt a twist of guilt again, about things he hadn't said. He shifted his feet, feeling he owed the lore master more honesty than he had given him. "As it happens, I had become aware of the trade, and since I am under Kuran's command, I've become involved in the investigation. And—" He paused and swallowed, "since Lord Kuran asked me directly if I knew anyone who might have knowledge relevant to this trade, I have told him your name and where to find you."

Fineas actually paled. "I hope you told him my story, Captain."

Nagaro made haste to reassure him. "Yes— at least to the extent of saying that you'd been sacked by Lord Madred's minister for refusing to obtain something from Jinara. I didn't specify what exactly you refused to get, although Kuran would probably suspect, and would surely ask you about it if he decides to seek information from you."

Master Fineas picked up the balance with hands that shook and bent to return it to its place under the counter. When he straightened, however, he looked resolute. His eyes behind his spectacles met Nagaro's directly and his voice didn't tremble when he spoke. "You haven't done ill in telling your commander what you know, Captain," he said. "It's more than possible that my... ah, experience... is relevant. And you may be sure that I will cooperate fully with Lord Kuran's investigation if he seeks me out. I shall, in fact, be very happy to do so." He paused, smiling wryly. "And I also thank you for telling me about the investigation. It would have been quite a shock to suddenly find the Lord of the Royal Fleet at my door. You may be sure that I will speak of this to no one else."

A minute later Nagaro was outside with the vial, and his little dried sprig of linjana in its leather folder, both tucked into his pocket. He stowed the packet of willow bark— it was quite a large packet— in his saddle bag. There were a number of people in the street by this time, but the morning was passing and he couldn't afford any more delay. So he put his hood back up, hoping it wouldn't seem odd in the warming air, before mounting the brown gelding and setting out at a brisk pace.

He was even more preoccupied as he left Brass Bell Lane than he had been when he'd entered it. He was relieved that Master Fineas had taken the news of the investigation in stride, but the thought occupied him only briefly. He could almost feel the little vial, like a bright, hot coal burning in his pocket.

Linjana! He was in possession of a potential miracle.

He was already wishing he'd paid the lore master more for the mind-restoring drug. How could one put a price on a man's sanity? Or on freedom from the abominable slavery of heskial? Five hundred rins seemed far too cheap.

More to the point was the question of how he might manage to *use* the precious medicine. His intended patient, Kale Fendred, was locked away very securely on an upper floor of the palace, his presence there a well-guarded secret. Nagaro frowned. *This wasn't going to be easy.* He could hardly approach Elgurn about it. He neither liked nor entirely trusted the king. Yet he was unlikely to be able to gain access to Kale directly by himself, and this meant he would have to enlist someone's aid. He couldn't go sneaking into the kitchen to try to discover when some drink was intended for Kale. It was likely the kitchen staff wouldn't even know, since Nevien had told him her father always dealt with Kale himself. For the same reason, it wouldn't serve him to try to enlist Nevien's assistance—

He frowned harder as his thoughts veered down a new path. He was riding along Market Street by now, still keeping his head down as he rode. He knew his way back to the Fleet Compound without thinking about it and so did the gelding. The horse needed no urging to quicken its pace.

He strongly suspected that his salvation had come from linjana, and it seemed likely that the drug had been in the glass of wine that Nevien had poured for him. It was shortly after he had drunk the wine that his head had seemed to explode with blinding light. In response, he had leaped to his feet, cried out aloud, and clutched his head— *all acts unbidden*, which should have been impossible under the will-enslaving influence of heskial.

He'd heard his chair hit the floor with a sound that had echoed in his ears— but he couldn't remember anything more. The sound of the chair falling seemed to fade away in his memory, as if it had been burned away by the battle between the spirit magic of linjana and that of heskial— the battle raging in his blood.

Still on Market Street, Nagaro struggled to solve the puzzle. The princess could have added the drug to his glass— her back had been turned towards him as she poured the wine. Or it could have already been in the bottle— which had arrived at her bedchamber in the hands of a servant, already uncorked. Nevien had explained the offering of wine by saying it would relax them both. She'd poured the two glasses and directed him to drink. She'd had to tell him twice because Dreigen had explicitly instructed him not to drink wine— perhaps worried about mixing wine with heskial. But Dreigen had also instructed him to obey the princess in all things, and the secpnd command had proven more potent. *Then*, after he'd drunk it, she had sat and *watched* him. He could picture her, across the table, with her own glass still full in her hand, making some nervous small talk while she waited.

She might have been waiting to see the effect of whatever she had added, or she might have just been waiting to see the effect of the wine. Either way, she must have been told what to do by whoever had been behind the plan. She certainly would *not* have been told what was really at stake. He was sure that Nevien hadn't known what her father was doing to him. She hadn't known at the time, and she clearly had learned nothing since. The dreadful conversation in the carriage had proven that. She would have behaved differently, spoken differently, if she'd known. So *someone* intent upon helping him must have used her, while keeping her mercifully in the dark. But who could it have been?

In these mental debates, Nagaro always came back to this question. It must have been someone who had known about the heskial— but also someone who knew about the properties of linjana. The first list was extremely short, consisting of the king and the three lords Nagaro thought of as his keepers— Bron Sobring, Kale Fendred, and Gillard Marchent. Of these, the only one likely to have wished to help him was Kale.

Kale had participated reluctantly in the beginning, and had continued out of loyalty to his friend, King Elgurn, but he'd clearly never liked what was going on. The difficulty, of course, was that there was no plausible reason why Kale, a Leithian, would have known about linjana. Kale had probably never been to Irvenen Wared— the only place where linjana grew. *How could Kale have found out about it?*

And then it struck him: *It might have been Rastyl Korven— the lord of Irvenen Wared.* The insight came with such blinding suddenness that Nagaro jerked in the saddle and the brown gelding stumbled a little and gave a snort of displeasure.

With the eyes of his mind, he could see Rastyl sitting across the table from him at that feast, talking to him, staring with his pale eyes. Nagaro had no idea what the man had been saying. He'd been too preoccupied with the fact that the most recent dose of heskial was wearing off and beginning to lose its grip. He'd been waiting for an opportunity to escape. But when at last he'd tried to run away, the Kelorin lord had come after him.

He remembered, also, being on the ground where he'd been thrown and pinned by Lord Bron. He'd begun to be wracked by the pain of heskial withdrawal, his limbs starting to shake. He had seen Kale stop Rastyl from coming any closer. Kale had needed to physically restrain the pale-eyed lord. What had Kale said to Rastyl? In his mind, Nagaro could hear the words: *"There is nothing you can do for him."* And in the next instant, he had felt the stab of the bladder-thorn and his mind had dropped into blackness as a fresh dose of heskial had coursed through his veins.

But what if Rastyl had answered, *"Perhaps there is."* What if the Kelorin lord had known something about linjana? He might have told Kale, and Kale might have pursued it on his own. Or perhaps Rastyl had guessed enough that Kale had been forced to confide in him, despite having been sworn to secrecy by Elgurn.

Nagaro's head spun. He might have had *two* benefactors rather than one! It was a conspicuous fact that Rastyl seemed to be the only person to recognize him from his days as Leyel Virden— the only one, that is, who hadn't known him before he'd been enslaved by heskial! Nor had Rastyl seemed at all surprised by the complete transformation in his behavior... Nagaro squirmed mentally at the thought that he might actually owe something to the pale-eyed man— *the man he had told rather pointedly to leave him alone.*

By this time, the gelding had brought him to the city's south gate, directly opposite the Fleet Compound, and he was jolted out of his thoughts when a passerby stumbled against his booted foot, jostling him.

Seeing that his destination was before him, he urged his horse forward and rode in through the gate of the Fleet Compound, hastily reordering his thoughts as he did so. He felt a wrench of guilt as he remembered Simion's predicament and Brandle's consequent distress.

Chapter 21

Well-Laid Plans

S ince it was nearly time for his meeting with Kuran, Nagaro rode directly to the Fleet Lord's quarters, where he dismounted and tied the gelding to the hitching rail. It was early, and Kuran's clerk, Estevad, hadn't yet reported for duty. It was the Lord of the Fleet himself who appeared in answer to Nagaro's knock.

"I have a report of my own to make," Nagaro informed him in response to his questioning look. "I hope you have time now to hear it."

Kuran shrugged resignedly as he stood aside to let Nagaro enter. "It seems I never have enough time to do all that I ought," he said wearily. "But I always have time for your reports, Captain. Come in and sit down."

Kuran listened gravely as Nagaro recounted the tale of Simion's disappearance, Geivian's sighting of him, and their adventure on the road the previous evening. When the story was complete, the Fleet Lord sat toying with his goose-quill and frowning. "How is it that you keep losing people?" he asked. "First Sindar and now Simion."

"I have no reason to believe the two are connected."

Kuran grimmaced. "Well, I would hope not! I was just struck by the coincidence, since I was preparing to write letters to Sindar's uncle and grandfather telling them what has happened. Your Turowan contacts have still had no word of Sindar, I assume?"

"No. None that I've heard. I put the word out through Kinu the stable hand to Omei's network, but it's as if he's vanished from the world."

Kuran sighed. "I intend to tell both Evran Marvenen and Burdal Korinos to keep an eye out for him. I hope he may simply have changed his mind and decided to return to one or the other of his relatives."

"I suppose it's possible he might have done that."

Nagaro did not, in fact, think it very likely, but he had no better idea and was grateful to be spared the need of writing to the two men himself. He would still have the painful duty of writing to Lissel. He intended to do so that very day, but right now he was concerned with Simion and Brandle.

"What do you make of Simion's situation?" he asked. "Brandle wants to go back to this road as soon as possible and continue the search. I persuaded him that he should wait at least until I could get your opinion."

Kuran put down his goose quill to massage his brow. "I'm glad that you did," he said. "The action Brandle proposes is precipitous under these circumstances— and dangerous. It could end with him having to contend with both Grimbold's forces and the highwaymen. And you don't really know what's happened, or why. This could still be unrelated to my investigation. All I did was write to Simion to inform him that he might be called upon to answer questions concerning what he knew. I didn't tell him to seek more information."

Kuran sighed. "But the truth is, I'm worried about his disappearance. We're clearly dealing with men who don't respect the law and aren't afraid to take serious risks. Simion's own respect for the law may have motivated him to try to discover how far his employer was involved, and that may have led to his falling afoul of dangerous men. Still I have no desire to see you and Brandle go down that isolated road and poke around in the private hunting forest of the Lord of Sobring Hold— at least not yet. Let me first make an inquiry in writing to the Elders of Sobring Hold. I can make it through the Crown, and say that I need to speak with Simion in connection with an important matter."

Nagaro sat frowning. "But the Elders are likely to simply claim that they don't have him."

"They may very well, and then you may have to take that ride down that road. But a royal request for information might just motivate them to let Simion go— after which they could claim they never had him, and that any tale he tells against them is a lie. In that case, we might never be able to prove anything, but at least Simion would be safe. Another possibility is that they'll produce some alternative tale to explain why they're holding him— something plausible and legitimate."

"It might appear legitimate, but still be false," Nagaro observed darkly.

"Of course it might, but at least we would then know what we had to deal with— what kind of evidence we'd need to have to counter their story, or to otherwise arrange to get Simion out of their clutches."

Nagaro's frown continued. "What you propose seems reasonable, My Lord, but Brandle won't be happy about the delay."

Kuran straightened in his chair. "Tell him that he should speak with Simion's family while we're waiting— explain the situation to them and enlist their aid. And, if he hasn't already done so, he should also speak to his own father. Lord Madred is Simion's employer, after all."

Nagaro shifted uncomfortably in his chair. "Madred may also be part of the plot, My Lord."

Kuran merely nodded. "I realize that. And if he is, he'll either be evasive or he'll tell Brandle to mind his own affairs. Even such answers as those, you see, would tell us something."

"Yes... I do see."

"That's decided then." Kuran tilted back his chair and clasped his hands behind his head. "As it happens, there's another reason why I can't afford right now to have you dashing off to rescue your friend, Captain. The new recruits need to have their first taste of seafaring. I've planned some introductory training maneuvers and the *Sword* and her captain will be part of them since you and your crew are among my best tutors. I want you to begin making your ship ready immediately. We should sail with the morning tide the day after tomorrow."

"Aye, Zirda." Nagaro knew that the previous subject was closed. "Is that why you summoned me here? To tell me that?"

"In part, yes, but chiefly for another matter. Vell will be going on a mission to Borlund Hold in connection with our investigation. He wondered if there was anything else you could tell him, since it was you who spoke directly to that Jinari translator. I've summoned him this morning as well, a little after you. He should be here soon."

Nagaro raised an eyebrow. "Why Vell Sobring for an investigation in Borlund?"

"You don't think him suitable? He may be Grimbold's nephew, but he's not of the same mind as his uncle, I assure you."

"I know that." Nagaro frowned. "But I would think he might find it a bit awkward, considering the involvement of Sobring Hold in all of this. And won't it appear odd to send a Fleet officer to investigate a case of illegal overland trading? Most would say it shouldn't be a Fleet matter."

"Which it isn't." Kuran rose and moved towards a cabinet that stood against one wall of the office. "It's just part of an investigation that's been put in my charge. But Vell isn't going as a captain of the Royal Fleet. He's going as a high-born Leithian whose allegiance to the Crown is beyond question. The King's Council chose him specifically."

"The Council, My Lord? I thought this was your investigation."

Kuran paused with his hand on one of the cabinet drawers and shot Nagaro a meaningful look. "*Officially* it is. Unofficially, the Council is taking an interest. Especially since there's a possible connection to Dreigen."

Nagaro's frown deepened. "All right. So why has the Council specifically chosen Lord Grimbold's nephew, then?"

Kuran smiled grimly. "They'd like to see Vell replace Grimbold as Lord of Sobring Hold. That choice is for the Sobring Elders to make, however, and the Council has no power to interfere in the Hold's internal affairs. I suppose they think that giving him a sensitive diplomatic mission may raise his stature in the Elders' eyes— if he acquits himself well." Kuran turned his attention back to the cabinet. "And now I really must find that map the Jinari made for us, since I can see Vell approaching through my office window."

Kuran opened a drawer and begun shuffling through its contents. He turned around with the rolled-up map in his hands just as a knock sounded at the front door. "And here is Vell now," he said as he re-crossed the room and settled himself in his chair.

Indeed they both heard the Leithian captain's voice in the hall speaking to Estevad, and presently Vell was ushered into the office where he took a seat at Kuran's invitation. The Leithian nodded an acknowledgment to each of them and then sat stiffly in the straight-backed chair, chewing his mustache and looking very sober. In fact, Nagaro thought he had never seen Vell look more tense.

Kuran had unrolled the map, and began weighting down the edges with an assortment of objects, an ink bottle, a ruler, a penknife. "I've just informed Captain Nagaro of the general nature of your mission," he said, addressing Vell. "I'm sure he'll do his best to answer your questions."

Vell nodded, cleared his throat, and turned to Nagaro. "My mission is partly diplomatic and, ah, partly investigational, Captain," he explained. "Diplomatic, because I'll have to present myself to Hilber Dorn, the current lord of Borlund Hold, and explain my mission to him in terms that are—" here Vell cast his eyes towards the ceiling and spoke as if reciting by rote, "— of sufficient delicacy as to secure his cooperation— or at least to minimize his interference." He brought his eyes back to his listeners and gave them a pained look. "Personally, I think I'll be lucky not to get my head taken off. I've never met Lord Hilber, and I've no idea what report of me my uncle may have given him."

Nagaro smiled with all his teeth, and said, "I don't envy you the task, Captain." He was surprised when Vell appeared disconcerted. He wondered if it had been the smile.

Kuran coughed. "Your noble status should give you some standing with the man, Vell, which is more than another man would have. I have every confidence in you. And it's the investigational aspect of your mission that concerns us here."

"Ah. Yes. Right." Vell seemed to collect himself. He turned to the map. "For the investigation, I'll have a small, hand-picked team of men. We'll be trying to determine whether the trafficking is still going on, by searching for evidence in the area, here, near the Jinari border." He indicated an area on the map adjacent to the X drawn by Utabala. "If I understand correctly," he added, putting his finger on the X, "this little mark represents the rendezvous point they've been using?" He cast Nagaro a questioning glance.

Nagaro nodded. "That's right. It was described to me as an abandoned woodcutter's hut."

"Ah?" Vell cast about. "My Lord, have you a pen and paper?"

Kuran grunted and produced the requested materials, which Vell used to jot down a quick note. The Leithian then turned back to Nagaro and asked, "Did your Jinari friend have anything else to say about the location?"

"Well," Nagaro considered. "He said the Jinari were using it for the rendezvous only, and not as a base. When they weren't there, they left nothing behind in that location that could identify or incriminate them."

"About how far is it from the Edroviran border? Do you know?"

Nagaro rose and bent over the map. "Utabala said it was located about a mile up the little stream that's drawn here." He pointed. "And the stream joins this larger one almost at the border, so I'd say it must be less than two miles."

Vell grimaced as he made more notes. "Anything else you can tell me?"

"Only that the Leithians who are crossing into Jinara have been wearing black wigs."

Vell stared at him. "Black wigs? Why would they do that?"

Nagaro shrugged. "I suppose because this trade has been associated with 'yellow-haired Leithians,' and they're trying not to fit that description."

Vell shook his head as he recorded the information. "But Borlund is a Leithian Hold," he objected. "Shouldn't be any Kelorin within miles. Trying to look like Kelorin would only make them more conspicuous."

"Only on the Edroviran side of the border," Kuran interjected. "The Jinari probably wouldn't think it strange."

"Ah." Vell nodded. "Yes, I see. They'd only don the wigs when they actually crossed the border then?"

Nagaro had already thought of this. "Very possibly," he said. "Do you intend to carry your investigation across the border, then, into Jinari territory?"

Vell's fingers strayed to his mustache as they tended to do when he was nervous or uncomfortable. "Only if necessary— in direct pursuit of Edroviran citizens who cross the border. Those are my instructions. I've a letter bearing the royal seal and signature that explains my purpose. Hopefully the Jinari will honor it."

"Since they want the trafficking stopped, they should." Nagaro rubbed his chin thoughtfully. "But if there's no objection," he added, "perhaps I could add a brief note to the bottom of that letter, addressed to my friend Utabala and with my signature. The Jinari High Council seems to trust Utabala, and he in turn trusts me."

Vell looked incredulous. "You're suggesting your signature would carry more influence than Elgurn's?"

Kuran laughed outright. "I'd take him up on it, if I were you, Vell. None of these Jinari have ever met the King of Edrovir."

Vell looked from one of them to the other. "Well, all right then," he said when he saw they were in earnest. "Can't see what harm it could do." He fished the letter out of his tirka and handed it to Nagaro.

Nagaro reached for Vell's borrowed pen.

"What are you going to write?"

Nagaro bent over the paper. "I'll say that I know you. That you're a man they can trust, and so forth."

Vell watched over his shoulder as the pen scratched decisively across the paper. "Ah... thank you, Captain," he said after reading the words. Then he looked at the floor as if embarrassed.

Once Nagaro had added his signature to the letter, there seemed to be nothing more to be communicated. The two captains accordingly took their leave, exiting Kuran's office together. On the porch, Nagaro moved to untie his horse and Vell paused, frowning and tapping his chin with the rolled-up map. "Ah, Captain," he began, then stopped and said, "Is it all right if I call you Nagaro?"

Nagaro halted with the reins in his hand, considering the other man. "Yes, Vell, of course."

Vell's pale blue eyes met his. "I want to thank you for your endorsement. On the letter. I can't help wondering, though whether you really meant everything you wrote."

"I'm not in the habit of writing things I don't mean."

Vell looked at the ground. "It's just that I... ah... don't think I ever told you properly how sorry I am about everything that led up to what happened at Osfaraad," he ventured. "And I've a confession to make. When they told me I was to be the true captain of the *Sword*, I was pleased— may the Gods forgive me." He raised his head, staring off across the compound. "I was so eager for a captain's posting, that at first I didn't care how I got it. But the more I thought about it— and the more I saw of you— the less I liked it." His eyes came back to meet Nagaro's. "It was a dirty trick to play on you, and I'm sorry for my part in it."

Nagaro sighed. "It wasn't your trick, Vell. I don't hold it against you that you followed your orders. And as for the rest, to begin with, you hardly knew me. And by the time we'd reached Osfaraad I could tell there was something bothering you. I just didn't know what it was."

Vell's relief showed plainly in his face. "Thank you," he said, with feeling. He put out his hand. "Are we friends, then?'

Nagaro grinned as he took the hand and shook it. "Yes. Friends." As he released the other man's hand, he added, "Could I ask you something?"

"Of course."

"Do you very often go to Sobring Hall?"

"As little as possible." Vell made a face. "I don't care for what my uncle does, and I'm afraid he knows it."

Nagaro's heart sank. "Then you wouldn't likely have heard anything about a man they're holding—. a Kelorin man named Simion?"

Vell shook his head. "Kuran has already learned that I'm of little use to his investigation as a source of inside information," he said ruefully. "But what's this about?"

Nagaro told him, briefly sketching the details of Simion's case.

Vell listened with a gathering frown. "Sounds like a bad business," he said when Nagaro stopped speaking. "And very much the sort of thing Grimbold is capable of. I could suggest that you work through Lord Madred, since the man is his clerk. But if Madred's a party to the plot, I suppose that won't help you. Still, I'm glad you told me about this. I'll not be going near the Hall before I leave on this mission, but if your friend is still missing when I get back, I'll be sure to keep my eyes and ears open."

Nagaro sighed and nodded. Vell's concern appeared completely genuine, so he thanked the other man and they parted.

***

He had little time to do any more thinking about anything that had been discussed in Kuran's study. He scarcely had time to write the letter to Lissel and to pen a brief explanation to Brandle, which he sent by courier. He didn't feel good about handling Brandle that way, knowing how distraught the man must be. Still, he could only advise the lieutenant to be patient and not to attempt anything on his own.

The rest of that day and the next were filled with preparations to sail. And then they were at sea and the days were filled with putting men through their exercises— rowing, following orders, and trimming the sails— with words of praise and encouragement balanced against necessary cautions and rebukes as the half dozen new recruits aboard the *Sword of Freedom* got their first taste of sea-craft.

During evenings, anchored among the isles, Nagaro, Taru, and Pavo had opportunities to talk. Nagaro tried several times to draw Taru out on the subject of his courtship, but the young Turo remained reticent, and Pavo would do no more than give Nagaro a long look with his narrow eyes and say, "Do not worry, Nagaro. All is in hand of Sheptuum."

When Nagaro mentioned the poem he had found at River House, his two friends clearly didn't know what to make of it. It didn't help that Nagaro could only imperfectly remember the words. Pavo at least appreciated the poignancy of what the verse suggested— the picture of two women writing letters back and forth and calling themselves "Lily" and "Rose", but he was noncommital on the possibility of any connection to Nagaro. Taru, on the other hand, didn't mince words. "If this Rose woman was your mother, wouldn't the poem ha' said something about you?" he demanded. "More likely the Lady Maramine was your mother. And since she was a high-born lady, I don't know why that's not good enough for ye. It'd be good enough for *me*, I can tell ye!"

On the subject of Simion, the two friends were even more sharply divided.

"I don't like to see ye takin' risks for that crossy, Nagaro," Taru declared flatly as they sat together over dinner in the *Sword*'s great cabin on the final evening of the training exercises. "Even if ye're just helping Brandle, it can only look bad. It's not like Simion was ever one of our crew."

Pavo, however, shook his shaggy head. "You are wrong, Taru," he said. "Simion was slave when we were slave. He have fought beside us when we became free man. And he have given his money to Nagaro when we had no more money to make ship ready to sail. He cannot help that he is crossed."

Nagaro was sitting, brooding and nursing a cup of sothiril. "I'm sorry, Taru," he said quietly. "But I agree with Pavo."

Taru scowled. "Well, just see that ye're careful if ye go with Brandle. And don't go spreading it about what ye mean t' do."

Nagaro sighed. "We're far more likely to be successful if we maintain secrecy anyway," he pointed out. "And maybe it won't be necessary to make the journey at all. Maybe we'll find when we get back to Lankura that the Leithians have let Simion go, and that he's safe and sound."

Nagaro's hope had been sincere when he'd spoken about Simion, but he wasn't really surprised when, upon their return to the Fleet Compoind, he rounded the corner of the long building that housed the captains' quarters and found Brandle sitting on the steps of his tiny front porch.

The big Leithian got to his feet as Nagaro approached. "I'm trying to be inconspicuous," he said with a forced smile. "I was going to wait for you at the dock, but I didn't want to spoil your reputation."

Nagaro smiled at what he recognized as attempted levity, but noted that it was belied by the look on the other man's face. Brandle looked as if he hadn't slept properly for some time. "You don't look very good, Brandle," Nagaro told him honestly. "And I imagine it's because there hasn't been any good news."

Brandle gloomily shook his head. "I've no one else to turn to but you, Captain. A man in need soon finds out how many friends he has, and I can tell you that an openly crossed man doesn't have many. I need to talk to Kuran right away. Can you arrange it?"

Nagaro frowned. He remembered Taru's advice and rejected it without hesitation. "I'll try, Lieutenant. Please come with me."

He struck off in the direction of Kuran's office, deliberately taking the most direct route— straight across the parade ground.

***

Kuran sat at his desk, eyeing Brandle with some concern from behind a small mountain of envelopes and papers. It appeared he was trying to listen to the lieutenant while continuing to examine the contents of the heap in front of him. In between encouraging nods and murmured words of sympathy, however, he had so far managed to pick up and examine only three items, transferring each to one of several smaller piles.

Brandle, for his part, was pacing the office floor, gesticulating as he vented his frustration. He had declared himself in no mood to sit, and clearly it hadn't been an exaggeration.

"They tell me nothing at the palace!" he raged. "*Nothing!* They can't understand that Simion is as dear to me as a wife might be to you, My Lord, or to the Captain, here. No, all they can say is that since Lord Kuran made the inquiry, the answer— whatever it is— must go to Lord Kuran. If you've received any information, My Lord concerning Simion, I beg you to tell me!"

Kuran tossed down an envelope and threw up his hands. "You must be patient, Lieutenant! I've only returned to my desk within the last half hour. If there's been any response to my inquiry, it will be somewhere here, amongst my mail." He indicated the pile of papers in front of him. "Which I'm attempting to go through as we speak. Now will you please sit down?"

Nagaro had taken a seat on one of the office chairs. He pushed a second one encouragingly in Brandle's direction. "What did Simion's parents say?" he asked, hoping to distract the Leithian so Kuran could concentrate on his mail.

"Ha!" Brandle dropped onto the chair, which creaked audibly under the impact of his large frame. "They hadn't even missed him! They haven't been in close communication, you see. But *now*, of course, they're distraught, because I told them what's happened! But they're not distraught enough, it seems, to open their arms or their hearts to me. I'm still treated as an outsider rather than a member of the family!"

"And your father?" Nagaro probed. "Did you speak to him?"

Brandle grimaced. "I couldn't even persuade him to look into it." Then he heaved a sigh. "Of course, to be fair, my father doesn't oversee the day-to-day management of his holdings here in Lankura in any detail. That's the task of Minister Torlung. It's not surprising that Father referred all my inquiries to him."

Nagaro frowned. He thought Brandle was making excuses for very callous behavior on his father's part. "Surely your father knows how you feel about Simion—"

"*Of course he knows!*" Brandle spat the words. "And he wishes I didn't! 'Speak to Minister Torlung.' That's all I got from him."

"*Have* you spoken to Torlung?" It was Kuran who asked, pausing in the act of picking up the next envelope.

Brandle shot him a look. "I did that before! When Simion first disappeared. His answer was that he knew nothing of any disappearance and that any employee who wasn't doing his work would lose his position! When I pressed him further, he told me very pointedly that it wasn't my concern! Which is very much the same as what I got from both Lord Odus and Lord Pendrik when I tried to ask about the inquiry you made!"

Nagaro shook his head. "This is unjust," he said. "If these gentlemen were confronted by a wife whose husband was missing, they wouldn't tell her it was none of her concern. They'd give her any information they had— or tell her that they had no information, if that was the case."

"I agree." Kuran sat poised with the next envelope in his hand. "It's to our shame that we aren't enlightened enough to recognize the kind of relationship that exists between Brandle and Simion as being the equivalent of marriage. But I can at least tell Brandle what's been communicated to *me*." He brandished the envelope. "This, I believe, is the response to my inquiry."

Brandle leaned forward avidly. "Open it, My Lord!"

Kuran did so, and his brow grew clouded as he read the paper within. "It appears to be a denial," he said. "The response is from the Elders of the Hold— after being told what Geivian saw. It says that they 'do not have specific information to indicate that a man named Simion Rudrin is being held in Sobring Hold'." He passed the document to Brandle, who snatched it from his hand and poured over it.

Nagaro rose to look over Brandle's shoulder, quickly confirming that Kuran had quoted the Elders correctly. "That's a rather cautious denial, wouldn't you say?"

Brandle sat stiffly, scowling. "You're right, Captain. It doesn't actually say that Simion *isn't there*."

Kuran rubbed his chin. "Yes. Those are the kind of words I would use if I weren't sure I had all the facts," he said thoughtfully, "especially if I wanted to be able to put the blame elsewhere if it turned out there was something I didn't know."

Brandle stood up and placed the paper on Kuran's desk. "Thank you, My Lord," he said with a small, stiff bow. "I mean to take a furlough tomorrow and go look for Simion if Captain Nagaro can be spared to accompany me and show me the place where the carriage disappeared."

Nagaro also rose. "I'd like to request leave to go with Lieutenant Brandle for that purpose, My Lord."

Kuran's expression was somber as he looked from one resolute face to the other. "I'm afraid I see no other choice," he said. "Though I hope you'll both be careful." He turned to Nagaro. "It will have to be a furlough, Captain, since this can't officially be Fleet business. I can, however, give you both permission to say that you're assisting me with my investigation if you run afoul of the authorities in Sobring Hold." He smiled grimly. "With any luck that should keep you from being shot for trespassing. Just don't take any unnecessary chances. Remember that I need you, Captain. We should be sailing to meet the Emperor at Chitaopa in a week."

Chapter 22

Into Sobring Hold

The horses picked their way gingerly along the sloping ground under the trees, treading carefully among the stones and tree roots that often lay concealed under a thick litter of dry leaves. Nagaro and Brandle were riding slowly. It was the sensible thing to do, given the uncertain footing, not to mention the sometimes dense undergrowth and the frequency of low-hanging branches. The going would have been much easier on the road, which ran parallel to their course some twenty feet below them and to their left, but the knowledge that there could be highwaymen about had led them to try a concealed approach once they were within about a mile of their destination.

The full heat of summer was upon the land. It was close to midday, and the temperature of the air under the trees was oppressive despite the shade they offered. The road, which could be glimpsed intermittently between the trunks, was a bleached-bright stripe of dusty earth baking under the rays of the sun.

Brandle, who was following Nagaro's lead, mopped his brow. "I wish I could see the sky," he said, "to see if there are any clouds gathering. The air feels like thunder."

Thunder-Heels gave a low wickering whinny, and Nagaro stroked the stallion's sleek gray neck. "He's not talking to you, lad," he said, speaking low. "He's just talking about the weather."

Brandle shook his head. "Kroneg's Blood!" he exclaimed. "I almost think you can converse with that animal. But when *I* only tried to touch his bridle, back in the stable yard, I swear he tried to kick and bite me at the same time!"

Nagaro laughed. "Thunder doesn't like strangers taking liberties."

"*Strangers?* He ought to know me by now! Or does 'stranger' mean anyone but you? I mean, I named this fellow True—" he slapped the neck of his chestnut gelding, "but he's nothing like as devoted as that beast of yours."

Nagaro smiled to himself. True, from what he had seen, was obedient and amiable, a handsome dark liver chestnut with a red-brown mane and a distinctive white star and snip. And Brandle, he had noticed, was much less agitated than he had been the day before— now that he was finally being allowed to take some action. He was, however, being unusually talkative, and some of his remarks were particularly unfettered. Nagaro was inclined to indulge the man. He'd heard that lack of sleep could act like strong drink, and he suspected the prolonged strain was wearing on the Leithian. "Thunder belongs to the Fleet, not to me," he offered by way of explanation. "Though everyone thinks of him as mine. And there *are* two grooms at the palace stables that he'll let saddle and bridle him, not to mention all of the Fleet stablemen. You've just never been granted the privilege."

"Granted? By whom?"

"Well it's Thunder-Heels who decides, of course, but he does seem to be influenced by my recommendation."

Brandle snorted. "What happens if anyone else tries to *ride* him?"

"No one has tried in quite a while, since he's been known to put up a fight about that." Nagaro drew rein, causing the big gray to come to a halt while Brandle's bay had to come up short to avoid colliding with the stallion's hind quarters. "I think we've come to the bend in the road," he said, pointing ahead through the trees.

From what they could see of the bright strip of earth that was the roadway, it appeared to swing sharply to the left rather than continuing the course it had been taking. Directly in front of them there was only hillside, shadowy tree trunks, and undergrowth.

"The bend that comes before the big rock?"

"Yes. Let's go down to the road's edge and see if we can get a view of what's up ahead on the road while staying under cover."

Dismounting, they led the horses as they cautiously descended towards the edge of the road and approached the bend until they reached a point where they should be able to see around it. Nagaro halted behind a clump of large bushes. Dropping Thunder-Heels' reins, he moved, crouching, to a good vantage point.

"By the blood of Kroneg's brow!" Brandle exclaimed. He'd found a vantage point of his own and he was leaning forward, staring.

Nagaro stared as well. The large beetling rock was clearly visible, and some fifty yards beyond it there was a carriage in the road— not moving along it, but standing still. "Bishka!" He reached for the spyglass that hung about his neck, its strap running diagonally across his chest.

"It's pointing this way," Brandle observed. "And someone's taken the horses. Probably that pack of highwaymen. By the Gods! I'd say old

Grimbold has some housecleaning to do if he's got a gang like that plying their trade just a few miles from his Hall."

Nagaro was studying the scene through the spyglass. "I don't see the driver—or anyone else, for that matter," he said. "And the left front wheel is missing."

"So they broke a wheel and took it off for repairs. And while they were gone, the carriage was set upon by horse-stealing brigands," Brandle interpreted.

"Or they took the horses, themselves, to ride back to Sobring Hall for a new wheel." Nagaro chewed his lip. "That carriage could be completely abandoned, or there could be people inside it, stranded and in need of help. The worst of it, for us, is that it's standing very near the spot where Geivian's little road leads off on the left-hand side. We'll have to go out into the roadway to get around the rock outcropping, and when we do that, we'll risk being visible to anyone hiding in the carriage."

"We could get a better look from the top of the rock," Brandle suggested. "I've been up and down this road, going and coming from Furthing Hold, and I know that rock now that I see it. You can get up onto the top of it by climbing one of the trees on this side."

Nagaro still had the spyglass to his eye. "There's something up on top of the carriage. Something light blue. Do you see it?"

"Aye," Brandle affirmed. "Some sort of bundle, do you think?"

"I thought I saw it move, but it could just be something covered with cloth that's blowing in the wind."

As if in confirmation, a sudden gust of wind ruffled the leaves of the trees above their heads.

"What did I tell you," Brandle muttered. "There's a thunderstorm on the way."

Nagaro glanced at what he could see of the sky. There were only a few streamers of cloud in the part that was visible from his hiding place, but summer thunderstorms usually blew up off the ocean to the west and that part of the sky was hidden from his view. "If you're right, we should hurry," he said. "Come on. Let's try the view from the rock."

Carefully they retraced their steps back up the slope under the trees, remounted, then rode forward again, following the curve of the road, until they could see a bright patch among the trees ahead of them where the sun was breaking through between two oaks and illuminating what looked like a shear wall of rock.

Nagaro urged Thunder-Heels forward. "That must be it. From up there we should be able to see past the carriage, and see if there are any travelers on the road beyond it."

"Or any highwaymen." Brandle grinned.

"*They* are more likely to be lying in wait among the trees where they won't be seen until they pounce on us. In fact, that rock might make a good lookout for highwaymen to use as well." Nagaro drew rein a little at the thought, and they moved forward cautiously under the trees.

Brandle sucked air between his teeth. "I still say you should have killed that bandit captain," he muttered. "Instead of just cutting his sword arm."

Nagaro similarly kept his voice low when he replied. "They'd only demanded our money and our horses, Brandle."

"They'd have had your swords, too. Don't doubt it. And they'd have left you stranded miles from any friendly hearth with night coming on. I hope you don't expect their captain to show you any gratitude for your leniency if you cross his path again!"

"I don't. He didn't seem the sort. But one of his men might—"

Nagaro pulled to a halt. The face of the rock rose before them, greater than the height of a man. Dense stands of laurel and sumac clustered about its feet and several large oak trees half overarched it, the trunk of one very nearly leaning against the gray stone. There was very clearly no one about. They both relaxed.

A number of lesser stones lay scattered close about the huge boulder like calves of some petrified whale, their gray backs hunched among the shrubbery or half-submerged in leaf litter. Brandle dropped True's reins, slid off the horse with a groan of relief, and sprawled his muscular frame at full length across one the smaller stones that happened to be aptly shaped to serve the purpose. There he lounged with his hands behind his head while Nagaro dismounted and stood studying the branches of the nearest oak, tracing a possible pathway to the summit of the large outcropping with his eyes.

"I think I see a way." Nagaro reached for the water flask that was slung behind his saddle, uncapped it, and tilted it up to take a swallow. Turning, he found Brandle eyeing him appreciatively.

"By the Gods," the Leithian said fervently. "You *are* a beautiful man. I can see why Simion first took you for some sort of angel."

"*What?*" Nagaro stood frozen in the act of re-stoppering the water flask.

"He'd just been pulled out of the sea, and dragged onto that wretched oar deck," Brandle explained. "Where he'd been sitting with his head down, wishing he were dead, when someone touched him on the arm, and he turned around, and there— sitting right beside him— was the most beautiful man he'd ever seen."

Nagaro could feel the blood in his face. He studiously gave his attention to re-capping the water flask, then very deliberately returned the flask to it place. Brandle had once declined to repeat something

Simion had said about him to spare him embarrassment and he suspected he had just heard it. The moment Brandle had just described hung vividly in his own memory. *He had stared at Simion a little too long, he knew. Because Simion's eyes were that rarest of colors, deep Kelorin blue. They had reminded him of the eyes of his sainted guardian, the Lady Maramine.*

"Simion had just been through a lot, as you say," he said quietly. "He'd had a ship sunk under him and nearly drowned, been stripped half naked, branded, and chained to a bench in a stinking hole. Any man might have imagined any number of things." He risked a look at Brandle.

The Leithian was still staring at him. "Yes, but in *this* case, that beautiful man turned out to have a spirit to match. That's what Simion said. I don't begrudge any of it, mind you. It gave him a reason to live. And there aren't many straight-sailing men who would do what you're doing today, Captain." Abruptly Brandle stopped and shook his head as if to clear it. "Gods, will you listen to me!" He rolled onto his elbow and scrambled to his feet with a hand to his forehead. "You'd best get up on that rock, Captain, before I make a worse ass of myself. And I'd best stay down here with the horses. The way my head feels I wouldn't trust myself not to fall off that thing and break my neck."

"Right." Nagaro hastily turned back to the oak he intended to climb. Brandle's praise embarrassed him even more than the revelation of Simion's words. It was best to pretend that the last few moments simply hadn't happened.

He tried to focus on the task at hand. After a little thought, he unbuckled his sword belt, re-buckled it into a loop, and hung it on his saddlebow. "Don't you lose that, Brother of the Wind," he told Thunder-Heels as he made sure the belt was secure.

"Could you put in a good word for me while you're about it?" Brandle spoke from behind him, with a return to his more usual jocularity. "If I'm to stay with the horses, we all have to get along."

Nagaro realized that the other man was right. "Well, come here then," he said.

Turning, he grasped Brandle's wrist as the lieutenant somewhat gingerly approached, then drew the other man toward the gray stallion. Placing the man's hand first against the horse's neck high up by the bridle and then lower on the animal's velvet-soft muzzle, he said, "Thunder, this is Brandle," in a serious tone as if formally introducing them. "He's a friend. You can trust him in anything, just as you trust me." The stallion's ears flicked backward and forward, and he lifted one forefoot and set it down again but showed no evidence of animosity.

"Is that all there is to it?" Brandle inquired incredulously. He rubbed the horse's muzzle and was rewarded by being blown on wetly as the big gray nuzzled back.

"Well, there's no guarantee that he'd really let you do everything he'd let me do," Nagaro admitted. "But I've just vouched for you, as it were. He should at least let you touch him or lead him by the bridle— provided you're not rough about it." He stepped back. "Now for the oak tree, and from there to the rock." He strode over to the oak and laid a hand on the trunk just as another gust of wind sept over the wood, tossing the branches overhead. Ignoring it, he began to climb.

Getting up into the tree presented no serious difficulties for a man possessed of reasonable strength and agility. Soon Nagaro was working his way around the trunk, making for a large limb that arced out across the curving surface of the rock, actually contacting it in several places.

"You be careful, Captain."

Brandle's voice came up from below with such an obvious note of concern that it made Nagaro wince. He recalled that Simion had been inclined to chafe under Brandle's protectiveness. "Don't worry, Lieutenant," he called back, speaking lightly. "I've always been good at physical tasks." Looking down, he saw that the big Leithian had followed him up into the tree and was standing on a branch about six feet above the ground while leaning on another. Farther below, the two horses were happily grazing on some tufts of grass and small herbs that had found enough sunlight in the area around the base of the rock.

In the pause that followed Nagaro's words, there came distinctly a rumble of distant thunder.

"If it starts to rain, it could get slippery up there."

"If it starts to rain, I'm coming down."

He reached the limb that gave access to the rock and worked his way out along it until he could get his feet onto the curving surface of the stone. From that point it was possible to more or less walk his way up, using the branch as a kind of very irregular balustrade. After a dozen feet, the branch became too thin to be trusted with his weight, but by that time the curve of the rock had leveled out and he was able to scramble the last few feet to a perch at the crest. There he paused, crouching, to look about him.

The top of the rock was entirely clear of the trees. The end of it that overhung the roadway was about twenty feet to his left, but the section of road where the carriage stood was plainly visible from the place he had reached. He also had a clear view of the western sky, and another stiff gust of wind now prompted him to look in that direction as he crouched just behind the rock crest. He wasn't surprised to see a mountainous mass of cloud rising behind the western hills. It was snowy-white above and deep blue-gray beneath and rather ominous looking. It was also moving in his direction at a significant rate of speed, judging its movement relative to the knife-sharp crest of the hills. "You're right about that storm," he called over his shoulder. "We're going to get wet before the afternoon is over."

Brandle had climbed a little higher, just enough to keep Nagaro in view. He smiled crookedly and saluted in acknowledgment. "What about the carriage?"

Nagaro nodded and turned around again, then crept forward slightly. Keeping his head low, he stretched out on his stomach on the sun-warmed stone and brought his spyglass into position. The image leaped to his eye across the distance. There was the carriage, missing a wheel, the naked axle propped up on some kind of forked wooden beam apparently designed for the purpose. He moved the spyglass carefully to right and then left. The carriage door was closed on the side that he could see, and he saw no one at the window. The angle was poor for looking inside, however, so this meant little. Slowly he angled the tip of the spyglass upward, his small circular field of view tracking towards the top of the carriage where the mysterious blue bundle lay. He found it and focused on it.

It took him a second to comprehend what he was seeing.

"*Keshaal!*" he murmured. He re-focused the glass and explored his discovery for several more seconds before twisting about so that he could see Brandle's anxious face below him, looking up. "That's not a bundle of cloth on the roof, Lieutenant ," he hissed. "It's a woman in a blue dress!"

"A *woman?* Kroneg's Blood! What's she doing up there?"

"If I had to make a guess, I'd say hiding. I'll have another look."

He re-located the splash of sky-blue and focused the spyglass. "She's lying down on her side, propped up on one elbow," he reported. "She's taking a drink now from some sort of flask. At least she has water. I can't quite see her face. No, wait! She just turned towards me." He nearly fumbled the glass in his astonishment. "By the Eyes of Vothra's Mind! It's the Lady Alisset!"

"*Alisset?* Are you sure?"

"Yes! What on earth is she doing here? I thought she was in Lankura."

"Well, she could be returning from home. You wouldn't have known, of course, but she left for a visit shortly after you sailed on your last mission."

"And she's the daughter of Bron Sobring— so she's been at Sobring Hall?"

"Actually, no. Home, for her, is in Furthing Hold since her father died. My father is her guardian. He's her maternal uncle."

Nagaro lowered the spyglass and twisted about again to look down at Brandle. "You mean she's your *cousin?*" he asked in astonishment. He'd known that Alisset was Vell's sister, but he hadn't known she was also related to Brandle Furthing. "You've never mentioned it."

Brandle made an ambivalent gesture that momentarily threatened to cause him to lose his balance. "I never had occasion to. I have rather a lot of cousins, actually. My mother has two sisters and a brother, and my father has two more sisters besides. So I have a lot of aunts too, besides Lady Merriel, and I don't generally have occasion to mention them either."

"Oh." Nagaro turned his attention back to the glass. "I really don't see any sign of anyone else about," he said. "What can have happened to have left her quite alone like this? Do you think we ought to go offer her our assistance? She's not in immediate danger, but with those highwaymen about—"

Without warning there was a sudden commotion on the ground below him.

There was a series of oaths and some startled snorts from the horses, followed by the sound of something large crashing through the bushes.

"*Here, you!*" Brandle shouted. "*Stop, thief!*" And something began noisily shaking the branches of the oak tree.

Nagaro spun around just in time to see Brandle hit the ground and vault into the saddle of his horse before striking off at a mad pace through the undergrowth. A motion some distance off among the trees drew his eye and he caught a glimpse of Thunder-Heels, making good speed in the general direction from which they had come. An unknown horseman flashed briefly into and out of view, in pursuit of the stallion, and was followed an instant later by Brandle on his chestnut.

"Come back, Brandle!" Nagaro cupped his hands to shout after the Leithian. "They'll never catch Thunder!"

"*Stay where you are! I'll fetch him back for you!*" Brandle's voice came back to him, already growing noticeably fainter with distance.

The diminishing sounds of the pursuit traced a path that diverged sharply from the road and led up into the hills. Before very long Nagaro could neither see nor hear any evidence of the whereabouts of the three horses.

"Bishka!" Nagaro swore under his breath. Thunder-Heels, he knew, was quite capable of leading his pursuer a merry chase. And he was quite as likely to run from Brandle as he was to stand still for the man Nagaro had so recently introduced to him. Nagaro shook his head. The irony was that the stallion would likely return to him of his own accord— if he weren't too badly frightened and the distance weren't too great. Alternatively, however, the big gray might take it into his head to return to his stable in the Fleet Compound, leaving Nagaro without a mount.

And he'd left his sword hanging from the saddlebow!

It dawned on Nagaro that the mishap had left him alone and unarmed, save for a knife that he wore at his belt, in potentially hostile territory.

Bloody bodgering Hel! Mentally cursing the horse thief, himself, the lieutenant, and ,Lokundas, he stretched himself out again on the sun-baked stone. It seemed that, for the moment at least, remaining where he was atop the rock was the wisest course. Or so he thought until he looked again in the direction of the carriage.

When he did so, he saw that Alisset was now sitting up and looking about, and he groaned inwardly. Most likely she had heard their shouts, and possibly some of the other sounds as well. Silently he willed her to lie down again, but she showed no signs of doing so, although she soon stopped actively looking about. Fortunately there was no sign of any other highwaymen. Neither his shouts nor Alisset's appearance on the carriage roof had brought any others out of the forest. He supposed it was possible that the horse thief who had tried to take Thunder-Heels had been acting alone, and if that were the case he might best stay where he was, since he was relatively safe and could keep an eye on Alisset.

So he lay in his high place with the sun beating down on his back, straining his ears for the sounds of returning horses and watching the road and the Lady Alisset as she sat sipping from her flask. The minutes ticked by. After perhaps a quarter of an hour he began to wish that he'd brought his own water flask to the top of the rock with him. The sun was making him sweat, and his throat was beginning to feel parched. He knew there was a stream somewhere on the other side of the road, but he'd have to leave his place of concealment and his vantage point to reach it.

There was still neither sight nor sound of Thunder-Heels nor of Brandle, and this he found increasingly worrying. He was in the process of mentally reviewing all the possible outcomes of Brandle's chase when a fresh gust of wind, stronger than any that had preceded it, swept across his hiding place, making the branch of the oak tree behind him thrash against the rock. The wind cut through his shirt, chilling the sweat on his body and causing him to glance anxiously skywards.

He immediately regretted not having given more attention to the approaching clouds. Already they towered over the hilltops on the western side of the valley. Their underbellies were purple-black now, heavy and swollen-looking, and they were drawing visibly closer by the second. He realized that he was very soon going to have to leave his perch and seek shelter. And in the next instant he thought of Alisset. She should be thinking of taking shelter as well. But when he looked, he saw her still sitting atop the carriage.

He realized that she was sitting with her back to the west. Was it possible that she was unaware of the approaching storm? A closer look with the spyglass showed that she was gesticulating as if talking to herself. When another brief gust of wind stirred her skirts, she put out a hand to smooth them, but nothing more. A rumble of thunder caused her to look up and to right and left, but she didn't turn around. At this point, he began to wonder a little about the contents of the flask from which she was drinking. When a second rumble, louder and more ominous, still failed to cause her to look over her shoulder, Nagaro decided he had to do something about the situation.

By now there was a constant breeze swaying the branches of the oak behind him. It didn't look dangerous, but he decided after a moment's consideration to descend from the rock on the opposite side, rather than by the way he had come, so that he wouldn't have to go out onto the roadway to get around the end of it. About thirty feet to his right, the outcropping merged with the hillside as the latter rose more steeply towards its summit. The distance from the rock crest to the ground was less at that uphill end than it was where he lay, and there were other trees there whose branches appeared likely to assist. As quickly as he dared, he crawled along the top of the rock, keeping low and just behind its crest.

Getting down in the place he had spotted turned out not to be very difficult. And once down, he had only to follow the side of the rock back to the road and then follow the edge of the road until he was opposite the position of the carriage. He went cautiously under the cover of the trees, casting his eyes warily about him. The rushing of the wind in the branches overhead made enough noise to cover the sound of leaves rustling underfoot or of a twig snapping, so that he had to rely on his eyes to check for the presence of lurking marauders. Of course, the rising wind also meant he didn't have to worry very much about the sounds made by his own feet.

When he presently caught sight of the carriage through an opening in the bushes that edged road, he crept stealthily down the slope and peered through the gap. Alisset was still there on top of the thing. From his new position he could see only her upper body, but it was evident that she was rocking back and forth and waving the flask in the air. When the wind dropped for a moment he heard her voice raised, high and sweet. She was singing a verse of *My love he was a Leithian.*

"*Vothra's Eyes and Ears,*" he murmured. "Is she out of her head?"

Clearly he had to get her down and into the carriage before the storm struck, though for propriety's sake he ought not to join her there. He would have to guard the door. He had no sword, but he still had his hands and his knife, and his body with which to block the entrance. Sooner or later someone was sure to come looking for Alisset, and they ought not to think too unkindly of him for aiding her, even if they were men of Sobring Hold.

He drew a breath as the thunder rumbled again, pushed his way through the bushes, and stepped out onto the roadway. Once there, he circled the carriage, moving around the front of it where the horses' traces lay on the ground. He kept at a little distance because he didn't want to startle Alisset if she should chance to notice him creeping about. She, however, continued singing to herself, quite oblivious. When he'd gotten around to a point where he knew he was clearly in her field of view, he raised his voice above the wind and called to her.

"Alisset!" My Lady!"

Her head swivelled towards him. Her mouth made a little round "O." Her flaxen hair had been disheveled by the wind and her face was flushed. Suddenly she laughed. "Oh, there you are, Capt'n Nagaro!" she exclaimed. "Now we can have a party!"

He stepped closer, trying to verify his impression that she was intoxicated. "What are you doing up there?"

"Hiding." She hiccuped, then put a dainty hand to her mouth and giggled.

"Yes, well, that would work better if you kept down low and if you didn't sing," he pointed out. "What are you hiding from?"

She waved the flask around vaguely. "Bad people."

"What happened to the carriage wheel? Has someone gone to fix it?"

She frowned. "Dorf and Driver went back to the Hall," she said as if reciting. "To get a new one."

"They took the old one? And the horses?"

This time she looked confused. "The old one's over there," she said, pointing with her free hand towards the trees on the farther side of the road.

It was his turn to frown, for this made no sense unless the wheel had gotten away from them and rolled across the road. He couldn't see any wheel in the place where she was pointing. He tried again. "Who took the horses?"

She looked at the empty traces. "Someone did," she said solemnly, with the air of stating a significant truth.

"Were there highwaymen? Bandits?"

"Oh yes!" She brightened. "There are bandits. Uncle's soldiers are chasing them."

"Soldiers. You mean your escort?"

This seemed to require some thought. "Yes?" she ventured.

"How many soldiers?"

More thought. "Three?"

"And how many bandits were there?"

"I don' know." She threw her hands in the air. "I di'nt see the bandits."

At this point a growl of thunder caused Nagaro to glance at the lowering clouds. He wanted very much to know exactly how this young woman had come to be left completely alone in such circumstances, but her wits were clearly befuddled by drink and he was running out of time. He needed to get her down and he needed to get the flask away from her.

"What's that you're drinking?"

"S'called apple scrum." She sloshed the bottle. "Driver keeps it un'er his seat. He says it's not for young ladies, but I don' see why not. It's yummy! Do you wan' some?"

"Ah, could I see it, please?"

"All right, Capt'n. Catch!"

She tossed the stoppered flask with a rather high loft and considerably more force than was necessary. He managed to catch it anyway, un-stoppered it, took one sniff, and re-stoppered it immediately. The contents smelled fruity and sweet, and strongly alcoholic. Judging by the weight of the bottle, most of it had already been consumed.

"This goes back under the seat," he told her, stowing it there. "And you had better come down from there and get inside. It's going to rain any minute. You don't want to get wet, do you?"

"No-o." She stared up at the sky, turning this way and that, but still not turning around to look behind her. "Where's the rain?"

As if to answer her, the clouds chose that exact moment to occlude the sun and a strong gust of wind swept across the road, scattering raindrops.

"Oh my!" She stared down at the sprinkling of darker blue dots that had just appeared on the skirt of her sky-blue gown.

"Please, My Lady," he said urgently. "You should come down right now."

"All right." The raindrops had apparently convinced her, for she began a rather unladylike crawl towards him across the carriage roof, moving on one hand and two knees and using the other hand to manage the skirt of her gown.

He was preparing to offer her his hand, but when she reached the edge of the roof she unexpectedly stood up and turned her back to him, swaying, her skirts billowing in the wind. "Catch me!" she cried. Then, flinging her arms wide, she pushed off and was airborne.

"*Bishka!*"

He caught her somehow, handling her as decorously as possible, and set her on her feet as quickly as he could. She was so unsteady, however, that he immediately offered her his arm. And when she didn't immediately take it, he captured her hand, placed it on his arm, and held it there. "Inside. Now." He tried to guide her to the carriage door.

She hung back. "That was fun! Can we do it again?"

"No!"

"Where's my apple scrum?"

"I don't think you should have any more of that, My Lady." He tugged her gently forward.

"Am I a little tipsy, Naga-ro?"

"Just a little." He pulled the carriage door open. "Please. Just get inside."

More raindrops spattered the dusty ground and this time they kept coming. To his immense relief, she climbed into the carriage. But when he tried to close the door, she stuck out her arm to block it.

"Oh, no, no, Naga-raro," she stumbled over his name. "Don' stay out there. Can I call you Naggy-woo?"

He winced. "I'd rather you didn't."

"But it's so much easier to say! You have t' come in too, Naggy-woo. You're getting all wet out there. And we're gonna have a party!"

"No," he said. "I'm not coming in. And we're not having a party."

"But we *have* to." She frowned. "I have some sweet spiced wine for us. See?" She fished under the seat of the carriage and brought forth another flask, larger than the one he'd already taken from her. "You have t' have some!"

"Could I see that?" He took it from her unresisting hand. "I think I had better put this with the other," he said. "I don't drink wine, and you've had enough already."

She blinked up at him. "But aren't you thirsty?"

He was thirsty, in fact— very thirsty. The rain was pelting his head, shoulders, and back, and soaking through his shirt, but it was doing nothing for the dryness in his mouth and throat. He might try turning his face up and opening his mouth, but he knew better than to think he could really slake his thirst that way. "Yes," he admitted. "Do you have any water in there?"

"Oh. No." She gave him a devastated look. "All I have is some soth'ril."

"That sounds fine," he said. "I'd like some sothiril."

"All right." She rummaged under the seat again and produced yet another flask, this one a bit smaller. But as he reached for it, she drew back her hand. A puzzled look crossed her face as if she were remembering something. "No," she said. "It's for after."

"After what?"

There was the puzzled look again. "After the wine. I think."

"Well in that case, I would have to wait a very long time," he said. "Since I don't drink wine. But I am very thirsty, and I'd be grateful for some of that sothiril."

She allowed him to take the flask from her hand when he reached for it a second time. He un-stoppered it, sniffed it, took a sip, and sighed appreciatively. It was Erantil Crimson and still noticeably below ambient temperature. He drank several swallows before recapping the flask and returning it to Alisset. "There," he said. "Thank you." She still looked worried, but he supposed it must be due to some confusion on her part.

"Can you lock this door?" he asked.

She shook her head. "I think the lock's broken."

"Well, lock the other one, then, and I'll stand guard outside this one," he said firmly, and he closed the door in the face of her renewed protests that he should join her so that he wouldn't get wet and they could have a party.

"It's a bit late to worry about getting wet," he muttered to himself. "I pretty much am already." The rain was coming down hard now, with a steady dull rush. It pelted his bare head and obscured the world more than a dozen feet away like a wet, gray curtain. The formerly dusty earth of the roadway was rapidly turning into thick, sucking mud.

He hunched his shoulders and tried leaning against the carriage to take some shelter in its lee, which only meant that whatever water was running off the roof of it came dripping down his neck. He heaved a rueful sigh, turned up his shirt collar, and tried to steel himself to take the dousing. At least it wasn't a cold rain, which was fortunate because most of him could already hardly be wetter if he'd gone for a swim with his clothes on.

He wondered where Brandle was— and Thunder-Heels, for that matter. He supposed they were trying to stay dry, somewhere. And, as if he didn't have enough reasons to regret the loss of his horse, he now remembered putting a cloak into his saddlebag that morning— a fine, thick, tightly-woven one with a hood.

The minutes passed as the rain continued to soak him. His thoughts began to wander. *It really wasn't cold at all. In fact, he felt quite warm... warm, and a little muzzy...* He shook his head to clear it, aware that a soporific lethargy seemed to be creeping over him. He tried to fight it, shaking his head again and stamping his feet, an action that splashed mud all over his boots. A moment later he caught himself with a jerk. He'd been slipping... had fallen against the carriage... He could hardly keep his eyes open— and it was getting worse! Soon he'd have to lie down. It was either that, or fall down.

A fear began to rise in him. This wasn't right, being suddenly so overcome with a need to sleep, in this place, under such conditions. *The only other times he'd felt like this had been when someone had given him a drug or a sleeping drought!* Desperately he turned around and yanked open the carriage door.

Alisset stared at him, round-eyed. "Oh," she said. "Did you decide t' come in, Naggy-woo?"

For answer he staggered up the little steps and all but fell onto the unoccupied carriage seat opposite her, sprawling on it at full length, dripping water. He managed somehow to turn himself more or less face up, struggling to keep a grip on consciousness. He felt hot, fevered. His head was spinning, but his limbs felt heavy and his eyes were doing their best to close of their own accord.

As if from a distance, he heard Alisset say, "You poor thing! You're soaking!"

"Drugged," he said, struggling with his tongue, which didn't seem to want to behave properly. "The soth'ril's drugged. Don' drink it!" *There. At least he'd warned her.*

He gave up trying to keep his eyes open.

As soon as he let them close, the space behind them became filled with swirling images— female images. When he tried to make the images hold still, it seemed to him that all of them were Nevien. She was standing beside him, or at a distance, or she was bending over him, her eyes shining with desire. A wave of heat rose in him and he felt that he might die for wanting her—

Suddenly he felt lips touch his.

They were warm, wet, and smelled of apple scrum. It seemed to him that it was Nevien's face that was bending over him, her lips seeking his, but when he tried to embrace her, he was struggling with arms that felt heavy and fingers that wouldn't properly obey him, as he groped for the form he seemed to see— which wasn't where he seemed to see it...

At last he touched something warm and yielding... *"Oh Nevien!"* he mumbled. *"I've been waiting s' long!"*

He heard a gasp of indrawn breath, and she was stiffening— pulling away! In dismay, he let his leaden arms drop and somehow managed to raise his eyelids. Groggily he stared up at the face that was bending over him. It was round and pink, framed by hair the color of corn silk, with eyes of cornflower blue...

He gasped for breath. "Al'sset?" His blood was still burning and his mind still trying to slide sideways into a dream, but the shock of what he was seeing jolted him in the direction of reality. "Did you try t' kiss me?"

Desperately she shook her head, even as one hand flew guiltily to her lips. "Oh, no, Capt'n! You're dreaming. Go back t' sleep!"

Her image receded in his blurred vision as she retreated to the opposite corner of the carriage and sat down, huddled, on the seat. For a moment longer he clung to what was real. He was in the carriage, the rain was drumming on the roof...

"Go back t' your dream!" Alisset said urgently.

The dream!

Yes, oh yes, the dream! Vothra, how he ached for Nevien! Trying to stay anchored in reality was much too hard. With a grateful sigh, he let his eyelids fall, and the dream was waiting for him, there, behind them.

She was waiting for him. *Standing before him, lips parted, eyes half-veiled by the shadow of dark lashes. Gloriously naked... perfect shoulders, throat, breasts, thighs... and he was sitting on the bed, fumbling with the buttons on his shirt.* "Here," she said, "Let me help you."

As his clothing fell away, he reached for her and took her willing body in his arms. His blood was afire in his veins as he pulled her down beside him. They were rolling together, intertwined upon the sheets. He was kissing her hungrily, caressing her body, desperately embracing this fever-fantasy— this sultry Turowan temptress wearing the face of his beloved princess.

Chapter 23

Caught!

He came to a half-awareness of himself, an awareness that included the sensation of being repeatedly jolted by the motion of a carriage rolling over uneven ground. It did not include the sound of water drumming on the roof. The latter fact evoked a little trickle of thought that suggested that the rain had stopped and he could therefore get out of the carriage and go home, but the thought trickled away again without engendering any action. His head was so very heavy and full of fog, and he had no desire to even try to open his eyes.

After an indefinite time, his awareness came to include the fact that his sodden clothing was sticking to him uncomfortably. Besides that, he was lying in an awkward position, twisted, half on his back and half on his side. The notion slowly took shape in his mind that he ought to try to do something about the latter fact, and this time he actually felt moved to do so. When he tried to shift to a more comfortable position, however, he encountered unexpected resistance to the movement of his arms.

Panic instantly jolted through him as a part of his brain screamed *drugged!* His heart began to race. Memories of his enslavement under heskial surged up, engulfing his drug-fogged consciousness in a tidal wave of terror. He struggled, desperately but weakly, against whatever it was that immobilized his arms and an instant later there came an intense wash of relief as his efforts informed him that he was merely bound at the wrists. *He was restrained, not paralyzed.*

The panic receded. His heartbeat eased its frantic gallop. The fog flowed back, but it wasn't as thick as it had been.

Bound at the wrists...

The thought nagged at him. This was not a good thing— was it? *No,* he decided after a while, *it wasn't.* It suggested... unfriendliness. Unfriendliness... Un-friend meant... enemy... but who were his enemies?

The highwaymen!

A new surge of alarm jerked him more fully awake behind his eyelids as he remembered finding Alisset in jeopardy, and all of his efforts to get her safely into the carriage. Had the highwaymen attacked the carriage while he lay unconscious? Was Alisset even now in their clutches? Had all of those things he'd been worried about as he approached the carriage come to pass anyway, because he hadn't been able to prevent them?

He had to know. With a monumental effort, he pried open his eyes.

The interior of the carriage swam blearily into partial focus. It did not contain a female figure in a sky-blue gown. There were, however, two male figures on the seat across from him, blond, wearing purple baldrics across their white tirkas. *Purple on white... colors of Sobring Hold... Sobring... Alisset Sobring...* That was all right then. Soldiers of Sobring Hold would take care of Alisset. In relief, he let his eyelids fall again.

"Hoy! I think he's comin' around."

The voice seemed somehow remote, and it required an effort to decipher the words.

"Naw. Just movin' in his sleep, I reckon. Like he did before."

"I tell ye, the filthy dog had his eyes open there for a bit."

Nagaro tried to frown. *Filthy dog?* The rest of it had sounded as if it might apply to him, but those two words seemed undeservedly unkind. *And there was still that part about being bound at the wrists.* With another heroic effort he got his eyes open again.

"There! See? I told ye."

His vision was so blurry that he could scarcely tell which of the men had spoken. Gathering his strength to fight the powerful lethargy that weighed on his limbs, he managed to raise his hands about six inches. He tried to speak. *"Whuh—"* He tried again. *"Whuh's th's?"* He couldn't even complete the question. His tongue felt as thick and heavy as a slab of wet shoe leather.

"That? That's a *rope*, mate." There followed some derisive laughter.

Anger stirred. *They shouldn't laugh at him.* Had the man deliberately misunderstood?

He made another effort. *"Whhy?"*

"Why? Why did we tie ye up? 'Cause ye've been a very bad boy, Capt'n-laddie."

"Aye. Ye're in trouble, right enough. We'll teach ye to lay hands on our Lady Alisset!"

Lay hands on the Lady Alisset?

He frowned. *He hadn't done that. The men had got it wrong.* He shook his head to tell them so. Speech was too difficult. So was keeping his eyes open. He let them close.

There had been a dream. He remembered now. A dream in which he'd lain with Nevien— or was it Jila? Really, now that he thought about it, it wasn't very clear. Remembering the dream made him squirm. It had been a strangely warped and fevered thing, and intensely pleasurable— yet, viewed from a distance in its entire context, not a pleasing memory at all.

And it *had* been only a dream— conjured by the drug, he supposed. So he hadn't done anything wrong. It was just a misunderstanding, and he would explain it— when the drug wore off and he could speak. Alisset would explain too. It would be all right... Thinking was still difficult, so he gave it up.

Time passed.

Perhaps he dozed. Or perhaps the drug reclaimed him for a while. In any event, he was suddenly jolted into wakefulness by the abrupt cessation of the motion of the carriage. He opened his eyes, and this time it wasn't nearly as difficult to do so. His head felt clearer, though it had begun to ache dully. His vision was clearer as well. The interior of the carriage, which he could now bring into proper focus, was consistent with what he remembered. Dark brown leather seat cushions and wood stained to match. The curtains had been drawn across the windows, but a glow of light came through the fabric, suggesting that it was still daylight and that the storm must have moved on—which agreed with the fact that he heard no drumming on the roof.

One of the two guards rose and came to stand over him. This one was broad-faced and burly, perhaps thirty or thirty-five years old. "Up with ye!" the man said, and added with a smirk, "If ye can stand."

"Aye. Move your sodden arse." This came from the other guard, whose face now appeared, looking over the shoulder of the first. This one was taller, thinner and younger than his fellow.

Nagaro made the effort to sit up, and succeeded, despite being hampered by his bound wrists. At least they'd tied his hands in front of him. With this success, however, came some unpleasant discoveries. The first was that sitting up made his headache worse. The second was that it also brought on a wave of nausea. And finally, he discovered that his boots were missing— a fact he had failed to notice previously in his general state of numbness. There could be no doubt of it now, however. When he swung his legs off of the carriage seat and set his feet on the floor he immediately felt the floorboards under his bare soles. If he'd needed any further proof, it was offered to him when the nausea doubled him over and he found himself staring at his naked toes while his gorge rose in his throat.

"Ha! Can't hold his drink! Look at him, he's going t' be sick."

"Aye, he's drunk as the dog that got into his master's beer barrel!"

Nagaro, swallowing bile, thought this last a rather poor metaphor. *How would a dog get into a barrel?* It was inaccurate in his case, besides. When he was able to raise his head, he fixed the speaker with a cold stare.

"Not drunk," he said carefully. "Drugged." His tongue still felt sluggish, but he was at least able to get the words out clearly this time, with an effort. Encouraged, he added, "In the sothiril."

The two guards exchanged looks that might have been either surprised or worried, but the older man rallied. "Not drunk?" The man sneered. "Then what's that on your shirt?"

Puzzled, Nagaro tucked his chin to look at the front of his shirt. To his surprise, he found there was a large reddish-pink stain across it that certainly looked as if it could have been spilled wine. The shirt was so generally damp that it was hardly surprising he hadn't noticed it sooner. He frowned. He didn't like the implications of this development. "I don't know how it got there," he said stiffly.

"Can't remember, eh?" The broad-faced guard jeered at him. "Drink'll do that. Up, now and out with ye!"

Nagaro gave the man a look like a dagger. He stood up cautiously, but not cautiously enough, as it turned out, to avoid pounding pains in his head and a fresh attack of nausea. Fighting both, he tottered toward the door, to the sound of sniggers from both of the Leithians. "Where are my boots?" he asked through teeth clenched against what his stomach was trying to do.

There was a derisive snort. "Seems there's a lot ye don't remember."

"Where's the Lady Alisset?"

"Ha! Ye'd like t' know, wouldn't ye?"

A hand seized his upper arm from behind as one of the men moved past him and flung open the door. Gazing through it, blinking in the sudden brightness, Nagaro got his first look at the place to which he had been brought.

The carriage had come to a halt in a kind of unpaved yard bathed in the rich, warm glow of late afternoon. By the lengths of the shadows, Nagaro estimated that he'd been unconscious for at least two hours—which wasn't encouraging. The rain had either stopped some time ago or else had been less heavy here, since the mud was beginning to dry. There were three more guards outside. They were waiting at the bottom of the carriage steps. One of them, a young man with a half-grown mustache, looked vaguely familiar, though Nagaro couldn't place him. Their eyes met briefly, but the young Leithian's glance flicked away.

Looking past the guards, Nagaro saw that the yard was encircled by several one- and two-story buildings, and a small pasture on one side. Beyond the buildings and the pasture, he could see nothing but trees—obviously a forest.

Nagaro stared at the buildings, the yard, the pasture. *He knew this place.* He and Taru had come here once, years ago, thinking it might be his half-remembered Averwin. The season then had been late winter or early spring instead of late summer, but he recognized it all the same. When he'd first seen it, it had been untenanted and he'd imagined that it was a hunting lodge, used in season by the lords of Sobring Hold, since it lay in the midst of Sobring Wood. Now, as he put the bits together, he deduced that he was standing at the other end of the road he and Brandle had come to investigate. He had meant to follow that road to its end if need be— but not like this.

"Go on! Move yer feet!"

The guards behind him had grown impatient. One of them now shoved him forward so forcefully that he nearly fell down the little steps, barely catching himself as his feet hit the ground by taking two rapid steps to regain his balance. The sudden exertion made his head throb violently, and the nausea that accompanied the pain was so severe that it was impossible to remain upright. He fell to his knees in the congealing mud, retching. He hadn't eaten for hours, and there was nothing in his stomach but sour liquid.

He spat, retched, and spat again.

Hands dragged him to his feet amid more derisive laughter, within which he again caught the word *drunk*. Angrily he twisted about in his captors' hands to glare at the stocky, broad-faced guard whose voice he recognized. "I'm not drunk!" he reiterated. "There was a drug in the sothiril. It's making me sick!" Past the man's shoulder, he caught sight of the carriage and his eyes lit upon the left front wheel. It was whole and undamaged, and a perfect match for the left rear wheel, down to the yellowing varnish and the amount of wear on the iron wheel rim. He had no time to consider the implications of this, however, because the guards who held him were dragging him towards the largest building at a pace that was undoubtedly much more comfortable for them than it was for him.

They took him into the building, by a side entrance, and dropped him onto a bench against one wall of a small room that was intended for servants' use, judging by the bare walls and rough-hewn wooden furniture. The tall, thin guard pulled a stool up a half dozen feet from Nagaro and sat down facing him with a smug expression and his arms folded across his chest. The man Nagaro had thought he recognized must have passed on along the hallway for he wasn't among the men in the room. The other guards seated themselves comfortably on the benches of a trestle table that occupied the center of the room.

The stocky broad-faced man was seated there, facing in Nagaro's direction, and he now raised his voice to call for some refreshment. "Hoy there, cook! Let's have some ale! And a bite t' eat for men what've put in a hard day's work."

Nagaro sat gratefully on the bench, leaning the back of his head against the wall, his eyes half closed. He was trying to recover, and also to think. *Simion might be here.* If he could get a glimpse of the young man, he would have accomplished what he'd set out to do— provided, of course, that he was able to get away, which didn't appear such an easy matter. The notion that he would simply explain himself and all would be well seemed increasingly naive. Still, he might hope that whoever was master of these guards would be more open-minded than the men he'd dealt with so far.

"Here ye are, Zirdas." A plump, red-faced, silver-haired man had entered through the room's third door, which apparently communicated with the kitchen based on the aromas that had accompanied the man into the room. He bore a tray laden with a pitcher, several cups, and plates of sliced sausage, bread, and cheese. He came to halt when he caught sight of Nagaro.

"What's this?" He gestured at the unexpected guest.

"That," came the broad-faced man's sneering reply, "Is the great Captain Nagaro! Caught him in *compromising circumstances* with the Lady Alisset, we did."

"Oh *my!*" The man regarded Nagaro with a mixture of shock and awe. "Do ye mean t' hold him *here?*"

"Aye. 'Til Lord Grimbold can deal with him. We'll put him upstairs. In the room. Ye're to feed him now. *If* he can eat."

The plump man, apparently the cook, had continued to stare at Nagaro. "He doesn't look well."

"Too much t' drink, that's all. 'Course he says different, but he would, wouldn't he?"

At this Nagaro sat up straight and gave the speaker a cold stare.

The cook deposited his tray on the table and approached Nagaro. "My name is Brun," he said. "And I'm the cook and the keeper o' this house. Is there anything I can get for ye, Zirda? Some soup, maybe?"

Nagaro returned him a look of gratitude. "Soup sounds good, Tor Brun. Thank you. The bread smells very good too." His tongue was working completely normally again.

"Bread and soup it is, then." The cook turned back toward the kitchen amid a sniggering chorus from the guards, which Nagaro studiously ignored.

He leaned back, allowing his throbbing head to rest against the wall once more, and closed his eyes. He was trying to understand what had happened. There had been a drug in the sothiril— a drug that had caused him to have dreams about lying with a woman. He knew that at least one such drug existed because he'd seen it on the list of items the Jinari had banned.

And this had happened in a situation involving a young woman, unattended and apparently in need of assistance. The drugged sothiril, together with other details, such as the apparently undamaged carriage wheel, suggested a plot or a trap, not just a mishap on the road. But he couldn't see how the trap could have been meant for him. How could they have known he was coming? Not to mention having put together such an elaborate scheme on such short notice. Perhaps it was a trap aimed at snaring the highwaymen then? *And he had wandered into it... Were these men making the most of having caught him because they'd failed to catch the game they'd really been after?*

A polite cough informed him that Brun had returned. He opened his eyes and watched as the cook placed a small folding table in front of him and set upon it a steaming bowl of soup, a spoon, and a plate bearing two generous slices of bread. He thanked the man again and set to, plying the spoon with some difficulty because of the way his hands were tied.

The soup tasted wonderful. So did the bread. His lingering queeziness evaporated in the face of hunger and the satisfaction of that hunger, leading him to conclude that his nausea had been caused by the action of the drug on an empty stomach. Brun stood by long enough to see that his offering was well-received, then went back to his kitchen.

The cook reappeared as Nagaro was sopping up the last bit of soup with the last bite of bread. "Something for ye t' drink, Zirda," he said, holding out an earthenware cup containing a dark liquid.

"Thank you." Nagaro took the cup, supposing it to contain a dark-brewed sothiril. He took a mouthful, choked, and spat it out into the empty soup bowl.

"Not *wine!* I don't drink wine!"

"Your pardon, Zirda, your pardon!" The cook snatched back the cup. "But it's good for the headache a man gets if he's had too much t' drink. I just thought—"

"I have *not* had too much to drink!" Nagaro checked himself, aware that he'd been shouting and that every eye in the room was on him. Brun was staring at him, looking quite terrified. He let out a breath, trying to untie the knot of his anger. "I'm sorry, Tor Brun," he said politely but firmly. "My headache is already better by virtue of your very good soup. I have *not* had too much to drink. I have not, in fact, had any wine at all. I don't drink wine—I keep the ban. And I'd be grateful if you didn't attempt to serve me wine or ale or anything of the kind."

The cook made him a nervous little bow, and said, "As ye wish, Zirda," then fled.

The room was very quiet. The tall thin guard had hitched his stool back a pace. His arms were no longer folded, and he was eyeing Nagaro warily. The other guards were suddenly busy with their sausage and cheese. For once, even the broad-faced fellow seemed to have no snide remark to make.

Nagaro leaned back against the wall once more. He felt very much better, both for the food and for his outburst. Even his clothes were beginning to dry. He began to consider options for escape, and he frowned as he took mental inventory. The lack of boots was an inconvenience, but he could manage barefoot. He also lacked so much as a knife. In fact, he noticed that his knife, its sheath, and even the belt that had carried it had been taken from him. His purse also was gone, so he had no money. Still, knowing where he was made a good deal of difference.

The border of Sobring Hold lay only a few miles to the west, over the crest of the range of hills. The town of Wotana was only another mile beyond that, and it was full of friends and people who were well-disposed towards him. He studied the other men in the room. They were all wearing swords. If he could somehow manage to wrest one away with his hands bound as they were, and then cut the rope...

His thoughts were interrupted yet again by the reappearance of Brun who came out of the kitchen again and approached him hesitantly with another cup. "I've brewed ye some sothiril, Zirda," he said. "It's just been cooling a bit." His tone and manner bespoke a desire to make amends for any earlier transgression.

The guards, who were nearly finished with their repast, all sat up at this, exchanging wary looks as if expecting another explosion. Nagaro, however, had no desire to make an enemy of the cook. He inclined his head to the man. "That was good of you, Tor Brun. Thank you."

He took the cup with one of his bound hands, took a sip and smiled appreciatively, then drank freely, draining it.

The cook, encouraged, returned his smile and turned back towards the doorway that led to the kitchen. Nagaro's eyes followed him, and so it was that he saw the two men who were standing inside the kitchen, just beyond the doorway. The man in front was a rough-looking fellow with grizzled stubble on his chin and a crooked nose. His eyes, riveted on Nagaro, were full of undisguised animosity and his face now twisted into an expression of vicious exultation.

With a jolt that seemed to hit him in the stomach, Nagaro realized that he'd seen both the face and the expression before— over the point of a sword, in the dusk on that stretch of the North Road that led to Sobring Hall. He almost dropped the cup as he leaped to his feet. "*You!*" he exclaimed, and then his glance flicked to the man standing behind the first man's shoulder. It was the young man with the half-grown mustache, wearing a look of horror. And seeing him now beside the other, Nagaro knew where he'd seen the young man before— on that same dusky stretch of road—

"—And *you?*" Nagaro took a step forward, but even as he did so, he felt a rising wave of dizziness. and grayness began to encroach upon his vision.

Brun had spun around to stare at him, then at the two men in the doorway, then back at Nagaro. A horrified expression was beginning also to overtake his ruddy features.

"*No!*" Nagaro shook his head violently. "*Not again!*"

The world was starting to spin, even as it faded. In a flash of rage, he launched himself past Brun, in the direction of the men in the doorway, bent on he knew not what. He never reached them, however, for a darkness descended on his eyes and he felt himself falling.

He must have been completely unconscious by the time he hit the floor.

Chapter 24

The Room

The chain rattled on the floor as Nagaro paced the room. For the sixth or seventh time, it pulled him up short of his stride. This was happening less frequently, but he still swore in annoyance as he bent over and rubbed his ankle where the iron shackle cut into the skin. At least they'd taken the rope off of his wrists. That, together with the fact that his ring was still around his neck, under his shirt, were the only bright spots in what was otherwise a very dismaying turn of events.

He assumed he was upstairs. In *the room.*

The room in question was roughly twelve feet by fifteen. It contained a narrow pallet bed against one wall with a lumpy straw mattress unadorned by pillow, blankets, or sheets. There was also a small, low table, a stool, and a chamber pot under the bed.

In locating the chamber pot, he'd discovered one additional object which he had deposited in his pocket— as evidence. Its presence there burned like a bit of red-hot iron. *It was a bladder-thorn.* The needle-like tip was damaged, blunting it, and it bore traces of blood, dried to a dark red-brown. His mind kept coming back to the thing, and every time it did, his thoughts went veering off in an alarming direction. *Was the blood Simion's? Had Simion been held in this very room? If so, what had they been doing to him, and where was he now?*

Nagaro shook himself in annoyance and yanked his thoughts back to his own predicament. His feet had stopped moving as he reached the end of his chain. Turning around, he resumed his pacing, hoping the physical motion might facilitate the turning of his mental wheels.

The room had a single door, which he'd already determined was kept locked, and a single window, which was barred. The chain didn't allow him to reach either one. The chain itself was forged of solid iron links. It was made fast at one end to a ring mounted securely in the wall at the foot of the bed. The other end was permanently attached to the iron shackle that encircled his right ankle. The shackle was hinged to open, and locked with a key.

As his feet reached the other end of their track, he turned, stepping over the chain as he did so. The action was becoming reflexive. The frown that had settled on his brow deepened. He was being treated like a condemned prisoner, not like a man merely suspected or accused of a crime. He was held as securely in this room as Pavo Maat had been held on the prison barge. And, as in Pavo's case, he saw no hope of escape without outside intervention.

The servant who brought him his food carried no weapon, and also apparently no keys. The door was unlocked by one of the guards, who remained outside while the servant, a lean, wiry, taciturn fellow, ventured in just far enough to put things down on the table, or to retrieve them. The table, in its turn, was placed at the extreme limit of Nagaro's chain and bolted to the floor. The arrangement had been well thought out, and he had to admire the intelligence involved, although it didn't make him feel the least bit better.

In fact, his mood was rapidly deteriorating. In addition to having concluded that escape was impossible, he had a headache. It was a new headache, and one that hadn't left him since he'd regained consciousness, lying on the straw mattress, chained to the wall. That re-awakening had occurred a little before dawn, and it was now nearing sunset on this first full day of his captivity— or so he judged by what little he was able to see through the window.

One reason for his persistent headache, he assumed, must be that he'd struck his head on the floor when he'd fallen the previous evening. The supporting evidence for this was a painful bump on his forehead above his left eye. The other reason, he suspected, was that he'd eaten nothing all day but some bread and had drunk nothing at all.

He paused in his pacing to pass a hand over his brow. He'd been drugged twice, and now his fear that it would happen again was getting the better of him. For breakfast they had brought him porridge and sothiril. The sothiril he'd found he couldn't bring himself to touch. Twice before, it had been sothiril that had betrayed him and his fear wouldn't allow him to trust it a third time. *Not in this place.* And when he'd picked up the spoon for the porridge, it had occurred to him that someone might have guessed he would avoid the sothiril. It was actually just as easy to put something into porridge as into a drink. And so he'd found that he couldn't bring himself to touch the porridge either.

What would they use on him the next time? Something that would make him start babbling? He told himself that such thinking was irrational— that they had no reason to drug him again. The second time had only been dedrel, or something like it, probably done to make it easier to chain him.

That was a reasonable supposition, except that he hadn't seen the guards plotting to do it, and he couldn't shake the notion that the broken-nosed highwayman hiding in the kitchen had done it to him for spite. *And that man might be hiding in the kitchen still.*

Standing still in the middle of the floor, he put both hands to his head and groaned. When his thoughts ran like this, it made him fear he was going mad— which in turn made him fear that the second drug had been more than dedrel.

He shook his head in rejection of the idea, and resumed his pacing. He was becoming very thirsty. He'd have to drink something, sooner of later. Lunch had been bread and soup. And sothiril. He could picture Tor Brun imagining that his "guest" was still feeling ill when the porridge had come back untouched, and therefore sending him soup again. He really didn't want to mistrust Brun, the only person in this place who had treated him with any respect or consideration. Yet he'd been unable to make himself eat the soup. He could picture someone adding a few drops of something to it when the cook's back was turned. He had drunk none of the sothiril, of course, and he'd only eaten the bread because he couldn't imagine how it could have been tampered with.

Keshaal! He had to try to think about something else!

With another groan, he stopped pacing and went to the bed and lay down on it. Pacing probably wasn't good for his headache. Maybe lying down would help. He tried again to puzzle out the story behind his misadventures, but all he seemed to have were questions. What was the bandit leader doing in the kitchen of the Lord of Sobring's hunting lodge? Why was another of the bandits wearing the uniform of Sobring Hold? Did these men lead double lives? Was that why Grimbold's soldiers had so far failed to apprehend them? That was plausible, but it didn't explain much else about what had happened on the North Road.

The most troubling thing was the part that Alisset had played. What had she been told to do, and by whom? He knew that younger Leithians obeyed their elders, and that Leithian women were expected to be obedient to their men, but had she really been placed there as a kind of bait? It was hard for him to imagine a man who had any kind of responsibility for a woman doing such a thing.

His train of thought was interrupted by a muffled sound of voices in the hallway outside the door of his cell. Hurriedly he sat up, turning to face the door and swinging his legs over the side of the bed to plant his feet firmly on the floor.

The voices drew nearer, halting outside the door, and a key grated in the lock. The door swung open and a man-at-arms stepped through, moved to one side of the open door, and stood stiffly to attention. A second man-at-arms followed and took up a similar stance on the other side of the door. Both men were beyond the reach of Nagaro's chain, both were clad in the uniform of Sobring Hold, and neither one appeared in any way familiar. The two men had no sooner taken up their places than a third man stepped through the door. Nagaro knew this man at once. He was none other than Grimbold Sobring.

The lord of Sobring Hold was a powerfully built man of about fifty years, red-faced, with cropped hair that had once been bronze-blond, but now appeared almost flaxen because it was so liberally peppered with silver. He strode into the room and stopped in a position between his two men-at-arms. Standing with belligerent nonchalance, he eyed Nagaro fiercely. He carried some rolled-up papers, held in one fist, which he now smacked absently against the opposite palm.

Nagaro had risen to his feet when the first soldier entered and had taken several steps in the direction of the door, stopping well short of the end of his chain. He could feel Lord Grimbold's disdain and he was very conscious of his bare feet, his stained shirt, and the fact that he hadn't bathed since the previous morning. All of which only made him determined to maintain what dignity he could. Accordingly, he held himself erect with his hands at his sides, trying to ignore his throbbing head and keep his expression neutral. He had given some thought to how he should approach the lord, whenever he finally arrived, and had decided to confine himself to the facts of which he was certain and to refrain from making accusations.

Grimbold stood raking him up and down with his gaze. The man's lip curled and there was a hint of cold satisfaction in his pale blue eyes. "Ah, Captain Nagaro," he said archly. "It seems you now show us your true colors."

"My Lord, I merely came to the aid of—"

"*Silence!*" The Leithian lord made a gesture and the two men-at-arms instantly assumed fighting poses directed at Nagaro, their hands on the hilts of their swords. "The prisoner will not speak until bidden!"

Nagaro stared at the grim-faced guards in frank astonishment. He couldn't see the point of this display. *Surely these Leithians wouldn't dishonor their blades by skewering an unarmed man simply for speaking out of turn? Surely Grimbold wouldn't order it?* Then he remembered how Anduar's man, Pedran, had perished at the hands of Lothard and his men. Frowning, he clamped his teeth shut.

Grimbold gestured again and the guards returned to attention. "The Elder Council of Sobring Hold has been informed of the nature of your crime, Captain," he intoned. "They have debated the matter of your punishment according to Leithian law. And, according to the law, they have pronounced their judgement—which I have here." He flourished the roll of papers.

Alarmed by the number of presumptions he had just heard, Nagaro would have spoken again at this point, but the Leithian Lord held up a warning hand. Then he ostentatiously unrolled the papers, and began to read from one of them.

"The prisoner, Nagaro Nareyo, having compromised the virtue of a high-born lady of the House of Sobring— to whit, the Lady Alisset Sobring— the which constitutes an offense against the honor of this House and Hold— and being himself a person of unknown and presumably common birth, and therefore incapable of satisfying the obligations of honor through single combat, said prisoner should properly be sentenced to atone for his crime through death by hanging."

Grimbold paused and once more held up a restraining hand to stifle the protest that sprang to Nagaro's lips. "*However—*"and the lord's lips twitched as if he were trying not to smile. "In view of the fact that the prisoner has committed no previous offense against this House or Hold, and that he is an officer in the service of the Crown who has distinguished himself to some degree in that service, it pleases this Council to be merciful and to commute the sentence of death in the event that the prisoner shall agree to the following: To wed the Lady Alisset Sobring, and to serve faithfully and honorably as her husband through all the days of their lives together, taking the name of Sobring as his own and submitting himself in all things to the will of the Lord of Sobring and to the judgements of this Council'."

Grimbold ceased speaking and lowered the paper. "So, Captain," he said sternly. "What have you to say?"

Nagaro stood, stunned. *Marry Alisset? Or be hanged?* He had a vision of thirty years of *Naggy-woo.* But what was worse, really, by far, was the idea of having to assume the hated name of Sobring and take orders from the likes of Lord Grimbold. He swallowed, trying to moisten a mouth and throat that had been dry even before Grimbold had delivered this outrageous ultimatum. "Surely there is no need for such extremity, My Lord," he ventured. "If you would carefully examine the facts of the case, I believe you will find that the lady's virtue has not been—"

"The facts have already been examined! It's not your place to dispute them."

Not my place? "How can I defend myself if I can't dispute what you believe to be the facts? You haven't even told me what you think the facts are!"

"The facts speak for themselves!" Grimbold's red face was getting redder, manifesting his displeasure. "You were found in the company of the Lady Alisset, she being in a giddy condition due to drink. You were partially undressed, smelling of wine, with wine on your shirt, and so much besotted that you couldn't be roused. *Do you deny this?*"

Nagaro frowned. "I can't answer for what may have happened while I was unconscious, My Lord, but I can say this: I did *not* drink the wine the lady offered me. It was not I who spilled it on my shirt. In order for a man to be drunk, in fact, the wine must be on the *inside* of him, not the outside. I also did not take off my own boots and belt."

Grimbold waved a dismissive hand. "Clearly you don't remember what you did. It's not uncommon when a man has had too much to drink."

Nagaro shook his head, which unfortunately made it throb painfully. "I remember quite well, My Lord. I drank only the sothiril. Then I stood *outside* the carriage, guarding the door, in the rain. But after a few minutes I was so overcome by the need to sleep that I judged I must have been drugged. I can only imagine that the sothiril contained a sleeping drought of some sort, though I don't know to what purpose. I took refuge in the carriage, rather than lie down in the mud, and the sleeping drug rapidly rendered me unconscious. I swear to you that I have done nothing improper with the Lady Alisset."

For a moment, something like uncertainty flickered in Grimbold's eyes as he listened, but then his eyes narrowed shrewdly. "Are you *sure* of that, Captain?"

"Yes!"

The eyes only narrowed further. "You don't perhaps remember doing something of an improper nature with the lady in what may have seemed to be a dream?"

At the mention of the word *dream*, Nagaro started. It struck him as suspicious that Grimbold should suggest the possibility. "A *dream*, My Lord?" he said carefully. "Surely you don't propose to convict me on the basis of what I do in my dreams."

The Leithian lord had caught his startled movement and his eyes gleamed exultantly. "You *do* remember something now, don't you, Captain," he said insinuatingly. "You *fancy* it was a dream, but drink confuses the mind so that memories can seem like dreams. What did you do in this so-called dream of yours?"

Nagaro felt icy fingers down his back. *It had all been a trap— a trap set for him— and Grimbold was privy to the plot!* He wished he could have said there had been no dream, but honesty wouldn't allow him to deny it. Still he stood his ground, his head up, and looked the Leithian lord in the eye. "As it happens, I did dream of being with a lady," he said levelly. "But it was a different lady. One who couldn't possibly have been there. And it *was* a dream, My Lord. You will not convince me otherwise."

Grimbold's impatience had apparently begun to mount as he listened to Nagaro's explanation, for his face twitched and his fingers worried the papers in his hands. Still, he managed a stiff grimace of a smile, apparently intended to be placating. "Come now, Captain, be sensible. You must admit that you may be mistaken. The Elder Council has been lenient, so why not make the best of it? A pretty young wife, an alliance with a noble House— this is not so bad, surely? I have a paper here for you to sign." He stepped forward to place one of the papers he held upon the little table.

Trying to maintain a calm facade despite rising anger that was making his head pound, Nagaro advanced to the limit of his chain and bent to examine the paper. It was a formal statement beginning with a confession to having committed a "grievous offense" against the virtue of the Lady Alisset and against the honor of the House of Sobring. It proceeded to an expression of contrition and then to a pledge to marry the lady, to take the name of Sobring, and to submit to the authority of the Lord and Council of Sobring Hold. It was so worded as to put all of these words into the mouth of whoever signed it. Frowning, he straightened and stepped back. "I have committed no such offense," he said evenly. "There is no reason I should sign this."

This time the Leithian lord scowled. "You're in no position to refuse, Captain!" he snapped. "Unless you wish to hang. You admit you cannot dispute the facts. You admit to having memories of a carnal nature—"

Nagaro's head was by now pounding cruelly. He cut across Grimbold's words. "I'm not convinced sufficient care was taken in determining the facts, My Lord," he said coldly. "What does the Lady Alisset say? Does she accuse me?"

At this, however, Grimbold gave a snorting laugh. "The Lady Alisset was in a confused state, and in any case the testimony of young women is of little value. They are giddy creatures, easily confused, and given to excesses of emotion. In Sobring Hold we do not consider women to be reliable witnesses."

Women not reliable witnesses? Nagaro stared in dismay. Alisset was his best, perhaps his only, witness! "This is not the way of things in the Court of Lankura!"

"We are not in Lankura, Captain!" Grimbold grated. "We're in Sobring Hold. *I am lord here!*"

Nagaro's head hurt so badly that his eyes would scarcely focus. He felt desperation rising. "But I'm not one of your subjects!" he protested. "I'm a citizen of Edrovir. I demand that my case be examined by the Crown—"

"*Silence!* By all the Gods, you will *not* make demands!" Grimbold's face was beet-red. He had leveled a finger at Nagaro and actually stamped his foot to emphasize the negative. The two men-at-arms who flanked him edged fractionally away from him.

Nagaro moved not an inch, and for a several heartbeats he and the Lord of Sobring Hold stood with gazes locked. Then Grimbold abruptly laughed harshly. "You have no House or Wared, Captain," he sneered. "No family. Who will bring suit for you?"

"I may not have a family, but I have friends—"

"And where are these *friends*, then, Captain? You've ventured into Sobring Hold, and Leithian law is sovereign here. You will sign the paper, or you will hang!"

Nagaro's mind raced. He swallowed, trying desperately to moisten his parched mouth and throat while the blood pounded excruciatingly in his brain. Then he remembered what Kuran had told him in parting. "You may hang me, My Lord, if you're quick about it," he said, speaking with all the dignity he could muster. "But there will be consequences. I am an officer of the Royal Fleet. I came here in connection with an official investigation, and Lord Kuran knows my objective. Besides that, my presence is required for an important mission that is to set sail at the end of the week. Lord Kuran will by now have learned of my disappearance and will make inquiries. He'll bring any suit that is necessary, and it will go ill with you if it's found that I was hanged on a trumped-up charge—"

"*Enough!* By the blood of Kroneg's brow, you will be silent, you insolent cur!" Grimbold had been growing redder and redder during Nagaro's recital and by now was literally spitting with rage. He gestured a command to the two men-at-arms.

The two men advanced threateningly, and stopped. Their hands were on their sword hilts, but their blades remained sheathed. Nagaro's gaze flicked from one to the other, reading their unwillingness in their eyes. For the space of two heartbeats all four men stood rigid. Then, very deliberately, Nagaro turned his back on the three Leithians. Dragging his chain, he walked the few steps to the bed, doing his best to ignore the fearful pricking between his shoulder blades.

Behind him, Grimbold uttered an oath, and there was a muttered exchange between the lord and his two guards. Then the man raised his voice, its tone taut with bridled rage. "You're being a fool, Captain! You'll change your mind when you've had time to think about it!"

Nagaro had sat down on the edge of the bed and now he stretched himself out on it and closed his eyes— still without having turned his gaze to the lord of Sobring Hold. "Time will not serve you, My Lord," he said wearily. "I will not sign that paper."

He heard an angry hiss of breath sucked past bared teeth, then, "We'll see about that! I give you three days!"

He heard the slick rustle of the paper being whisked from the table, the sound of booted feet withdrawing, the door being closed and locked, and finally the sound of footsteps retreating down the hallway. He drew a shuddering sigh. Clearly there was no point in trying to reason with Grimbold Sobring over this, but he didn't like having had to bluff. He was uncomfortable with having touted his own importance. He hoped he hadn't overstated it too grossly, but the truth was that he couldn't imagine how he would be saved without the intervention of someone like Lord Kuran.

He was a little surprised that Grimbold had given him three days, rather than just declaring he would hang him on the spot. Had he really given the man pause with his talk of inquiries, the Crown, and the Lord of the Fleet? The idea was encouraging, but it didn't quite ring true. From the document Grimbold had read, it sounded as if the Elders of Sobring Hold didn't really want to execute him. That might be what was restraining the lord of the Hold. But it had also seemed to Nagaro that Grimbold preferred the idea of having him alive and under his control. And that *might* mean that he could bargain for more time when the three days were up— or it might only mean that he could expect more drastic forms of coercion.

How long could he hold out? Would anyone come to help him?

He thought about Kuran, who was his best hope. He thought he'd seen a subtle dilation of Grimbold's eyes at his mention of someone making an inquiry, and he dared to hope this meant that the inquiry had already been made. But how much more could Kuran do?

He thought of Brandle. It seemed likely that the attempted horse theft had been a ruse to draw Brandle away— to separate them. He hoped the lieutenant was all right, that he'd gotten safely away. The lieutenant would want to help Nagaro if he could, and he was a Leithian, but he had little standing since his father had disinherited him. In fact, there was probably little that Brandle could do, and he might only put himself in danger if he tried. In which case Nagaro had to hope that being Lord Madred's son would protect him even if Brandle wasn't high in his father's good graces.

And finally, he thought of Simion, hoping that the young Kelorin was still alive, somewhere. If Simion was alive, and could get away— and if he somehow learned of Nagaro's plight— he would certainly try to summon aid. But Simion had even less standing in the world than Brandle. Just his merchant family...

About half an hour after Grimbold's departure, the taciturn servant brought Nagaro's dinner. It consisted of bread and water. This, Nagaro reflected, was probably intended as a punishment, an expression of the lord's anger. He smiled bitterly to himself, wondering whether the man were even aware that he'd already been eating nothing but bread. He examined the cup of water, sniffed it, tasted it. When he still felt no ill effects a quarter of an hour later, he gratefully drank the rest of it, draining the cup quickly before fear could again get the better of him. He ate the bread then, finding it easier to swallow once his mouth wasn't so dry, and lay down, feeling somewhat better for the food— and especially for the drink. His headache eased a little. He closed his eyes to sleep. All he had to do was wait this out. *After all, they couldn't make him sign the paper.*

***

He awoke in the black of night, out of a dream in which Bron Sobring had been sitting on his chest while Dreigen's bony fingers probed along the inside of his forearm, seeking a promising spot to insert a bladder-thorn. His mind was screaming *heskial!*

"Bloody bodgering Hel!" He swore aloud, sitting bolt upright on the narrow bed, sweating, his heart pounding. They *could* make him sign the paper— *with heskial!* They could force him to marry Alisset! With Heskial, they could make him do whatever they wanted. And he had every reason to believe that Grimbold Sobring had access to heskial and knew how to use it!

He couldn't lie down and sleep again after that. Not with the image burning in his brain of men creeping into the room... stealing across the floor... *one of them holding ready the accursed bladder-thorn...*

He sat cross-legged instead, near the foot end of the bed, his back against the wall. In this position he could do no more than doze, but he told himself he would awaken quickly if anyone came into the room... *If anyone were to touch him...*

When morning came at last, suffusing the room with a dreary light, he prayed that the servant would again bring him bread and water. The taste of sothiril he knew would easily mask the taste of heskial— of many drugs, in fact. But he *knew* the taste of heskial in water. He could take just the tiniest amount onto his tongue and he would be able to tell.

Breakfast, when it finally came, was sothiril and porridge.

Both were steaming hot, the aromas maddeningly wholesome and enticing— or they would have been, if not for the whisperings of his tortured mind: *Either one could contain heskial.*

He groaned aloud. *Why, oh why, couldn't it have been water?*

But no... even water wouldn't be safe! Some drugs had no taste. A tasteless drug in his food or drink could render him unconscious. *And then... the bladder-thorn, and the heskial...*

Chapter 25

Lord Madred

Nagaro jerked himself awake. He had been drifting... dozing... he could tell. The room's window faced roughly west, and he could mark the passage of time in the afternoon by the movement of the rectangular splash of sunlight on the opposite wall.

It was afternoon of the second day of the three days that Grimbold had given him.

He spent almost all of his time now sitting on the bed, leaning against the wall. The practice conserved his energy and kept the pain in his head to a low, dull throbbing that was so constant he could almost ignore it. His thirst was harder to ignore. His throat was dry, his mouth pasty. His tongue felt thick and heavy. But it didn't matter what liquid they brought him— sothiril, water, soup— he couldn't bring himself to touch any of it.

***

There was a sound of voices outside in the hall. Nagaro frowned. It was too early, by about an hour, for them to be bringing his dinner. One of the voices he hadn't heard before in this place, though it seemed familiar. For an instant his heart leaped, but he knew Kuran's voice and it wasn't Kuran.

The key grated in the lock. The door opened. To Nagaro's surprise, the man who appeared in the doorway was Madred Furthing.

Like Brandle, Lord Madred was tall, blond, broad-shouldered, and handsome— amply endowed with nature's gifts. Unlike his eldest son, however, Madred Furthing was also a master of hauteur. His usual manner was that of one who considers himself superior to nearly everyone else around him. On this occasion, Lord Madred stepped into the room, dressed as for a day at court, and swept the dismal cell with a disdainful glance. Turning, he spoke to the guard in the hallway.

"Give me that chair, Zirda. And you may close the door. No, I don't need anyone in here with me. This man will not do me any harm."

The chair in question was a simple wooden one with a high back and no arms. Lord Madred carried it two paces past the little table and set it down in front of Nagaro's place on the bed, at a comfortable distance for conversing, well within the reach of the iron chain. As the door clicked shut behind him, he seated himself on the chair and regarded Nagaro with a cool, steady gaze.

Nagaro returned the look in silence. The silence lengthened. Eventually it was Madred who broke it.

"You don't look very well, Captain."

Nagaro made no answer. He wasn't prepared to dispute the other man's observation.

Madred tried again. "The cook tells me you've eaten nothing but bread, and drunk nothing, since the day before yesterday, and then it was only a cup of water. He is rather distraught about this."

Nagaro swallowed painfully. "I don't mistrust Tor Brun." Speech wasn't easy, and his voice came out hoarse and husky. "But food can be... tampered with, before or after it leaves the kitchen."

"Surely you don't think someone is trying to poison you."

Nagaro gave the lord a cold stare, and rasped, "I don't trust anything in this place!"

Lord Madred sighed heavily. "This won't do at all," he said with an expression as if he were tasting something mildly unpleasant. "I can't have a civil conversation with you in this condition." He stood up, went to the door, and opened it. "Will you have someone fetch us a pitcher of water, please? A large one. See that it's full. And also fetch two glasses." He started to turn back, then added, "And please be sure everyone understands that I intend to share this refreshment with your, ah, guest."

The Leithian lord left the door open and proceeded to make a perambulation of the room while awaiting the result of his request. Nagaro ignored him and closed his eyes. He didn't know what Madred's purpose here might be. The water would be very welcome, but the fact that the man wanted to talk rather than simply ordering the manacle unlocked was not encouraging.

When the water arrived— in an earthenware pitcher with a pair of cups to match— Lord Madred moved the stool close to the bed so that it stood between them and could serve as a table. He filled both cups and placed them on the stool before returning to his chair. Then, seeing that Nagaro still made no move, he sighed, and taking up his own cup, drank from it.

Only when the lord had set the cup down again, and he could see that it was visibly less full, did Nagaro shift his position. He edged himself forward on the mattress and reached for his cup. Raising it, he took an experimental swallow. It was cool, without any trace of inappropriate flavor. Gratefully he drained it, and it was as if he could feel life flowing down his throat and out into his veins. There was an immediate, though modest, easing of his headache. His throat and tongue felt better as well.

He set the cup down with a heartfelt sigh. "Thank you, My Lord," he said fervently.

Lord Madred gave him a barely perceptible nod of acknowledgment, then took up the pitcher and refilled the empty cup, gesturing for Nagaro to drink more if he wished. Nagaro seized the cup again unabashedly and drank about half of the contents. At that point he felt satisfied, at least for the moment, and he set the cup down. "*Vothra*," he murmured, "that was good." He bent his head to massage the still-tender spot above his eye.

Lord Madred considered him. "I must say that I am disappointed, Captain," he said at length, "to see you fallen so low."

Nagaro's head came up sharply. "Not half so disappointed as I shall be, My Lord," he retorted, "if I learn that you are a party to this abominable scheme."

Madred looked taken aback. "Abominable scheme? Come now, Captain. The circumstances may have provided the opportunity for you to trip yourself up, but it's still you who have done the tripping. You're not the first man to be undone by drink, I might add." Here the man's tone was mildly patronizing. "Your lack of familiarity with such things has surely contributed, and I dare say it also explains why you're having so much difficulty accepting the situation."

Nagaro reached for his cup again to cover his rising anger. He took a swallow and lowered the cup, still holding it in his hand. "Are you familiar with the tale of Nevrath and Hindrath, My Lord?" he asked.

Madred looked puzzled. "The older son wandered too close to the edge of the cliff at the falls of Vered Mahir, as I recall, and fell. We Leithians use the tale to illustrate how an older son may lose the rule of his Hold to a younger son if he isn't careful."

Nagaro set the cup down and passed a hand over his eyes. "You're a poor scholar of Kelorin history, My Lord," he said. "In the first place, Nevrath was the younger brother, not the elder. The people of the Wared chose him over Hindrath, because, of the two, he was the more like his father and more suited to lead. So the story illustrates how Kelorin folk choose the best leader, rather than passing the rule automatically to the eldest son. But all of that is beside the point I was trying to make. Which is this: Nevrath did *not* wander too close to the edge. He did *not* 'trip himself up.' He ended up at the bottom of the cliff because he was pushed."

"Well… I suppose it depends upon what you mean by the word—"

"I mean *pushed!*" Nagaro made a shoving gesture with his free hand. He was not in a mood to be patient, and it took all his effort to curb his annoyance as he tried to explain. "His enemies lured him to the top of the cliff, and when he failed to fall over the edge as they had hoped, one of them stepped in and gave him a shove. *That* is what I mean by 'pushed.' And then that enemy went back to Hindrath and told him that his brother had tripped and fallen. The point I was trying to make is that he did *not* trip, and his enemy *lied* about what had happened to make it appear that Nevrath had come to harm by his own carelessness."

"And you think your case is similar?" Madred looked down his long patrician nose. "You cast yourself in the role of Nevrath. And I, I suppose, am the brother?"

"You, or the Elder Council." Nagaro gestured in the air. "Anyone who is being lied to."

"And who is your enemy then? Who do you think is telling these supposed lies?"

Nagaro regarded the other man coldly. "Why are you here, My Lord?" he asked. "I hoped you had come out of a desire to know the truth. But perhaps you're only here to try to negotiate my capitulation?"

Lord Madred gave him a haughty glance. "Since you ask, I was returning from Furthing Hold and stopped at Sobring Hall, where Lord Grimbold informed me that he was holding you here— and under what circumstances. And, in fact, I am necessarily concerned, since the Lady Alisset is my ward and will not be wedded without my approval. I could have awaited the outcome of Grimbold's actions. Instead, I have come now to see what may be done, and this is because I believe you to be a good man, however badly you may have stumbled. I would like to see this matter resolved amicably if at all possible."

…may have stumbled…

Nagaro managed to contain his outrage. "That's a fair beginning, My Lord," he said levelly. "And I also would prefer to believe that *you* are good man— however ill-considered may be the company you keep."

This time Madred stiffened and he drew himself up. "*Ill-considered? The company I keep?* I should punish you, Zirda, for such insolence!"

"Why? Because I speak to you as you just spoke to me? If you don't like it, I suggest you reconsider your tone, My Lord." The words were out before Nagaro could stop them. Perhaps his state of exhaustion had undermined his control. Nor did he stop there, though he did try to curb the anger in his voice. "My Lady Guardian didn't teach me to grovel, My Lord. Neither did she teach me to dominate. She was a Kelorin Lady and a devoted Vothrin, and she taught me to treat every person with respect— at least until they prove by their actions that they don't deserve it."

"Prove by their actions? What are you implying?" The Leithian lord was trying to look down his nose as if it were beneath him to be rattled, but the touch of angry color in his cheeks betrayed him. "Do you presume," he added, "to judge the actions of men of the noble class? Of those who are your betters?"

This was too much altogether. Nagaro was off of the bed and on his feet amid an alarming rattle of chain. His eyes fairly blazed, and when he spoke it was with ice-cold fury.

"My Lord, I have been tricked, and trapped. I have been drugged twice! I have been robbed. I've been bound, imprisoned, and chained! Falsely accused, threatened with hanging, and denied the right to present any kind of defense! All because I stopped to give aid to a young woman who appeared to have been left abandoned on the road on top of a broken-down carriage! And *now* you presume to judge me on hearsay, and claim that your noble birth gives you the right to do so? If this is an example of Leithian honor— of the honor of what you call men of the *noble class*— I can tell you, *I am not impressed!*"

Nagaro stopped speaking because the combination of having stood up so suddenly and the intensity of his emotion was causing his head to pound afresh, almost blinding him with pain. Stooping, he groped for the half-empty cup, got his hand around it, and retreated stumblingly to the bed. Once sitting on it, he pressed his back against the wall, gulped water, and shut his eyes. As the pain began to recede, there arose in his mind the image of the stunned expression on Lord Madred's face, and he remembered belatedly that it was this man who had brought him the water.

"I beg your pardon, My Lord," he murmured, "if I have misjudged you in any way."

There was silence for several heartbeats, and then Madred spoke.

"I have to say, I'm quite impressed, Captain." The Leithian lord's tone was surprisingly mild. "And I will never believe you to be a mere commoner. Some high-born Kelorin man has surely fathered you— out of wedlock, perhaps, but that is hardly your fault."

Nagaro's eyes snapped open in surprise. "Why do you say so, My Lord?" he asked sharply. "Because I lost my temper?"

Madred was regarding him appraisingly. "You did it with admirable forcefulness, and eloquence— giving your words the ring of judgement. Clearly you were born to command lesser men."

Nagaro shook his head emphatically, though the action made it throb. "Being more eloquent than another man does not make me better," he protested. "My Lady Guardian taught me to read, and encouraged me to do so— and she had an excellent library. But that doesn't make me better than my friend Taru who speaks like a fisherman because his father was a fisherman. I once laughed at Lothard for not knowing the meaning of the word 'immaterial', not because of his ignorance, but because he fancied himself superior while demonstrating an inferior vocabulary—"

"A man of the high blood is not defined by the reading of books." Madred cut him off, then dismissed the matter with a gesture. "But you have made some serious allegations, Captain. If I promise to hear you out, will you swear to speak the truth?"

This sounded hopeful, and Nagaro responded accordingly. "Upon my honor and in Vothra's name, I will tell you nothing false. I have no oath more binding."

"Very good." Madred stood up. "A moment, please." He went to the door, which he opened, and then spoke to the guard outside. "Have the cook send dinner up to us— in a common serving dish, with separate plates and utensils. Make it clear that we will share the meal."

The Leithian lord returned to his seat.

Nagaro had shifted back to a seat at the edge of the bed and picked up the pitcher. "Thank you for that, My Lord," he said very sincerely, as he poured himself another cup of water.

Madred gave him a stern look. "I can't have you starving yourself." He leaned back in his chair. "Now tell me your tale, Captain. Omit no significant detail, but try otherwise to be brief. You may begin with the state in which you found the carriage and the Lady Alisset."

Nagaro described how he had found the carriage standing abandoned in the road, the missing wheel, and the absence of horses, driver, chaperon, and escort. "The Lady Alisset was sitting on top of the carriage, drinking from a flask and singing. And there was a thunderstorm fast blowing up over the western hills."

"She was on *top* of the carriage... *singing?*"

"Yes. She was quite drunk, My Lord."

Madred bridled. "That's not a word to employ when speaking of young ladies!"

"It's a straightforward word, My Lord. And accurate. A less straightforward word might be misconstrued."

Madred considered this. "I suppose there's some truth to that," he conceded. "Are you going to tell me, then, that she had begun consuming the wine we see splashed on your shirt?"

"No, My Lord. She had found something else. She called it 'apple scrum' and said that the driver kept it under his seat."

"You're saying that *my* driver keeps apple scrum under his seat?"

"*She* said it, My Lord. And I don't know that it was *your* driver. It might have been Grimbold's. I couldn't get anything very coherent from her concerning what had happened. She said the driver and chaperon had gone back to the Hall for a new wheel, but that the old wheel was in the woods on the other side of the road. Her uncle's soldiers were chasing bandits, but she'd seen no bandits. That sort of thing. From what she said, I gather it was her first experience with the apple scrum, and I doubt she had any idea how strong it was. I got her to toss the flask down to me. The contents smelled very strongly fermented and there wasn't much left. I put it back under the driver's seat. I don't blame her so much for what happened as I blame whoever it was that left her alone in such a situation."

Lord Madred's high brow was creased by a frown. "If it is as you say, I would tend to agree," he said, and sniffed. "Apple scrum is an unrefined concoction, favored by common laborers. But we must return to your tale. You say it was threatening rain. I assume you both took shelter in the carriage?"

Nagaro shook his head. "I persuaded her to come down, and to get into the carriage, but I intended to stay outside for the sake of propriety. It was by that time already raining, and she invited me into the carriage. I declined. She talked about 'having a party' and said that she had some wine. When she produced a flask from inside the carriage, I took it from her, since I don't drink wine and she'd already had more than enough of such things."

"Did you open it? Did you perhaps spill some?"

"No, My Lord. I took the Lady Alisset at her word as to the contents. I stowed it under the driver's seat with the apple scrum, and that is the last I saw of it. I swear it to you in Vothra's name."

Lord Madred sighed. Then he reached into the front of his tirka and produced a folded paper, which he opened and laid on the little table. "Your account leaves a number of points unexplained when compared to the detailed charges I obtained from Lord Grimbold," he observed dryly, bending over the paper.

"I don't doubt that, My Lord."

"For example, it says here that, 'following an attack upon the carriage by bandits,' the lady's escort returned to find you *inside* the carriage. How did you come to be inside?"

Nagaro sighed. "The explanation for that, by implication, explains a number of other things."

"Very well, Captain, proceed."

Nagaro took another swallow of water, and began to describe how he'd come to drink some of the sothiril and the events that had followed. When he reached the description of how he had opened the carriage door and fallen upon the carriage seat in a half-conscious state, the Leithian lord raised a hand.

"You're quite sure it was only sothiril you drank? Could it not have been sothiril laced with some strong spirit, which in fact overcame you?"

"It was sothiril, My Lord. Erantyl Crimson, to be exact. And it had neither taste nor smell of fermentation. I *have* been drunk once in my life, and I remember what it felt like. This experience was quite different."

Lord Madred hadn't taken his eyes from Nagaro's face. "And so you contend that this sothiril was drugged?"

"My Lord, I cannot know it with certainty, but it's the only reasonable explanation," Nagaro answered earnestly. "I drank only a few swallows, and I began to feel the effect within a few minutes afterwards. It was no natural sleep that overtook me. I have been drugged to make me sleep before, at the hands of a healer. This felt very like a sleeping drought in the beginning, but it also gave me vivid dreams. I was unconscious under it for at least two hours. When I came to myself, I found the Lady Alisset gone and two guards wearing Sobring livery there in her place. My wrists were bound. My boots, belt, knife, and purse were missing. Also there was this stain on my shirt."

"I'm afraid I'm not as familiar with such... drugs... as you seem to be, Captain." Lord Madred had listened with a gathering frown and now he spoke with apparent care. "I understand the nature of a sleeping drought, and that any manner of thing might have been done without your knowledge while you were unconscious. But is there really such a thing as a drug that can give men dreams as you describe?"

"Oh yes." Nagaro spoke with confidence that came from personal experience. "Opa, I know gives dreams. They're rather fanciful and frequently very pleasant. But this drug gave me dreams of what Grimbold was pleased to call a 'carnal nature'."

At this, Madred's eyes narrowed ever so slightly. "Meaning," he said, "that you dreamed of lying with a woman?"

Nagaro felt the blood in his face, but he answered without hesitation. "Yes, My Lord. And I know there is at least one drug that has that effect. With a little research I could tell you the name of it. And I find it suspicious that such a drug was used in such a circumstance, and even more suspicious that Lord Grimbold brought up the subject of such a dream before I made any mention of it. He then proceeded to suggest that it had been a real experience, a drunken one, that only seemed to be a dream."

"And you're quite certain it was not?" Lord Madred was frowning harder, and his cool blue glance was probing.

"Yes. I'm quite sure of it for several reasons."

"And these are?"

Nagaro ticked the items off on his fingers, doing his best not to flinch under the lord's unrelenting gaze. "First, the woman I dreamed about was not the Lady Alisset. Second, the drug was very nearly paralyzing. As I was falling under it, my arms felt so heavy I could scarcely lift them.

I couldn't have physically *done* the things I dreamed about doing. And finally, there is... ah... the exact nature of the things I dreamed." Nagaro ceased speaking. He could once again feel the blood burning in his face.

"Meaning?" Still the blue eyes skewered him.

Not allowing his glance to waver, Nagaro took a breath. "Let's say that I don't think an innocent, high-born young lady would know the tricks of a Turowan tavern woman."

"I *see*." Madred's tone as well as his glance revealed his distaste. "Are you in the habit of availing yourself of such... tricks... Captain?"

Nagaro stiffened. "No, I am not, My Lord. I've had only one such encounter. It was on the occasion I have already mentioned, when I was drunk, and it resulted in the begetting of my daughter. I have sworn not to repeat the mistakes I made on that occasion, and it's an oath that I have kept."

"Ah." Lord Madred leaned back in his chair. "I didn't require all the details, Captain, but it speaks well of you that you've offered them so freely."

It was at this moment that the dinner arrived, heralded by the sound of voices outside in the hallway and the opening of the door. The silent servant, accompanied by another, brought in the small folding table that Nagaro had previously seen downstairs, and placed upon it a steaming tureen of savory rabbit stew, a basket of bread, and a pitcher of what turned out to be sothiril. A small stack of dishes and utensils was also produced and deposited on the table as well. Following this, the two servants withdrew without comment.

The plates, cups and forks were quickly distributed, the stew ladled out, and the sothiril poured. The two men spoke little while they ate. Nagaro moved from the bed to the stool, which was of a better height for eating, and he devoured his food without any pretense of concealing his eagerness. He was quite capable of displaying impeccable table manners when required, but in this case he was very hungry and not inclined to give the Leithian lord any new excuse to suggest that he carried noble blood in his veins.

Madred ate with precise, fastidious movements, watching Nagaro narrowly all the while. As Nagaro was sopping up the last drop of gravy from his plate, the Leithian lord spoke.

"You eat like a soldier on campaign who doesn't know when his next meal may come to him."

Nagaro gave him a baleful look. "I feel embattled here, My Lord. I don't expect you to stay long, and once you're gone, the people here will again be free to follow whatever orders they may have been given, or to do whatever they imagine might please their lord."

"I cannot but think that you are being overly suspicious—"

"*Still?*" Nagaro cut the other man off. "Listen, then, while I tell you how I was drugged the second time." Returning to his seat on the edge of the bed, he proceeded to do so.

Madred had appeared annoyed at first at the interruption, but he listened attentively and with a gathering frown. He had put the folded paper back into his tirka during the meal but he brought it out again as Nagaro finished speaking. "It's told rather differently here," he said with a trace of irony. "This has you spitting out sothiril and calling for wine instead, and then becoming drunk enough again that you had to be carried upstairs."

Nagao's brows knit fiercely. His gray eyes flashed. "In every way in which it differs from what I've just told you, it is a lie, My Lord! There were men enough there to witness, who could tell you so if they could be persuaded to tell the truth."

"It also says that you attacked the cook."

"I did nothing of the sort!"

"It says you made a run at him."

Nagaro groaned in frustration and took his head in his hands. "Not at the *cook!* Though he was in the way, and so it might have seemed so. I was going for the two men behind him— the highwaymen— standing in kitchen doorway."

"Highwaymen? *In the kitchen?*" Madred's voice was laden now with mingled indignation and disbelief. "Come now, Zirda, this is absurd!"

Nagaro's head had come up. "There were two men there. A roughly-dressed, older, heavyset man with a crooked nose, and a slim young man in Grimbold's livery who is trying to grow a mustache. And I swear that I had seen them both before, together with five others, on the North Road not much more than a week ago when I came with another man. They tried to steal our money and our horses."

An expression of outrage had been growing in Madred's face, and he regarded Nagaro coldly when the latter ceased speaking. "The second man you describe is unknown to me," he said sternly. "But the first description matches Grimbold's gamekeeper, Grobend, who looks after this part of Sobring Wood. I hardly think it likely it was he who tried to rob you on the road!"

Nagaro lifted his chin. "I know what I saw, My Lord. It was the same man. And *he* knew *me* as well. He gave such a look of gleeful spite as would curdle cream. He had good reason, too. Not only did Geivian and I get cleanly away, but I cut him as well. If you want the proof of it, bid him roll up his right shirt sleeve and you'll see the healing wound on his sword arm— so!" Nagaro marked his own right biceps with a slashing motion of his hand.

"Oh, but Captain, this makes no sense." Madred had passed from outrage to condescension. "Why would a man who has a good position under Lord Grimbold be out among these highwaymen?"

"*I* don't know!" Nagaro gestured wearily. "I don't pretend to be able to untangle the twisted workings of this place. But I have sworn to speak only truth, and I'm telling you what I saw."

Madred was shaking his head, but his disbelief seemed now to give way to curiosity, for he asked, "You have been *twice* at that place upon the North Road within a week?"

"Yes, My Lord."

"To what purpose? What was your business in Sobring Hold?"

At this, Nagaro drew breath, aware that the truth, here, could get him into trouble if Lord Madred had any involvement in Simion's disappearance. Making a swift decision, however, he decided to take the chance.

"We were looking for a missing man both times— Simion Rudrin. You may recall the name, My Lord, since he's been employed as your clerk."

There was a little twitch in the muscles around Lord Madred's mouth. "Yes," he said sourly. "I know the name. But you said *'we'*, Captain, and *both times'*, and mentioned another man, I believe. Please elaborate."

"The first time I came with Simion's cousin, Geivian. He'd seen Simion's face in the window of a carriage escorted by men in Grimbold's livery earlier that day, and followed it. That carriage turned down a side road just at the spot where the abandoned carriage was. The second time, I was with Brandle Furthing."

There was a more significant twitch of Lord Madred's facial muscles. "So my less-than-favored son is involved in this?" he said tartly. "I notice you didn't mention him when you described how you approached the carriage."

"You asked me to be brief, My Lord, and we had become separated earlier."

Nagaro went on to describe how Brandle had disappeared in pursuit of the horse thief while he had been scouting from the top of the rock. He finished by adding, "He will likely have reported my disappearance to Lord Kuran. And if so, Kuran will have made an inquiry. Kuran approved our search, My Lord, because Simion had been a source of information in his investigation into illicit trading in substances banned by the High Council of Jinara."

"Oh, *that*." Madred made a disdainful flick of his hand. "Elgurn has circulated an edict about it. I've seen it. It doesn't concern me."

Nagaro frowned. The man sounded sincere, as if he really didn't think the illicit trade had anything to do with him. Nagaro suspected the situation to be otherwise, although possibly unbeknownst to Lord Madred. He decided the time was probably not opportune to pursue the issue directly, since the evidence was circumstantial. Still, he thought he might gain some information.

"If this place lies at the end of the road I was investigating, as I believe it does, then it's possible that Simion may have been held here. He may be here still."

Madred shifted in his chair and sniffed. "I've seen no sign of him," he observed coldly. "And, really, it's inappropriate for me to pry into Lord Grimbold's affairs."

"Even when your own clerk is involved?"

Madred's lip curled in distaste. "I don't concern myself with the detailed activities of my Lankura staff," he said haughtily. "I have a man, Minister Torlung, who takes care of that." He waved the matter aside, then continued with a milder expression and in a tone that bordered on didactic."I am here concerning *you*, Captain, and because the Lady Alisset is involved in your case. It would behoove you to forget about Simion Rudrin, and attend to your own situation— which is precarious. While these things that you've told me have raised doubts in my mind regarding how much you were at fault, the fact remains that you *were* alone in the company of a young lady of the House of Sobring. The matter therefore concerns the honor of the House of Sobring, and of Sobring Hold. Honor must be upheld, Captain. And it is Lord Grimbold and the Elder Council of the Hold who must be satisfied that it has been."

"I'm well aware of my situation." Nagaro had waited with growing irritation for the Leithian lord to finish, and he spoke rather sharply. "Grimbold has indicated that he will return tomorrow to see whether I have changed my mind about signing his precious paper. Since I have not, he'll be left with the alternative, which according to him is to hang me."

Madred responded to this with a short laugh. "Come now, Captain," he said. "It surely needn't come to that."

"I will not sign the paper, My Lord! Have you seen it?"

The Leithian lord's expression remained mild and he gave the slightest inclination of his head. "It happens that I have."

"Would you sign it if you were in my place?"

Madred continued to regard him calmly, although there was perhaps the slightest flicker of something in his eyes. "If I were in your position, Captain, I would consider the advantages of marrying into a noble family and of allying myself with a respected House," he said sententiously. "As a man who presently lacks the protection of House or Hold, you have much to gain by such an alliance."

At this, Nagaro was again on his feet. "But *at what cost*, My Lord?" he demanded. "I've told you my story! I have done no harm to the Lady

Alisset— to her person, or to her honor— as she would surely tell you if you'd trouble to ask her! I doubt you would have done any differently than I if you had encountered a broken-down carriage on the road and a young lady apparently left to her own devices. Having done no wrong whatsoever, would you truly put your name to a letter that put such dishonoring lies into your mouth?"

In response to this tirade, Lord Madred permitted himself the slightest of frowns. "The wording is perhaps unfortunate," he observed smoothly. "But there is still the appearance of a breach of the honor of the House of Sobring which can be put right by an honorable marriage—"

"Honorable marriage! Appearance of a breach of honor! *Appearance?*" The chain clinked ominously as Nagaro took a step forward, his gray eyes ablaze. "I have been tricked, and drugged, and trapped, to create this *appearance!* And you speak to me of the honor of the House of Sobring—"

"*Enough!*" Madred's face had been darkening and now he rose as if jerked to his feet by the force of his anger. He raised a hand commandingly. "By the Mark! You will not speak to me in this way!"

Nagaro stood his ground. "I speak as the situation warrants, *My Lord,*" he said coldly. "And I fail to see how you are the injured party here." And with that he returned once again to the bed, taking up his cross-legged seat upon it and deliberately and noisily arranging the chain so that it gave him as little inconvenience as possible. Returning his attention to Lord Madred, he found the man still standing as if frozen in shock, staring fixedly at him, his face pale.

Nagaro remained seated on the bed, his back straight and his head erect. "Have you anything else to say, My Lord, that would better serve the cause of justice?" He made his voice as even and as he could, though he was unable to keep a certain coolness out of it.

Lord Madred shifted then. Apparently realizing that he was still standing, he seated himself once more on the chair he had brought into the room for the purpose. The color began to come back into his proud patrician face. "Who are you *really?*" he asked, his eyes fixed upon Nagaro and a trace of something more than curiosity in his voice. "I must know which of the noble lines of Kelor has sired you. You're not half Turowan as so many folk believe. I can't but notice that the skin of your feet and ankles is fair, not dark like that of your face and hands..." He let the sentence dangle suggestively.

Nagaro felt a surge of panic at the lord's words. *The truth! Take refuge in the truth... as much as you dare.* He drew a breath. "I don't know who my parents were," he said, trying to force into those words the weariness that he tended to feel whenever he had to repeat them. "I use kuma stain to darken my skin. It protects against sunburn at sea. I'm not concerned with what folk believe about my parentage. Like every other man, I stand or fall by my deeds."

Madred continued to stare at him. "You don't perceive your own worth," he said. "I believe the House of Sobring stands to gain as much as you do by this marriage that is proposed. Grimbold and the Elder Council must see it as well. This surely explains the urgent desire for you to sign the paper."

"If you ask me," Nagaro observed dryly, "Grimbold is motivated by a desire to have me under his thumb. The prospect of being able to give me orders makes him gleeful, though I fear he would be disappointed. I'm not good at following bad orders."

Lord Madred's mouth twitched. "Do you allude to what happened at Loros Hall?" he asked, but he didn't wait for an answer. "Grimbold can become rather hot at times," he continued, and now his voice was cool and smooth. "He takes altogether too simple a view of the world. But the Elders of Sobring Hold are broader in their thinking and more measured in their actions. If they don't perceive your value now, I believe I can persuade them of it."

Nagaro heaved an exasperated sigh. "I would rather, My Lord, that you used your influence to persuade the guard outside that door to unlock this chain and let me go. If you perceive my virtue, you should also perceive that justice is ill-served here. And, having perceived the injustice, honor should prompt you to put it right."

At this, Madred's face froze. "I am not lord here," he said stiffly. "This is not my Hold. The servants may answer my requests for food and drink, because they understand that I'm an honored guest, but it would be improper for me to countermand their master's orders."

Nagaro stared back at him, unimpressed. "So in Leithian lands, propriety is a greater virtue than justice or honor?" he observed.

"Obviously you don't understand, Captain. There is a certain order to the world. Without it everything dissolves into chaos."

Again Nagaro sighed. "Then we are at an impasse, My Lord. You will not rescue me, and I will not sign the paper."

At this, strangely, Lord Madred seemed to relax a little. He had rolled up the paper he held in his hands and he now tapped the table with it. "What if I could persuade the Elders to dispense with the paper, Captain? Suppose, for a moment, that I could prevail upon them to be satisfied with the marriage?"

"Be satisfied with the marriage?" Nagaro bridled. "*Satisfied?*" he repeated, incredulously. *Did this man understand nothing?*

Lord Madred however apparently took his incredulity for incomprehension. He elaborated. "If you were simply to agree to wed the Lady Alisset, Captain," he explained. "The appearance of impropriety and possible dishonor to Sobring Hold would be satisfied, even without the paper. A mutually beneficial alliance could be made, and you wouldn't have to set your name to anything you find objectionable. I am prepared to bring my influence to bear on your behalf to bring this about."

Nagaro suppressed a groan. "My Lord," he said carefully, "It would still be a forced marriage."

"But it need not be, surely, Captain." Madred leaned forward now, speaking earnestly, reasonably. "If you will but consider the matter carefully. After all, it would appear thus: You have proven your merit to the Elders of the Hold by coming to the aid of a distressed young lady, and in turn are offered marriage into a noble House. Marriage, I might add, to a fair, obedient, and sweet-tempered young wife. Why should anyone believe the marriage to be forced?"

Nagaro saw that Madred was sincere. He frowned harder, searching for a diplomatic way to set the other man straight. "I am sorry, My Lord," he ventured. "But I have no desire to wed the Lady Alisset, and— more importantly from your point of view as her guardian— she has no desire to wed *me.*"

Lord Madred's expression didn't change. Rather, he dismissed Nagaro's protest with a wave of his hand. "It's high time you considered marriage, Captain," he said. "And this is an excellent opportunity. As for the Lady Alisset, you needn't be concerned. She is dutiful and will accept whatever choice I make for her."

"I've done the lady no harm up to this point, My Lord," Nagaro protested. "And I don't wish to begin now! I happen to know that her heart lies with Nile Fendred. I have no desire to ruin whatever chance she still has for happiness, particularly since I happen to know he feels the same way about her."

"Your concern is admirable, Captain, but you must understand that it isn't necessary." Madred was condescending again. "Duty must, and will, prevail over foolish romantic notions. There is no advantage to a match between Nile and the Lady Alisset. Nile knows his duty and will do what is required of him, and Alisset is dutiful, as I have said. Once the thing is done, she may mope for a time, but then she'll accept it. A man shouldn't let concern for a woman's feelings interfere with making a practical decision. You have much to learn about the responsibilities and burdens borne by men of the noble class, but once you are well-married, I'm sure we can work on your instruction."

Nagaro jaw tightened. His headache was threatening to make a resurgence. *A practical decision...* He wondered how Madred's wife contrived to put up with him! But then, he supposed it must be her duty. It might have been wise to let the matter drop, since Madred was obviously firmly entrenched in his opinion, but Nagaro couldn't risk letting his silence to be taken for agreement. "I have no intention of being 'well-married,' as you put it, My Lord," he said tightly. "I'm sorry if I didn't make that clear." He paused to run a hand through his hair and tried to measure his words carefully. "I mean no disrespect to you, My Lord. You've shown me some kindness, and have been good enough to hear me out. But I am not interested in the 'opportunity' you are offering. I cannot in honor accept it."

This time a frown creased Lord Madred's handsome brow. "You refuse the marriage as well as the paper?" he asked incredulously. "Explain this, Captain."

Nagaro sighed and made an effort. "You asked why anyone should believe the marriage was forced, My Lord, since it might appear a good match. But the point is, *I* would *know* it was forced. To pretend otherwise would be a lie. I would dishonor myself by accepting."

Comprehension was dawning in Lord Madred's eyes. "You value honor more than you value position." he said. "But consider. You're a man without the protection of a Hold or Wared. You haven't even a family. Setting aside the question of the lady's feelings, is the match really so distasteful that you couldn't consider entering into it freely?"

Again Nagaro sighed. "I have nothing to say against the Lady Alisset, My Lord," he said earnestly. "She is gentle, kind-hearted, and very pretty after the manner of Leithian women, but I have no wish to ally myself with the House of Sobring. Even without signing the paper, marrying into the House of Sobring would make me subject to the lord and Elders of that House. Isn't this so?"

"Well, yes." Madred frowned. "But Grimbold won't be lord of Sobring Hold forever."

Nagaro had to pause at that, remembering that Grimbold's successor might well be Vell Sobring, whom he had recently called a friend. But it had been Bron Sobring who had given Dreigen permission to use heskial. It was too much to ask Nagaro to live under the name of Sobring. This wasn't negotiable, though he couldn't explain it to Lord Madred.

"I have reasons of my own not to love Sobring Hold, My Lord, that I don't care to discuss," he said. "And whether you understand it or not, I *am* concerned with the Lady Alisset's feelings in this matter. Since I'm innocent of any harm to her, and the 'appearance' you're so concerned about was arranged by trickery, I shouldn't have to marry her. And I will not do so willingly."

The light from the room's only window had been gradually fading for some time, as the afternoon drew towards evening. As Nagaro finished speaking, the sun must have dipped behind the tops of the trees in the surrounding forest, for there was a noticeable darkening that seemed to creep from the corners of the room.

Lord Madred sat still, his face doubly clouded by the gloom and by his darkening frown. "I see," he said. "An impasse, after all, then. Still I hope you'll think about it and perhaps reconsider."

Nagaro shook his head. "Grimbold gave me three days to reconsider, under threat of hanging. Tomorrow will be the third day, and I haven't changed my mind. I may not have the protection of a Hold or Wared, but I do have friends. I told Grimbold there would likely be consequences if he were to execute me."

"There is some controversy over whether the King's law supercedes the laws of the Holds and Wareds in the matter of capital crimes," Madred observed gravely. "Grimbold may risk putting the issue to the test. Being right is of little use to you if you are dead."

"Perhaps I don't value my life as highly as you think, My Lord."

At this point, there came a tap at the door, and it swung open, allowing light to stab into the room. The taciturn serving man entered, bowing to Lord Madred even as he held a lantern aloft in his hand. He hung the thing on a hook to one side of the doorway and its light flooded the room, casting a lurid glow on the stark walls and sparse furnishings, making shadows leap and dance. "Very sorry to interrupt ye, My Lord," he said obsequiously. "But I've come for the dishes."

Lord Madred inclined his head to the man and watched in silence as the servant transferred the dishes from the table to the tray. Nagaro, noticing the half-full pitcher of water, which had been left standing on the floor beside the table, made a sudden cat-like lunge and scooped it up in his hands. He retreated again, then, to his place on the bed, sitting cross-legged with the pitcher cradled protectively in his lap.

The servant had jumped in alarm at Nagaro's sudden movement. Now he stood, frowning his disapproval. He made a tentative motion as if he were considering trying to reclaim the pitcher, but Lord Madred stopped him with a raised hand. "Leave it 'til the morning," the Leithian lord admonished. "There's no harm in a pitcher— or in allowing the Captain the means of satisfying his thirst if he should wake in the night."

"As ye wish, My Lord." The servant sounded a little sullen, but he bobbed a fawning bow nevertheless. He then took up the laden tray and made his way hastily to the door. Before going out, he turned back to again address Lord Madred.

"If it please ye, My Lord, I'd be obliged if ye'd fetch out the lamp when ye're finished."

He bowed yet again as he exited.

Lord Madred had risen as the door closed behind the servant. He stood looking down at Nagaro. "You make it difficult for me to help you, Captain," he observed soberly.

"Not so difficult, really." Nagaro indicated the pitcher with a gesture. "I am grateful for this, My Lord. And for dinner, and for your patience."

This time the Leithian lord shook his head sadly. "I'm sure your distrust is misplaced, Captain."

Nagaro regarded him coolly. "I want you to remember what I've told you, My Lord," he said levelly. "I will not, of my own free will, sign that paper or consent to marry the Lady Alisset. If it comes to your ears in the future that I have done either one, you should suspect that a way has been found to compel me."

"Compel you?" Lord Madred frowned. "When the fear of death doesn't move you? How could you be compelled?"

Nagaro's hand had slid into his pocket as the other man was speaking and he raised it now, holding up the bladder-thorn to the lamplight. "There are ways, My Lord. I found this under the bed. Do you know what it is?"

Madred advanced a step, peering at the object in Nagaro's hand. "I've seen them before," he said. "Healers use them, I believe, to tend to the sick."

"Does this look like a sickroom?" Nagaro gestured at his prison cell. "Healers use them, certainly, because healers sometimes need to introduce a medicine directly into a man's blood— if the man isn't able to drink it, for example. But the bladder-thorn can also be used to introduce a drug in the same way— a drug that has no medical value whatsoever."

Lord Madred stood very still. He had turned so that the lamp was behind him and his face was shadowed. His expression was difficult to read. "What sort of drug do you mean?" he asked in a voice that carried no inflection.

"It could be various things, depending on the purpose, but there is one in particular that can be used to compel a man." Nagaro paused fractionally to gather his will to speak of the thing. "It is called... *heskial*," he managed, and it seemed to him that there might have been a little flinch in Madred's face in response to the name. He forced himself to go on. "It was created by the Jinari... to be used as a truth drug. But they soon discovered that a man under its influence would do... anything he was commanded – *anything at all*. It completely subverts the will." He swallowed. "The Jinari call it an abomination and have banned its use. To buy or sell it is forbidden under their law. It was the discovery of trading in this drug that led the High Council of Jinara to complain to the King of Edrovir."

Nagaro stopped speaking. In the silence Madred shifted a little, turning so that the lamplight partially illumined his face, and Nagaro saw that he was frowning. "But surely it is a great leap," the Leithian ventured, "to imagine that this... *heskial*, as you call it... is to be found in this house."

Nagaro saw a chance to probe a little. "Not so great a leap, My Lord," he said. "The men who bought the heskial were described as yellow-haired Droviri, and such men have been carrying on a secret trade with Jinara for several years at least. There is evidence that implicates the House of Sobring— among others."

Lord Madred made a small movement. "What others?" he asked sharply.

"The House of Hurn, My Lord, and the House of Furthing."

Now the Leithian lord stiffened visibly. "This is either an error or a deceit, Captain," he said coldly. "At least as far as the House of Furthing is concerned. Such activities did go on during my father's time, but I put a stop to them when I became lord— nearly a dozen years ago."

Nagaro leaned against the wall, his hands on the earthenware pitcher in his lap. He hadn't taken his eyes from the figure of the Leithian lord, standing erect before him, silhouetted by the lamplight. "I believe you speak the truth, My Lord," he said. "As far as you know it. But I will let you be the judge of where the error or deceit may lie." And he proceeded to relate how the drawings of the seals of those three houses had come into his possession. "The Jinari agent who made the drawings of the seals couldn't have known their significance— and I thought they were merchants' marks," he concluded. "Simion showed me the proof of what they were in the pages of a book called the *Noble Houses of Edrovir*."

"When was this?" Madred asked, his voice tight.

"A little more than two months ago, and it appears that the trafficking has continued. We believe it's going overland now, through Borlund Hold."

Lord Madred lowered his head, his handsome profile limned by the lamplight. His expression was very grave. "*There must be some explanation*," he murmured, as if speaking to himself.

"Oh yes." Nagaro's hands caressed the smooth, hard curve of the water pitcher. "There is always an explanation, My Lord. The question is whether it is one that would please *you*— or one that would justify my fears."

Madred straightened. "I must think on this," he said tersely. "I regret I cannot be of more help to you, but since you seem determined to be stubborn about this marriage, I suppose there's nothing you can do but wait and see what Grimbold will do with you. Good evening, Captain."

With that, the Leithian lord inclined his head, a gesture that Nagaro gravely returned. Then Madred turned to go, pausing only long enough to take down the lamp from its hook beside the door. After that, the door opened and swung shut behind him, the key clicked in the lock, and Nagaro was left alone with his fears as the room was plunged into the gloom of gathering twilight.

Chapter 26

The Honor Of Sobring Hold

H e struggled in the grip of Bron Sobring's beefy hands. *"Let go of me! What are you doing?"*

"Be silent, you ungrateful whelp! You'll find out soon enough." The big man snarled as he forced his victim down onto the cold flagstones of the back hallway, just outside the kitchen door. Beyond the red-faced Leithian, floated the cruelly smiling face of Gillard Marchent. The younger Leithian lord held up a candle to illuminate the darkened hall—

A candle—

Nagaro jerked awake, sitting on the pallet bed, and aimed a reflexive kick at the silent serving man, who was stooping over the narrow bed, holding a candle aloft with one hand while the other reached for the earthenware pitcher. His bare heel connected with the man's arm and the candle spun away, its light extinguished as it arced through the air. The snuffing of the flame was accompanied by a startled oath coming out of the sudden darkness.

Nagaro's movement hadn't taken account of the pitcher, still cradled between his knees. In the last fraction of a second of illumination he'd seen it tipping dangerously. He grabbed desperately for it in the dark with his hands, seeking to catch it and right it— and succeeded, with only a half cupful of precious liquid spilling onto the mattress.

There were scuffling sounds in the blind blackness after the light was gone, coming from near the floor and moving in the direction of the door of the room. Nagaro heard the door open, saw the brief rectangle of lamplight appear and become occluded by the moving shape of a man's body.

"Ye told me he was asleep!" The servant sounded deeply aggrieved.

"I tell ye, he was!" The answering voice sounded like that of the younger of the two guards who had ridden in the carriage and railed at him so unkindly.

The lamp-lit rectangle narrowed and vanished as the door closed. The key turned in the lock. Nagaro sat tensely, listening. Muffled sounds of unintelligible speech in the hall outside came faintly to his ears, then ceased. Footsteps retreated down the hall and died away.

The silence lengthened.

At last, Nagaro decided that he was to be left alone once more. It seemed that the man had only meant to reclaim the pitcher. Probably the servant feared Grimbold's wrath if the thing were found in Nagaro's possession when the lord returned. He shifted his body to settle himself more comfortably against the wall. After some internal debate, he drank as much of the remaining water as he had any desire to drink, tipping up the pitcher very carefully lest a single drop be wasted. He might be thirstier later and wish he had saved it, but right at that moment he was more worried that the water would be spilled in the dark before that time arrived.

After that, he sat, trying to relax again so he could sleep.

He needed rest, and decided that sleeping sitting up should be safe, since he couldn't sleep very soundly in that position. He frowned as he tried to settle his mind. The man had been very quiet. He'd been awakened, not by any sound, but by the light of the candle flame glowing crimson, through his closed eyelids. Right now the room was black as pitch. Anything could be out there... waiting silently.

But it wasn't, he told himself. He had seen no other threats, in the brief glimpse he'd gotten of the room before the candle went out. But the glimpse had been so brief... and he'd been distracted. *What if he had missed something?*

Every muscle he had was tense, every nerve on edge.

How could he sleep like this? And how could he keep his wits and his sanity if he didn't sleep? A thought occurred to him then, and he wondered why he hadn't thought of it before.

He spoke softly into the darkness. "Vothra?"

I am here, Spirit that calls itself Nagaro.

The answer came so swiftly— entering Nagaro's mind like a breath of fresh air flowing into a catacomb— that he sucked in his breath. Tears of relief and gratitude sprang in his eyes. "Oh Vothra! Thank you! I'm so afraid... I've been so alone here..."

It has been a sore trial for you, but one you have borne well.

"*Well?*" Nagaro laughed, and the sound had an edge of hysteria. "Several times I think I was been on the verge of not bearing it at all! I should have thought to call you long before this."

There was just the slightest pause before the Spirit spoke again: *I have not been far from you. And I have seen your suffering. It has not been easy to withhold my hand, yet as long as you were not actually breaking, I have done so. Understand that there was no secret purpose in this, beyond my resolve to intervene as little as possible. Yet it may have served one none-the-less. Would you have spoken quite so freely or so forcefully to the one called Madred if you had been more comfortable?*

Again Nagaro could only laugh. "What did my words avail me?"

Only the unfolding of time will tell. The one called Madred is possessed of an uncommon capacity for certitude, self-approval, and self-justification— well beyond what is warranted. You scratched his armor. You gave him pause. He knows more than he has told you— Here the Spirit seemed to break off, and paused again before adding: *Was there a reason why you called me now, beyond the desire for company?*

Nagaro felt abashed at what he had planned to ask. "I... I'm afraid I was hoping you could... well... watch over me for a time, so I could feel safe enough to sleep."

And then Vothra laughed, a sound like a gentle arpeggio of harp strings. *Dwelling as I do in the Void,* the Spirit told him, *I am poorly placed to play watchdog for spirits bound to flesh. It would be difficult to follow all the spirits that are in your vicinity. Your own spirit's familiarity makes you shine like a beacon on a hilltop, while the others are but flickering candles. Their thoughts do not shout to me as yours do. Nor can I tell how close to you they truly are in the world of flesh, nor whether there may be a wall in between. And yours is not the only spirit that is troubled this night.*

Nagaro was instantly contrite. "Forgive me, Vothra. I'm being selfish."

How should you not be? The voice was ineffably gentle. *Flesh is by nature hungry. You are in need, and in no position to help anyone else.* Once more the Spirit paused, then added, *Your spirit is a beacon, remember that. If I become aware of a danger that I am certain of, I will warn you. And for your comfort, I will also tell you this: Among the spirits near you, there are some that mean you well. In that, there is hope. And now, Spirit that calls itself Nagaro, you must try to sleep.*

And it was a little easier after that. He lay down and stretched himself on the narrow bed with the pitcher between him and the wall, cradled against his side, and closed his eyes.

***

What woke him was not a warning, spoken by the Benevalent Spirit in his mind, but the real, physical sound of metal grating on metal. Whatever dream he had been in the middle of, fled in an instant.

Someone was trying to unlock the door, and fumbling about in the process.

Nagaro swore silently as he sat up, guarding the pitcher, and tensed himself in the darkness. He had slept— for quite some time. He knew this because there was a faint gleam of silver light from the room's one window, and a rectangular splash of moonlight on the opposite wall. The bright moon, Talebra, must have passed its zenith and was arcing down the western sky.

The key-in-lock sounds ceased, then started again after a brief interval in which he thought he caught the jingle of the keys on a ring. *It almost sounded as if someone was trying to find the right key.*

The key ground metalically, and the lock clicked, loudly, in the silence.

He held his breath as he heard the key being awkwardly withdrawn, and at last the door swung open. To his astonishment, the figure outlined by the rectangle of light was obviously female, with a long skirt, slender waist, and hair flowing over narrow shoulders.

The woman raised one graceful arm, her hand holding a lighted candle which now shed its glow upon her face. Her wide blue eyes blinked at him.

"*Lady Alisset?*" He gazed at her, stunned. "What on earth are *you* doing here?"

"I've come to help you," she said, taking one step forward into the room.

He set the pitcher aside and was up and off of the bed in one lithe movement, the chain clattering across the floor behind him. "Oh no!" he said, backing away from her. *She* might mean him well, but— "*Please, no! I don't want any more trouble!*"

He saw her gaze go to the chain, then sweep over the stark contents of the room and come back to him. Her eyes were wide with shock and distress.

"Oh, this is horrible!" she cried. "See what they've done to you, poor Captain! And they've made you afraid of me, too. But you *must* let me help you! I can't put things *right* if you won't let me help! I've come to let you out. See? I've got the keys." She held up a heavy metal ring in her other hand and shook it so that the keys hanging from it jingled.

Nagaro's gaze locked onto the ring of keys. *Was this another trap... or a test?* She sounded sincere. And he would clearly be in a better position to free himself without the chain on his ankle.

He moistened his lips. "Toss them to me," he said.

She did so. It wasn't a deft toss, but his catch made up for it.

Then he was sitting on the bed swiftly going through the half dozen keys, finding the one with the right sort of shape. It turned with a grating sound and a sharp clink. The metal cuff came open and dropped to the floor.

He stood up, stepping clear of the thing. He looked at her, where she still stood just inside the doorway. "Where did you get these?" he asked, gesturing with the key ring. "And what's happened to the guard?"

"Oh, he's right out there," she said brightly, and motioned towards the doorway behind her. "Tolbert put something in his drink and he's asleep. The keys were lying right beside him."

For a moment he studied her narrowly. "Who is Tolbert?" he asked as he retrieved the pitcher from the bed and hastily drained the last of its contents.

"He's another one of the guards," she offered. "He said you'd know him if you saw him but he wasn't sure you would trust him, so he said I should do this part. Besides, I can say that I found the guard asleep and decided to let you out because I didn't think it was right to keep you. Uncle Grimbold will be angry, but Uncle Madred will make sure he doesn't hurt me." After a pause, she added, "Uncle Madred's my good uncle."

Nagaro smiled wryly. "Relatively speaking," he said, and when he saw her blank look he decided not to enlighten her. It sounded like a good plan, provided she was right enough about that 'good uncle.' He sincerely hoped that she was, but he had another concern. "Is... Tolbert out there?" he asked. "In the hallway?"

"Oh, no. He's downstairs in the kitchen. With the cook, I think."

Nagaro frowned. He thought the cook was probably a good man, but he didn't know who the guard named Tolbert was. "You'd best go back out into the hall, My Lady," he said. "If there's no sort of chaperon about... and anyone were to see us..."

Alisset dutifully retreated several steps, but she made a gesture of annoyance as she went. "I thought about bringing Julivel, my serving woman, for a chaperon," she said. "But I didn't want to get her into trouble, and I don't need a chaperon with you, anyway, Captain." Her expression and her tone embodied innocent sincerity. "Not after the way you treated me out there on the road! You were ever so kind, and *ever* so patient. And I was so *very* tipsy. It was kind of you to say I was only a little bit tipsy, though I'm sure you knew better. I've never been so tipsy in my *life*, and I'm terribly, terribly sorry about all of this!"

Nagaro had advanced as she retreated, though staying at least a half dozen feet from her. He now stood in the doorway where he could see the guard for himself, clearly illuminated by a lamp hanging from a hook on the wall beside the doorframe. The man was sprawled with his back against the wall, his legs splayed out across the floor. The way his head lolled made it clear that he was indeed unconscious. Nagaro also saw that the guard was the older, heavy-set man who'd given him so much grief during the carriage ride. The sight offered him some reassurance— and a certain amount of satisfaction.

He turned his attention back to Alisset. "But what are you doing *here*, My Lady?" he asked again. "I thought they would have taken you to Sobring Hall."

"Oh, they did! But Uncle Madred brought me here with him. He's asleep downstairs. He wants very much to see us betrothed. But of course that would be all *wrong*." She dropped her eyes and he thought he saw in the lamplight that she was blushing. "I... I'm sorry I started to... to kiss you, Captain." She began haltingly, then continued in a rush. "Uncle Grimbold said you were to be my husband, and I thought, if it must be so, then at least I should be sure you'd be faithful. Lady Lissafel says that a kiss— 'innocent and freely given'— is a powerful charm, and so I thought I would do it. But when I heard you say *her* name... When I knew you were mistaking me for *her*..."

Alisset had raised her eyes, and she faltered to a halt when she saw the look on his face.

When I heard you say her name...

Nagaro felt as if his heart had stopped, then started again, pounding like a hammer. "*Vothra!*" he murmured in horrified dismay. "Did I say that *aloud?*"

She nodded, eyes wide, flaxen hair bobbing.

"Oh Vothra!" He clutched at the doorframe for support. "Vothra help me!" He'd suspected that the little half-kiss had been real, despite Alisset's earlier denial, but he'd thought his own words had been spoken in the dream. He stared at Alisset, who was blinking at him, round-eyed as an owl. "Please don't tell her," he begged. "You mustn't tell her! *You mustn't tell anyone!*"

"Oh, I won't!" Her eyes were round and blue and earnest, and she shook her head vigorously. "Not a living soul. I swear it by all the Gods. As I hope to wed my sweet Nile, I swear it!"

She looked so serious and sounded so solemn that he might have laughed if he'd been at all inclined to take the matter lightly. As it was, he decided he should trust her. There was probably no oath that Alisset would find more binding. *Vothra had said there were people nearby who meant him well.*

As his panic ebbed, he recovered enough presence of mind to glance up and down the hall and confirm his impression that it was empty except for himself, the lady, and the sprawled figure of the single guard. The room he had occupied was near one end of the hall, and there were a number of other doors along it on both sides— all closed— and a curtained window at either end. The top of a stairway, leading down, lay a little more than halfway along the length of the hallway.

As he relaxed, some of the other things she had said began to penetrate. "What did you think was going on out there on the road?" he asked curiously. "What did Grimbold tell you?"

"He said I was to be sure that you drank some of the wine, and some of the sothiril." Alisset's brow puckered painfully. "That was supposed to make you dream about... being with a woman... I think. He... he said I must endure whatever you might do." Since the hanging lamp gave plenty of light, she had set the candle down on a little self beside the door. Her hands were thus free, and she now began wringing them. "And when it was all over, he said you and I would be wed. It was my duty, and all for the good of Sobring Hold— but it would have been wrong! Don't you see? Lissafel has marked you for Nevien. And Nile and I are promised to each other in the name of the Lady. And Lissafel will have her way!"

This recital confirmed much of what Nagaro had already guessed. It also plainly embarrassed Alisset as much as it did him. "You think Lissafel is stronger than Kroneg, then?" he asked, stooping to examine the drugged guard so that he didn't have to meet her eyes. The man was very still, his jaw was slack, his breathing heavy.

"Oh, yes!" Alisset's confidence was unassailable. "This is her time! Talebra is starting to take Naru in her arms. Didn't you see the moons last night?"

Nagaro grimaced. It was several weeks since he'd troubled to note of the progress of the approaching conjunction. "Not from in there," he said as he closed and locked the door of the room that had been his prison. Stooping, he placed the ring of keys on the floor beside the sleeping guard's hand. "If we make it look as if nothing's amiss, it may take them longer to realize that I'm gone," he explained. "If Tolbert didn't give him too strong a dose, the guard may even think he just fell asleep. What did Tolbert dose this man with? Do you know?"

She took two steps closer and peered at the recumbent figure. "I... I think it was the same thing they put in the sothiril they gave you to drink downstairs," she said.

Nagaro nodded, frowning. A simple sleeping drought, then. Not what he'd drunk that had sent him crawling into the carriage. Remembering what *that* drug had done to him sparked anger. *Oh yes, he had dreamed about being with a woman...* It galled him to have been so manipulated. With an effort, he shook off the thought. "Where is Tolbert now?" he asked. "And why is he trying to help me?"

"He's downstairs somewhere." She waved vaguely. "And he wants to put everything right, just as I do. He said he put your boots and things in the kitchen. You can go there and get them."

Nagaro glanced along the hall. "Which way is the kitchen? I was unconscious when they brought me up here."

"Oh." She frowned. "You have to turn right when you get to the bottom of the stairs. Then it's the first door on the left, I think. Anyway, I'll show you. But we should go now, before the guard wakes up!"

Nagaro was in complete agreement. He set off for the top of the stairs, padding as silently as a cat on his bare feet. He had no idea how long the guard might sleep, since it depended on the potency of the drought. There would be a guard for the next shift coming, probably around dawn in any case. Dawn, he imagined, was not that far off.

He could hear Alisset a half dozen paces behind him, her shoes making little soft scuffing sounds. She'd picked up her candle again, and as they left the stronger light of the lamp behind them, the candle flame threw their shadows onto the paneled walls of the hallway.

As Nagaro passed a closed door, a guilty thought occurred to him and he turned back to whisper urgently to the Lady Alisset. "I came here looking for another man. A young Kelorin. Do you know if he's here somewhere?" He gestured at the closed doors.

She shook her head, blue eyes wide, and wrinkled her brow. "Tolbert said this whole floor was empty— except for you. I think there was another man in there where you were, but they moved him. Maybe Tolbert knows where he is."

They had reached the stairs, which descended into darkness. The lamp outside the door of the prison room seemed to be the only one lit, upstairs or down, and Nagaro was glad of Alisset's candle, though it shed much less light than the lamp. He started down the stairs, with Alisset a few steps behind him. Candlelight wavered and flickered and cast his own shadow before him so that it half obscured the steps and he had to feel his way. He went very warily, knowing that the bottom of the poorly lit stairway provided a perfect opportunity for an ambush. Even were Alisset as innocent as she seemed, others in this house might have less benign intentions. *And Alisset might be an unknowing pawn.* He tried not to dwell on that thought.

Despite his fears, they reached the bottom of the stairs without incident, and he let out a sigh of relief. He was in a hallway similar to the one above, but longer, the building being larger on the ground floor. This hall was also more dimly lit, for there was no lamp in it. Alisset's candle was only a flicker.

Off to his right, towards the end of the hall, an open doorway on the right-hand side cast a wavering strip of light across the floor and up the opposite wall. As his eyes adjusted further, he became aware of a third source of illumination, paler and more silver than the other two. It came from a pair of windows, one to the left and one to the right, and he realized it must be moonlight.

"That light is the kitchen." Alisset whispered as she pointed past him towards the illuminated open door."Tolbert and the cook will be there, but I have to go back to my room before Julivel misses me."

He nodded. "Thank you, My Lady," he said earnestly, keeping his own voice low. "I won't forget your kindness— or your courage."

But she shook her head and waved his words aside. "What else could I possibly do? What Uncle Grimbold is doing is *wrong!* I've bound myself to Lissafel— with charms and prayers— and I *know* she is with me. And she must have her hand on you, too, Captain. If we tried to go against her now, one of us would surely die!"

Die? From marrying the wrong person? That sounded rather excessive. "The Leithian men I've talked to say that when the moons come together, Lissafel and Kroneg have an equal chance of winning," he ventured.

"Men say that because all they ever think about is war and fighting," she responded impatiently. "Lissafel *has* to win! Because life comes before death, and love is what makes life! Love always has to win— unless it's the end of the world. You don't think it's the end of the world, do you, Captain?"

"No, of course not—"

"Then you must have faith!" In the candle's weakly flaring light her face glowed with ecstatic fervor. "The Lady has marked you for Nevien! And I'm so glad it's you. You're the perfect one for her!"

Bitterly he turned away to start along the hallway in the direction of the lighted kitchen door. "It's no use," he muttered. "She's beyond my reach."

Alisset must have heard him, for her words floated back to him, spoken low and urgently. "Do not despair, Captain! Trust in the Lady— and I will keep you in my prayers!"

He resisted the urge to tell her not to bother. There was nothing in his life's experience to convince him of the existence of the Leithian gods, or the power of prayer. He'd been told that he must bear Kroneg's mark because of his skill in battle, or that Hrathgard must be watching over him when the weather worked in his favor. He rejected both notions. He was a reluctant warrior, uncomfortable with how easy it was to take a man's life. And weather was just weather. The storm that had driven him into the carriage two days ago had hardly served him well, after all. And he was scarcely any more comfortable with the idea of having Lissafel's favor than Kroneg's.

But there was no harm in prayers, he reminded himself. An innocent, and a true believer, Alisset meant him well. If it made her feel good to pray, let her pray.

He had moved very cautiously down the hall, careful not to make a sound, and hadn't gotten far when a figure suddenly appeared in the open doorway he was moving towards. For a moment, his heart nearly stopped. But even with what little light there was, it was easy to identify Brun, the cook. The stout little man stood in the doorway, light spilling around him, and turned to survey the hall with an air of over-done nonchalance that made Nagaro wince. When he turned his face in Nagaro's direction he further spoiled the effect by starting visibly. Then he beckoned frantically, put a finger to his lips, and ducked back into the kitchen.

Nagaro sighed. He moved forward more quickly, but no less silently. There didn't appear to be any enemies abroad in the house at this hour, but it still seemed wise to be cautious. He passed a short side hall on his left, which he recognized as the entryway through which he'd been brought into the building two days before. This told him what he needed to know of the layout of the place. The room in which he'd been fed— and drugged a second time— must now lie behind the wall on his left, and the kitchen door he was approaching must stand at right angles to the one through which he'd caught sight of the two highwaymen.

By the time he'd completed this assessment, he had reached the open kitchen door. He paused, hoping very sincerely that this wasn't a trap. Still, there was the promise of the return of his boots and knife, and the only other course would be to go back to the entryway and try to slip out, unarmed and barefoot, into the darkness. He drew a breath, and stepped into the kitchen where Tor Brun stood waiting.

"Welcome, Captain, welcome!" The cook beamed at him. "I'm glad t' see ye free and looking well in yourself. The lady must ha' done her part proper!" He stopped, then, looking abashed.

Nagaro put out his hand. "Well met, friend Brun," he said, putting all his good will into the smile he gave the man. "And I want you to know that I've never tasted a better rabbit stew."

"Oh, well..." Tor Brun scuffed the floor with his foot as he took Nagaro's hand. "Hunger's the best seasoning, they say."

Nagaro looked past the man he'd just greeted, to survey the room. The cook was alone, and the light he had seen, which was none too bright after all, came from a combination of a fire burning vigorously on the hearth and a lighted candle in a candlestick on a table in the middle of the room. The lamp that hung from the ceiling was unlit.

Also on the table, he could see his belt, his knife in its sheath, and his purse. His boots were standing on the floor next to a short bench, one of two that were drawn up to the table on either side. "Ah," he said, "There's a sight for weary eyes, indeed!" Moving around Tor Brun, he was soon seated on one of the benches, putting on his boots. The socks, he was glad to find, had been stuffed inside of them.

As he donned the boots, he watched the cook, who was nervously looking from him to the door he'd just come through, and back again. "So what is your part in this little conspiracy, Tor Brun?" he inquired.

"Oh, it's little enough." The red-faced little man kneaded his hands nervously. "Besides puttin' my kitchen at your service, Zirda, I'm what ye might call the man in the middle."

"The man in the middle?" Nagaro had finished with the boots and stood up to buckle on the belt with the sheath and knife secured to it.

Brun hastened to explain. "It's like this, Zirda: Young Tolbert came in with some firewood and overheard me muttering t' meself about how I don't care for anyone mucking about with my good sothiril— and behind my own back too! And when he heard that, he up and told me that he'd had enough o' what was goin' on and wished he could put a stop to it. And then the young lady come in later with her serving woman— to be gettin' some o' my tea cakes— and she was all teary about how Grimbold shouldn't force ye t' marry her, on account o' yer bein' innocent. Well, when I heard *that*, I remembered what Tolbert had said, and I... ah... told each one o' them about the other, so to speak."

Nagaro nodded. "Well, that was certainly important."

"Aye, but it was young Tolbert what came up wi' the plan." Brun was apparently encouraged by Nagaro's approva,l for he proceeded to supply more details. "We would ha' set it in motion an hour sooner if it weren't for that bloody Tofle decidin' he wanted t' get the pitcher back. We had t' wait for the ruckus ye kicked up to settle down. And then we had t' wait for Tofle to go to bed, and 'til he was sleepin' soundly. That's when Tolbert took a nip o' ale up to Fendle— with a bit of an extra nip in it, if ye understand me."

"I do. But where is Tolbert now?"

Brun twisted his hands together, nervous again. "He went t' be sure that all's clear outside, Captain. I expect he'll be back any minute."

Nagaro accepted this with another nod. He'd begun to guess who Tolbert was, and hearing the man referred to as 'young' all but confirmed his suspicion. The final confirmation came a moment later when the young guard with the half-grown mustache appeared in the kitchen doorway. Nagaro looked up from counting the money in his recovered purse, which contained only a fraction of what had been there when he'd lost it. "Ah," he said, rising and advancing to extend his hand. "You must be Tolbert— the reluctant highwayman."

The young man took the hand awkwardly and shook it. "I hope ye don't think too ill o' me, Captain, for what I did that evening," he said shamefacedly. "I was following orders. Orders I didn't much like."

"Orders from whom? Old crooked-nose? The man I'm told is the gamekeeper?"

"Aye." Tolbert nodded. "Of course, Grobend says the orders come from Lord Grimbold. I don't know that it's true, but I'd not be surprised."

Tolbert might not be surprised, but Nagaro was. "I thought the lords were charged by the Crown with keeping the roads in their territories clear of thieves. Why would Grimbold set his own men to robbing people?"

Tolbert shrugged. "To raise money for his army. He needs money and horses, and that's what Grobend's band is taking." He paused, noticing the purse in Nagaro's hand. "I'm sorry about your money, Captain," he added. "And your spyglass. Grobend kept the spyglass and shared the money out among the men what helped t' trap ye. What's there is just my share and the little I could spare from my last week's pay."

"I see, and it's very good of you. You have my thanks." Nagaro slipped the purse into his pocket. He'd all but forgotten about the spyglass, which was worth more than the money, although the money was likely to be of more immediate use to him. Thinking of the spyglass reminded him of why he had brought it, however. "I came here looking for a man who's gone missing. Lady Alisset thought you might know where he is."

"A Kelorin man? About my size, but a bit older? Dark blue eyes and curly hair?

Nagaro felt a surge of hope. "That sounds like him."

"They've got him out in one o' the sheds. He was in the room upstairs, but they moved him when they brought ye in. As long as I've gone this far, I might as well turn him loose too— if ye'll swear that he's done no crime, that is. Begging your pardon, Zirda."

"I swear on my honor that he's done no crime that I know of. His mistake may have been taking too much interest in the crimes of others."

Tolbert made a rueful face. "That doesn't surprise me. But if ye're ready, Captain, we should go. I'll take ye to him, first, and then I'll be bidding ye both farewell."

As he spoke, Tolbert beckoned Nagaro towards the door by which he had entered, but before Nagaro could follow, Brun approached him bearing a large leather pouch in one hand and a flask in the other, each with a shoulder strap. "I took the liberty o' packing ye some food and drink for the road, Captain," he said. "Some bread and cheese and cold meat. And a flask of my best sothiril— without anything extra added this time."

Nagaro took the pouch and the flask and made a small bow. "Thank you, Tor Brun," he said. "I will remember you well."

Tolbert then led him out into the hall and turned towards the end of it, away from the stairs. There was a small door there that opened out into the night air. Nagaro took a deep breath as he passed through, relishing his freedom. Tolbert had brought neither lamp nor candle, but there was no need. The light from the kitchen had been enough to guide their steps in the hallway and outside there was moonlight, pure and silver, washing over everything it could reach.

Wherever it couldn't reach, was inky darkness. Tolbert paused once outside. The end of another building stood directly before them, about twenty feet away. It was a long, single-story buileing with a peaked roof that loomed, casting a moon-shadow.

"That's the stable," Tolbert informed him, nodding at the building. "I'll leave it up to ye what use to make of it."

"It's not guarded?"

"Nothing's guarded. Except the room upstairs. Grimbold fancies he's safe on his own land, I guess."

"Then all the guards I've seen here in Sobring livery are—"

"Kept here t' play at being highwaymen. That and any other mischief old Grobend or Lord Grimbold can dream up. The man that we're going t' rescue is part of some o' that other mischief, I guess. Come on— this way."

Nagaro followed the young Leithian around the corner of the building they had just exited. From there, Tolbert made for a small, dark, square silhouette about fifteen yards away in the direction of the forest. It looked like a small outbuilding, about ten feet by twelve.

"I hope you and Tor Brun aren't taking too big a risk by helping me, Tolbert," Nagaro ventured, keeping his voice low as they crossed the open space. "The Lady Alisset has the advantage of being a woman and high-born— and having Lord Madred to look out for her— but I'm sure that you and Brun will both be in a great deal of trouble if Grimbold finds out what you've done."

Tolbert paused at the nearest corner of the shed they'd been approaching, stopping in the building's moon-shadow and turning around to answer. "We can claim that Brun wasn't any part of it, and the Lady'll cover for us as best she can," he said. "I tried not t' give Fendle too big a dose, but if he swears he was drugged, I know I'm the first one they'll come after. I don't mean t' stay here if things get too hot, though," he added. "I never liked robbing folk in the first place. I didn't want to lose my position, but after that day when we tried to rob ye and that other man, I got t' thinking that *you* don't follow bad orders, and neither should I. After that, I asked Grobend to give me some other duty. He set me t' fetching and carrying for Brun, just t' spite me, but I don't care as long as it's honest work. Still, I'll wager ye wouldn't ha' done the wrong thing in the first place."

Nagaro couldn't make out the young man's face in the darkness. "It's important to be sure you understand the situation," he said. "When I saw you standing behind Grobend in the kitchen doorway, I was ready to take your head off for being a highwayman. That wouldn't have been a good thing to do, would it?"

"Well, no," Tolbert conceded. "I'd seen Grobend put the drops in that sothiril, and I was trying to catch your eye so's I could make ye a sign not t' drink it. But I can't blame ye for not knowing that."

"No, you can't, but my point is that knowing the right thing to do isn't always easy."

"Oh." Tolbert shifted in the darkness. "Am I doing the right thing now, Captain?"

Nagaro sighed. "I believe you are, Tolbert. But please be careful. And once you've bidden me farewell tonight, don't take any more chances for me. I'm very grateful to both you and Brun, but you've done enough." He hesitated as a thought struck him. "I gave your description to Lord Madred," he added. "Along with Grobend's, because I'd seen you both among the highwaymen. He didn't want to believe me about Grobend, and he said he didn't know you, but I know he won't forget what I said. If he questions you about it, you'll know why."

"I'd not be afraid to tell Lord Madred the truth. He's a man of honor, and anyway, he's not my master."

"That's up to you, of course, but he may pass information to Lord Grimbold. I don't think he entirely approves of Grimbold, but he seems to feel it's important to preserve the 'proper order of things.' He wasn't willing to countermand Grimbold's orders concerning me."

"Oh." Tolbert's hand came up to his mouth in a furtive gesture. "Maybe I should forget about growing this mustache?"

"I'd say that's a good idea."

"All right, then. Come on." Tolbert turned decisively and started moving again, skirting the side of the shed.

Turning the corner of it, he stopped in front of a door, which was barred with a beam of wood. Where they stood, they were out of the moon-shadow, and Nagaro could see quite clearly what needed to be done. He set his hands to the beam and started to lift it. Tolbert spoke behind him in an urgent whisper.

"Farewell to ye, Captain. And good luck!"

Before Nagaro could answer, Tolbert was gone. The young man's light footsteps faded rapidly as he hurried away in the direction from which they had come. Nagaro drew a breath and finished unbarring the door. Setting the beam aside, he carefully opened the door and peered inside.

Some of the moonlight spilled in to illuminate a small fraction of the shed's interior. In that narrow triangular swath of pale light, a pair of booted feet were visible, bound around the ankles with several windings of stout cord. Nagaro crouched and began feeling with his hands, investigating how the prisoner was lying. Abruptly the man stiffened under his touch and emitted a muffled, half-strangled sound of alarm.

"Simion?" Nagaro spoke the name in an urgent whisper.

"Mnrr-nhh?"

Nagaro had already discovered that the man's wrists were also bound with cord. Now he reached for the source of the sound in the darkness and discovered a gag. Hurriedly he yanked at the twisted rag, pulling it out from between the prisoner's teeth.

"*Nagaro?*" It was Simion's voice, and the young Kelorin sounded on the verge of tears with relief.

"Yes, Simion. It's me. Hold your hands still while I cut the rope."

"Nagaro! *Oh, Vothra!*" Simion gasped. "Praise to Lokundas! Here I thought they'd trapped you, and now you've come to rescue me! But of course it would be you—"

Nagaro was plying his knife to good effect. He'd already cut the cord that bound the other man's wrists and was at work on the one that encircled his ankles. He winced at Simion's gush of words. "I'm no heaven-sent savior, Simion." he said. "I *was* trapped— for two days— and in need of rescue myself. I'd still be chained up there in that room if it weren't for the courage of three people who took it upon themselves to right a wrong. *They're* the angels this time."

The knife bit through the last of the cord, and Simion immediately rolled into a sitting position. He bent over his hands, rubbing his wrists, the moonlight silvering his disheveled hair and revealing the heavy growth of stubble on his cheeks. "So Brandle's been telling tales on me, has he," he said. He sounded painfully chagrined.

"Brandle can be forgiven. He's been under a lot of strain."

Simion's head instantly came up, his face tilting to the light so that the moon made stars in his dark eyes. "Where is he?" he demanded anxiously. "Is he with you? *Is he all right?*"

"No, he's not with me. We got separated before I was taken in their trap. Can you stand up?"

Nagaro extended a hand, which Simion leaned on heavily as he struggled to his feet. Once on them, the young Kelorin continued to stand, his head down, his right hand clasping his left wrist where Nagaro had seen a dark mark. For a moment Nagaro thought the other man was focused on his injury, but then he began to speak.

"It's my fault they were able to set a trap for you, Nagaro!" he cried in anguish. They *knew* you would help Brandle— knew you'd come for me! And they got everything from me— everything they wanted! It was that horrible drug! I couldn't stop myself! I had no control— It was as if... as if—"

"I know." Nagaro felt the chill of ice-cold memory mixed with the horror of a near escape. So there *was* heskial here in this place!

"— as if there was someone else inside of me that was answering—" Simion's voice babbled on.

"I know!"

"I couldn't even *move* unless they told me to! And Grimbold was there with that horrible smile, saying 'you will answer all our questions. You will tell us everything.' And then they'd ask— And... and I would *answer*... I didn't *want* to, but—"

"Simion, *I know!*" Desperate to staunch the flow of words, Nagaro took the other man by shoulders and shook him. "It was heskial! I *know* about heskial! *It's not your fault!*"

Simion had raised his head. He was staring at Nagaro, his dark eyes wide with alarm. "*Oh, Vothra!*" he whispered. "That's what they used on you! Oh, Nagaro, I'm *sorry!* I shouldn't have gone on about it!"

Nagaro realized that his hands were clenched on Simion's shoulders. With an effort. he uncurled his fingers, releasing the other man. "Let it go," he said, turning away before he could further betray the intensity of his emotion. "Come on. We need to get out of here!"

He struck off at a fast pace, rounding the corner of the shed and making in the direction of the stable. He wasn't sure which made him angrier, the thought of what they'd done to Simion or the fact that the mere memory of things that had been done to *him* almost ten years before still had the power to turn his soul to ice and his guts to water. He'd gone at least a dozen strides before he realized that Simion wasn't with him, and stopped to look back.

The young man had all but come to a halt, several paces behind him. He was still standing in the pool of shadow cast by the shed.

Nagaro backtracked. "What's the matter," he asked, trying to keep the tenseness out of his voice. He couldn't wait to be far away from this place.

"It's not just the trap, Nagaro. They know everything I know!"

"*What?*" Nagaro felt his chest tighten. The moonlight seemed to dim.

Simion saw the stricken look on his face. "No, no, not *that!*" he said, hurriedly. "Not what you told me on Pakoa. But only because they didn't command me to tell them about your *past*. If they had, it would have come spilling out like everything else!"

Nagaro did his best to breathe again. "Then what *did* you tell them?" he asked, because Simion was so obviously distraught. "What did they want to know?"

"All about Lord Kuran's investigation. Everything you found out. Everything *I* found out. Things I know they're doing that I haven't told Kuran yet."

"Well, that's all right. We'll go tell him, and then we'll all know everything too. And we'll know what they know about us." Nagaro tried to be reassuring, desperate to calm Simion down. "Now let's go!" He turned around and started forward again.

"Where are we going?" Simion gasped, stumbling along beside him. "We need horses, or we won't get far before they come after us!

Nagaro jerked his head at the building ahead of them. "That's the stable. I mean to borrow a pair of horses."

"*Borrow?*" Simion stumbled, caught himself, and hopped to catch up. "How do you mean to return them?"

"I'll find a way. I don't want anyone to be able to call me a horse thief, though I'm sure Grimbold will anyway. I wish I had my sword," he added, thinking how little he'd like to be caught in the act of making off with the mounts.

"Your heaven-sent saviors didn't give it back to you?"

"They never had it. I lost it— along with Thunder-Heels— before I walked into that bloody trap." *And the thief who'd frightened the horses had probably been part of the trap.*

The building was indeed the stable. Its big double doors were barred, but not locked, and the bar was quickly removed and the door swung wide. Inside the high-vaulted structure, there was a reassuring smell of leather, hay, and horses. And also the sound of the big animals shifting their weight from hoof to hoof in the shadowy stalls and making occasional low snuffing noises. Two rows of windows high on the walls on either side gave them enough light to see by once their eyes grew accustomed to the new conditions.

Nagaro's glance swept the two rows of stalls. At least eight of them were tenanted. "We'll need saddles and bridles," he muttered, looking around for a tack room. He could ride bareback, but he wasn't sure if Simion could, and it wasn't the best choice if one needed to ride fast or over rough country. He remembered two low extensions on the side of the building, and noted two corresponding doorways opening on his left. "You check that one," he said, gesturing towards one of the doorways. "I'll check the other."

The room he stepped into turned out to be a small smithy, mostly for the shoeing of horses, but there was evidence that some repair or manufacture of smaller pieces of iron-work was done there as well. Various bits of rusted or dented metal lay on low shelves or scattered on the floor, only half-identifiable by the light from a single window. Nagaro was turning to go when something caught his eye. It was a metal rod a little more than three feet long, leaning against a wall. On closer inspection, it turned out to be a somewhat rusty spit for roasting meat. As thick as his little finger, it was pointed at one end and bore a three-inch diameter metal disk about six inches from the other. The disk must have been part of a pulley arrangement for turning the spit from outside of the fireplace, but to Nagaro's eye it resembled the hand-guard on a sword hilt. With a hungry smile, he picked up the object and hefted it. It was scarcely heavier than his own sword, and no worse in balance than some of the cruder blades he'd used. He took it with him when he returned to the stable.

Simion had found the saddles. The young Kelorin eyed the spit skeptically, but refrained from commenting. Setting one saddle on the floor, he went to get another, and the bridles as well.

Nagaro thrust the spit through his belt and set about choosing two of the horses. He recognized Lord Madred's white charger, but left the beast in its stall and brought out a black mare instead, choosing the dark color on purpose. He got a surprise when he went back for a dark chestnut. The horse's markings were familiar.

"This is Brandle's horse!" he exclaimed.

"Are you sure?" Simion stood with a bridle in his hands. In the dim light his face was hard to read, but his voice and stance registered alarm.

"Yes. And I don't like that. When I last saw Brandle, he was riding away on this horse in pursuit of a would-be horse thief— and now this."

Simion approached the chestnut and put out his hand. "Hello there, True," he coaxed. "Remember me?"

The horse wuffled at him and nuzzled his hand, the small white snip on its muzzle plainly visible even in the dim light.

Nagaro pictured Brandle having to walk the twenty miles back to Lankura. "Let's get that bridle on him," he said. "The sooner we get out of here, the better."

They divided the work, Simion dealing with the bridles and Nagaro the saddles. Simion had nearly completed his task and Nagaro was just cinching the second saddle, when he caught a movement out of the corner of his eye and spun around to face the open stable door. A figure stood there, just outside the threshold, illuminated by the moonlight.

It was Lord Madred and he held his sword naked in his hand.

"What's going on here?" the Leithian lord demanded.

Nagaro almost laughed at the absurdity of the question. "Why, Simion and I were just borrowing a pair of horses for our ride back to Lankura," he replied smoothly. "That bit of courtesy seems the least we're due under the circumstances, since the hospitality here has been so unsatisfactory— although it will only be necessary to return this mare, since I believe *that* horse belongs to your son Brandle." With a jerk of his head, he indicated the dark liver chestnut that Simion was holding by the bridle.

Madred took a step forward, his sword-point up and ready. "I know Grimbold hasn't arrived yet," he said. "And it doesn't appear that you've been freed by this... *man*." The way he said the last word sounded as if applying it to Simion caused him physical difficulty. "So there must be some treachery here—"

"Treachery!" Nagaro had let go of the saddle girth and his hand hovered near his belt where the end of the spit protruded. "*I* would say the honor of Sobring Hold has been redeemed this night— and not by any man of noble blood! I advise you not to interfere with us, My Lord. As you've pointed out, this isn't your Hold."

"The will of the Lord of Sobring should not be thwarted!" Madred had taken another step forward, bringing him under the stable's roof.

Nagaro advanced to meet him, drawing the spit from his belt with a fluid motion and holding it almost negligently. "It was the Lord of Sobring who dragged the honor of his Hold in the mud, My Lord," he said evenly. "And right now, it's *my* will that you should be concerned about thwarting. I won't go back to that room, nor do I intend to return Simion to the shed where I found him, bound and gagged." He brought the point of the spit up and came on his guard.

Madred stared in disbelief. "What *is* that?" he asked, frowning at the spit. "Surely you don't intend—"

Nagaro didn't let the lord finish. Instead, he made his intentions abundantly clear. With a quick lunge and a deft twist and flick of the spit, he sent Lord Madred's sword flying.

Simion had been moving, slowly beginning to circle the Leithian lord. With an exultant cry, he now sprang to retrieve the blade as it skidded across the floorboards and came to a stop inches from the stable's threshold. Though he moved a little stiffly, he had hold of the blade before Madred could overcome his astonishment at having been disarmed with a piece of kitchen hardware.

The young Kelorin quickly continued his circle so as to plant himself between Madred and the door. He leveled the blade at the Leithian lord's torso. "Go ahead and finish with that saddle, Nagaro," he said grimly. "I'll keep this one out of mischief."

Lord Madred had turned, and his gaze was now locked on Simion, his expression somewhere between apprehension and outrage. Simion appeared deadly serious.

Nagaro cautiously returned the spit to his belt and finished buckling the saddle girth, taking his eyes from the other two men as little as possible. "Don't do anything you'll regret, Simion," he admonished.

Simion laughed mirthlessly. "Oh, if I do it, I won't regret it."

"Now see here, Zirda!" Madred spoke with outraged indignation. "I've done you no injury!"

"No injury?" Simion stabbed the man with his eyes. "It was *your* gold that paid for the heskial they put into me, *My Lord!*"

"That's impossible! I've not authorized any such purchase."

"I believe he's sincere, Simion." Nagaro had finished with the girth and was adjusting the stirrups, still glancing as often as he could at the other two men. His words apparently forestalled Simion's hot rejoinder.

Simion frowned. "Then he ought to keep a closer eye— and hand— on that Minister Torlung of his, because the man's been making purchases behind his back!"

"How dare you make that accusation!"

"I've been keeping your books, My Lord! I know where the money goes— whatever's spent in Lankura!"

"You'll not be keeping my books anymore! Not after this!"

"Do you think I'd want to? After what I've seen in them?"

By this time Madred was livid. "I will not tolerate this, you little rogue! He advanced a step, impelled by his anger, only to check himself when Simion made a menacing movement with the sword. He then turned upon Nagaro. "Captain, I'm astonished that you tolerate this... this... *creature!* Let alone that you permit him to threaten me and make false accusations!"

Nagaro had finished with the stirrups. "I've known Simion much longer than I've known you, My Lord," he observed coldly. "And I've learned to trust him. If he says your gold has been going to buy heskial, I'm sure the account books will show it." Taking the two horses by their bridles, he led them past Madred and Simion to a spot in the open doorway of the stable. There he stopped, and added. "Simion was one of the six swordsmen who led the fight to capture the Mautep war galley on which we'd both been slaves. I know I can count on him to keep my enemies off my back. While *you*, My Lord, seem only inclined to aid and abet them. All things considered, I'd rather count Simion among my friends than some of the men you number among yours."

Madred frowned darkly. "To whom are you referring, Captain?"

"To Grimbold— and to Lothard Hurn."

Lord Madred's mouth twitched, and he looked as if he were tasting something bitter. "Even the fairest tree occasionally produces a twisted twig," he said stiffly. "But the ways of our fathers must be upheld! Traditions honored by time are more important than individual men. And the Brothers of the Blood include better men than these. Hilber Dorn of Borlund, for one."

"I'm glad to hear it, My Lord. Since Vell Sobring has been sent to question Lord Hilber about the illicit trade with Jinara that appears to be passing across his border."

Nagaro was gratified to read shock on Madred's face, but he was eager to be away. Setting his foot in the stirrup, he swung up lightly onto the back of the black mare. Once there, he said, "Would you please hand me the sword now, Simion?"

For a moment, Simion appeared reluctant to comply. But the moment passed and he proffered the hilt of Lord Madred's sword to Nagaro without comment, then stiffly mounted True. Nagaro sat astride the mare, the point of the sword leveled at its owner.

"What are you going to do, Captain?" Still standing under the stable roof, Madred's face was too shadowed to read easily, but the haughtiness had left his voice. The question had been an honest one. "Will you keep my sword?"

"That I will not!" Nagaro raised the blade and flung it in a high arc over Lord Madred's head, deep into the interior of the dark stable. The blade flashed briefly in a shaft of moonlight and fell with a distant metallic clatter that elicited startled stamps and snorts from the remaining horses.

Madred made no move to retrieve the blade. He stood with his hands spread. "And you mean to just ride away?" he asked.

"I thought I'd made that clear from the outset, My Lord."

"It could go ill with you if Grimbold brings a public charge— saying you refused to give satisfaction for dishonoring the Lady Alisset, and that you fled from custody." It almost seemed that Madred's voice held a note of genuine concern.

Nagaro smiled so that his teeth flashed. "I'd rather take my chances with what the world might think of me than risk what Grimbold might do to me," he said grimly. "The man doesn't wish me well."

"It would seem not." The Leithian lord heaved a sigh, and when he spoke again there was a hopeful lift to his words. "If you stay and let me intervene with Grimbold, I believe I can offer you the hand of a woman of Furthing Hold. One who would be more pleased with the match than the Lady Alisset seems to be."

Nagaro heard Simion's intake of breath. For a moment he could only stare at Madred. Then he shook his head. "I must give you the same answer I once gave the Emperor of the Mahuk Baar under similar circumstances, My Lord," he said earnestly. "You honor me by the offer, but my heart lies elsewhere. And in any case, we are not in Furthing Hold. Farewell, My Lord." And with that, he turned the mare about and set his heels to her flanks so that the animal sprang away in a clatter of iron-shod hooves.

Lord Madred's words came after him. "If ever you find your father, he'll be a man of noble blood. Mark my words!"

Nagaro made no answer.

Simion had spun his mount as well, spurring after Nagaro. As he sped into the night, the young Kelorin flung parting words of his own over his shoulder. "Take a look at your own books, My Lord, but don't tell Torlung you mean to do it!"

They were just passing the little fenced pasture and weren't even fairly out onto the narrow rutted road when the sound of shouts broke out behind them.

Chapter 27

Flight

At first Nagaro pressed the mare to a gallop, glad of the moonlight that made such speed possible without great risk of a fall. Well before the animal was winded, however, he drew rein and motioned Simion to follow him as he turned off into the trees on the right-hand side of the road. Under the arching canopy of boughs, they were immediately plunged into deep shadow, their nostrils full of the smells of vegetation and damp earth.

"What's your plan, Nagaro?" Simion asked breathlessly.

"I mean to go west. Over the crest of these hills. There's another road on the other side that joins the North Road at the border of Sobring Hold."

"Good idea."

Nagaro caught the eager light in the other man's dark eyes. "I hope they'll expect us to take the North Road all the way, because it's more direct, " he added. "The coast road will take us longer to get to that crossroads by an hour or two, but if we had stayed on the North Road we'd have been racing them all the way— risking breaking our necks in the dark. There's a chance they'd catch us, and we're unarmed— except for this roasting spit."

"You should have kept Madred's sword."

"No, Simion. He never actually used it against me, and I'm not a thief even if I *am* a pirate."

They picked their way up the slope in the darkness among the trunks and tree roots. Moonlight only occasionally penetrated to the forest floor, in small patches or dappled specks like spattered drops of quicksilver. As they went, they paused at intervals to listen. All too soon they heard the hoofbeats and harness-jingle of the pursuing party. They were some way clear of the road by that time, but still stood holding their breaths while the horsemen passed by below them. The rutted track they had left still showed clearly as an irregular strip of moonlit earth at the bottom of the slope. It's path was easy to follow, and they caught a glimpse of the pursuing party through the trees. Nagaro counted eight riders.

They pressed ahead up the slope after that, without speaking, until they came to a break in the trees that afforded a view of the hill's crest above them.

"How are we going to get over that?" Simion wondered aloud, for it looked high and jagged and imposing.

"See that notch?" Nagaro pointed. "That's what we're making for. Taru and I crossed over that way from the other side— and back again— years ago. The very top is a bit steep and we'll have to dismount, but it's not a difficult pass, really. And once on the other side, the going will be easier."

Half an hour later they reached the summit. There was a last vigorous scramble, leading the horses, and then they were standing just over the crest, gazing across the moonlit land and sea, and breathing salt air as they caught their breath. The ground that dropped away before them was more sparsely clad with cedar and pine than the slope they had just climbed. They could look over the nearest treetops all the way to where the moon-silvered sea met the jet black of the western sky. Eastward, behind them, the sky was lightening to deepest blue, heralding the coming dawn.

Below them, the long arc of the shore of Wotana Bay was marked by the pale gleam of sea-foam where the waves were breaking. Out across the water, the long, low shapes of several islands were dark silhouettes that seemed to float in molten silver. Above them, the sky was dominated by the two moons, Naru and Talebra, the latter so bright that her face dimmed the stars. And now at last Nagaro could clearly see what Alisset had meant when she'd said that Talebra was beginning to take Naru into her arms.

The long-anticipated conjunction had begun. The moons were nearly full, the trailing edge of Talebra's brilliant disk still a little ragged. Naru, chasing her down the sky, had just begun to pass in front of the larger moon. His smaller, dimmer disk— dull steel to Talebra's gleaming silver— was sharply etched against the brightness of her face where he clipped a little curving sliver from Talebra's trailing edge.

"It's a sight to see, isn't it," said Simion, beside him.

"Yes it is. And of course Leithian folk-lore sees it as a confrontation between Lissafel, their goddess of love, and Kroneg, the god of war."

"How's that supposed to work, then?" Simion was gingerly rubbing his left wrist where the rope that had bound him had left an open sore.

"I'm not sure. Naru passes in front, but Talebra is larger, so there must come a time when she encircles him. I've heard some call that an embrace."

Simion laughed. "So what is this, a kiss?" he asked archly. "I'd say mighty Kroneg is riding for a fall."

"Alisset thinks so too. But come on. It'll be dawn soon and we've a long way to go. And I'd like to stop somewhere down there and tend that wound of yours if we can."

The trees quickly began to gather more thickly as they descended, and they were soon riding through a forest once more, weaving their way between trunks under a canopy of overarching branches, the air heavy with the scents of growing things. Still they were aware that, even under the trees, the gloom was lessening, and by the time they emerged from the eaves of the wood and came down onto the coast road, the sky was lavender, tinted rose in the east, the stars had faded, and the two contentious or amorous moons were dipping towards the western horizon. Birds could be heard coming to life in the forest, and light and color were returning to the world.

Nagaro drew rein at the edge of the road and demanded that Simion let him examine his wrist in the dawning light.

"I don't like it," he said, shaking his head. "These red puffy places and the crustiness along this edge look like it's starting to fester. I learned enough from Tredhold to be able to clean it for you if we can get boiled water. But it's up to you, of course, if you'd rather wait for a real healer to do it. I don't think you'll come to serious harm from it before we can reach Lankura."

"Of course I'll let you do it, Nagaro." Simion's eyes were wide and trusting. "But where will we get boiled water?"

"We can try down there." Nagaro pointed to a small stone house some distance farther down the slope, below the road and close to the shore of the bay. "Taru's family used to live there, and I know the family who holds it now, a little." In fact he'd met Gudo and Lanei only once and had found he had too little in common with either of them to make much conversation, but for this purpose they should do well enough.

Despite the earliness of the hour, they spied Gudo as they approached the house, just leaving the woodshed with an armful of firewood. Nagaro hailed the young fisherman. Gudo looked harried. A stocky, broad-faced young man, his eyes kept darting in the direction of the little makeshift pier where his fishing boat was moored as Nagaro explained what they wanted.

Still, boiled water was a simple thing and the truth was that Nagaro's reputation in Wotana was such that there probably wasn't a man, woman, or child anywhere in the vicinity who would have refused any request of his if they had power to grant it.

"Hot water?" Gudo asked, when Nagaro had finished. "Oh, aye. Just go down to the door an' ask my Lanei. She'll see t' whatever ye need. But

I can't stay. I've my boat to make ready. Times are lean, and the day's a-wasting."

Lanei was even more accommodating. She was a buxom, sloe-eyed young Turowa with an inclination to plumpness. It was also evident that she was carrying what would be the couple's third child.

She poured the last of the morning's sothiril into chipped earthenware cups for them while they sat at the main room's small table, and then refilled the kettle and set it on the fire to boil. She also brought them some scraps of rag. She swung her hips and made eyes at both Nagaro and Simion whenever she passed them, despite her swelling belly and the fact that her two children were asleep in the little room that Nagaro and Taru had once shared.

Her behavior amused Simion, but Nagaro found it embarrassing. He was reminded of how hard Taru's father had worked to keep his son away from Lanei because of her reputation for wantonness. Gudo's marriage had, in fact, been forced by his having gotten her with child. Taru had expressed sympathy for Gudo over that on account of Lanei being not much of a cook, and Nagaro wondered whether Gudo knew how his wife carried on in front of strangers when he was out of the house. He did his best to ignore Lanei's flirtatiousness, focusing on Simion and grasping at any topic of conversation he could find.

As they waited for the water, Simion rubbed his chin ruefully, and said, "If only I had a razor I'd take advantage of the hot water to shave."

At that Nagaro laughed. "You won't find a razor here. Not in a Turowan house. Besides, I think the beard becomes you."

"You do?" Simion's dark eyes were suddenly wide and eager.

Nagaro mentally kicked himself for making what he had intended to be an entirely innocent remark. He was very glad when, a moment later, the water boiled and he could give his attention to treating the other man's wound.

The interior of the house was dim, the dawn light that entered by an open window being still pale and watery. A lamp on the table sputtered as it burned, suggesting poor-quality oil, but still cast the best light available. Working by its erratic glow, Nagaro cleaned the wound thoroughly using a bit of rag soaked in the water. He then asked Lanei if she had any salt.

"Salt?" Lanei left off batting her eyelashes at Simion to turn suddenly worried eyes to Nagaro. "Oh, Tor Nagaro, we've so little left! An' there's no money right now to buy more."

"I'll pay you for it," Nagaro put in quickly. "Five rins, for the salt and for your trouble." He knew that five rins would buy an entire bag of precious salt in Wotana.

Her mouth dropped open and her eyes widened. "Oh, aye, Zirda! I'll fetch it right away!"

"It's going to sting, Simion—" Nagaro began apologetically.

"You think I don't know that?" Simion gave him a rueful look. "I've taken worse wounds than this."

The little wooden salt box that Lanei brought was indeed very nearly empty. Simion managed not to wince as Nagaro applied the white crystals sparingly to the worst-looking areas and returned the box to their hostess. All that remained then was to tear some of the rag into strips and bandage the wrist with several snug turns of cloth.

Having finished, Nagaro pulled out his purse and counted out the five rins, laying the coins in Lanei's outstretched hand. He couldn't help noticing how hungrily her eyes followed the copper pieces. Nor could he help noticing that the room they were in seemed dingier to him than when Taru's mother, Olomi, had kept it. The oiled skin on one of the two windows had been patched rather than replaced, and the back of the chair Simion was sitting in had been inexpertly mended, probably by Gudo. The shelves on the wall looked less well-stocked with crockery and cooking utensils. The children's toys that lay scattered on the floor near the hearth were poor things— a crude horse made of sticks tied together, a rag ball, a doll made of sticks rapped in a dirty rag with a lump of painted clay for a head.

Remembering Gudo's words about the times being lean, Nagaro added two more rins, nominally for the cloth he had used, though the scraps were too small and ragged to have any real value. Then he thanked Lanei and rose to go, beckoning Simion to follow him.

He didn't get far, however, before Lanei called urgently after him. "Wait, Tor Nagaro! Please! Ye used t' live in this house. Can ye tell me what's in this box? We can't get it open."

Nagaro was eager to be gone but he felt he couldn't refuse to look at the thing. He was hoping to be able to give a quick negative response, but when he followed Lanei's gesture and saw the small wooden chest tucked against the wall in a corner of the room, he recognized it immediately. It was about sixteen inches long, less than twelve inches in each of its other two dimensions, with brass hinges and a brass plate with a keyhole at the front.

"That's Olomi's sewing box!" he exclaimed in surprise. "Why is it still here?" He could picture the contents. The box had held Olomi's greatest treasures: needles and pins, a scissors, a thimble, spare buttons, and remnants of cloth folded up at the bottom.

Lanei squirmed uncomfortably. All her flirtatiousness had vanished and she looked quite miserable and a little desperate. "We took the house an' everything in it," she said, "Gudo an' me— after Taru's Hama had kept what she wanted, o' course. She left the box, an' I thought maybe I'd sell what's in it, only I never found the key. I don't s'pose ye'd be knowing where it is?"

"Olomi always wore it on a string around her neck…" Nagaro's words trailed. He didn't need to finish with the obvious conclusion. When the bodies of Taru's murdered parents had been found, the immediate concern must have been to get them decently buried as quickly as possible. The key had surely gone with Olomi to her final resting place.

"Oh." Lanei twisted her fingers together. "Then I'll never get the things out of it!" She sounded completely crestfallen.

"A locksmith could open it easily," Simion ventured. "He'd just make a new a key."

Lanei looked blank. Simion, in turn, looked taken aback by her apparent mystification.

Nagaro offered an explanation. "I don't suppose they have any locksmiths in Wotana. Hardly anyone around here ever locks anything— or needs to." It was true. Folk in Wotana looked out for each other. Theft was rare, and Olomi's lockable box had been something special, a wedding gift. She'd kept it locked for no other reason than that she could.

Nagaro stood for a moment, uncertain. He hadn't enough rins left in his purse to make a reasonable bid for the sewing box, nor any wish to be encumbered by it on his ride to Lankura. While it saddened him to think of Olomi's prized possessions being sold off to whoever might be willing to buy them, they had plainly already passed to Lanei and Gudo, and the family needed the money. "Look," he said. "Why don't you talk to Goran the trader about it? The box is probably worth at least as much as what's in it, and Goran might well buy it from you without seeing what's inside if he thinks he can sell it for a profit in Galenor or Lankura."

Lanei brightened immediately. "D' ye really think so?" She looked from one of them to the other.

Simion, the merchant's son, was immediately intrigued. "It's a fair notion, Zirdyn," he told her. "It sounds as if there's no market for that locked box here in Wotana, but in Lankura it could easily fetch twenty rins. Perhaps twenty-five, with what's inside. The trader will have the trouble of transporting it, and of course he needs his profit, but you might get as much as eighteen rins from him. Don't let him have it for less than fourteen—"

Nagaro rolled his eyes. "Come *on*, Simion. She'll get whatever Goran is willing to give her, surely. And we should be gone."

***

Eager though he was to be on their way, Nagaro still insisted on stopping at the spot at the edge of the woods above the house where a large gray stone painted with faded spirit signs marked the grave of Jomo and Olomi Nareyo. "They were good to me during a bad time," he said in response to Simion's raised eyebrow. He didn't dismount, but sat in the saddle with his head bowed, remembering the kindness and decency of those two very ordinary people— and the courage with which they had both faced their final moments. He would always be grateful for the way they had taken him into their house and into their lives at a time when he had lost even the memory of his own history and the knowledge of who he was.

The sun was just clear of the crest of the hills they had crossed earlier that morning when they rode on, south, following the coast road as it ran between the forest and the sea. The road was all but deserted, partly because of the hour but also because the land flanking the road was nearly untenanted. They rode at first at a dogged pace, alternating bursts of speed with intervals when they dropped to a walk to allow the horses to rest. It was during the latter periods that they had the opportunity to talk, and to share the details of their experiences at the hands of their captors.

Simion was amazed to hear the history behind Lord Madred's remarkable offer. He fretted at the tale of Brandle's disappearance, and smiled a little at the antics of Alisset. He was outraged by the rough handling that Nagaro had received, though he'd been handled no less roughly himself.

The wound on his wrist was evidence of the fact that his hands had been bound almost continuously since the day he'd been taken in the street behind Lord Madred's house in Lankura by three armed Leithians. They had approached him on a pretense of asking directions to a nearby street address, then grabbed him and forced him into a carriage and driven off with him, bound and gagged. He had been subjected repeatedly to interrogation under heskial— several times while being held at some unidentified location in Lankura, and again while he'd been held in the same room where Nagaro had found himself chained.

"In Lankura the questions were mostly about Lord Kuran's investigation," he explained. "What he knew and how he knew it. And of course they also wanted to know what else I had learned— or guessed. When they discovered that I'd gotten information from you, they were very keen to know how you'd come by it."

"They know about Utabala, then?" Nagaro asked.

"I'm afraid so, but I don't think he's in any danger. It doesn't seem that these Brothers of the Blood have any agents that they trust among the Jinari— just men they do business with. In fact, they spoke disparagingly of the Jinari people in general, because their skins are dark. They were really much more interested in you— how they could lure you to the hunting lodge. That's all they asked me about after they brought me to *that* place. They wanted to know, first, whether you would come to my aid. And then they wanted all the details of that retched affair involving Jila."

Nagaro made a rueful face. "Did they think that if I'd done such a thing once, I would do it again?"

"Obviously. I could have told them you'd never make the same mistake twice, but they didn't try to get my opinion. The part of my brain that was giving them answers seemed to be dense as a brick. It only talked about *exactly* what they told it to, and in the most simple-minded way. It was really rather stupid, when I think about it."

Dense as brick... simple-minded... stupid...

Nagaro fixed his gaze on the road ahead, not trusting himself to meet Simion's eyes. "Yes," he said through his teeth. *"I know."* He didn't need Simion's description of the stupidity of what he had called the 'puppet part' of his mind. *He'd been worse than a village idiot... or a palace idiot. He'd been the idiot of all Edrovir!* Driven by his rising anger, he dug his heels into the mare's flanks, sending the horse plunging forward in a full gallop and leaving Simion to follow as best he could.

When Simion caught up, he made no attempt to return to the subject, and when Nagaro eventually slowed his pace to rest the horses, the young Kelorin kept the conversation confined to harmless topics. Nagaro was glad of it, though he felt the irony— that Simion, whose experiences with heskial were fresh and raw, could talk about them more easily than he could talk about his own, which had happened nearly a decade ago. It felt to him like weakness, and he found it galling.

The road turned inland, running through wild, unpeopled country, mostly wooded but with stretches of meadowland interspersed. As they left the cooling influence of the sea behind and the sun rode higher, the day grew warm— though not as hot as the day when Grimbold's men had set their trap. Nagaro knew the way well enough to know when they were approaching the place where their road joined the old North Road. When they were less than a mile from the crossroads, he suggested they stop to rest a little and share the food that Tor Brun had packed for him.

They chose the edge of a small grove of trees on the south side of the road, beside a bit of meadow where the horses could graze while the two men sat in the shade and ate. They did so with focused intensity at first. It was only a little past midmorning, but they had missed breakfast and were both very hungry. As their hunger eased, however, they both began to relax. It was a peaceful spot. There were flowers in the meadow and bees buzzed lazily. Birds called among the trees. A squirrel scampered noisily along a branch over their heads and chattered down at them.

"Are we still in Sobring Hold, do you think?" Simion asked presently, between bites of bread and cheese.

Nagaro took a swallow of sothiril from the flask, and shook his head. "It's over there." He gestured at the woods on the other side of the road. "Where we're sitting is Crown lands. This road marks the boundary."

"Ah." Simion nodded and his deep blue eyes grew wistful. "This would be the edge of the old Loros Wared, then. Where does it become Kel Wared?"

"Very near the crossroads up ahead. The marker is overgrown with weeds and easy to miss, but I've seen it when I've come this way before."

"Going to Wotana?"

"Yes. Going to Wotana."

For a moment more they sat in silence as they ate. Nagaro was thinking of the stop they had made on Wotana Bay and wondering whether they'd taken longer about it than they should.

Simion's thoughts must have been running in a similar vein, for he asked, "Do you think they're still looking for us?"

Nagaro frowned. "It depends on how far they're willing to go without direct orders from their lord. They could easily have reached the crossroads by now. If they didn't find us on the way, they might turn back at the border of their Hold. Or they might ride on into Kel Wared."

"Then they'd be ahead of us." Simion hunched his shoulders and glanced worriedly at the road.

Nagaro tried to hide his own concern. "Yes, but that stretch of the North Road running south of the crossroads is less lonely— there are farms. The Sobring men might be reluctant to try taking us where someone could see and come to our aid. We should be careful, though ... get off the road if necessary."

Simion glanced at the road again. Having finished the last of his bread, he stood up. "What if they're waiting for us at the crossroads?"

"Then we'll have to leave the road and strike off across country," Nagaro said matter-of-factly. He picked up the empty pouch and flask, and stood up as well. "I don't think we can afford to wait for them to leave. We should scout the crossroads before we come to it."

Simion nodded grimly. "Right," he said. "I'll catch the horses."

The last stretch of road leading to the crossroads was winding. They went cautiously, keeping to the south side of the roadway, their eyes focused ahead of them, as stands of trees often blocked their view of what was immediately ahead.

They passed the weed-covered marker for the border of Kel Wared, and Nagaro knew they were very close.

Just as he thought they were approaching the last bend, the wind— which had been from their backs— shifted, and he caught the sound of raised voices. Immediately he turned and rode off of the road into a stand of birch and alder, beckoning Simion to follow.

"It sounds as if there's someone at the crossroads," he said. "We'll have to try to use these trees for cover."

Simion nodded agreement.

They dismounted for better concealment and began threading their way between the slender trunks. Nagaro went first, leading the black mare by the bridle. The fickle wind carried more snatches of the voices to their ears, but it was impossible to make out the words.

At last, Nagaro reached the other end of the stand of trees and pushed through the last of the undergrowth and low-hanging branches. The crossroads that marked the meeting of the Coast Road they'd been following and the North Road lay about fifty yards ahead.

There were more than a score of horsemen at the crossroads.

They were clearly in two groups, facing each other in what had every appearance of a standoff. The group on the north side was mainly composed of men in the purple and white of Sobring Hold. The group on the south was dominated by men in the dark blue of the Royal Fleet. Nagaro thought he saw two riderless horses, one of which looked like Thunder-Heels.

"And *there* is Kuran," he muttered under his breath, as he identified the distinctive bearded figure of the Lord of the Fleet on his long-legged bay, front and center among the men in blue.

"*And* Lord Madred." Simion had come up behind Nagaro and was standing looking over his shoulder, holding True's bridle. He extended his free hand to point out the Lord of Furthing Hold among Grimbold's men, hanging back a little and flanked by two men in a different livery. "He's brought two of his own men! What should we do, Nagaro?"

Nagaro had the answer ready. "Backtrack a little through these trees, get back out onto the road, and ride up to them as if it's the most natural thing in the world."

"Are you *sure*, Nagaro?" Simion obviously wasn't. "*They're* all armed, and we're not!"

Nagaro had already started to back up and to turn the mare around. "If you've done nothing wrong, Simion, the best thing to do is not to act as if you had."

"*Huh!*" Simion was doing his best to follow with True. "Now I *know* you're not crossed, talking like that."

Nagaro frowned. "If things get too hot for you personally, Simion, don't hesitate to make a run for it. And don't worry about me if you do."

Chapter 28

At The Crossroads

Less than a minute later they were back on the road, rounding the last curve that brought them into view of the crossroads, moving at an easy trot. Simion was hanging back a little, warily, letting Nagaro take the lead. They weren't inclined to talk in any case. Their full attention was on the men up ahead.

The two groups of riders were milling about tensely, their collective attention on the obviously heated discussion that was going on between Kuran and one of the men in Grimbold's livery, presumably the leader of the Sobring force. Nagaro was fairly sure he could guess the topic of that conversation. Trying to avoid being seen by these horsemen, he felt, wasn't really an option, however much Simion might have preferred it. He doubted the argument would come to any satisfactory conclusion if he didn't show himself, and he feared there could be violence.

They had advanced to within thirty-five yards of the horsemen before they were noticed, and then it was Taru's voice that rang out above the others.

"There he is! There's Nagaro!"

Other voices followed in a tangled jumble. The men of Sobring Hold wheeled their horses and started in Nagaro's direction, only to be cut off when Kuran's force quickly spread out to block the Coast Road.

"And there's Simion!"

The new voice was Brandle's cutting through the commotion, and a horse bearing a big blond man out of uniform broke from the rear of the group of Fleet men.

Simion gave a cry and kicked True into a gallop.

Nagaro heaved a sigh and urged his own horse into a canter, following in the other man's wake. *So much for Simion's fears.*

Simion and Brandle met about thirty feet from the line of Fleet riders. Nagaro swept past them without stopping, though he noted that Brandle was sporting a lingering black eye— its colors progressing from purple to yellow and green— and several healing cuts on his face. There was a story there, but since the man was on a horse, it was likely he would live, Nagaro reasoned, and Simion was paying the big Leithian enough attention for both of them in any case.

Nagaro glimpsed a number of familiar faces among the Fleet men, Taru, Pavo, Landros, and Tredhold were all there, but Nagaro made straight for Thunder-Heels. The stallion— saddled and bridled, but not on a lead rein— tossed his head in greeting. Nagaro was off of the black mare and onto the big gray in seconds. All eyes were on him as he grabbed the mare's bridle with one hand and Thunder's reins with the other. Taru tried to say something, but Nagaro muttered *"later"* under his breath and steered his mount towards Kuran. Reining to a halt beside the Lord of the Fleet, he sent the mare on past him with a slap on the rump, into the space between the two groups of riders. Then he raised his voice for the Sobring men to hear.

"There's the horse I borrowed!"

The mare trotted about three paces before dropping to a disinterested walk and then coming to a halt, oblivious to the tension between the men surrounding her. She stood in the middle of the open space, showing no preference for either group of horses.

Kuran had returned his attention to the Leithian soldier he'd been arguing with. Nagaro didn't recognize the man, an older Leithian with a military bearing and close-cropped graying hair the color of rusty iron. Among the other four men in white and purple, he noticed two— one stocky, one tall and weedy— who had been among the men at the table in the room next to the kitchen when he'd been brought in, still sick from the drug in the sothiril that Alisset had given him. The stocky fellow, in his thirties with sweat-slicked white-blond hair, pressed his horse close to his sergeant and spoke some words to him in a low voice.

The sergeant scowled. "I'm told there were *two* horses taken."

"Well you're not having mine!" Brandle pushed his horse to the front of the line with Simion, still mounted on True, close behind him. "I was set upon by horse thieves in your forest, and now Simion tells me they found *my* horse in *your* stable!"

The sergeant drew himself up. *"How dare you imply—"*

"I'll do more than imply! Two of the men who pulled me off my horse and beat me are right *there*, and *there!"* Brandle stabbed his finger at the two men Nagaro had recognized.

The two Leithians immediately began to protest their innocence while their sergeant went red in the face and began to sputter.

Kuran loudly cleared his throat and raised his voice. "Give them the other spare horse, Pavo," he said in a level tone that belied the steel glint in his eye. "I don't have time to argue about trivialities."

Pavo's "Aye, Zirda" was spoken with typical Hashtep deadpan. The young Fleet officer unhooked the lead rein of the strawberry roan he'd been leading and shooed the animal out into the empty space where the black mare stood mouthing her bit.

The iron-haired sergeant barked a directive to his men to collect the animals, but before they could finish, he refocused his ire on Kuran. "You see, My Lord?" he growled, pointing a finger at Nagaro. "I told you we didn't have him!"

"Seeing the proof of that, Sergeant, I concede the point," Kuran responded coldly. "But I'll concede nothing else without equally convincing evidence."

"I told you he was arrested, My Lord, and escaped from our custody!"

Kuran turned to Nagaro. "Is this true, Captain?"

"As far as it goes, yes, My Lord," Nagaro responded levelly.

The sergeant appeared encouraged. "He was being held under a judgement from our Council of Elders, My Lord, for compromising the honor of the Lady Alisset. He must be retaken and held until he marries her— or he must face execution!"

This drew indignant cries from the Fleet men, which Kuran silenced with a gesture. Not taking his eyes off the sergeant, he said, "I assume there's no truth to *that* charge, Captain?"

Nagaro's response was loud and firm. "I swear on my honor and in Vothra's name that I have done no harm to the Lady Alisset— neither her person nor her honor. The lady will confirm it if anyone asks her. I was trapped and drugged, and evidence was concocted to create the appearance of a compromising situation. I was given no chance to present my case, and Lord Grimbold clearly wasn't interested in the truth. I can only assume that the Elders based their judgement on the concocted evidence."

Nagaro had been watching the expressions of Grimbold's men as he spoke, noting the sergeant's innocent outrage and the much less innocent shock on the faces of the two men he'd seen at the hunting lodge. "If the sergeant wasn't privy to the plot," he added quickly, "he might be forgiven for assuming that he's in the right." He hoped that Kuran had seen what he'd seen.

Again Nagaro's words drew outraged exclamations from the Fleet men, which Kuran gestured into silence.

Behind the men of Sobring Hold, Lord Madred still sat on his horse, as he had from the beginning, stone-faced, his eyes taking in everything.

The sergeant, however, exploded, flinging his wrath first at Nagaro, with a sputtered, "That's completely preposterous!" He then turned his anger on Kuran. "You can't believe these vile slanders, My Lord! The charge against Captain Nagaro comes from the Elders of Sobring Hold. It can't be ignored. I have orders from Lord Grimbold to hold him!"

"And *I* have orders from the King of Edrovir," Kuran shot back, "to use whatever force is necessary to secure the captain's release. Since he's already free, I'll use whatever force I must to keep him so. I mean to sail with tomorrow's tide to meet the Emperor of the Mahuk Baar and secure the release of a hundred Edroviran citizens who've been held as galley slaves. Captain Nagaro was instrumental in arranging the release, and the Emperor has specifically requested his presence."

"You would completely ignore the charge, My Lord?" The sergeant was incredulous. "An official pronouncement from the Elders of a Hold?"

"I rather think the King's will outweighs that of your Elders," Kuran observed dryly. "If they continue to believe they have a grievance, they can take it up with the Crown. I warn you, however, that I've never known Captain Nagaro to speak falsely, and it seems to me that he has charges of his own."

Nagaro cleared his throat. "Charges that include kidnaping Simion Rudrin and holding him without cause."

"I second that charge! And I add horse theft!" Brandle interjected.

"I would also point out," Kuran continued without missing a step, "that we are at present on the public road, and not even within the borders of Sobring Hold. You therefore have no jurisdiction."

The sergeant opened his mouth, but apparently could find no answering argument because he shut it again, then said stiffly, "Very well, My Lord— if that's how you're going to be about this. I'll just make my report to Lord Grimbold, and we'll see what he has to say!"

Kuran made a sardonic half bow from his horse's saddle. "By all means, do that, Sergeant," he said, and then he sat stonily while the Leithian ordered his men to turn their horses around and the five of them rode off up the North Road in the direction of Sobring Hall with the two riderless horses in tow.

Lord Madred and the two men in his livery made no move to follow the men of Sobring Hold. The three of them had been doing a fair imitation of statues throughout the whole encounter, and Madred continued to sit his horse with unstudied hauteur. As soon as the departing men were plausibly out of earshot, however, the Leithian lord addressed Nagaro.

"So, Captain, *this* is the protection you have chosen?" He flicked a hand to indicate Lord Kuran. "It may be more... familiar... but I fear not nearly as strong as what you have been offered."

Nagaro met Madred's gaze. "Strength isn't everything, My Lord," he said. "Or should I say that it isn't always what it seems."

Kuran pointedly cleared his throat. "May I ask what your purpose is here, My Lord Madred?"

Madred transferred his attention. "I came to witness, My Lord Kuran," he said. "To verify that nothing improper occurred in the apprehension of an escaped prisoner. You may be sure that I will make my own report to all relevant parties."

Nagaro still had his eyes on Madred. "I trust that report will include the testimony I have given you, My Lord?"

Madred favored him with a condescending glance. "Such of it as I shall deem appropriate, Zirda. The welfare of my ward, the Lady Alisset, is my first concern."

At this, Brandle spurred his horse forward a pace beyond the line of Fleet men. "Then it should concern you, Father, that the captain and I found her abandoned on the top of a carriage— lacking horses, driver, and its left front wheel— on a wild stretch of road in Sobring Forest!"

Lord Madred appeared to be experiencing some mild discomfort. He raised a blond eyebrow and spoke, using his words like pins puncturing a series of bubbles. "The captain has said that you and he became separated *before* he approached the carriage."

Brandle sat up straighter, wincing. "We were separated *after* we'd both seen it from a distance! *He* climbed the rock to get a better view with his spyglass, and *I* stood with the horses. He'd only just told me that what had looked like a bundle of cloth was my cousin Alisset when a sneak-thief tried to make off with the captain's horse. I mounted mine and gave chase!"

Madred was plainly unimpressed. "So now it is *one* horse thief, Brandle? I thought it was supposed to be a whole a band of—"

"*The others were lying in ambush!* There were five of them all together— including the two I just saw in the sergeant's company! They pulled me from my horse, beat me senseless, and left me half a mile from the road! I've a cracked skull, two cracked ribs, and a dozen cuts and bruises— some of which you can see on my face! And before you ask how I managed to get back to Lankura in that condition— *Father*— I'll tell you! It was Captain Nagaro's horse! They couldn't catch him— or maybe they didn't try. All I know is, I came 'round with that horse standing over me. I got onto his back from a fallen log, and he carried me all the way to the Fleet Compound!"

Brandle stopped speaking, head up, back straight, as if daring his father to disbelieve him.

But Madred's face registered only scorn. "It's as good a tale as any, I suppose," he said, "to explain why you weren't there to help your cousin— or the captain, for that matter, after dragging him into your affairs. Bringing him low—"

"Kroneg's Blood!" The words were wrenched from Brandle.

Simion urged his horse forward to come up beside his lover, leaning across the space between to murmur words that Nagaro couldn't hear.

"And there's your doxy, the little *snake!*" Lord Madred spoke with sudden and uncharacteristic venom as he leveled a finger at Simion. "I should have known better than to shelter him under any roof of mine! He's not welcome back, I can tell you! He shan't cross my threshold again, nor you either, Brandle, if you won't renounce him!"

Simion froze as if pinned by a thrown knife.

Brandle went pale under his bruises. "You would cast me out, Father?" he asked. "Well then, so be it! *I* was always taught that a good man doesn't abandon the people he loves! And I will not! Even if *you* do!"

Madred had apparently mastered his spate of rage for he merely shook his head and said, with an air of aggrievement, "You could have been lord of Furthing Hold one day, Brandle, if that boy hadn't ruined you—"

"That's all you care about?" Brandle shot back. "Who inherits the lordship? What a pity my mother's honor is above reproach. If it weren't for that, you could blame my begetting on some other man. *And I might claim a better father!*" And with that, Brandle wheeled his horse around, ignoring the shock on his father's face. "Come on, Simion," he said. "We're finished here."

Simion turned True about to follow Brandle. The line of Fleet men parted to let them through, and they rode away side by side, taking the road south towards Lankura.

Nagaro watched them go with sorrow in his heart. He turned back just in time to catch the fleeting hurt in Lord Madred's eyes.

"I wouldn't throw away such a son if I had one," Kuran observed almost casually.

Madred had already recovered himself. "Fortunately I have another," he said as if he were talking about a spare cloak. His attention was on Kuran. "Do you intend to give protection to Simion Rudrin, My Lord?" he asked with cool courtesy.

Kuran's response was equally cool. "Is there some charge against him? Lord Grimbold's sergeant made no effort to detain him."

Madred sniffed. "He has made brazen and slanderous accusations against my House and Hold. I won't know the full extent of his mischief until I've made my own investigation."

"The Rudrin family are citizens in good standing of Kel Wared, My Lord." Kuran observed mildly. "Which lies *there.*" His gesture took in the land to the south of the crossroads. "And Simion is a former Fleet man who gave honorable service. I have no reason to doubt his honesty, and I won't allow him to be taken without some evidence of wrongdoing."

This time the twist of Lord Madred's mouth was distinctly sour. "In many places, a crossed man has no standing, My Lord, as you may discover. When a man is crooked in one thing, he's likely crooked in other ways as well. Consider yourself warned."

Kuran's answering smile was hard-edged. "I find myself warned in more respects than one, Lord Madred. And now I think we are all finished here."

"Indeed." Madred looked down his patrician nose. "But I wouldn't assume that Sobring Hold is finished with Captain Nagaro." With that, he signed to his two guardsmen, who had remained so still and silent that Nagaro had all but forgotten them.

The three men wheeled their mounts in perfect unison and rode away up the North Road, spurring their horses to a canter.

Kuran sat still on his horse long enough to see the three Leithians disappear around the first bend in the road before directing the Fleet party to depart the crossroads in the opposite direction.

The Lord of the Fleet took the lead, beckoning Nagaro to his side. When Taru and Landros tried to crowd in close, Kuran waved them back. "Not yet," he told them. "I want to hear the Captain's report—in private."

Accordingly, he and Nagaro pressed ahead at a trot, opening a little space between themselves and the rest of the company, before Kuran reined his mount back to a walk to facilitate their conversation.

"I must say I was relieved when you made your appearance, Captain," he said. "And I'm curious to know what Madred meant when he said you'd been offered 'other protection'."

Nagaro took a breath and told his tale. He began with the carriage trap, then his interviews with Grimbold and Madred, and finally his escape with Simion. He included an accounting of what Alisset, Tolbert, and Simion had told him about what they knew. "So it appears that Grimbold has some of his men posing as highwaymen to obtain horses for an army that he's building," he concluded. "And Simion was kidnaped because he'd found out about the unlawful trade and Grimbold wanted to know who else was involved in the investigation and what we knew. The trap with Alisset and the carriage was a separate plot, I think, that was hatched after they saw that Geivien and I had come looking for Simion. Based on what Grimbold got from Simion with the truth drug, he must have reasoned that I would come back, and so he set a trap for me. Lord Madred called the offered marriages 'protection'. I think Grimbold just wanted to have me under his control. But Madred did appear more sincere."

Kuran shook his head. "It's possible that they both want you out of play if it comes to a factional war," he said. "They wouldn't want to see men rallying behind you, or your sword raised against Lothard's."

Nagaro stiffened in the saddle. "Why not just kill me then?"

Kuran shot him a look. "Probably because there would have been an outcry. You're very popular with the common folk, Captain. Even if they made it look as though you'd been killed by highwaymen, many would still have thought it was murder. And if it happened in Sobring Hold, they'd have had a pretty good idea of who to blame."

Nagaro frowned. "Are you saying that Grimbold's threat of execution was a bluff? And you think Madred wasn't being honest with me?" He was beginning to think that he'd been excessively naive, and worrying about how candidly he had spoken to the Lord of Furthing. A glance at Kuran caught the Fleet Lord's brow furrowed in thought.

"It's hard to be certain with Grimbold," Kuran admitted after a moment. "He's a mean-spirited, intemperate man. And I don't doubt that he got a judgement from the Elders of the Hold, or that execution is the established punishment for the supposed crime. But I believe the purpose of it all was to frighten you into signing the paper. The Elders would have expected you to sign it. They wouldn't have wanted to risk hanging you. And it's possible that you *did* impress Madred— that he truly imagines you were fathered by some high-born Kelorin. And marrying into a Hold *would* give you some protection from charges brought by other Holds. But I find it hard to believe that Madred would risk bringing your uncertain blood into a Leithian House solely out of concern for your safety, and Grimbold could hardly have used Alisset in his scheme without getting some kind of permission from Madred."

This made Nagaro feel mildly vindicated concerning his handling of the situation in some respects, though not at all reassured in others. "I don't believe that Madred knew about the plan to drug me," he said. "He talked as if it were all some kind of test, and he was surprised I hadn't passed it."

Kuran shot him a significant look. "Then it's likely that Grimbold deceived Madred about his exact intentions. That could work to your advantage— *if* Madred discovers it."

Nagaro sighed. "The lady Alisset will set him straight if he bothers to ask her."

Kuran frowned. "Then let's hope that he does."

They rode on in silence while Nagaro digested all of this. "I'm very grateful that you came looking for me with a show of force, My Lord," he ventured after a moment. "And that both Grimbold's men and Lord Madred saw it. They may at least believe that I have *some* friends."

Kuran laughed shortly. "You have many friends, Captain. I asked for volunteers, and I could have easily brought twice this number. I thought it best to limit it to ten because, after recent events, I didn't want us to look like an invading force. And I would have come for you regardless of what Elgurn said, though I'm glad I took the time to speak to him." Kuran sighed grimly. "It took me half a day to get that order from him, and that was after having to wait two days for Brandle to be well enough to ride." He shot Nagaro a look. "You can imagine what a stir it made when *your* horse came walking up to the gate of the compound, with *your* sword hanging from the saddlebow and that big Leithian clinging to the saddle with blood all over him. The rumor that you'd been slain started spreading like wildfire. Of course Brandle's story gave the lie to it, more or less, when he came around and was able to tell it."

Nagaro winced. "I'm sorry—"

"It wasn't your fault, and I don't want to hear any more of that! You're safe for the moment, and we have an important mission— starting tomorrow morning. That's what you should be thinking about."

They rode on through summer countryside now dotted with farms, each thinking his own thoughts, until Kuran called for an increase in speed, saying that he wished to overtake Simion and Brandle. "I want to ask Simion some questions," he told Nagaro before urging his horse to a canter.

A mile farther down the road, they found Brandle and Simion, dismounted and resting in the shade of an ample oak. The two men rose when they saw the party approaching, Simion springing to his feet with a start and Brandle rising more slowly, with a degree of care that suggested the movement was painful. The impression was supported by the fact that he let the much smaller Simion help him get into the saddle of his own horse.

Kuran called for Simion to ride with him, again setting a moderate pace so that he could talk easily to the young Kelorin.

Nagaro dropped back. But before he could join Taru and Pavo, Brandle reined True into the position at his right hand. The big Leithian looked pale under his bruises and sat his horse with apparent discomfort. Nagaro was about to make a solicitous inquiry, but Brandle spoke first.

"That horse of yours may have saved my life, Captain. I'm grateful for the 'introduction' you gave me."

Nagaro leaned forward to rub Thunder-Heels' neck. "I'm very glad he was of service, though I'm a little surprised he let you ride him like that, even *with* my introduction."

Brandle laughed, and grimaced. "Old training reasserting itself, I expect. He was Lord Bron's warhorse. Bron would have had him trained to carry a wounded rider, gently— and to bring him safely home. I'm just lucky that 'home' to him didn't mean his old stable at Sobring Hall. It was a lot closer than the Fleet Compound."

Nagaro frowned at this reminder that Thunder-Heels had once belonged to Bron Sobring— and had apparently been abused by

Grimbold. *He* understood the horse's choice. "Home to a horse is a place that feels safe," he said. "A place where he gets shelter and feed and gentle handling."

Brandle attempted a shrug and winced. "I guess that's so."

"Are the cracked ribs bothering you?"

This time Brandle grimaced unashamedly. "Yes. I expect to have Master Tredhold after me at any minute. He wanted me to wait another day at least. He was probably right as far as the ribs are concerned. He was just wrong about what I had to do."

Nagaro understood about that... and other things. What he'd seen pass between Brandle and Lord Madred at the crossroads disturbed him deeply. "I'm sorry that those men beat you," he ventured. "And I'm also sorry that your father was so indifferent to what you'd suffered. He shouldn't have dismissed your story like that."

Brandle kept his eyes straight ahead, his mouth set into a hard line. "He thinks crossed men have no honor," he said bitterly, "because they were made wrong. Crooked. Distorted."

This time it was Nagaro who winced. "He said as much after you'd gone. It surprised me, because you'd told me your father was a fair-minded man. I spoke candidly to him at the hunting lodge because I expected him to be fair."

Brandle's mouth set even harder. His eyes remained fixed on the road. "You needn't worry, Captain," he said, his voice tight. "*You're* not crossed. My father is the fairest man in the world until he comes up against one of his blind spots— and then he's a pig."

Nagaro swallowed. "You cut your father at the end. I read it in his eyes."

Brandle gave a furious snort, flicking a glowering glance at Nagaro. "He cuts *me* all the time! He acts like there's some virtue in it—" Brandle cut himself short, drawing a breath that made him grimace. "There's nothing new about this, Captain," he continued more calmly. "It just went further this time than usual. I don't mind that the lordship will pass to my brother. It makes sense. The lord is expected to produce an heir and I'm not likely to have any children. What bothers me is that my father thinks I should have denied my nature— forced myself to act like a... *normal man...* for the sake of appearances— for the sake of the Hold. What did the Gods make crossed men for, then? So we could suffer in a way that other men don't have to suffer? What's the point of that?"

Nagaro didn't believe in the Leithian gods— or any other gods for that matter— but he didn't feel it was a good time to point this out. "I believe things are as they are," he said. "And we all should try to be kind—"

"*Brandle! It's going to be all right!*"

Simion's excited voice cut in before Nagaro could think of anything else to say. Kuran must have finished interrogating the young Kelorin, since both men had reined in their horses enough to let those behind them catch up. Simion maneuvered his horse to a place on Brandle's other side. His unshaven face wore a wide grin. "Kuran has work for me!" he explained in answer to Brandle's questioning look. "He says he trusts me, and he's been thinking of hiring another clerk for some time."

Nagaro didn't know whether the last part was true, but it was at least plausible, judging by the usual state of Kuran's desk. "That's wonderful, Simion," he offered.

"Yes, it is wonderful!" Brandle's voice rang with gratitude. The Leithian looked past Simion to where Kuran rode on his bay. "It's lucky that you had an open position, My Lord."

"*And* fortuitous that Simion became available," Kuran interjected with a lupine smile. "The position also includes lodgings in the Fleet Compound."

"Even better!" The relief was painfully written on Brandle's ravaged face. "Simion's family would have taken him in, I'm sure, but—" Brandle caught a look from Simion and broke off.

Nagaro could guess what the Leithian was thinking. If Grimbold sent his men to try to recapture Simion— or to silence him— they'd have to get past the guards at the Fleet's front gate.

Before any more could be said, Tredhold pushed his way in beside Brandle, riding on a little buckskin that made True look like a racehorse, and began bombarding Brandle with questions regarding the status of his injuries.

And then Taru, Pavo, Landros, and several others pressed forward on their mounts, demanding to hear the tale of Nagaro's and Simion's escape.

Kuran promptly advised caution in the telling, since there were likely to be charges and countercharges. The tale Nagaro told was accordingly rather thin on details. He didn't specify the nature of the drugs he and Simion had been subjected to, or name any of the Leithians who had aided them. He also tried to gloss over the final confrontation in the barn with Lord Madred, only to have Taru ask how they'd gotten out of such a tight spot without any swords.

At this, Simion laughed outright. "What makes you think Nagaro needs a sword?" he demanded. "The captain disarmed Madred as neat as you please with a roasting spit— the very one he's still got stuck in his belt!"

This drew whoops of laughter from the Fleet men, who insisted that Simion give them the details, and then demanded that Nagaro demonstrate the unorthodox weapon.

Nagaro had completely forgotten the spit. He sheepishly drew it and brandished it before thrusting it back into his belt. "I took Madred by surprise," he explained. "I'm sure I wouldn't succeed as easily a second time."

"And don't go spreading the tale about," Kuran admonished the grinning men.

"But it's such a good story, My Lord!" Landros protested.

Kuran's mouth twitched. "It is that," he admitted. "But there's no good can come, just now, from letting the world know that Madred Furthing was humiliated at the hands of Captain Nagaro."

This sobering thought brought an end to the mirth.

They were passing farms more frequently now in any case, and there were beginning to be significant numbers of people traveling on the road— common folk going about their business. So the Fleet men continued without much talk for the remaining dozen miles of their journey.

It was well into the afternoon by the time they reached the Fleet Compound. With a mission looming in the morning, and duties that had been interrupted, the men dispersed quickly. Simion disappeared with Kuran. Taru and Pavo went to get something to eat and Tredhold ordered Brandle back to the Fleet infirmary, before he and Landros disappeared about some other errand.

Nagaro helped the injured Brandle dismount at the stable and walked to the infirmary with the wincing Leithian.

"Shouldn't you be in the palace infirmary?" he asked as he offered a hand under Brandle's elbow.

Brandle grimaced. "Master Tredhold sent a message to Commander Worling about that," he replied. "And Worling told him he should finish what he'd started. Tredhold doesn't seem to mind. He's been very decent to me, really."

This last didn't surprise Nagaro. "Tred is a very decent man," he said.

Brandle shot him a look. "So are you, Captain. I won't forget this. It's a bodjering shame, the mess it got you into. Simion and I will bear witness to anything we saw, if need be, though the word of a pair of crossed men may not be worth much."

Nagaro didn't know what to say to this, and they had reached the door of the infirmary in any case, so he merely said, "I don't suppose you saw what happened to the carriage."

Brandle shook his head. "It was gone when your horse brought me back to the road. I was half fainting, but I remember that much. The rest of the ride is a blur." He paused in the infirmary doorway. "It's a funny thing," he continued. "While I was lying there, beaten and soaking wet from the rain I never felt, I thought I heard Simion's voice say, '*Wake up, spirit that calls itself Brandle. You should get up and mount the horse before it gets dark'*. It must have been a dream, of course, because Simion wasn't there. But I opened my eyes, and there was Thunder-Heels with his nose two inches from my face! I don't know how much longer I might have lain there if not for that. It didn't *feel* like a dream, that voice, but it must have been. I can't see Kroneg, the Lord of Battle, bothering to talk to me about a horse!"

Nagaro was doing his best to suppress a smile. "Maybe Kroneg wouldn't," he said. "But Vothra would. That wording, *"Spirit that calls itself*, in front of your name, is the way Vothra addresses one of the living."

Brandle stared at him. "You think *Vothra* spoke to me? A *Leithian?* I don't even believe in Vothra!"

"That doesn't matter," Nagaro explained earnestly. "Whether you believe or not, or whether you're Kelorin or not, Vothra sometimes sees a need and just helps someone. The Spirit can see what name you use— in your mind— but that's only what your name is in *this* life. Your spirit has lived, or will live, many others. So Vothra says *'Spirit that calls itself Brandle'*, or maybe *'Spirit called Brandle'* if it's in a hurry." Nagaro read Brandle's growing skepticism in his eyes. "I'm not making this up," he added. "It's all explained in the Vothrin Writings. And the Spirit can sound like whatever it wants because the voice is in your head. Simion's voice is one you would trust, and a voice you'd pay attention to."

"And Vothra would talk to a crossed man?"

Nagaro laughed. "Vothra doesn't care two rins about that either."

"Huh!" Brandle shook his head. "Maybe I should become Vothrin," he mused, then added with a bitter twist to his mouth, "That would just *kill* my father!"

"I can lend you my copy of the Book of Vothra," Nagaro told him, "if you're serious. But I'm afraid it says you shouldn't do a thing just to hurt someone else."

"Of course not—" Brandle broke off and his gaze slid away. Then he straightened, painfully, and brought his eyes back to meet Nagaro's. "I'd like to borrow that book," he said. "And I'd be doing it for myself."

Chapter 29

The Meeting At Chitaopa

"Their banners are brown and gold." Nagaro lowered the spyglass and stood frowning on the captain's platform of the *Sword of Freedom.*

"So it's Angkat!" Taru's voice came up from the oar deck via the speaking tube. "What's he doing here?"

Which was, of course, a very good question. Nagaro's gaze swept over the eight war galleys that were arrayed across their intended course like a string of floats on a fisherman's net. It was the fifth morning since they'd left Lankura, sailing south with four ships along the coast, making for the point where Kuran intended to turn west and head directly for Chitaopa. They'd been nearing that point as evening fell, but the light of dawn had revealed the Mahuk galleys, and Kuran had ordered all oars kept shipped while he assessed the situation. Such canvas as the Edroviran fleet had spread was providing little forward way with the light breeze.

It was a glorious morning, of the kind that comes at the end of summer, and the menace of the apparent blockade belied the serenity of every other aspect of the scene. The breeze blew lightly from the mainland shore that lay astern of the Edroviran Fleet. The swells were long and easy. The sky was a misty blue. A faint haze hung in the air, turning the coast of Jinara into a long blue-gray silhouette under the orb of the rising sun.

The island of Judaba, off their port bow, was darker and greener, but just as featureless. The line of Mahuk ships began there, at the northern tip of Judaba, and arced northward into the open sea with the last ship well away to the *Sword*'s starboard. There wasn't a single Jinari merchant vessel or fishing boat in sight. The *Pride of Lankura*, bearing the Lord of the Fleet, was nosing through the water some fifty feet off the *Sword*'s starboard beam, with the other two Edroviran warships following to stern.

"Angkat's ship are blocking way for us to sail," Pavo observed from his place beside Nagaro at the *Sword*'s stern castle rail.

"Aye, but *why?*" Taru's question came to them hollowly from below. "Has the Emperor changed his mind, d' ye think?"

Nagaro shook his head. "He gave us his promise, and this action would dishonor him. More likely this is Angkat acting on his own, but still the question is why?"

"Maybe he do not want us to meet with Emperor?" Pavo suggested.

Nagaro's eyes narrowed. "Or maybe he doesn't want us to recover a hundred freed slaves." He studied the line of ships. They remained motionless, waiting. Angkat had been Baalkir's chief rival in the recent struggle for the imperial throne, but why would Angkat choose to defy the Emperor's orders in this particular way? Edrovir, with it's puny fleet, was no threat to the Mautep warlord, even if Emperor Baalkir and King Elgurn were to forge an alliance— a possibility that had never even been broached.

Nagaro frowned as his thoughts ran on. Angkat would likely not be happy with the Emperor's ban on taking Droviri gold and slaves. If they could reach Chitaopa, the Emperor would hand over to them a hundred such slaves, hopefully with more to follow. And Baalkir would draw those slaves from where, exactly? How many Droviri slaves were aboard the eight warships that were arrayed in front of them?

The *Pride of Lankura* had steered a little closer to the *Sword*, and now Kuran raised his voice to shout across the distance.

"Is Baalkir playing games with us?"

"Not Baalkir!" Nagaro cupped his hands to shout back. There was so little wind that a speaking trumpet was unnecessary at such close range. "It's Angkat. Baalkir's rival."

"We didn't come to fight. Should we try to go around them?" Kuran gestured to the north, whence they had come.

Nagaro shook his head emphatically. "They'll only move the line north, to match us."

Across the water, he saw Kuran raise both hands in frustration.

"What's your counsel?"

Nagaro smiled one of his feral pirate smiles. "I say we row right through the middle!" His out-flung arm indicated the two-hundred-foot gap between the central pair of warships.

"They outnumber us! I don't want a fight—"

"There won't be one if their slaves know who we are! There's not enough wind to maneuver without oars."

Kuran's bark of laughter carried across the swells. "Lead on, Captain!" he cried. "On my signal." And turning about he began to give orders— to be passed from ship to ship— to extend the oars and adjust the sails to take the best advantage of what little breeze there was. On the

Sword's stern castle, Nagaro echoed the commands, and Pavo descended to the main deck to oversee the trimming of the sails.

"Sail right up the middle, Nagaro?" Taru, below on the oar deck could only imagine what lay before them. "You think they won't attack?"

"Oh, their captains will try," Nagaro answered grimly. "But I don't think their slaves will let them."

Nagaro grabbed the speaking trumpet from its hooks just under the rail and tossed it down to Pavo on the main deck. "Once we get close enough, Pavo, make sure every man on those oar decks knows who we are and what we're here to do."

"Aye, Zirda!" Pavo saluted. His habitually impassive face broke briefly into a broad grin before he turned and strode across the deck.

A short time later, Kuran gave the order: "*Forward!* Best speed for a long row!"

The oars bit the water, and the Edroviran fleet surged ahead. The four ships moved in close formation, oars dipping and flashing, sails bellying gently as the ship's prows clove the placid sea. Slowly at first, then more and more rapidly as they gained speed, the Edroviran craft began to close the distance between them and the ships of the waiting blockade.

Nagaro, standing tensely on the captain's platform, had his spyglass to his eye once more and was closely studying the movements of the deck crews on the two central Mahuk war galleys. He knew their captains would be watching his crew and Kuran's, trying to interpret their adversary's intent. Smiling slightly, he imagined their speculations: *Did the Droviri fools take the blockade for an honor guard? Or was this some feint, a simulated attack? It couldn't be a real attack, four against eight?* They would be watching for signs that the Droviri captains understood their danger and were losing their nerve.

The Edroviran ships maintained their heading and their pace. Nagaro did not intend to blink.

It wasn't until the distance had dwindled to less than half a mile that Nagaro saw telltale signs of impending action through his spyglass. Mautep crewmen were beginning to move about the decks more urgently. Some were going up the rigging. Oar ports opened, and the blades of the oars protruded. Still he waited another full minute, while the distance continued to diminish, before he cupped his hands to his mouth and shouted, "*Now, Pavo!*"

Pavo immediately sprang up the ladder to the deck of the forecastle and raised the speaking trumpet to his mouth. "Make way!" he cried. "Make way for Captain Nagaro! And for Lord of Fleet of Edrovir! We come to take home hundred Droviri slaves!" He repeated the message, then switched to Hashti and repeated it twice in that tongue before pausing to catch his breath.

In the silence, the sound of shouts from the Mahuk vessels could be heard wafting across the water. The two central ships had started to turn in the water and to begin to close the gap between them, using their oars to maneuver, but some of those oars had stopped moving. Some were being withdrawn, some worked at cross-purposes. Beyond the closest pair of ships, the other Mahuk craft had also begun to move, and were still moving along courses that would place them either ahead of or behind the tight cluster of Droviri ships, surrounding them.

The intended trap was now obvious, but the Edroviran ships held steady to their course. The *Sword* and the *Pride*, in the lead, were rapidly approaching the line of the blockade. Pavo raised the speaking trumpet once again and bellowed his message, alternately to port and to starboard. When he paused again, the shouts of the Mautep crewmen had grown louder.

Frustration was giving way to anger among the crews aboard the two nearest ships, who were finding it all but impossible to make way by means of rowing. Only the ship with the best angle to the wind was still approaching at a significant rate of speed under the power of her sails, but her helmsman was struggling increasingly to maintain her course against the effects of oars thrust out every which-way. Beyond the central pair, the next nearest pair of Mahuk galleys were also beginning to flounder. Ragged chants rose on the air.

"Kiraam! Kiraam! Kiraam!"

As the Edroviran ships began to run the faltering gauntlet, Pavo delivered his message one more time, though he scarcely needed to. The cries of the slaves were alerting one another, the chant spreading from ship to ship. The more distant warships were all failing to complete their planned maneuvers, slowing and turning from their courses. The closest Mahuk ship, immediately to windward, had turned nearly broadside, not fifty feet from the *Pride*, and was still rotating. The curses of her crewmen blended with the chanting of her slaves.

Through the spyglass, Nagaro could read the rage and disbelief on the face of the nearest Mautep captain. *How could this be happening? Slaves were supposed to do as they were told! They were supposed to fear the whip!*

A cheer went up from the Fleet warriors as the Edroviran ships pulled clear of the floundering Mahuk war galleys and swept on, putting the enemy craft to stern and setting their course for Chitaopa. They had done it!

But Nagaro's mood was somber. He had rejected using a similar ploy on the fateful day when he'd surrendered at Osfaraad, because he couldn't have offered the slaves any immediate salvation. And he had known they would be punished by their masters. The situation had changed since then, of course. *These* slaves weren't rebelling against their Emperor, but against being used by Angkat to thwart the Emperor's will. Still, he knew they would likely be put to the lash before the Emperor had any chance to intervene. Some might even pay with their lives for giving him what would otherwise have been a bloodless victory.

The Emperor was about to turn over a hundred Droviri slaves, so any Droviri slaves on the ships they had just passed might hope eventually to be freed as well and returned to Edrovir. But the shouts of *"Kiraam"* suggested that most of those chanting had been Hashtep. What salvation could Hashtep slaves hope for?

***

It was mid afternoon by the time Lord Kuran's small fleet reached the island of Chitaopa. They found that Emperor Baalkir had arrived before them with four war galleys, escorting a merchant vessel that actually carried the freed slaves. All were anchored in the island's little cove. The four Edroviran ships joined them there, crowding the small anchorage.

An exchange of diplomatic pleasantries followed, held on the deck of the Emperor's flagship. Compared to their previous meeting, this one was notably cordial. Each leader formally greeted the other, Baalkir in halting Common Speech, Kuran in hastily-rehearsed Hashti. Hands were extended and grasped in the ritual gesture of good will.

The ensuing conversation relied heavily on the linguistic talents of Pavo Maat and the Emperor's nephew, Roheed jir-Akaan. The upshot was that the actual return of the promised hundred slaves would occur on the following day. The freed men would first be transferred to the island's shore from the Mahuk ship that carried them, commencing at an hour after dawn. After the former slaves had been reviewed there, they would be transferred to the Edroviran craft for their journey home.

Nagaro listened with only half an ear to this exchange. He was thinking about how far his efforts on behalf of the galley slaves of the Mahuk Baar had come— and how far there was yet to go. Kuran had decided to refrain from mentioning their encounter with Angkat's ships, not wishing to embarrass the Emperor. Nagaro would have liked to hear Baalkir's reaction to the incident, but he supposed that Kuran's caution was wise. Baalkir would probably not appreciate hearing about the disobedience of one of his warlords from an emissary of the King of Edrovir.

The following day dawned a little misty, the towering rock that formed the bulk of Chitaopa looming out of the sun-gilded morning vapors. It took several hours to transfer the newly freed men from the

Mahuk ship to the shore, but by midday, the hundred former slaves finally all stood together on a rough turf of dune grass just beyond the beach. They were loosely surrounded by a dozen Mautep sea warriors— there to "assist" the former slaves, not to guard them, despite the fact that the Mautep wore swords. Similarly armed Fleet warriors stood ready with the longboats drawn up on the sand, waiting to bear the men to the waiting ships.

Kuran and Nagaro stood before the ranks of former slaves, with Pavo and half a dozen other fleet officers. They were met there by the regal figure of Emperor Baalkir jir-Akaan— an imposing man of fifty-five, resplendent in red, gold, and black— and his uniformed retinue. The latter included his nephew, Roheed.

Behind them in the cove, the Mahuk and Edroviran war galleys rocked side by side on languid turquoise swells. The dark mass of the island's central bastian stood crisp and clear, now, as it beetled overhead. The gently stirring air bore mingled scents of sea and cedar. The high, keen cries of sea birds punctuated the murmur of waves breaking on the pale sand as Kuran and Baalkir faced one another.

Nagaro felt his heart swell within him. Kuran was about to receive custody of these men, whose freedom they had come to claim. It was the moment they had been awaiting since their arrival in Chitaopa's harbor, the culmination of their mission.

The freed slaves stood in three ranks, not to attention, but straight and tall with heads up and faces expectant. Nagaro, surveying them, was pleasantly surprised. Kuran evidently was as well, for he turned to address the Emperor.

"I am pleased to see them in such good condition. When I have seen freed slaves before, they have been in a deplorable state. Were these men chosen for their good health and robust spirit?"

Pavo quickly rendered this utterance into Hashi and translated the Emperor's response.

"He says these that were chosen were not most strong, but they have all been treated very well for six week or more, which have made big difference. They have had good food, and hair-cutting, and new clothes to wear. And *dakatar* have tended them."

While Pavo was speaking, Nagaro approached the front rank of men to examine them more closely. Roheed moved at his side. The evidence of the special treatment the men had received was clear in the well-scrubbed skin, the trimmed beards or clean-shaven faces. The men were still barefoot and bare-chested, but most wore obviously new mid-calf length cotton pants, rough-woven but clean. Only those whose own garments were still serviceable had apparently declined the new clothing, though their old garments had obviously been washed.

As he moved along the lines, Nagaro met the eyes of each man in turn and gave each of them a reassuring smile and nod. Some murmured his name appreciatively. More than two thirds of them were brown-skinned Turo, but there were a good number of dark-haired, fair-skinned Kelorin, and here and there the blond head of a Leithian stood out in a blaze of pale gold. Near the end of the last rank of men, one of these rare Leithians was fidgeting as Nagaro approached, and when at last his turn came, he suddenly fell to his knees and prostrated himself at Nagaro's feet.

"Mercy!" he cried. "Mercy, Captain, I beg of you!"

Nagaro stared down at the abject figure in astonishment. "Get up, friend," he said. "There's plenty of mercy here for everyone."

"But no one needs it so much as I! Not when you know what I've done—"

The man raised his face and Nagaro felt a sudden disorienting jolt of recognition. "*Commander Strad?*" he cried in astonishment. "We thought you were dead!"

At this point Roheed, who had all the while been standing at Nagaro's elbow, spoke in Hashti. "He would be dead man if I had not told my crew to pull him out of water. He was captain of ship that left you behind to die at Osfaraad, is it not so? I have made him row to punish him."

"He was my commander." Nagaro, still struggling with his astonishment, now also struggled to find words in Hashti. "He gave order that if one ship— either ship— escaped, it would not turn back to help other one. *His* ship got past because all of your man wanted to catch *me!* And then his ship was lost in battle at Paktaar."

Roheed looked taken aback. "You are not pleased that I have punished him?"

Nagaro shook his head. "I am pleased you saved his life, but not that you made him be slave. No man should be slave."

Strad had remained on his knees, looking back and forth from one to the other of them during this exchange in Hashti, which he clearly could not understand. Now he reached out to touch Nagaro's boot. "I should have listened to you, Captain!" he cried. "*I should have trusted you!*"

Nagaro reached down to seize the man's arm and pull him to his feet. "You listened to men who you did trust, Strad, but they weren't men who trusted me. That's all. But your ordeal is over now. You're free like all of these others."

Strad staggered to his feet. He was gazing at Nagaro, tears actually running down his cheeks. "Oh, you are merciful!" he blubbered. "The Gods be praised for this salvation! First I thought it was their will that I should die on that oar deck! Then I thought you would take just revenge on me! But you are merciful!"

Embarrassed for the man, Nagaro hastily moved along the line. Roheed still followed, though he now looked chastened and a little puzzled. When Nagaro had finished the review, he went immediately to tell Kuran of his discovery.

"*Strad here?* Among *these?*" Kuran spun to confront the Emperor. "I thought there were no prisoners taken at Paktaar! Why was this man not ransomed? Why was this not spoken of when we met at Osfaraad?"

Baalkir, however, when he understood Pavo's translation, looked as surprised as the Lord of the Fleet. Nagaro gave Roheed a significant look.

The young Mautep's unease was apparent but he held his head up as he cleared his throat. "It was I give order to take that man from water. And to make him slave," he explained, in mingled Common Speech and Hashti. "I thought to punish man to please Kiraam Shaku-Tal. But he is not so pleased."

Baalkir had been watching the Edroviran faces. His sharp black eyes flicked back and forth as he listened, and a frown gathered on his brow. When his nephew finished, he addressed Kuran with a serious tone and deferential manner.

Pavo translated. "Emperor say he did not know of this thing and asks whether he should punish *Heerukan* Roheed for it."

Nagaro immediately shook his head. "I do not wish it, My Lord," he said, speaking quickly to Kuran. "Roheed clearly thought he had witnessed a dishonorable or cowardly act when he saw Commander Strad leave us at Osfaraad. And he did rescue the man."

Kuran snorted. "And we should be glad to have Strad back, eh?" he observed in a low tone intended for Nagaro's ears alone. "Even if he's a fool? Still," he added archly, "a dead man cannot learn from his mistakes."

The official explanation the Lord of the Fleet gave to the Emperor was rather more diplomatic. "Punishment is not necessary, Lord Emperor. Our two peoples, yours and mine, are still learning each other's ways. We are grateful for the rescue, grateful to have one of our officers restored to us, when we had thought him dead."

The Emperor bowed in acknowledgment of this magnanimity. Roheed, however, leaned over and spoke into his uncle's ear, and Baalkir frowned fleetingly, then addressed Nagaro.

"Your Lord of Fleet is gracious, Nagaro Kiraam, but Heerukan Roheed tells me he heard man beg mercy from you. I think maybe this man knows he has not been your friend. Can you tell me, plain-speaking man, why officer of royal fleet should ask for mercy from Nagaro, Kiraam Shaku-Tal?"

Nagaro squirmed inwardly as Pavo translated. A plain-speaking answer must touch upon internal Edroviran politics that it wouldn't please the King or Council of Edrovir to have discussed. But Kuran was waiting with a carefully neutral expression, if somewhat tensely, trusting him to speak. He frowned as he searched for words that would be true yet tread as carefully as possible around the delicate issues. He answered in Hashti.

"Man had two different order, Lord Emperor. Order from Lord Kuran say to trust me. Other order say not to trust me. Not to take my counsel."

"So he followed wrong order?" The Emperor's eyes had narrowed shrewdly. "But who is there in Edrovir who does not trust Nagaro Kiraam? Who does not trust honor of plain-speaking man?"

Nagaro sighed. Kuran, having heard Pavo's line-by-line translation, was now looking distinctly pained. But Nagaro had come to Chitaopa hoping to build trust between two nations, and it was his conviction that trust was most firmly based on understanding. He did his best to explain. "In Edrovir, we have three different kind of people trying to be one people. Different people have different idea about honor. Some man say honor must have vengeance—"

"And you have counseled against vengeance." The Emperor finished his thought. "I know you, Kiraam. Man who thought my punishment of Urchak was too harsh."

Nagaro nodded. "I follow path of Vothra, who teaches us that vengeance makes more vengeance. This one strikes that one. That one strikes back. There is no end unless someone say, *enough*."

Baalkir gestured at Strad. "And that man did not take your counsel, Nagaro Kiraam? That is his crime for which he begs your mercy?"

"Not crime, Lord Emperor. He was my commander. But if he had taken my counsel, you would not have caught me at Osfaraad."

The Emperor regarded him with black eyes that were hard and sharp as flints. "And if King of Edrovir had taken your counsel, there would have been no battle at Paktaar? No plan to attack my capital? No vengeance?"

Nagaro met those hard, dark eyes. He didn't look at Kuran, though he caught a little movement from the corner of his eye as Pavo's translation caught up with the Emperor's words. He drew a breath. "Yes, that also is true."

"Is King of Edrovir also one of those who like vengeance?"

This time there was more than a little movement from Kuran. There was an audible intake of breath. Nagaro frowned and switched to the Common Speech, choosing his words with care.

"King Elgurn is Leithian, of the same people as the man who begs for my mercy. But his mind is open. He is not set on the old ways of thinking. I have said there are three peoples in Edrovir, but that only begins to explain our politics. There are men of my people, Kelorin, who would speak for vengeance, at least sometimes, and there are Leithian men who would speak against it. And the Turo, the dark-skinned folk, are mostly fishermen who wish to be left in peace, yet many of them would fight for what is theirs."

Baalkir listened, stone-faced, to the translation, which Pavo did justice to, and then abruptly laughed. It was a low rumble in his throat. "So," he said. "It is more complicated. Always more complicated. Thank you, plain-speaking man. I had to punish you at Osfaraad, because all my man were watching, but I am glad, once again, that I did not let Urchak kill you."

The Emperor paused to flick a glance at Kuran, then addressed himself to Pavo. "Tell your Lord of Fleet that I am sorry for rudeness of my warlord, Angkat, who tried yesterday to stop all your ship."

Nagaro started. Without waiting for Pavo to translate, he exclaimed in Hashti, "You have heard of this already, Lord Emperor? How?"

"I have... ways." The Emperor's handsome face remained impassive. Only his eyes seemed to hold a smile. "You have given Angkat good lesson in value of my new order."

"Your... new order, Lord Emperor?"

This time Baalkir's lips smiled ever so slightly. "I have decided that, by end of this new year that comes, all warship of Mahuk Baar that sail on sea shall be rowed by free man."

Nagaro stared at the Emperor. *Free men at the oars of all the warships of the Mahuk Baar?* A surge of hope was rising in him that he scarcely dared to let himself acknowledge. "Do you mean there will be an end to slavery in the Mahuk Baar?" In his astonishment he spoke in the Common Speech. Since Pavo was still catching Kuran up with the conversation, Roheed stepped in to translate Nagaro's words for the Emperor.

Baalkir raised a hand in a gesture of equivocation. "Still there will be other kind of slave. A few. But greatest number by far are galley slave, and there will be no more of them by new year's end. After that, I will think what should be done with other kind of slave."

The Emperor ceased speaking.

Nagaro stood still, speechless with emotion.

Kuran, once he understood the Emperor's words, asked a question. Vaguely Nagaro heard the Emperor explaining why he had made the decision.

"I have watched these Droviri slave that we have made free. When first they were brought from oar deck, they were like beaten dog. But after we have treated them like man for little time, I saw how they have become man again. I thought of how Droviri ship are rowed by man, and I thought, why should Mahuk ship be rowed by beaten dog? It is not fitting. And I remembered those word that Nagaro Kiraam spoke to me when first we met at Osfaraad. That free man row better than slave, because they want same thing their captain wants."

The Emperor paused to turn to Nagaro. "Often I have wondered, Nagaro Kiraam, why you chose to say such word to me at such time, when I had said I meant to kill you."

Nagaro managed to find his voice. Overwhelmed as he was, putting words together in Hashti at that moment was beyond him, so he again used the Common Speech. "It... was the most important thing I could think of that I wanted to tell you. If I was going to die, there would be no other chance to say it."

He had imagined, on that day, how things might change— sometime— in the future. He'd spoken hypothetically of an end to slavery. Of words being stronger than swords if only men would listen. Such dreams! He had dared to hope they might come true one day. He hadn't expected to live to see it...

And now this!

His spirit rose as if a wind had come to lift it up, up and out of him, to carry it high and far above the world.

He only half heard the discussion that followed between the two leaders, regarding the number of Droviri still held— the Emperor estimated it at close to a thousand— and the number to be relinquished at the next meeting to be held early the following spring.

The other Fleet men who had come ashore, meanwhile began the process of transferring the first hundred slaves, a few at a time, to the waiting Edroviran ships, making repeated trips back and forth in longboats.

As Nagaro stood next to Kuran, watching the transfer proceed, he seemed to be seeing it from a distance. A distance of time and space. His heart was too full.

They would carry these men to freedom, the first galley slaves ever to be voluntarily yielded up. And if all went well, little by little, all the others who were Edroviran-born would follow. And the Hashtep— even the Hashtep— would be free in their own land. If only nothing happened to interfere or to stop this plan of the Mautep Emperor, this astonishing man who could deal out such cruelty and then turn around and do such a thing— to give his warlords such an order!

He was so deep in the well of his own thoughts that he didn't realize that the transfer of the men was nearly complete. He had just watched Strad climb into a longboat for what would be its final trip across the water, when he became aware that Kuran and Baalkir had moved away, but that someone else was standing beside him, waiting. Turning, he found that it was Roheed.

The young Mautep, seeing that he at last had Nagaro's attention, spoke in the Common Speech. "Emperor wishes I ask you how is made Droviri king."

"Made? Droviri king?"

"Yes. King. How you do make new king."

Nagaro stared distractedly. Had Kuran mentioned something about this in speaking to Baalkir? "There's... a Council." He frowned. "Four men. When the time comes, they will decide." He wondered if that would sound as inadequate and implausible to Roheed as it did to him. The method hardly seemed worthy of the nation or her people. *And whoever marries Nevien is expected to be the Council's choice. Or, whoever their choice is, he will be expected to marry Nevien....*

"Man do not fight for it?" Roheed's brow was puckered in concentration. He was trying to understand.

"No." This time Nagaro shook his head, his own frown deepening. "At least, I hope not. A lot of people are trying very hard to keep that from happening." *But there was so little openness in how the choice was made. So many people had a stake in it, yet most were denied any role in the decision.*

"Ah." Roheed nodded as if he understood. "You do not like to see man fight. To see man be killed."

Well, that was true. Nagaro could think of nothing more to add.

A moment more they stood in silence, watching the boat that carried Strad and several other freed men as it bumped against the side of the *Pride of Lankura,* watching as the former slaves started, one by one, to clamber up the dangling rope ladder.

"You are pleased, Nagaro Kiraam, with new order of Emperor?" Roheed ventured at last. He was studying Nagaro's face uncertainly. "You have hear it, but you do not speak."

Nagaro managed a smile. "Yes, I am pleased, Roheed. I am more pleased than I have words to say. I was worried about the Hashtep galley slaves. I am glad they will be free as well."

Roheed shook his head. "Never I have met man like you. Who cares so much about man who are not of his kind."

There was another pause while the two men gazed again out across the cove and Nagaro's heart swelled with elation at the turning of events, the unpredictable workings of Lokundas, at the wonders of the world that could make a dream perhaps come true. Then Roheed turned to him one final time and asked one last question.

"When are you go to be married, Nagaro Kiraam?"

From the heights to which his spirit had soared, it plummeted like a bird struck by a sling-stone. His heart beat on, but he couldn't meet the other man's eyes. Yet he knew that Roheed was innocently waiting for an answer to his well-intentioned query.

He swallowed and gave the only answer that he could.

"I do not know."

Roheed did not pursued the matter. Nor did he object when Nagaro took the first opportunity that arose, after that, to return to the *Sword of Freedom,* leaving Kuran and Baalkir to take their meal together and continue their diplomatic discussions without him, until the sun sank and the stars came out, and Talebra rose with Naru gnawing the perfect curve of her shining flank.

Roheed's parting question weighed heavily on Nagaro's mind that evening as the ships of Kuran's little fleet beat their way northward along the coast, carrying their precious human cargo home to Edrovir— to Lankura, where Nevien faced her own marriage woes. He knew he couldn't have Nevien, and he wondered whether he might eventually marry Hamani... or whether he would live a lonely, loveless life, never marrying at all.

Nor could he keep the feelings he had for Nevien from rising out of the depths of his soul. Images drawn from the drug-induced "carnal" dream he'd had in the carriage also preyed upon him, and these two threads— of love and lust— twined together as fever-images invaded his dreams on that first night of the voyage home. Waking in a sweat, he hoped the dream had been only a chance occurrence that would not be repeated, only to have it recur the next night, and the next.

Chapter 30

A Proposition

She stood in the luminous gloom of the bedchamber. Light from a lamp turned very low shown behind her through the filmy fabric of her nightdress, revealing the form beneath. The swelling curve of her breast was clearly outlined as she raised her arm to draw the comb through her hair, a curtain of rich honey-gold in the lamplight, spilling over her shoulders and down her back.

Nevien! He was moving towards her, drawn by the sweet promise of her body, driven by hot desire. He reached for her, eagerly grasping her arm, pulling the comb from her fingers and letting it fall unheeded. He drew her to the bed... pushed her down onto the mattress, kneeling, fumbling with her nightdress with hands that shook... struggling with his own nightshirt. Now pressing his body against hers, feeling the softness of her skin and the yielding firmness of feminine flesh beneath...

Oh, Nevien!

He pressed harder, pinning her, moving with an awkwardness combined of urgency and ignorance of exactly how to do the thing he was so desperate to do.

Nevien! Oh, Nevien!

He was unmindful of her resistance, overwhelmed by the fever of his need, insensitive to her struggling, her stiffening...

Until at last she cried out, *"Stop! Stop! You're scaring me!"* And he froze, his fever turned instantly to ice, his muscles gone as rigid as stone.

"Please, Leyel! Get off of me!"

Obedient to her voice as a puppet to its strings, he rolled to one side. Lying there, staring up at the carved designs that decorated the underside of the wooden bed canopy, he waited for what inevitably would follow— *the sound of her muffled sobs*— waited while he drowned in a rising tide of anger and self-loathing—

"No!"

Gasping, he sat up in bed. The cry that had been wrung from his soul and had forced its way to his lips had awakened him from his nightmare.

Uttering a sound that was somewhere between an oath and a sob, he struggled free of the damp, tangled sheet, casting it off of his sweating body. The great cabin would have been very dark if not for the moonlight that streamed in through the large stern windows. He judged that dawn was still at least an hour away.

A continuous undulating motion told him that the ship was making good way over long, even swells. Still, it was a wonder that he hadn't fallen out of the narrow captain's bed, as troubled as his sleep had been. There was a squat earthenware pitcher on a little table by the head of the bed. The water in it was meant for drinking, since bathing was a luxury at sea, but he picked the pitcher up and poured as much of its contents as he dared over his face and hair, welcoming the cold, clean shock of it. Then he lay down again and tried to quiet his mind.

If these these dreams continued, they would drive him mad!

The fleet was three nights out from Chitaopa, and each of those nights had brought dreams of Nevien. They always began benignly— sitting with her, or walking with her— but they always came around to the same place: to the palace bedchamber that he had intermittently shared with the sixteen-year-old princess— to the scenes of forced, unnatural intimacy that were the crowning horror of that travesty of a marriage.

He dashed a hand across his eyes and tried to push the memories back into the recesses of his mind where they had lain buried for so long. *He needed to think about something else.*

He couldn't blame Roheed's innocent question about his marriage for setting off these nightmares. It was more satisfying, by far, to blame Grimbold and his minions for dosing him with a drug that had roused the smoldering fire of his blood— long kept safely damped— and linked that fire to his feelings for Nevien. But while it might be satisfying to lay blame in that way, it wasn't entirely fair. The drug had long since been washed from his body, after all, and he couldn't deny the nature of his feelings.

Did he want Nevien in that way? Of course he did, but if he were ever in a position to follow his desire, he would never be so ungentle. Not if he were in control...

Lying in the dark cabin, he shook his head violently, as if he could shake out the unwanted thoughts. But it was no use. He hadn't been gentle, years ago. There'd been a different drug in his veins then, and he hadn't been in control, but there had been the same feelings, even then. His thoughts conjured memories, now— vivid ones, that burst into his brain. He groaned and squeezed his eyes tight shut in a vain attempt to blot them out.

His actual experiences from that distant time had involved less mindless lust, and more awareness of the princess's reactions, but his actions had been every bit as clumsy and inept as in his nightmares. And he could still hear Dreigen's voice with the ears of memory: *"When you see her body, you will feel lust. It is an animal thing— quite natural. You will allow that animal nature to guide your actions. You will do what it is natural to do..."*

When he had first heard those words, he'd dared to hope that it wouldn't be so. It was only his will to do things that was a slave under heskial— a slave to whoever might command him. The drug couldn't be used to control his thoughts or feelings. He might be made to smile, but not to feel pleasure— to laugh or cry, but not to feel joy or sorrow. The Lore Master's words couldn't cause him to act on feelings of lust that he didn't have. He'd hoped that Dreigen's intended command could not become a true command because it was based on a prediction that would prove false.

Unfortunately, however, it had proven all too true. The sight of Nevien's body, intimately revealed, had aroused exactly the animal response that Dreigen had spoken of with such confidence. The Lore Master had also provided some anatomical instructions that had been crudely explicit, if not entirely accurate— Dreigen clearly had no personal experience to draw upon. The bitter irony was that without the rising of his blood, those instructions would have been completely useless. With it, they could eventually have brought success— the begetting of Elgurn's precious heir. But Dreigen's efforts had fallen short of achieving that end, partly because of Nagaro's awkward ignorance, but mostly because of Nevien's resistance to everything he'd tried to do. *And who could blame her?*

What woman would wish to be assaulted by a clumsy, panting, sweating idiot? If only his blood hadn't risen to the call! But it had, over and over again, every night that he'd been sent to her. He'd loathed the experience every time— watched himself in horror as his hands had seized her... groped her... as he'd incompetently tried to plant his seed. He'd shuddered in relief when the word "stop," falling from her lips, had inevitably put and end to each episode. *And then he'd lain there, drowning in a poisonous sea of rage and shame— while lying beside him, Nevien had begun silently to weep.*

Nagaro gnashed his teeth, tossing on the narrow mattress. His chest seemed to constrict so that he couldn't breathe, while his brain was full of excruciating images. Emotions every bit as raw as they had been ten years ago were flooding through him— until he feared he was losing himself—

In a rising panic, he cried out. *"Vothra! Help me!"*

The answer came immediately: *Spirit called Nagaro, I am here. What is your need?*

"Help me to stop remembering!" He twisted frantically as if still trying to free himself from the entangling sheets, although it was something else, something less substantial and yet terribly real, that was ensnaring him.

That is not so easy. Do you wish to talk about these things that trouble you? The voice that spoke inside his head was gentle and calm— too calm, by far.

"No! I have to think about something else! But I *can't!* Why did I have to fall in love with her?"

Well, that would at least be something else to think about. Why did you fall in love with the one called Nevien?

At that, confusion momentarily derailed his panic. Startled, he thought that he opened his eyes, but all he saw was the silvery sign of Vothra hanging in the air above him like the after-image of a light too bright for the eye to bear. He drew a ragged breath that seemed still to leave him breathless. He shut his eyes again, but the sign still hung there, and he wasn't sure if they'd ever been open. His heart was still racing as he struggled to focus on the Spirit's words. "I... I couldn't help it. It just happened! And now I'm caught! I'm trapped!"

Yes, the love of the world is like that. But how did you come to be so moved?

"I didn't mean to! I only meant to be her friend!"

So you sought to befriend her. But why undertake such a thing? Not because you lusted after her body?

"Of course not!" His heart, that had begun to slow its beat, jolted again in his chest. "She was a good person, that's all— a good person, caught in a bad place!"

And who could understand that better than you? How good a person she was, and how bad a place she was in. And there should be no one better than she, to understand you—

"No, she wouldn't!" Nagaro's spirit writhed as if skewered on a red-hot spit. "It was *horrible! I* was horrible! *You don't understand*—" He choked on the last word, then gasped as he felt the world begin to turn with a sickening lurch, felt himself falling—

Suddenly he felt a touch on his brow.

Peace...

The word settled over him like a soothing cloud, interrupting his mind's spiraling descent into chaos, slowing the wild careening of his heart. And again it came:

Peace...

His breath came easier. His blood no longer thudded in his ears. His thoughts ceased their mad gyration as his mind wrapped itself gratefully around the single syllable. Yet a third time, the Spirit spoke the word.

Peace...

And now his mind was adrift. His chest rose and fell gently, and the blood moved in a soft, silken whisper through his veins. The last thing he remembered as he drifted into slumber's embrace were more words, spoken ever so gently.

Three things I would have you remember when you wake, spirit called Nagaro. The first is that you can only be held responsible for what you choose to do, and then only to the extent that your choice is truly free. The second is that lust and love are different things. One is of the flesh, the other of the spirit. Either can exist alone, but they come often hand in hand. You should not feel guilty that your body lusts for what your spirit loves. And the third thing you should remember is that it would serve you well to find someone you can talk to about the things that give you pain.

***

"Please sit down, Captain."

Nodding his acceptance, Nagaro dropped onto the chair across the table from where the Lord of the Fleet was seated. "I've come as you requested," he said. "I thought the other captains would be here..." He let the thought dangle.

He'd come to the great cabin of the *Pride of Lankura*, fully expecting to be part of a general meeting of the captains of the little fleet, perhaps called to discuss how the former slaves would be handled when the ships reached the Edroviran capital. Instead he found that he and Kuran were the only occupants of the room.

"There's a matter I wish to discuss with you privately. Would you like some sothiril?" Kuran didn't wait for a response, but rose briefly to retrieve a steaming pot and a pair of china cups, which he proceeded to fill.

"I... yes, thank you." Nagaro was puzzled. The meeting was only possible because the ships were anchored in the harbor at Kel Tierna. They had stopped to take on fresh water, and Kuran had issued orders that they would stay the night, to "rest all hands," even though it would delay their return to Lankura by at least six hours. The ordered rest had not seemed strictly necessary to Nagaro, but he'd seen no need to question it. And then the summons had come.

Not knowing what to expect, he followed the older man's example by picking up his cup of sothiril. He blew on the contents and waited for the other man to speak, reflecting that at least he was able to wait calmly.

He hadn't been troubled by nightmares last night or the night before— not since Vothra had visited him. When he awakened, his dreams slipped away, leaving no recollection. And when awake, he had no difficulty keeping his thoughts from sliding down treacherous slopes. It was as if he had stepped back a distance, away from a brink. The edge was still there, and he knew perfectly well what gulf lay beyond it, but he couldn't see it from where he stood, and he felt no compulsion to step closer to the abyss— or to look down. He was much calmer than he had been, though he was having some trouble staying focused on things, as if thinking about *something else* had become a reflex.

At least he could think about Nevien, as she was now, without fearing the intrusion of memories from years before— which was a good thing, since he thought about her more and more as the *Sword* drew nearer to Lankura. Unfortunately, it meant that the feeling of emptiness that tended to plague him whenever he was far from his beloved had returned, distracting him at times and making him inclined to melancholy.

He shifted, now, under Kuran's gaze. The Lord of the Fleet was regarding him intently, and he thought the man seemed unusually tense as he swirled the sothiril in his cup.

At last the older sea warrior broke the silence.

"I've had an opportunity to speak at some length with Strad." The casualness of Kuran's tone belied the intensity of his gaze. "I've never seen a man more changed by an experience. He used to be confident and ambitious— driven— completely focused on the progress of his career in the Fleet. Now he speaks of going to the Temple Compound when we reach Lankura and entering the service of the Leithian gods. He seems sincere."

Nagaro frowned. "Did he say why?"

Kuran grunted. "Not in so many words, but he clearly sees the gods at work, both in his fall and in his salvation. He spoke in particular of the hand of Hrathgard."

"Ah." Nagaro bared his teeth in a rueful smile. "The lord of wind and weather." *And the patron of kings...*

Nagaro thought he understood. Vell, who had witnessed the events on that fateful day at Osfaraad, had seen them in much the same way. And Nagaro knew that the Hashtep slaves had all heard the tale, and they saw the hand of Sheptuum in it. Strad must have heard the stories, told and retold, as he languished in chains on a Mahuk oar deck. Nagaro winced. He was getting used to finding himself at the center of such notions, but he still didn't like it. Different men called their gods by different names, but the desire to see higher powers and purposes at work in the world seemed to be nearly universal. Weather happened everywhere, all the time, and went largely unregarded. But let the weather impinge upon men's lives in a significant way, and suddenly they saw the work of gods...

Nagaro checked his wandering thoughts, aware that he ought to make some response. "I've heard such things said before," he said wearily. "I've never found them very convincing." Unlike the extremely convincing existence of Vothra— who had never claimed to be a god. Three nights ago, Vothra had made the mistake of trying to lead him into understanding when he'd been in no condition to participate. The Spirit had apparently realized its mistake and abandoned the effort. *Vothra was neither all-wise nor all-powerful, but fallible and limited, and refreshingly honest about it.*

"Strad was also prepared to talk freely about who had given him his secret orders."

Nagaro blinked, realizing that Kuran had just spoken to him again. He hoped he hadn't missed anything. "Who, then?" he asked, hastily taking a gulp of sothiril to cover his confusion.

Kuran brandished his cup dramatically. "None other than Madred Furthing."

"Oh." Nagaro frowned. The news was disconcerting. He would have liked to think better of the Lord of Furthing Hold. On the other hand, this news reflected something that had occurred quite some time ago. Much had happened since then. "He... seemed to think *somewhat* better of me when he spoke to me in Sobring Hold," he ventured cautiously.

Kuran set down his cup with an emphatic clunk and leaned across the table. "You say this because he was willing to offer you a wife and a place in the House of Furthing?" The older man made a gesture of dismissive annoyance. "The more I think about it, the more sure I am that he wanted to have you beholden to him. Grimbold was more heavy-handed— and more transparent— trying to force you into a subordinate position under him. But all of it was about getting you in some measure under the control of the Brothers of the Blood— or of the Leithian Faction. Enough so that, in the event of a civil war, you would face conflicting loyalties and be forced to remain neutral. You wouldn't then be able to participate in any move the Council might wish to make against the House of Sobring or Furthing— or their allies. You may have escaped Grimbold's clutches without taking any help from Madred, but I doubt that you've heard the end of the matter!"

Nagaro found himself shaken, in spite of himself, by Kuran's sudden vehemence, and also by the cogency of the other man's argument. He realized that this must be why he'd been summoned. This was what the Lord of the Fleet had wished to speak to him about. Strad had merely provided a convenient preamble.

He cleared his throat. "I hadn't assumed the affair was over. And I made clear to Grimbold that I would demand a proper investigation, and a hearing, by an impartial power—"

"But therein lies the difficulty." Kuran's eyes bored into him. "You might try to appeal to the Crown, but Elgurn doesn't like to take positions on behalf of commoners against the lords of the noble Houses. He told me to secure your release with force if necessary, because he wanted those hundred freed slaves too much to risk letting anything stand in the way. But I wouldn't take wagers on what might happen now that our mission is complete."

Kuran paused to draw breath, then continued, still speaking with the same grim intensity. "You're not in a position to make demands, Nagaro— not if Grimbold is prepared to press the limits of his rights. The supposed offense involved a woman of his House and took place entirely within his jurisdiction. You have no means— as a commoner lacking family or Wared Lord to speak for you— to ensure that any demand you make will be heard, let alone acted upon!"

Nagaro swallowed. He dropped his eyes, studying his hands that held his cup of sothiril. "I had hoped that you, as my commander— as Lord of the Fleet— would speak for me. I thought I had been of some service to Edrovir..."

"Ah!"

There was such satisfaction in the single syllable that Nagaro jerked his eyes back up to the face of the man seated across from him. He surprised a look of eagerness— or was it hope? — before Kuran scooped up his own cup and took what seemed an unnecessarily long time blowing on the liquid in it and taking a sip. At last, the Lord of the Fleet leaned back in his chair.

Still holding the cup in both hands, Kuran regarded Nagaro over the rim of it, his expression neutral. "Actually," he said without obvious inflection, "I had something a bit different in mind."

Nagaro was instantly wary. "What do you mean, My Lord?"

Kuran regarded him narrowly, toying with his cup. "There's only so much I can do for you in my capacity as Lord of the Fleet. Please don't mistake me. You *have* been of service to Edrovir— great service. I was prepared, when I went to look for you, to argue that your presence was urgently needed on a matter of great importance to the Crown, and to rescue you by force if necessary. And I would certainly argue strongly— if permitted to speak in any hearing— that your death would be a great loss to the nation. But Grimbold and the Elders of Sobring Hold are not fools. They won't demand your execution. They will press for the marriage. And there is no easy way for me to argue against *that*. Not as the Lord of the Fleet."

At this, Nagaro felt a welling of anger, sharp and bitter as bile. The legs of his chair scraped the floor as he jerked erect in outrage. "I shouldn't be forced to marry Alisset! She doesn't wish it, and neither do I! And I've done nothing wrong!"

Kuran held up one hand to silence him, holding the cup in the other. "*I* understand that," he said. "But to the most traditional minds, your presence with her in that carriage without a chaperon is cause enough to require marriage. And others who are less strict in their thinking will see a wedding as a harmless way of placating the Elders of Sobring Hold. Many will say it's a good marriage, too, though little to your liking. Your status simply leaves you vulnerable in such a situation. Which is why I began some time ago to see what I could do about changing that status."

"I... don't understand, My Lord." Nagaro had felt his anxiety rise as the older man presented his assessment. Now he perceived a spark of hope, but he wasn't sure what the other man was driving at.

Kuran set his cup on the table, his dark eyes never leaving Nagaro's face. "I have a proposition, to which I hope you will agree," he said earnestly. "It is this: I propose to adopt you as my heir."

Nagaro stared. His anxiety and wariness gave way in an instant to pure astonishment. It was a moment before he found his voice. "You... you're willing to do this?"

"I'm more than willing." Kuran's eyes held an eager gleam. "As I said, I've been considering it for some time. It required approval from both the Crown and the Council, because I'm lord of a Wared, but all of that was accomplished a week before you and Brandle made your ill-fated venture into Sobring Hold. The paper has been drawn up and is waiting in my study at the Fleet Compound. It requires only our two signatures. I'd been waiting for the right moment, but... well... I seem to have run out of time..."

A paper... a signature... to be Kuran's heir! Oh Vothra! Did he really merit such a thing?

Nagaro had great respect for Kuran Kell. More than that, he liked the man— and he'd been given reason to believe the affection was mutual, long before this. Kuran had given him advice and support, had proven his friend on more than one occasion. Still he could scarcely believe what he was being offered. Even Varsyl's offer to take him into the House of Virden hadn't been so extravagant a gift as this.

And yet, as he sat there tongue-tied, clutching his cup, the doubts began to come, creeping at first, and then crowding thick and fast. *Kuran didn't know what he would be taking on... didn't know Nagaro's secrets— because he hadn't told him— couldn't tell him— that he wasn't what he seemed. And if Kuran ever found out...*

He found he couldn't continue to meet Kuran's eyes. He looked at his hands instead, still holding the cup. Then he set the thing down, not trusting himself not to spill it's contents. He swallowed. "You... honor me, My Lord. But I'm—"

"Don't you dare say you aren't worthy!" Kuran's interruption was swift and emphatic. "There's no man alive that wouldn't be proud to have you for a son!"

Nagaro's eyes leaped back to Kuran's face, meeting that glance, so open, so direct. He bit back the words the older man had anticipated. "But, you... you don't really know very much about me..."

"I know enough. And I take the rest on trust."

Nagaro winced. *Trust.* It wasn't a comfortable concept just then. The legs of his chair scraped the floor again as he rose and made for the windows, in search of air. This time, Kuran let him go.

He needed to breathe— and to escape from the look in the older man's eyes. The great cabin, though generous quarters by shipboard standards, was not a large room. It took only three strides to reach the row of windows set across the rear of the *Pride's* stern castle. They were standing open to the early evening, to the smell of tar and seaweed and brine, and the sounds of little waves licking the ship's hull. He put his hands on the frame of the middle window, steadying himself, and drew a breath, trying to find words. At length he spoke, haltingly.

"There are things— secrets. That I... that I keep."

"I know that." Kuran's voice was unperturbed. "Some day I hope you will choose to confide in me, but that's for you to decide. I won't press you. And don't imagine that I think you must be without faults. We all have faults."

Nagaro sighed heavily, tightening his fingers on the window frame. Faults were only part of it. There was also danger in the secrets that he kept. *Still, if Kuran was prepared to let him keep his secrets...* "What would it mean?" he asked warily. "What would be expected of me?"

"Not a great deal. I wouldn't expect you to call me 'Father,' for example. 'Kuran' will suffice. You're not a child in need of nurturing, after all. I *would* expect you to attend me and support me in any time of need, as a son would do. You would be entitled to bear the name of Kel, though you needn't abandon the name Nareyo, if you don't wish to. And you would, of course, stand to inherit whatever lands or worldly goods I leave behind when my time comes. And, if I were to sire any natural sons or daughters, you would share equally with them as if they were your brothers or sisters."

Kuran ceased speaking, and Nagaro turned to face him, aware that the light from the window behind him would make it hard to read his face. He found that Kuran was regarding him with both hopefulness and genuine sympathy.

"What is more to the point in your current situation," the Lord of the Fleet continued from his seat at the table, "is that you would become a citizen of Kel Wared. I would thus become both the head of your House and your Wared Lord. As such, I would be able to offer you much more protection than I can as your commander."

"You, spoke of changing my... *status*."

Kuran shrugged. "Such 'noble' status as I have would extend to you as well. I inquired about that specifically. While Kelorin folk don't have a well-defined notion of nobility, and don't traditionally consider rank or status to be hereditary, Leithians do. In fact, they insist upon it. So, out of fairness, the children of a Wared Lord share his status just as do the children of the Lord of a Hold— at least in the eyes of the King and the Council. In your case it would be a somewhat dubious honor, I confess. Most of the Leithians consider me an upstart, and they would look upon you the same way— perhaps more so. Still, my status was conferred by the Crown, and the Crown recognizes it. "

"I see."

Nagaro gnawed his lip. He had never cared about noble status, but Kuran's offer of protection was attractive. And he was touched by the older sea warrior's obvious concern. *Did he dare to do this? Should he allow Kuran to tie their fates together in this way?*

"What about Narei?" he asked. "If I were to become one of your family—"

"Your daughter would as well." Kuran finished for him. "That isn't required as part of the adoption process, but she's flesh of your flesh, and I would welcome her."

Still Nagaro stood uncertain.

Kuran sighed. "You needn't give me your answer here and now," he said. "I want you to be comfortable with your decision. Please think about it. Take whatever time you need— or what time Lokundas will allow you." His face twitched into a rueful smile. "I'm not sure what you'll find waiting for you when we reach Lankura."

Nagaro doubted that more time would make the decision any easier. He moved back towards the table, away from the window and into the warm glow of the oil lamp hanging from a hook set into one of the timbers overhead.

"I don't mean to seem ungrateful, My Lord," he began. "But there are circumstances... risks... that you don't understand—"

At that moment there came a sound of excited voices from the deck above, followed by loud steps in the passageway and an urgent knocking at the door.

"My Lord! There is news! News from Lankura!" Captain Ruald's voice penetrated the wooden planks of the door.

Kuran had risen at the first sounds, and now crossed the cabin in few strides to fling the door wide. "What news?"

Ruald, the captain of the *Pride of Lankura*, had been ashore overseeing the taking-on of supplies. Apparently he had just returned. His honest, earnest face registered deep distress as he stood revealed in the doorway.

"There have been rumors coming in all afternoon, My Lord," he explained breathlessly. "Into Kel Tierna, I mean. We hardly wished to believe them. But then we learned— from Lord Rathdar, himself— that there's been an official messenger from Lankura." He gulped air. "Ferenan Eyilas is dead! Murdered on the road— just like young Fargil of Galenor all those years ago. It was made to look like the work of thieves— of highwaymen. But of course no one believes that! Not for a moment!"

Chapter 31

A Pledge

Ruald's news put an immediate end to Nagaro's conversation with Kuran. The Lord of the Fleet muttered a parting admonition to "think about it," and bade him return to his ship. Numbly, Nagaro descended to his waiting longboat and rowed himself the short distance to the *Sword of Freedom*. There was but a single thought in his mind.

The man who had been chosen to marry Nevien was dead— almost certainly for no other reason than that he was to have been her husband.

Almost as soon as he reached the deck of the *Sword*, the order came, shouted across the water, amplified by speaking trumpet: "*All ships prepare to weigh anchor! We sail within the hour!*"

Apparently they would not be spending the night at Kel Tierna after all.

Nagaro gathered himself enough to ascend to the deck of the stern castle and issue the appropriate commands. Moments later, Taru and Pavo found him at the stern castle rail.

"What's this, Nagaro?" Taru demanded. "I thought we were going t' anchor here for the night, and now the word is we're to sail? I've had enough of cold rations, and Rubo was going to cook something hot for dinner! What's going on?"

Nagaro shook himself. "It's the news from shore. Ferenan has been slain. Murdered., we assume."

"So... Ferenan was go to marry princess... and he is dead?" Pavo's voice betrayed his dismay. "That is not good thing, is it?"

Nagaro was staring blindly across the water of the harbor. "No, it isn't."

Taru waved this aside. "They'll just find somebody else. They always do."

Nagaro shook his head. "They may not be able to this time." *They were running out of candidates. There was just Nile...*

"Well, so what if they can't?" Taru was impatient. "Why should we sail? What does Kuran think he's going to do about it?"

Nagaro turned at last to give his friend a reproachful look. "I imagine he thinks he should be there."

"For what? So they can send a ship-full o' sea warriors riding all over the country again?"

Pavo had been watching and listening to the words flung back and forth. "What did Kuran say at meeting of all his captain?" he asked.

Again Nagaro shook his head. "There was no meeting of captains. Kuran wanted to talk to me. Alone."

"About all of slaves that will be free? Or about what Emperor want?"

"No." Nagaro turned back to the view of the harbor. "He wants to make me his heir. For my protection."

"His *heir?*" Taru sounded stunned.

"So then you will be lord?" Pavo asked. "After Kuran?"

"No, it doesn't work like that," Nagaro explained. "The people of Kel Wared would have to choose me."

"But ye know they would!" Taru grabbed his arm. "Ye said yes— didn't ye?"

Nagaro tried to shrug off his friend's hand. "I'm supposed to think about it."

"What's there t' think about?" Taru tightened his grip.

"Well... it's pretty much the same argument that Madred made."

"Aye, but it's a better offer!"

"He is right, Nagaro," Pavo put in. "Kuran is better than Madred. And you do not have to marry woman you do not want."

Nagaro twisted out of Taru's grasp and turned on his friends, frowning. "Shouldn't you both be getting the ship ready to sail?"

Taru gave an exasperated shrug of his shoulders. "In a minute! Nagaro, ye can't let this chance slip away!"

Pavo spread his hands. "Do you not like Lord Kuran?"

"Of course I do!" Nagaro caught himself as he realized that his voice had risen. He hastily glanced around, but there were no other crewmen nearby. All the same, he lowered his voice when he continued. "Of *course* I like Kuran, Pavo, but he doesn't know about... about my past."

"Then it is maybe time you tell him—"

"*I can't!*" Nagaro gulped air, searching for a valid reason. "Kuran and King Elgurn are friends! Remember? They talk."

Taru threw up his hands. "Fine, then! *Don't* tell him. Ye've been *not* telling him for two years, so that's nothing new!"

Nagaro shut his eyes, clamping his mouth shut. He mastered himself with an effort, and when he opened his eyes again, he found that both of his friends were watching him warily. "Of *course* I would have to go on *not* telling him," he said, speaking deliberately. "But it doesn't seem fair for me not to tell him, if he makes me his heir. *That's* the problem. That's why I have to think about it. And now, Taru, *you* need to be on the oar deck. And *you*, Pavo, should be down on the main deck getting ready for the order to weigh anchor."

They both went, after that, without another word.

***

The rest of the voyage to Lankura passed under a cloud, or so it seemed to Nagaro. It had nothing to do with the weather, which continued fair—unconscionably so, he thought. It seemed unjust that the much-vaunted gods should be so unmoved as not to spare even a few celestial tears for Ferenan, out of respect for the man's sacrifice.

Nagaro knew he should be trying to think about Lord Kuran's offer during those two days, but his mind shied away from the subject. Fear and guilt lay down that path. Instead, he thought about Nevien a great deal. A man was dead for merely having agreed to marry her. It had happened once before. But still, how must that feel? And what would be next for her? The choice of Ferenan had been a carefully balanced compromise. Could the Council find another such? Would they sacrifice young Nile, Alisset's true love? And if Nile was named, how long would the young man live after the announcement? Or would the king decide to wed his young daughter to the aging Lord Devral in an effort to remove her playing piece from the game board?

When it all became too much for him, Nagaro would remind himself that the fair weather was at least good for the newly freed slaves. The *Sword*'s share of these freed men were quartered on the main deck because there was no other place. They didn't seem to mind the accommodations, being glad just to be in the open air. Nagaro found walking among them a welcome distraction. Ferenan meant nothing to these men. Many were dismayed to learn that the queen had died several months ago. Yet they'd all heard some version of the tale of how the Emperor had captured Nagaro and tested him and let him go, and how Nagaro had saved his innocent Hashtep friend from execution. Their heartfelt praise and gratitude warmed him even as it embarrassed him, and he had to point out that he'd done very little of it alone. And the end result would have been far different if Baalkir jir-Akaan had been a man of a different character.

Seeing these men was a reminder that the world was changing. There would very soon be no more need for piracy of the kind he had once practiced— that still was being practiced by two of his captains and their men. What would those men do? Timegar, the former Fleet warrior, could easily resume his interrupted retirement and return to fishing. And Moraga could likely be hired as a merchant captain. Nagaro could easily imagine the former merchant seaman growing rich as the master of his own merchant ship. It occurred to Nagaro to wonder whether he might follow the same course himself, if continuing in the Fleet became untenable. It should be possible. The difficulty was, of course, that he didn't want to.

On the morning of the third day, the four ships arrived in Lankura. They docked at the wharf just outside the Fleet Compound with very little fanfare. The inhabitants of Edrovir's capital city quite understandably had other things on their minds, having recently seen Ferenan's funeral procession wind its way through the streets and out by the East Gate, bearing the body of the slain lord away on the road that would carry him home to where he would be laid to rest beside his dear wife in the Wared of his birth.

Nagaro stood on the forecastle and watched as twenty-five men who had been slaves only weeks before filed down the gang plank and set their feet upon the shore of Edrovir. Many of them raised their hands in triumph as they did so, and shouted words expressing their joy and gratitude.

Taru came to stand beside his friend, and for a time they watched together in silence. But Taru eventually couldn't resist saying what was on his mind.

"Have ye given Kuran your answer yet?"

"No." Nagaro kept his eyes on the freed men. The question wasn't unexpected, even if it was unwelcome.

"He's going t' ask ye again, Nagaro— now that the mission's over. If he doesn't do it today, it'll be tomorrow. And he won't wait forever for ye to say yes."

Nagaro shot a look at the young Turo. He'd been trying not to think about these rather obvious facts, and almost succeeding. "I don't know that I *will* say yes," he said stiffly. "And right now, we're needed down there on the dock. The last of the men have just stepped off and there must be some plan for what's to be done with them."

There was a plan, of course. It had been devised before Kuran's ships had even set out on their mission, and was now duly carried out. It consisted of ceremonially escorting the freed men through the streets of Lankura to temporary quarters in pavilions set up for them in the large courtyard separating the city from the palace and royal gardens. In the days to come, the men's names would be catalogued, along with information regarding where each had made his home, or where he wished to make a new one. There would be some stipend given to each to facilitate his reentry into society, and transportation would have to be arranged, and so on.

Nagaro declined the use of a horse for the short journey through the town, pointing out that the former slaves would have to walk— and suddenly all the other officers and dignitaries involved declared that *they* would be walking as well. Any hope Nagaro had of being inconspicuous was thereby frustrated, and he found himself and Kuran placed at the head of the procession for a march that was rather less triumphal in feeling than it should have been.

The streets were lined with citizens, and more were leaning from upper story windows and balconies, but the cheering was decidedly subdued. Ferenan's funeral had simply been too recent, and folk didn't wish to appear disrespectful of the dead. Even so, Nagaro felt a modest satisfaction upon hearing cries of "Free men! Free men!" on the lips of men, women, and children belonging to all of the country's peoples, Kelorin, Leithian, and Turo, in addition to repetition of his own name and Kuran's. Subdued though it was, it was nevertheless a joyous homecoming for the former galley slaves, and he was glad to have played a role in bringing it about.

As he stood among the Fleet officers in the palace courtyard, watching as the freed men were assigned to their tents, Nagaro's thoughts turned again to Nevien. She was nearby, presumably, in the palace. She might even be watching through a window, though he supposed it was unlikely. The original plan had called for a royal presence to welcome the men, but that obviously had changed under the circumstances. It was likely that the members of the royal household, as well as the members of the King's Council, had other more pressing things to attend to.

The journey back to the wharf was more sober, especially for Nagaro. The king had ordered a number of carriages to carry the Fleet officers back to the docks, and the rattling ride over the cobblestones, sequestered with the other captains behind curtained windows, left Nagaro nothing to think about but his impending need to give Kuran an answer, and the fact that he still didn't know what that answer should be.

In due course, the carriages came to a stop outside the front gate of the Fleet Compound, disgorged their passengers, and pulled away, leaving a milling group of uniformed men. Many of them were quickly hailed and embraced by family members who had followed the carriages. Others broke into smaller groups, talking as they moved towards the gate with it's flanking pair of guards standing stiffly at attention.

Nagaro looked around for Taru and Pavo, who had been assigned to a different carriage, but before he could spot them in the crowd, Kuran appeared at his elbow.

"Will you walk with me, Captain?"

There was nothing for him to do but nod and fall in beside the older man. They had gone only a few steps, however, and neither had ventured to say anything, when they were startled by a clatter of hooves and a breathless hail.

"Kuran! My Lord! Let me through, Zirdas, I have urgent business!"

The rider was Vell, who pushed his horse through the crowd right up to Kuran's side before dismounting.

"What's this?" Kuran was taken aback. "I see that you have returned from your mission, Vell, but if this is about your report, it can surely wait an hour or two."

Vell was out of breath and looked flustered. "The mission went much as we expected," he said. "And I can give you my report whenever you like. This is something different. Something worse!"

The Leithian had a leather satchel slung on a strap across his chest and he now seized it and began to unfasten the flap. "The Council sent me to bring this to you, My Lord," he continued as he pulled a large, formal-looking, sealed envelope from the satchel. "It's a... a court summons—" He shot a nervous look at Nagaro and quickly looked away again to glance about at the thinning crowd. He lowered his voice. "It concerns the captain, here, My Lord, but it was sent to you, because he's under your command. I'm sorry, but my uncle Grimbold has charged him with the rape of my sister—"

"*Rape!*" Nagaro stared at Vell in consternation. The word cut a flaming gash across his soul. "I *didn't!* I swear it!"

"I know, I know!" Vell met Nagaro's eyes this time and he looked as if he would gladly have bitten out his own tongue. "I've talked to Alisset, and she says it never happened. She has nothing but praise for you. The Council insisted that *I* must deliver the formal charge. Never mind that it makes me feel like crawling under a rock!"

Kuran was scowling thunderously, but had yet to speak.

Nagaro shook his head in dismay. His knees felt weak. "I-I don't understand," he stammered. "Why does Grimbold say *rape* now? He never used that word to me! It wasn't in the paper he tried to make me sign!"

"Not so loud!" Kuran hissed. "Grimbold must have decided to raise the stakes. Though I don't know why, if the Lady Alisset can be counted on to speak in your favor."

Nagaro groaned. "He won't let her testify," he said wretchedly. "He said the testimony of young women isn't considered reliable under Leithian law."

"But it won't *be* Leithian law." Kuran gestured at the envelope in Vell's hands. "It will be Edroviran law. That bears the king's seal!"

The king's seal? Hope sprang in Nagaro's heart, until he saw the sick look on Vell's face.

The young scion of the House of Sobring was shaking his head. "Alisset *will* testify," he said hollowly. "She told me that Grimbold is counting on it. He has some way to make her say whatever he wants! She'd never willingly do anything to hurt Nagaro, but she says she won't be able to help herself— and she's terrified!"

"What can Grimbold do besides threaten her?" Kuran was plainly skeptical.

But Nagaro felt a coldness grip him like hands of ice. *Whatever he wants her to say... Won't be able to help herself...* The words had a too-familiar ring.

"*Heskial!*" he murmured. "*Grimbold has heskial—*" He had a mental image of Alisset, standing before a court, pale and stiff, while false words— words that damned him— fell from her lips. "*No!*" he moaned. "*Vothra, no—*"

The world began to dim— though the sun still shone brightly in the western sky. The clamor of the quay grew fainter in his ears. He staggered, and he might have fallen if Kuran hadn't swiftly moved to grip his arm.

As if from a distance he heard Kuran saying, in voice that seemed to be raised for the benefit of anyone in earshot, "Of course I'll hear your report, Captain Vell. But not here. My office is the place for that. Come!"

And then he heard other voices— Taru's and Pavo's— but the words were lost in the pounding of blood in his ears. He only just made out the voice of someone close beside him— it must have been Vell— saying, "Bring my horse—"

Fortunately, it wasn't far to the gate of the Fleet Compound, or from there to Kuran's quarters. Nagaro traversed the distance in a daze, vaguely aware of Kuran on one side of him and Vell on the other, steering him, steadying him.

All he could think of was Alisset. *That innocent of innocents, who hadn't an ill-intentioned bone in her body. Alisset, who had said she would pray for him...* The idea of that gentle, harmless creature being subjected to heskial... and on his account...

Inside the building, he found himself being pushed into a chair. He gratefully sank down onto it. Bending his head, he hid his face in his hands. "*They mustn't do it,*" he murmured huskily. "*They can't—*"

But he knew that Grimbold could. Grimbold would.

"Is there anything to drink?" *That was Kuran.* "He's sensitive to being confronted by evil. Here! Simion! Fetch us some water."

Simion had already assumed his new position as Kuran's clerk, and he must have had a pitcher somewhere very close, because the next thing Nagaro knew, someone was pressing a brimming cup into his hands.

He raised his head a little, grasped the cup, and took a swallow from it because he knew it was expected of him. Then he took another, and another, because it actually did help. He hadn't realized how tight his throat was until he felt the cool water ease the clenching of it.

He was suddenly embarrassed, aware that Kuran, Vell, and Simion were all standing around him— worried, puzzled, solicitous— as if he were a sick child or a fainting woman. *In fact he very nearly had fainted, back there on the quay.* They were asking each other questions, trying to understand what had happened. *He had to say something... try to explain.* With an effort, he focused on Simion— the one among those present whom knew the most, the one who would understand— and managed, brokenly, to convey what it was that he feared.

Simion translated for the benefit of the other two men. "They have a drug called heskial, Vell, that uses spirit magic. It does just what your sister said. I know— because they used it on me! With it, I'm afraid that Grimbold can make it look very bad for Nagaro. He'll trot out what happened in Pakoa, years ago, when Nagaro's daughter was begotten. Nagaro has never tried to deny any of that. And then Grimbold will bring out Alisset, and she'll say whatever she's been told to say. She won't look or sound quite like herself, of course, but folk will put it down to her being distressed... or ashamed— uncomfortable, maybe, with talking about it in front of a tribunal."

"But... if we know all this," Vell began, "then, when she speaks, all we have to do is explain—"

"*No!*" Desperately Nagaro shook his head. "I can't let him do it! I don't want to give Grimbold the opportunity! I'll go away! I'll leave Lankura... leave the country—"

"*Flee the charge?*" Kuran was outraged. "No, Nagaro, you mustn't do that! It will make you look guilty!"

"I don't care! I can't let him do that to her!"

Abruptly Kuran bent over him, fixing Nagaro with his sharp black eyes. "You mustn't run away, Nagaro," he said sternly. "It speaks well of you that you're willing to sacrifice your career to spare a young lady from being forced to tell lies, but it won't be necessary. There's a better way. If you will just accept my offer— sign the inheritance document I've prepared— I can help you!"

Nagaro hesitated, pinned by the older man's gaze, teetering on the brink of indecision. *If only there weren't so much that Kuran didn't know!*

The Lord of the Fleet put a hand on his shoulder. "It's not as if it can't be undone," he said. "If we decide it was a mistake for some reason, it's not irrevocable."

And with that, the balance tipped. Nagaro swallowed. "All right," he said weakly. "I accept your offer. I'll sign. And... and thank you."

"Good enough!" Kuran snapped his fingers and signed to Simion. "Bring us the paper," he said. "You know the one I mean."

Simion gave Nagaro an encouraging look, mouthed some reassurance, and scurried away. He came back quickly with a paper, supported on a polished board that Nagaro could lay across his knees.

While Vell looked on, Kuran dipped a pen and brought it to him, and Nagaro inscribed his signature where Simion indicated. The Lord of the Fleet then added his own, and the deed was done. Nagaro had pledged himself to the House of Kel.

Kuran didn't even wait for the ink to dry. "Right," he said, turning to Vell. "Let's have that summons."

Vell handed over the envelope.

Kuran unsealed it and extracted the paper it contained, which he unfolded and read through grimly. "Ha!" he said. "We'll soon see about this! There's a right to challenge in Edroviran law— it was a concession to the Leithians." He flashed a brief, wicked smile, then strode to his desk, where he found a blank sheet of paper, re-dipped the pen, and wrote out a short statement, signing it with a flourish. "There," he said with satisfaction as he presented the paper to Vell. "You can take that answer back to the Council and bid them convey it to Grimbold. And I hope they find someone else to carry it, this time. They've used you quite enough."

Nagaro shifted in his seat. "What does it say, Vell?" he asked with some misgivings.

Vell, who'd been reading the paper, had begun to smile broadly. He cleared his throat and gleefully read aloud:

"*Be it known that all accusations brought by Lord Grimbold, Lord of the House of Sobring, against Captain Nagaro, now of the House of Kel, concerning misconduct of any kind with respect to the Lady Alisset Sobring, on or about the twenty-third day of Oteyin in the year 560 of the new calendar, are wholly and entirely false. Let Lord Grimbold be informed that Captain Nagaro hereby asserts his Right of Challenge. He will be pleased to prove his innocence in a challenge bout, to be fought with swords, against no other person than Lord Grimbold Sobring, at any time that said lord may find convenient.*" He looked up, grinning. "*Signed, Kuran Kel, Lord of Kel Wared and of the House of Kel.*"

Nagaro was out of his chair in an instant. "A *challenge!*" he cried in dismay. "I don't want to fight Grimbold over this! That isn't how justice should be sought— with the decision going to whoever is the better swordsman! There should be a hearing... a tribunal—"

Kuran shook a finger at him. "You didn't want the tribunal, remember?" he said. "You didn't want to give Grimbold the opportunity to use the heskial. Look at it this way: What Grimbold is trying to do would be a perversion of justice. All we are doing is preventing that perversion."

Nagaro sagged, even as he shook his head. "I still don't like the idea of a challenge bout."

Kuran smiled a smile that would have done any pirate proud. "The bout isn't going to *happen*, Nagaro! Grimbold is no more than a middling swordsman. He'd be a fool to fight you, so he'll have to back down."

"That's right!" Vell was obviously enjoying himself. "The traditional Leithian Trial by Challenge is based on the idea that the Gods will intervene— See to it that right prevails, and all that. But Grimbold knows he isn't in the right! He won't dare risk fighting you because he knows how good you are and he knows he'll lose. And if he tries to cry foul because you're a better swordsman, he's as good as admitting that the Gods wouldn't favor him! He'll have to withdraw the charge. It's brilliant!"

Kuran cut an elegant bow. "Thank you, Captain Vell," he said. "I did rather think so. And now that we have solved Nagaro's immediate problem, if there is no further objection, I would like to move on to the matter of that report of yours."

Nagaro tried to listen to Vell's report because he knew he should. The heskial was likely coming through Borlund Hold, after all. It was important to know, and he was able to focus enough to understand that Vell's experiences in Borlund broadly supported that notion, although there was nothing to prove it beyond any doubt.

After that, his mind wandered back to Kuran's plan to avoid a trial by substituting a challenge that Grimbold couldn't hope to win. He wondered if Kuran's merchant upbringing might explain the man's willingness to take advantage of possessing something that others lacked. To Nagaro, it still felt unjust, even though it was being done in the service of justice.

He felt drained, and a little light-headed. A crushing weight that had nearly struck him down had been miraculously lifted, but another had descended in its place— a weight not so heavy, perhaps, but heavy enough. *What would come of signing the paper? What would it mean to be Kuran's heir?*

Eventually he pleaded weariness, and Kuran let him go. He left the other two men to finish their discussion and went out into the late autumn afternoon. As he stepped onto Kuran's porch, he found Vell's horse tethered to the hitching rail and Taru and Pavo sitting on the bench beside the front door. His two friends immediately stood up and eagerly closed around him.

"What's this all about, Nagaro?" Taru demanded. "What's going on?"

"Yes, Nagaro." Pavo was less strident, but no less curious. "What is in envelope that Vell have given to Kuran?"

So, standing there on the porch in front of Kuran's quarters, Nagaro gave his two friends as succinct a summary as he could manage of what had just transpired concerning the summons, Vell's conversation with Alisset, and Lord Kuran's solution to the problem.

"Praise Hakura Kili and the Spirits!" Taru chortled, when Nagaro came to the end of the tale. The young Turo addressed the heavens. "The blister-headed barnacle has signed the paper!"

Pavo's reaction was more respectful, and more cautious. "Are you sure it will work, Nagaro? Will Grimbold really take charge away?"

Nagaro ran a weary hand through his hair. "Kuran and Vell both seem certain of it. Kuran knows the law, and Vell knows Grimbold."

"That is good then." Pavo nodded approvingly.

"And if Grimbold *doesn't* withdraw the charge," Taru added gleefully, "Nagaro can fight him! He's sure to win."

Nagaro winced. "*Nothing* is ever sure, Taru."

"It's sure if the Spirits are with ye!" Taru's grin was impishly smug.

"Or if Shepuum is with you," Pavo added with the unswerving confidence of the true believer.

Nagaro suppressed a groan and managed to refrain from comment. "I only hope that Kuran will let me keep my secrets," he muttered. "Because if he won't, I may have to turn my back on him. And he deserves better."

Pavo placed a large brown hand on Nagaro's shoulder. "Kuran is good man," he said seriously. "You should trust him."

Which of course did nothing to make Nagaro feel any better.

"And besides," Taru put in, "he said ye could always tear up the paper. Now, come on, both o' ye! We should celebrate with some *food!*"

It was well past noon, and Nagaro hadn't eaten since breakfast, so he made no objection, and the three of them struck off across the parade ground in the direction of the dining hall. Eating, he told himself, would probably do him good.

As he walked, he reflected that, while he couldn't believe in the favor of Sheptuum or of the Turowan World Spirits, he did believe in his friends. Taru was striding along on his right, and Pavo on his left. He could always depend on them. And Kuran also seemed to be a friend. Even Vell was on his side. The Leithian had accepted Nagaro's innocence without question. Things could be a good deal worse.

He thought of words from the Vothrin Writings: *Rejoice in the days you are given, and celebrate what victories you can, be they large or small.* It was good advice and he resolved to try to follow it. The afternoon was fine and fair. The parade ground basked in the light of a westering sun whose rays were warm upon his shoulders. The breeze from the sea was cool and kissed with salt. The future might hold uncertainty for him, for Nevien, and for Edrovir, but on this particular day, and in this hour, he could celebrate the small victory of having been delivered from the clutches of the Brothers of the Blood.

And there was the larger victory to celebrate as well, the one that he had witnessed only days ago on the island of Chitaopa— one hundred galley slaves set free. As the three friends reached the door of the dining hall, Nagaro took a deep breath and murmured words of gratitude, addressed, as usual, to no one in particular.

Glossary

Alisset (A-lihs-seht): Alisset Sobring. A high-born young Leithian woman. One of the princess's ladies. Daughter of Bron Sobring and sister of Vell.

Anduar Tyronin (AHN-doo-ar teer-O-nihn): A Kelorin lord. One of the Signers of the Pact of Lankura and a member of the King's Council. Also ruling lord of Tyronin Wared.

Angkat (AHNG-kaht): A powerful Mautep warlord whose men have twice attacked Lankura.

anim (AH-nihm): That of which spirit is composed: spirit energy.

Animara (ah-nee-MAR-ah): A Torowan woman. Jila's sister and therefore Narei's aunt, who raised her. Called "Ani" for short.

Arlinas (AR-lihn-ahs): The "shadowed" land to the east of the Goreitha Mountains from which the Kelorin and Leithian people fled when they founded Edrovir during the cataclysm known as the "Time of Fire and Water."

Atadalba (ah-tah-DAHL-bah): One of the larger outer Jinari islands, south of the island of Janidi.

Averwin (AV-er-wihn): A small country estate in Virden Wared. Nagaro's boyhood home, now belonging to the Crown and known as River House.

Baalkir jir-Akaan (BAHL-keer jeer-ah-KAHN): Emperor Baalkir. A powerful Mautep warlord who has become Emperor of the Mahuk Baar. Uncle of Roheed.

Baku (BAH-koo): Bloody-Hand Baku. A Turowan man, leader of a band of highway thieves.

Beloras (BEHL-or-ahs): A Kelorin man, Maramine's murdered love.

Berinar Sundorin (BEHR-ih-nar SUHN-dor-ihn): A Kelorin lord. One of the Signers of the Pact of Lankura. Former ruling lord of Sundorin Wared. Father of Rathdar. Author of *Rule of Loros*, his mysterious death is often attributed to the hand of the master poisoner Dreigen.

bishka (BIHSH-kah): A relatively mild but expressive expletive in Hashti.

bladder-thorn: A device used to inject a liquid directly into a person's vein, made by attaching a hollow thorn from the *scapala* tree to a bladder obtained from the marsh-bladder plant.

bodjer (BAH-jer): An expletive derived from a Leithian expression that was originally much cruder. It means roughly to "do an injury to" as commonly used in the Common Speech.

Borlund Hold) BOR-luhnd hold): A Leithian territory ruled by Lord Hilber Dorn, the southern-most coastal territory claimed by Edrovir. It shares an often-disputed border with Jinara.

Brandle Furthing (BRAND-l FUR-dhing): A young Leithian, lieutenant, the commander of the Princess's Guard. A "crossed man," the older son of Lord Madred Furthing. ("dh" denotes the voiced "th" sound in "this")

Bron Sobring (brahn SO-bring): A Leithian lord and former ruling lord of Sobring Hold. One of Leyel Virden's "keepers." Father of Vell and Alisset, he was killed in the border war.

Brun (broon): Tor Brun. A Leithian man, cook and keeper at a hunting lodge in Sobring Wood.

Burdal Korinos (BUR-dahl KOR-ih-nos): An elderly Kelorin merchant from Vered Mahir. Patriarch of the Korinos family. Grandfather of Sindar.

Chitaopa (chih-TAOW-pah): A small uninhabited island off the coast of Jinara, not claimed by any nation.

Chula (CHOO-lah): A elderly Turowan man, gardener at Averwin. He taught Leyel how to plant things and make things out of sticks and string.

Clarimel (CLAR-ih-mehl): A high-born young Leithian woman. One of the princess's ladies.

crossed: English translation of a word in the Common Speech used as a term for homosexual.

Darion (DEHR-ee-ahn): King Darion, called "Darion the Great." Ruling lord of the House of Loros and of Loros Wared. Chosen to be the first king of Edrovir. Son of Nevrath and Minowei. Father of Tevren.

dedrel (DEH-drehl): A soporific drug used as a general anesthetic.

Delasin Virden (DEHL-ah-sihn VER-dehn): A high-born young Kelorin woman newly added to the princess's ladies. Youngest daughter of Varsyl.

Delvin (DEHL-vihn): A Kelorin youth. A member of the Palace Guard, well known to Landros whom Nagaro met during the second Mautep attack on Lankura.

Devral Sedras (DEHV-rahl SEHD-rahs): An aging Kelorin Lord. One of the Signers of the Pact of Lankura and a member of the King's Council. Also ruling lord of Sedras Wared.

dokan (do-KAHN): A gold coin of Edrovir. There are ten trokins to the dokan, and one hundred rins to the trokin.

Dreigen (DREHY-gehn): A man of mixed Kelorin and Jinari heritage. The king's Lore Master, an expert on poisons.

Droviri (dro-VEER-ee): Name used by the inhabitants of Jinara and the Mahuk Baar for the Edroviran language (the Common Speech), or the people of Edrovir. Also an adjective meaning "pertaining to Edrovir."

Duleyin (doo-Lay-ihn): Seventh month of the Edroviran calendar, equivalent to July.

Dunrel (DOON-rehl): Sixth month of the Edroviran calendar, equivalent to June.

Edro (EHD-ro): River Edro. Largest river in Edrovir, flowing roughly northeast to southwest and emptying into the sea at Lankura where its mouth forms a major port.

Edrovir (EHD-ro-veer): Country inhabited by the Kelorin, Leithians, and Turowans, stretching from the Gorietha mountains in the east to the western sea, and from the Kor Vaskol mountains in the north to its borders with Jinara and Hran in the south.

Elgurn Harlind (EHL-gurn HAR-lihnd): King Elgurn. A Leithian lord chosen by the Pact Signers to be the third king of Edrovir. Also the ruling lord of Harlind Hold. Father of Nevien.

Elyan (EHL-ee-ahn): Prince Elyan. A high-born Kelorin man, third husband of Princess Nevien, he was fatally wounded while defending Lankura during the second Mautep attack.

Erantil (EHR-ahn-tihl): Erantil Crimson. A rare and costly variety of sothiril having ruby-red color and superior flavor and fragrance.

Estevad (EHS-teh-vahd): A Kelorin man. Clerk to Kuran Kel, the Lord of the Royal Fleet of Edrovir.

Evran Marvenen (EHV-rahn mar-VEHN-ehn): A Kelorin merchant from Harmoth. Maternal uncle of Sindar.

Evrel (EHV-rehl: Fourth month of the Edroviran calendar, equivalent to April.

Fargil (FAR-gihl) of Galenor (GAL-eh-nor): A Kelorin youth, son of the Lord of Galenor Wared, who is believed to have been murdered because he was courting the Princess Nevien.

farusia (fah-ROO-see-ah): A plant bearing large white trumpet-shaped flower, or the flower itself.

Fendar (FIHN-dar): A Kelorin swordmaster who was Leyel Virden's instructor, now serving as Swordmaster to the Royal Fleet.

Ferenan Eyilas (FEHR-eh-nahn AY-ih-las): A middle-aged high-born man of mixed Kelorin and Leithian blood. One of Princess Nevien's suitors.

Filora (fih-LOR-ah): An older Kelorin woman, Mistress of the Royal Kitchens in the palace of Lankura.

Fineas (FIHN-ay-ahs): Master Fineas. A young Kelorin lore master employed at one time by Lord Madred Furthing but now keeping an apothecary shop in Brass Bell Lane.

Finorel (FIHN-or-ehl): Twelfth month of the Edroviran calendar, equivalent to December.

Furthing Hold (FER-dhing hold). The territory governed by the Leithian lord Madred Furthing. ("dh" denotes the "th" sound in the word "this")

Gama (GAH-ma): An old Turowan woman, Taru's grandmother. (The word *gama* means "grandmother" in the Turowan tongue.)

Geivian (GAY-vee-ahn): A young high-born Kelorin man who has a seat at the "match table" because he is courting one of the princess's ladies (Currently Kendira, though previously Rianine).

Genorel (GUEHN-or-ehl): First month of the Edroviran calendar, equivalent to January.

Gillard Marchent (GIHL-ard MAR-chehnt): A high-born Leithian man, second husband of Princess Nevien who went mad and jumped from a balcony. Also called "Gill". One of Leyel Virden's "keepers."

Grimbold Sobring (GRIHM-bold SO-brihng): A Leithian lord. Brother, and successor of, Bron Sobring as ruling lord of Sobring Hold. Uncle of Vell and Alisset. A member of the Leithian Faction and one of the Brothers of the Blood.

Grobend (GRO-behnd): A Leithian man. Leader of a band of highwayman in Sobring Wood.

Groft (grawft) : A young Leithian man, a member of the Palace Guard. A suitor of Kendira.

Gudo (GOO-do): A young Turo, childhood friend of Taru in Wotana , married to Lanei. He bought the house Taru grew up in from Gama after the death of Taru's parents.

Hakura Kili (hah-KOOR-ah KEE-lee): Guiding Spirit of the Turo. Turowans often swear by Hakura Kili. The exclamation "Hakura!" expresses awe, excitement, or gratitude.

hamanei mata noa (hah-MAH-nay MAH-tah NO-ah): A Turowan exclamation, literally meaning 'Spirits protect us.' Also shortened to just "Hamanei!" It expresses alarm.

Hamani (hah-MAH-nee): A young Turowan woman who lives across the road from Taru's grandmother in Wotana. Her name means "spirit". Older sister of Jitali, she is enamored of Taru.

Hanuroa (HAH-noo-RO-ah): Turowan name for the afterlife. Equivalent to heaven.

Harmoth (HAR-mahth): Southern-most major port city in Edrovir.

Haruda (hah-ROO-dah): A former Turowan merchant seaman from Pakoa Island, a follower of Nagaro. One of those who also joined the Royal Fleet.

Hashtep (HAHSH-tehp): The common folk of the Mahuk Baar. Also the general word for their race, which includes the Mautep or warlord class.

Hashti (HAHSH-tee): Language of the people of the Mahuk Baar (both Hashtep and Mautep).

heerukan (HEER-oo-kahn): A Mautep sea warrior rank roughly equivalent to "commander" in the Royal Fleet.

Hel (hehl): In Leithian belief, a place of punishment for the spirits of those who have transgressed in life.

Hendrel (HEHN-drehl): A young highborn Kelorin man who has a seat at the "match table" because he is courting one of the princess's ladies (Currently Delasin, previously Rianine).

heskial (hehs-kee-AHL): A Jinari drug that enslaves the will while sparing conscious awareness. Derived from the heskia vine, it derives its power from "spirit magic."

Hilber Dorn (HIHL-ber dorn): A Leithian man, ruling Lord of Borlund Hold. A member of the Leithian Faction and one of the Brothers of the Blood.

Hranji (HRAHN-jee): An inhabitant of Hran. Also used as the plural, or to denote the people of Hran.

Hrathgard (HRAHTH-gard): Patriarchal god of the Leithians, King of the Heavens and Lord of the Wind. He is the patron of kings and rulers.

Hurn Hold (hern hold): The territory governed by the Leithian Lord Lothard Hurn.

Idrin (IHD-rihn): Seven-day-long thirteenth month of the Edroviran calendar, surrounding the winter solstice and marking the 'turning of the year'. Commonly considered unlucky.

Indrid (IHN-drihd): A highborn Leithian woman. Kuran's wife who died of the plague, along with their young son.

Irvenen Wared (ir-VEHN-ehn WAH-rehd): The territory governed by Lord Rastyl Korven, lying in the extreme north of Edrovir.

Jaamra (JAHM-rah): Strait of Jaamra. A passage between two islands of the Mahuk Baar. Site of a sea battle between two rival Mautep warlords, Baalkir and Angkat, during which Nagaro led his fellow slaves and seized the *Fist of Death* to make their escape.

Janidi (jah-NEE-dee): One of the more northerly of the outer Jinari islands, lying north of Atadalba and south of Judaba.

Jila (JEE-lah): A beautiful and notorious Turowan woman. Animara's sister. Mother of Narei.

Jinara (jih-NAH-rah): A coastal country lying between Edrovir and the Mahuk Baar, involved in a long-running border dispute with Edrovir.

Jinari (jih-NAH-ree): Edrovirin name for the inhabitants of Jinara. Also their language and an adjective meaning "pertaining to Jinara".

Jitali (jee-TAH-lee): A young Turowan woman living in Wotana. Younger, prettier sister of Hamani and Taru's latest romantic interest.

Judaba (joo-DAH-bah): Northernmost major island of the Jinari isles. The port of Patamtala is near its northen tip.

Kale Fendred (kayl FEHN-drehd): A Leithian, boyhood friend of King Elgurn. One of Leyel Virden's "keepers" who is now insane.

Kasadrin (KAH-sah-drihn): Also known as "King's Men". A Kelorin board game similar to chess.

Kel Tierna (kel tee-EHR-nah): Port city on the southern coast of Edrovir, south of Lankura and north of Harmoth.

Kel Wared (kehl WAH-rehd): Territory governed by Lord Kuran Kel, it was part of the former Loros Wared, granted to Kuran by the Crown. (The Kelorin word "kel" means "mountain,")

Kelorin (KEL-or-in): A fair-skinned, dark-haired people originally from the isles of Kelor in the far western sea. Also their language, or an adjective meaning "pertaining to Kelor or the Kelorin people".

Kendira (kehn-DEER-ah): A young Kelorin woman. One of the princess's ladies. Nagaro had been paired with her at the match table. She was subsequently paired with Geivian.

Kenthos (KEHN-thos): Kenthos of Irvenen. A young Kelorin blacksmith mistakenly believed by some members of the Kelorin Faction to be the long lost heir of King Darion, through his son Tevren Loros.

keshaal (keh-SHAHL): An expletive in Hashti, fairly strong.

Kinu (KEE-noo): A Turowan man, working as a stableman at the stable in the Fleet Compound.

Kiraam Shaku-Tal (KEER-ahm SHAH-koo-TAHL): Name given to Nagaro by Roheed. In Hashti, it means "one who takes slaves." Rendered in the Common Speech as "Thief of Slaves."

Kroneg (KRON-ehg): Leithian god of war. Arbiter of the outcome of armed conflict and ruler of the dark moon, Naru.

kuma (KOO-mah): Kuma stain or ointment. The ointment stains the skin brown and is made from the nuts of the kuma plant. Used by fair-skinned seamen to prevent sunburn.

Kuran Kel (KOOR-ahn kehl): Lord of the Royal Fleet of Edrovir. A man of mixed Kelorin and Turowan blood, from a merchant family but elevated by King Elgurn to the status of Lord of the House of Kel. Also ruling lord of Kel Wared, a territory the king created for him from part of the former Loros Wared.

Landros Torenin (LAN-dros tor-EHN-ihn): An older Kelorin sea warrior, former officer of the Royal Fleet of Edrovir, then a slave and one of Nagaro's followers who rejoined the Fleet. Captain of the *Sea Eagle*.

Lanei (LAH-nay): A young Turowan woman of Wotana, married to Gudo.

Lankura (LAHN-koor-ah): Capital city of Edrovir, located at the mouth of the River Edro.

Leithians (LAY-thee-ens): Fair-skinned, light-haired people originally from a land called Leith. "Leithian" denotes either a single individual or is used as an adjective meaning "pertaining to Leithians."

Leyel Virden (LEHY-ehl VER-dehn) Name given to Nagaro by the Lady Maramine Virden, under which he was ridiculed as the "idiot prince" during his marriage to Princess Nevien while under the influence of heskial..

Lindra (LIHN-drah): Queen Lindra. A Kelorin woman, wife of King Tevren. Killed, supposedly accidentally, along with her husband by Reith Hurn.

linjana (lihn-JAH-nah): A Kelorin medicinal drug used to cure mental disorders such as addiction or madness. It is distilled from the leaves and stems of a small herb of the same name and derives its virtue from "spirit magic."

Lissafel (LIHS-ah-fehl): "The Lady," Maiden Goddess of the Leithians. Ruler of the hearts of men and women, and of the pale moon, Talebra.

Lissel (lih-SEHL): A young Kelorin woman. Youngest daughter of the merchant Gedras of Pakoa Island. She is enamored of Sindar.

Lokundas (lo-KOON-dahs): The "Turner of Worlds," Kelorin personification of fate. One of the old gods of the Cloud Mountain People from before the founding of Kelor.

Loros Wared (LOR-os WAH-rehd): A formerly-existing wared, lying on the northern bank of the River Edro, near its mouth. Founded by Nevrath of Loros, father of Darion and grandfather of Tevren, it was cut into pieces after Tevren's death.

Lothard Hurn (LO-thard hurn): A Leithian lord, son of one of the Signers of the Pact of Lankura (Reith Hurn) and currently ruling lord of Hurn Hold and lord of the House of Hurn. A member of the Leithian Faction and one of the Brothers of the Blood.

Luka (LOO-ka): An old Turowan medicine woman known to Nagaro from his childhood at Averwin. Mother of Omei.

Madred Furthing (MAH-drehd FUR-dhing): A highly respected Leithian Lord, the ruling lord of Furthing Hold. Father of Brandle and a leader of the Leithian Faction. ("dh" denotes the "th" sound in the word "this")

Madrel (MAH-drehl): Third month of the Edroviran calendar, equivalent to March.

Mahuk Baar (MAH-huke BAR): A coastal country, and islands, lying beyond Jinara to the south of Edrovir. Inhabited by the Hashtep people with their Mautep warlords and ruled by an emperor. "Mahuk" is often used for the nationality, as in "Mahuk warships" or "Mahuk waters". It is also used (ignorantly) for the people of the Mahuk Baar.

Maramine Virden (mar-ah-MEEN VER-dehn): A Kelorin lady, former mistress of the estate of Averwin, estranged from her family. Nagaro's lady guardian, she was smothered by Elgurn to end her suffering during what would have been fatal heskial withdrawal.

Matapili (MAH-tah-PEE-lee): A Jinari man with a small boat who often carries messages for Utabala.

Mautep (MAH-oo-tehp): Ruling warrior class of the Hashtep people of the Mahuk Baar.

Medrin (MEHD-rihn): Fifth month of the Edroviran calendar, equivalent to May.

Merriel (MEHR-ee-ehl): Lady Merriel. A high-born Leithian woman, formerly one of Queen Semorel's ladies and chaperon to Princess Nevien and her ladies.

Minowei (mih-NO-way): Princess Minowei. A Turowan chief's daughter who married Nevrath, founding the House of Loros. Mother of Darion.

Moraga (mor-AH-gah): A Turowan former merchant seaman and freed slave. One of Nagaro's followers who did not join the Royal Fleet. Captain of the *Tiger*.

Nagaro (nah-GAR-o): Captain Nagaro, also known as Nagaro the Pirate, and Kiraam Shaku-Tal (Hashti for "Thief of Slaves").

Narei (NAR-ay): Daughter of Nagaro and Jila. Animara is her aunt.

Naru (NAR-oo): The dark moon, smaller of the world's two moons. It travels slightly faster than the bright moon, Talebra, overtaking her at times in what the Leithians consider a portentious conjunction.

Nevien Harlind (NEHV-ee-ehn HAR-lihnd): Princess Nevien, daughter of King Elgurn and Queen Semorel.

Nevrath (NEV-rahth): A Kelorin man who left the House of Tyronin and founded the House of Loros after a falling-out with his brother Hindrath. Nevrath married the Turowan Princess Minowei. Darion was their first-born son. First ruling lord of Loros Wared.

Nile Fendred (nile FEHN-drehd): A young high-born Leithian, in love with Alisset but courting Princess Nevien. Son of Kale Fendred.

Nondorin (NOAN-dor-ihn): Eleventh month of the Edroviran calendar, equivalent to November.

Obiari (o-bee-AR-ee): Master Obiari. A highly-regarded Jinari lore master of the past.

Odus Morbern (O-duhs MOR-burn): A Leithian lord. One of the Signers of the Pact of Lankura and a member of the King's Council. Ruling lord of Morbern Hold.

Olomi (o-LO-mee): A Turowan woman, Taru's mother. She and Taru's father (Jomo) were both killed by Mautep sea raiders when Taru and Nagaro were taken as slaves.

Omei (O-may): Tira Omei. A Turowan woman, one of Minowei's people who lived in the former Loros Wared and one of the "ku taihana" who hold the names of all living members of Minowei's clan in their memories. Daughter of Luka. She does menial work for several Leithian Houses in Lankura and looked after Nagaro's daughter Narei during the latter's abduction.

opa (O-pah): A potent drug used to relieve pain, noted for giving vivid "opa dreams."

Orl (orl): A Leithian member of the Princess's Guard.

Osfaraad (ose-far-AHD): An island belonging to the Mahuk Baar, near the northern border of Mahuk waters, where Nagaro's ships had put freed Hashtep slaves ashore. Site of Nagaro's surrender to Emperor Baalkir that led to the torture of three Edroviran Fleet officers, one of whom betrayed the Fleet's mission to the Emperor.

Oskampo (os-KAHM-po): A table game played with pictured cards and small wooden counters.

Oteyin (oh-TAY-ihn): Eighth month of the Edroviran calendar, equivalent to August.

Pakoa (pah-KO-ah): An island off the southern coast of Edrovir where Nagaro made his home during his pirate period. Southern-most inhabited isle of the Lomoas. Pakoa Town, on Pakoa Harbor, is its only significant town.

Paktaar (pahk-TAR): An island belonging to the Mahuk Baar, close to Emperor Baalkir's capital port city of Sar Tipaal. Site of the disastrous battle in which the Edroviran Fleet's mission to attack Sar Tipaal ended in defeat at the hands of the Emperor's sea warriors.

Patamtala (PAH-tahm-TAH-lah): A trading port on the northernmost Jinari island of Judaba.

Pavo Maat (PAH-vo MAHT): A Hashtep fisherman's son and former slave. Follower and close friend of Nagaro who also joined the Royal Fleet. Not tortured by the Emperor at Osfaraad, he was falsely convicted of treason and rescued by Nagaro and Taru, resulting in their emporary exile.

Pedran (PEHD-rahn): A Kelorin man, a tracker working for Lord Anduar, mercilessly slain by Lothard Hurn and his men.

Peldred Gilforn (PEHL-drehd Gihl-forn): A young high-born Leithian Fleet officer, assigned to Nagaro's crew as third mate. One of those tortured by Emperor Baalkir at Osfaraad. He divulged the mission plan to the Emperor and later sought his own death in battle to reclaim his honor.

Pendrik Glenmark (PEHN-drihk glehn-MARK): A Leithian lord, one of the Signers of the Pack of Lankura and a member of the King's Council. Also ruling lord of Glenmark Hold.

Rastian Korven (rahs-tee-AHN KOR-vehn): A young Kelorin officer in the Royal Fleet of Edrovir. Son of Lord Rastyl Korven.

Rastyl Korven (rahs-TEEL KOR-vehn): A Kelorin man with unusually pale gray eyes. Ruling lord of Irvenen Wared. Father of Rastian.

Rathdar Sundorin (RAHTH-dar SUN-dor-ihn): A Kelorin man, son of the deceased Pact Signer Berinar Sundorin. Current ruling lord of the Sundorin Wared. One of the leaders of the Kelorin faction.

Reineth (RAY-neth): Lady Reineth. A high-born Kelorin woman, a friend of Lady Merriel and one of the former queen's ladies.

Reith Hurn (rayth hurn): A Leithian lord, previous ruling lord of Hurn Hold. Father of Lothard. A Signer of the Pact of Lankura and former member of the King's Council, he was killed in the border war with Jinara.

Rese (rees): A young high-born Leithian man, suitor first of Alisset, then Clarimel. One of those seated at the "match table."

Rianine (REE-ah-neen): A young Kelorin woman, called Rian for short. One of Princess Nevien's ladies and her frequent confidant.

rin (rihn): A small copper coin, the base unit of Edroviran currency. There are one hundred rins in one trokin and one thousand rins in one dokan.

Roheed jir-Akaan (ro-HEED jeer-ah-KAHN): A young Mautep officer, Emperor Baalkir's nephew. He speaks some Droviri, having been raised by the Kelorin slave woman, Emril. The apparent death of Emril's infant son, Sindar, formed the basis of a "blood debt" requiring Roheed to save the life of someone who was orphaned.

Ruald Grinard (roo-AHLD grihn-ARD): A Leithian officer in the Royal Fleet of Edrovir. Captain of Lord Kuran's flagship, the *Pride of Lankura*.

Rubo Ataya (ROO-bo ah-TAH-yah): An older Turowan man, once retired as a sea warrior/cook with the Royal Fleet of Edrovir. One of Nagaro's followers who re-joined the Fleet as a first mate under Landros.

Sar Tipaal (sar tih-PAHL): A major sea port of the Mahuk Baar and the country's capital under Emperor Baalkir. Site of his famed shipyard.

Sedrin (SEHD-rihn): Ninth month of the Edroviran calendar, equivalent to September.

Semorel (SEHM-or-ehl): Queen Semorel. A Kelorin woman, wife of King Elgurn and therefore queen of Edrovir. (Deceased.)

Seralind (sehr-ah-LIHND): Name for the place of reward after death in Leithian religious belief. Equivalent to paradise or heaven.

shapas (SHAH-pahs) and **shilka** (SHIHL-kah): Kelorin style women's riding clothes. The shapas are a kind of pantaloons, the shilka an upper garment.

Sheptuum (shehp-TOOM): God of the Hashtep people, including the Mautep class.

Simion Rudrin (SIHM-ee-ahn ROOD-rihn): A young Kelorin crossed man, Brandle Furthing's lover. Former Fleet warrior and galley slave who escaped in the slave mutiny led by Nagaro. He has been working as a book-keeper for Lord Madred at a building on Broad Street in Lankura.

Sindar (SIHN-dahr): A young Kelorin man held captive from infancy in the Mahuk Baar who escaped and has been under Nagaro's guidance. Grandson of of Burdal Korinos and nephew of Evran Marvenen.

Sobring Hold(SO-bring hold): The territory governed by the Leithian Lord Grimbold Sobring.

Solbrid (SOL-brihd): The Leithian Mother Goddess. Ruler of Earth and giver of life.

sothiril (SO-thur-ihl): Kelorin tea-like drink made by steeping the dried berries of the plant of the same name.

Strad Olbern (strahd OL-burn): A high-born Leithian who was a commander in the Royal Fleet of Edrovir during the incident at Osfaraad. Believed lost at Paktaar.

Talebra (tah-LEHY-brah): The bright moon, larger of the world's two moons.

Tambali (tahm-BAH-lee): A major port city near the northern border of Jinara, Utabala's home.

Taru Nareyo (TAR-roo nar-AY-o): A Turowan fisherman's son. Nagaro's first friend from Wotana Bay who was enslaved with him by the Mautep sea raiders, freed in the slave mutiny. Nagaro's first mate, he joined the Fleet but went into exile for a time with Nagaro.

Tenepti (tehn-EHP-tee): A young Hashtep woman of Pakoa. Wife of Pavo Maat.

Tevren Loros (TEHV-rehn LOR-os): King Tevren. Lord of Loros Wared and the young second king of Edrovir, killed by Reith Hurn in an event that sparked a civil war. Son of Darion the Great, he was mostly Kelorin but carried some Turowan blood through his grandmother, Minowei.

Thenden (Thehn-dehn): A Kelorin man. An innkeeper and Jila's husband.

Timegar (TIH-may-gar): A Kelorin man from Pakoa. A former Fleet warrior, retired, who joined Nagaro's followers and became captain of the pirate ship *North Wind*.

Tira (TEER-rah): Respectful from of address for a woman, roughly equivalent to "Mrs.", but with no implied marital status. Always used before a given name.

tirka (TUR-kah): A men's short-sleeved upper outer garment, opening down the front, and cut long enough to cover the hips. Generally worn over a long-sleeved shirt and usually belted.

Todrin (TOE-drihn): Tenth month of the Edroviran calendar, equivalent to October.

tokabi (to-KAH-bee): A Jinari tea-like drink or the plant whose dried leaves are used to brew it.

Tolbert (TOL-bert): A young Leithian man seen among a troop of highwaymen in Sobring Wood.

Tor (tor): Respectful form of address for a man, roughly equivalent to "Mr." Always used before a given name.

Torlung (TOR-luhng): Minister Torlung. A Leithian of the House of Furthing, Chief Minister to Lord Madred.

Tredhold Ferth (TRED-hold furth): A Leithian healer, called Tred for short. A former Fleet warrior and ship's doctor who was held as galley slave, freed in the slave mutiny led by Nagaro. One of Nagaro's followers who rejoined the Fleet. Ship's doctor on the *Sword of Freedom*.

trokin (TRO-kihn): A silver coin worth one hundred rins. There are ten trokins to the dokan.

Turo (TOOR-o): The Turo. Turowan name for their people, also use to refer to a Turowan man.

Turowa (toor-O-wah): Word for a woman of the Turowan people. The female equivalent Turo.

Turowans (toor-O-ahns): A brown-skinned, dark-haired people native to the coastal region and islands of Edrovir. Called by themselves "the Turo". The word "Turowan" can refer to a single male individual and is also used as an adjective to describe anything relating to the Turo.

Urchak tok-Faar (UR-chahk toke-FAHR): Captain of the Mautep war galley *Fist of Death*, taken in the slave mutany led by Nagaro and re-christened the *Sword of Freedom*. Emperor Baalkir set him to punish Nagaro when he was captured at Osfaraad.

Utabala (OO-tah-BAH-lah): A Jinari merchant's agent and interpreter, a freed galley slave who returned to the service of his employer and sometimes also serves the Jinari High Council.

Vanhold (VAN-hold): A young high-born Leithian man, suitor of first Clarimel, then Alisset, and therefore one of those with a seat at the "match table."

Varsyl Virden (vahr-SEEL VER-dehn): A Kelorin man, brother of Maramine, who slew her love, Beloras, in a sword challenge. He is now ruling lord of Virden Wared.

Vedorel (VEHD-or-ehl): Second month of the Edroviran calendar, equivalent to February.

Vell Sobring (vehl SO-bring): A young Leithian officer in the Royal Fleet of Edrovir. Son of Bron Sobring. Nephew of Grimbold Sobring who is currently the lord of Sobring Hold since Bron's death in the border war. One of three officers tortured at Osfaraad.

Venerev (VEHN-er-ehv): A Kelorin man, a follower of Kenthos.

Vered Mahir (VEHR-ehd mah-HEER): A city on the upper reaches of the River Edro above a large waterfall. Also the "bitter place" where the brothers Nevrath and Hindrath quarreled, leading to the founding of the House of Loros by splitting it from the House of Tyronin.

Vothra (VO-thrah): The Benevolent Spirit of the Kelorin, an entity composed of the combined spirits of many individuals all of whom have lived multiple lives. Vothra's wisdom, collectively referred to as "the Path" is recorded in the Vothrin Writings. Vothra has an unusually strong connection to Nagaro's spirit.

Wared (WAH-rehd): Kelorin word for the territory governed by a lord. Equivalent to a Leithian "Hold".

Worling (WOR-lihng): Commander Worling, a Leithian man. Commander of the Palace Guard.

Wotana (wo-TAH-nah): A small town on the bay of the same name, located on the Edroviran coast about twenty miles north of Lankura. Taru's home town.

Yuna (YOO-nah): Yuna River (also called the Tenorin). It flows past Averwin and ultimately joins the River Edro.

Zirda (ZUR-dah): A respectful masculine form of address, roughly equivalent to "Sir" in modern casual usage.

Zirdyn (zur-DEEN): A respectful feminine form of address, roughly equivalent to "Madame" in modern casual usage.

Acknowledgements

I remain ever grateful to my fans, who give me hope that I am on the right track, and to my first reader, Kristie McCue. And of course I must thank those who gave me input on the manuscript including especially my test readers for the final version, Suzanne Coulter, Paul Wilde, Louise Wilde, and Gerald Wuenschell. As for other works in this series, the members of ScHoFan, a critique group under the auspices of the Greater Los Angeles Writers Society (GLAWS), gave me feedback on versions of the early chapters. In alphabetical order, they are Carol Ann Alves, Ken Hughes, Scott Kilburn, Carmen Mendivil, Robin Reed, and Taguhi Tavitian.

I continue to be grateful for the support of my husband and the other members of my family, who by now have gotten used to this. I'm also grateful for the continuing support and encouragement of my dear friends, Suzanne Coulter and Anne Bannon. Anne's technical knowledge and expertise were also indispensible during the task of formatting this latest volume.

About the Author

Carol Louise Wilde is the author of the books of the seven books comprising the fantasy saga of the Nagaro Chronicle. She long led a double life: biology reseach scientist by day, and by night, chief archivist for the nation of Edrovir and its neighboring states. The Nagaro Chronicle covers but one brief period in long and eventful history of this world and its inhabitants. Ms. Wilde lives in Southern California with her husband of more than forty years. They have two sons to carry on the family tradition..

www.ingramcontent.com/pod-product-compliance
Lightning Source LLC
Chambersburg PA
CBHW070342170726
48291CB00001B/148